DIARY OF A DRUG FIEND

Diary of a Drug Fiend

AND OTHER WORKS BY

Aleister Crowley

SIRIUS

The text reflects the time in which it was written and the author's own views, not those of the publisher.

SIRIUS

This edition published in 2021 by Sirius Publishing, a division of Arcturus Publishing Limited,
26/27 Bickels Yard, 151–153 Bermondsey Street,
London SE1 3HA

Cover design: Peter Ridley
Design: Catherine Wood, Mike Reynolds

ISBN: 978-1-78828-559-9
AD006162UK

Printed in China

CONTENTS

INTRODUCTION

"DO WHAT THOU WILT
SHALL BE THE WHOLE OF THE LAW"

INTRODUCTION

Aleister Crowley (1875–1947) was a living contradiction. A shameless self-publicist, he revelled in shocking polite society and living up to his image as "the wickedest man in the world". And yet, for all his baiting of those he despised and goading of those he considered his intellectual inferiors, he professed and exhibited a profound understanding of practical magic which few occultists of his era could equal. Furthermore, he possessed the courage to venture beyond the visualization exercises and Masonic/Rosicrucian rituals practised by his contemporaries in order to cross "the abyss", the symbolic chasm between the Conscious and Unconscious, and explore the realms of the inner and upper worlds.

His knowledge of practical "magick" (his spelling), and his understanding of the other realms and realities described in the texts collected between these covers, reveals that he was not a man to be satisfied with speculative theories and assumptions. He craved direct personal experience of the Mysteries as the Western esoteric tradition was known at that time, and he risked his life, and some might say his sanity, in pursuit of the secrets of life and death that can only be glimpsed during heightened states of awareness.

He was largely responsible for making the process and practices of ceremonial magic accessible to succeeding generations, whose secrets had been concealed between the covers of arcane grimoires since the Middle Ages. He also redefined magic for the modern age in stating, "Magick is the Science and Art of causing Change to occur in conformity with Will." [*Magick In Theory and Practice*] It is a definition that is universally accepted to this day.

Crowley's uncompromising character was formed during his comparatively privileged childhood. He was born Edward Alexander Crowley in the Warwickshire town of Leamington Spa on 12 October 1875. The only child of strict, puritanical parents, he was the focus of their attention and yet grew to despise his mother, Emily, a religious

hysteric whom he later described as a "brainless bigot". His father, Edward, died in March 1887 when Aleister was entering his teens, leaving the adolescent unchecked by paternal influence and free to practise his new-found philosophy of amoral self-indulgence.

The death of Crowley's father drove his mother to seek succour in religion, her zeal serving to compound his belief that religious mania was a form of insanity. It was his mother who reviled him as "The Beast of Revelation" after she caught him seducing their maid. He was just 14 at the time, if his account is to be believed, but it is impossible to distinguish fact from fiction when it comes to the Crowley myth, for so much of it was of his own making.

Sex, his mother warned him, was the devil's creation and he would be eternally damned if he succumbed to temptation. Absolving herself of responsibility, she sent him off to boarding school, first at Malvern then at Tonbridge in Kent, where he explored his burgeoning bisexuality and wrote reams of morbidly pornographic poetry. As no self-respecting British publisher was willing to publish the poems, Crowley paid to have them printed abroad, as he was to do with several later works included in this present collection, ensuring that the first editions became highly valued and sought after collector's items.

Fortunately, he had the means to indulge his passions, having inherited a small fortune from the family brewery business, Crowley's Alton Ales, which he spent freely during his early years as a Cambridge undergraduate. He entered Cambridge in 1895, having finished his public school education in July the previous year at Eastbourne College.

At Cambridge, he discovered occultism, devouring A. E. Waite's *The Book of Black Magic and Of Pacts* and MacGregor Mathers' translation of *The Kabbalah Unveiled* in a single sitting, or so he claimed. Both books had a profound influence on Crowley's own writings, although characteristically he later dismissed them as "pretentious". Success in magic as in all things, he believed, depended on the ability to "awaken one's creative genius" by visualizing what one wished for and then bringing it into being.

One of his earliest attempts at ceremonial magic saw him cursing a Cambridge professor who had refused to allow his headstrong student to stage a bawdy play. According to Crowley, he gathered a group of

fellow scholars on the night of the full moon to witness the ritual which involved sticking pins into a wax effigy of the academic. However, one of his fellow students lost his nerve and tried to seize the doll. The pin stuck in its foot and the next day the master tripped on the stairs and broke his ankle. Crowley's development as a magician was swift and remarkable, due mainly to his unwavering self-belief and his single-minded desire to attain recognition as an adept.

In November 1898, he paid the 10 shilling membership fee and was accepted into the outer circle of the most fashionable fraternity of practising occultists in Victorian England, the Hermetic Order of the Golden Dawn. The Order boasted several eminent members of the establishment, among them the visionary poet W. B. Yeats, who later described Crowley as "an unspeakable person", and senior member Allan Bennett who would be influential in introducing Buddhism to Britain. Bennett became Crowley's mentor and live-in private tutor in a luxury flat they shared in Chancery Lane, London. It was Bennett who introduced Crowley to the use of drugs in ceremonial rites and who in vain tried to persuade his pupil to follow his ascetic regime. But Crowley refused to moderate his behaviour to the consternation of the elder members who found his egotism intolerable and who disapproved of his open bisexuality.

Crowley was unapologetic. He soon despaired of learning the ageless secrets from his elders on finding that the membership was composed largely of former freemasons who were as dogmatic in their rituals as any organized religion or private club. They in turn resisted his persistent demands to be initiated into the inner Second Order to which he believed himself entitled and in 1904 in a fit of pique he disregarded the oath of secrecy he had sworn before the brotherhood and dragged the Order's leader S. L. MacGregor Mathers into open court to the amusement of the tabloid press and their scandal-hungry readers. The resulting publicity led to the dissolution of the Golden Dawn to the revulsion of his former associates, who never forgave him for going against the central tenet of their magical craft, which required initiates "To Know, To Dare, To Will and To Remain Silent".

A year after joining the Golden Dawn, Crowley had purchased the Scottish estate Boleskine House on the shore of Loch Lomand and declared

himself "Laird of Boleskine". He intended to make it his private sanctuary where he could perform ceremonial magic far from prying eyes. But he was too restless to settle and was soon on his travels, journeying to Mexico, Ceylon, Burma and India, where he studied Yoga and in 1902 attempted an ascent of K2 (Kanchenjunga), the world's third-highest mountain in the company of the eminent climber Oscar Eckenstein.

From Nepal, he made his way to Paris where he established himself as a painter, becoming acquainted with sculptor Auguste Rodin and befriending Gerald Kelly, a future President of the Royal Academy. On returning to Boleskine, he became enamoured of Kelly's recently widowed sister Rose, an emotionally unstable young woman whose family was intent on arranging a second marriage of convenience. She begged Crowley to help her and he agreed to elope with her. They were married on 12 August, 1903. During their honeymoon in Cairo, Rose demonstrated an unexpected ability as a medium, channelling the text of what would comprise the first three chapters of *The Book of the Law* in April 1904.

Crowley claimed it had been partly dictated by the Egyptian God Horus and the remainder by his own guardian angel Aiwass. It was to form the basis of his new religion, Thelema, but this found few converts at the time. It became a cult text during the occult revival of the late 1960s when its appeal to "take your fill and will of love as ye will, when and with whom ye will" was adopted by the hippies who interpreted it as an endorsement of Free Love. For this reason, Crowley appears on the cover of The Beatles' *Sgt Pepper* album along with Gandhi and W. C. Fields among others. A decade later in the cynical 1970s, it was adopted as the credo of the Church of Satan, which saw its advocacy of self-gratification and disregard for the sufferings of one's fellow man as a validation of their own nihilistic philosophy.

But Rose's usefulness was short-lived and she became an alcoholic after she had given birth to their "magical child", which died in infancy. A second child survived, but Crowley had no interest in her, cruelly predicting that the little girl, Lola Zaza (1907–1990), would become an "ordinary little whore". He had her mother committed to an asylum in 1911, two years after he divorced her. Rose died there in 1932.

Relieved of any responsibility he might have felt towards his wife and child, Crowley was free to pursue "The Great Work" which he had begun during his third year in Cambridge and which he defined as the process of "becoming a Spiritual Being free from the constraints, accidents and deceptions of material existence". [*Magick In Theory and Practice*]

His wilful disregard for those he considered had outlived their usefulness was, however, no hindrance to his progress as a magician. He soon attracted a circle of slavishly devoted admirers who were seduced by his charismatic personality and an ideology which centred on the psychic energy generated during the sexual act.

Crowley was not the only modern magician to advocate the harnessing of one's vital life force for magical purposes. He shared this conviction with the German Ordo Templis Orientis, who in 1912 were incensed to see their secret rites and doctrine published in Crowley's privately printed periodical *The Equinox* and *The Book of Lies* (1912 or 1913). The dispute was settled out of the public gaze, with Crowley being granted permission to set up a branch of the OTO in Britain, which provided an official endorsement of his magical activities and helped to attract new devotees.

The Book of Lies is arguably the most mystifying, exasperating and ultimately rewarding magical text he wrote. Essentially an initiation manual for "Babes of the Abyss", it consists of 93 single page "chapters" containing secrets and insights into the nature of reality which only reveal themselves with intense study and contemplation: Zen-like *koans* which frustrate and fascinate in equal measure but promise to reveal universal truths depending on how hard the reader is prepared to work at untangling the wilfully obscure cryptic clues.

When war was declared in 1914, Crowley decamped for America where he remained for five years, spreading anti-British propaganda to spite the country which had refused to recognize his peculiar genius. In exile, he penned his most accomplished and compelling novel *Moonchild* (1917), which centres on the struggle within a sect of white and black magicians for the soul of a young girl destined to give birth to the avatar of a new age. All of the major characters are thinly disguised portraits of his friends and adversaries, while Crowley himself appears as the girl's seducer, white magician Cyril Grey. Its chief purpose was to

disseminate its author's occult philosophy, though for a fuller understanding of the book it is necessary to have a working knowledge of
Crowley's theories and a familiarity with esoteric concepts. It failed to
find a publisher and remained among Crowley's manuscripts until 1929,
when small press publisher Mandrake Press offered to issue it. When
they floundered, Crowley stepped in to self-finance its publication, but
it did not sell and Mandrake Press folded the following year.

By war's end, he had spent the last of the family fortune and was
sponging off friends who soon tired of his unrelenting demands for funds
and his boorish behaviour.

Determined to establish himself as an avatar of the New Age, he
emigrated to Sicily in 1920 with his clique of admiring disciples and there
established "The Abbey of Thelema" in an old farmhouse in Cefalu. It
was there that he wrote his commentary on *The Book of the Law* and also
the fevered, semi-biographical confession *Diary of a Drug Fiend* (1922).

Thelema was a sect over which he could be sure to exercise
unchallenged authority, and assume the role he was born to play – the
dark guru and messiah for the New Age of Horus, the age of cynicism,
self-obsession and glorious excess, which he proclaimed would dawn in
the latter half of the 20th century.

There was a lively atmosphere in Sicily to say the least, with his two
mistresses, Leah Hirsig (whom he named "the Ape of Thoth") and Ninette
Shumway (his former housekeeper) often coming to blows to the evident
amusement of their lover and spiritual guru. Their feud intensified when
guests began to arrive at the "Abbey" and the male acolytes offered to
share their wives with the master. Crowley had a talent for attracting
self-destructive personalities to him, but he found himself powerless to
prevent inevitable tragedy when one young disciple, Raoul Loveday, drank
the blood of a sacrificed cat and died on 16 February 1923. The Abbey
was immediately closed on the orders of Mussolini and its inhabitants
deported. It was this incident which earned Crowley the title of "the
wickedest man in the world", a reputation he exploited for the last twenty
years of his life.

Those years were blighted by an increasing dependency on drugs and
alcohol and desperate attempts to fund his habits and fend off bankruptcy.

Abandoning Leah and their 5-year-old chain-smoking son Dionysus in Tunis along with Ninette and an infant daughter he had sired, he headed for France. He had no scruples about leaving his nearest and dearest. His only obligation, he declared, was to himself and completion of the Great Work.

In Paris, he performed a rite that was to have been the consummation of his magical career – an invocation of Pan. But when he and his assistant failed to reappear the morning after the ceremony, his anxious followers broke down the door and found the assistant dead and Crowley cowering in a corner gibbering. He never recovered and retired to Hastings on Britain's southeast coast where he lived in a seedy boarding house, a shadow of his former self and allegedly frightened of the dark. He died on 1 December 1947. His final words were "I am perplexed".

A practising magician of my acquaintance once remarked that Crowley had put "just enough chocolate in his books to make them taste like chocolate cake" but also pitted them with traps to ensnare the uninitiated. Such tactics are not the work of a true teacher, but rather of one who jealously guards his secrets. But Crowley's masterful generating of his own image has ensured that he continues to exert a profound and lasting effect on those seeking forbidden knowledge

But it is Crowley's enduring and pervading influence on popular culture and specifically rock music, which has ensured his name lived on into the Age of Horus and beyond. Both Black Sabbath and Led Zeppelin, the two leviathans of Heavy Rock, paid homage to Crowley in song and even David Bowie, who professed no particular interest in the occult, name-checked Crowley in an early song 'Quicksand' (1970). Zeppelin guitarist Jimmy Page became so obsessed with Crowley that he bought Boleskine House and spent a fortune acquiring the largest collection of original Crowley manuscripts and first editions in private hands.

Crowley's wilful disregard for the secrecy of the magical orders to which he belonged led to his estrangement from occult circles, but had he not done so future generations would have been deprived of the texts which are collected here.

—**Paul Roland**

DIARY OF A DRUG FIEND

TO ALOSTRAEL
Virgin Guardian of the Sangraal in
the Abbey of Thelema in "Telepylus"

and to

ASTARTE LULU PANTHEA
its youngest member, I dedicate this story
of its Herculean labours toward releasing
Mankind from every form of bondage.

PREFACE

This is a true story.

It has been rewritten only so far as was necessary to conceal personalities.

It is a terrible story; but it is also a story of hope and of beauty.

It reveals with startling clearness the abyss on which our civilisation trembles.

But the self-same Light illuminates the path of humanity: it is our own fault if we go over the brink.

This story is also true not only of one kind of human weakness, but (by analogy) of all kinds; and for all alike there is but one way of salvation.

As Glanvil says: Man is not subjected to the angels, nor even unto death utterly, save through the weakness of his own feeble will.

Do what thou wilt shall be the whole of the Law.

—Aleister Crowley

CONTENTS

BOOK I
PARADISO

CHAPTER I
A KNIGHT OUT

Yes, I certainly was feeling depressed.

I don't think that this was altogether the reaction of the day. Of course, there always is a reaction after the excitement of a flight; but the effect is more physical than moral. One doesn't talk. One lies about and smokes and drinks champagne.

No, I was feeling quite a different kind of rotten. I looked at my mind, as the better class of flying man soon learns to do, and I really felt ashamed of myself. Take me for all in all, I was one of the luckiest men alive.

War is like a wave; some it rolls over, some it drowns, some it beats to pieces on the shingle; but some it shoots far up the shore on to glistening golden sand out of the reach of any further freaks of fortune.

Let me explain.

My name is Peter Pendragon. My father was a second son; and he had quarrelled with my Uncle Mortimer when they were boys. He was a struggling general practitioner in Norfolk, and had not made things any better for himself by marrying.

However, he scraped together enough to get me some sort of education, and at the outbreak of the war I was twenty-two years old and had just passed my Intermediate for M.D. in the University of London.

Then, as I said, the wave came. My mother went out for the Red Cross, and died in the first year of the war. Such was the confusion that I did not even know about it till over six months later.

My father died of influenza just before the Armistice.

I had gone into the air service; did pretty well, though somehow I was never sure either of myself or of my machine. My squadron commander used to tell me that I should never make a great airman.

"Old thing," he said, "you lack the instinct," qualifying the noun with an entirely meaningless adjective which somehow succeeded in making his sentence highly illuminating.

"Where you get away with it," he said, "is that you have an analytic brain."

Well, I suppose I have. That's how I come to be writing this up. Anyhow, at the end of the war I found myself with a knighthood which I still firmly believe to have been due to a clerical error on the part of some official.

As for Uncle Mortimer, he lived on in his crustacean way; a sulky, rich, morose, old bachelor. We never heard a word of him.

And then, about a year ago, he died; and I found to my amazement that I was sole heir to his five or six thousand a year, and the owner of Barley Grange; which is really an awfully nice place in Kent, quite near enough to be convenient for the prosperous young man about town which I had become; and for the best of it, a piece of artificial water quite large enough for me to use for a waterdrome for my seaplane.

I may not have the instinct for flying, as Cartwright said; but it's the only sport I care about.

Golf? When one has flown over a golf course, those people do look such appalling rotters! Such pigmy solemnities!

Now about my feeling depressed. When the end of the war came, when I found myself penniless, out of a job, utterly spoilt by the war (even if I had had the money) for going on with my hospital, I had developed an entirely new psychology. You know how it feels when you

are fighting duels in the air, you seem to be detached from everything. There is nothing in the Universe but you and the Boche you are trying to pot. There is something detached and god-like about it.

And when I found myself put out on the streets by a grateful country, I became an entirely different animal. In fact, I've often thought that there isn't any "I" at all; that we are simply the means of expression of something else; that when we think we are ourselves, we are simply the victims of a delusion.

Well, bother that! The plain fact is that I had become a desperate wild animal. I was too hungry, so to speak, even to waste any time on thinking bitterly about things.

And then came the letter from the lawyers.

That was another new experience. I had no idea before of the depths to which servility could descend.

"By the way, Sir Peter," said Mr. Wolfe, "it will, of course, take a little while to settle up these matters. It's a very large estate, very large. But I thought that with times as they are, you wouldn't be offended, Sir Peter, if we handed you an open cheque for a thousand pounds just to go on with."

It wasn't till I had got outside his door that I realised how badly he wanted my business. He need not have worried. He had managed poor old Uncle Mortimer's affairs well enough all those years; not likely I should bother to put them in the hands of a new man.

The thing that really pleased me about the whole business was the clause in the will. That old crab had sat in his club all through the war, snapping at everybody he saw; and yet he had been keeping track of what I was doing. He said in the will that he had made me his heir "for the splendid services I had rendered to our beloved country in her hour of need".

That's the true Celtic psychology. When we've all finished talking, there's something that never utters a word, but goes right down through the earth, plumb to the centre.

And now comes the funny part of the business. I discovered to my amazement that the desperate wild animal hunting his job had been after all a rather happy animal in his way, just as the desperate god battling in the air, playing pitch and toss with life and death, had been happy.

Neither of those men could be depressed by misfortune; but the prosperous young man about town was a much inferior creature. Everything more or less bored him, and he was quite definitely irritated by an overdone cutlet. The night I met Lou, I turned into the Cafe Wisteria in a sort of dull, angry stupor. Yet the only irritating incident of the day had been a letter from the lawyers which I had found at my club after flying from Norfolk to Barley Grange and motoring up to town.

Mr. Wolfe had very sensibly advised me to make a settlement of a part of the estate, as against the event of my getting married; and there was some stupid hitch about getting trustees.

I loathe law. It seems to me as if it were merely an elaborate series of obstacles to doing things sensibly. And yet, of course, after all, one must have formalities, just as in flying you have to make arrangements for starting and stopping. But it is a beastly nuisance to have to attend to them.

I thought I would stand myself a little dinner. I hadn't quite enough sense to know that what I really wanted was human companions. There aren't such things. Every man is eternally alone. But when you get mixed up with a fairly decent crowd, you forget that appalling fact for long enough to give your brain time to recover from the acute symptoms of its disease – that of thinking.

My old commander was right. I think a lot too much; so did Shakespeare. That's what worked him up to write those wonderful things about sleep. I've forgotten what they were; but they impressed me at the time. I said to myself, "This old bird knew how dreadful it is to be conscious."

So, when I turned into the cafe, I think the real reason was that I hoped to find somebody there, and talk the night out. People think that talking is a sign of thinking. It isn't, for the most part; on the contrary, it's a mechanical dodge of the body to relieve oneself of the strain of thinking, just as exercising the muscles helps the body to become temporarily unconscious of its weight, its pain, its weariness, and the foreknowledge of its doom.

You see what gloomy thoughts a fellow can have, even when he's Fortune's pet. It's a disease of civilisation. We're in an intermediate stage

between the stupor of the peasant and – something that is not yet properly developed.

I went into the cafe and sat down at one of the marble tables. I had a momentary thrill of joy – it reminded me of France so much – of all those days of ferocious gambling with Death.

I couldn't see a soul I knew. But at least I knew by sight the two men at the next table. Every one knew that grey ferocious wolf – a man built in every line for battle, and yet with a forehead which lifted him clean out of the turmoil. The conflicting elements in his nature had played the devil with him. Jack Fordham was his name. At sixty years of age he was still the most savage and implacable of publicists. "Red in tooth and claw", as Tennyson said. Yet the man had found time to write great literature; and his rough and tumble with the world had not degraded his thought or spoilt his style.

Sitting next him was a weak, good-natured, working journalist named Vernon Gibbs. He wrote practically the whole of a weekly paper – had done, year after year with the versatility of a practised pen and the mechanical perseverance of an instrument which has been worn by practice into perfect easiness.

Yet the man had a mind for all that. Some instinct told him that he had been meant for better things. The result had been that he had steadily become a heavier and heavier drinker.

I learnt at the hospital that seventy-five per cent of the human body is composed of water; but in this case, as in the old song, it must have been that he was a relation of the McPherson who had a son,

> "That married Noah's daughter
> And nearly spoilt the flood
> By drinking all the water. And this he would have done,
> I really do believe it,
> But had that mixture been
> Three parts or more Glen Livet."

The slight figure of a young-old man with a bulbous nose to detract from his otherwise remarkable beauty, spoilt though it was by years of

insane passions, came into the cafe. His cold blue eyes were shifty and malicious. One got the impression of some filthy creature of the darkness – a raider from another world looking about him for something to despoil. At his heels lumbered his jackal, a huge, bloated, verminous creature like a cockroach, in shabby black clothes, ill-fitting, unbrushed and stained, his linen dirty, his face bloated and pimpled, a horrible evil leer on his dripping mouth, with its furniture like a bombed graveyard.

The cafe sizzled as the men entered. They were notorious, if nothing else, and the leader was the Earl of Bumble. Every one seemed to scent some mischief in the air. The earl came up to the table next to mine, and stopped deliberately short. A sneer passed across his lips. He pointed to the two men.

"Drunken Bardolph and Ancient Pistol," he said, with his nose twitching with anger.

Jack Fordham was not behindhand with the repartee.

"Well roared, Bottom," he replied calmly, as pat as if the whole scene had been rehearsed beforehand.

A dangerous look came into the eyes of the insane earl. He took a pace backwards and raised his stick. But Fordham, old campaigner that he was, had anticipated the gesture. He had been to the Western States in his youth; and what he did not know about scrapping was not worth being known. In particular, he was very much alive to the fact that an unarmed man sitting behind a fixed table has no chance against a man with a stick in the open.

He slipped out like a cat. Before Bumble could bring down his cane, the old man had dived under his guard and taken the lunatic by the throat.

There was no sort of a fight. The veteran shook his opponent like a bull-dog; and, shifting his grip, flung him to the ground with one tremendous throw. In less than two seconds the affair was over. Fordham was kneeling on the chest of the defeated bully, who whined and gasped and cried for mercy, and told the man twenty years his senior, whom he had deliberately provoked into the fight, that he mustn't hurt him because they were such old friends!

The behaviour of a crowd in affairs of this kind always seems to me very singular. Every one, or nearly every one, seems to start to interfere; and nobody actually does so.

But this matter threatened to prove more serious. The old man had really lost his temper. It was odds that he would choke the life out of the cur under his knee.

I had just enough presence of mind to make way for the head waiter, a jolly, burly Frenchman, who came pushing into the circle. I even lent him a hand to pull Fordham off the prostrate form of his antagonist.

A touch was enough. The old man recovered his temper in a second, and calmly went back to his table with no more sign of excitement than shouting, "Sixty to forty, sixty to forty."

"I'm on," cried the voice of a man who had just come in at the end of the cafe and missed the scene by a minute. "But what's the horse?"

I heard the words as a man in a dream; for my attention had suddenly been distracted.

Bumble had made no attempt to get up. He lay there whimpering. I raised my eyes from so disgusting a sight, and found them fixed by two enormous orbs. I did not know at the first moment even that they were eyes. It's a funny thing to say; but the first impression was that they were one of those thoughts that come to one from nowhere when one is flying at ten thousand feet or so. Awfully queer thing, I tell you – reminds one of the atmospherics that one gets in wireless; and they give one a horrible feeling. It is a sort of sinister warning that there is some person or some thing in the Universe outside oneself: and the realisation of that is as frankly frightening as the other realisation, that one is eternally alone, is horrible.

I slipped out of time altogether into eternity. I felt myself in the presence of some tremendous influence for good or evil. I felt as though I had been born – I don't know whether you know what I mean. I can't help it, but I can't put it any different.

It's like this: nothing had ever happened to me in my life before. You know how it is when you come out of ether or nitrous-oxide at the dentist's – you come back to somewhere, a familiar somewhere; but the place from which you have come is nowhere, and yet you have been there.

That is what happened to me.

I woke up from eternity, from infinity, from a state of mind enormously more vital and conscious than anything we know of otherwise, although one can't give it a name, to discover that this nameless thought of nothingness was in reality two black vast spheres in which I saw myself. I had a thought of some vision in a story of the middle ages about a wizard, and slowly, slowly, I slid up out of the deep to recognise that these two spheres were just two eyes. And then it occurred to me – the thought was in the nature of a particularly absurd and ridiculous joke – that these two eyes belonged to a girl's face.

Across the moaning body of the blackmailer, I was looking at the face of a girl that I had never seen before. And I said to myself, "Well, that's all right, I've known you all my life." And when I said to myself "my life", I didn't in the least mean my life as Peter Pendragon, I didn't even mean a life extending through the centuries, I meant a different kind of life – something with which centuries have nothing whatever to do.

And then Peter Pendragon came wholly back to himself with a start, and wondered whether he had not perhaps looked a little rudely at what his common sense assured him was quite an ordinary and not a particularly attractive girl.

My mind was immediately troubled. I went hastily back to my table. And then it seemed to me as if it were hours while the waiters were persuading the earl to his feet.

I sipped my drink automatically. When I looked up the girl had disappeared.

It is a trivial observation enough which I am going to make. I hope at least it will help to clear any one's mind of any idea that I may be an abnormal man.

As a matter of fact, every man is ultimately abnormal, because he is unique. But we can class man in a few series without bothering ourselves much about what each one of them is in himself.

I hope, then, that it will be clearly understood that I am very much like a hundred thousand other young men of my age. I also make the remark, because the essential bearing of it is practically the whole story of this book. And the remark is this, after that great flourish of trumpets:

although I was personally entirely uninterested in what I had witnessed, the depression had vanished from my mind. As the French say, "*Un clou chasse l'autre.*"

I have learnt since then that certain races, particularly the Japanese, have made a definite science starting from this fact. For example, they clap their hands four times "in order to drive away evil spirits". That is, of course, only a figure of speech. What they really do is this: the physical gesture startles the mind out of its lethargy, so that the idea which has been troubling it is replaced by a new one. They have various dodges for securing a new one and making sure that the new one shall be pleasant. More of this later.

What happened is that at this moment my mind was seized with sharp, black anger, entirely objectless. I had at the time not the faintest inkling as to its nature, but there it was. The cafe was intolerable – like a pest-house. I threw a coin on the table, and was astonished to notice that it rolled off. I went out as if the devil were at my heels.

I remember practically nothing of the next half-hour. I felt a kind of forlorn sense of being lost in a world of incredibly stupid and malicious dwarfs.

I found myself in Piccadilly quite suddenly. A voice purred in my ear, "Good old Peter, good old sport, awfully glad I met you – we'll make a night of it."

The speaker was a handsome Welshman still in his prime. Some people thought him one of the best sculptors living. He had, in fact, a following of disciples which I can only qualify as "almost unpleasantly so".

He had no use for humanity at the bottom of his heart, except as convenient shapes which he might model. He was bored and disgusted to find them pretending to be alive. The annoyance had grown until he had got into the habit of drinking a good deal more and a good deal more often than a lesser man might have needed. He was a much bigger man than I was physically, and he took me by the arm almost as if he had been taking me into custody. He poured into my ear an interminable series of rambling reminiscences, each of which appeared to him incredibly mirthful.

For about half a minute I resented him; then I let myself go and found myself soothed almost to slumber by the flow of his talk. A wonderful

man, like an imbecile child nine-tenths of the time, and yet, at the back of it all, one somehow saw the deep night of his mind suffused with faint sparks of his genius.

I had not the slightest idea where he was taking me – I did not care. I had gone to sleep, inside. I woke to find myself sitting in the Cafe Wisteria once more.

The head waiter was excitedly explaining to my companion what a wonderful scene he had missed.

"Mr. Fordham, he nearly kill' ze Lord," he bubbled, wringing his fat hands. "He nearly kill' ze Lord."

Something in the speech tickled my sense of irreverence. I broke into a high-pitched shout of laughter.

"Rotten," said my companion. "Rotten! That fellow Fordham never seems to make a clean job of it anyhow. Say, look here, this is my night out. You go 'way like a good boy, tell all those boys and girls come and have dinner."

The waiter knew well enough who was meant; and presently I found myself shaking hands with several perfect strangers in terms which implied the warmest and most unquenchable affection. It was really rather a distinguished crowd.

One of the men was a fat German Jew, who looked at first sight like a piece of canned pork that has got mislaid too long in the summer. But the less he said the more he did; and what he did is one of the greatest treasures of mankind.

Then there was a voluble, genial man with a shock of grey hair and a queer twisted smile on his face. He looked like a character of Dickens. But he had done more to revitalise the theatre than any other man of his time.

I took a dislike to the women. They seemed so unworthy of the men. Great men seem to enjoy going about with freaks. I suppose it is on the same principle as the old kings used to keep fools and dwarfs to amuse them. "Some men are born great, some achieve greatness, some have greatness thrust upon them."

But whichever way it is, the burden is usually too heavy for their shoulders.

You remember Frank Harris's story of the Ugly Duckling? If you don't, you'd better get busy and do it.

That's really what's so frightful in flying – the fear of oneself, the feeling that one has got out of one's class, that all the old kindly familiar things below have turned into hard monstrous enemies ready to smash you if you touch them.

The first of these women was a fat, bold, red-headed slut. She reminded me of a white maggot. She exuded corruption. She was pompous, pretentious, and stupid. She gave herself out as a great authority on literature; but all her knowledge was parrot, and her own attempts in that direction the most deplorably dreary drivel that ever had been printed even by the chattering clique which she financed. On her bare shoulder was the hand of a short, thin woman with a common, pretty face and a would-be babyish manner. She was a German woman of the lowest class. Her husband was an influential Member of Parliament. People said that he lived on her earnings. There were even darker whispers. Two or three pretty wise birds had told me they thought it was she, and not poor little Mati Hara, who tipped off the Tanks to the Boche.

Did I mention that my sculptor's name was Owen? Well, it was, is, and will be while the name of Art endures. He was supporting himself unsteadily with one hand on the table, while with the other he put his guests in their seats. I thought of a child playing with dolls.

As the first four sat down, I saw two other girls behind them. One I had met before, Violet Beach. She was a queer little thing – Jewish, I fancy. She wore a sheaf of yellow hair fuzzed out like a Struwwelpeter, and a violent vermilion dress – in case any one should fail to observe her. It was her affectation to be an Apache, so she wore an old cricket cap down on one eye, and a stale cigarette hung from her lip. But she had a certain talent for writing, and I was very glad indeed to meet her again. I admit I am always a little shy with strangers. As we shook hands, I heard her saying in her curious voice, high-pitched and yet muted, as if she had something wrong with her throat:

"Want you to meet Miss –"

I didn't get the name; I can never hear strange words. As it turned out, before forty-eight hours had passed, I discovered that it was Laleham

– and then again that it wasn't. But I anticipate – don't try to throw me out of my stride. All in good time.

In the meanwhile I found I was expected to address her as Lou. "Unlimited Lou" was her nickname among the initiates.

Now what I am anxious for everybody to understand is simply this. There's hardly anybody who understands the way his mind works; no two minds are alike, as Horace or some old ass said; and, anyhow, the process of thinking is hardly ever what we imagine.

So, instead of recognising the girl as the owner of the eyes which had gripped me so strangely an hour earlier, the fact of the recognition simply put me off the recognition – I don't know if I'm making myself clear. I mean that the plain fact refused to come to the surface. My mind seethed with questions. Where had I seen her before?

And here's another funny thing. I don't believe that I should have ever recognised her by sight. What put me on the track was the grip of her hand, though I had never touched it in my life before.

Now don't think that I'm going off the deep end about this. Don't dismiss me as a mystic-monger. Look back each one into your own lives, and if you can't find half a dozen incidents equally inexplicable, equally unreasonable, equally repugnant to the better regulated type of mid-Victorian mind, the best thing you can do is to sleep with your forefathers. So that's that. Goodnight.

I told you that Lou was "quite an ordinary and not a particularly attractive girl". Remember that this was the first thought of my "carnal mind" which, as St. Paul says, is "enmity against God".

My real first impression had been the tremendous psychological experience for which all words are inadequate.

Seated by her side, at leisure to look while she babbled, I found my carnal mind reversed on appeal. She was certainly not a pretty girl from the standpoint of a music-hall audience. There was something indefinably Mongolian about her face. The planes were flat; the cheek-bones high; the eyes oblique; the nose wide, short, and vital; the mouth a long, thin, rippling curve like a mad sunset. The eyes were tiny and green, with a piquant elfin expression. Her hair was curiously colourless; it was very abundant; she had wound great ropes about her head. It reminded me of

the armature of a dynamo. It produced a weird effect – this mingling of the savage Mongol with the savage Norseman type. Her strange hair fascinated me. It was that delicate flaxen hue, so fine – no, I don't know how to tell you about it, I can't think of it without getting all muddled up.

One wondered how she was there. One saw at a glance that she didn't belong to that set. Refinement, aristocracy almost, were like a radiance about her tiniest gesture. She had no affectation about being an artist. She happened to like these people in exactly the same way as a Methodist old maid in Balham might take an interest in natives of Tonga, and so she went about with them. Her mother didn't mind. Probably, too, the way things are nowadays, her mother didn't matter.

You mustn't think that we were any of us drunk, except old Owen. As a matter of fact, all I had had was a glass of white wine. Lou had touched nothing at all. She prattled on like the innocent child she was, out of the sheer mirth of her heart. In an ordinary way, I suppose, I should have drunk a lot more than I did. And I didn't eat much either. Of course, I know now what it was – that much-derided phenomenon, love at first sight.

Suddenly we were interrupted. A tall man was shaking hands across the table with Owen. Instead of using any of the ordinary greetings, he said in a very low, clear voice, very clear and vibrant, as though tense with some inscrutable passion:

"Do what thou wilt shall be the whole of the Law."

There was an uneasy movement in the group. In particular, the German woman seemed distressed by the man's mere presence.

I looked up. Yes, I could understand well enough the change in the weather. Owen was saying: "That's all right, that's all right, that's exactly what I do. You come and see my new group. I'll do another sketch of you – same day, same time. That's all right."

Somebody introduced the newcomer – Mr. King Lamus – and murmured our names.

"Sit down right here," said Owen, "what you need is a drink. I know you perfectly well; I've known you for years and years and years, and I know you've done a good day's work, and you've earned a drink. Sit right down and I'll get the waiter."

I looked at Lamus, who had not uttered a word since his original greeting. There was something appalling in his eyes; they didn't focus on the foreground. I was only an incident of utter insignificance in an illimitable landscape. His eyes were parallel; they were looking at infinity. Nothing mattered to him. I hated the beast!

By this time the waiter had approached.

"Sorry, sir," he said to Owen, who had ordered a '65 brandy.

It appeared that it was now eight hours forty-three minutes thirteen and three-fifth seconds past noon. I don't know what the law is; nobody in England knows what the law is – not even the fools that make the laws. We are not under the laws and do not enjoy the liberties which our fathers bequeathed us; we are under a complex and fantastic system of police administration nearly as pernicious as anything even in America.

"Don't apologise," said Lamus to the waiter in a tone of icy detachment. "This is the freedom we fought for."

I was entirely on the side of the speaker. I hadn't wanted a drink all evening, but now I was told I couldn't have one, I wanted to raid their damn cellars and fight the Metropolitan Police and go up in my 'plane and drop a few bombs on the silly old House of Commons. And yet I was in no sort of sympathy with the man. The contempt of his tone irritated me. He was inhuman, somehow; that was what antagonised me.

He turned to Owen.

"Better come round to my studio," he drawled; "I have a machine gun trained on Scotland Yard." Owen rose with alacrity.

"I shall be delighted to see any of you others," continued Lamus. "I should deplore it to the day of my death if I were the innocent means of breaking up so perfect a party."

The invitation sounded like an insult. I went red behind the ears; I could only just command myself enough to make a formal apology of some sort.

As a matter of fact, there was a very curious reaction in the whole party. The German Jew got up at once – nobody else stirred. Rage boiled in my heart. I understood instantly what had taken place. The intervention of Lamus had automatically divided the party into giants and dwarfs; and I was one of the dwarfs.

During the dinner, Mrs. Webster, the German woman, had spoken hardly at all. But as soon as the three men had turned their backs, she remarked acidly:

"I don't think we're dependent for our drinks on Mr. King Lamus. Let's go round to the Smoking Dog."

Everybody agreed with alacrity. The suggestion seemed to have relieved the unspoken tension.

We found ourselves in taxis, which for some inscrutable reason are still allowed to ply practically unchecked in the streets of London. While eating and breathing and going about are permitted, we shall never be a really righteous race!

CHAPTER II
OVER THE TOP!

It was only about a quarter of an hour before we reached "The Dog"; but the time passed heavily. I had been annexed by the white maggot. Her presence made me feel as if I were already a corpse. It was the limit.

But I think the ordeal served to bring up in my mind some inkling of the true nature of my feeling for Lou.

The Smoking Dog, now ingloriously extinct, was a night club decorated by a horrible little cad who spent his life pushing himself into art and literature.

The dancing room was a ridiculous, meaningless, gaudy, bad imitation of Klimt.

Damn it all, I may not be a great flyer, but I am a fresh-air man. I detest these near-artists with their poses and their humbug and their swank. I hate shams.

I found myself in a state of furious impatience before five minutes had passed. Mrs. Webster and Lou had not arrived. Ten minutes – twenty – I fell into a blind rage, drank heavily of the vile liquor with which the place was stinking, and flung myself with I don't know what woman into the dance.

A shrill-voiced Danish siren, the proprietress, was screaming abuse at one of her professional entertainers – some long, sordid, silly story of sexual jealousy, I suppose. The band was deafening. The fine edge of my sense was dulled. It was in a sort of hot nightmare that I saw, through the smoke and the stink of the club, the evil smile of Mrs. Webster.

Small as the woman was, she seemed to fill the doorway. She preoccupied the attention in the same way as a snake would have done. She saw me at once, and ran almost into my arms excitedly. She whispered something in my ear. I didn't hear it.

The club had suddenly been, so to speak, struck dumb. Lou was coming through the door. Over her shoulders was an opera cloak of deep rich purple edged with gold, the garment of an empress, or (shall I say?) of a priestess.

The whole place stopped still to look at her. And I had thought she was not beautiful!

She did not walk upon the ground. "*Vera incessu paluit dea,*" as we used to say at school. And as she paced she chanted from that magnificent litany of Captain J. F. C. Fuller, "Oh Thou golden sheaf of desires, that art bound by a fair wisp of poppies adore thee, Evoe! I adore thee, I A O!"

She sang full-throated, with a male quality in her voice. Her beauty was so radiant that my mind ran to the breaking of dawn after a long night flight.

"In front the sun climbs slow, how slowly, but westward, look! the land is bright!"

As if in answer to my thought, her voice rolled forth again:

"O Thou golden wine of the sun, that art poured over the dark breasts of night! I adore Thee, Evoe! I adore Thee, I A O!"

The first part of the adoration was in a sort of Gregorian chant varying with the cadence of the words. But the chorus always came back to the same thing.

I adore Thee, Evoe! I adore Thee, I A O!

EE-AH-OH gives the enunciation of the last word. Every vowel is drawn out as long as possible. It seemed as if she were trying to get the last cubic millimetre of air out of her lungs every time she sang it.

"O Thou crimson vintage of life, that art poured into the jar of the grave! I adore Thee, Evoe!

I adore Thee, I A O!"

Lou reached the table, with its dirty, crazy cloth, at which we were sitting. She looked straight into my eyes, though I am sure she did not see me.

"O Thou red cobra of desire, that art unhooded by the hands of girls! I adore Thee, Evoe! I adore Thee, I A O!"

She went back from us like a purple storm-cloud, sun-crested, torn from the breasts of the morning by some invisible lightning.

"O Thou burning sword of passion, that art torn on the anvil of flesh! I adore Thee, Evoe! I adore Thee, I A O!"

A wave of almost insane excitement swept through the club. It was like the breaking out of anti-aircraft guns. The band struck up a madder jazz.

The dancers raved with more tumultuous and breathless fury.

Lou had advanced again to our table. We three were detached from the world. Around us rang the shrieking laughter of the crazy crowd. Lou seemed to listen. She broke out once more.

"O Thou mad whirlwind of laughter, that art meshed in the wild locks of folly! I adore Thee, Evoe! I adore Thee, I A O!"

I realised with nauseating clarity that Mrs. Webster was pouring into my ears an account of the character and career of King Lamus.

"I don't know how he dares to come to England at all," she said. "He lives in a place called Telepylus, wherever that is. He's over a hundred years old, in spite of his looks. He's been everywhere, and done everything, and every step he treads is smeared with blood. He's the most evil and dangerous man in London. He's a vampire, he lives on ruined lives."

I admit I had the heartiest abhorrence for the man. But this fiercely bitter denunciation, of one who was evidently a close friend of two of the world's greatest artists, did not make his case look blacker. I was not impressed, frankly, with Mrs. Webster as an authority on other people's conduct.

"O Thou Dragon – prince of the air, that art drunk on the blood of the sunsets! I adore Thee, Evoe! I adore Thee, I A O! "

A wild pang of jealousy stabbed me. It was a livid, demoniac spasm. For some reason or other I had connected this verse of Lou's mysterious chant with the personality of King Lamus.

Gretel Webster understood. She insinuated another dose of venom.

"Oh yes, Mr. Basil King Lamus is quite the ladies' man. He fascinates them with a thousand different tricks. Lou is dreadfully in love with him."

Once again the woman had made a mistake. I resented her reference to Lou. I don't remember what I answered. Part of it was to the effect that Lou didn't seem to have been very much injured.

Mrs. Webster smiled her subtlest smile.

"I quite agree," she said silkily, "Lou is the most beautiful woman in London tonight."

"O Thou fragrance of sweet flowers, that art wafted over blue fields of air! I adore Thee, Evoe! I adore Thee, I A O!"

The state of the girl was extraordinary; it was as if she possessed two personalities in their fullest possibilities – the divine and the human. She was intensely conscious of all that was going on around her, absolute mistress of herself and of her environment; yet at the same time she was lost in some unearthly form of rapture of a kind which, while essentially unintelligible to me, reminded me of certain strange and fragmentary experiences that I had had while flying.

I suppose every one has read *The Psychology of Flying* by L. de Giberne Sieveking. All I need do is to remind you of what he says:

"All types of men who fly are conscious of this very obscure, subtle difference that it has wrought in them. Very few know exactly what it is. Hardly any of them can express what they feel. And none of them would admit it if they could. . . . One realises without any formation into words how that one is oneself, and that each one is entirely separate and can never enter into the recesses of another, which are his foundation of individual life."

One feels oneself out of all relation with things, even the most essential. And yet one is aware at the same time that everything of which one has ever been aware is a picture invented by one's own mind. The Universe is the looking-glass of the soul.

In that state one understands all sorts of nonsense.

"O Thou foursquare Crown of Nothing, that circlest the destruction of Worlds! I adore Thee, Evoe! I adore Thee, I A O!"

I flushed with rage, understanding enough to know what Lou must be feeling as she rolled forth those passionate, senseless words from her volcanic mouth. Gretel's suggestion trickled into my brain.

"This beastly alcohol brutalises men. Why is Lou so superb? She has breathed the pure snow of Heaven into her nostrils."

"O Thou snow-white chalice of Love, that art filled up with the red lusts of man! I adore Thee, Evoe! I adore Thee, I A O!"

I tingled and shivered as she sang; and then something, I hardly know what, made me turn and look into the face of Gretel Webster. She was sitting at my right; her left hand was beneath the table, and she was looking at it. I followed her glance.

In the little quadrilateral of the veins whose lower apex is between the first and middle fingers, was a tiny heap of sparkling dust. Nothing I had ever seen before had so attracted me. The sheer bright infinite beauty of the stuff! I had seen it before of course, often enough, at the hospital; but this was quite a different thing. It was set off by its environment as a diamond is by its setting. It seemed alive. It sparkled intensely. It was like nothing else in Nature, unless it be those feathery crystals, wind-blown, that glisten on the lips of crevasses.

What followed sticks in my memory as if it were a conjurer's trick. I don't know by what gesture she constrained me. But her hand slowly rose not quite to the level of the table; and my face, hot, flushed, angry and eager, had bent down towards it. It seemed pure instinct, though I have little doubt now that it was the result of an unspoken suggestion. I drew the little heap of powder through my nostrils with one long breath. I felt even then like a choking man in a coal mine released at the last moment, filling his lungs for the first time with oxygen.

I don't know whether this is a common experience. I suspect that my medical training and reading, and hearing people talk, and the effect of all those ghoulish articles in the newspapers had something to do with it.

On the other hand, we must make a good deal of allowance, I think, for such an expert as Gretel Webster. No doubt she was worth her wage

to the Boche. No doubt she had picked me out for part of "Die Rache". I had downed some pretty famous flyers.

But none of these thoughts occurred to me at the time. I do not think I have explained with sufficient emphasis the mental state to which I had been reduced by the appearance of Lou. She had become so far beyond my dreams – the unattainable.

Leaving out of account the effect of the alcohol, this had left me with an intolerable depression. There was something brutish, something of the baffled rat, in my consciousness.

"O Thou vampire Queen of the Flesh, wound as a snake around the throats of men! I adore Thee, Evoe! I adore Thee, I A O!"

Was she thinking of Gretel or of herself? Her beauty had choked me, strangled me, torn my throat out. I had become insane with dull, harsh lust. I hated her. But as I raised my head; as the sudden, the instantaneous madness of cocaine swept from my nostrils to my brain – that's a line of poetry, but I can't help it – get on! – the depression lifted from my mind like the sun coming out of the clouds.

I heard as in a dream the rich, ripe voice of Lou.

"O Thou fierce whirlpool of passion, that art sucked up by the mouth of the sun! I adore Thee, Evoe! I adore Thee, I A O!"

The whole thing was different – I understood what she was saying, I was part of it. I recognised, for one swift second, the meaning of my previous depression. It was my sense of inferiority to her. Now I was her man, her mate, her master!

I rose to catch her by the waist but she whirled away down the floor of the club like an autumn leaf before the storm. I caught the glance of Gretel Webster's eyes. I saw them glitter with triumphant malice; and for a moment she and Lou and cocaine and myself were all inextricably interlocked in a tangled confusion of ruinous thought.

But my physical body was lifting me. It was the same old, wild exhilaration that one gets from rising from the ground on one's good days. I found myself in the middle of the floor without knowing how I had got there. I, too, was walking on air. Lou turned, her mouth a scarlet orb, as I have seen the sunset over Belgium, over the crinkled line of shore, over the dim blue mystic curve of sea and sky; with the thought

in my mind beating in tune with my excited heart. We didn't miss the arsenal this time. I was the arsenal too. I had exploded. I was the slayer and the slain. And there sailed Lou across the sky to meet me.

"O Thou outrider of the Sun, that spurrest the bloody flanks of the wind! I adore Thee, Evoe! I adore Thee, I A O!"

We came into each other's arms with the inevitableness of gravitation. We were the only two people in the Universe – she and I. The only force that existed in the Universe was the attraction between us. The force with which we came together set us spinning. We went up and down the floor of the club; but, of course, it wasn't the floor of the club, there wasn't the club, there wasn't anything at all except a delirious feeling that one was everything, and had to get on with everything. One was the Universe eternally whirling. There was no possibility of fatigue; one's energy was equal to one's task.

"O Thou dancer with gilded nails, that unbraidest the star hair of the night! I adore Thee, Evoe! I adore Thee, I A O!"

Lou's slim, lithe body lay in my arm. It sounds absurd, but she reminded me of a light overcoat. Her head hung back, the heavy coils of hair came loose. All of a sudden the band stopped. For a second the agony was indescribable. It seemed like annihilation. I was seized with an absolute revulsion against the whole of my surroundings. I whispered like a man in furious haste who must get something vital done before he dies, some words to the effect that I couldn't stick this beastly place any longer –

"Let's get some air."

She answered neither yes nor no. I had been wasting words to speak to her at all.

"O Thou bird-sweet river of Love, that warblest through the pebbly gorge of Life! I adore Thee, Evoe! I adore Thee, I A O!"

Her voice had sunk to a clear murmur. We found ourselves in the street. The chucker-out hailed us a taxi. I stopped her song at last. My mouth was on her mouth. We were driving in the chariot of the Sun through the circus of the Universe. We didn't know where we were going, and we didn't care. We had no sense of time at all. There was a sequence of sensations; but there was no means of regulating them. It was as if one's mental clock had suddenly gone mad.

I have no gauge of time, subjectively speaking, but it must have been a long while before our mouths separated, for as this happened I recognised the fact that we were very far from the club.

She spoke to me for the first time. Her voice thrilled dark unfathomable deeps of being. I tingled in every fibre. And what she said was this:

"Your kiss is bitter with cocaine."

It is quite impossible to give those who have no experience of these matters any significance of what she said.

It was a boiling cauldron of wickedness that had suddenly bubbled over. Her voice rang rich with hellish glee. It stimulated me to male intensity. I caught her in my arms more fiercely. The world went black before my eyes. I perceived nothing any more. I can hardly even say that I felt. I was Feeling itself! I was O the possibilities of Feeling fulfilled to the uttermost. Yet, coincident with this, my body went on automatically with its own private affairs.

She was escaping me. Her face eluded mine.

"O Thou storm-drunk breath of the winds, that pant in the bosom of the mountains! I adore Thee, Evoe! I adore Thee, I A O!"

Her breast sobbed out its song with weird intensity. I understood in a flash that this was her way of resistance. She was trying to insist to herself that she was a cosmic force; that she was not a woman at all; that a man meant nothing to her. She fought desperately against me, sliding so serpent-like about the bounds of space. Of course, it was really the taxi – but I didn't know it then, and I'm not quite sure of it now.

"I wish to God," I said to myself in a fury, "I had one more sniff of that Snow. I'd show her!"

At that moment she threw me off as if I had been a feather. I felt myself all of a sudden no more good. Quite unaccountably I had collapsed, and I found myself, to my amazement, knocking out a little pile of cocaine from a ten-gramme bottle which had been in my trousers' pocket, on to my hand, and sniffing it up into my nostrils with greedy relish.

Don't ask me how it got there. I suppose Gretel Webster must have done it somehow. My memory is an absolute blank. That's one of the funny things about cocaine. You never know quite what trick it is going to play you.

I was reminded of the American professor who boasted that he had a first-class memory whose only defect was that it wasn't reliable.

I am equally unable to tell you whether the fresh supply of the drug increased my powers, or whether Lou had simply tired of teasing me, but of her own accord she writhed into my arms; her hands and mouth were heavy on my heart. There's some more poetry – that's the way it takes one – rhythm seems to come natural – everything is one grand harmony. It is impossible that anything should be out of tune. The voice of Lou seemed to come from an enormous distance, a deep, low, sombre chant –

"O Thou low moan of fainting maids, that art caught up in the strong sobs of Love! I adore Thee, Evoe! I adore Thee, I A O!"

That was it – her engine and my engine for the first time working together! All the accidents had disappeared. There was nothing but the unison of two rich racing rhythms.

You know how it is when you are flying – you see a speck in the air. You can't tell by your eyes if it is your Brother Boche coming to pot you, or one of our own or one of the allied 'planes. But you can tell them apart, foe from friend, by the different beat of their engines. So one comes to apprehend a particular rhythm as sympathetic – another as hostile.

So here were Lou and I flying together beyond the bounds of eternity, side by side; her low, persistent throb in perfect second to my great galloping boom.

Things of this sort take place outside time and space. It is quite wrong to say that what happened in the taxi ever began or ended. What happened was that our attention was distracted from the eternal truth of this essential marriage of our souls by the chauffeur, who had stopped the taxi and opened the door.

"Here we are, sir," he said, with a grin.

Sir Peter Pendragon and Lou Laleham automatically reappeared. Before all things, decorum!

The shock bit the incident deeply into my mind. I remember with the utmost distinctness paying the man off, and then being lost in absolute blank wonder as to how it happened that we were where we were. Who had given the address to the man, and where were we?

I can only suppose that, consciously or subconsciously, Lou had done it, for she showed no embarrassment in pressing the electric bell. The door opened immediately. I was snowed under by an avalanche of crimson light that poured from a vast studio.

Lou's voice soared high and clear:

"O Thou scarlet dragon of flame, enmeshed in the web of a spider! I adore Thee, Evoe! I adore Thee, I A O!"

A revulsion of feeling rushed over me like a storm for in the doorway, with Lou's arms round his neck, was the tall, black, sinister figure of King Lamus.

"I knew you wouldn't mind our dropping in, although it is so late," she was saying.

It would have been perfectly simple for him to acquiesce with a few conventional words. Instead, he was pontifical.

"There are four gates to one palace; the floor of that palace is of silver and gold; lapis-lazuli and jasper are there; and all rare scents; jasmine and rose, and the emblems of death. Let him enter in turn or at once the four gates; let him stand on the floor of the palace."

I was unfathomably angry. Why must the man always act like a cad or a clown? But there was nothing to do but to accept the situation and walk in politely.

He shook hands with me formally, yet with greater intensity than is customary between well-bred strangers in England. And as he did so, he looked me straight in the face. His deadly inscrutable eyes burned their way clean through to the back of my brain and beyond. Yet his words were entirely out of keeping with his actions.

"What does the poet say?" he said loftily. "Rather a joke to fill up on coke – or words to that effect, Sir Peter."

How in the devil's name did he know what I had been taking?

"Men who know things have no right to go about the world," something said irritably inside myself. But something else obscurely answered it.

"That accounts for what the world has always done – made martyrs of its pioneers."

I felt a little ashamed, to tell the truth; but Lamus put me at my ease. He waved his hand towards a huge arm chair covered with Persian

tapestries. He gave me a cigarette and lighted it for me. He poured out a drink of Benedictine into a huge curved glass, and put it on a little table by my side. I disliked his easy hospitality as much as anything else. I had an uncomfortable feeling that I was a puppet in his hands.

There was only one other person in the room. On a settee covered with leopard skins lay one of the strangest women I had ever seen. She wore a white evening dress with pale yellow roses, and the same flowers were in her hair. She was a half-blood negress from North Africa.

"Miss Fatma Hallaj," said Lamus.

I rose and bowed. But the girl took no notice. She seemed in utter oblivion of sublunary matters. Her skin was of that deep, rich night-sky blue which only very vulgar eyes imagine to be black. The face was gross and sensual, but the brows wide and commanding.

There is no type of intellect so essentially aristocratic as the Egyptian when it happens to be of the rare right strain.

"Don't be offended," said Lamus, in a soft voice, "she includes us all in her sublime disdain."

Lou was sitting on the arm of the couch; her ivory-white, long crooked fingers groping the dark girl's hair. Somehow or other I felt nauseated; I was uneasy, embarrassed. For the first time in my life I didn't know how to behave.

A thought popped into my mind: it was simply fatigue – I needn't bother about that.

As if in answer to my thought, Lou took a small cut-glass bottle with a gold-chased top from her pocket, unscrewed it and shook out some cocaine on the back of her hand. She flashed a provocative glance in my direction.

The studio suddenly filled with the reverberation of her chant:

"O Thou naked virgin of love, that art caught in a net of wild roses! I adore Thee, Evoe! I adore Thee, I A O!"

"Quite so," agreed King Lamus cheerfully. "You'll excuse me, I know, if I ask whether you have any great experience of the effects of cocaine."

Lou glowered at him. I preferred to meet him frankly. I deliberately put a large dose on the back of my hand and sniffed it up. Before I had finished, the effect had occurred. I felt myself any man's master.

"Well, as a matter of fact," I said superciliously, "tonight's the first time I ever took it, and it strikes me as pretty good stuff."

Lamus smiled enigmatically.

"Ah, yes, what does the old poet say? Milton, is it?"

"Stab your demoniac smile to my brain, Soak me in cognac, love, and cocaine."

"How silly you are," cried Lou. "Cocaine wasn't invented in the time of Milton."

"Was that Milton's fault?" retorted King Lamus. The inaptitude, the disconnectedness, of his thought was somehow disconcerting.

He turned his back on her and looked me straight in the face.

"It strikes you as pretty good stuff, Sir Peter," he said, "and so it is. I'll have a dose myself to show there's no ill-feeling."

He suited the action to the words.

I had to admit that the man began to intrigue me. What was his game?

"I hear you're one of our best flying men, Sir Peter," he went on.

"I have flown a bit now and then," I admitted.

"Well, an aeroplane's a pretty good means of travel, but unless you're an expert, you're likely to make a pretty sticky finish."

"Thank you very much," I said, nettled at his tone. "As it happens, I'm a medical student."

"Oh, that's all right, then, of course."

He agreed with a courtesy which somehow cut deeper into my self-esteem than if he had openly challenged my competence.

"In that case," he continued, "I hope to arouse your professional interest in a case of what I think you will agree is something approaching indiscretion. My little friend here arrived tonight, or rather last night, full up to the neck with morphia. Dissatisfied with results, she swallowed a large dose of Anbalonium Lewinii, reckless of the pharmaceutical incompatability. Presumably to pass away the time, she has drunk an entire bottle of Grand Marnier Cordon Rouge; and now, feeling herself slightly indisposed, for some reason at which it would be presumptuous to guess, she is setting things right by an occasional indulgence in this pretty good stuff of yours."

He had turned away from me and was watching the girl intently. My glance followed his. I saw her deep blue skin fade to a dreadful pallor. She had lost her healthy colour; she suggested a piece of raw meat which is just beginning to go bad.

I jumped to my feet. I knew instinctively that the girl was about to collapse. The owner of the studio was bending over her. He looked at me over his shoulder out of the corners of his eyes.

"A case of indiscretion," he observed, with bitter irony.

For the next quarter of an hour he fought for the girl's life. King Lamus was a very skilled physician, though he had never studied medicine officially.

But I was not aware of what was going on. Cocaine was singing in my veins. I cared for nothing. Lou came over impulsively and flung herself across my knees. She held the goblet of Benedictine to my mouth, chanting ecstatically:

"O Thou sparkling wine-cup of light, whose foaming is the heart's blood of the stars! I adore Thee, Evoe! I adore Thee, I A O!"

We swooned into a deep, deep trance. Lamus interrupted us.

"You mustn't think me inhospitable," he said.

"She's come round all right; but I ought to drive her home. Make yourselves at home while I'm away, or let me take you where you want to go."

Another interruption occurred. The bell rang.

Lamus sprang to the door. A tall old man was standing on the steps.

"Do what thou wilt shall be the whole of the Law," said Lamus.

"Love is the law, love under will," replied the other.

It was like a challenge and countersign.

"I've got to talk to you for an hour."

"Of course, I'm at your service," replied our host. The only thing is –" He broke off.

My brain was extraordinarily clear. My self-confidence was boundless. I felt inspired. I saw the way out.

A little devil laughed in my heart: "What an excellent scheme to be alone with Lou!"

"Look here, Mr. Lamus," I said, speaking very quickly, "I can drive any kind of car. Let me take Miss Hallaj home."

The Arab girl was on her feet behind me.

"Yes, yes," she said, in a faint, yet excited voice. "That will be much the best thing. Thanks awfully."

They were the first words she had spoken.

"Yes, yes," chimed in Lou. "I want to drive in the moonlight."

The little group was huddled in the open doorway. On one side the dark crimson tides of electricity; on the other, the stainless splendour of our satellite.

"O Thou frail bluebell of moonlight, that art lost in the gardens of the stars! I adore Thee, Evoe! I adore Thee, I A O!"

The scene progressed with the vivid rapidity of a dream. We were in the garage – out of it – into the streets – at the Egyptian girl's hotel – and then –

CHAPTER III
PHAETON

Lou clung to me as I gripped the wheel. There was no need for us to speak. The trembling torrent of our passion swept us away. I had forgotten all about Lamus and his car. We were driving like the devil to Nowhere. A mad thought crossed my mind. It was thrown up by my "Unconscious", by the essential self of my being. Then some familiar object in the streets reminded me that I was not driving back to the studio. Some force in myself, of which I was not aware, had turned my face towards Kent. I was interpreting myself to myself. I knew what I was going to do. We were bound for Barley Grange; and then, eh, the wild moonlight ride to Paris.

The idea had been determined in me without any intervention of my own. It had been, in a way, the solution of an equation of which the terms were firstly, a sort of mad identification of Lou with all one's romantic ideas of moonlight; then my physical habit as a flying man; and thirdly, the traditional connection of Paris with extravagant gaiety and luxuriant love.

I was quite aware at the time that my moral sense and my mental sense had been thrown overboard for the moment but my attitude was simply: "Goodbye, Jonah!"

For the first time in my life I was being absolutely myself, freed from all the inhibitions of body, intellect, and training which keep us, normally, in what we call sane courses of action.

I seem to remember asking myself if I was insane, and answering, "Of course I am – sanity is a compromise. Sanity is the thing that keeps one back."

It would be quite useless to attempt to describe the drive to Barley Grange. It lasted barely half a second. It lasted ageless aeons.

Any doubts that I might have had about myself were stamped under foot by the undeniable facts. I had never driven better in my life. I got out the sea-plane as another man might get out a cigarette from his case. She started like an eagle. With the whirr of the engine came Lou's soft smooth voice in exquisite antiphony:

"O Thou trembling breast of the night, that gleamest with a rosary of moons! I adore Thee, Evoe! I adore Thee, I A O!"

We soared towards the dawn. I went straight to over three thousand. I could hear the beat of my heart. It was one with the beat of the engine.

I took the pure unsullied air into my lungs. It was an octave to cocaine; the same invigorating spiritual force expressed in other terms.

The magnificently melodious words of Sieveking sprang into my mind. I repeated them rapturously. It is the beat of the British engine.

"Deep lungfuls! Deep mouthfuls! Deep, deep mental mouthfuls!"

The wind of our speed abolished all my familiar bodily sensations. The cocaine combined with it to anaesthetise them. I was disembodied; an eternal spirit; a Thing supreme, apart.

"Lou, sweetheart! Lou, sweetheart! Lou, Lou, perfect sweetheart!"

I must have shouted the refrain. Even amid the roar, I heard her singing back.

"O Thou summer softness of lips, that glow hot with the scarlet of passion! I adore Thee, Evoe! I adore Thee, I A O!"

I could not bear the weight of the air. Let us soar higher, ever higher! I increased the speed.

"Fierce frenzy! Fierce folly! Fierce, fierce, frenzied folly!"

"O Thou tortured shriek of the storm, that art whirled up through the leaves of the woods! I adore Thee, Evoe! I adore Thee, I A O!"

And I felt that we were borne on some tremendous tempest. The earth dropped from beneath us like a stone into blind nothingness. We were free, free for ever, from the fetters of our birth!

"Soar swifter! Soar swifter! Soar, soar swifter, swifter!"

Before us, high in the pale grey, stood Jupiter, a four-square sapphire spark. "O Thou bright star of the morning, that art set betwixt the breasts of the Night! I adore Thee, Evoe! I adore Thee, I A O!"

I shouted back.

"Star seekers! Star finders! Twin stars, silver shining!"

Up, still up, I drove. There hung a mass of thunder-cloud between me and the dawn. Damn it, how dared it! It had no business to be there. I must rise over it, trample it under my feet.

"O Thou purple breast of the storm, that art scarred by the teeth of the lightning! I adore Thee, Evoe! I adore Thee, I A O!"

Frail waifs of mist beset us. I had understood Lou's joy in the cloud. It was I that was wrong. I had not had enough cocaine to be able to accept everything as infinite ecstasy. Her love carried me out of myself up to her triumphal passion. I understood the mist.

"O Thou unvintageable dew, that art moist on the lips of the Morn! I adore Thee, Evoe! I adore Thee, I A O!"

At that moment, the practical part of me asserted itself with startling suddenness. I saw the dim line of the coast. I knew the line as I know the palm of my hand. I was a little out of the shortest line for Paris. I swerved slightly to the south.

Below, grey seas were tumbling. It seemed to me (insanely enough) that their moving wrinkles were the laughter of a very old man. I had a sudden intuition that something was wrong; and an instant later came an unmistakable indication of the trouble. I was out of gas.

My mind shot back with a vivid flash of hatred toward King Lamus. "A case of indiscretion!" He'd as good as called me a fool to my face. I thought of him as the sea, shaking with derisive laughter.

All the time I had been chuckling over my dear old squad commander. Not a great flyer, am I? This will show him! And that was true enough. I was incomparably better than I had ever been before. And yet I had omitted just one obvious precaution.

I suddenly realised that things might be exceedingly nasty. The only thing to be done was to shut off, and volplane down to the straits. And there were points in the problem which appalled me.

Oh, for another sniff! As we swooped down towards the sea in huge wide spirals, I managed to extract my bottle. Of course, I realised instantly the impossibility of taking it by the nose in such a wind. I pulled out the cork, and thrust my tongue into the neck of the bottle.

We were still three thousand feet or more above the sea. I had plenty of time, infinite time, I thought, as the drug took hold, to make my decision. I acted with superb aplomb. I touched the sea within a hundred yards of a fishing smack that had just put out from Deal.

We were picked up as a matter of course within a couple of minutes. They put back and towed the 'plane ashore.

My first thought was to get more gas and go on, despite the absurdity of our position. But the sympathy of the men on the beach was mixed with a good deal of hearty chaff. Dripping, in evening dress, at four o'clock in the morning! "Like Hedda Gabler, one doesn't do these things."

But the cocaine helped me again. Why the devil should I care what anybody thought?

"Where can I get gas?" I said to the captain of the smack.

He smiled grimly. "She'll want a bit more than gas."

I glanced at the 'plane. The man was perfectly right. A week's repairs, at the least.

"You'd better go to the hotel, sir, and get some warm clothes. Look how the lady's shivering."

It was perfectly true. There was nothing else to be done. We went together slowly up the beach.

There was no question of sleeping, of course. Both of us were as fresh as paint. What we needed was hot food and lots of it.

We got it.

It seemed as if we had entered upon an entirely new phase. The disaster had purged us of that orchestral oratorio business; but, on the other hand, we were still full of intense practical activity.

We ate three breakfasts each. And as we ate we talked; talked racy, violent nonsense, most of it. Yet we were both well aware that the whole

thing was camouflage. What we had to do was to get married as quickly as we could, and lay in a stock of cocaine, and go away and have a perfectly glorious time for ever and ever.

We sent for emergency clothes in the town, and went stalking a parson. He was an old man who had lived for years out of the world. He saw nothing particularly wrong with us except youth and enthusiasm, and he was very sorry that it would take three weeks to turn us off.

The good old boy explained the law.

"Oh, that's easy," we said in a breath. "Let's get the first train to London."

There are no incidents to record. We were both completely aneasthetised. Nothing bothered us. We didn't mind the waiting on the platform, or the way the old train lumbered up to London.

Everything was part of the plan. Everything was perfect pleasure. We were living above ourselves, living at a tremendous pace. The speed of the 'plane became merely a symbol, a physical projection of our spiritual sublimity.

The next two days passed like pantomime. We were married in a dirty little office by a dirty little man. We took back his car to Lamus. I was amused to discover that I had left it standing in the open half over the edge of the lake.

I made a million arrangements in a kind of whirling wisdom. Before forty-eight hours had passed we were packed and off for Paris.

I did not remember anything in detail. All events were so many base metals fused into an alloy whose name was Excitement. During the whole time we only slept once, and then we slept well and woke fresh, without one trace of fatigue.

We had called on Gretel and obtained a supply of cocaine. She wouldn't accept any money from her dear Sir Peter, and she was so happy to see Lou Lady Pendragon, and wouldn't we come and see her after the honeymoon?

That call is the one thing that sticks in my mind.

I suppose I realised obscurely somehow that the woman was in reality the mainspring of the whole manoeuvre.

She introduced us to her husband, a heavy, pursy old man with a paunch and a beard, a reputation for righteousness, and an unctuous way of saying the right kind of nothing. But I divined a certain

shrewdness in his eyes; it belied his mask of ostentatious innocence.

There was another man there too, a kind of half-baked Nonconformist parson, one Jabez Platt, who had realised early in life that his mission was to go about doing good. Some people said that he had done a great deal of good – to himself. His principle in politics was a – very simple one: If you see anything, stop it; everything that is, is wrong; the world is a very wicked place.

He was very enthusiastic about putting through a law for suppressing the evil of drugs.

We smiled our sympathetic assent, with sly glances at our hostess. If the old fool had only known that we were full of cocaine, as we sat and applauded his pompous platitudes!

We laughed our hearts out over the silly incident as we sat in the train. It doesn't appear particularly comic in perspective; but it's very hard to tell, at any time, what is going to tickle one's sense of humour. Probably anything else would have done just as well. We were on the rising curve. The exaltation of love was combined with that of cocaine; and the romance and adventure of our lives formed an exhilarating setting for those superb jewels.

"Every day, in every way, I get better and better."

M. Coué's now famous formula is the precise intellectual expression of the curve of the cocaine honeymoon. Normal life is like an aeroplane before she rises.

There is a series of little bumps; all one can say is that one is getting along more or less. Then she begins to rise clear of earth. There are no more obstacles to the flight.

But there are still mental obstacles: a fence, a row of houses, a grove of elms or what not. One is a little anxious to realise that they have to be cleared. But as she soars into the boundless blue, there comes that sense of mental exhilaration that goes with boundless freedom.

Our grandfathers must have known something about this feeling by living in England before the liberty of the country was destroyed by legislation, or rather the delegation of legislation to petty officialdom.

About six months ago I imported some tobacco, rolls of black perique, the best and purest in the world. By-and-by I got tired of

cutting it up, and sent it to a tobacconist for the purpose.

Oh, dear no, quite impossible without a permit from the Custom House!

I suppose I really ought to give myself up to the police.

Yes, as one gets into the full swing of cocaine, one loses all consciousness of the bumpy character of this funny old oblate spheroid. One is really very much more competent to deal with the affairs of life, that is, in a certain sense of the word.

M. Coué is perfectly right, just as the Christian Scientists and all those people are perfectly right, in saying that half our troubles come from our consciousness of their existence, so that if we forget their existence, they actually cease to exist!

Haven't we got an old proverb to the effect that "what the eye doesn't see, the heart doesn't grieve over"?

When one is on one's cocaine honeymoon, one is really, to a certain extent, superior to one's fellows. One attacks every problem with perfect confidence. It is a combination of what the French call elan and what they call insouciance.

The British Empire is due to this spirit. Our young men went out to India and all sorts of places, and walked all over everybody because they were too ignorant to realise the difficulties in their way. They were taught that if one had good blood in one's veins, and a public school and university training to habituate one to being a lord of creation, and to the feeling that it was impossible to fail, and to not knowing enough to know when one was beaten, nothing could ever go wrong.

We are losing the Empire because we have become "sicklied o'er with the pale cast of thought". The intellectuals have made us like "the poor cat in the adage". The spirit of Hamlet has replaced that of Macbeth. Macbeth only went wrong because the heart was taken out of him by Macduff's interpretation of what the witches had said.

Coriolanus only failed when he stopped to think. As the poet says, "The love of knowledge is the hate of life."

Cocaine removes all hesitation. But our forefathers owed their freedom of spirit to the real liberty which they had won; and cocaine is merely Dutch courage. However, while it lasts, it's all right.

CHAPTER IV
AU PAYS DE COCAINE

I can't remember any details of our first week in Paris. Details had ceased to exist. We whirled from pleasure to pleasure in one inexhaustible rush. We took everything in our stride. I cannot begin to describe the blind, boundless beatitude of love. Every incident was equally exquisite.

Of course, Paris lays herself out especially to deal with people in just that state of mind. We were living at ten times the normal voltage. This was true in more senses than one. I had taken a thousand pounds in cash from London, thinking as I did so how jolly it was to be reckless. We were going to have a good time, and damn the expense!

I thought of a thousand pounds as enough to paint Paris every colour of the spectrum for a quite indefinitely long period; but at the end of the week the thousand pounds was gone, and so was another thousand pounds for which I had cabled to London; and we had absolutely nothing to show for it except a couple of dresses for Lou, and a few not very expensive pieces of jewellery.

We felt that we were very economical. We were too happy to need to spend money. For one thing, love never needs more than a pittance, and I had never before known what love could mean.

What I may call the honeymoon part of the honeymoon seemed to occupy the whole of our waking hours. It left us no time to haunt Montmartre. We hardly troubled to eat, we hardly knew we were eating. We didn't seem to need sleep. We never got tired.

The first hint of fatigue sent one's hand to one's pocket. One sniff which gave us a sensation of the most exquisitely delicious wickedness, and we were on fourth speed again!

The only incident worth recording is the receipt of a letter and a box from Gretel Webster. The box contained a padded kimono for Lou, one of those gorgeous Japanese geisha silks, blue like a summer sky with dragons worked all over it in gold, with scarlet eyes and tongues.

Lou looked more distractingly, deliriously glorious than ever.

I had never been particularly keen on women. The few love affairs which had come my way had been rather silly and sordid. They had not revealed the possibilities of love; in fact, I had thought it a somewhat overrated pleasure, a brief and brutal blindness with boredom and disgust hard on its heels.

But with cocaine, things are absolutely different.

I want to emphasise the fact that cocaine is in reality a local anaesthetic. That is the actual explanation of its action. One cannot feel one's body. (As every one knows, this is the purpose for which it is used in surgery and dentistry.)

Now don't imagine that this means that the physical pleasures of marriage are diminished, but they are utterly etherealised. The animal part of one is intensely stimulated so far as its own action is concerned; but the feeling that this passion is animal is completely transmuted.

I come of a very refined race, keenly observant and easily nauseated. The little intimate incidents inseparable from love affairs, which in normal circumstances tend to jar the delicacy of one's sensibilities, do so no longer when one's furnace is full of coke. Everything soever is transmuted as by "heavenly alchemy" into a spiritual beatitude. One is intensely conscious of the body. But as the Buddhists tell us, the body is in reality

an instrument of pain or discomfort. We have all of us a subconscious intuition that this is the case; and this is annihilated by cocaine.

Let me emphasise once more the absence of any reaction. There is where the infernal subtlety of the drug comes in. If one goes on the bust in the ordinary way on alcohol, one gets what the Americans call "the morning after the night before". Nature warns us that we have been breaking the rules; and Nature has given us common sense enough to know that although we can borrow a bit, we have to pay back.

We have drunk alcohol since the beginning of time; and it is in our racial consciousness that although "a hair of the dog" will put one right after a spree, it won't do to choke oneself with hair.

But with cocaine, all this caution is utterly abrogated. Nobody would be really much the worse for a night with the drug, provided that he had the sense to spend the next day in a Turkish bath, and build up with food and a double allowance of sleep. But cocaine insists upon one's living upon one's capital, and assures one that the fund is inexhaustible.

As I said, it is a local anaesthetic. It deadens any feeling which might arouse what physiologists call inhibition. One becomes absolutely reckless. One is bounding with health and bubbling with high spirits. It is a blind excitement of so sublime a character that it is impossible to worry about anything. And yet, this excitement is singularly calm and profound. There is nothing of the suggestion of coarseness which we associate with ordinary drunkenness. The very idea of coarseness or commonness is abolished. It is like the vision of Peter in the Acts of the Apostles in which he was told, "There is nothing common or unclean."

As Blake said, "Everything that lives is holy." Every act is a sacrament. Incidents which in the ordinary way would check one or annoy one, become merely material for joyous laughter. It is just as when you drop a tiny lump of sugar into champagne, it bubbles afresh.

Well, this is a digression. But that is just what cocaine does. The sober continuity of thought is broken up. One goes off at a tangent, a fresh, fierce, fantastic tangent, on the slightest excuse. One's sense of proportion is gone; and despite all the millions of miles that one cheerily goes out of one's way, one never loses sight of one's goal.

While I have been writing all this, I have never lost sight for a moment of the fact that I am telling you about the box and the letter from Gretel.

We met a girl in Paris, half a Red Indian, a lovely baby with the fascination of a fiend and a fund of the foulest stories that ever were told. She lived on cocaine. She was a more or less uneducated girl; and the way she put it was this: "I'm in a long, lovely garden, with my arms full of parcels, and I keep on dropping one; and when I stoop to pick it up, I always drop another, and all the time I am sailing along up the garden."

So this was Gretel's letter.

> "My DARLING Lou, – I could not begin to tell you the other day how delighted I was to see you My Lady and with such a splendid man for your husband. I don't blame you for getting married in such a hurry; but, on the other hand, you mustn't blame your old friends for not being prophets! So I could not be on hand with the goods. However, I have lost no time. You know how poor I am, but I hope you will value the little present I am sending you, not for its own sake, but as a token of my deep affection for the loveliest and most charming girl I know. A word in your ear, my dear Lou: the inside is sometimes better than the outside. With my very kindest regards and best wishes to dear Sir Peter and yourself, though I can't expect you to know that I even exist at the present,
>
> Yours ever devotedly,
> "GRETEL."

Lou threw the letter across the table to me. For some reason or no reason, I was irritated. I didn't want to hear from people like that at all. I didn't like or trust her.

"Queer fish," I said rather snappily.

It wasn't my own voice; it was, I fancy, some deep instinct of self-preservation speaking within me.

Lou, however, was radiant about it. I wish I could give you an idea of the sparkling quality of everything she said and did. Her eyes glittered, her lips twittered, her cheeks glowed like fresh blown buds in spring. She

was the spirit of cocaine incarnate; cocaine made flesh. Her mere existence made the Universe infinitely exciting. Say, if you like, she was possessed of the devil!

Any good person, so-called, would have been shocked and scared at her appearance. She represented the siren, the vampire, Mclusine, the dangerous, delicious devil that cowards have invented to explain their lack of manliness. Nothing would suit her mood but that we should dine up there in the room, so that she could wear the new kimono and dance for me at dinner.

We ate grey caviare, spoonful by spoonful. Who cared that it was worth three times its weight in gold? It's no use calling me extravagant; if you want to blame any one, blame the Kaiser. He started the whole fuss; and when I feel like eating grey caviare, I'm going to eat grey caviare.

We wolfed it down. It's silly to think that things matter.

Lou danced like a delirious demon between the courses. It pleased her to assume the psychology of the Oriental pleasure-making woman. I was her Pasha-with-three-tails, her Samurai warrior, her gorgeous Maharaja, with a scimitar across my knee, ready to cut her head off at the first excuse.

She was the Ouled Ndil with tatooed cheeks and chin, with painted antimony eyebrows, and red smeared lips.

I was the masked Toureg, the brigand from the desert, who had captured her.

She played a thousand exquisite crazy parts.

I have very little imagination, my brain runs entirely to analysis; but I revel in playing a part that is devised for me. I don't know how many times during that one dinner I turned from a civilised husband in Bond Street pyjamas into a raging madman.

It was only after the waiters had left us with the coffee and liqueurs – which we drank like water without being affected – that Lou suddenly threw off her glittering garment.

She stood in the middle of the room, and drank a champagne glass half full of liqueur brandy. The entrancing boldness of her gesture started me screaming inwardly. I jumped up like a crouching tiger that suddenly sees a stag.

Lou was giggling all over with irrepressible excitement. I know "giggling all over" isn't English; but I can't express it any other way.

She checked my rush as if she had been playing full back in an International Rugger match.

"Get the scissors," she whispered.

I understood in a second what she meant. It was perfectly true – we had been playing it a bit on the heavy side with that snow. I think it must have been about five sniffs. If you're curious, all you have to do is to go back and count it up – to get me to ten thousand feet above the poor old Straits of Dover, God bless them! But it was adding up like the price of the nails in the horse's shoes that my father used to think funny when I was a kid. You know what I mean – Martingale principle and all that sort of thing. We certainly had been punishing the snow.

Five sniffs! it wasn't much in our young lives after a fortnight.

Gwendolen Otter says:

"Heart of my heart, in the pale moonlight, Why should we wait till tomorrow night?"

And that's really very much the same spirit.

"Heart of my heart, come out of the rain, let's have another go of cocaine."

I know I don't count when it comes to poetry, and the distinguished authoress can well afford to smile, if it's only the society smile, and step quietly over my remains. But I really have got the spirit of the thing.

"Always go on till you have to stop, Let's have another sniff, old top!"

No, that's undignified.

"Carry on! Over the top!" – would be better. It's more dignified and patriotic, and expresses the idea much better. And if you don't like it, you can inquire elsewhere.

No, I won't admit that we were reckless. We had substantial resources at our command. There was nothing whatever of the "long firm" about us.

You all know perfectly well how difficult it is to keep matches. Perfectly trivial things, matches – always using them, always easy to replace them, no matter at all for surprise if one should find one's box empty; and I don't admit for one moment that I showed any lack of proportion in the matter.

Now don't bring that moonlight flight to Paris up against me. I admit I was out of gas; but every one knows how one's occupation with one's

first love affair is liable to cause a temporary derangement of one's ordinary habits.

What I liked about it was that evidently Gretel was a jolly good sport, whatever people said about her. And she wasn't an ordinary kind of good old sport either. I don't see any reason why I shouldn't admit that she is what you may call a true friend in the most early Victorian sense of the word you can imagine.

She was not only a true friend, but a wise friend. She had evidently foreseen that we were going to run short of good old snow.

Now I want all you fellows to take it as read that a man, if he calls himself a man, isn't the kind of man that wants to stop a honeymoon with a girl in a Japanese kimono of the variety described, to have to put on a lot of beastly clothes and hunt all around Paris for a dope peddler.

Of course, you'll say at once that I could have rung for the waiter and have him bring me a few cubic kilometres. But that's simply because you don't understand the kind of hotel at which we were unfortunate enough to be staying, We had gone there thinking no harm whatever. It was right up near the Etoile, and appeared to the naked eye an absolutely respectable first-class family hotel for the sons of the nobility and gentry.

Now don't run away with the idea that I want to knock the hotel. It was simply because France had been bled white; but the waiter on our floor was a middle-aged family man and probably read Lamartine and Pascal and Taine and all those appalling old bores when he wasn't doing shot drill with the caviar. But it isn't the slightest use my trying to conceal from you the fact that he always wore a slightly shocked expression, especially in the way he cut his beard. It was emphatically not the thing whenever he came into the suite.

I am a bit of a psychologist myself, and I know perfectly well that that man wouldn't have got us cocaine, not if we'd offered him a Bureau de Tabac for doing it.

Now, of course, I'm not going to ask you to believe that Gretel Webster knew anything about that waiter – beastly old prig! All she had done was to exhibit wise forethought and intelligent friendship. She had experience, no doubt, bushels of it, barrels of it, hogsheads of it, all those measures that I couldn't learn at school.

She had said to herself, in perfectly general terms, without necessarily contemplating any particular train of events as follows:

"From one cause or another, those nice kids may find themselves shy on snow at a critical moment in their careers, so it's up to me to see that they get it."

While these thoughts were passing through my mind, I had got the manicure scissors, and Lou was snipping the threads of her kimono lining round those places where those fiercely fascinating fingers of hers had felt what we used to call in the hospital a foreign body.

Yes, there was no mistake. Gretel had got our psychology, we had got her psychology, everything was going as well as green peas go with a duck.

Don't imagine we had to spoil the kimono. It was just a tuck in the quilting. Out comes a dear little white silk bag; and we open that, and there's a heap of snow that I'd much rather see than Mont Blanc.

Well, you know, when you see it, you've got to sniff it. What's it for? Nobody can answer that. Don't tell me about "use in operations on the throat". Lou didn't need anything done to her throat. She sang like Melba, and she looked like a peach; and she was a Pêche-Melba, just like two and two makes four.

You bet we sniffed! And then we danced all round the suite for several years – probably as much as eight or nine minutes by the clock – but what's the use of talking about clocks when Einstein has proved that time is only another dimension of space? What's the good of astronomers proving that the earth wiggles round 1000 miles an hour, and wiggles on 1000 miles a minute, if you can't keep going?

It would be absolutely silly to hang about and get left behind, and very likely find ourselves on the moon, and nobody to talk to but Jules Verne, H. G. Wells, and that crowd.

Now I don't want you to think that that white silk packet was very big.

Lou stooped over the table, her long thin tongue shot out of her mouth like an ant-eater in the *Dictionary of National Biography* or whatever it is, and twiddled it round in that snow till I nearly went out of my mind.

I laughed like a hyena, to think of what she'd said to me. "Your kiss is bitter with cocaine." That chap Swinburne was always talking about bitter kisses. What did he know, poor old boy?

Until you've got your mouth full of cocaine, you don't know what kissing is. One kiss goes on from phase to phase like one of those novels by Balzac and Zola and Romain Rolland and D. H. Lawrence and those chaps. And you never get tired! You're on fourth speed all the time, and the engine purrs like a kitten, a big white kitten with the stars in its whiskers. And it's always different and always the same, and it never stops, and you go insane, and you stay insane, and you probably don't know what I'm talking about, and I don't care a bit, and I'm awfully sorry for you, and you can find out any minute you like by the simple process of getting a girl like Lou and a lot of cocaine.

What did that fellow Lamus say?

"Stab your demoniac smile to my brain,

Soak me in cognac, kisses, cocaine."

Queer fish, that chap Lamus! But seems to me that's pretty good evidence he knew something about it. Why, of course he did. I saw him take cocaine myself. Deep chap! Bet you a shilling. Knows a lot. That's no reason for suspicion. Don't see why people run him down the way they do. Don't see why I got so leary myself. Probably a perfectly decent chap at bottom. He's got his funny little ways – man's no worse for that.

Gad, if one started to get worried about funny little ways, what price Lou! Queerest card in the pack, and I love her.

"Give me another sniff off your hand."

Lou laughed like a chime of bells in Moscow on Easter morning. Remember, the Russian Easter is not the same time as our Easter. They slipped up a fortnight one way or the other – I never can remember which – as long as you know what I mean.

She threw the empty silk bag in the air, and caught it in her teeth with a passionate snap, which sent me nearly out of my mind again. I would have loved to be a bird, and have my head snapped off by those white, small, sharp incisors.

Practical girl, my Lady Pendragon! Instead of going off the deep end, she was cutting out another packet, and when it was opened, instead of the birds beginning to sing, she said in shrill excitement, "Look here, Cockie, this isn't snow."

I ought to explain that she calls me Cockie in allusion to the fact that my name is Peter.

I came out of my trance. I looked at the stuff with what I imagine to have been a dull, glazed eye. Then my old training came to my rescue.

It was a white powder with a tendency to form little lumps rather like chalk. I rubbed it between my finger and thumb. I smelt it. That told me nothing. I tasted it. That told me nothing, either, because the nerves of my tongue were entirely anaesthetised by the cocaine.

But the investigation was a mere formality. I know now why I made it. It was the mere gesture of the male. I wanted to show off to Lou. I wished to impress upon her my importance as a man of science; and all the time I knew, without being told, what it was.

So did she. The longer I have known Lou, the more impressed I am with the extent and variety of her knowledge.

"Oh, Gretel is too sweet," she chirped. "She guessed we might get tired of coco, 'grateful and comforting' as it is. So the dear old thing sent us some heroin. And there are still some people who tell us that life is not worth living!"

"Ever try it?" I asked, and delayed the answer with a kiss.

When the worst was over, she told me that she had only taken it once, and then, in a very minute dose, which had had no effect on her as far as she knew.

"That's all right," I said, from the height of my superior knowledge. "It's all a question of estimating the physiological dose. It's very fine indeed. The stimulation is very much better than that of morphine. One gets the same intense beatific calm, but without the languor. Why, Lou, darling, you've read De Quincey and all those people about opium, haven't you? Opium's a mixture, you know – something like twenty different alkaloids in it. Laudanum: Coleridge took it, and Clive – all sorts of important people. It's a solution of opium in alcohol. But morphia, is the most active and important of the principles in opium. You could take it in all sorts of ways. Injection gives the best results; but it's rather a nuisance, and there's always danger of getting dirt in. You have to look out for blood-poisoning all the time. It stimulates the imagination marvellously. It kills all pain and worry like a charm. But at the very moment

when you have the most gorgeous ideas, when you build golden palaces of what you are going to do, you have a feeling at the same time that nothing is really worth doing, and that itself gives you a feeling of terrific superiority to everything else in the world. And so, from the objective point of view, it comes to nothing. But heroin does all that morphia does. It's a derivative of morphia, you know – Diacetyl–Morphine is the technical name. Only instead of bathing you in philosophical inertia, you are as keen as mustard on carrying out your ideas. I've never taken any myself. I suppose we might as well start now."

I had a vision of myself as a peacock strutting and preening. Lou, her mouth half open, was gazing at me fascinated with enormous eyes; the pupils dilated by cocaine. It was just the male bird showing off to his mate. I wanted her to adore me for my little scraps of knowledge; the fragments I had picked up in my abandoned education.

Lou is always practical; and she puts something of the priestess into everything she does. There was a certain solemnity in the way in which she took up the heroin on the blade of a knife and put it on to the back of her hand.

"My Knight," she said, with flashing eyes, "our Lady arms you for the fight."

And she held out her fist to my nostrils. I snuffed up the heroin with a sort of ritualistic reverence. I can't imagine where the instinct came from. Is it the sparkle of cocaine that excites one to take it greedily, and the dullness of the heroin which makes it seem a much more serious business?

I felt as if I were going through some very important ceremony. When I had finished, Lou measured a dose for herself. She took it with a deep, grave interest.

I was reminded of the manner of my old professor at U.C.H. when he came to inspect a new case; a case mysterious but evidently critical. The excitement of the cocaine had somehow solidified. Our minds had stopped still. And yet their arrest was as intense as their previous motion.

We found ourselves looking into each other's eyes with no less ardour than before; but somehow it was a different kind of ardour. It was as if we had been released from the necessity of existence in the ordinary

sense of the word. We were both wondering who we were and what we were and what was going to happen; and, at the same time, we had a positive certainty that nothing could possibly happen.

It was a most extraordinary feeling. It was of a kind quite unimaginable by any ordinary minds. I will go a bit further than that. I don't believe the greatest artist in the world could invent what we felt, and if he could he couldn't describe it.

I'm trying to describe it myself, and I feel that I'm not making out very well. Come to think of it, the English language has its limitations. When mathematicians and men of science want to exchange thoughts, English isn't much good. They've had to invent new words, new symbols. Look at Einstein's equations.

I knew a man once that knew James Hinton, who invented the fourth dimension. Pretty bright chap, he was, but Hinton thought, on the most ordinary subjects, at least six times as fast as he did, and when it came to Hinton's explaining himself, he simply couldn't do it.

That's the great trouble when a new thinker comes along. They all moan that they can't understand him; the fact annoys them very much; and ten to one they persecute him and call him an Atheist or a Degenerate or a Pro-German or a Bolshevik, or whatever the favourite term of abuse happens to be at the time.

Wells told us a bit about this in that book of his about giants, and so does Bernard Shaw in his *Back to Methuselah*. It's nobody's fault in particular, but there it is, and you can't get over it.

And here was I, a perfectly ordinary man, with just about the average allowance of brains, suddenly finding myself cut off from the world, in a class by myself – I felt that I had something perfectly tremendous to tell, but I couldn't tell even myself what it was.

And there was Lou standing right opposite, and I recognised instinctively, by sympathy, that she was just in the same place.

We had no need of communicating with each other by means of articulate speech. We understood perfectly; we expressed the fact in every subtle harmony of glance and gesture.

The world had stopped suddenly still. We were alone in the night and the silence of things. We belonged to eternity in some indefinable

way; and that infinite silence blossoms inscrutably into embrace.

The heroin had begun to take hold. We felt ourselves crowned with colossal calm. We were masters; we had budded from nothingness into existence! And now, existence slowly compelled us to action. There was a necessity in our own natures which demanded expression and after the first intense inter-penetration of our individualities, we had reached the resultant of all the forces that composed us.

In one sense, it was that our happiness was so huge that we could not bear it; and we slid imperceptibly into conceding that the ineffable mysteries must be expressed by means of sacramental action.

But all this took place at an immense distance from reality. A concealed chain of interpretation linked the truth with the obvious commonplace fact that this was a good time to go across to Montmartre and make a night of it.

We dressed to go out with, I imagine, the very sort of feeling as a newly made bishop would have the first time he puts on his vestments.

But none of this would have been intelligible to, or suspected by, anybody who had seen us. We laughed and sang and interchanged gay nothings while we dressed.

When we went downstairs, we felt like gods descending upon earth, immeasurably beyond mortality.

With the cocaine, we had noticed that people smiled rather strangely. Our enthusiasm was observed. We even felt a little touch of annoyance at everybody not going at the same pace; but this was perfectly different. The sense of our superiority to mankind was constantly present. We were dignified beyond all words to express. Our own voices sounded far, far off. We were perfectly convinced that the hotel porter realised that he was receiving the orders of Jupiter and Juno to get a taxi.

We never doubted that the chauffeur knew himself to be the charioteer of the sun.

"This is perfectly wonderful stuff," I said to Lou as we passed the Arc de Triomphe. "I don't know what you meant by saying the stuff didn't have any special effect upon you. Why, you're perfectly gorgeous."

"You bet I am," laughed Lou. "The king's daughter is all-glorious within; her raiment is of wrought gold, and she thrusts her face out to be kissed,

like a comet pushing its way to the sun. Didn't you know I was the king's daughter?" She smiled, with such seductive sublimity that something in me nearly fainted with delight.

"Hold up, Cockie," she chirped. "It's all right. You're it, and I'm it, and I'm your little wife."

I could have torn the upholstery out of the taxi. I felt myself a giant. Gargantua was a pigmy. I felt the need of smashing something into matchwood, and I was all messed up about it because it was Lou that I wanted to smash, and at the same time she was the most precious and delicate piece of porcelain that ever came out of the Ming dynasty or whatever the beastly period is.

The most fragile, exquisite beauty! To touch her was to profane her. I had a sudden nauseating sense of the bestiality of marriage.

I had no idea at the time that this sudden revulsion of feeling was due to a mysterious premonition of the physiological effects of heroin in destroying love. Definitely stimulating things like alcohol, hashish and cocaine give free range to Cupid. Their destructive effect on him is simply due to the reaction. One is in debt, so to speak, because one has outrun the constable.

But what I may call the philosophical types of dope, of which morphine and heroin are the principal examples, are directly inimical to active emotion and emotional action. The normal human feelings are transmuted into what seem on the surface their spiritual equivalents. Ordinary good feeling becomes universal benevolence; a philanthropy which is infinitely tolerant because the moral code has become meaningless for it. A more than Satanic pride swells in one's soul. As Baudelaire says: "Hast thou not sovereign contempt, which makes the soul so kind?"

As we drove up the Butte Montmartre towards the Sacré Coeur, we remained completely silent, lost in our calm beatitude. You must understand that we were already excited to the highest point. The effect of the heroin had been to steady us in that state.

Instead of beating passionately up the sky with flaming wings, we were poised aloft in the illimitable ether. We took fresh doses of the dull soft powder now and again. We did so without greed, hurry or even desire. The sensation was of infinite power which could afford infinite

deliberation. Will itself seemed to have been abolished. We were going nowhere in particular, simply because it was our nature so to do. Our beatitude became more absolute every moment.

With cocaine, one is indeed master of everything; but everything matters intensely.

With heroin, the feeling of mastery increases to such a point that nothing matters at all. There is not even the disinclination to do what one happens to be doing which keeps the opium smoker inactive. The body is left to itself so perfectly that one is not worried by its natural activities.

Again, despite our consciousness of infinity, we maintained, concurrently, a perfect sense of proportion in respect of ordinary matters.

CHAPTER V
A HEROIN HEROINE

I stopped the taxi in the Place du Tertre. We wanted to walk along the edge of the Butte and let our gaze wander over Paris.

The night was delicious. Nowhere but in Paris does one experience that soft suave hush; the heat is dry, the air is light, it is quite unlike anything one ever gets in England.

A very gentle breeze, to which our fancy attributed the redolence of the South, streamed up from the Seine. Paris itself was a blur of misty blue; the Pantheon and the Eiffel Tower leapt from its folds. They seemed like symbols of the history of mankind; the noble, solid past and the mechanical efficient future.

I leant upon the parapet entranced. Lou's arm was around my neck. We were so still that I could feel her pulses softly beating.

"Great Scott, Pendragon!"

For all its suggestion of surprise, the voice was low and winsome. I looked around.

Had I been asked, I should have said, no doubt, that I should have resented any disturbance; and here was a sudden, violent, unpleasant disturbance; and it did not disturb me. There was a somewhat tentative smile on the face of the man who had spoken. I recognised him instantly, though I had not seen him since we were at school together. The man's name was Elgin Feccles. He had been in the mathematical sixth when I was in the lower school.

In my third term he had become head prefect; he had won a scholarship at Oxford – one of the best things going. Then, without a moment's warning, he had disappeared from the school. Very few people knew why, and those who did pretended not to. But he never went to Oxford.

I had only heard of the man once since. It was in the club. His name came up in connection with some vague gossip about some crooked financial affair. I had it in my mind, vaguely enough, that that must have had something to do with the trouble at school. He was not the sort of boy to be expelled for any of the ordinary reasons. It was certainly something to do with the subtlety of his intellect. To tell you the truth, he had been a sort of hero of mine at school. He possessed all the qualities I most admired – and lacked – in their fullest expansion.

I had known him very slightly; but his disappearance had been a great shock. It had stuck in my mind when many more important things had left no trace.

He had hardly changed from when I had last seen him. Of middle height, he had a long and rather narrow face. There was a touch of the ecclesiastic in his expression. His eyes were small and grey; he had a trick of blinking. The nose was long and beaked like Wellington's; the mouth was thin and tense; the skin was fresh and rosy. He had not developed even the tiniest wrinkle.

He kept the old uneasy nervous movement which had been so singular in him as a boy. One would have said that he was constantly on the alert, expecting something to happen, and yet the last thing that any one could have said about him was that he was ill at ease. He possessed superb confidence.

Before I had finished recognising him, he had shaken hands with me and was prattling about the old days.

"I hear you're Sir Peter now, by the way," he said. "Good for you. I always picked you for a winner."

"I think I've met you," interrupted Lou. "Surely, it's Mr. Feccles."

"Oh, yes, I remember you quite well. Miss Laleham, isn't it?"

"Please let's forget the past," smiled Lou, taking my arm.

I don't know why I should have felt embarrassed at explaining that we were married.

Feccles rattled off a string of congratulations.

"May I introduce Mademoiselle Haidé Lamoureux?"

The girl beside him smiled and bowed.

Haidé Lamoureux was a brilliant brunette with a flashing smile and eyes with pupils like pin-points. She was a mass of charming contradictions. The nose and mouth suggested more than a trace of Semitic blood, but the wedge-shaped contour of the face betokened some very opposite strain. Her cheeks were hollow, and crows' feet marred the corners of her eyes. Dark purple rims suggested sensual indulgence pushed to the point of weariness. Though her hair was luxuriant, the eyebrows were almost non-existent. She had pencilled fine black arches above them. She was heavily and clumsily painted. She wore a loose and rather daring evening dress of blue with silver sequins, and a yellow sash spotted with black. Over this she had thrown a cloak of black lace garnished with vermilion tassels. Her hands were deathly thin. There was something obscene in the crookedness of her fingers, which were covered with enormous rings of sapphires and diamonds.

Her manner was one of vivid languor. It seemed as if she always had to be startled into action, and that the instant the first stimulus had passed she relapsed into her own deep thoughts.

Her cordiality was an obvious affectation; but both Lou and myself, as we shook hands, were aware of a subtle and mysterious sympathy which left behind it a stain of inexpressible evil.

I also felt sure that Feccles understood this unspoken communion, and that for some reason or other it pleased him immensely. His manner changed to one of peculiarly insinuating deference, and I felt that he was somehow taking command of the party when he said –

"May I venture to suggest that you and Lady Pendragon take supper with us at the Petit Savoyard?"

Haidé slipped her arm into mine, and Lou led the way with Feccles.

"We were going there ourselves," she told him, "and it will be perfectly delightful to be with friends. I see you're quite an old friend of my husband's."

He began to tell her of the old school. As if by accident, he gave an account of the circumstances which had led to his leaving.

"My old man was in the city, you know," I heard him say, "and he dropped his pile 'somewhere in Lombard Street'" (he gave a false little laugh), "where he couldn't pick it up, so that was the end of my academic career. He persuaded old Rosenbaum, the banker, that I had a certain talent for finance, and got me a job as private secretary. I really did take to it like a duck to water, and things have gone very well for me ever since. But London isn't the place for men with real ambition. It doesn't afford the scope. It's either Paris or New York for yours sincerely, Elgin Feccles."

I don't know why I didn't believe a word of the tale; but I didn't. The heroin was working beautifully. I hadn't the slightest inclination to talk to Haidé.

In the same way she took no notice of me. She never uttered a word.

Lou was in the same condition. She was apparently listening to what Feccles was saying; but she made no remark, and preserved a total detachment. The whole scene had not taken three minutes. We reached the Petit Savoyard and took our seats.

The patron appeared to know our friends very well. He welcomed them with even more than the usual French fussiness. We sat down by the window.

The restaurant overhangs the steep slopes of the Montmartre like an eyrie. We ordered supper, Feccles with bright intelligence, the rest of us with utter listlessness. I looked at Lou across the table. I had never seen the woman before in my life. She meant nothing whatever to me. I felt a sudden urgent desire to drink a great deal of water. I couldn't trouble to pour myself out a glass. I couldn't trouble to call the waiter, but I think I must have said the word "water", for Haidé filled my goblet. A smile wriggled across her face. It was the first sign of life she had given. Even the shaking hands had been in the nature of a mechanical reflex rather

than of a voluntary action. There was something sinister and disquieting in her gesture. It was as if she had the after-taste in her mouth of some abominable bitterness.

I looked across at Lou. I saw she had changed colour.

She looked dreadfully ill. It mattered nothing to me. I had a little amusing cycle of thoughts on the subject. I remembered that I loved her passionately; at the same time she happened not to exist. My indifference was a source of what I can only call diabolical beatitude.

It occurred to me as a sort of joke that she might have poisoned herself. I was certainly feeling very unwell. That didn't disturb me either.

The waiter brought a bowl of mussels. We ate them dreamily. It was part of the day's work. We enjoyed them because they were enjoyable; but nothing mattered, not even enjoyment. It struck me as strange that Haidé was simply pretending to eat, but I attributed this to preoccupation.

I felt very much better. Feccles talked easily and lightly about various matters of no importance. Nobody took any notice. He did not appear to observe, for his own part, any lack of politeness.

I certainly was feeling tired. I thought the Chambertin would pick me up, and swallowed a couple of glasses.

Lou kept on looking up at me with a sort of anxiety as if she wanted advice of some kind and didn't know how to ask for it. It was rather amusing.

We started the entré. Lou got suddenly up from her seat. Feccles, with pretended alarm on his face, followed her hastily. I saw the waiter had hold of her other arm. It was really very amusing. That's always the way with girls – they never know what's enough.

And then I realised with startling suddenness that the case was not confined to the frailer sex. I got out just in time.

If I pass over in silence the events of the next hour, it is not because of the paucity of incident. At its conclusion we were seated once more at the table.

We took little sips of very old Armagnac; it pulled us together. But all the virtue had gone out of us; we might have been convalescents from some very long and wasting illness.

"There's nothing to be alarmed about," said Feccles, with his curious little laugh. "A trifling indiscretion."

I winced at the word. It took me back to King Lamus. I hated that fellow more than ever. He had begun to obsess me. Confound him!

Lou had confided the whole story to our host, who admitted that he was familiar with these matters.

"You see, my dear Sir Peter," he said, "you can't take H. like you can C., and when you mix your drinks there's the devil to pay. It's like everything else in life; you've got to find out your limit. It's very dangerous to move about when you're working H. or M., and it's almost certain disaster to eat."

I must admit I felt an awful fool. After all, I had studied medicine pretty seriously; and this was the second time that a layman had read me the Riot Act.

But Lou nodded cheerfully enough. The brandy had brought back the colour in her cheeks.

"Yes," she said, "I'd heard that all before, but you know it's one thing to hear a thing and another to go through it yourself."

"Experience is the only teacher," admitted Feccles. "All these things are perfectly all right, but the main thing is to go slow at first, and give yourself a chance to learn the ropes."

All this time Haidé had been sitting there like a statue. She exhaled a very curious atmosphere. There was a certain fascination in her complete lack of fascination.

Please excuse this paradoxical way of putting it. I mean that she had all the qualities which normally attract. She had the remains of an astonishing, if bizarre, beauty. She had obviously a vast wealth of experience. She possessed a quiet intensity which should have made her irresistible; and yet she was absolutely devoid of what we call magnetism. It isn't a scientific word – so much the worse for science. It describes a fact in nature, and one of the most important facts in practical affairs. Everything of human interest, from music hall turns to empires, is run on magnetism and very little else. And science ignores it because it can't be measured by mechanical instruments!

The whole of the woman's vitality was directed to some secret interior shrine of her own soul.

Now she began to speak for the first time. The only subject that interested her in this wide universe was heroin. Her voice was monotonous.

Lou told me later that it reminded her of a dirge droned by Tibetan monks far off across implacable snow.

"It's the only thing there is," she said, in a tone of extraordinary ecstatic detachment. One could divine an infinite unholy joy derived from its own sadness. It was as if she took a morbid pleasure in being something melancholy, something monstrous; there was, in fact, a kind of martyred majesty in her mood.

"You mustn't expect to get the result at once," she went on. "You have to be born into it, married with it, and dead from it before you understand it. Different people are different. But it always takes some months at least before you get rid of that stupid nuisance – life. As long as you have animal passions, you are an animal. How disgusting it is to think of eating and loving and all those appetites, like cattle! Breathing itself would be beastly if one knew one were doing it. How intolerable life would be to people of even mediocre refinement if they were always acutely conscious of the process of digestion."

She gave a little shiver.

"You've read the Mystics, Sir Peter?" interrupted Feccles.

"I'm afraid not, my dear man," I replied. "Fact is, I haven't read anything much unless I had to."

"I went into it rather for a couple of years," he returned, and then stopped short and flushed.

The thought had apparently called up some very unpleasant memories. He tried to cover his confusion by volubility, and began an elaborate exposition of the tenets of St. Teresa, Miguel de Molinos, and several others celebrated in that line.

"The main point, you see," he recapitulated finally, "is the theory that everything human in us is before all things an obstacle in the way of holiness. That is the secret of the saints, that they renounce everything for one thing which they call the divine purity. It is not simply those things which we ordinarily call sins or vices – those are merely the elementary forms of

iniquity, exuberant grossness. The real difficulty hardly begins till things of that sort are dismissed for ever. On the road to saintship, every bodily or mental manifestation is in itself a sin, even when it is something which ordinary piety would class as a virtue. Haidé here has got the same idea."

She nodded serenely.

"I had no idea," she said, "that those people had got so much sense. I've always thought of them as tangled up with religious ideas. I understand now. Yes, it's the life of holiness, if you have to go to the trouble of putting it in the terms of morality, as I suppose you English people have to. I feel that contact of any sort, even with myself, contaminates me. I was the chief of sinners in my time, in the English sense of the word. Now I've forgotten what love means, except for a faint sense of nausea when it comes under my notice. I hardly eat at all – it's only brutes that want to wallow in action that need three meals a day. I hardly ever talk – words seem such waste, and they are none of them true. No one has yet invented a language from my point of view. Human life or heroin life? I've tried them both; and I don't regret having chosen as I did."

I said something about heroin shortening life. A wan smile flickered on her hollow cheeks. There was something appalling in its wintry splendour. It silenced us.

She looked down at her hands. I noticed for the first time with extreme surprise that they were extraordinarily dirty. She explained her smile.

"Of course, if you count time by years, you're very likely right. But what have the calculations of astronomers to do with the life of the soul? Before I started heroin, year followed year, and nothing worthwhile happened. It was like a child scribbling in a ledger. Now that I've got into the heroin life, a minute or an hour – I don't know which and I don't care – contains more real life than any five years' period in my unregenerate days. You talk of death. Why shouldn't you? It's perfectly all right for you. You animals have got to die, and you know it. But I am very far from sure that I shall ever die; and I'm as indifferent to the idea as I am to any other of your monkey ideas."

She relapsed into silence, leaned back and closed her eyes once more.

I make no claim to be a philosopher of any kind but it was quite evident to the most ordinary common sense that her position was

unassailable if any one chose to take it. As G. K. Chesterton says, "You cannot argue with the choice of the soul."

It has often been argued, in fact, that mankind lost the happiness characteristic of his fellow-animals when he acquired self-consciousness. This is in fact the meaning of the legend of "The Fall". We have become as gods, knowing good and evil, and the price is that we live by labour, and "In his eyes foreknowledge of death."

Feccles caught my thought. He quoted with slow emphasis:

> "He weaves and is clothed with derision,
> Sows and he shall not reap.
> His life is a watch or a vision,
> Between a sleep and a sleep."

The thought of the great Victorian seemed to chill him. He threw off his depression, lighting a cigarette and taking a strong pull at his brandy.

"Haidé," he said, with assumed lightness, "lives in open sin with a person named Baruch de Espinosa. I think it's Schopenhauer who calls him '*Der Gott-betrunkene Mann*'."

"The God-intoxicated man," murmured Lou faintly, shooting a sleepy glance at Haidé from beneath her heavy blue-veined eyelids.

"Yes," went on Feccles. "She always carries about one of his books. She goes to sleep on his words; and when her eyes open, they fall upon the page."

He tapped the table as he spoke. His quick intuition had understood that this strange incident was disquieting to us. He wriggled his thumb and forefinger in the air towards the waiter. The man interpreted the gesture as a request for the bill, and went off to get it.

"Let me drive you and Sir Peter back to your hotel," said our host to Lou. "You've had a rather rough time. I prescribe a good night's rest. You'll find a dose of H. a very useful pick-me-up in the morning, but, for Heaven's sake, don't flog a willing horse. Just the minutest sniff, and then coke up gradually when you begin to feel like getting up. By lunch time you'll be feeling like a couple of two-year-olds."

He paid the bill, and we went out. As luck would have it, a taxi had just discharged a party at the door. So we drove home without any trouble.

Lou and I both felt absolutely washed out. She lay upon my breast and held my hand. I felt my strength come back to me when it was called on to support her weakness. And our love grew up anew out of that waste of windy darkness. I felt myself completely purged of all passion; and in that lustration we were baptised anew and christened with the name of Love.

But although nature had done her best to get rid of the excess of the poison we had taken, there remained a residual effect. We had arrived at the hotel very weary, though as a matter of course we had insisted on Feccles and Haidé coming upstairs for a final drink. But we could hardly keep our eyes open; and as soon as they were gone we made all possible haste to get between the sheets of the twin beds.

I need hardly tell my married friends that on previous nights the process of going to bed had been a very elaborate ritual. But on this occasion, it was a mere attempt to break the record for speed. Within five minutes from the departure of Feccles and Haidé the lights were out.

I had imagined that I should drop off to sleep instantly. In fact, it took me some time to realise that I had not done so. I was in an anaesthetic condition which is hard to distinguish from dreaming. In fact, if one started to lay down definitions and explained the differences, the further one got the more obscure would the controversy become.

But my eyes were certainly wide open; and I was lying on my back, whereas I can never sleep except on my right side, or else, strangely enough, in a sitting position. And the thoughts began to make themselves more conscious as I lay.

You know how thoughts fade out imperceptibly as one goes to sleep. Well, here they were, fading in.

I found myself practically deprived of volition on the physical plane. It was as if it had become impossible for me to wish to move or to speak. I was bathed in an ocean of exceeding calm. My mind was very active, but only so within peculiar limits. I did not seem to be directing the current of my thoughts.

In an ordinary way that fact would have annoyed me intensely. But now it merely made me curious. I tried, as an experiment, to fix my mind on something definite. I was technically able to do so, but at the same time I was aware that I considered the effort not worth making. I noticed, too, that my thoughts were uniformly pleasant.

Curiosity impelled me to fix my mind on ideas which are normally the source of irritation and worry. There was no difficulty in doing so, but the bitterness had disappeared.

I went over incidents in the past which I had almost forgotten by virtue of that singular mental process which protects the mind from annoyance.

I discovered that this loss of memory was apparent, and not real. I recollected every detail with the most minute exactitude. But the most vexatious and humiliating items meant nothing to me any more. I took the same pleasure in recalling them as one has in reading a melancholy tale. I might almost go so far as to say that the unpleasant incidents were preferable to the others.

The reason is, I think, that they leave a deeper mark on the mind. Our souls have invented our minds, so to speak, with the object of registering conscious experiences, and therefore the more deeply an experience is felt the better our minds are carrying out the intention of our souls.

"*Forsitan haec olim meminisse juvabit*," says Aeneas in Virgil when recounting his hardships. (Quaint, by the way! I haven't thought of a Latin tag a dozen times since I left school. Drugs, like old age, strip off one's recent memories, and leave bare one's forgotten ideas.)

The most deeply seated instinct in us is our craving for experience. And that is why the efforts of the Utopians to make life a pleasant routine always arouse subconscious revolt in the spirit of man.

It was the progressive prosperity of the Victorian age that caused the Great War. It was the reaction of the schoolboy against the abolition of adventure.

This curious condition of mind possessed an eternal quality; the stream of thoughts flowed through my brain like a vast irresistible river. I felt that nothing could ever stop it, or even change the current in any

important respect. My consciousness had something of the quality of a fixed star proceeding through space by right of its eternal destiny. And the stream carried me on from one set of thoughts to another, slowly and without stress; it was like a hushed symphony. It included all possible memories, changing imperceptibly from one to another without the faintest hint of jarring.

I was aware of the flight of time, because a church clock struck somewhere far off at immense incalculable intervals. I knew, therefore, that I was making a white night of it. I was aware of dawn through the open French windows on the balcony.

Ages, long ages, later, there was a chime of bells announcing early Mass; and gradually my thought became more slow, more dim; the active pleasure of thinking became passive. Little by little the shadows crept across my reverie, and then I knew no more.

CHAPTER VI
THE GLITTER ON THE SNOW

I woke to find Lou fully dressed. She was sitting on the edge of my bed. She had taken hold of my hand, and her face was bending over mine like a pallid flower. She saw that I was awake, and her mouth descended upon mine with exquisite tenderness. Her lips were soft and firm; their kiss revived me into life.

She was extraordinarily pale, and her gestures were limp and languid. I realised that I was utterly exhausted.

"I couldn't sleep at all," she said, "after what seemed a very long time in which I tried to pull myself together. My mind went running on like mad – I've had a perfectly ripping time – perfectly top-hole! I simply couldn't get up till I remembered what that man Feccles said about a hair of the dog. So I rolled out of bed and crawled across to the H. and took one little sniff, and sat on the floor till it worked. It's great stuff when you know the ropes. It picked me up in a minute. So I had a bath, and got these things on. I'm still a bit all in. You know we did overdo it, didn't we, Cockie?"

"You bet," I said feebly. "I'm glad I've got a nurse."

"Right-o," she said, with a queer grin. "It's time for your majesty's medicine."

She went over to the bureau, and brought me a dose of heroin. The effect was surprising! I had felt as if I couldn't move a muscle, as if all the springs of my nerves had given way. Yet, in two minutes, one small sniff restored me to complete activity.

There was in this, however, hardly any element of joy. I was back to my normal self, but not to what you might call good form. I was perfectly able to do anything required, but the idea of doing it didn't appeal. I thought a bath and a shower would put me right; and I certainly felt a very different man by the time I had got my clothes on.

When I came back into the sitting-room, I found Lou dancing daintily round the table. She went for me like a bull at a gate; swept me away to the couch and knelt at my side as I lay, while she overwhelmed me with passionate kisses.

She divined that I was not in any condition to respond.

"You still need your nurse," she laughed merrily, with sparkling eyes and flashing teeth and nostrils twitching with excitement. I saw on the tip of one delicious little curling hair a crystal glimmer that I knew.

She had been out in the snowstorm!

My cunning twisted smile told her that I was wise to the game.

"Yes," she said excitedly, "I see how it's done now. You pull yourself together with H. and then you start the buzz-wagon with C. Come along, put in the clutch."

Her hand was trembling with excitement. But on the back of it there shimmered a tiny heap of glistening snow.

I sniffed it with suppressed ecstasy. I knew that it was only a matter of seconds before I caught the contagion of her crazy and sublime intoxication.

Who was it that said you had only to put salt on the tail of a bird, and then you could catch it? Probably that fellow thought that he knew all about it, but he got the whole thing wrong. What you have to do is to get snow up your own nose, and then you can catch the bird all right.

What did Maeterlinck know about that silly old Blue Bird?

Happiness lies within one's self, and the way to dig it out is cocaine.

But don't you go and forget what I hope you won't mind my calling ordinary prudence. Use a little common sense, use precaution, exercise good judgment. However hungry you may happen to be, you don't want to eat a dozen oxen *en brochette*. *Natura non facit saltum*.

It's only a question of applying knowledge in a reasonable manner. We had found out how to work the machine, and there was no reason in the world why we shouldn't fly from here to Kalamazoo.

So I took three quite small sniffs at reasonable intervals, and I was on the job once more.

I chased Lou around the suite; and I dare say we did upset a good deal of the furniture, but that doesn't matter, for we haven't got to pick it up.

The important thing was that I caught Lou; and by-and-by we found ourselves completely out of breath; and then, confound it, just when I wanted a quiet pipe before lunch, the telephone rang, and the porter wanted to know if we were at home to Mr. Elgin Feccles.

Well, I told you before that I didn't care for the man so much as that. As Stevenson observes, if he were the only tie that bound one to home, I think most of us would vote for foreign travel. But he'd played the game pretty straight last night; and hang it, one couldn't do less than invite the fellow to lunch. He might have a few more tips about the technique of this business anyhow. I'm not one of those cocksure fellows that imagine when they have one little scrap of knowledge, that they have drained the fount of wisdom dry.

So I said, "Ask him to be good enough to come up by all means."

Lou flew to the other room to fix her hair and her face and all those things that women always seem to be having to fix, and up comes Mr. Feccles with the most perfect manner that I have ever observed in any human being, and a string of kind inquiries and apologies on the tip of his tongue.

He said he wouldn't have bothered us by calling at all so soon after the case of indiscretion, only he felt sure he had left his cigarette case with us, and he valued it very much because it had been given him by his Aunt Sophronia.

Well, you know, there it was, right on the table, or rather, under the table, because the table was on top of it.

When we got the table on its legs again, we saw, quite plainly that the cigarette case had been under it, and therefore must have been on top of it before it was overturned.

Feccles laughed heartily at the humorous character of the incident. I suppose it was funny in a sort of way. On the other hand, I don't think it was quite the thing to call attention to. However, I suppose the fellow had to have his cigarette case, and after all, when you do find a table upside down, it's not much good pretending that you don't notice it. And very likely, on the whole, the best way to pass over the incident pleasantly is to turn it into a kind of joke.

And I must say that Feccles showed the tact of a perfect gentleman in avoiding any direct allusion to the circumstances that caused the circumstances that were responsible for the circumstances that gave rise to the circumstances which it was so difficult to overlook.

Well, you know, this man Feccles had been a perfect dear the night before. He had seen Lou through the worst of the business with the utmost good taste at the moment when her natural protector, myself, was physically unable to apply the necessary what-you-may-call-it.

Well, of course, the way things were at the moment, I wished Feccles in the place that modern Christianity has decided to forget. But the least I could do was to ask him to lunch. But before I had time to put this generous impulse into words, Lou sailed in like an angel descending from heaven.

She went straight up to Feccles, and she positively kissed him before my eyes, and begged him to stay and have lunch. She positively took the words out of my mouth.

But I must admit that I wanted to be alone with Lou – not only then, but for ever; and I was most consumedly glad when I heard Feccles say:

"Why, really, that's too kind of you, Lady Pendragon, and I hope you repeat the invitation some other day, but I've got to lunch with two birds from the Bourse. We have a tremendous deal coming off. Sir Peter's got more money already than he knows what to do with, otherwise I'd be only too glad to let him in on the *rez-de-chaussée*."

Well, you know, that's all right about my being a millionaire, and all that. It's one thing being a single man running round London perfectly happy with a shilling cigar and a stall at the Victoria Palace, and it's quite another being on a honeymoon with a girl whom her most intimate friends call "Unlimited Lou."

Feccles did not know that I had spent more than a third of my annual income in a fortnight. But, of course, I couldn't tell the man how I was situated. We Pendragons are a pretty proud lot, especially since Sir Thomas Malory gave us that write-up in the time of Henry VIII. We've always been a bit above ourselves. That's where my poor old dad went gaga.

However, the only thing to do was to beg the man to find a date in the near future to fight Paillard to a finish.

I think Paillard is the best restaurant in Paris, don't you?

So out comes a little red pocket-book, and there is Mr. Feccles biting his pencil between his lips, and then cocking his head, first on one side and then on the other.

"Confound Paris," he said at last. "A man gets simply swept away by social engagements. I haven't a thing for a week."

And just then the telephone rang. Lou did a two-step across to the instrument.

"Oh, it's for you, Mr. Feccles," she said. "However did any one know you were here?"

He gave his funny little laugh.

"It's just what I've been telling you, Lady Pendragon," he said, as he walked over to the receiver. "I'm a very much wanted man. Every one seems to want me but the police," he giggled, "and they may get on to me any minute now, the Lord knows."

He became suddenly serious as he talked on the phone.

"Oh, yes," he said to the caller. "Very annoying indeed. What's that? Four o'clock ? All right, I'll be round."

He hung up. He came back to us radiant, holding out his hands.

"My dear friends," he said. "This is a special providence – nothing less. The lunch is off. If your invitation holds, I shall be the happiest man in Europe."

Well, of course, there couldn't be two men like that in Europe. I was

infernally bored. But there was nothing to do except to express the wildest joy.

It didn't add to my pleasure to see that Lou was really pleased. She broke out into a swift sonata.

"Let's lunch up here," she said. "It's more *intime*. I hate feeding in public. I want to dance between the courses."

She rang down for the head waiter while I gave Feccles a cigarette, lamenting my lack of forethought in not having insinuated a charge of trinitro-toluol amid the tobacco.

Lou had a passionate controversy with the head waiter. She won on points at the end of the sixth round. Half an hour later we started the grey caviare.

I don't know why every one has to rejoice on grey caviare; but it's no use trying to interfere with the course of civilisation. I ate it; and if I were in similar circumstances tomorrow, I would do it again.

In the immortal words of Browning, "You lied. D'Ormea, I do not repent." Beside which, this was no ordinary lunch. It was big with the future.

It was an unqualified success from the start. We were all in our best form. Feccles talked freely and irresponsibly with the lightness of champagne. He talked about himself and his amazing luck in financial matters; but he never stayed long enough on any subject to make a definite impression or, you might say, to allow of a reply. He interspersed his remarks with the liveliest anecdotes, and apologised towards the end of the meal for having been preoccupied with the deal which he had on at the moment.

"I'm afraid it's literally obsessing me," he said. "But you know it makes, or rather will make, a big difference to my prospects. Unfortunately, I'm not a millionaire like you, old thing. I've been doing very well, but somehow, it's gone as easy as it came. But I've scraped up twenty thousand of the best to buy an eighth share in this oil proposition that I told you about."

"No," put in Lou, "you didn't tell us what it was."

"I made sure I had," he laughed back; "I've got it fairly on the brain, especially since that lunch was put off. I need another five thou', you see,

and I was going to dig it out of those birds. The only difficulty was that I can't exactly borrow it on my face, can I? And I don't want to let those birds into 'the know' – they'd simply snap the whole thing up for themselves. By the way, that reminds me of a very good thing I heard of the other day – " and he rattled off an amusing story which had no connection with what he had been saying before.

I didn't listen to what it was. My brain was working very fast with the champagne on top of the other things. His talk had brought to my mind that I should have to wire for another thousand today or tomorrow. I was aware of a violent subconscious irritation. The man's talk had dealt so airily with millions that I couldn't help recognising that I was a very poor man indeed, by modern standards. Five or six thousand a year, and perhaps another fifteen hundred from the rents of the Barley Grange estate, and that infernal income tax and so on – I was really little better than a pauper, and there was Lou to be considered.

I had always thought jewellery vulgar; a signet ring and a tie pin for a man – for a woman, a few trinkets, very quiet, in good taste – that was the limit.

But Lou was absolutely different. She could wear any amount of the stuff and carry it off superbly. I had bought her a pair of ear-rings in Cartier's yesterday afternoon – three diamonds in a string, the pendant being a wonderful pear-shaped blue-white, and as she ate, and drank, and talked, they waggled behind the angle of her jaw in the most deliciously fascinating way, and it didn't vulgarise her at all.

I realised that, as a married man, it was my duty to buy her that string of pearls with the big black pearl as a pendant, and there was that cabochon emerald ring! How madly that would go with her hair. And then, of course, when we got back to England, she must be presented at Court, not but what we Pendragons don't feel it a little humiliating – that meant a tiara, of course.

And then you know what dressmakers are!

There's simply no end to the things that a civilised man has to have when he's married! And here was I, to all intents and purposes, a case for out-door relief.

I came out of my reverie with a start. My mind was made up.

Lou was laughing hysterically at some story of a blind man and a gimlet.

"Look here, Feccles," I said. "I wish you'd tell me a little more about this oil business. To tell you the truth, I'm not the rich man you seem to think –"

"My dear fellow – " said Feccles.

"In fact, I assure you," said I. "Of course, it was all very well when I was a bachelor. Simple tastes, you know. But this little lady makes all the difference."

"Why, certainly," replied Feccles, very seriously. "Yes, I see that perfectly. In fact, if I may say so, it's really a duty to yourself and your heirs, to put yourself on Easy Street. But money's been frightfully tight since the war as you know. What with the collapse in the foreign exchanges, the decrease in the purchasing power of money, and the world's gold all locked up in Washington, things are pretty awkward. But then, you know, it's just that sort of situation which provides opportunities to a man with real brains. Victorian prosperity made us all rich without our knowing anything about it or doing anything for it."

"Yes," I admitted, "the gilt edges seem to have come off the ginger-bread securities."

"Well, look here, Pendragon," he said, pulling his chair half round so as to face me squarely, and making his points by tapping his Corona on a plate, "the future lies with just two things as far as big money's concerned. One's oil, and the other is cotton. Now, I don't know a thing about cotton, but I'll give any sperm whale that ever blew four thousand points in twelve thousand up about oil, and you can lay your shirt on the challenger."

"Yes, I see that," I replied brightly. "Of course, I don't know the first thing about finance; but what you say is absolutely common sense. And I've got a sort of flair for these things, I believe."

"Why, it's very curious you should say that," returned Feccles, as in great surprise. "I was thinking the same thing myself. We know you've got pluck, and that's the first essential in any game. And making money is the greatest game there is. But beside that, I've got a hunch that you've got the right kind of brain for this business. You're as

shrewd as they make 'em, and you've got a good imagination. I don't mean the wild fancies that you find in a crank, but a good, wholesome, sound imagination."

In the ordinary way, I should have been embarrassed by so direct a compliment from a man who was so evidently in the know, a man who was holding his own with the brightest minds all over the world. But in my present mood I took it as perfectly natural.

Lou laughed in my ear. "That's right, Cockie, dear," she chirruped. "This is where you go right in and win. I've really got to have those pearls, you know."

"She's quite right," agreed Feccles. "When you're through with this honeymoon, come round with me, and we'll take our coats off and get into the game for all we're worth and a bit more, and when we come out, we'll have J. D. Rockefeller as flat as a pancake."

"Well," said I, "no time like the present. I don't want to butt in, but if I could be any use to you about this deal of yours – "

Feccles shook his head.

"No," he said, "this isn't the sort of thing at all. I'm putting my last bob into the deal; but it's a risky business at the best, and I wouldn't take a chance on your dropping five thou' on the very first bet. Of course, it is rather a good thing if it comes off!"

"Let's have the details, dear boy," I said, trying to feel like a business man bred in the bone.

"The thing itself's simple enough," said Feccles.

It's just a case of taking up an option on some wells at a place called Sitka. They used to be all right before the war – but in my opinion they were never properly developed. They haven't been worked ever since, and it might take all sorts of money to put them on the map again. But that's the smaller point. What I and my friends know and nobody else has got on to is that if we apply the Feldenberg process to the particular kind of oil that Sitka yields, we've got practically a world's monopoly of the highest class oil that exists. I needn't tell you that we can sell it at our own price."

I saw in a flash the magnificent possibilities of the plan.

"Of course, I needn't tell you to keep it as dark as a wolf's mouth," continued Feccles. "If this got out, every financier in Paris would buy

the thing over our heads. I wouldn't have mentioned it to you at all except for two things. I know you're on the square – that goes without saying; but the real point is this, that I told you I rather believe in the Occult."

"Oh, yes," cried Lou, "then, of course, you know King Lamus."

Feccles started as if he had received a blow in the face. For a moment he was completely out of countenance. It seemed as if he were going to say several things, and decided not to. But his face was black as thunder. It was impossible to mistake the meaning of the situation.

I turned to Lou with what I suppose was rather a nasty little laugh.

"Our friend's reputation," I said, "appears to have reached Mr. Feccles."

"Well," said Feccles, recovering himself with a marked effort, "I rather make a point of not saying anything against people, but as a matter of fact, it is a bit on the thick side. You seem to know all about it, so there's no harm in my saying the man's an unspeakable scoundrel."

All my hatred and jealousy surged up from the subconscious. I felt that if Lamus had been there I would have shot him like a dog on sight.

My old school-fellow skated away from the obnoxious topic.

"You didn't let me finish," he complained. "I was going to say I have no particular talent for finance and that sort of thing in the ordinary way, but I have an intuition that never lets me down – like the demon of Socrates, you remember, eh?"

I nodded. I had some faint recollection of Plato.

"Well," said Feccles, tapping his cigar, with the air of a Worshipful Master calling the Lodge to order, "I said to myself when I met you last night, 'It's better to be born lucky than rich, and there's a man who was born lucky.'"

It was perfectly true. I had never been able to do anything of my own abilities, and after all I had tumbled into a reasonably good fortune.

"You've got the touch, Pen," he said, with animation. "Any time you're out of a job, I'll give you ten thousand a year as a mascot."

Lou and I were both intensely excited. We could hardly find the patience to listen to the details of our friend's plan. The figures were convincing; but the effect was simply to dazzle us. We had never dreamed of wealth on this scale.

I got the vision for the first time in my life of the power that wealth confers, and I realised equally for the first time how vast were my real ambitions.

The man was right, too, clearly enough, about my being lucky. My luck in the war had been prodigious. Then there was this inheritance, and Lou on the top of that; and here I'd met old Feccles by a piece of absolute chance, and there was this brilliant investment. That was the word – he was careful to point out that it was not a speculation, strictly speaking – absolutely waiting for me.

We were so overjoyed that we could hardly grasp the practical details. The amount required was four thousand nine hundred and fifty pounds.

Of course, there was no difficulty in getting a trifle like that, but as I told Feccles, it would mean my selling out some beastly stock or something which might take two or three days. There was no time to lose; because the option would lapse if it weren't taken up within the week, and it was now Wednesday.

However, Feccles helped me to draft a wire to Wolfe to explain the urgency, and Feccles was to call on Saturday at nine o'clock with the papers.

Meanwhile, of course, he wouldn't let me down, but at the same time he couldn't risk pulling off the coup of his life in case there was a hitch, so he would get a move on and see if he couldn't raise five thousand on his own somewhere else, in which case he'd let me have some of his own stock anyway. He wanted me in the deal if it was only for a sovereign, simply because of my luck.

So off he ran in a great hurry. Lou and I got a car and spent the afternoon in the Bois du Boulogne. It seemed as if the cocaine had taken hold of us with new force, or else it was the addition of the heroin.

We were living at the same terrific speed as on that first wild night. The intensity was even more extraordinary; but we were not being carried away by it.

In one sense, each hour lasted a fraction of a second, and yet, in another sense, every second lasted a lifetime. We were able to appreciate the minutest details of life to the full.

I want to explain this very thoroughly.

"William the Conqueror, 1066, William Rufus, 1087."

One can sum up the whole period of the reign of the Duke of Normandy in a phrase. At the same time, an historian who had made a special study of that part of English History might be able to write ten volumes of details, and he might, in a sense, have both aspects of his knowledge present to his mind at the same moment.

We were in a similar condition. The hours flashed by like so many streaks of lightning, yet each discharge illuminated every detail of the landscape; we could grasp everything at once. It was as if we had acquired a totally new mental faculty as superior to the normal course of thought as the all-comprehending brain of a great man of science is to that of a savage, though the two men are both looking with the same optical instruments at the same black beetle.

It is impossible to convey, to any one who has not experienced it, the overwhelming rapture of this condition.

Another extraordinary feature of the situation was this; that we seemed to be endowed with what I must call the power of telepathy, for want of a better word. We didn't need to explain ourselves to each other.

Our minds worked together like those of two first-class three-quarters who are accustomed to play together.

Part of the enjoyment, moreover, came from the knowledge that we were infinitely superior to anything we might happen to meet. The mere fact that we had so much more time to think than other people assured us of this.

We were like a leash of greyhounds, and the rest of the world so many hares, but the disproportion of speed was immensely increased. It was the airman against the wagoner.

We went to bed early that night. We had already got a little tired of Paris. The pace was too slow for us. It was rather like sitting at a Wagner opera. There were some thrilling moments, of course, but most of the time we were bored with long and monotonous passages like the dialogue between Wotan and Erde. We wanted to be by ourselves; no one else could keep up with the rush.

The difference between sleep and waking, again, was diminished, no, almost abolished. The period of sleep was simply like a brief

distraction of attention, and even our dreams continued the exaltation of our love.

The importance of any incident was negligible. In the ordinary way one's actions are to a certain extent inhibited. As the phrase goes, one thinks twice before doing so and so. We weren't thinking twice anymore. Desire was transformed into action without the slightest check. Fatigue, too, had been completely banished.

We woke the next morning with the sun. We stood on the balcony in our dressing-gowns and watched him rise. We felt ourselves one with him, as fresh and as fervent as he. Inexhaustible energy!

We danced and sang through breakfast. We had a phase of babbling, both talking at once at the top of our voices, making plans for the day, each one as it bubbled in our brains the source of ecstatic excitement and inextinguishable laughter.

We had just decided to spend the morning shopping when a card was brought up to the room.

I had a momentary amazement as I read that our visitor was the confidential clerk of Mr. Wolfe.

"Oh, bother the fellow," said I, and then remembered my telegram of the day before.

I had a swift pang of alarm. Could something be wrong? But the cocaine assured me that everything was all right.

"I'll have to see the fellow, I suppose," I said, and told the hall-boy to send him upstairs.

"Don't let him keep you long," said Lou, with a petulant pout, and ran into the bedroom after a swift embrace, so violent that it disarranged my new Charvet necktie.

The man came up. I was a little bored by the gravity of his manner, and rather disgusted by its solemn deference. Of course, one likes being treated as a kind of toy emperor in a way, but that sort of thing doesn't go with Paris. Still less does it go with cocaine.

It annoyed me that the fellow was so obviously ill at ease, and also that he was so obviously proud of himself for having been sent to Paris on important business with a real live knight.

If there's one thing flying teaches one more than another, it is to hate

snobbery. Even the Garter becomes imperceptible when one is flying above the clouds.

I couldn't possibly talk to the man till he was a little more human. I made him sit down and have a drink and cigarette before I would let him tell me his business.

Of course, everything was perfectly in order. The point was simply this, that the six thousand pounds wasn't immediately available, so, as I needed it urgently, it was necessary for me to sign certain papers which Mr. Wolfe had drawn up at once, on receipt of my wire, and it would be better to have it done at the consulate.

"Why, of course, get a taxi," I said; "I'll be down in a minute."

He went downstairs. I ran in to Lou and told her that I had to go to the consul on business: I'd be back in an hour and we could do our shopping.

We took a big sniff of snow and kissed goodbye as if I were starting on a three years' expedition to the South Pole. Then I caught up my hat, gloves, and cane, and found my young man at the door.

The drink and the air of Paris had given him a sense of his own dignity. Instead of waiting humbly for me to get into the car, he was sitting there already; and though his greeting was still solemnly deferential, there was a little more of the ambassador about it. He had repressed the original impulse to touch his hat.

I myself felt a curious sense of enjoyment of my own importance. At the same time, I was in a violent hurry to get back to Lou. My brain was racing with the thought of her. I signed my name where they told me, and the consul dabbed it all over with stamps, and we drove back to the hotel, where the clerk extracted a locked leather wallet from a mysterious inside hip pocket and counted me out my six thousand in hundred-pound notes.

Of course, I had to ask the fellow to lunch, it was only decent, but I was very glad when he excused himself. He had to catch the two o'clock train back to town.

"Good God, what a time you've been," said Lou, and I could see that she had been filling it in in a wonderful way. It was up to her neck. She danced about like a crazy woman with little jerky movements which I

couldn't help seeing signified nervous irritability. However, she was radiant, beaming, glowing, bursting with excitement.

Well, you know, I don't like to be left in the lurch. I had to catch up. I literally shovelled the snow down. I ought to have been paid a shilling an hour by the County Council. The world is full of injustice.

However, we certainly didn't have any time to have questions asked in Parliament. There was Lou almost in tears because she had nothing to wear; practically no jewellery – the whole idea of being a knight is that when you see a wrong it is your duty to right it.

Fortunately, there was no difficulty at the present moment. All we had to do was to drive down to the Rue de la Paix. I certainly almost fell down when I saw all those pearls on her neck. And that cabochon emerald! By George, it did go with her hair!

These shop men in Paris are certainly artists. The man saw in a moment what was wrong. There was nothing to match the blue of her dress, so he showed us a sapphire and diamond bracelet and a big marquise ring that went with it in a platinum setting. That certainly made all the difference! And yet he seemed to be very uneasy. He was puzzled; that's what it was.

Then his face lightened up. He had got the idea all right. You can always trust these chaps when you strike a really good man. What was missing was something red!

I told you about Lou's mouth; her long, jagged, snaky, scarlet streak always writhing and twisting as if it had a separate life of its own and were perpetually in some delicious kind of torture!

The man saw immediately what was necessary. The mouth had to be repeated symbolically. That's the whole secret of art. So he fished out a snake of pigeon's blood rubies.

My God! it was the most beautiful thing I had ever seen in my life, except Lou herself. And you couldn't look at it without thinking of her mouth, and you couldn't think of her mouth without wanting to kiss it, and it was up to me to prove to Paris that I had the most beautiful woman in the world for my wife, and that could only be done in the regular way by showing her off in the best dresses and the most wonderful jewellery. It was my duty to her as my wife, and I could afford it perfectly well

because I was a tolerably rich man to start with anyhow, and besides, the five thousand I was putting into Feccles' business would mean something like a quarter of a million at least, on the most conservative calculations, as I had seen with my own eyes.

And that was all clear profit, so there was no reason in the world why one shouldn't spend it in a sensible way. Mr. Wolfe himself had emphasised the difficulty of getting satisfactory investments in these times.

He told me how many people were putting their money into diamonds and furs which always keep their value, whereas government securities and that sort of thing are subject to unexpected taxation, for one thing, depreciation for another, with the possibility of European repudiation looming behind them all.

As a family man, it was my duty to buy as many jewels for Lou as I could afford. At the same time, one has to be cautious.

I bought the things I mentioned and paid for them. I refused to be tempted by a green pearl tie pin for myself, though I should have liked to have had it because it would have reminded me of Lou's eyes every time I put it on. But it was really rather expensive, and Mr. Wolfe had warned me very seriously about getting into debt, so I paid for the rest of the stuff, and we went off, and we thought we'd drive out to the Bois for lunch, and then we took some more snow in the taxi and Lou began to cry because I had bought nothing for myself. So we took some more snow, we had plenty of time, nobody lunches before two o'clock. We went straight back to the shop and bought the green pearl, and that got Lou so excited that the taxi was like an aeroplane; if anything, more so.

It's stupid to hang back. If you start to do a thing, you'd much better do it. What's that fellow say? "I do not set my life at a pin's fee." That's the right spirit. "Unhand me, gentlemen, I'll make a ghost of him that lets me."

That's the Pendragon spirit, and that's the flying man's spirit. Get to the top and stay at the top and shoot the other man down!

CHAPTER VII
THE WINGS OF THE OOF-BIRD

The lunch at the Restaurant de la Cascade was like a lunch in a dream. We seemed to be aware of what we were eating without actually tasting it. As I think I said before, it's the anaesthesia of cocaine that determines the phenomena.

When I make a remark like that, I understand that it's the dead and gone medical student popping up.

But never you mind that. The point is that when you have the right amount of snow in you, you can't feel anything in the ordinary sense of the word. You appreciate it in a sort of impersonal way. There's a pain, but the pain doesn't hurt. You enjoy the fact of the pain as you enjoy reading about all sorts of terrible things in history at school.

But the trouble about cocaine is this; that it's almost impossible to take it in moderation as almost any one, except an American, can take whisky. Every dose makes you better and better. It destroys one's power of calculation.

We had already discovered the fact when we found that the supply we had got from Gretel, with the idea that it would last almost indefinitely, was running very short, when the dressing-gown came to solve the problem.

We had only been a few days on the stunt, and what we had got from three or four sniffs, to begin with, meant almost perpetual stoking to carry on. However, that didn't matter, because we had an ample supply. There must have been a couple of kilograms of either C. or H. in that kimono. And when you think that an eighth of a gain is rather a big dose of H., you can easily calculate what a wonderful time you can have on a pound.

You remember how it goes – twenty grains one penny-weight, three penny-weights one scruple – I forget how many scruples one drachm, eight drachms one ounce, twelve ounces one pound.

I've got it all wrong. I could never understand English weights and measures. I have never met any one who could. But the point is you could go on a long time on one-eighth of a grain if you have a pound of the stuff.

Well, this will put it all right for you. Fifteen grains is one gramme, and a thousand grammes is a kilogramme, and a kilogramme is two point two pounds. The only thing I'm not sure about is whether it's a sixteen-ounce pound or a twelve-ounce pound. But I don't see what it matters anyway, if you've got a pound of snow or H. you can go on for a long while, but apparently it's rather awkward orchestrating them.

Quain says that people accustomed to opium and its derivatives can take an enormous amount of cocaine without any bother. In the ordinary way, half a grain of cocaine can cause death, but we were taking the stuff with absolute carelessness.

One doesn't think of measuring it as one would if one took it by hypodermic. One just takes a dose when one feels one needs it. After all, that's the rule of nature. Eat when you're hungry. Nothing is worse for the health than settling down to a fixed ration of so many meals a day.

The grand old British principle of three meat meals has caused the supply of uric acid to exceed the demand in a most reprehensible manner.

Physiology and economics, and, I should think, even geology, combine to protest.

Now we were living an absolutely wholesome life. We took a sniff of cocaine whenever the pace slackened up, and one of heroin when the cocaine showed any signs of taking the bit in its teeth.

What one needs is sound common sense to take reasonable measures according to the physiological indications. One needs elasticity. It's simply spiritual socialism to tie oneself down to fixed doses whether one needs them or not. Nature is the best guide. We had got on to the game.

Our misadventure at the Petit Savoyard had taught us wisdom. We were getting stronger on the wing every hour.

That chap Coué is a piker, as they say in America. "Every day, in every way, I get better and better," indeed? The man must simply have been carried away by the rhyme. Why wait for a day? We had got to the stage where every minute counted.

As the Scotchman said to his son, halfway through the ten-mile walk to kirk, when the boy said, "It's a braw day the day." "Is this a day to be ta'king o' days?"

Thinking of days makes you think of years, and thinking of years makes you think of death, which is ridiculous.

Lou and I were living minute by minute, second by second. A tick of the clock marked for us an interval of eternity.

We were the heirs of eternal life. We had nothing to do with death. That was a pretty wise bird who said, "Tomorrow never comes."

We were out of time and space. We were living according to the instruction of our Saviour "Take no thought for the morrow."

A great restlessness gripped us. Paris was perfectly impossible. We had to get to some place where time doesn't count.

The alternation of day and night doesn't matter so much; but it's absolutely intolerable to be mixed up with people who are working by the clock.

We were living in the world of the Arabian Nights; limitations were abhorrent, Paris was always reminding us of the Pigmies, who lived, if you call it living, in a system of order.

It is monstrous and ridiculous to open and close by convention. We had to go to some place where such things didn't annoy us. . .

An excessively irritating incident spoilt our lunch at the Cascade. We had made a marvellous impression when we came in. We had floated in like butterflies settling on lilies. A buzz went round the tables. Lou's beauty intoxicated everybody. Her jewellery dazzled the crowd.

I thought of an assembly of Greeks of the best period unexpectedly visited by Apollo and Venus.

We palpitated not only with our internal ecstasy but with the intoxicating sense that the whole world admired and envied us. We made them feel like the contents of a wastepaper basket.

The head waiter himself became a high priest. He rose to the situation like the genius he was. He was mentally on his knees as he ventured to advise us in the choice of our lunch.

It seemed to us the tribute of inferior emperors. And there was that fellow King Lamus five or six tables away!

The man with him was a Frenchman of obvious distinction, with a big red rosette and a trim aristocratic white moustache and beard. He was some minister or other. I couldn't quite place him but I'd seen him often enough in the papers: somebody intimate with the president. He had been the principal object of interest before we came in.

Our arrival pricked that bubble.

Lamus had his back to us, and I supposed he didn't see us, for he didn't turn round, though everyone else in the place did so and began to buzz.

I didn't hate the man any more; he was so absurdly inferior. And this was the annoying thing. When he and his friend got up to leave, they passed our table all smiles and bows.

And then, the deuce! The head waiter brought me his card. He had scribbled on it in pencil: "Don't forget me when you need me."

Of all the damned silly impertinence! Absolutely gratuitous insufferable insolence! Who was going to need Mr. Gawd Almighty King Lamus?

I should have handed out some pretty hot repartee if the creature hadn't sneaked off. Well, it wasn't worth while. He didn't count any more than the grounds in the coffee.

But the incident stuck in my mind. It kept on irritating me all the afternoon. People like that ought to be kicked out once and for all.

Why, hang it, the man was all kinds of a scoundrel. Every one said so. Why did he want to butt in? Nobody asked him to meddle.

I said something of the sort to Lou, and she told him off very wittily.

"You've said it, Cockie," she cried. "He's a meddler, and his nature is to be rotten before he's ripe."

I remembered something of the sort in Shakespeare. That was the best of Lou; she was brilliantly clever, but she never forced it down one's throat.

At the same time, as I said, the man stuck in my gizzard. It annoyed me so much that we took a lot more cocaine to get the taste out of our mouths.

But the irritation remained, though it took another form. The bourgeois atmosphere of Paris got on my nerves.

Well, there was no need to stay in the beastly place. The thing to do was to hunt up old Feccles and pay him the cash, and get to some place like Capri where one isn't always being bothered by details.

I was flooded by a crazy desire to see Lou swim in the Blue Grotto, to watch the phosphorescent flames flash from her luminous body.

We told the chauffeur to stop at Feccles's hotel, and that was where we hit a gigantic snag.

Monsieur Feccles, the manager said, had left that morning suddenly. Yes, he had left his heavy baggage. He might be back at any moment. No, he had left no word as to where he was going.

Well, of course, he would be back on Saturday morning to get the five thousand. It was obvious what I was to do. I would leave the money for him, and take the manager's receipt, and tell him to send the papers on to the Caligula at Capri.

I started to count out the cash. We were sitting in the lounge. A sense of absolute bewilderment and helplessness came over me.

"I say, Lou," I stammered, "I wish you'd count this. I can't make it come right. I think I must have been going a bit too hard."

She went through the various pockets of my portefeuille.

"Haven't you some money in your pocket?" she said.

I went through myself with sudden anxiety. I had money in nearly every pocket; but it only amounted to so much small change. A thousand francs here and a hundred francs there, a fifty-pound note in my waistcoat, a lot of small bills –

In the meanwhile, Lou had added up the contents of my portefeuille. The total was just over seventeen hundred.

"My God! I've been robbed," I gasped out, my face flushing furiously with anger.

Lou kept her head and her temper. After all, it wasn't her money! She began to figure on a scrap of the hotel note paper.

"I'm afraid it's all right," she announced, "you dear, bad boy."

I had become suddenly sober. Yes, there was nothing wrong with the figures. I had paid cash to the jeweller without thinking.

By Jove, we were in a hole! I felt instinctively that it was impossible to telegraph to Wolfe for more money. I suppose my face must have fallen; a regular nose dive. Lou put her arm around my waist and dug her nails into my ribs.

"Chuck it, Cockie," she said, "we're well out of a mess. I always had my doubts about Feccles, and his going off like this looks to me as if there were something very funny about it."

My dream of a quarter of a million disappeared without a moment's regret. I had been prudent after all. I had invested my cash in something tangible. Feccles was an obvious crook. If I had handed him that five thousand, I should never have heard of him or of it again.

I began to recover my spirits.

"Look here," said Lou, "let's forget it. Write Feccles a note to say you couldn't raise the money by the date it was wanted, and let's get out. We ought to economise, in any case, Let's get off to Italy as we said. The exchange is awfully good, and living's delightfully cheap. It's silly spending money when you've got Love and Cocaine."

My spirit leapt to meet hers. I scribbled a note of apology to Feccles, and left it at the hotel. We dashed round to the Italian consulate to have our passport vise'd, got our sleeping cars from the hotel porter, and had the maid pack our things while we had a last heavenly dinner.

CHAPTER VIII

VEDERE NAPOLI E POI - PRO PATRIA - MORI

We had just time to get down to the Gare de Lyon for the train de luxe. A sense of infinite relief enveloped us as we left Paris behind; and this was accompanied with an overwhelming fatigue which in itself was unspeakably delicious. The moment our heads touched the pillows we sank like young children into exquisite deep slumber, and we woke early in the morning, exhilarated beyond all expression by the Alpine air that enlarged our lungs; that thrilled us with its keen intensity; that lifted us above the pettiness of civilisation, exalting us to communion with the eternal; our souls soared to the primaeval peaks that towered above the train. They flowed across the limpid lakes, they revelled with the raging Rhone.

Many people have the idea that the danger of drugs lies in the fact that one is tempted to fly to them for refuge whenever one is a little bored

or depressed or annoyed. That is true, of course; but if it stopped there, only a small class of people would stand in real danger.

For example, this brilliant morning, with the sun sparkling on the snow and the water, the whole earth ablush with his glory, the pure keen air rejoicing our lungs; we certainly did say to ourselves, our young eyes ablaze with love and health and happiness, that we didn't need any other element to make our poetry perfect.

I said this without a hint of hesitation. For one thing, we felt like Christian when the burden of his sins fell off his back, at getting away from Paris and civilisation and convention and all that modern artificiality implies.

We had neither the need to get rid of any depression, nor that to increase our already infinite intoxication; ourselves and our love and the boundless beauty of the ever changing landscape, a permanent perfection travelling for its pleasure through inexhaustible possibilities!

Yet almost before the words were out of our mouths, a sly smile crept over Lou's loveliness and kindled the same subtly secret delight in my heart.

She offered me a pinch of heroin with the air of communicating some exquisitely esoteric sacrament and I accepted it and measured her a similar dose on my own hand as if some dim delirious desire devoured us. We took it not because we needed it; but because the act of consummation was, so to speak, an act of religion.

It was the very fact that it was not an act of necessity which made it an act of piety.

In the same way, I cannot say that the dose did us any particular good. It was at once a routine and a ritual. It was a commemoration like the Protestant communion, and at the same time a consecration like the Catholic. It reminded us that we were heirs to the royal rapture in which we were afloat. But also it refreshed that rapture.

We noticed that in spite of the Alpine air, we did not seem to have any great appetite for breakfast, and we appreciated with the instantaneous sympathy which united us that the food of mortals was too gross for the gods.

That sympathy was so strong and so subtle, so fixed in our hearts, that we could not realise the rude, raw fact that we had ever existed as separate

beings. The past was blotted out in the calm contemplation of our beatitude. We understood the changeless ecstasy that radiates from statues of the Buddha; the mysterious triumph on the mouth of Mona Lisa, and the unearthly and ineffable glee of the attitude of Haidé Lamoureux.

We smoked in shining silence as the express swept through the plains of Lombardy. Odd fragments of Shelley's lines on the Euganean hills flitted through my mind like azure or purple phantoms.

> "The vaporous plain of Lombardy
> Islanded with cities fair."

A century had commercialised the cities for the most part into cockpits and cesspools. But Shelley still shone serene as the sun itself.

> "Many a green isle needs must be
> In this wide sea of misery."

Everything he had touched with his pen had blossomed into immortality. And Lou and I were living in the land which his prophetic eyes had seen.

I thought of that incomparable idyll, I will not call it an island, to which he invites Emilia, in Epipsychidion.

Lou and I, my love and I, my wife and I, we were not merely going there; we had always been there and should always be. For the name of the island, the name of the house, the name of Shelley, and the name of Lou and me, they were all one name – Love.

> "The winged words with which my song would pierce
> Into the heights of love's rare universe
> Are chains of lead about its flight of fire,
> I pant, I sink, I tremble, I expire."

I noticed, in fact, that our physical selves seemed to be acting as projections of our thought. We were both breathing rapidly and deeply. Our faces were flushed, suffused with the sunlight splendour of our bloods that beat time to the waltz of our love.

Waltz? No, it was something wilder than a waltz. The Mazurka, perhaps. No, there was something still more savage in our souls.

I thought of the furious fandango of the gypsies of Granada, of the fanatical frenzy of the religious Moorish rioters chopping at themselves with little sacred axes till the blood streams down their bodies, crazily crimson in the stabbing sunlight, and making little scabs of mire upon the torrid trampled sand.

I thought of the maenads and Bacchus; I saw them through the vivid eyes of Euripides and Swinburne. And still unsatisfied, I craved for stranger symbols yet. I became a Witch-Doctor presiding over a cannibal feast, driving the yellow mob of murderers into a fiercer Comus-rout, as the maddening beat of the tom-tom and the sinister scream of the bull-roarer destroy every human quality in the worshippers and make them elemental energies; Valkyrie-vampires surging and shrieking on the summit of the storm.

I do not even know whether to call this a vision, or how to classify it psychologically. It was simply happening to me – and to Lou – though we were sitting decorously enough in our compartment. It became increasingly certain that Haidé, low-class, commonplace, ignorant girl that she was, had somehow been sucked into a stupendous maelstrom of truth.

The normal actions and reactions of the mind and the body are simply so many stupid veils upon the face of Isis.

What happened to them didn't matter. The stunt was to find some trick to make them shut up.

I understood the value of words. It depended, not on their rational meaning, but upon their hieratic suggestion.

> "In Xanadu did Kubla Khan
> A stately pleasure-house decree."

The names mean nothing definite, but they determine the atmosphere of the poem. Sublimity depends upon unintelligibility.

I understood the rapture of the names in Lord Dunsany's stories. I understood how the "barbarous names of evocation" used by magicians,

the bellowings and whistlings of the Gnostics, the Mantras of Hindoo devotees, set their souls spinning till they became giddy with glory.

Even the names of the places that we were passing in the train excited me just as far as they were unfamiliar and sonorous.

I became increasingly excited by the sight of the Italian words, "*E pericoloso sporgersi*". That wouldn't mean much, no doubt, to any one who spoke Italian. To me, it was a master-key of magic. I connected it somehow with my love for Lou. Everything was a symbol of my love for Lou except when that idiotic nuisance, knowledge, declared the contrary.

We were whirling in this tremendous trance all the morning. There kept on coming into my mind the title of a picture I had once seen by some crazy modern painter: "Four red monks carrying a black goat across the snow to Nowhere."

It was obviously an excuse for a scheme of colour but the fantastic imbecility of the phrase, and the subtle suggestion of sinister wickedness, made me pant with suppressed exaltation.

The "first call for lunch" came with startling suddenness. I woke up wildly to recognise the fact that Lou and I had not spoken to each other for hours, that we had been rushing through a Universe of our own creation with stupendous speed and diabolical delight. And at the same time I realised that we had been automatically "coking up" without knowing that we were doing so.

The material world had become of so little importance that I no longer knew where I was. I completely mixed up my present journey with memories of two or three previous Continental excursions.

It was the first time that Lou had ever been farther than Paris, and she looked to me for information as to time and place. With her, familiarity had not bred contempt, and I found myself unable to tell her the most ordinary things about the journey. I didn't even know in which direction we were travelling, whether the Alps came next, or which tunnel we were taking; whether we passed through Florence, or the difference between Geneva and Genoa.

Those who are familiar with the route will realise how hopelessly my mind was entangled. I hardly knew morning from evening. I have described things with absolute confidence which could not possibly have taken place.

We kept on getting up and looking at the map on the panels of the corridor, and I couldn't make out where we were. We compared times and distances only to make confusion worse confounded.

I went into the most obstruse astronomical calculations as to whether we ought to put our watches on an hour or back an hour at the frontier; and I don't know to this day whether I came to any correct conclusion. I had an even chance of being right; but there it stopped.

I remember getting out to stretch our legs at Rome, and that we had a mad impulse to try to see the sights during the twenty minutes or so we had to wait.

I might have done it; but on the platform at Rome I was brought up with a shock. An impossible thing had happened.

"Great Scot," cried a voice from the window of a coach three ahead of our own. "Of all the extraordinary coincidences! How are you?"

We looked up, hardly able to believe our ears. Who should it be but our friend Feccles!

Well, of course, I'd rather have seen the devil himself. After all, I'd behaved to the man rather shabbily; and, incidentally, made a great fool of myself. But what surprised me on second glance was that he was travelling very much incognito. He was hardly recognisable.

I don't think I mentioned he had fair hair with a bald patch, and was clean shaven. But now his hair was dark; and a toupe silently rebuked Nature's inclemency. A small black moustache and imperial completed the disguise. But in addition, his manner of dressing was a camouflage in itself. In Paris he had been dressed very correctly. He might have been a man about town of very good family.

But now he was dressed like a courier, or possibly a high-class commercial traveller. His smartness had an element of commonness very well marked. I instinctively knew that he would prefer me not to mention his name.

At this moment the train began to move, and we had to hop on. We went at once to his compartment. It was a coupé, and he was its sole occupant.

I have already described the shock which the reappearance of Feccles had administered to my nerves.

Normally, I should have felt very awkward indeed, but the cocaine lifted me easily over the fence.

The incident became welcome; an additional adventure in the fairy tale which we were living. Lou herself was all gush and giggles to an extent which a month earlier I should have thought a shade off. But everything was equally exquisite on this grand combination honeymoon.

Feccles appeared extremely amused by the encounter. I asked him with the proper degree of concern if he had had my note. He said no, he'd been called suddenly away on business, I told him what I had written, with added apologies.

The long journey had tired me deep down. I took things more seriously, though the cocaine prevented my realising that this was the case.

"My dear fellow," he protested. "I'm extremely annoyed that you should have troubled yourself about the business at all. As a matter of fact, what happened is this. I went round to see those men at four o'clock, as arranged on the 'phone, and they were really so awfully decent about the whole thing that I had to let them in for five thousand, and they wrote me their cheque on the spot. Now, of course, you mustn't imagine that I'd let an old pal down. Any time you find yourself with a little loose cash, just weigh in. You can have it out of my bit."

"Well, that's really too good of you," I said, "and I won't forget it. It'll be all right, I suppose, now you've got the thing through, to wait till I get back to England."

"Why, of course," he replied. "Don't think about business at all. It was really rotten of me to talk shop to a man on his honeymoon."

Lou took up the conversation. "But do tell us," she began, "why this thusness. It suits you splendidly, you know. But after all, I'm a woman."

Feccles suddenly became very solemn. He went to the door of the coupé and looked up and down the corridor; then he slid the door to and began to speak in a whisper.

"This is a very serious business," he said, and paused. He took out his keys and played with them, as if uncertain how far to go. He thrust them back into his pocket with a decisive gesture.

"Look here, old chap," he said, "I'll take a chance on you. We all know

what you did for England during the war – and take one thing with another, you're about my first pick."

He stopped short. We looked at him blankly, though we were seething with some blind suppressed excitement whose nature we could hardly describe.

He took out a pipe, and began to nibble the vulcanite rather nervously. He drew a deep breath, and looked Lou straight in the face.

"Does it suggest anything to you," he murmured, almost inaudibly, "a man's leaving Paris at a moment's notice in the middle of a vast financial scheme, and turning up in Italy, heavily camouflaged?"

"The police on your track!" giggled Lou.

He broke into hearty, good-natured laughter. "Getting warm," he said. "But try again."

The explanation flashed into my mind at once. He saw what I was thinking, and smiled and nodded.

"Oh, I see," said Lou wisely and bent over to him and whispered in his ear. The words were:

– *"Secret Service"*.

"That's it," said Feccles softly. "And this is where you come in. Look here."

He brought out a passport from his pocket and opened it. He was Monsieur Hector Laroche, of Geneva, so it appeared; by profession a courier.

We nodded comprehensively.

"I was rather at my wits' end when I saw you," he went on. "I'm on the trail of a very dangerous man who has got into the confidence of some English people living in Capri. That's where you're going, isn't it?"

"Yes," we said, feeling ourselves of international importance.

"Well, it's like this. If I turn up in Capri, which is a very small place, without a particularly good excuse, people will look at me and talk about me, and if they look too hard and talk too much, it's ten to one I'm spotted, not necessarily for what I am, but as a stranger of

suspicious character. And if the man I'm after gets on his guard, there'll be absolutely nothing doing."

"Yes," I said, "I see all that, but – well, we'd do anything for good old England – goes without saying, but how can we help you out?"

"Well," said Feccles, "I don't see why it should put you out very much. You needn't even see me. But if I could pose as your courier, go ahead and book your rooms and look after your luggage and engage boats and that sort of thing for you, I shouldn't need to be explained. As things are, it might even save you trouble. They're the most frightful brigands round here; and anything that looks like a tourist, especially of the honeymoon species, is liable to all sorts of bother and robbery."

Well, the thing did seem almost providential; as a matter of fact, I had been thinking of getting a man to keep off the jackals, and this was killing two birds with one stone.

Lou was obviously delighted with the arrangement. "Oh, but you must let us do more than that," she said. "If we could only help you spot this swine!"

"You bet I will," said Feccles heartily, and we all shook hands on it. "Any time anything happens where you could be useful, I'll tell you what to do. But of course you'll have to remember the rules of the service – absolute silence and obedience. And you stand or fall on your own feet, and if the umpire says 'out', you're out, and nobody's going to pick up the pieces."

This honeymoon was certainly coming out in the most wonderful way. We had left the cinema people at the post. Here we were, without any effort of our own, right in the middle of the most fascinating intrigues of the most mysterious kind. And all that on the top of the most wonderful love there was in the world, and heroin and cocaine to help us make the most of the tiniest details.

"Well," said I to Feccles, "this suits me down to the ground. I'm trying to forget what you said about my brain, because it isn't good for a young man to be puffed up with intellectual vanity. But I certainly am the luckiest man in the world."

M. Hector Laroche gave us a delightful hour, telling of some of his past exploits in the war. He was as modest as he was brave; but for all

that, we could see well enough what amazing astuteness he had brought to the service of our country in her hour of peril. We could imagine him making rings round the lumbering minds of the Huns with their slow pedantic processes.

The only drawback to the evening was that we couldn't get him to take any snow. And you know what that means – you feel the man's somehow out of the party. He excused himself by saying that the regulations forbade it. He agreed with us that it was rotten red-tape, but "of course, they're right in a way, there are quite a lot of chaps that wouldn't know how to use it, might get a bit above themselves and give something away – you know how it is."

So we left him quietly smoking, and went back to our own little cubby and had the most glorious night, whispering imaginary intrigues which somehow lent stronger wing to the real rapture of our love. We neither of us slept. We simply sailed through the darkness to find the dawn caressing the crest of Posilippo and the first glint of sunrise signalling ecstatic greetings to the blue waters of the Bay of Naples.

When the train stopped, there was Hector Laroche at the door, ordering everybody about in fluent Italian. We had the best suite in the best hotel, and our luggage arrived not ten minutes later than we did, and breakfast was a perfect poem, and we had a box for the opera and our passages booked for the following day for Capri, where a suite was reserved for us at the Caligula. We saw the Museum in the morning and automobiled out to Pompeii in the afternoon, and yet M. Laroche had managed everything for us so miraculously well that even this very full day left us perfectly fresh, murmuring through half-closed lips the magic sentence "*Dolce far niente.*"

The majority of people seem to stumble through this world without any conception of the possibilities of enjoyment. It is, of course, a matter of temperament.

But even the few who can appreciate the language of Shelley, Keats and Swinburne look on those conceptions as Utopian.

Most people acquiesce in the idea that the giddy exaltation of *Prometheus Unbound*, for example, is an imaginary feeling. I suppose, in fact, that one wouldn't get much result by giving heroin and cocaine,

however cunningly mixed, to the average man. You can't get out of a thing what isn't there.

In ninety-nine cases out of a hundred, any stimulant of whatever nature operates by destroying temporarily the inhibitions of education.

The ordinary drunken man loses the veneer of civilisation. But if you get the right man, the administration of a drug is quite likely to suppress his mental faculties, with the result that his genius is set free. Coleridge is a case in point. When he happened to get the right quantity of laudanum in him, he dreamed Kubla Khan, one of the supreme treasures of the language.

And why is it incomplete? Because a man called from Porlock on business and called him back to his normal self, so that he forgot all but a few lines of the poem. Similarly, we have Herbert Spencer taking morphia very day of his life, decade after decade. Without morphia, he would simply have been a querulous invalid, preoccupied with bodily pain. With it, he was the genius whose philosophy summarised the thought of the nineteenth century.

But Lou and I were born with a feeling for romance and adventure. The ecstasy of first love was already enough to take us out of ourselves to a certain extent. The action of the drugs intensified and spiritualised these possibilities.

The atmosphere of Capri, and the genius of Feccles for preventing any interference with our pleasure, made our first fortnight on the island an unending trance of unearthly beauty.

He never allowed us a chance to be bored, and yet, he never intruded. He took all the responsibilities off our hands, he arranged excursions to Anacapri, to the Villa of Tiberius and to the various grottos. Once or twice he suggested a wild night in Naples, and we revelled in the peculiar haunts of vice with which that city abounds.

Nothing shocked us, nothing surprised us. Every incident of life was the striking of a separate note in the course of an indescribable symphony.

He introduced us to the queerest people, drove us into the most mysterious quarters. But everything that happened wove itself intoxicatingly into the tapestry of love.

We went out on absurd adventures. Even when they were disappointing from the ordinary standpoint, the disappointment itself seemed to add piquancy to the joke.

One couldn't help being grateful to the man for his protecting care. We went into plenty of places where the innocent tourist is considered fair game; and his idiomatic Italian invariably deterred the would-be sportsman. Even at the hotel, he fought the manager over the weekly bill, and compelled him to accept a much lower figure than his dreams had indicated.

Of course, most of his time was occupied with keeping watch on the man he was trailing; and he kept us very amused with the account of his progress.

"I shall never be grateful enough to you, if I bring this off as I think I shall," he said. "It will be the turning point in my official career. I don't mind telling you they've treated me rather shabbily at home about one or two things I've done. But if I bag this bird, they can hardly say no to anything I may ask."

At the same time, it was clear that he took a genuine friendly interest in his love-birds, as he called us. He had had a disappointment himself, he said, and it had put him off the business personally, but he was glad to say it hadn't soured his nature, and he took a real pleasure in seeing people so ideally happy as we were.

The only thing, he said, that made him a little uneasy and discontented was that he hadn't got in touch with the people who ran the Gatto Fritto, which was an extremely exciting and dangerous kind of night club which indulged in pleasures of so esoteric a kind that no other place in Europe had anything to compare with it.

CHAPTER IX
THE GATTO FRITTO

It was about the end of the third week, I discover from Lou's Diary (I had lost all count of time myself), that he came in one day with a smile of subtle triumph in his eyes.

"I've got on to the ropes," he said, "but I think I ought in fairness to warn you that the Gatto Fritto is a pretty hot place. I wouldn't mind taking you as long as you go in disguise and have a gun in your pocket, but I really can't take it on my conscience to have Lady Pendragon along."

I was so full up with cocaine I hardly knew what he was saying. It was the easiest way out to nod assent and watch the clouds fighting each other to get hold of the sun.

I was betting on that big white elephant on the horizon. There were two black cobras and a purple hippopotamus against him; but I couldn't help that. With those magnificent tusks he ought to be able to settle their business, and only to look at his legs you could see the old sun hadn't got a dog's chance. I can't see why people haven't the sense to

keep still when a fight of this kind is in progress. What's the referee for, anyway?

It was extremely annoying of Lou to protest in that passionate shrill voice of hers that she was going to the Gatto Fritto, and if she didn't she'd take to keeping cats herself, and fry them, and make me eat them!

I don't know how long she went on. It was perfectly gorgeous to hear her. I knew what it meant just as soon as we could get rid of that swine Feccles.

Hang it all, one doesn't want another man on one's honeymoon!

So there was Feccles turning to me in a sort of limp, helpless protest, imploring me to put my foot down about it.

So I said, "Feccles, old top, you're the right sort. I always liked you at school; and I shall never forget what you've done for me these last thirty or forty years or whatever it is we've been in Capri, and Lloyd George can trust you to nip that blighter you're after, why shouldn't I trust you to see us through this fun at the Gatto Fritto?"

Lou clapped her hands, screaming with merriment, but Feccles said:

"Now, that's all right. But this is a very serious business. You're not going about it in the right spirit. We've got to go about it very quietly and soberly, and then open up when the word comes over the top."

We pretended to pull ourselves together to please him, but I couldn't blind my eyes to the fact that I was likely to lose my money, because the white elephant had turned into a quite ordinary Zebu or Brahman cow, or at the best a two-humped or Bactrian dromedary, in any case, an animal entirely unfitted by nature to carry the money of a cautious backer.

Agitated by this circumstance, I was hardly in a condition to realise the nature of the proposals laid before the meeting by Worshipful Brother Feccles, Acting Deputy Grand Secretary General.

But roughly they were to this effect: That we were to lock up all our money and jewellery, except a little small change, as an act of precaution, and Feccles would arrive in due course, with disguises for me and Lou as Neapolitan fisherfolk, and we were to take nothing but a revolver apiece and a little small change, and we were to slip off the terrace of the hotel after dark without any one seeing, and there would be a motor-boat across to Sorrento; and there would be an automobile, so we could get into

Naples at about one o'clock in the morning, and then we were to go to a certain drinking place, the Fauno Ebbrio, and as soon as the coast was clear he would pick us up and take us along to the Gatto Fritto, and we would know for the first time what life was really like.

Well, I call that a perfectly straight, decent, sensible programme. It's the duty of every Englishman to learn as much of foreign affairs as he can without interfering with his business. That sort of knowledge will always come in useful in case of another European War. It was knowing that sort of thing that had put Feccles where he was in the Secret Service, the trusted confident of those mysterious intelligences that watch over the welfare of our beloved country.

Thank you, that will conclude the evening's entertainment.

I will say this for Feccles. He always understood instinctively when he wasn't wanted. So immediately the arrangements were made, he excused himself hastily, because he had to go down to the Villa where his victim was staying, and fix a dictaphone in the room where he was going to have dinner.

So I had Lou all to myself until he came with the disguises the next day in the afternoon. And I wasn't going to waste a minute.

I admit I was pretty sick about the way the white cloud let me down. I'd have gone after the silly old sun myself if I hadn't been a married man.

However, there we were alone, alone for ever, Lou and I in Capri, it was all much too good to be true! Sunlight and moonlight and starlight! They were all in her eyes. And she handed out the cocaine with such a provocative gesture! I knew what it was to be insane. I could understand perfectly well why the silly fools that aren't insane are afraid of being insane. I'd been that way myself when I didn't know any better.

This rotten little race of men measures the world by its own standard. It is lost in the vastness of the Universe, and is consequently afraid of everything that doesn't happen to fit its own limits.

Lou and I had discarded the miserable measures of mankind. That sort of thing is all right for tailors and men of science; but we had sprung in one leap to be conterminous with the Universe. We were as incommensurable as the ratio of a circle to its diameter. We were as imaginary and unreal from their point of view as the square root of minus one.

We didn't ask humanity to judge us. It was simply a case of mistaken identity to regard us as featherless bipeds at all. We may have looked like human beings to their eyes; in fact, they sent in bills and things as if we had been human beings.

But I refuse to be responsible for the mistakes of the inferior animals. I humour them to some extent in their delusions, because they're lunatics and ought to be humoured. But it's a long way between that and admitting that their hallucinations have any basis in fact.

I had been in their silly world of sense a million years or so ago, when I was Peter Pendragon.

But why recall the painful past? Of course, one doesn't come to one's full strength in a minute. Take the case of an eagle. What is it as long as it's in the egg? Nothing but an egg with possibilities. And the first day it's hatched you don't expect it to fly to Neptune and back. Certainly not!

But every day, in every way, it gets better and better. And if I was ever tempted to flop and remember my base origin as a forked radish, why all I needed was a kiss from Lou, or a sniff of cocaine to put me back in Paradise.

I can't tell you about those next twenty-four hours. Suffice it to say that all world's records were broken and broken again. And we were simply panting like two hungry wolves when Feccles turned up with the disguises and the guns!

He repeated those instructions, and added one word of almost paternal counsel in a very confidential tone.

"You'll excuse me, I know; I'm not suggesting for a moment you're not perfectly capable of taking care of yourself, but you haven't been in these parts before, and you must never forget the quick, violent tempers of these Southern Italians. It's like one of these sudden gusts that the fishermen are so afraid of. It doesn't mean anything in particular; but it's often ugly enough at the moment, and what you have to do is to keep out of any kind of a row. There may be a lot of drunken ruffians in the Fauno Ebbrio. Sit near the door; and if anybody starts scrapping, slip out quietly and walk up and down till it's over. You don't want to get mixed up with a fuss."

I could see the wisdom of his remarks, although, on the other hand, I was personally spoiling for a fight. The one fly in the apothecary's

ointment of the honeymoon, though I didn't notice it, was that something in me missed the excitement of the daily gambling with death to which the war had accustomed me.

The slightest reminder of the wilder passions – a couple of boatmen quarrelling, or even a tourist protesting about some trifle, sent the blood to my head. I only wanted a legitimate excuse for killing a few hundred people.

But nature is wise and kind, and I was always able to take it out of Lou. The passions of murder and love are inseparably connected in our ancestry. All civilisation has done is to teach us to pretend to idealise them.

The programme went off without the slightest hitch. Our room opened on to a terrace in deep shadow. At this time of year there was hardly any one in the hotel, of course. A little flight of steps at the side of the terrace took us under an arch of twisted vines into the barely more than mule-path that does duty for a road in Capri.

No one took any notice of us. There were only strolling lovers, parties of peasants singing as they walked to the guitar, and two or three tired happy fishermen strolling home from the wine-shop.

We found the motor-boat at the quay, and lay lapsed in delight. It seemed hardly a minute later when we found ourselves in Sorrento couched in a huge roadster. Without a word spoken, we were off at top speed.

The beauty of the drive is notorious; and yet:

> "We were the first that ever burst
> Into that silent sea."

The world had been created afresh for our sakes. It was an ever-changing phantasmagoria of rapturous sounds and sights and scents; and it all seemed a mere ornamentation for our love, the setting for the jewel of our sparkling passion.

Even the last few miles into Naples, where the road runs through tedious commercialised suburbs, took on a new aspect. The houses were a mere irregular skyline. Somehow they suggested the jagged contour of a score of Debussy.

But all this, exquisite as it was, gripping as it was, was in a way superficial. At the bottom of our hearts there seethed and surged a white hot volcanic lake of molten, of infernal, metal.

We did not know what hideous, what monstrous abominations were in store for us at the Gatto Fritto.

I have set down how the action of the drugs had partially stripped off the recent layers of memory. It had achieved a parallel result much more efficiently on the moral plane. The toil of countless generations of evolution had been undone in a month. We still preserved, to a certain extent, the conventions of decency; but we knew that we did so only from ape-like cunning.

We had reverted to the gorilla. No action of violence and lust but seemed a necessary outlet for our energies!

We said nothing to each other about this. It was, in fact, deeper and darker than could be conveyed by articulate speech.

Man differs from the lower animals indeed, first of all, in this matter of language. The use of language compels one to measure one's thoughts. That is why the great philosophers and mystics, who are dealing with ideas that cannot be expressed in such terms, are constantly compelled to use negative adjectives, or to rebuke the mind by formulating their thoughts in a series of contradictory statements. That is the explanation of the Athanasian Creed. Its clauses puzzle the plain man.

One must oneself be divine to comprehend divinity,

The converse proposition is equally true. The passions of the pit find outlet only in bestial noises.

The automobile stopped at the end of the dirty little street where the Fauno Ebbrio lurks. The motorman pointed to the zig-zag streak of light that issued from it, and cast a sinister gleam on the opposite wall.

A bold, black-haired, short-skirted girl with a gaudy shawl and huge gold ear-rings was standing in the door. What with the long journey and the drugs and other things, we were a little drunk – just enough to realise that it was part of our policy to pretend to be a little more drunk than we were.

We let our heads roll from side to side as we staggered to the door. We sat down at a little table and called for drink. They served

us one of those foul Italian imitations of liqueurs that taste like hair-wash.

But instead of nauseating us, it exalted us; we enjoyed it as part of the game. Dressed as low-class Neapolitans, we threw ourselves heartily into the part.

We threw the fiery filth down our throats as if it had been Courvoisier '65. The drink took effect on us with surprising alacrity. It seemed to let loose those swarming caravans of driver ants that eat their way through the jungle of life like a splash of sulphuric acid flung in a woman's face.

There was no clock in the den, and of course we had left our watches at home. We got a little impatient. We couldn't remember whether Feccles had or had not told us how long he was likely to be. The air of the room was stifling. The lowest vagabonds of Naples crowded the place. Some were jabbering like apes; some singing drunkenly to themselves; some shamelessly caressing; some sunk in bestial stupor.

Among the last was a burly brute who somehow fascinated our attention.

We thought ourselves quite safe in speaking English; and for all I know we were talking at the top of our voices. Lou maintained that this particular man was English himself.

He was apparently asleep; but presently he lifted his head from the table, stretched his great arms, and called for a drink, in Italian.

He drained his glass at a gulp, and then came suddenly over to our table and addressed us in English.

We could tell at once from his accent that the man had originally been more or less of a gentleman, but his face and his tone told their own story. He must have been going downhill for many years – reached the bottom long ago, and found it the easiest place to live.

He was aggressively friendly in a brutal way, and warned us that our disguises might be a source of danger; any one could see through them, and the fact of our having adopted them might arouse the quick suspicion of the Neapolitan mind.

He called for drinks, and toasted King and Country with a sort of surly pride in his origin. He reminded me of Kipling's broken-down Englishman.

"Don't you be afraid," he said to Lou. "I won't let you come to any harm. A little peach like you? No blooming fear!"

I resented the remark with almost insane intensity, To hell with the fellow!

He noticed it at once, and leered with a horrible chuckle.

"All right, mister," he said. "No offence meant," and he threw an arm round Lou's neck, and made a movement to kiss her.

I was on my feet in a second, and swung my right to his jaw. It knocked him off the bench, and he lay flat.

In a moment the uproar began. All my old fighting instincts flashed to the surface. I realised instantly that we were in for the very row that Feccles had so wisely warned us to avoid.

The whole crowd – men and women – were on their feet. They were rushing at us like stampeding cattle. I whipped out my revolver. The wave surged back as a breaker does when it hits a rock.

"Guard my back!" I cried to Lou.

She hardly needed telling. The spirit of the true Englishwoman in a crisis was aflame in her.

Fixing the crowd with my eyes and my barrel, we edged our way to the door. One man took up a glass to throw; but the Padrone had slipped out from behind the bar, and knocked his arm down.

The glass smashed to the floor. The attack on us degenerated into a volley of oaths and shrieks. We found ourselves in the fresh air – and also in the arms of half a dozen police who had run up from both ends of the street.

Two of them strode into the wine-shop. The uproar ceased as if by magic.

And then we found that we were under arrest. We were being questioned in voluble, excited Italian. Neither Lou nor I understood a word that was said to us.

The sergeant came out of the dive. He seemed an intelligent man. He understood at once that we were English.

"*Inglese?*" he asked. "*Inglese?*" and I forcibly echoed "*Inglese, Signore Inglese,*" as if that settled the whole matter.

English people on the Continent have an illusion that the mere fact of their nationality permits them to do anything soever. And there is a

great deal of truth in this, after all, because the inhabitants of Europe have a settled conviction that we are all harmless lunatics. So we are allowed to act in all sorts of ways which they would not tolerate for a moment in any supposedly rational person.

In the present instance, I have little doubt that, if we had been dressed as ourselves, we should have been politely conducted to our hotel or put into an automobile, without any more fuss, perhaps, than a few perfunctory questions intended to impress the sergeant's men with his importance.

But as it was, he shook his head doubtfully.

"*Arme vietate*," he said solemnly, pointing to the revolvers which were still in our hands.

I tried to explain the affair in broken Italian. Lou did what was really a much more sensible thing by taking the affair as a stupendous joke, and going off into shrieks of hysterical laughter.

But as for me, my blood was up. I wasn't going to stand any nonsense from these damned Italians. Despite the Roman blood that is legitimately the supreme pride of our oldest families, we always somehow instinctively think of the Italian as a nigger.

We don't call them "dagos" and "wops", as they do in the United States, with the invariable epithet of "dirty"; but we have the same feeling.

I began to take the high hand with the sergeant and that, of course, was quite sufficient to turn the balance against us.

We found ourselves pinioned. He said in a very short tone that we should have to go to the Commissario.

I had two conflicting impulses. One to shoot the dogs down and get away; the other to wish, like a lost child, that Feccles would turn up and get us out of the mess.

Unfortunately for either, I had been very capably disarmed, and there was no sign of Feccles.

We were marched to the police station and thrown into separate rooms.

I cannot hope to depict the boiling rage which kept me awake all night. I resented ill-temperedly the attempts of the other men to be sympathetic. I think they recognised instinctively that I had got into trouble through no fault of my own, and were anxious to show kindness in their own rough way to the stranger.

The worst of the whole business was that they had searched us and removed our stand-by, the dear little gold-topped bottle! I might have got myself into a mood to laugh the whole thing off, as had so often happened before; and I realised for the first time the dreadful sinking of heart that comes from privation.

It was only a hint of the horror so far. I had enough of the stuff in me to carry me through for a bit. But, even as things were, it was bad enough.

I had a feeling of utter helplessness. I began to repent having repulsed the advances of my fellow prisoners. I approached them and explained that I was a "*Signor Inglese*" with "*molto danaro*"; and if any one could oblige me with a sniff of cocaine, as I explained by gesture, I should be practically grateful.

I was understood immediately. They laughed sympathetically with perfect comprehension of the case. But as it happened, nobody had managed to smuggle anything in. There was nothing for it but to wait for the morning. I lay down on a bench, and found myself the prey of increasingly acute irritation.

The hours passed like the procession of Banquo's heirs before the eyes of Macbeth; and a voice in me kept saying, "Macbeth hath murdered sleep, Macbeth shall sleep no more!"

I had an appallingly disquieting sensation of being tracked down by some invisible foe. I was seized with a perfectly unreasonable irritation against Feccles, as if it were his fault, and not my own, that I was in this mess.

Strangely enough, you may think, I never gave a thought to Lou. It mattered nothing to me whether she were suffering or not. My own personal physiological sensations occupied the whole of my mind.

I was taken before the Commissario as soon as he arrived. They seemed to recognise that the case was important.

Lou was already in the office. The Commissario spoke no English, and no interpreter was immediately available. She looked absolutely wretched.

There had been no conveniences for toilet, and in the daylight the disguise was a ridiculous travesty.

Her hair was tousled and dirty; her complexion was sallow, mottled with touches of unwholesome red. Her eyes were bleared and bloodshot. Dark purple rims were round them.

I was extremely angry with her for her unprepossessing appearance. It then occurred to me for the first time that perhaps I myself was not looking like the Prince of Wales on Derby Day.

The commissary was a short, bull-necked individual, evidently sprung from the ranks of the people. He possessed a correspondingly exaggerated sense of his official importance.

He spoke almost without courtesy, and appeared to resent our incapacity to understand his language.

As for myself, the fighting spirit had gone out of me completely. All I could do was to give our names in the tone of voice of a schoolboy who has been summoned by the head master, and to appeal for the "*Consule, Inglese*".

The commissary's clerk seemed excited when he heard who we were, and spoke to his superior in a rapid undertone. We were asked to write our names.

I thought this was getting out of it rather nicely. I felt sure that the "Sir" would do the trick, and the "V-C., K.B.E." could hardly fail to impress.

I'm not a bit of a snob; but I really was glad for once to be of some sort of importance.

The clerk ran out of the room with the paper. He came back in a moment, beaming all over, and called the attention of the commissary to one of the morning newspapers, running his finger along the lines with suppressed excitement.

My spirits rose. Evidently some social paragraph had identified us.

The commissary changed his manner at once. His new tone was not exactly sympathetic and friendly, but I put that down to the man's plebeian origin.

He said something about "*Consule*", and had us conducted to an outer room. The clerk indicated that we were to wait there – no doubt, for the arrival of the consul.

It was not more than half an hour; but it seemed an eternity. Lou and I had nothing to say to each other. What we felt was a blind ache to get away from these wretched people; to get back to the Caligula; to have a bath and a meal; and above all, to ease our nerves with a good stiff dose of heroin and a few hearty sniffs of cocaine.

CHAPTER X
THE BUBBLE BURSTS

We felt that our troubles were over when a tall bronzed Englishman in flannels and a Panama sauntered into the room.

We sprang instinctively to our feet, but he took no notice beyond looking at us out of the tail of his eye, and twisting his mouth into a curious little compromise between a smile and a query.

The clerk bowed him at once into an inner room. We waited and waited. I couldn't understand at all what they could have been talking about in there for so long.

But at last the soldier at the door beckoned us in. The vice-consul was sitting on a sofa in the background. With his head on one side, he shot a keen fixed glance out of his languid eyes, and bit his thumbnail persistently, as if in a state of extreme nervous perplexity.

I was swept by a feeling of complete humiliation. It was a transitory feverish flush; and it left me more exhausted than ever.

The commissario swung his chair around to our saviour, and said something which evidently meant, "Please open fire."

"I'm the vice-consul here," he said. "I understand that you claim to be Sir Peter and Lady Pendragon."

"That's who we are," I replied, with a pitiful attempt at jauntiness.

"You'll excuse me, I'm sure," he said, "if I say that – to the eyes of the average Italian official – you don't precisely look the part. Have you your passports?"

The mere presence of an English gentleman had a good effect in pulling me together.

I said, with more confidence than before, that our courier had arranged to take us to see some of the shows in Naples that the ordinary tourist knows nothing about, and in order to avoid any possible annoyance, he had advised us to adopt this disguise – and so on for the rest of the story.

The vice-consul smiled – indulgently, as I thought. "I admit we have some experience," he said slowly, "of young people like yourselves getting into various kinds of trouble. One can't expect every one to know all the tricks; and besides, if I understand correctly, you're on your honeymoon."

I admitted the fact with a somewhat embarrassed smile. It occurred to me that honeymoon couples were traditionally objects of not unkindly ridicule from people in a less blessed condition.

"Quite so," replied the vice-consul. "I'm not a married man myself; but no doubt it is very delightful. How do you like it in Norway?"

"Norway?" I said, completely flabbergasted.

"Yes," he said. "How do you like Norway; the climate, the *lax*, the people, the fiords, the glaciers?"

There was some huge mistake somewhere.

"Norway?" I said, with a rising inflection.

I was on the brink of hysteria.

"I've never been to the place in my life. And if it's anything like Naples, I don't want to go!"

"This is a rather more serious matter than you seem to suppose," returned the consul, "If you're not in Norway, where are you?"

"Why, I'm here, confound it," I retorted with another weak flush of anger.

"Since when, may I ask?" he replied.

Well, he rather had me there. I didn't know how long I'd been away from England. I couldn't have told him the day or the month on a bet.

Lou helped me out.

"We left Paris three weeks ago tomorrow," she said positively enough, though the tone of her voice was weak and weary, with a sub-current of irritation and distress. I hardly recognised the rich, full tones that had flooded my heart when she chanted that superb litany in the "Smoking Dog".

"We spent a couple of days here," she said, "at the Museo-Palace Hotel. Since then, we've been staying at the Caligula at Capri; and our clothes, our passports, our money, and everything are there."

I couldn't help being pleased by the way in which she rose to the crisis; her practical good sense, her memory of those details that are so important in business, though the male temperament regards them as a necessary nuisance.

These are the things that one needs in an official muddle.

"You don't know any Italian at all?" asked the consul.

"Only a few words," she admitted, "though, of course, Sir Peter's knowledge of French and Latin help him to make sense out of the newspapers."

"Well," said the consul, rising languidly, "as it happens, that's just the point at issue."

"I know the big words," I said. "It's the particles that bother one."

"Perhaps then it will save trouble," said the consul, "if I offer you a free translation of this paragraph in this morning's paper."

He reached across, took it from the commissario, and began a fluent even phrasing.

"England is always in the van when it comes to romance and adventure. The famous ace, Sir Peter Pendragon, V.C., K.B.E., who recently startled London by his sudden marriage with the leading society beauty, Miss Louise Laleham, is not spending his honeymoon in any of the conventional ways, as might be expected from the gentleman's bold and adventurous character. He has taken his bride for a season's guideless climbing on the Jostedal Brae, the largest glacier in Norway."

I could see that the commissario was drilling holes in my soul with his eyes. As for myself, I was absolutely stupefied by the pointless falsehood of the paragraph.

"But, good God!" I exclaimed. "This is all absolute tosh."

"Excuse me," said the consul, a little grimly, "I have not finished the paragraph."

"I beg your pardon, sir," I answered curtly.

"Taking advantage of these facts," he continued to read, "and of a slight facial resemblance to Sir Peter and Lady Pendragon, two well-known international crooks have assumed their personalities, and are wandering around Naples and its vicinity, where several tradesmen have already been victimised."

He dropped the paper, put his hands behind his back, and stared me square in the eyes.

I could not meet his glance. The accusation was so absurd, so horrible, so unexpected! I felt that guilt was written on every line of my face.

I stammered out some weakly, violent objurgation. Lou kept her head better than I.

"But please, this is absurd," she protested. "Send for our courier. He has known Sir Peter since he was a boy at school. The whole thing is shameful and abominable. I don't see why such things are allowed."

The consul seemed in doubt as to what to do. He played with his watch-chain nervously.

I had sunk into a chair – I noticed they hadn't offered us chairs when we came in – and the whole scene vanished from my mind. I was aware of nothing but a passionate craving for drugs. I wanted them physically as I had never wanted anything in my life before. I wanted them mentally, too. They, and they only, would clear my mind of its confusion, and show me a way out of this rotten mess. I wanted them most of all morally. I lacked the spirit to stand up under this sudden burst of drum fire.

But Lou stuck to it gamely. She was on her mettle, though I could see that she was almost fainting from the stress of the various circumstances.

"Send for our courier, Hector Laroche," she insisted. The consul shrugged his shoulders. "But where is he?"

"Why," she said, "he must be looking for us all over the town. When he got to the Fauno Ebbrio and found we weren't there, and heard what had happened, he must have been very anxious about us."

"In fact, I don't see why he isn't here now," said the consul. "He must have known that you were arrested."

"Perhaps something's happened to him," suggested Lou. "But that would really be too curious a coincidence."

"Well, these things do happen," admitted the consul. He seemed somehow more at his ease with her, and better disposed, than when he was talking to me. Her magnetic beauty and her evident aristocracy could not help but have their effect.

I found myself admiring her immensely, in quite a new way. It had never occurred to me that she could rise to a situation with such superb aplomb.

"Won't you sit down?" said the consul, "I'm sure you must be very tired."

He put a chair for her, and went back to his seat on the sofa.

"It's a little awkward, you see," he went on. "I don't, as a matter of fact, believe all I read in the papers. And there are several very curious points about the situation which you don't seem to see yourself. And I don't mind admitting that your failure to see them makes a very favourable impression."

He paused and bit his lip, and pulled at his neck.

"It's very difficult," he continued at last. "The facts of the case, on the surface, are undeniably ugly. You are found in disguise in one of the worst places in Naples, and you have actually arms in your hands, which is *strengst verboten*, as they say in Germany. On the other hand, you give an account of yourself which makes you out to be such utter fools, if you will forgive the frankness of the expression, that it speaks volumes for your innocence, and there's no doubt about your being British – " he smiled amiably, "and I think I must do what I can for you. Excuse me while I talk to my friend here."

Lou turned on me with a triumphant smile; one of her old proud smiles, except that it was wrung, so to speak, out of the heart of unspeakable agony.

Meanwhile, the commissario was gesticulating and shouting at the consul, who replied with equal volubility but an apparently unsurmountable languor.

Then the conversation stopped suddenly short. The two men rose to their feet.

"I've arranged it with my friend here on the basis of his experience of the bold, bad, British tourist. You will come with me to the consulate under the protection of two of his men," he smiled sarcastically, "for fear you should get into any further trouble. You can have your things back except the guns, which are forbidden."

How little he knew what a surge of joy went through us at that last remark!

"I will send one of my clerks with you to Capri," he said, "and you will get your passports and money and whatever you need, and come back to me at once and put the position on a more regular footing."

We got our things from the sergeant, and made excuses for a momentary disappearance.

By George, how we did want it!

Five minutes later we were almost ourselves again. We saw the whole thing as an enormous lark, and communicated our high spirits to our companion. He attributed them, no doubt, to our prospects of getting out of the scrape.

Lou rattled on all the way about life in London, and I told the story – bar the snow part – of our elopement.

He thawed out completely. Our confidence had reassured him.

We shook hands amid all-round genial laughter when we left under the guidance of a very business-like Italian, who spoke English well.

We caught the boat to Capri with plenty of time to spare, and regaled the consul's clerk with all sorts of amusing anecdotes. He was very pleased to be treated on such a friendly footing.

We went up to the Piazza in the Funicular with almost the sensation of soaring. It had been a devil of a mess; but five minutes more would see it at an end. And, despite my exaltation, I registered a vow that I would never do anything so foolish again.

Of course, it was evident what had happened to Feccles. He had somehow failed to learn of our arrest, and was waiting at the hotel with impatient anxiety for our return.

At the same time, it was rather ridiculous in that costume in broad daylight to have to ask the porter for one's key.

I could not at all understand his look of genuine surprise. That wasn't simply a question of clothes – I felt it in my bones. And there was the manager, bowing and scraping like a monkey. He seemed to have lost his self-possession. The torrent of his words of welcome ran over a very rough bed.

I couldn't really grasp what he was saying for a moment, but there was no mistaking the import of his final phrase.

"I'm so delighted that you've changed your mind, Sir Peter, but I felt sure you could never bear to leave Capri so soon. Our beautiful Capri!"

What the deuce was the fellow talking about? Change my mind? What I wanted to do was to change my clothes!

The consul's clerk made a few rapid explanations in Italian, and it almost hit me in the eye to watch the manager's face as he lifted his eyes and saw the two obvious detectives in the doorway.

"I don't understand," he said with sudden anxiety. "I don't understand this at all," and he bustled round to his desk.

"Where's our courier?" called out Lou. "It's for him to explain everything."

The manager became violently solemn.

"Your Ladyship is undoubtedly right," he broke out.

But the conventional words did not conceal the fact that his mental attitude was that of a man who has suddenly fallen through a trap-door into a cellar full of something spiky.

"There's some mistake here," he went on. "Let me see."

He called to the girl at the desk in Italian. She fished about in a drawer and produced a telegram.

He handed it over to me. It was addressed to Laroche.

"*Urgent bisnes oblige live for Roma night. Pay bill packup join me Museo Palace Hotel Napls in time to cach miday train. Pendragon.*"

The words were mostly mis-spelt; but the meaning was clear enough. Some one must be playing a practical joke. Probably that paragraph in the paper was part of the same idea. So I supposed Laroche was in the hotel in Naples wondering why we didn't turn up.

"But where's our luggage?" cried Lou.

"Why," said the manager, "your Ladyship's courier paid the bill as usual. The servants helped him to pack your luggage, and he just managed to catch the morning boat."

"But what time was this?" cried Lou, and scanned the telegram closely.

It must have been received within a few minutes of our leaving the hotel.

The girl handed over another telegram addressed to the manager.

"*Sir Petre add Lady Pendragom espress ther regrets at having so leve so sudenl and will always have the warmest remembrances of the hapy times they had at the Caligula and hop so riture at the earliest possibile opportunity. Courier till attend to busines details.*"

It suddenly dawned on my mind that there was one scrap of fact imbedded in this fantastic farrago. The courier had attended to business details with an efficiency worthy of the best traditions of the profession.

The thing seemed to sink into Lou's mind like a person seeing his way through a chess problem. Her face was absolutely white with cold and concentrated rage.

"He must have watched us in Paris," she said.

If he must have known that we had spent the money we were going to put into his swindle, and made up his mind that his best course was to get the jewellery and the rest of the cash.

She sat down suddenly, collapsed; and began to cry. It developed into violent hysterics, which became so alarming that the manager sent for the nearest doctor.

A knot of servants and one or two guests had gathered in the atrium of the hotel. The outside porter had become the man of the moment.

"If why, certainly," he announced triumphantly in broken English. "If Mr. Laroche, he went off this morning on the seven o'clock boat. I tink you never catch him."

The events of the last few hours had got me down to my second wind, so to speak. I turned to the consul's clerk; and I spoke. But my voice seemed to come not so much from me as from the animal inside me, the original Pendragon, if you know what I mean, the creature with blind instincts and an automatic apparatus of thought.

"You see how it is," I heard myself saying, "no passports, no cash, no clothes – nothing!"

I was speaking of myself in the third person. The whole process of human life and action had stopped automatically as far as the hotel was concerned. The knot of babbling gossipers was like a swarm of mosquitoes.

The consul's clerk had taken in the situation clearly enough; but I could see that the detectives had become highly suspicious. They were itching to arrest me on the spot.

The clerk argued with them garrulously for an interminable time. The manager seemed the most uncomfortable man in Capri. He protested silently to heaven – there being nobody on earth to listen to him.

The situation was set going again by the reappearance of Lou on the arm of a chambermaid, followed by the doctor, who wore the air of a man who has once more met the King of Terrors in open combat, and knocked the stuffing out of him.

Lou was exceedingly shaky, paling and flushing by turns. I hated her. It was she who had got me into all this mess.

"Well," said the clerk, "we must simply go back to the consulate and explain what has happened."

"Don't be distressed, Lady Pendragon," he said. "There can be no doubt at all that this man will be caught in a very few hours, and you'll have all your things back."

Of course I had sense enough to know that he didn't believe a word of what he was saying. The proverb, "Set a thief to catch a thief", doesn't apply to Italy. If a thief were worth stealing, that would be another story.

There was no boat back to Naples that night. There was nothing to do but to wait till the morning. The manager was extremely sympathetic. He got us some clothes, if not exactly what we were accustomed to, at least better than the horrible things we were wearing. He ordered a special dinner with lots of champagne, and served it in the best suite but one in the house.

His instinctive Italian tact told him not to put us in the rooms we had had before.

He looked in from time to time with a cheery word to see how we were, and to assure us that telegraphic arrangements had been made to catch Mr. Laroche Feccles.

We managed to get pretty drunk in the course of the evening; but there was no exhilaration. The shock had been too great, the disillusion too disgusting. Above all, there was the complete absence of what had, after all, been the mainspring of our lives; our love for each other.

That was gone, as if it had been packed in our luggage. The only approach to sympathetic communion between us was when Lou, practical to the last, brought out our pitifully small supply of heroin and cocaine.

"That's all we've got," she whispered in anguish of soul, "till God knows when."

We were frightfully afraid, into the bargain, of its being taken from us. We were gnawed by fierce anxiety as to the issue of our affair with the police. We were even doubtful whether the consul wouldn't turn against us and scout our story as a string of obvious falsehoods.

The morning was chill. We were shaking with the reaction. Our sleep had been heavy, yet broken, and haunted by abominable dreams.

We could not even stay on deck. It was too cold, and the sea was choppy. We went down in the cabin, and shivered, and were sea-sick.

When we reached the consulate we were physical wrecks. One bit of luck, however, was waiting for us. Our luggage had been found in a hotel at Sorrento. Everything saleable had, of course, been removed by the ingenious Mr. Feccles, including our supply of dope.

But at least we had our passports, and some clothes to wear; and the finding of the luggage in itself, of course, confirmed our story.

The consul was extremely kind, and returned with us himself to the commissario, who dismissed us genially enough, obviously confirmed in his conviction that all English people were mad, and that we in particular ought to travel, if travel we must, in a bassinette.

It took three days to telegraph money from England. It was utterly humiliating to walk about Naples. We felt that we were being pointed at as the comic relief in a very low-class type of film.

We borrowed enough money to get on with, and, of course, we had only one use for it. We stayed in our room in a little hotel unfre-

quented by English, and crawled out by night to try to buy drugs.

That in itself is a sordid epic of adventure and misadventure. The lowest class of so-called guide was our constant companion. Weary in spirit, we dragged ourselves from one dirty doubtful street to another; held long whispered conferences with the scavenger type of humanity, and as often as not bought various harmless powders at an exorbitant price, and that at the risk of blackmail and other things possibly worse.

But the need of the stuff drove us relentlessly on. We ultimately found an honest dealer, and got a small supply of the genuine stuff. But even then we didn't seem to pick up. Even large doses did hardly more than restore us to our normal, by which I mean, our pre-drug selves. We were like Europe after the war.

The worst and the best we could do was to become utterly disgusted with ourselves, each other, Naples, and life in general.

The spirit of adventure was dead – as dead as the spirit of love. We had just enough moral courage after a very good lunch at Gambrinus, to make up our minds to get out of the entire beastly atmosphere.

Our love had become a mutual clinging, like that of two drowning people. We shook hands on the definite oath to get back to England, and get back as quick as we could.

I believe I might have fallen down even on that. But once again Lou pulled me through. We got into a *veittura* and took our tickets then and there.

We were going back to London with our tails between our legs, but we were going back to London!

BOOK II
INFERNO

CHAPTER I
SHORT COMMONS

AUGUST 17

We are at the Savoy. Cockie has gone to see his lawyer. He is looking awfully bad, poor boy. He feels the disgrace of having been taken in by that Feccles. But how was he to know?

It was all really my fault. I ought to have had an instinct about it.

I feel rotten myself. London is frightfully hot; much hotter than it was in Italy. I want to go and live at Barley Grange. No, I don't; what I want is to get back to where we were. There's frightfully little H. left. There's plenty of C.; only one wants so much.

I wonder if this is the right stuff. The effect isn't what it used to be. At first everything went so fast. It doesn't any more.

It makes one's mind very full; drags out the details; but it doesn't make one think and talk and act with that glorious sense of speed. I think the truth is that we've got tired out.

Suppose I suggest to Cockie that we knock off for a week and get our physical strength back and start fresh.

I may as well telephone Gretel and arrange for a really big supply. If we're going to live at Barley Grange, we'll have to be cocaine hogs and lay in a big stock. There wouldn't be any chance of getting it down there; and besides one must take precautions. . . .

Bother August! Of course Gretel's out of town – in Switzerland, the butler said. They don't know when she'll be back. I wonder when Parliament meets.

Cockie came back for lunch with a very long face. Mr. Wolfe gave him a good talking-to about money. Well, that's perfectly right. We had been going the pace.

Cockie wanted to take me out and buy me some jewellery to replace what was stolen; but I wouldn't let him, except a new watch and a wedding ring.

I've got a horrid feeling about that. It's frightfully unlucky to lose your wedding ring. I feel as if the new one didn't belong to me at all.

We had a long talk about Gretel being away. We tried one or two places, but they wouldn't give us any. I wish Cockie had taken out his diploma.

The papers are disgusting. It's the silly season, right enough. Every time one picks one up, there's something about cocaine. That old fool Platt is on the war-path. He wants to "arouse public opinion to a sense of the appalling danger which threatens the manhood and womanhood of England."

One paper had a long speech of his reported in full. He says it's the plot of the Germans to get even with us.

Of course, I'm only a woman and all that; but it sounds to me rather funny.

We went to tea with Mabel Black. Every one was talking about drugs. Every one seemed to want them; yet Lord Landsend had just come back from Germany and he said you could buy it quite easily there, but nobody seemed to want to.

Then is the whole German people in a silent conspiracy to destroy us? I never took much stock in all those stories about the infernal cunning of the Hun.

We heard a lot about the underground traffic, though, and I think we ought to be able to get it pretty easily. . . .

I don't know what's the matter with us both. It made us a bit better to meet the old crowd, and we thought we'd celebrate.

It didn't come off.

We had a wonderful dinner; and then a horrible thing happened, the most horrible thing in my life. Cockie wanted to go to a show! You might have hit me on the head with a poker. I don't attract him any more; and I love him so much!

He went to the box office to see about tickets, and while he was gone – this was the really horrible thing – I found I was simply telling myself, "I love him so much."

Love is dead. And yet that's not true. I do love him with all my heart and soul; and yet, somehow, I can't. I want to be able to love until I get back. Oh, what's the good of talking about it!

I know I love him, and yet I know I can't love any one.

I took a whole lot of cocaine. It dulled what I felt. I was able to fancy I loved him.

We went to the show. It was awfully stupid. I was thinking all the time how I wanted to love, and how I wanted dope, and how I wanted to stop dope so that the dope might do me some good.

I couldn't really feel. It was a dull, blind sense of discomfort. I was awfully nervous, too. I felt as if I were somehow caught in a trap; as if I had got into the wrong house by mistake and couldn't get out again. I didn't know what might be behind all those doors; and I was quite alone. Cockie was there; but he couldn't do a thing to help me. I couldn't call to him. The link between us was broken.

And yet apart from all the fear I had for myself, there was an even deeper fear on his account. There is something in me that loves him, something deeper than life; but it won't talk to me.

I sat through the show like being in a nightmare. I was clinging desperately to him; and he didn't seem to understand me and my need. We were strangers.

I think he was feeling rather good. He talked in a charming, light, familiar way; but every smile was an insult, every caress was a stab.

We got back to the Savoy, utterly worn out and wretched. We kept on taking H. and C. all night; we couldn't sleep, we talked about the drugs. It was just a long argument about how to take them. We felt we were somehow doing it wrong.

I had been so proud of his medical knowledge, and yet it didn't seem to throw any light.

It seems that in the medical books, they speak of what they call "Drug virginity". The thing was to get it back; and according to the books the only way to do it is to take nothing for a long time.

He said it was really just the same as any other appetite. If you have a big lunch, you can't expect to be hungry at tea-time.

But then, what is one to do in the meanwhile?

AUGUST 18

We lay in bed very late. I didn't seem to miss my sleep; but I was too weak to get out of bed.

We had to buck ourselves up in the usual way, and manage to get downstairs for lunch.

London is quite empty and terribly dull. We met Mabel Black by accident walking in Bond Street. She is looking frightfully ill. I can see she dopes too hard. Of course, the trouble with her is she hasn't got a man. She has a lot of men round her. She could marry any day she liked.

We talked about it a bit. She hasn't got the energy, she said, and the idea of men disgusts her.

She wears the most wonderful boots. She has a new pair almost every day, and hardly ever puts the same pair on twice. I think she's a little bit crazy. . . .

London seems different somehow. I used to be interested in every funny little detail. I want to get back to myself. Drugs help me to get almost there; but there is always one little corner to turn and they never take one round. . . .

AUGUST 19

We got back from Bond Street bored and stupefied. We went off unexpectedly to sleep; and when we woke it was this morning. I can't understand why a long sleep like that doesn't refresh one. We're both absolutely fagged.

Cockie said a meal would put us right, and he rang down for breakfast in bed. But when it came, we couldn't either of us eat it.

I remember what Haidé said about the spiritual life. We were being prepared to take our places in the new order of Humanity. It's perfectly right that one should have to undergo a certain amount of discomfort. You couldn't expect anything else. It's nature's way. . . .

We picked ourselves up with five or six goes of heroin. It's no use taking cocaine unless you're feeling pretty good already. . . .

The supply is really awfully small. Confound this silly holiday habit. It really isn't fair of Gretel to let us down like this.

We went to the Cafe Wisteria. Somebody introduced us to somebody that said he could get all he wanted.

But now there was a new nuisance. The police find it troublesome and dangerous to attend to the crime wave. Besides they're too busy enforcing regulations. England's altogether different since the war. You never know where you are. Nobody takes any interest in politics in the way they used to, and nobody bothers any more about the big ideas.

I was taught about Magna Charta and the liberty of the individual, and freedom slowly broadening down from precedent to precedent, and so on and so forth.

All sorts of stupid interference with the rights of the citizen gets passed under our noses without our knowing what it is. For all I know, it may be a crime to wear a green hat with a pink dress.

Well, it would be a crime; but I don't think it's the business of the police.

I read in a paper the other day that a committee of people in Philadelphia had decided that a skirt must be not less than seven and a half inches from the ground – or not more. I don't know which and I don't know why. Anyhow, the net result is that the price of cocaine has

gone up from a pound an ounce to anything you like to pay. So of course everybody wants it whether they want it or not, and anybody but a member of parliament would know that if you offer a man twenty or thirty times what a thing is worth in itself, he'll go to a lot of trouble to make you want to buy it. . . .

Well, we found this man was a fraud. He tried to sell us packets of snow in the dark. He tried to prevent Cockie examining the stuff by pretending to be afraid of the police.

But as it happened, Cockie's long suit was chemistry. He was the wrong man to try to sell powdered borax to at a guinea a sniff. He told the man he'd rather have Beecham's Pills.

What I love about Cockie is the witty way he talks. But somehow or other, the flashes don't come like they did – not so often, I mean. Besides which, he seems to be making his jokes to himself.

Most of the time, I don't get what he means. He talks to himself a great deal, for another thing. I get a feeling of absolute repulsion.

I don't know why it is. The least thing irritates me absurdly. I think it's because every incident, even the things that are pleasant, distracts my mind from the one thing that matters – how to get a supply and go down to Kent and lay off for a bit and have a really good time like we used to last month. I am sure love would come back if we did, and love's the only thing that counts in this world or the next.

I feel that it's only round the corner; but a miss is as good as a mile. It makes it somehow worse to be so near and yet so far. . . .

A very funny thing has just struck me. There's something in one's mind that prevents one from thinking of the thing one wants to.

It was perfectly silly of us to be hunting round London for dope and getting mixed up with a rotten crowd like we did in Naples. It never struck us till tonight that all we had to do was to go round to King Lamus. He would give us all we needed at the proper price.

Funny, too, it was Cockie that thought of that. I know he hates the man, though he never said so except in an outburst which I knew didn't mean anything. . . .

We went to the studio in a taxi. Curse the luck, he was out! There was a girl there, a tall, thin woman with a white face like a wedge. We gave

several hints; but she didn't rise, and wretched as we were, we didn't want to spoil the market by telling her outright.

Lamus would be there in the morning, she said.

We said we'd be there at eleven o'clock.

We drove back. We had a rotten night economising. We didn't dare tell each other what we really feared: that somehow he might let us down. . . .

I can't sleep. Cockie is lying awake with his eyes wide open, staring at the ceiling. He doesn't stir a muscle. It maddens me that he takes no interest in me. But after all, I take no interest in him. I am as restless as the wandering Jew. At the same time, I can't settle down to anything. I keep on scribbling this stuff in my diary. It relieves me somehow to write what I feel.

What is so utterly damnable is that I understand what I am doing. This complaining rambling rubbish is the substitute which has taken the place of love.

What have I done to forfeit love? I feel as if I had died and got forgotten in some beastly place where there was nothing but hunger and thirst. Nothing means anything any more except dope, and dope itself doesn't really mean anything vital.

AUGUST 20

I am so tired, so tired, so tired I . . .

My premonition was right about Lamus. There was a very unpleasant scene. We were both frightfully wretched when we got there. (I can't get my hands and feet warm, and there's something wrong with my writing).

Peter Pan thought it best to remind him in a jocular way about his remark that we were to come when we needed him, and then introduced the subject of what we needed.

But he took the words brutally out of our mouths.

"You needn't tell me what you need," he said. "The lack is only too obvious."

He said it in a non-committal way so that we couldn't take offence; but we knew instinctively he meant brains.

However, Peter stuck to his guns, like the game little devil he is. That's why I love him.

"Oh, yes, heroin," said Lamus, "cocaine. We regret exceedingly to be out of it for the moment."

The brute seemed unconscious of our distress. He gave an imitation of an apologetic shop-walker.

"But let me show you our latest lines on morphine."

Cockie and I looked at each other wanly. Morphine would no doubt be better than nothing. And then, if you please, the beast pulled a review with a blue cover out of a revolving bookcase and read aloud a long poem. His intonation was so dramatic, he gave so vivid a picture that we sat spell-bound. It seemed as if he had long pincers twisted in our entrails, and were wrenching at them. He gave me the verses when he had finished.

"You ought to paste these," he said, "in your Magical Diary."

So I have. I hardly know why. There's a sort of pleasure in torturing oneself. Is that it?

Thirst!
Not the thirst of the throat
Though that be the wildest and worst
Of physical pangs – that smote
Alone to the heart of Christ,
Wringing the one wild cry
"I thirst!" from His agony,
While the soldiers drank and diced:
Not the thirst benign
That calls the worker to wine;
Not the bodily thirst
(Though that be frenzy accurst)
When the mouth is full of sand,
And the eyes are gummed up, and the ears
Trick the soul till it hears

Water, water at hand,
When a man will dig his nails
In his breast, and drink the blood
Already that clots and stales
Ere his tongue can tip its flood,
When the sun is a living devil
Vomiting vats of evil,
And the moon and the night but mock
The wretch on his barren rock,
And the dome of heaven high-arched
Like his mouth is and and parched,
And the caves of his heart high-spanned
Are choked with alkali sand!

Not this! but a thirst uncharted
Body and soul alike
Traitors turned black-hearted,
Seeking a space to strike
In a victim already attuned
To one vast chord of wound
Every separate bone
Cold, an incarnate groan
Distilled from the icy sperm
Of Hell's implacable worm;

Every drop of the river
Of blood aflame and a-quiver
With poison secret and sour –
With a sudden twitch at the last
Like certain jagged daggers.
(With bloodshot eyes dull-glassed
The screaming Malay staggers
Through his village aghast).
So blood wrenches its pain
Sardonic through heart and brain.

Every separate nerve
Awake and alert, on a curve
Whose asymptote's name is never
In a hyperbolic "for ever!"
A bitten and burning snake
Striking its venom within it,
As if it might serve to slake
The pain for the tithe of a minute.

Awake, for ever awake!
Awake as one never is
While sleep is a possible end,
Awake in the void, the abyss
Whose thirst is an echo of this
That martyrs, world without end,
(World without end, Amen!)
The man that falters and yields
For the proverb's month and an hour
To the lure of the snow-starred fields
Where the opium poppy's aflower.

Only the prick of a needle
Charged from a wizard well!
Is this sufficient to wheedle
A soul from heaven to hell?
Was man's spirit weaned
From fear of its ghosts and gods
To fawn at the feet of a fiend ?
Is it such terrible odds, –

The heir of ages of wonder,
The crown of earth for an hour,
The master of tide and thunder
Against the juice of a flower?
Aye in the roar and the rattle

Of all the armies of sin,
This is the only battle
He never was known to win.

Slave to the thirst – not thirst
As here it is weakly written,
Not thirst in the brain black-bitten,
In the soul more sorely smitten!
One dare not think of the worst!
Beyond the raging and raving
Hell of the physical craving
Lies, in the brain benumbed,
At the end of time and space,
An abyss, unmeasured, unplumbed –
The haunt of a face!

She it is, she, that found me
In the morphia honeymoon;
With silk and steel she bound me,
In her poisonous milk she drowned me,
Even now her arms surround me,
Stifling me into the swoon
That still – but oh, how rarely! –
Comes at the thrust of the needle,
Steadily stares and squarely,
Nor needs to fondle and wheedle
Her slave agasp for a kiss,
Hers whose horror is his
That knows that viper womb,
Speckled and barred with black
On its rusty amber scales,
Is his tomb –
The straining, groaning, rack
On which he wails – he wails!
Her cranial dome is vaulted,

155

Her mad Mongolian eyes
Aslant with the ecstasies
Of things immune, exalted
Far beyond stars and skies,
Slits of amber and jet –
Her snout for the quarry set
Fleshy and heavy and gross,
Bestial, broken across,
And below it her mouth that drips
Blood from the lips
That hide the fangs of a snake,
Drips on venomous udders
Mountainous flanks that fret,
And the spirit sickens and shudders
At the hint of a worse thing yet.

Olya! the golden bait
Barbed with infinite pain,
Fatal, fanatical mate
Of a poisoned body and brain!
Olya, the name that leers
Its lecherous longing and knavery,
Whispers in crazing ears
The secret spell of her slavery.

Horror indeed intense,
Seduction ever intenser,
Swinging the smoke of sense
From the bowl of a smouldering censer!
Behind me, behind and above,
She stands, that mirror of love.
Her fingers are supple-jointed;
Her nails are polished and pointed,
And tipped with spurs of gold:
With them she rowels the brain.

Her lust is critical, cold;
And her Chinese cheeks are pale,
As she daintily picks, profane

With her octopus lips, and the teeth
Jagged and black beneath,
Pulp and blood from a nail.

One swift prick was enough
In days gone by to invoke her
She was incarnate love
In the hours when I first awoke her.
Little by little I found
The truth of her, stripped of clothing,
Bitter beyond all bound,
Leprous beyond all loathing.
Black, the plague of the pit,
Her pustules visibly fester,
Cancerous kisses that bit
As the asp caressed her.

Dragon of lure and dread,
Tiger of fury and lust,
The quick in chains to the dead,
The slime alive in the dust,
Brazen shame like a flame,
An orgy of pregnant pollution
With hate beyond aim or name –
Orgasm, death, dissolution!
Know you now why her eyes
So fearfully glaze, beholding
Terrors and infamies
Like filthy flowers unfolding?
Laughter widowed of ease,
Agony barred from sadness,

157

Death defeated of peace,
Is she not madness?
She waits for me, lazily leering,
As moon goes murdering moon;
The moon of her triumph is nearing;
She will have me wholly soon.

Who have missed the morphia craving,
Cry scorn if I call you brothers,
Curl lip at my maniac raving,
Fools, seven times beguiled,
You have not known her? Well!
There was never a need she smiled
To harry you into hell

Morphia is but one
Spark of its secular fire.
She is the single sun –
Type of all desire!
All that you would, you are –
And that is the crown of a craving.
You are slaves of the wormwood star.
Analysed, reason is raving.
Feeling, examined, is Pain.
What heaven were to hope for a doubt of it!
Life is anguish, insane;
And death is – not a way out of it

"Olya," too, reminds me of myself. I have a morbid wish to be an impossible monster of cruelty and wickedness.

Lamus had told me that long ago. He said it was the phantasm which summed up my longing to – "revert to type". *La nostalgie de la boue.* Cockie lost all his dignity. He pleaded for just one sniff. We weren't really very bad, but the description of the thirst in that horrible poem had made us feel thirsty.

"My dear man," said Lamus very brutally. "I'm not a dope peddler. You've come to the wrong shop."

Cockie's head was drooping, and his eyes were glassy. But the need of dope drove him desperately to try every dodge.

"Hang it all," he said with a little flash of spirit. "You encouraged us to go on,"

"Certainly," admitted Lamus, "and now, I'm encouraging you to stop."

"I thought you believed in do what you like; you're always saying it."

"I beg your pardon," came the sharp retort. "I never said anything of the kind. I said, 'Do what thou wilt,' and I say it again. But that's a horse of quite a different colour."

"But we need the stuff," pleaded Peter. "We've got to have it. Why did you induce us to take it?"

"Why," he laughed subtly, "it's my will to want you to do your will."

"Yes, and I want the stuff."

"Acute psychologist as you are, Sir Peter, you have failed to grasp my meaning. I fear I express myself badly."

Cockie was boiling inwardly, yet he was so weak and faint that he was like a lamb. I myself would have killed Lamus if I had had the means. I felt that he was deliberately torturing us for his own enjoyment.

"Oh, I see," said Cockie, "I forgot what you were. What's your figure?"

The point blank insult did not even make him smile. He turned to the tall girl who was at the desk, correcting proofs.

"Note the characteristic reaction," he said to her, as if we had been a couple of rabbits that he was vivisecting. "They don't understand my point of view. They misquote my words, after hearing them every time we have met. They misinterpret four words of one syllable, 'Do what thou wilt.' Finally realising their lack of comprehension, they assume at once that I must be one of the filthiest scoundrels unhanged."

He turned back to Cockie with a little bow of apology.

"Do try to get some idea of what I'm saying," he said very earnestly.

I was bursting with hatred, brimming with suspicion, aghast with contempt. Yet he forced me to feel his sincerity. I crushed down the realisation with furious anger.

"I encourage you to take drugs," he went on, "exactly as I encourage you to fly. Drugs claim to be every man's master."

> 'Is it such terrible odds –
> The heir of ages of wonder,
> The crown of earth for an hour,
> The master of tide and thunder
> Against the juice of a flower?
> Ay I in the roar and the rattle
> Of all the armies of sin,
> This is the only battle
> He never was known to win.'

"You children are the flower of the new generation. You have got to fear nothing. You have got to conquer everything. You have got to learn to make use of drugs as your ancestors learnt to make use of lightning. You have got to stop at the word of command, and go on at the word of command according to circumstances."

He paused. The dire need of the drug kept Peter alert. He followed the argument with intense activity.

"Quite," he agreed, "and just at the moment, the word of command is 'go on.'"

The face of King Lamus flowered into a smile of intense amusement; and the girl at the desk shook her thin body as if she were being deliciously tickled.

Intuition told me why. They had heard the argument before.

"Very cleverly put, Sir Peter. It would look well in a broad frame, very plain, of dark mahogany, over the mantelpiece, perhaps."

For some reason or other, the conversation was pulling us together. Though we had had no dope, we both felt very much better. Cockie fired his big gun.

"It's the essence of your teaching, surely, Sir. Lamus, that every man should be absolute master of his own destiny."

"Well, well," admitted the Teacher with an exaggerated sigh, "I expected to be beaten in argument. I always am. But I, too, am the master of mine.

'If Power asks Why, then is Power weakness,' as we read in the *Book of the Law*; and it's not my destiny to give you any drugs this morning."

"But you're interfering with my Will," protested Cockie, almost vivaciously.

"It would take too long to explain," returned Lamus, "why I think that remark unfair. But to quote the *Book of the Law* once more, 'Enough of Because, be he damned for a dog.' Instead, let me tell you a story."

We tactfully expressed eagerness to hear it.

"The greatest mountaineer of his generation, as you know, was the late Oscar Eckenstein."

He went through a rather complicated gesture quite incomprehensible; but it vaguely suggested to me some ceremonial reverence connected with death.

"I had the great good fortune to be adopted by this man; he taught me how to climb; in particular, how to glissade. He made me start down the slope from all kinds of complicated positions; head first and so on; and I had to let myself slide without attempting to save myself until he gave the word, and then I had to recover myself and finish, either sitting or standing, as he chose, to swerve or to stop; while he counted five. And he gave me progressively dangerous exercises. Of course, this sounds all rather obvious, but as a matter of fact, he was the only man who had learnt and who taught to glissade in this thorough way.

"The acquired power, however, stood me in very good stead on many occasions. To save an hour may sometimes mean to save one's life, and we could plunge down dangerous slopes where (for example) one might find oneself on a patch of ice when going at high speed if one were not certain of being able to stop in an instant when the peril were perceived. We could descend perhaps three thousand feet in ten minutes where people without that training would have had to go down step by step on the rope, and perhaps found themselves benighted in a hurricane in consequence.

"But the best of it was this: I was in command of a Himalayan expedition some years ago; and the coolies were afraid to traverse a snow slope which overhung a terrific cliff. I called on them to watch me, flung

myself on the snow head first, swept down like a sack of oats, and sprang to my feet on the very edge of the precipice.

"There was a great gasp of awed amazement while I walked up to the men. They followed me across the *mauvis pas* without a moment's hesitation. They probably thought it was magic or something. No matter what. But at least they felt sure that they could come to no harm by following a man so obviously under the protection of the mountain gods."

Cockie had gone deathly white. He understood with absolute clarity the point of the anecdote. He felt his manhood shamed that he was in the power of this blind black craving. He didn't really believe that Lamus was telling the truth. He thought the man had risked his life to get those coolies across. It seemed impossible that a man could possess such absolute power and confidence. In other words, he judged King Lamus by himself. He knew himself not to be a first-rate airman. He had flattered himself that he had dared so many dangers. It cut him like a whip that Lamus should despise what people call the heroic attitude; that he looked upon taking unnecessary risks as mere animal folly. To be ready to take them, yes. "I do not set my life at a pin's fee."

Lamus had no admiration for the cornered rat. His ideal was to make himself completely master of every possible circumstance.

Cockie tried to say something two or three times; but the words wouldn't come. King Lamus went to him and took his hand.

"Drugs are the slope in front of us," he said, "and I'm wily old Eckenstein, and you're ambitious young Lamus. And I say 'stop!' and when you show me that you can stop, when you have picked yourself together and are standing on the slope laughing, I'll show you how to go on."

We knew at the back of our minds that the man was inexorable. We hated him as the weak always hate the strong, and we had to respect and admire him, detesting him all the more for the fact.

CHAPTER II
INDIAN SUMMER

We went out gritting our teeth with mingled rage and dejection. We walked on aimlessly in silence. A taxi offered itself. We climbed into it listlessly and drove back here. We threw ourselves on our beds. The idea of lunch was disgusting. We were too weak and too annoyed to do anything. We could not trust ourselves to speak; we should have quarrelled. I fell into a state of sleepless agony. Our visit to the studio had burnt itself into my mind. I imagined the flesh of my soul sizzling beneath the white hot branding iron of Lamus's Will.

I reached out my hands for this diary. It has relieved me to write it down in all this detail.

I found myself on fire with passionate determination to fight H. and C. to a finish; and my hands were tied behind my back, my feet were fettered by a chain and ball. I wouldn't be made to stop by that beast. We'd get it despite him. We wouldn't be treated like children; we'd get as much as we wanted and we'd take it all the time, if it killed us.

The conflict in myself raged all the afternoon. Cockie had gone to sleep. He snored and groaned. He was like one's idea of a convict. He

hadn't shaved for two days. My own nails were black. I felt sticky and clammy all over. I hadn't dressed myself. I had thrown my clothes on carelessly.

Cockie woke about dinner-time. We couldn't go down as we were. We were suddenly stung by the realisation that we were making ourselves conspicuous in the hotel. We had a horrible fear of being found out. They might do something. It was all the worse that we didn't quite know what. And we felt so helpless, almost too weak to move a finger.

Oh, couldn't we find some anywhere! . . .

My God! what a bit of luck. What a fool I am. There was one packet of H. in the pocket of my travelling dress. We crawled towards each other and shared it. After the long abstention, the effect was miraculous.

Cockie picked himself up almost fiercely. The desperate anguish of our necessity drove him to swift resolute action. He sent for the barber and the waiter. We had the maid pack our things. We paid the bill and left our heavy trunks in the hotel, explaining that we had been called away suddenly on business. We put our dressing cases into a taxi and said, "Euston, main line."

Cockie stopped the man at Cambridge Circus.

"Look here," he said in an eager whisper, "we want some rooms in Soho. Some French or Italian place."

The man was equal to the problem. He found us a dirty dark little room on the ground floor in Greek Street. The landlady was some kind of Southerner with a dash of black blood. Her face told us that she was exactly the kind of woman we wanted.

We paid the taxi. Cockie was very restless. He wanted to get the man to do what we wanted. He was itching all over, but he was afraid. We sat down on the bed, and began to make plans.

AUGUST 21

I don't remember anything. I must have gone off suddenly to sleep as I was. Cockie is out. . . .

He has been going round town all night; the clubs and that. He got two sniffs from Mabel Black; but she was shy herself. He and Dick Wickham went down to Limehouse. No luck! They nearly got into a row with some sailors. . . .

Madame Bellini has brought breakfast. Horrible, beastly food. We must eat some; I'm so weak. . . .

She came in to clear it away and do the room. I got her talking about her life. She has been in England nearly thirty years, I worked round to the interesting subject. She doesn't know much about it. She thinks she can help. One of the women lodgers injects. She asked could we pay. It's really rather comic. Eight thousand a year and one of the most beautiful houses near London. And here we are in this filthy hole being asked "can we pay!" by a hag that never saw a sovereign in her life unless she stole it from some drunken client.

Cockie seems to have lost his sense. He flashed a fifty-pound note in her face. It was because he was angry at her attitude. She rather shut up. Either she thinks we're police spies or she's made up her mind to rob us.

The sight of the cash knocked her out of time! It destroyed her sense of proportion. It put all her ideas of straight dealing out of her mind. Her manner changed. She went off.

Peter told me to go and see the dope girl myself. It's the first time he ever spoke to me like that. All sexual feeling is dead between us. We've tried to work up the old passion. It was artificial, horrible, repulsive; a degradation and a blasphemy. Why is it? The snow intensified love beyond every possibility. Yet I love him more than ever. He's my boy. I think he must be ill. I wish I weren't so tired. I'm not looking after him properly, and I can't think about anything except getting H. I don't seem to mind so much about C. I never liked C. much. It made me dizzy and ill.

We have no amusements now. We get through the day in a dark, dreary dream. I can't fix my mind on anything. The more I want H. the less I am able to think and act as I should to get anything else I wanted.

Cockie went out slamming the door. It swung open again.

I couldn't go to the woman like this. I've written this to try to keep from crying.

But I am crying, only the tears won't come.

I'm snivelling like a woman I once saw when I visited the hospital.

I haven't got a handkerchief.

I can't bring myself to wash in that dirty cracked basin. We've brought no soap. The towel's soiled and torn. I must have some H. . . .

I've just been to see Lillie Fitzroy. How can men give her money? Her hair is grey, crudely dyed. She has wrinkles and rotten teeth. She was in bed, of course. I shook her roughly to wake her. I've lost every feeling for others, and people see it, and it spoils my own game. I must pretend to have the kindness and gentleness which I used to have so much; which used to make people think me an amiable fool.

Someone told me once that adjectives spoilt nouns in literature, and you can certainly cut out that one.

She's a good sort, all the same, poor flabby old thing. She only takes M., and only gets that in solution ready to inject. She saw I was all in, and gave me a dose in the thigh. It doesn't touch the spot like H., but it stops the worst of the suffering. She never gets up till tea-time. I left her a fiver. She promised to see what she could do that night with the man who gets it for her.

She got very affectionate in a sentimental, motherly style, told me the story of her life, and so on, for ever it seemed. Of course, I had to pretend to be interested to keep her in good humour. Everything might depend on that.

But it was awful to have to let her kiss me when I went away. I wonder if I should get like that if I went on with dope.

What absolute nonsense! For all I know, it may have prevented her going faster still. She must have had a beastly rotten life. The way she clawed at that five quid was the clue to her troubles; that and her ignorance of everything but the nastiest kind of vice and the meanest kind of crime.

The morphine has certainly done me a world of good. I am quite myself. I feel it by the way I am writing this entry. I have a quiet impersonal point of view.

I have got back my sense of proportion. I can think of things consecutively and I feel physically much stronger, but I've got very sleepy again. . . .

Joy! Cockie has just come in full of good news. He looks fine – as fine as he feels. He had a sample from a pedlar he met in the Wisteria. It's absolutely straight stuff. Pulled him round in a second. There are two of them in it; the man with the dope and the sentry. They talk business in the lavatory, and if another man comes in, the pedlar disappears. In case of real danger, he gets rid of his sample in a flash beyond any possibility of being traced. The loss is trifling; they can buy the stuff at a few shillings an ounce and sell it for I don't know how many times its weight in gold.

We shall have a great night tonight!

AUGUST 22

A hellish night!

Cockie kept his date with the pedlar, got ten pounds' worth of H. and fifteen of C., and the H. was nothing at all, and the C. so adulterated that we took the whole lot and it was hardly worth talking about.

What filthy mean beasts people are!

How can men take advantage of the bitter needs of others? It was the same in the war with the profiteers. It's always been the same.

I am writing this in a Turkish bath. I couldn't stand that loathsome house any more. It has done me lots of good. The massage has calmed my nerves. I slept for a long while, and a cup of tea has revived me.

I tried to read a paper, but every line opens the wound. They seem to have gone mad about dope. . . .

I suppose it's really quite natural. I remember my father telling me once that the inequality of wealth and all the trickery of commerce arose from artificial restriction.

Last night's swindle was made possible by the great philanthropist Jabez Platt. His Diabolical Dope Act has created the traffic which he was trying to suppress. It didn't exist before except in his rotten imagination. . . .

I get such sudden spells of utter weariness. Dope would put me right. Nothing else has any effect. Everything that happens makes me want a sniff; and every sniff makes something happen. One can't get away from the cage, but the complexity makes me . . . there, I can't think what I started to say.

My mind stops suddenly. It's like dropping a vanity bag. You stop to pick it up and the things are all over the place and it always seems as if something were missing. One can never remember what it is, but the feeling of annoyance is acute. It's mixed up with a vague fear. I've often forgotten things before – every one does all the time, but it doesn't bother one.

But now, every time that I remember that I've forgotten something, I wonder whether it's H. or C. or mixing the two that is messing up my mind.

My mind keeps on running back to that American nigger we met in Naples. He said snow made people "flighty and sceptical". It was such a queer expression. By sceptical he meant suspicious, I think. Anyhow, I've got that way. Flighty – I can't keep my mind on things like I could, except, of course, the one thing. And even that is confused. It's not a clear thought. It's an ache and a fear and a pain – and a sinister rapture. And I am suspicious of everybody I see.

I wonder if they think I'm taking it, and if they can do something horrid. I'm always on the look-out for people to play me some dirty trick, but that isn't a delusion at all. I've seen more meanness and treachery since the night I met Cockie than I knew in the rest of my life.

We seem to have got into a bad set somehow. And yet, my oldest friends – I can't trust them like I did. They're all alike. I wonder if that's a delusion? How can I tell? They do act funnily. I'm unsettled. How can one be sure of anything? One can't. The more one thinks of it, the more one sees it must be so.

Look how Feccles let us down. For all I know, there may be some motive at the back of even a really nice woman like Gretel – or Mabel Black. I'm really suspicious of myself. I think that's it.

I must go home. I hope to God Cockie's found some somewhere!

I met Mabel Black coming out of the Burlington Arcade. She looked fine, all over smiles, a very short, white skirt and a new pair of patent leather boots almost up to her knees. She must find them frightfully hot. She rushed me into a tea place, awfully smart with rose-shaded lights reflected up to a blue ceiling; the combination made a most marvellous purple.

We got an alcove shut off by canary-coloured curtains and a set of the loveliest cushions I ever saw. Two big basket chairs and a low table. They have the most delightful tea in egg-shell china and Dolly cigarettes with rose leaves.

Mabel talked a hundred miles a minute. She has struck the biggest kind of oil – a romantic boy of sixty-five. He had bought her a riding crop with a carved ivory handle; the head of a race horse with ruby eyes and a gold collar.

I asked her laughingly if it was to keep him in order. But what she was really keen on was H. She had got a whole bottle and gave me quite a lot in an envelope.

The first go, oh, what joy! And then – how strange we all are! The minute I had it in my bag – in my blood – a nightmare – a nightmare of suffocation – and it came to me with the force of a blow that the effect was not due to the H. at all, or hardly at all. When we got it again in Naples, it didn't do us much good.

Why was I translated into heaven this afternoon? Why had I found my wings?

The answer came as quick as the question. It's the atmosphere of Mabel and the relief of my worry. With that came a rational fear of the drug. I asked her if she hadn't had any troubles from taking it.

"You can't sleep without it," she said, but not as if it mattered much, "and it rather gets on one's nerves now and then."

She had to rush off to meet her beau for dinner. I went back to our dirty little den, brimming over with joy. I found Cockie sprawling on the bed in the depth of dejection. He did not move when I came in. I ran to him and covered him with kisses. His eyes were heavy and swollen and his nose was running.

I gave him my handkerchief and pulled him up.

His clothes were all rumpled and of course he hadn't shaved. I couldn't resist the temptation of teasing my darling. My love had come back in flood. I tingled with the pain of feeling that he did not respond. I hugged the pain to my heart. My blood beat hard with the joy of power. I held him in my hand. One dainty act, and he was mine. I hadn't the strength to enjoy myself to the full. Pity and tenderness

brought the tears to my eyes. I shook out a dose of the dull white wizardry.

He sniffed it up with stupid lethargy like a man who has lost hope of life, yet still takes his medicine as a routine. He came up gradually, but was hardly himself till after the third dose.

I took one, too, to keep him company, not because I needed it. I sent him out to get shaved and buy clean linen.

I take a curious delight in writing this diary. I know now why it is and it has rather startled me. It's just that chance phrase of King Lamus: "Your magical diary."

I have flirted a lot with Lamus, but it was mostly swank. I dislike the man in many ways.

By Jove, I know why that is, too. It's because I feel that he despises me intellectually, and because I respect him. Despite my dislike, I am eager to show him that I am not such a rotter after all.

One of his fads is to make his pupils keep these magical diaries. I feel that I've gone in for a competition; that I have to produce something more interesting than, anything they do, whoever they are.

Here comes Peter Pan. He hasn't grown old after all. . . .

We had a gorgeous feed at the dear old cafe. King Lamus came up to our table but he only said a few words.

"So you got it, I see." Cockie gave him one back.

"I hate to injure your reputation as a prophet, Mr. Lamus, but it isn't stopping when you have to stop. I've got it, as you say, and now, with your kind permission, I'm going to show you that we can stop."

Lamus changed his manner like a flash. His contemptuous smile became like sunrise in spring.

"That's talking," he said. "I'm glad you've got the idea. Don't think I'm trying to put you off, but if you should find it more difficult than you imagine, don't be too proud to come to me! I really do know some fairly good tips."

I was glad that Peter took it in good part. Being in good form, he realised, I suppose, that it was a serious business. We might strike a snag.

AUGUST 23

The night has been a miracle!

We went on taking H. pretty steadily. I think the C. spoils it. Our love bloomed afresh as if it was a new creation. We were lapsed in boundless bliss!

> "Awake, for ever awake!
> Awake as one never is
> While sleep is a possible end,
> Awake in the void, the abyss."

But not in the unutterable anguish of which the poet was writing. It is a formless calm. But love! We had never loved like this before. We had defiled love with the grossness of the body.

The body is an instrument of infinite pleasure; but excitement and desire sully its sublimity. We were conscious of every nerve to the tiniest filament; and for this one must be ineffably aloof from movement.

H. makes one want to scratch, and scratching is infinite pleasure. But that is only a relic of animal appetite.

After a little while, one is able to enjoy the feeling that makes one want to scratch in itself. It is an impersonal bliss perfectly indescribable and indescribably perfect.

I cannot measure the majesty of my consciousness; but I can indicate the change in the whole character of my consciousness.

I am writing this in the mood of the recording angel. I am living in eternity, and temporal things have become tedious and stupid symbols. My words are veils of my truth. But I experience quite definite delight in this diary.

King Lamus is always at the root of my brain. He is Jupiter and I have sprung from his thought: Minerva, Goddess of Wisdom!

The most tremendous events of life are unworthy trifles. The sublimity of my conceptions sweeps onward from nowhere to nowhere. Behind my articulate anthem is a stainless silence.

I am not writing for any reason, not even for myself to read; the action is automatic.

I am the first-born child of King Lamus without a mother. I am the emanation of his essence.

I lay all night without moving a muscle. The nearness of my husband completed the magnetic field of our intimacy. Act, word, and thought were equally abolished. The elements of my consciousness did not represent me at all. They were sparks struck off from our Selves. Those Selves were one Self which was whole. Any positive expression of it was of necessity partial, incomplete, inadequate. The Stars are imperfection of Night; but at least these thoughts are immeasurably faster and clearer than anything I have thought all my life.

If I were ever to wake up – it seems impossible that I ever should – this entry will probably be quite unintelligible to me. It is not written with the purpose of being intelligible or any other purpose. The idea of having a purpose at all is beneath contempt. It is the sort of thing a human being would have.

How can a supreme being inhabiting eternity have a purpose? The absolute, the all, cannot change; how then could it wish to change? It acts in accordance with its nature; but all such action is without effect. It is essentially illusion; and the deeper one enters into one's self the less one is influenced by such illusions.

As the night went on, I found myself less and less disturbed by my own exquisite emotions. I felt myself dissolving deliciously into absence of interruption to the serenity of my soul. . . .

I think writing this has reminded me of what I used to think was reality. It was time to go out and have lunch. The luxurious lethargy seems insuperable. . . .

It isn't hunger; it's habit. Some instinct, some obscure and obscene recollection of the lurking brute drives one to get up and go out. The dodge for doing this is to take three or four rather small sniffs in quick succession. C. would be much better, but we haven't got any.

SEPTEMBER 1

What ages and ages have passed! These filthy lodgings have been Eden without the snake. Our lives have been Innocence; no toil, no thought. We did not even eat, except the little food the woman brought in.

We scared her, by the way. She can't or won't get us any H. or C. The morphine girl has disappeared.

I'm not sure and it doesn't matter, but I think the landlady – I can never remember the woman's name, she reminds me of those dreadful days in Naples – told us that she stole some things from a shop and went to jail. It was a great nuisance, because I had to put my clothes on and call on Mabel. Luckily, she was in and had a whole lot of it.

We must have been increasing the dose very fast; but I can't be sure, because we don't keep track of it or of the days either. Counting things is so despicable. One feels so degraded. Surely that's the difference between spirit and matter. It's bestial to be bounded.

Cockie agrees with me about this. He thinks I'm writing rather wonderful things. But as soon as we come down to ordinary affairs, we quarrel all the time. We snap about nothing at all. The reason is evident.

Having to talk destroys the symphony of silence. It's hateful to be interrupted; and it interrupts one to be asked to pass a cigarette.

I wasn't going to be bothered to go out again, so I made Mabel give me all she could spare. She promised to get some more and send it round next Sunday. . . .

We're not very well, either of us. It must be this dark, dirty room and the bad atmosphere; and the street noises get on my nerves.

We could go to Barley Grange, but it's too much trouble. Besides, it might break the spell of our happiness. We're both a little afraid about that.

It happened once before, and we don't want to take any chances. It wants a lot of clever steering to keep the course. For instance, we took too much one night and made ourselves sick. It took three or four hours to get back, and that was absolute hell. My heart is a little fretful at times. It's certainly great, Peter Pan having medical knowledge. He went out and got some strychnine and put me right.

Champagne helps H. quite a lot. You mustn't drink it off. The thing to do is to sip it very slowly. It helps one to move one's hands.

We sent out a boy and got in three dozen small bottles.

SEPTEMBER 5

The world is a pig. It keeps on putting its nose where it isn't wanted. We are overdrawn at the bank. Cockie had to write to Mr. Wolfe.

"It ought to be stopped," he cried, "it amounts to brawling in church!"

A flash of the old Peter Pan!

SEPTEMBER 8

The woman says it's Tuesday, and we're running awfully short. Why can't people keep their promises? I'm sure Mabel said Sunday.

CHAPTER III
THE GRINDING OF THE BRAKES

SEPTEMBER

Peter and I have had a long, nasty quarrel, and I had to pull his hair for him. It broke one of my nails. I've let them go very long. I don't know when I was manicured last.

For some reason, they're dry and brittle. I must have them done. I'd send the boy out, but I don't like the idea of a strange girl coming here. One never knows what may go wrong. It doesn't really matter, either. The body is merely a nuisance, and it hurts.

"So blood wrenches its pain
Sardonic through heart and brain."

I am beginning to hate that horrible poem. It haunts me. I don't know why I should remember it like I do.

Have I been reading it, I wonder? Or perhaps it is the incredible access

of intellectual power which heroin gives that has improved my memory. Anyhow, the fact is that odd bits of it come swimming into my mind like goldfish darting in and out among streaming seaweed.

Oh, yes, my quarrel with Cockie. He said we mustn't risk being absolutely short of the suit; and I must go and get a new supply from Mabel before we ran clean out. I can't help seeing that Cockie is degenerating morally. He ought to be ashamed of himself. He ought to have made proper arrangements for a regular supply instead of relying on me.

He lies there all the time perfectly useless. He hasn't washed or shaved in a month, and he knows perfectly well that I detest dirt and untidiness. One of the things that attracted me most about him was his being so spruce and well-groomed and alert. He has changed altogether, since we came to London. I feel there is some bad influence at work on him. . . .

This place is full of vermin. I found what had been annoying me. I think I shall bob my hair. I'm awfully proud of its length, but one must be practical. . . .

I am lying down for a bit. It was a frightful nuisance getting ready to go out. Cockie nagged and bullied all the time.

I'm stiff all over, and it seems such waste of time to wash and dress, besides, the irritation of the interruption, and my clothes are impossible. I've been sleeping in them. I wish we'd brought some trunks from the Savoy. No, I don't, it would have been a lot of trouble, and interfered with our heroin honeymoon.

It's best the way it is. I wish I had Jacqueline here all the same. I need a maid, and she could have gone out and got things. But we both felt that any one at all would be a pill. The old woman doesn't bother us, thank goodness. I'm sure she still thinks we're spies. Bother, what's this? . . .

Damn! It's a letter from Basil!

(*Note. The original of this letter was destroyed. It is now printed from the carbon copy in the files of Mr. King Lamus. Ed.*)

"Dear Unlimitted Lou, – Do what thou wilt shall be the whole of the Law. You will, I am sure, forgive me for boring you with a letter; but you know what a crank I am, and it

is my mania just now to collect information about the psychology of people who are trying to advance spiritually in the way we spoke about when you so charmingly dawned on my studio the other morning."

"Do you find, in particular, that there is any difficulty in calling a halt? If so, is it not perhaps because you hear on all sides – especially from people quite ignorant of the subject, such as journalists, doctors and parrots – that it is in fact impossible to do so? Of course, I don't doubt that you immediately killed any such 'pernicious suggestion' by a counter-suggestion based on my positive statement, from experience, that people of strong character and high intelligence like yourself and Sir Peter – to whom please give my most cordial greetings! – were perfectly well able to use these things in moderation as one does soap."

"But, apart from this, do you find that the life of a 'Heroine' makes you abnormally 'suggestible'?"

"As you know, I object to the methods of Coué and Baudouin. They ask us deliberately to abandon free will and clear mentality for the semi-hypnotic state of the medieval peasant; to return like 'the sow that was washed to her wallowing in the mire' from which we have been extricated by evolution."

"Now, doesn't waltzing with the Hero's Bride or making Snow Men tend to put you into a state of mind which is too dreamy to resist the action of any strenuous idea which is presented to it strongly enough, is too dead to feeling to wish to resist, or so excitable that it is liable to be carried away by its admiration for any fascinatingly forceful personality?"

"I should be so glad to have your views on these points; and, of course, your personal confirmation of my theory that people like you and Sir Peter can use these substances with benefit to yourselves and others, without danger of becoming slaves. I have trained myself and many others to stop at Will;

but every additional affidavit to this effect is of great value to me in my present campaign to destroy the cowardly superstition that manhood and womanhood are incapable of the right and proper use of anything whatever in nature. We have tamed the wild lightning, after all; shall we run away from a packet of powder?"

Love is the law, love under will.
With my kind regards to Sir Peter, Yours ever,
"BASIL KING LAMUS."

Satirical, sneering stupidity – or is he a devil incarnate, as Gretel told us he was? Does he gloat? I loathe the beast – and I thought – once – well, never mind! Peter took the letter. Anything, anything to distract the mind from its boredom! Yet we haven't the energy to do anything: we take whatever comes to us, and clutch at it feebly. "It's true," said Cockie, to my amazement, "and we've got to be able to tell him we've won." There was a long quarrel – as there is over every incident of any sort. That is natural, with this eternal insomnia and sleeping at the wrong time. I hated Peter (and K.L.) the more because I knew all the time he was right. If K.L. is a Devil, it's up to us to get the last laugh. I tore the beastly letter into shreds. Peter has gone out – I hope he has gone to kill him. I want to be thrilled – just once more – if I had to be hanged for it myself.

Our watches have run down. It doesn't matter. I can call on Mabel any time I like. I may as well go now. I'll drink a small bottle and go along. . . .

It is night. Cockie has not returned. just when I needed him most! I'm frightened of myself. I'm stark staring sober. I went to the glass to take my hat off. I didn't know who I was. There is no flesh on my face. My complexion's entirely gone. My hair is lustreless and dry, and it's coming out in handfuls. I think I must be ill. I've a good mind to send for a doctor. But I daren't. It has been a frightful shock!

I must pull myself together and write it up.

It was about five o'clock when I got to Mount Street. If Mabel wasn't in, I could wait.

A strange man answered the door. It annoyed me. I felt frightened. Why had she changed Cartwright? I felt faint. Had something told me?

It embarrassed me to ask "Is Mrs. Black at home?" The man answered as if he had been asked the time.

"Mrs. Black is dead."

Something inside me screamed. "But I must see her," I cried insanely, feeling the ground cut suddenly from under my feet.

"I'm afraid it's impossible, madame," he said, misunderstanding me altogether. "She was buried yesterday morning. "

So that was why she hadn't sent the stuff! I stood as if I was in a trance. I heard him explaining, mechanically. I did not take in what he was saying. It was like a record being made on a gramophone.

"She was only ill two days," the man said. "The doctors called it septic pneumonia."

I suppose I thanked him, and went away automatically. I found myself at home without knowing how I got here. Something told me that the real cause of her death was heroin, though, as a matter of fact, septic pneumonia can happen to any one at any moment.

I've known two or three people go off like that.

As my Uncle John used to say, conscience makes cowards of us all.

King Lamus was always saying that as long as one has any emotion about any thing, love or fear or anything else, one can't observe things correctly. That's why a doctor won't attend his own family, and I can see coldly and clearly like a drowning man that whenever the idea of H. comes into my mind, I begin to think hysterically and come to the most idiotic conclusions; and heroin has twined itself about my life so closely that everything is connected with it one way or another.

My mind is obsessed by the thought of the drug. Sometimes it's a weird ecstasy, sometimes a dreadful misgiving.

> "Not thirst in the brain black-bitten
> In the soul more sorely smitten!
> One dare not think of the worst!
> Beyond the raging and raving
> Hell of the physical craving,

Lies, in the brain benumbed,
At the end of time and space,
An abyss, unmeasured, unplumbed –
The haunt of a face."

SEPTEMBER 12

Peter came in just as I had finished writing this account. He seemed much more cheerful, and his arms were full of books.

"There," he said, throwing them on the bed, "that will refresh my memory, in case we have any trouble in stopping. I'll show Mr. King Lamus what it means to be a Pendragon."

I told him about Mabel. And now a strange thing happened. Instead of being depressed, we felt a current of mysterious excitement, rippling at first, then raging and roaring in every nerve. It was as if the idea of her death exhilarated us. He took me in his arms for the first time in – is it weeks or months? His hot breath coiled like a snake about my ear, and thrilled my hair like an electric machine. With a strange ghastly intensity his voice, trembling with passion, strummed the intoxicating words:

"Olya! the golden bait
Barbed with infinite pain,
Fatal, fanatical mate
Of a poisoned body and brain!
Olya, the name that leers
Its lecherous longing and knavery,
Whispers in crazing ears
The secret spell of her slavery."

The room swam before my eyes. We were wreathed in spirals of dark blue smoke bursting with crimson flashes.

He gripped me with epileptic fury, and swung me round in a sort of savage dance. I had an intuition that he was seeing the same vision as I was. Our souls were dissolved into one; a giant ghost that enveloped us.

I hissed the next lines through my teeth, feeling myself a fire-breathing dragon.

> "Horror indeed intense,
> Seduction ever intenser,
> Swinging the smoke of sense
> From the bowl of a smouldering censer!"

We were out of breath. My boy sat on the edge of the bed. I crept up behind him. I shook out my hair all over his face, and dug my nails into his scalp.

We were living the heroin life, the life of the world of the soul. We had identified ourselves with the people of the poem. He was the poet, wreathed with poppies, with poisonous poppies that corrupted his blood, and I was the phantom of his delirium, the hideous vampire that obsessed him.

Little drops of blood oozed from his scalp and clotted to black under my greedy nails. He spoke the next lines as if under some cruel compulsion. The words were wrenched from him by some overwhelming necessity. His tone was colourless, as if the ultimate anguish had eaten up his soul. And all this agony and repulsion exercised a foul fascination. He suffered a paroxysm of pleasure such as pleasure itself had never been able to give him. And I was Olya, I was his love, his wife, world without end, the demon whose supreme delight was to destroy him.

> "Behind me, behind and above,
> She stands, that mirror of love.
> Her fingers are subtle-jointed
> Her nails are polished and pointed,
> And tipped with spurs of gold:
> With them she rowels the brain.
> Her lust is critical, cold;
> And her Chinese cheeks are pale,
> As she daintily picks, profane

181

With her octopus lips, and the teeth
Jagged and black beneath,
Pulp and blood from a nail."

I jerked his head back, and fastened my mouth on his. I sucked his breath into my lungs. I wanted to choke him; but there was time enough for that. I would torture him a few years longer first.

I leapt away from him. He panted heavily. When he got his breath back, he glared at me horribly with the pin-point pupils of his sightless eyes.

He began with romantic sadness, changing to demoniac glee.

"She was incarnate love
In the hours when I first awoke her.
Little by little I found
The truth of her, stripped of clothing,
Bitter beyond all bound,
Leprous beyond all loathing."

We shouted with delight, and fell into a fit of hysterical laughter. We came out of it completely exhausted.

I must have slept for a while.

When I woke he was sitting at the table under the yellow gas jet, reading the books he had bought.

Somehow, the past had been washed out of us. We found ourselves intent on the idea of stopping H.; and the books didn't help very much. They were written in a very positive way. The writers quarrelled among themselves like a Peace Conference.

But they all agreed on two points: that it was beyond the bounds of human possibility to break off the habit by one's own efforts. At the best, the hope was pitifully poor. The only chance was a "cure" in a place of restraint. And they all gave very full details of the horrors and dangers of the process. The physician, they said, must steel his heart against every human feeling, and refuse inexorably the petitions of the patient. Yet he must always be ready with his syringe, in case of a sudden collapse threatening life itself.

There were three principal methods of cure: Cutting the drug off at once, and trust to the patient's surviving; then there was a long tedious method of diminishing the daily dose. It was a matter of months. During the whole of the time, the agony of the patient continues in a diluted form. It was the choice between plunging into boiling oil and being splashed with it every day for an indefinite period. Then there was an intermediate method in which the daily amount was reduced by a series of jerks. As Peter said, one was to be sentenced to be flogged at irregular intervals without knowing exactly when. One would be living in a state of agonising apprehension which would probably be more morally painful than in either of the other ways.

In all cases alike there was no hint of any true comprehension of the actual situation. There was no attempt to remove the original causes of the habit; and they all admitted that the cure was only temporary, and that the rule was relapse.

There was also a horribly disquieting impression that the patient could not trust the honesty of the doctor. Some of them openly advocated attempts to deceive the patient by injecting plain water. Others had a system of giving other drugs in conjunction with the permitted dose, with the deliberate intention of making the patient so ill that he would rather bear the tortures of abstention than those devised by his doctor.

I felt too, that if I went to one of those places, I should never know what trick might be played on me next. They were cruel, clumsy traps set by ignorant and heartless charlatans. I began to understand the intensity of jealousy with which the regular physician regards the patent-medicine vender and the Christian scientist.

They were witch-doctors with a licence from government to torture and kill at extravagant prices. They guarded their prerogatives with such ferocity because they were aware of their own ignorance and incompetence; and if their victims found them out their swindle would be swept away. They were always trying to extend their tyranny. They were always wanting new laws to compel everybody, sick or well, to be bound to the vivisection table, and have some essential organ of the body cut out. And they were brazen enough to give the reason. They didn't understand what use it was! And everybody must be injected with all

sorts of disgusting serums and vaccines ostensibly to protect them against some disease which there was no reason whatever to suppose they were likely to get. . . .

The last three days have been too dreadful. This is the first time I have felt like writing, and yet I have been itching insanely to put down that hideously luxurious scene when our love broke out like an abscess. All the old fantastic features were there. They had assumed a diabolical disguise; but my mind has been in abeyance. We shut the medical books with a shudder, and slung them out of the window into the street. A little crowd gathered; they were picked up, and the passers-by began talking about what was to be done. We realised the rashness of our rage. The last thing was to attract attention! We pulled the frowsy old curtains across, and put out the light.

The reaction of our reading was terrific. We venomously contrasted the calm confidence of King Lamus with the croaking clamour of the "authorities".

Cockie summed up the situation with a quotation.

"Quoth the Raven, 'Nevermore!'"

Our thoughts splashed to and fro like an angry sea in a cave. These three days have been a flux of fugitive emotion. We are resolved to stop taking H.; and there the memory of Lamus's letter was like a rope held by a trustworthy leader for a novice on some crumbling crag.

If we could only have relied on that! But our minds were shaken by panic.

Those cursed medical cowards! Those pompous prophets of evil! Every time we came back to the resolution to stop, they pulled us off the rock.

"It's beyond human power."

But they know which side their bread's buttered. it's their game to discourage their dupes.

But they had over-played their hand. They had painted their picture in too crude colours. They revolted us.

Again, the effect of Mabel's death, and the fact that our supplies were so short, combined to drive us into the determination to stop at whatever cost.

We struggled savagely hour by hour. There were moments when the abstinence itself purged us by sheer pain of the capacity to suffer. Our

minds began to wander. We were whirled on the wings of woe across the flaming skies of anguish.

I remember Peter standing at the table, lost to all sense of actuality. He cried in a shrill, cracked voice:

> "Her cranial dome is vaulted,
> Her mad Mongolian eyes
> Aslant with the ecstasies
> Of things immune, exalted
> Far beyond stars and skies,
> Slits of amber and jet –"

I heard him across abysses of aching inanity. A thrill of Satanic triumph tingled in my soul, and composed a symphony from its screams. I leapt with lust to recognise myself in the repulsive phantasm pictured by the poet.

> "Her snout for the quarry set
> Fleshy and heavy and gross,
> Bestial, broken across,
> And below it her mouth that drips
> Blood from the lips
> That hide the fangs of the snake,
> Drips on venomous udders
> Mountainous flanks that fret,
> And the spirit sickens and shudders
> At the hint of a worse thing yet."

We had, on the other side, some spasms of weakness; a ghastly sensation of the sinking of the spirit. It's the same unescapable dread that seizes one when one is in a lift which starts down too quickly, or when one swoops too suddenly in a 'plane. Waves of weakness washed over us as if we were corpses cast up by the sea from a shipwreck. A shipwreck of our souls.

And in these hideous hours of helplessness, we drifted down the dark and sluggish river of inertia towards the stagnant and stinking morass of insanity.

We were obsessed by the certainty that we could never pull through. We said nothing at first. We were sunk in a solemn stupor. When it found voice at last, it was to whimper the surrender. The Unconditional Surrender of our integrity and our honour!

We eked out our small allowance of H. with doses of strychnine to ward off the complete collapse of all our physical faculties, and we picked ourselves up a bit on the moral plane by means of champagne.

In these moments of abdication we talked in fragile whispers, plans for getting supplies. We had both of us a certain shame in admitting to each other that we were renegades. We felt that in future we should never be able to indulge frankly and joyously as we had hitherto done. We should become furtive and cunning; we should conceal from each other what we were doing, although it was obvious to us both.

I slipped out this afternoon on tiptoe, thinking Peter was asleep, but he turned like a startled snake just as I made for the door.

"Where are you going, Lou?"

His voice was both piteous and harsh. I had not thought of inventing a pretext; but a lie slipped ready-made from my tongue.

"I am going to Basil, to see if he can't give me something to help us out."

I knew he didn't believe me, and I knew he didn't care where I went or what I did. He was not shocked at my lying to him – the first time I had ever done so.

I took a taxi round to the studio. My lie was half truth. I was going to ask him to help in the cure; but my real object was to induce him, no matter how, to give me at least one dose. I didn't care how I got it. I would try pretending illness. I would appeal to our old relations, and I would look about slyly to see if I couldn't find some and steal it. And I didn't mean to let Peter know.

On the top of everything else was the torture of shame. I had always been proud of my pride. A subtle serenity made my brain swim when I got into the street. It delighted me to be alone – to have got rid of Peter. I felt him as a restraining influence, and I had shaken him off. I despised myself for having loved him. I wanted to go to the devil my own way.

I found Basil in, and alone. What luck! That hateful tall thin girl was out of the way.

Basil received me with his usual greeting. It stung me to the quick like an insult. What right had he to reproach me? And why should "Do what thou wilt" sound like a reproach?

As a rule he added something to the phrase. He slid into ordinary conversation with a kind of sinuous grace. There was always something feline about him. He reminded me of a beautiful, terrible tiger winding his way through thick jungle.

But today, he stopped short with dour decision. It was as if he had fired a shot, and was waiting to see the effect. But he motioned me silently into my usual armchair, lit a cigarette for me and put it into my mouth, switched in the electric kettle for tea, and sat on the corner of his big square table swinging his leg. His eyes were absolutely motionless; yet I felt that they were devouring my body and soul inch by inch.

I wriggled on my chair as I used to do at school when I didn't feel sure whether I had been found out in something or not.

I tried to cover my confusion by starting a light conversation; but I soon gave it up. He was taking no notice of my remarks. To him they were simply one of my symptoms.

I realised with frightful certitude that my plans were impossible. I couldn't fool this man, I couldn't play on his passions, I couldn't steal in his presence.

Despite myself, my lie had become the truth. I could only do what I said I was coming to do; to ask him to help me out. No, not even that. I had not got rid of Peter after all.

With King Lamus, I found I couldn't think of myself. I had to think of Peter. I was absolutely sincere when I said with a break in my voice, "Cockie's in an awful mess."

I had it in my mind to add, "Can't you do something to help him?" and then I changed it to "Won't you?" and then I couldn't say it at all. I knew it was wasting words. I knew that he could and he would.

He came over and sat on the arm of my chair, and took down my hair, and began playing with the plaits. The action was as absolutely natural and innocent as a kitten playing with a skein of wool.

It stabbed my vanity to the heart for a second to realise that he could

do a thing like that without mixing it up with sexual ideas. Yet it was that very superiority to human instincts that made me trust him.

"Sir Peter's not here," he said lightly and kindly,

I knew that it had pleased him that I had not mentioned my own troubles.

"But it's you, my dear girl, that I see in my wizard's spy-glass, on a lee shore with your masts all gone by the board, and the Union Jack upside down flying from a stump, and your wireless hero tapping out S.O.S."

He dropped my hair and lighted his pipe. Then he began to play with it again.

"And some on boards, and some on broken pieces of the ship, they all came safe to land."

One's familiarity with the New Testament makes a quotation somehow significant, however little one may believe in the truth of the book.

I felt that his voice was the voice of a prophet. I felt myself already saved.

"You take some of this," he went on, bringing a white tablet from a little cedar cabinet, and a big glass of cold water. "Throw your head back, and get it well down, and drink all this right off. Here is another to take home to your husband, and don't forget the water. It will calm you down; your nerves have all gone west. I've got some people coming here in a few minutes. But this will help you through the night, and I'm coming round in the morning to see you. What's the address?"

I told him. My face blazed with the disgrace. A house where the top social note was a fifth-rate musician in a jazz-band, and the bottom where we don't give it a name.

He jotted it down as if it had been the Ritz. But I could feel in my over-sensitive state the disgust in his mind. It was as if he had soiled his pencil.

The tablet made me feel better; but I think that the atmosphere of the man did more than its share of the work. I felt nearly normal when I got up to go.

I didn't want his friends to see me. I knew too well what I was looking like.

He stopped me at the door.

"You haven't any of that stuff, I take it?" he said.

And I felt an inexpressible sense of relief. His tone implied that he had taken charge of us.

"No," I said, "we used up the last grain some time ago."

"I won't ask you to remember when," he replied.

"I know too well how muddled one gets. And besides, when one starts this experiment, the clock doesn't tell one much, as you know."

My self-respect came back to me with a rush. He insisted on our regarding ourselves as pioneers of science and humanity. We were making an experiment; we were risking life and reason for the sake of mankind.

Of course, it wasn't true. And yet, who can tell the real root of one's motives? If he chose to insist that we were doing what the leaders of thought have always done, how could I contradict him?

A buoyant billow of bliss bounded in my brain. It might not be true; but, by God, we'd make it come true.

I suppose a light leapt in my eyes, and enabled him to read my thought.

"*Respice finem!* judge the end;
The man, and not the child, my friend!"

he quoted gaily.

And then, to my absolute blank amazement, he took me back into the studio, got a bottle of heroin from the cedar cabinet and shook out a small quantity on to a scrap of paper. He twisted it up, and put it in my hand.

"Don't be surprised," he laughed, "your face tells me that it's all right. You hadn't got that look of a dying duck in a thunderstorm which shows that you're wholly enslaved. As Sir Peter very cleverly pointed out the other day, you can't stop unless you've got something to stop with. You're keeping your magical diary, of course."

"Oh, yes," I cried gladly; I knew how important he thought the record was.

He shook his head comically.

"Oh, no, Miss Unlimited Lou, not what I call a magical diary. You ought to be ashamed of yourself for not knowing the hours, minutes, and

seconds since the last dose. *Nous allons changer tout cela.* You can take this if you like, and when you like. I merely put it up to you as a sort of sporting proposition that you should see how long you can manage to keep off it. But I trust you to make a note of the exact time when you decide on a sniff, and I trust you to tell me the truth. Get it out of your mind once and for all that I disapprove of your taking it. It's entirely your business, not mine. But it's every one's business to be true to himself; and you must regard me as a mere convenience, an old hand at the game whose experience may be of use to you in training for the fight."

I hurried home a different woman. I didn't want to save myself. I felt myself as a suit of armour made for the purpose of protecting Peter. My integrity was important not for my own sake but for his.

Peter is out, so I have written this up. How surprised he will be. . . .

I wonder why he is so long, and where he has gone. It is very uncomfortable, waiting, with nothing to do. I should like a dose. The tablet has not made me sleepy; it seems to have calmed me. It has taken the edge off that hateful restlessness. I can bear it as far as that goes, if only I had something to do to take my mind off things. My mind keeps prowling around the little packet of paper in my bag. I turn a thousand corners; but it is always waiting behind all of them. There is something terrifying about the fatality of the stuff. It seems to want to convince you that it's useless to try to escape. One's thoughts always recur to lots of other subjects which we don't think of as obsessing. Why should we have this idea in connection with dope and be unable to do anything to throw it off? What's the difference?

CHAPTER IV
BELOW
THE BRUTES

SEPTEMBER 13

I wonder how I have lived through this. Peter came in last night just after I had closed my diary. I had never seen him like it before; his eyes were half out of his head, bloodshot and furious. He must have been drinking like a madman. He was trembling with rage. He came straight up to me, and hit me deliberately in the face.

"That'll teach you," he shouted, and called me a foul name.

I couldn't answer. I was too hurt, not by the blow, but by the surprise. I had pictured it so differently.

He staggered back into the middle of the room and pointed to the blood that was running down my face. The edge of his ring had cut the corner of my eye. The sight sent him into fits of hysterical laughter.

The only feeling in my mind was that he was ill that it was my duty to nurse him. I tried to go to the door to get help. He thought I was

escaping, and flung me back right across the room on to the bed, howling with rage.

"You can get away with it at once," he said, "but that's enough. You wait right here, and see whether Mr. Bloody King Lamus will come to fetch you. Don't fret; I expect he will. He likes dirt, the filthy beast!"

I burst out crying. The contrast between the two men was too shocking. And I belonged to this screaming swearing bully with his insane jealousy and his senseless brutality!

I would rather have swept out Basil's studio for the rest of my life than be Lady Pendragon.

What masters of irony the gods are! I had been swimming in a glowing flood of glory; I had been almost delirious to think I was the wife of a man in whose veins ran the blood of England's greatest king; of him whose glamour had gilded the centuries with romance; to think that I might hold such royal heirship under my heart. What radiant rapture!

And Peter himself had shown himself worthy of his ancestry. Had not he too beaten back the heathen and saved England?

So this was the end of my dream! This brawling ruffian was my man!

I sat stupefied while his incoherent insults battered my brain; but my indignation was not for myself. I had deserved all I was getting; but what right had this foul-mouthed coward to take in his mouth the name of a man like King Lamus?

My silence seemed to exasperate him more than if I had taken up the quarrel. He swayed and swore with blind ferocity. He didn't seem to know where I was. It was getting dark. He groped his way round the room looking for me; but he passed me twice before he found me. The third time he stumbled up against me, gripped me by the shoulder, and began to strike.

I sat as if I were paralysed. I could not even scream. Again and again he swore and struck me savagely, yet so weakly that I could not feel the blows. Besides, I was dulled to all possible pain. Presently he collapsed, and rolled over on the bed. I thought for a moment he was dead, and then he was seized by a series of spasms; his muscles twisted and twitched; his hands clawed at the air; he began to mutter rapidly and unintelligibly. I was horribly frightened.

I got up and lit the gas. The poor boy's face was white as death; but small, dark crimson flushes burnt on the cheek-bones.

I sat at the table for some time and thought. I didn't dare send for a doctor. He might know what was the matter and take him away from me; take him to one of those torture-traps, and he'd never get out.

I knew what he wanted, of course; a little heroin would bring him round all right. I told him I had some. I had to tell him several times before he understood.

When he did, the mere thought helped to restore him but there remained an ort of rage, and he told me to give it him, with a greedy snarl. If I had wanted to keep it from him, I shouldn't have let him know I had it.

I brought him the stuff, sitting down by his side and lifting his head with one hand while I gave it to him on the back of the other. My heart sank like a stone in deep water. The old familiar attitude, the old familiar act! – and yet how different in every point!

The convulsive movements stopped immediately. He sat up almost at once on one elbow. The only sign of distress was that he still breathed heavily. All his anger, too, had disappeared. He seemed tired, like a convalescent, but as tractable as a child. He smiled faintly. I don't know if he had any consciousness or memory of what had passed. He talked as if there had been no quarrel at all. The colour came back to his face, the light to his eyes.

"One more go like that, Lou," he said, "and I'll be all right."

I wasn't at all sure what King Lamus would have said; but it was my own responsibility, and I couldn't refuse him.

He went off to sleep very soon after. In the morning I found out what had happened to him. He had been round to some of the men he used to know in the hospital to get them to give him some H., but they hadn't dared to do it. They were suffering from a sense of insult about the new law, the Diabolical Dope Act. They had undergone a long and expensive training and had diplomas which made them responsible for the health of the community; and now they weren't allowed to prescribe for their own patients. It was natural enough that they should be indignant.

The fourth man to whom Peter had gone told the same story, but had been very cordial. He thought he'd help things by standing Peter a dinner and filling him up with alcohol, with the idea that that would help him to support the lack of the other stimulant.

It seems that I had to pay for the prescription.

No, Lou, you're a naughty girl. You mustn't be bitter like that. It's your fault for getting born into a world where ignorance and folly are in constant competition for the premiership of the minds of the educated classes. The commonest ploughman would have had more horse-sense than that doctor.

I gave Peter the tablet with plenty of water when he began to get restless. It soothed him a great deal. I wished I had one for myself. I felt my irritability returning; but I didn't break out because it couldn't be long till Basil came round. I looked forward to his coming as to a certain end to all our troubles. . . .

What actually happened was quite different. I hardly know how to write it down. The shame and the disappointment are blasting. I feel that the doors of hope have been slammed in my face. I can imagine the grinding of the key as it turns in the lock, the screech of the rusty bolt as it is driven home.

The moment Basil appeared, Peter's insanity blazed up. He poured out a stream of insults, and accused Basil to his face of trying to get me away.

If Basil had only known how eagerly I would have gone! A man in sexual mania is not fit to consort with human beings. I never realised before why women despise men in their hearts so deeply. We respect men who have mastered their passions, if only because we are ourselves ultimately nothing but those passions. We expect a man to show himself superior. It will not do to kill passion, like Klingsor; the sexless man is even lower than "the wounded king", Amfortas, the victim of his virility. The true hero is Parsifal, who feels the temptations. "A man of like passions with ourselves." The more acutely alive he is to love, the greater are his possibilities. But he must refuse to surrender to his passions; he must make them serve him. "*Dienen! Dienen!*"

Who would kill a horse because he was afraid to ride him? It is better to mount, and dare the brute to bolt.

After the man is thrown, we pick him up and nurse him, but we don't adore him. Most men are like that. But what every woman is looking for is the man with the most spirited horse and the most complete mastery of him. That's most symbolic in The Garden of Allah, where the monk who cannot ride takes a stallion out into the desert, determined to fight the thing out to a finish.

Basil was not moved by the savage spite of Peter.

He refused to be provoked. Whenever he got a chance to put a word in, he simply asserted the purpose of his visit. He did not even take the trouble to deny the main accusation.

It tired Peter to dash himself so uselessly against the cliff of Basil's contempt. I don't mean that it was contempt, either, but his calm kindness was bound to be felt as contempt because Peter couldn't help knowing how well he deserved disdain. He was aware of the fact that his abuse became weaker and emptier with every outburst. He simply pulled himself together with a last effort of animosity toward the friend who could have saved us, and ordered him out of the house. He made himself more ridiculous by posing as an outraged husband.

Lofty morality is the last refuge when one feels oneself to be hopelessly in the wrong.

It was the first time I had ever known Peter play the hypocrite. His professions of propriety were simply the measure of his indignity.

There was nothing for Basil to do but to go. Peter pretended to have scored a triumph. It would not have deceived anybody, but – if there had been a chance – he cut away the pulpit from under his own feet when he swung back into the room and snapped with genuine feeling:

"God damn it, what a fool I am! Why didn't you tip me the wink? We ought to have played up to him and got some heroin out of him. . . ."

This morning has taken everything out of me. I don't care about saving myself. I know I can't save Peter. Why must a woman always have a man for her motive? All I want is H. Both Cockie and I need it hellishly.

"Look here, Lou," he said with a cunning grin I'd never seen before, quite out of keeping with his character. "You doll yourself up and try the doctors. A man told me last night that there were some who would give you a prescription if you paid them enough. A tenner ought to do the trick."

He pulled some dirty crumpled notes out of his trousers' pocket.

"Here you are. For God's sake, don't be long."

I was as keen as he was. All the will to stop had been washed out of me when Basil went. My self-respect was annihilated.

Yet I think it was reluctance to go that kept me hanging about on the pretence of attending to my toilet.

Peter watched me with approval. There was a hateful gleam in his eye, and I loved it. We were both degraded through and through. We had reached the foul straw of the sty. There was something warm and comfortable about snuggling up to depravity. We had realised the ideal of our perversion. . . .

I went to my own doctor. Peter had put me up to symptoms; but he wasn't taking any. He talked about change of climate and diet and the mixture to be taken three times a day. I saw at once it was no good by the way he jumped when I mentioned heroin first.

All I could do was to get out of the old fool's room without losing face. . . .

I didn't know what to do next. I felt like Morris What's-his-name in *The Wrong Box* when he had to have a false death certificate, and wanted a "venal doctor".

It annoyed me that it was daylight, and I didn't know where to go. Suddenly, out of nowhere, there came the name and address of the man who had helped Billy Coleridge out of her scrape. It was a long way off, and I was horribly tired. I was hungry, but the thought of lunch made me sick. I felt that people were looking at me strangely. Was it the scar by my eye?

I bought a thick veil. The girl looked surprised, I thought. I suppose it was rather funny in September, and might attract still more attention; but it gave me a sense of protection, and it was a very pretty veil – cream lace with embroidered zig-zags.

I took a taxi to the doctor's. Doctor Collins, it was, 61 or 71 Fairelange Street, Lambeth.

I found him at home; a horrid, snuffy old man with shabby clothes; a dingy grimy office as untidy as himself.

He seemed disappointed at my story. It wasn't his line, he said, and

he didn't want to get into trouble. On the other hand, he was frightened of me because of what I knew about Billy. He promised to do what he could; but under the new law, he couldn't do more than prescribe ten doses of an eighth of a grain apiece. Four or five sniffs, the whole thing! And he wouldn't dare to repeat it in less than a week.

However, it was better than nothing. He told me where to get it made up.

I found a cloak-room where I could put the packets into one, and started.

The relief was immense. I went on, dose after dose. Cockie could get his own. I should tell him I had drawn blanks. I felt I could eat again, and had some light food and a couple of whiskies and sodas.

I felt so good that I drove straight back to Greek Street, and poured out a mournful tale of failure. It was delicious to deceive that brute after he'd struck me.

It was keen pleasure to see him in such pain; to imitate his symptoms with minute mimicry; to mock at his misery. He was angry all the same, but his blows gave me infinite pleasure. They were the symbols of my triumph.

"Here, you get out of this," he said, "and don't come back without it. I know where you can get it. Andrew McCall is the man's name. I know him to the bottom of his rotten soul."

He gave me the address.

It was a magnificent house near Sloane Square. He had married a rich old woman, and lived on the fat of the land.

I had met him once myself in society. He was a self-made Scot, and thought evening dress *de rigueur* in Paradise.

Peter sent me off with a sly snigger. There was some insane idea at the back of his mind. Well, what did I care? . . .

Dr. McCall was a man of fifty or so, very well preserved and very well dressed, with a gardenia in his buttonhole. He recognised me at once, and drew me by the hand into a comfortable armchair. He began to chatter about our previous meeting; about the duchess of this and the countess of that.

I wasn't listening, I was watching. His tact told him that I wasn't interested. He stopped abruptly.

"Well, well, excuse me for running on like this about old times. The point is, what can I do for you today, Miss Laleham?"

I instantly saw my advantage. I shook my head laughingly.

"Oh, no," I said, "it's not Miss Laleham."

He begged my pardon profusely for the mistake.

"Can it be possible? Two such beautiful girls so much alike?"

"No," I smiled back, "it's not as bad as that. I was Miss Laleham, but now I am Lady Pendragon."

"Dear, dear," he said, "where can I have been? Quite out of the world, quite out of the world!"

"Oh, I'm not quite such an important person as that, and I only married Sir Peter in July."

"Ah, that accounts for it," said the doctor. "I've been away all the summer in the heather with the Marchioness of Eigg. Quite out of the world, quite out of the world. Well, I'm sure you're very happy, my dear Lady Pendragon."

He always mentioned a title with a noise like a child sucking a stick of barley sugar.

I saw at once the way to appeal to him.

"Well, of course, you know," I said, "in really smart circles one has to offer heroin and cocaine to people. It's only a passing fashion, of course, but while it's on, one's really out of it if one doesn't do the right thing."

McCall got out of the chair at his desk, and drew up a little tapestried stool close to mine.

"I see, I see," he muttered confidentially, taking my hand and beginning to stroke it gently, "but you know, it's very hard to get."

"It is for us poor outsiders," I lamented, "but not for you."

He rolled back my sleeve, and moved his hand up and down inside of my forearm. I resented the familiarity acutely. The snobbishness of the man reminded me that he was the son of a small shopkeeper in a lowland village – a fact which I shouldn't have thought of for a second but for his own unctuous insistence on Debrett.

He got up and went to a little wall safe behind my back. I could hear him open and shut it. He returned and leant over the back of my chair, stretching out his left arm so that I could see what was in his hand.

It was a sealed ten-gramme bottle labelled "Heroini Hydrochlorid", with the quantity and the maker's name. The sight of it drove me almost insane with desire.

Within a yard of my face was the symbol of victory. Cockie, Basil, the law, my own physical pangs: they were all in my power from the moment my fingers closed over the bottle.

I put out my hand; but the heroin had disappeared in the manner of a conjuring trick.

McCall leant his weight on the back of my chair and tilted it slightly. His ugly shrewd false face was within a foot of mine.

"Will you really let me have that?" I faltered. "Sir Peter's very rich. We can afford to pay the price, whatever it is."

He gave a funny little laugh. I shrank from the long wolf-like mouth hanging over me greedily open, with its bared two white rows of sharp, long fangs.

I was nauseated by the stale whisky in his breath.

He understood immediately; let my chair back to its normal position, and went back to his desk. He sat there and watched me eagerly like a man stalking game. As if inadvertently, he took out the bottle and played with it aimlessly.

In his smooth varnished voice he began to tell me what he called the romance of his life. The first time he saw me he had fallen passionately in love with me; but he was a married man, and his sense of honour prevented his yielding to his passion. He had, of course, no love for his wife, who didn't understand him at all. He had married her out of pity; but for all that he was bound by his sense of right feeling, and above all by realising that to give rein to his passion, God-given though it was, would mean social ruin for me, for the woman he loved.

He went on to talk about affinities and soul-mates and love at first sight. He reproached himself for having told me the truth, even now, but it had been too strong for him. The irony of fate! The tragic absurdity of social restrictions!

At the same time, he would feel a certain secret pleasure if he knew that I, on my part, had had something of the same feeling for him. And

all the time, he went on playing with the heroin. Once or twice he nearly dropped it in his nervous emotion.

It made me jump to think of the danger to that precious powder. But there was clearly only one thing to be done to get it: to fall in with the old fellow's humour.

I let my head fall on my breast and looked at him sideways out of the corners of my eyes.

"You can't expect a young girl to confess everything she has felt," I whispered with a deep sigh, "especially when she has had to kill it out of her heart. It does no good to talk of these things," I went on. "I ought really not to have come. But how could I guess that you, a great doctor like you, had taken any notice of a silly kid like me?"

He jumped to his feet excitedly.

"No, no," I said sadly, with a gesture which made him sit down again, very uneasily. "I should never have come. It was absolutely weakness on my part. The heroin was only my excuse. Oh, don't make me feel so ashamed. But I simply must tell you the truth. The real motive was that – I wanted to see you. Now, let's talk about something else. Will you let me have that heroin, and how much will it cost?"

"One doesn't charge one's friends for such slight services," he answered loftily. "The only doubt in my mind is whether it's right for me to let you have it."

He took it out again and read the label. He rolled the bottle between his palms.

"It's terribly dangerous stuff," he continued very seriously. "I'm not at all sure if I should be justified in giving it to you."

What absolute rubbish and waste of time, this social comedy! Every one in London knew McCall's hobby for intrigues with ladies of title. He had invented the silly story of love at first sight on the spur of the moment. It was just a gambit.

And as for me, I loathed the sight of the man, and he knew it. And he knew, too, that I wanted that heroin desperately badly. The real nature of the transaction was as plain as a prison plum-pudding.

But I suppose it does amuse one in a sort of way to ape various affected attitudes. He knew that my modesty and confusion and blushes

were put on like so much paint on the cheeks of a Piccadilly street walker. It didn't even hurt his vanity to know that I thought him an offensive old ogre. He had the thing I wanted, I had the thing he wanted, and he didn't care if I drugged myself to death tomorrow, provided I had paid his price today.

The callous cynicism on both sides had one good effect from the moral point of view. It prevented me wasting my time in trying to cheat him.

He went on with his gambit. He explained that my marriage made a great difference. With reasonable caution, for which we had every facility, there was not the slightest risk of scandal.

Only one thing stuck in my conscience, and fought the corrosive attack of the heroin-hunger. After King Lamus had gone this morning, Peter and I had quarrelled bitterly. I had given up Basil, I had given up all idea of living a decent life, I had embraced the monster in whose arms I was struggling, gone with my eyes wide open into his dungeon, devoted myself to drugs, and why? I was Sir Peter's wife. The loss of my virtue, independence, self-respect, were demanded by my loyalty to him. And already that loyalty demanded disloyalty of another kind.

It was a filthy paradox. Peter had sent me to McCall with perfect foresight. I knew well enough what he expected of me, and I gloried in my infamy – partly for its own sake, but partly, unless I am lying to myself, because my degradation proved my devotion to him.

I no longer heard what McCall was saying, but I saw that he had taken a little pocket-knife and cut the string of the bottle. He had levered out the cork, and dipped the knife into the powder. He measured out a dose with a queer cunning questioning smile in his eyes.

My breath was coming quickly and shallowly. I gave a hurried little nod. I seemed to hear myself saying, "A little bit more". At least, he added to the heap.

"A little mild stimulant is indicated," he said, with an imitation of his bedside manner. He was kneeling in front of my chair, and held up his hand like a priest making an offering to his goddess.

The next thing I remember is that I was walking feverishly, almost running, up Sloane Street. I had a feeling of being pursued. Was it true, that old Greek fable of the Furies? What had I done? What had I done?

My fingers worked spasmodically on the little amber-tinted bottle of poison. I wanted to get away from every one and everything. I didn't know where I was going. I hated Peter from the depths of my soul. I would have given anything in the world – except the heroin – to be able never to see him again. But he had the money, why shouldn't we enjoy our abject ruin as we had enjoyed our romance? Why not wallow in the moist, warm mire?

CHAPTER V
TOWARDS MADNESS

I found I was attracting attention in the street by my nervous behaviour. I shuddered at the sight of a policeman. Suppose I were arrested, and they took it away from me?

And then I remembered how silly I was. Maisie Jacobs had a flat in Park Mansions. I knew she would stand for anything, and keep her mouth shut.

She was in, thank goodness. I don't know what tale I told her. I don't know why I was stupid enough to trouble my head to invent one. She's a real good sport, Maisie, and doesn't care what you do as long as you don't interfere with her.

She had some white silk, and we sewed up the H. in little packets, and stitched them in the flounces of my dress. I kept about half, and put it in an old envelope she had. That was to make my peace with Peter. But I needed two or three good goes on the spot.

I had a fit of hysterical crying and trembling. I must have fainted

for a bit. I found myself on the sofa with Maisie kneeling by me and holding a glass of champagne to my lips.

She didn't ask any questions. It wasn't her business if my story was all lies.

I felt a bit better after a while. She began to talk about King Lamus. She had fallen for him the first time she met him, about a year ago, and had become an enthusiastic pupil. She could do what she liked; she was free, plenty of money of her own, no one to interfere.

In a way, I hated her for her independence. It was really envy of her freedom.

I felt that Basil was the only man that mattered, and I had missed my chance with him through not being worthy. I had ended by losing him altogether; and the irony of it was terrible, for I had lost him through loyalty to Peter at the very moment when I thoroughly loathed and despised him.

Yet I knew that Basil would admire and love me for that very loyalty itself. It was the first thing that I had ever had to show him. My only asset had made me bankrupt for ever!

Maisie had been talking quietly while I was thinking these things. I slid out of my concentration to hear her voice once more. She was in the middle of an explanation of her relations with Basil.

"He claims to be utterly selfish," vibrated her tense tones, "because he includes every individual in his idea of himself. He can't feel free as long as there are slaves about. Of course, there are some people whose nature it is to be slaves; they must be left to serve. But there are lots of us who are kings and don't know it; who suffer from the delusion that they ought to bow to public opinion, all sorts of alien domination. He spends his life fighting to emancipate people in this false subjection, because they are parts of himself. He has no ideas about morality. His sense of honour, even, means nothing to him as such. It is simply that he happened to be born a gentleman. 'If I were a dog,' he said to me once, 'I should bark. If I were an owl, I should hoot. There's nothing in either which is good or bad in itself. The only question is, what is the natural gesture?' He thinks it his mission in the world to establish this Law of Thelema."

She saw my puzzled look.

"Do what thou wilt shall be the whole of the Law," she quoted merrily. "You must have heard those words before!"

I admitted it. We laughed together over our friend's eccentricity.

"He says that to every one he meets," she explained, not only to influence them, but to remind himself of his mission and prevent himself wasting his time on anything else. He's not a fanatic; and in the year that I have known him, I've certainly got on more with my music than I ever did in any five years before. He proved to me – or, rather, showed me how to prove to my own satisfaction – that my true Will was to be a singer. We began by going through all the facts of my life from my race and parentage to my personal qualities, such as my ear and my voice being physiologically superior to that of the average musician, and my circumstances enabling me to devote myself entirely to training myself to develop my powers to the best advantage. Even things like my guardian being a great composer! He won't admit that was an accident."

"He claims that the coincidence of so many circumstances affords evidence of design; and as so many of these are beyond the control of any human intelligence, it leads one to suppose that there is some individual at work somewhere beyond our limitations of sense who has made me a singer instead of a milliner."

"Oh, yes, Maisie," I interrupted, "but that's the old argument that the design of the Universe proves the existence of God; and people have stopped believing in God chiefly because the design was shown to be incompatible with a consistent character."

"Oh, certainly," she admitted without a qualm. "The evidence goes to show that there are many different gods, each with his own aim and his own method. Whether their conflicting ambitions can be reconciled (as seems necessary from a philosophical point of view) is practically beyond the scope of our present means of research. Basil implored me not to bother my head about any such theories. He simply laughed in my face and called me his favourite nightingale. 'Thou wast not born for death, immortal bird,' he chuckled, 'but neither wast thou born to take a course of Neo-Platonism.' His whole point is that one mustn't leave the rails. If I had convinced myself that I was a singer, would I kindly refrain from meddling with other affairs?"

"I know," I put in, "as the captain said when the first officer interrupted him, – 'What I want from you, Mr. Mate, is silence, and precious damned little of that!'"

Again we found ourselves laughing together. It was really very extraordinary the way in which talking to Basil or his pupils exhilarated the mind. I began to see why he was so distrusted and disliked. People always pretend to want to be lifted out of themselves, but in reality they're terribly afraid of anything happening to them. And Basil always strikes at the root of one's spiritual oak. He wants one to be oneself, and the price of that is to abandon the false ideas that one has of oneself. People like the sham teachers that soothe them with narcotic platitudes. They dread having to face reality in any form. That is the real reason for persecuting prophets.

Of course, I was full of H., but Maisie had made me forget all about it for a moment.

"Who's that thin girl that's always there?" I asked her.

It was an automatic spurt of jealousy.

"Oh, Lala," said Maisie, "she's rather a dear. She's a queer girl, one of the queerest ever. Swiss or something, I fancy. He's trained her for the last three years. He met her, I don't know how, and asked her to pose for him. She told me once how startled she was at the reason he gave. 'Did you write that psalm,' he asked her, '"I can tell all my bones, they look and stare upon me?"' "You know the girl hasn't got an ounce of flesh on her body. She's perfectly healthy; she's just a freak of nature. And while he sketched her he asked her to suggest a title for the picture. 'Paint me as a dead soul,' she answered. He caught up the phrase with fiery enthusiasm, and began to work on an enormous screen, a triptych with the strangest beasts and birds and faces, all arranged to lead up to her as the central figure. She is standing naked with a disproportionately large head grinning detestably. The body is almost a skeleton covered with greenish skin. It made a perfectly grisly sensation. I wonder you haven't seen it."

As a matter of fact, I had seen a photograph of it in some newspaper, and now I remembered that Bill Waldorf had pointed her out, roaring with laughter, as the Queen of the Dead Souls. Basil had said that London was full of dead souls.

"It's nothing to do with that story of Gogol's," said Maisie. "Basil thinks – and it's only too ghastly true – that most of the people we see walking about, and eating and drinking and dancing, are really dead – 'dead in trespasses and sins,' as my old uncle used to say – in the sin of not knowing themselves to be Stars, True and Living Gods Most High – "

I sighed with sadness. I, too, was a dead soul – and I had given up the Lord of Resurrection that morning out of loyalty to another dead soul. And – the same afternoon! Faugh! What a charnel-house Life is! How chill and damp and poisonous is the air! How the walls sweat the agony of the damned!

"And look at Lala now!" Maisie went on. "He had to put her through the most frightful ordeals – for she was very dead indeed – but she got to the other end of the tunnel all right. She's a Great Soul, if ever there was one in the world, and he has raised her mortal into immortality. Her corruptibility has put on incorruption – and she radiates light and life and love, leaping through the years in utter liberty – "

"But what does she do now?" I asked with a dull pain at my heart.

"Why, her True Will, of course," came back the flaming answer. "She knows that she came to this planet to bear witness to the Law of Thelema in her own person, and to help her Titan in his task!"

Maisie was really stupefying. Every one knows that she was in love with Basil from the first, and is, and always will be. How was it that she could speak of another woman who loved him without jealousy, and, as things were, without envy? It was true, perhaps, after all, that he had some huge hypnotic power, and held them helpless, filed away like so many letters. But Maisie was bubbling over with energy and joy; it was absurd to think of her as vampirised, as a victim. I asked her about it point-blank.

"My dear Lou," she laughed, "don't be too utterly gaga! My Will is to sing, and Lala's is to help him in his work – why should we clash? Why should there be any ill-feeling? She's helping me by helping him to help me; and I'm helping her by showing that his Law has helped me, and can help others. We're the best friends in the world, I and Lala; how could anything else be possible?"

Well, of course, she was herself doing a notoriously impossible feat.

The point of view of Basil and his crowd is simply upside down to all ordinary people. At the same time, one can't deny that the result is amazingly invigorating to contemplate. I could quite understand his idea of developing mankind into what is practically a new species, with new faculties, and the old fears, superstitions, and follies discarded for ever.

I couldn't stand it another second. Maisie had given him – and herself – up, and yet she possessed both herself and him: I had clung to him and to myself, and I had lost both – Lost, lost for ever! I got up to go home; and before I reached the street I realised with desolate disgust and despair the degree of my degradation, of my damnation; and I hugged desperately my hideous perverse pride in my own frightful fate, and rejoiced as the horrible hunger for heroin made itself known once more, gnawing at my entrails. I licked my lips at the thought that I was on my way to the man whom my love had done so much to destroy – and myself with him.

To begin with, no more of this diary why should I put myself out for King Lamus? "Every step he treads is smeared with blood," as Gretel once said.

Yes, in some infernal way he had made me one of his victims. "All right – you shall get enough magical diary to let you know that I'm out of your clutches – I'll put down just those things which will tell you how I hate you – how I have outwitted you – and you shall read them when my Dead Soul has got a Dead Body to match it."

SEPTEMBER 14

I expected Peter would be in; impatient to know if I'd wangled McCall. Instead, he turned up after twelve, full of champagne and – SNOW!

My aunt, what a lucky day!

He was boiling with passion, grabbed me like a hawk.

"Well, old girl," he shouted, "what luck with McCall?"

I produced my package.

"Hurrah, all our troubles are over!"

We opened our last three half-bottles of fizz to celebrate the occasion,

and he gave me some coke. And I thought I didn't like it! It's the finest stuff there is. A sniff to the right and a sniff to the left and a big heap right on my tongue; and that wasn't all.

"I tell you what's been wrong," he said in the morning. "Who the hell could expect to be right in a place like this? I've got right on to the ropes. We need never run short any more. We'll go down to Barley Grange and have another honeymoon. You're my honeysuckle, and I'm your bee."

He went and flung open the door and shouted for the woman to pack our things while we went out to breakfast, and have the bill ready.

"What infernal fools we are," he cried as we went sailing down the street to the Wisteria where you can get real French coffee and real English bacon.

We looked at ourselves in the long mirror. We could see how ill we had been, but all that was gone.

Decision and self-confidence had come back; and love had come back with them. I could feel love mingling its turbulent torrent with my blood like the junction of the Rhone and the Arve in Geneva.

We walked into a shop and bought a car on the spot, and took it away then and there. There was one at the Grange, but we wanted a racer.

We drove back to Greek Street in a flood of delight. It was a bright, fresh autumn morning; everything had recovered its tone. Winter could never come. There was no night except as a background for the moon and the stars, and to furnish the scenery of our heavenly hell.

SEPTEMBER 17

The Grange is certainly the finest house in the world. There is only one drawback. We didn't want callers. County society is all right in its way; but tigers don't hunt in packs, especially on the honeymoon. So we had to send the word around that the precarious state of my health made it impossible for us to receive. Rather an obvious lie, motoring the way we were. The 'plane had come back from Deal, but we didn't do any flying.

Cockie gave various reasons; but they were unconvincing. We roared with laughter at their absurdity.

The truth was that he was nervous.

It didn't make us ashamed. After what he had done, he could rest on his oars. It was only temporary, of course. We'd made ourselves rottenly ill in that gaga place in Greek Street. We couldn't expect to get back to the top of our form in a week.

Besides, we didn't want that kind of excitement. We had enough in other ways. We found we could see things. That ass, Basil, was always talking about the danger of magic, and precaution, and scientific methods and all that bunk. We were seeing more spirits and demons every day than he ever saw in ten years. They are nothing to be afraid of. I should like to see the old Boy himself. I'd –

SEPTEMBER 18

We found a book in the library one rainy afternoon. It told us how to make the Devil appear.

Cockie's grandfather was great on that stuff. There's a room in the north tower where he did his stunts.

We went up after dinner. Everything had been left more or less the way it was. Uncle Mortimer never troubled to alter anything.

There was a legend about this room too. For one thing, grandfather was a friend of Bulwer Lytton's. We found a first edition of *A Strange Story*, with an inscription.

Lytton had taken him for the model of Sir Philip Derval, the white magician who gets murdered. Lytton said so in this copy.

It was all very weird and exciting. The room was full of the strangest objects. There was a table painted with mysterious designs and characters and a huge cross-hilted sword; two silver crescents separated by two copper spheres and a third for the pommel. The blade was two-edged, engraved with Arabic or something.

Cockie began to swing it about. We thought flashes of light came from the point, and there was a buzzing, crackling sound.

"Take this," said Cockie, "there's something devilish rum about it."

I took it out of his hand. Of course, it was only my fancy; but it seemed

to weigh nothing at all, and it gave a most curious thrill in one's hand and arm.

Then there was a golden cup with rubies round the brim. And always more inscriptions.

And there was a little wand of ebony with a twisted flame at the top; three tongues, gold, silver, and some metal we'd never seen before.

And there were rows and rows of old books, mostly Latin, Greek, and Hebrew.

There was a big alabaster statue of Ganesha, the elephant god.

"This is the place," I said, "to get hold of the devil."

"That's all right," said Cockie, "but what about a little she-devil for me?"

"Oh," I said, "if I'm not satisfactory, you'd better give me a week's salary in lieu of notice."

We laughed like mad.

Something in the room made our heads swim. We began kissing and wrestling.

It's all very well to laugh at magic, but after all certain ideas do belong to certain things; and you can get an idea going, if you're reminded of it by a place like this. . . .

(Lady Pendragon's Diary is interrupted by a note written on some later occasion in the handwriting of Mr. Basil King Lamus. Ed.)

Lou means all right, bless her! She makes me think of Anatole France – La Rotisserie de la Reine Pédauque – old Coignard has been warned by the Rosicrucian not to pronounce the word Agla, and the moment he does so, a wheel comes off his carriage, with the result that he gets murdered by Moses.

Then, again, all the Rosicrucian's Predictions come true; and he himself goes up in a flame like the Salamander he has been invoking. He looks upon his own death as the crown of his career – the climax towards which he has been working.

Anatole France is, in fact, compelled to write as if the Rosicrucian theories were correct, although his conscious self is busily exposing the absurdity of magic.

It looks as if the artist's true self were convinced of the actuality of magic,

and insisted on expressing itself despite every effort of the sceptical intellect to turn the whole thing into ridicule. There are numerous other examples in literature of the same conflict between the genius and the mind which is its imperfect medium. For instance – at the other end of the scale – Mr. W. S. Maugham, in "The Magician", does his malignant utmost to make the "villain" objectionable in every way, an object of contempt, and a failure. Yet in the very moment when his enemies succeed in murdering him and destroying his life's work, they are obliged to admit that he has "Accomplished the Great Work" – of creating Living Beings! "Every man and every woman is a star." – B. K. L.

I don't like that room. I said nothing about it to Peter; but the old man was there walking about as large as life. You have to be specially prepared to see these things.

Cockie was never spiritually minded.

SEPTEMBER 18

An alarm of burglars last night. We roused the house – but no traces could be found. The servants here are frightfully stupid. They irritate me all the time.

One can't sleep in this house. It's too old. The wood cracks all the time. just as one is on the verge of sleep some noise makes one more wide-awake than ever.

I can't bear the idea of being touched. My skin is very sensitive. It's part of the spiritualising of my life, I suppose.

I'm glad, though, that the new honeymoon didn't last more than three or four days.

It is irritating to one's vanity. But that is merely a memory. How can vanity co-exist with the spiritual life?

I saw the Spirit of heroin today when I went up to the magic room. It is tremendously tall and thin, with tattered rags fluttering round it, and these turn into little birds that fly off it, that come and burrow in one's skin!

I just feel the prick of the beak, and then it disappears. They were

messengers from the other world. There is a little nest of them in my liver. It is very curious to hear them chirping when they want food.

I don't know what they'll do so far away from their mother.

It is horrible not being able to sleep. That, too, must be a preparation for the new life.

I wandered up all alone to the magic room, and sat with my hands on the table opposite the old man, trying to get him to talk.

His lips move, but I can't hear what he says.

I was disturbed, of course. I always am being disturbed. I am so tired. Why won't they let me alone?

This time it was a shot. The magic room has windows all around it.

I went to see who could have fired. It was very bright moonlight; but I could see nothing.

Then there came another flash and report. I went round to the side it came from, and watched. It was by the lake. I watched a long time. Then a crouching figure hidden among the reeds sprang up, put a gun to its shoulder and fired twice in rapid succession. Then it screamed, and ran to the house throwing away its gun. I wonder what it could be.

SEPTEMBER 20

I have found a manuscript in grandfather's room that tells you how to invoke the Devil. It needs two people, and I don't feel sure about Peter.

He can't see into the spiritual world at all. On the contrary, he is getting a little queer in the head, and imagines he sees things which don't exist at all. He's constantly scratching himself.

He behaved very strangely at dinner. I think the butler noticed it.

At midnight we went up to the old man's room and began to go through the ritual. A lot of it seems silly, but the climax is fine.

You keep on saying, over and over

"Io Pan Pan! Io Pan Pan! Ai Pan Pan!
Io Pan Pan! Io Pan Pan! Pan Pan Pan!

Aegipan, Aegipan, Aegipan, Aegipan, Aegipan,
Aegipan, Io Pan Pan!"

You go on till something comes. We used two black robes that we
found hanging up there.

They were lovely silk robes with hoods.

You take candles in both hands and dance while you make the
incantations.

We got frightfully excited. It was as if a strange force had got hold of
us. It seemed to lead us all round the house and then into the grounds.

We were shouting at the top of our voices.

Once or twice we saw a servant putting out a nose through a chink
of a door. It would always be shut with a little squeal, and we could hear
keys turning and bolts being pushed.

We wanted to roar with laughter, but we had to keep on with the
invocation. The book said you mustn't stop it while you were outside the
magic room, or the Devil could get you.

The strange thing is that I don't remember at all what happened. Did
the Devil come or not?

I don't even remember getting back to the magic room. I must have
gone to sleep, for I've woken up frightfully hungry.

Cockie's awake too. He's kneeling at the window with a shot gun. He
aimed it two or three times, but didn't fire. He came back to me after
putting the gun in a corner.

He said, "It's no good. They're too spry. The only chance to get them
is at night."

He was hungry too. We rang for some food. Nobody answered the bell.

We rang again and again.

Then Peter got angry and went to see what was wrong. "There isn't a
soul in the place!"

It's perfectly incomprehensible. What could have happened to them all?

Peter says it's the Germans. Part of a plot to persecute him for what
he did in the war. But I don't think so at all.

It says in a book that you have to get rid of every one if you're going
to start the spiritual life.

I expect my spiritual guide put it into their minds to go, but I'm very doubtful about Cockie. He's not ready for any high development. Men are always revoltingly gross.

Think how they are even about love. I must say this for Cockie, he's all right about that. The very flower of purity – a perfect knight!

Yet we went through a period of a very evil character. No doubt we had to be purged of all our baser elements.

There is a great sympathy between us at times, and it is not soiled by any animality.

The only thing is I'm not sure whether it hasn't been too great a strain for his mind – the process of purification.

He certainly has some very queer ideas. Sometimes I catch him looking at me with some deep suspicion in his eyes. His mind is harping on the Germans. He broke out just now into a denunciation of Gretel Webster as a German spy, and rambled on from that to say something that I couldn't properly understand. But the gist of it was apparently that as Gretel had introduced us more or less, I was being used to do him some harm.

Of course ideas like this come to one when one's hungry, and all this sprang up owing to the mysterious disappearance of the servants.

There was nothing for it but for Peter to go to the inn and have food sent in. But I had the devil's own job to get him to do it. His character lacks decision.

I made him take two or three sniffs of snow. That put him right, and now he's gone off to the inn.

I'm very glad to be alone. I always felt those servants were spying. The house is delightfully quiet.

As I write there are two beautiful people looking over my shoulder. They have been sent to watch over me and guide me, and prepare me for the great destiny which is in store for me.

Here comes Peter with the waiter and a tray. I must hide this book. The secrets of the spiritual life must be kept from the profane.

It's all right. Peter is my soul-mate after all. We couldn't eat much. It's only natural; all base appetites have to be killed out before one is ready to go on. Peter ate very little himself; and then he said:

"I know why we couldn't get the Devil to come the other night. It was having those servants about. I remember now that grandfather only had two in the house, and he used to send them away when he had anything big on. Let's see what we can do tonight."

That was delightful. That was his old self.

We thought it would be a good plan to coke up pretty hard before starting.

CHAPTER VI
COLD TURKEY

SEPTEMBER 23

I don't remember what happened. I know why. Basil told me long ago that the mind only kept count of material things. So these spiritual events are recorded in a higher kind of mind of which we are not conscious until we get accustomed to spiritual life. So all I can put down is that we had a complete success.

The Devil, of course, needs a human interpreter if he is to communicate with this world, and so he took possession of Peter. He has been preparing Peter to represent him. He will make Peter pope, and I am to be in the Vatican disguised, to help him because he can't do without me.

My own spiritual guide is named Keletiel. She is a wonderful being, wears peacock blues and greens. She has white wings like a swan, and carries a sheaf of many-coloured flowers. She has long, loose, black curling hair down to her waist. There is a golden band round her forehead, studded with sapphires, with her name on it. I can always tell her by this.

There has to be a token, because she changes her size so much. Sometimes she is a tiny thing, not up to my knee, and sometimes she is two or three times as high as the North Tower.

Peter and I are covered with blood. We came out of the circle before the Devil had gone, and he scratched us all to pieces. Luckily we got back before he killed us, but we lost consciousness and woke up a long while later. That's why we can't remember what happened.

I have some idea that I had a terrible quarrel with Peter, but I can't remember any details. I think he does, though, but he won't tell me.

I don't know why he should act like that. The only thing I can think is that Gretel Webster may have come down to see him perhaps in her astral body, and put him against me somehow. . . .

He was lying on the sofa in his pyjamas. I wanted to be kissed, and went over to him with some cocaine. But he didn't move. He looked at me with wide open eyes. There was some dreadful fear in them, and he said –

"Black, the plague of the pit,
Her pustules visibly fester."

Of course, I knew he didn't mean it, but I was hurt. I gave him the cocaine.

It roused him. He sat up and then he held me by the shoulders and looked straight at my face and said:

"Dragon of lure and dread,
Tiger of fury and lust,
The quick in chains to the dead,
The slime alive in the dust,
Brazen shame like a flame
An orgy of pregnant pollution
With hate beyond aim or name –
Orgasm, death, dissolution!"

And then he began shrieking, and ran out of the house down to the lake and dived right in. He swam a few strokes and then came out and walked slowly up to the house.

I found some towels in the linen chest. I was afraid of his catching a chill, so I rubbed him hard all over. He seemed to have forgotten everything. He was quite nice and normal but just a little scared.

I can't make out what's the matter with him. He acts as if he had learnt some terrible secret which he had to keep from me. He always seems afraid of being spied on or overheard.

I went up to the magic room tonight. Peter was sitting in the old man's chair writing in a book. I couldn't understand it at first. I had come straight up, and he was fast asleep downstairs! Then, of course, the whole mystery became clear.

While he's asleep, his astral double comes up and does magic. I knew it was very dangerous to disturb any one's astral double, so I tiptoed out of the room; but the double followed me noiselessly. Every time I looked over my shoulder he was there, though he was very quick at dodging back round the corner or into a doorway. . . .

Peter has been very preoccupied for some time. He writes out telegrams on forms, and then tears them up; and then he seems to think that isn't safe, and picks the pieces up and burns them. I asked him about it; but he would say nothing, and got very angry.

I think I know what it is, though. I found a sheet of paper which he had forgotten to destroy – a letter to the War Office, warning them against German plots, and telling some things that have happened down here. I could hardly read it; his handwriting is absolutely gaga.

He talks a great deal to himself. I overheard some of it. He thinks there may be a German spy in the War Office and is afraid to trust the post or telegraph.

He kept on saying, "I'm at my wits' end." Then he went off into muttering about the plots against him.

I am sure I could help him out if he would only trust me. I wonder if it's all delusion on his part. He certainly has some funny ideas.

For one thing, he pretends to see spiritual guides, which is impossible, because he is not pure enough. Besides, the things he says he sees are all horrible and disgusting.

But he says nothing at all now, any more. He begins to speak to me and checks himself. . . .

It is very dark tonight. Rain is falling. Peter has gone down to the lake with his gun.

I have taken this book from its hiding place. I am horribly frightened.

I had no appetite at lunch, and Peter wouldn't eat. He burst out in a hysterical appeal to me, reminded me of our love, and said he couldn't believe it was all a sham. Why had I gone into the plot to drive him to death? He doesn't eat, because he thinks the food is poisoned; and when he saw that I wasn't eating, it convinced him that I was in the plot against him.

I tried to tell him this was all nonsense. I told him that I was not in any plot against him. It didn't set his mind at ease. I had to tell him my great secret that I am the woman clothed with the sun in the Book of Revelations, and that he must protect me.

I proved to him that this was the only explanation.

The reason why he couldn't live with me as my husband was that my angel had told me that I was going to bring the Messiah into the world.

We went into a heated argument. I don't remember what happened; but as usual, it turned into a quarrel.

One must be concentrated on the spiritual life, so the slightest interruption from the senses, if it's only the wind in the trees, is a terribly irritating thing.

"Satan is the prince of the power of the air," it says in the Bible, so he sends these noises in the air to disturb my mind.

How can I give birth to the Messiah if I am not caught up into the Seventh Heaven, and unconscious of material things?

The world, the flesh, and the Devil. One in three and three in one. This evil trinity must be abolished. It knows that; and that's why it tries to interrupt me either by means of Peter or the pains of the body, or the sights and sounds of nature.

Nature is under a curse because of sex, and so this world is in the power of the Evil One. But I am chosen to redeem it, and the Holy Spirit overshadows me and sends angels to guard me. That is how we got rid of the servants.

Peter suddenly attacked me. He got me down, and put his knee on my chest, and tried to strangle me. But the angel smote him suddenly, and all his muscles relaxed and he rolled over.

His eyes were wide open, but I could only see the whites. That is a sign that he is possessed by the Devil, and that the angels are protecting me.

He has fired two or three times, and now I see him coming up from the lake. I must hide this book, and then I will go to the garage, and hide till the morning.

Keletiel tells me that this is the critical night. I will get into the big car under the sheet. He won't look for me there, and the angels will be on the watch. . . .

It came out all right. I slept on the seat of the car. I had a dreadful nightmare, and woke sweating all over. Then I went to sleep again. I was with six angels who carried me through the air to a place which I mustn't describe. It is a great and wonderful mystery.

It is awful and miraculously wonderful to be the woman clothed with the sun. The sublimity of it would have frightened me only a few weeks ago. I have been gently and wisely prepared for my exalted position.

This vision initiated me into the most marvellous secrets.

When I woke Keletiel came and told me that the crisis was over. I was shivering with cold, and went into the house for some heroin. That's the only thing that keeps one warm however hot the weather is. This is because what keeps the body warm is the rush of animal life, and when one has got to the stage where one becomes wholly spiritual, the body becomes cold like a corpse. . . .

A dreadful thing has happened. We have used up all the heroin, and there is hardly any cocaine. I remembered what I had sewn away in my white frock, and went to get it. It was on the floor in a corner of the drawing-room.

It was all shrunk and rumpled and dirty, and it was still quite wet. I suppose I must have gone a long walk in the rain, though I don't remember anything about it.

All the heroin was washed away. There wasn't a grain left. Peter came in and found me crying. He understood at once what had happened. All he said was:

"You'll have to go back to McCall."

I couldn't even be angry. Men are too grossly animal to understand. How could I do such a thing, seeing who I was?

He wanted some H. badly; finding it gone, made him want it insanely.

He took one of the packets and began to chew it. "Thank God," he said, "it's quite bitter. There must be a lot in the dress."

I was shivering and faint. I got another packet, and put it in my mouth. He went wild and clutched me by the hair, and forced open my jaws with his finger and thumb. I struggled and kicked and scratched; but he was too strong. He got it out and put it in his own mouth. Then he hit me in the face as I sat. I went flat and limp, and began to howl. He picked up the dress and the packets, and started to go. I caught at his ankles desperately; but he kicked himself free, and went out of the room with the dress.

I was too weak and hurt to go after him, and my nose was bleeding.

But I had got some H., and I remembered who I was. This was all part of the ordeal. At any moment I might manifest my glory, and he would fall down at my feet and worship me. After all, he has a wonderful destiny himself; like St. Joseph – or else perhaps he may be the Dragon that will try to destroy me and the Messiah.

In my position the actual H. isn't really necessary any more than food is. The spiritual idea is sufficient. That I suppose is the lesson I had to learn. I had been relying on the stuff itself. It says in the Bible "Angels came and ministered unto him." My angels will bring me the manna that cometh down from heaven.

I am perfectly happy. It is sublime not to be dependent any more on earthly things. Keletiel came and told me to go and prophesy to Peter, so I will hide away the diary. I must think of a new place every time, else Peter will find out where I keep it, or the old man may be hunting around in his astral body and take it away. I have been very careful what I wrote; but he might discover some of the secrets and ruin everything.

There's another trouble. I can only remember spiritual things clearly. The material world is fading out. It would be disaster if I forgot where I hid it.

Basil would never forgive me.

I will hide it in the chimney, then I can always look up where I put it. . . .

What is dreadful is the length of time. With H. or C. or both, there

is never a dull moment; without them the hours, the very minutes, drag. It's difficult to read or write. My eyes won't focus properly. They have been open to the spiritual world, they can't see anything else. It's hard, too, to control the hands. I can't form the letters properly.

This waiting is hellish. Waiting for something to happen! I can think of nothing but H. Everything in the body is wrong. It aches intolerably. Even a single dose would put everything right.

It makes me forget who I am, and the wonderful work to be done. I have become quite blind to the spiritual world. Keletiel never comes. I must wait, wait, wait for the Holy Spirit; but that's a memory so far, far off!

There are times when I almost doubt it, yet my faith is the only thing that prevents my going insane. I can't endure without H.

The sympathy of suffering has brought Peter closer. We lie about and look at each other; but we can't touch, the skin is too painful. We are both restless as it is impossible to describe. It irritates us to see each other like this, and we can't do anything; we constantly get up with the idea of doing something, but we sit down again immediately. Then we can't sit, we have to lie down. But lying down doesn't rest us; it irritates me more, so we get up again, and so on for ever. One can't smoke a cigarette; after two or three puffs it drops from one's fingers. The only respite I have is this diary. It relieves me to write of my sufferings; and besides, it is important for the spiritual life. Basil must have the record to read.

I can't remember dates, though. I don't even know what year it is. The leaves in the park tell me it is autumn, and the nights are getting longer. The night is better than the day; there is less to irritate. We don't sleep, of course, we fall into a torpor. Basil told me about it once. He called it the dark night of the soul. One has to go through it on the way to the Great Light.

The light of day is torture. Every sense is an instrument of the most devilish pain. There is no flesh on our bones.

This perpetual craving for H! Our minds are utterly empty of everything else. Rushing into the void come tumbling the words of that abominable poem:

> "A bitten and burning snake
> Striking its venom within it,
> As if it might serve to slake
> The pain for the tithe of a minute."

It is like vitriol being thrown in one's face. We have no expression of our own. We cannot think. The need is filled by these words. . . .
The impact of light itself is a bodily pain.

> "When the sun is a living devil
> Vomiting vats of evil,
> And the moon and the night but mock
> The wretch on his barren rock,
> And the dome of heaven high-arched
> Like his mouth is and parched,
> And the caves of his heart high-spanned
> Are choked with alkali sand!"

We are living on water. It seems for the moment to quench the thirst, at least part of it. Peter's nervous state is very alarming. I feel sure he has delusions.

He got up and staggered to the mantelpiece and leant against it with his arms stretched out. He cried in a hoarse, dry voice:

> "Thirst
> Not the thirst of the throat,
> Though that be the wildest and worst
> Of physical pangs that smote
> Alone to the heart of Christ,
> Wringing the one wild cry
> 'I thirst' from His agony,
> While the soldiers drank and diced."

He thought he was Jesus on the Cross instead of the Dragon, as he really is. It makes me very nervous about him.

When he had finished reciting, his strength suddenly failed him, and he collapsed. The clatter of the fire-irons was the most hideous noise that I had ever heard. . . .

When I can summon up enough strength to write in my diary, the pain leaves me. I see that there are two people here. I, myself, am the Woman clothed with the Sun, writing down my experiences. The other is Lou Pendragon, an animal dying in agony from thirst.

I said the last word aloud, and Peter caught it up.

He crawled away from the grate towards me croaking out,

> "Not the thirst benign
> That calls the worker to wine;
> Not the bodily thirst
> (Though that be frenzy accurst)
> When the mouth is full of sand,
> And the eyes are gummed up, and the ears
> Trick the soul till it hears
> Water, water at hand,
> When a man will dig his nails
> In his breast, and drink the blood
> Already that clots and stales
> Ere his tongue can tip its flood."

His mind had gone back to infancy. He thought that I was his mother, and came to me to be nursed.

But when he came near, he recognised me and crawled away again, hurriedly, like a wounded animal trying to escape from the hunter. . . .

Most of the time, when we have energy to talk at all, we discuss how to get more H. and C. The C. has been finished long ago. It's no good without the H. We could go to Germany and get it; or even to London, but something keeps us from decision.

I, of course, know what it is. It is necessary for me to undergo these torments that I may be purified completely from the flesh.

But Peter doesn't understand at all. He blames me bitterly. We go over

the whole thing again and again. Every incident since we met is taken in turn as the cause of our misery.

Sometimes his brutal lust revives in his mind. He thinks I am a vampire sent from Hell to destroy him; and he gloats over the idea. I cannot make him understand that I am the woman clothed with the sun. When he gets those ideas, they arouse similar thoughts in me. But they are only thoughts.

I am afraid of him. He might shoot me in a mad fit. He has got a target pistol, a very old one with long, thin bullets, and carries it about all the time. He never mentions the Germans now. He talks about a gang of hypnotists that have got hold of him, and put evil thoughts in his mind. He says that if he could shoot one of them it would break the spell. He tells me not to look at him as I do; but I have to be on the watch lest he should attack me.

Then he mixes up my hypnotic gaze with ideas of passion. He keeps on repeating:

> "Steadily stares and squarely,
> Nor needs to fondle and wheedle
> Her slave agasp for a kiss,
> Hers whose horror is his
> That knows that viper womb,
> Speckled and barred with black
> On its rusty amber scales,
> Is his tomb –
> The straining, groaning rack
> On which he wails – he wails!"

He takes an acute delight in the intensity of his suffering. He is wildly proud to think that he has been singled out to undergo more atrocious torments than had ever been conceived of before.

He sees me as the principal instrument of the torture, and loves me with perverse diabolical lust for that reason, yet the whole thing is a delusion on his part, or else it is a necessary consequence of his changing into the Dragon.

It is only natural that there should be strange incidents in a case of that sort, especially as it never happened before. It is wonderful and terrible to be unique. But, of course, he is not really unique in the way that I am. . . .

We have lighted a huge fire in the billiard-room. We sleep there so far as we sleep at all. We got the waiter to bring down blankets and quilts from the bedroom, and he leaves the food on the table.

But fires are no good. The cold comes from inside us. We sit in front of the blaze, roasting our hands and faces; but it makes no difference. We shiver.

We try to sing like soldiers round a camp fire, but the only words that come are the appropriate ones. That poem has obsessed us. It fills our souls to the exclusion of everything else except the thirst.

> "Every separate bone
> Cold, an incarnate groan
> Distilled from the icy sperm
> Of Hell's implacable worm."

We repeated them over and over. . . .

I don't know how one thing ever turns into another. We are living in an eternity of damnation. It is a mystery how we ever get from the fire to the table or the two big Chesterfields. Every action is a separate agony rising to a climax which never comes. There is no possibility of accomplishment or of peace.

> "Every separate nerve
> Awake and alert, on a curve
> Whose asymptote's name is 'never'
> In a hyperbolic 'for ever!'"

I don't know what some of the words mean. But there is a fascination about them. They give the idea of something without limit. Death has become impossible, because death is definite. Nothing can really ever happen. I am in a perpetual state of pain. Everything is equally anguish.

I suppose one state changes into another to prevent the edge being taken off the suffering. It would be incredibly blissful if one could experience something new, however abominable. The man that wrote that poem has left out nothing. Everything that comes into my mind is no more than an echo of his groans.

> "Body and soul alike
> Traitors turned black-hearted,
> Seeking a place to strike
> In a victim already attuned
> To one vast chord of wound."

The rhythm of the poem, apart from the words, suggests this *moto perpetuo* vibration. Yet the nervous irritability tends to exhaust itself as such. It is so unendurable; the only escape seems to be if one could transform it into action. The poison filters through into the blood. I am itching to do something horrible and insane.

> "Every drop of the river
> Of blood aflame and a-quiver
> With poison secret and sour –
> With a sudden twitch at the last
> Like certain jagged daggers."

When Peter crosses the room, I see him

> "With blood-shot eyes dull-glassed
> The screaming Malay staggers
> Through his village aghast."

It is natural and inevitable that he should murder me. I wish he were not so weak. Anything to end it all.

The medical books said that if one didn't die outright from abstention, the craving would slowly wear off. I think Peter is already a little stronger. But I am so young to die! He complains constantly of vermin under his

skin. He says he could bear that; but the idea of being driven mad by the hypnotists is more than any man can be expected to stand. . . .

I felt I should scream if I went on a moment longer; and by scream I don't mean just an ordinary scream, I mean that I should scream and scream and scream and never stop.

The wind is howling like that. The summer has died suddenly – without a warning, and the world is screaming in agony. It is only the echo of the wailing for my own lost soul. The angels never come to me now. Have I forfeited my position? I am conscious of nothing but this tearing, stabbing, gnawing pain, this restless raging trembling of the body, this malignant groping of a mad surgeon in the open wound of my Soul.

I am so bitter, bitter cold. Yet I can't stand the room. Peter is lying helplessly on the couch. He follows me about with his eyes. He seems to be afraid that he will be caught out in something. It's like it was when we had dope. Though we knew we were taking it, offering it to each other openly, yet whenever we took it ourselves, we were afraid lest the other should know.

I think he has something that he wants to hide away, and is trying to get me out of the room so that I shan't know where he has put it.

Well, I don't care, I'm not interested in his private affairs. I'll go out and give him a chance. I'll hide this book in the magic room, if I have strength to get there. The old man might be able to give me some elixir. I wouldn't mind if it killed my body; if my spirit were free I could fulfil my destiny. . . .

Just as I closed the book I heard an answering shot. It must have been the door, for the old man has come in. He has a marvellous light in his eyes, and he radiates rainbow colours throughout the world. I understand that my ordeal is over. He stands smiling and points downwards. I think he wants me to go back to the billiard-room. Perhaps there is some one waiting for me; some one to take me away to fulfil my destiny.

I know now what it was that I thought was a shot, or a door closing. It was really both of these things in a mystical sense; for I know now who the old man is, and that he is the father of the Messiah. . . .

CHAPTER VII
THE FINAL PLUNGE

SUNDAY

The church bells tell me the day. I have been through another terrible ordeal. I don't know how long ago since I came down from the north tower. The noise was really a shot. I found Peter on the floor with the pistol by his side, and blood pouring from a wound in his breast.

I understood immediately what I had to do. It was impossible to send for a doctor. The scandal of the suicide would make life impossible ever after, and he would immediately discover that it was due to dope. The burden must be on my own shoulders. I must nurse my boy back to life.

I remember that I had been too weak to walk down from the north tower. I climbed to the balustrades and gasped, and slid myself, sitting, from step to step. I was almost blind, too. My eyes seemed unable to focus on anything.

But the moment I saw what had happened, my strength came back to me, at least, not my strength but the strength of nature. It flowed through me like the wind blowing through a flimsy ragged curtain.

The cartridges were very old, and the powder must have lost its strength; for the bullet turned on his breast bone and ran round the ribs. It was really a trifling wound; but he was so weak that he might have died from loss of blood. I got some water, and washed the wounds, and bound them up as best I could. When the waiter came, I sent him for proper things from the chemist, and some invalid food. For the first time I was glad of the war. My Red-Cross training made all the difference.

There was a little fever, due to his intense weakness, and occasionally he had delirium. The obsession of the poem still enthralled him. While I was dressing the wounds he said feebly and dreamily:

> "She it is, she, that found me
> In the morphia honeymoon;
> With silk and steel she bound me
> In her poisonous milk she drowned me,
> Even now her arms surround me."

"Yes," I said, "but it's your wife who loves you and is going to nurse you through this trouble, and we're going to live happy ever afterwards."

He smiled very faintly and sweetly and dozed off. . . .

WEDNESDAY

I count the days now. We are having an Indian summer. Nature is lovely. I go out for little walks when Peter is asleep.

FRIDAY

There have been no complications, or I should have had to get a doctor in at whatever risk. What troubles me is that as he gets stronger, the

delusions of persecution have begun to return. I know now how deeply I was myself obsessed by ideas of grandeur, and how my need to be a mother determined their form.

But is it a delusion that I should be thinking constantly of Basil? I seem to hear him saying that I was cured from the moment that I forgot myself altogether in the absorption of my love for Peter; the work of bringing him back to life.

And now that I have ceased to look at myself and feel for myself, I have become able to see him and feel for him with absolute clearness. There is not the slightest possibility of error.

All the time he has been able to realise dimly that he was slipping down the dark slope to insanity. He has mixed it all up with the idea of me. He had begun to identify me with the phantom of murderous madness which he recognised as destroying him. A look of trouble comes into his face every now and then; and he begins to repeat plaintively in a puzzled voice with his eyes fixed on mine:

> "Know you now why her eyes
> So fearfully glaze, beholding
> Terrors and infamies
> Like filthy flowers unfolding?
> Laughter widowed of ease,
> Agony barred from sadness,
> Death defeated of peace,
> Is she not madness?"

Over and over again he said it, and over and over again I told him the answer. I had indeed been a personification of the seductress, of the destroying angel. But it had been a nightmare. I had awakened, and he must awake.

But he saw not me any more, but his ideal enveloping me congealed into my form. No matter what I said, his fixed idea became constantly stronger as his physical strength came back.

> "She waits for me, lazily leering,
> As moon goes murdering moon;

> The moon of her triumph is nearing;
> She will have me wholly soon."

The rhythm of the poem was still in my own blood; but it seemed to have worked itself out into another channel. I had forgotten the acute personal anguish of the earlier part of the poem. I could not even remember the lines any more. I was wholly occupied by the last two paragraphs where the subject changes so suddenly.

I began to realise what my governess used to call *Weltschmertz*; the universal sorrow wherein "Creation groaneth and travaileth until now."

I understood Basil's wish that we should undertake the fearful experiment which had brought us to such extremity. My insanity had been the result of my selfish vanity. I was not singled out for a unique destiny. The realisation of my own suffering had led me to understand that every one else was in the same boat. I could see even the false note of the contempt of the poet for those who had not experienced his own sublimity of horror.

> "And you, you puritan others,
> Who have missed the morphia. craving,
> Cry scorn if I call you brothers,
> Curl lip at my maniac raving,
> Fools, seven times beguiled,
> You have not known her? Well!
> There was never a need she smiled
> To harry you into hell!"

The pride of Satan, in the deepness of damnation, has a fall when he realises that others are in a same calamity – without having been at such perverse pains to get there. He only attains the truth when he becomes wholly impersonal, in the final paragraph.

> "Morphia, is but one Spark of its secular fire.
> She is the single sun –
> Type of all desire!

All that you would you are –
And that is the crown of a craving.
You are slaves of the wormwood star.
Analysed, reason is raving.
Feeling, examined, is pain.
What heaven were to hope for a doubt of it!
Life is anguish, insane;
And death is – not a way out of it."

I saw that all feeling, however it might seem to casual scrutiny, must be of the nature of pain, because it implied duality and imperfection; and that the nature of thought of whatever kind, must ultimately be insanity, because it expresses the relations between things, and never the things in themselves.

It became evident that the sorrow of the Universe was caused by the desire of manifestation, and that death could not do more than suppress one form of existence in favour of another. Of course, the impasse is complete. There seems to be no solution of the problem. It is a vicious circle.

At the same time, by acquiescence in actuality, the insane insistence on one's individual anguish is abated. Sympathy with universal suffering brings one into a certain sombre serenity. It does not show us the way of escape, if such there be, but at least it makes the idea of escape thinkable. As long as one is trying to get out of the burning theatre for one's own sake, the panic makes concerted action impossible. "Every man for himself and the devil take the hindmost" is not the kind of order that is likely to secure victory. It does not even ensure the safety of any one man.

How quickly I had recovered my own well-being when I was forced to forget about it!

Peter is still desperately striving to save himself. "He that loveth his life shall lose it." I must dedicate my miraculously restored faculties to his salvation. Only I don't see how to set to work.

If only Basil were here. He would know. He has worked out the technique. All I can do is to love and labour blindly. After all, there must

have been angels looking after me in some sense which I don't pretend to understand. Why should they not be even more vigilant on his behalf?

I am only a foolish flapper not worth throwing into the waste-paper basket. He is a splendid man with a glorious past and endless possibilities for the future.

It won't do to let him go under; and they must know that.

I won't trouble my silly head about it, I'll keep on loving and trusting.

OCTOBER 26

I have forgotten about my diary all this time. I have been too busy with Peter. My memory is frightfully bad. I don't seem able to fix things at all. Peter got stronger all the time. He is practically quite well now, and took me out and taught me to shoot pheasants this morning. It was terribly exciting. I actually got one, my very first day. I got a man and wife and their daughter to come in and do for us, so we're really very comfortable, in a countrified way. I couldn't have any one while Peter was raving.

The waiter from the inn is a Swiss. He kept his mouth shut; and I saw to it that he had no reason to regret the policy.

What I can't remember is how Peter began to get better: mentally, I mean. I ought to have kept this diary properly, I know; but as he improved, he took up more and more of my time, and then I had to do so many things to have things ready for him when he was able to get up.

And now, I can't think how it came about; but I believe the first sign of improvement was that the poem dropped out. He began to talk naturally about ordinary affairs. He was terribly weak and ill, and it had scared him. He was like an ordinary convalescent, I suppose signs of returning interests in the affairs of life. I had ceased to be a symbol. I was just his nurse.

Part of the time he had forgotten who I was. He was back in the base hospital; the time they winged him.

Our honeymoon and its sequel is mostly blotted out. I can't say how much he knows. He says things sometimes which make me think it's quite a lot.

And then again, other things which make me think he doesn't even remember that I am his wife. This morning, for instance, he said: "I must go to London to see about a settlement I'm making in case I ever get married."

And then, not half an hour afterwards, he referred to an incident of our life in Capri. I am careful not to contradict him or alarm him about the state of his mind, but it's very difficult to know what to do. There are so many things I forget myself.

"How did we get down here?" Then again, "Where is Alice?" The name keeps on popping up, and yet I don't know any one at all intimately or importantly with that name.

I had forgotten this diary – I found it by accident and immediately began to read it through to refresh my memory.

Most of the handwriting is unreadable. I puzzled and puzzled before I could make out the words. And then when I got the words, they were so senseless. I can't believe that all that happened to me. Some of it came back slowly; curiously, the unimportant things came first.

I was amazed to find that Mabel Black was dead. I wrote her a letter only yesterday. Poor old girl!

The part, too about Dr. McCall. I could swear quite honestly that never happened. And yet it must have; for I found scraps of the dress in the cushions of the blue Chesterfield chewed to a pulp......

OCTOBER 27

We have been shooting again; but it was cold and damp. We were neither of us interested and we were too weary to walk. Peter said nothing; but all the time I can feel how disgusted he is. We're so rottenly let down. This afternoon I picked up the article of Sieveking's. He is talking about the sensation of walking after a flight.

"One has an infinitely distressing sensation of being clamped down to the ground – manacled by the very grass-blades!"

We have been living so long at such a terrific bat, life is intolerable on any other terms.

I don't feel any physical need of drugs any more. On the contrary, I feel a delightful bodily buoyancy at having got free. It's an extraordinary thing, too, how normal appetite has returned. We've been eating five meals a day, one feeding like forty instead of Wordsworth's forty feeding like one. We had been starving ourselves for months, and we had to make up for it. The most delicious sensation of all is the re-birth of healthy human love. Spring coming back to the earth!

But it doesn't satisfy, even so. The intervals between one's emotions are appallingly long. I think drugs intensify the high lights for one thing; but for another, and this is really more important, they fit up the interstices of shadow.

It's hard, I imagine, in the ordinary way, to come off one's honeymoon back into regular life. I often wonder how a poet feels when he isn't absorbed in the ecstasy of inspiration. That may be why so many of them go off the deep end, the interstices bore them.

I may as well face the facts. We've had a pretty narrow escape. We've got out of the mess more by good luck than by good judgment. But if it weren't for that, I'm not sure that we shouldn't be inclined to take another chance. Of course, as things are, it's quite out of the question. It may not be the least of our luck that the lesson was so severe at it was.

OCTOBER 30

The fact is, we're too young. We don't think of the obvious thing. Of course we're bored stiff down here with the leaves all fallen, and the mist steaming up from the lake and swamping the house like a gas attack. We ought to be in London, and do the theatres, and look up a few of the old crowd. I ought really to see Maisie Jacobs and tell her how grateful I am.

Funny, I can't think what I have to be grateful about. But luckily it's in the diary.

Peter has got more silent and morose every day, like the weather. He seems to have something on his mind. I wish he'd tell me what it is.

He brightened up at dinner. "Let's go to town tomorrow, Lou," he said.

"We'll just take small bags. We needn't be away more than two or three days. What we need is a few decent meals in a restaurant, and take in a show or two, and perhaps get a bunch down here to liven us up a bit. The birds are pretty good this year after all."

OCTOBER 31

It only struck us when we got into the train that we couldn't possibly go to the Savoy with no clothes. Peter thought it would be a joke to go round to that place of ours in Greek Street.

It certainly will be amusing to look at it from the new point of view. He will take the bags on there, while I get one or two nice people together. We ought to give a little dinner to celebrate.

Here's London at last. I'll lock this up in my dressing case. . . .

Later – I can pocket the creature's insolence at the price. It must have been on my mind. The first address I gave to the chauffeur was McCall's. He looked shocked when I was announced.

"My dear Lady Pendragon," he almost shouted at me very fast. "I know you'll forgive me. I'm frightfully busy this afternoon."

(There wasn't a soul in his waiting-room.)

"If you'll allow me, I think this is what you want, and I hope you will come and see me again soon. Always at your service, dear Lady Pendragon."

While he was talking he half emptied a ten-gramme bottle into a piece of paper, twisted it up like a grocer, thrust it almost rudely into my hand, and bowed me out volubly and effusively into the street.

I went faint all over. The taxi was still there. I called him, and drove to Mme. Daubignac's. I don't know why, but I felt that I needed a treatment. I was trembling all over. It was worse when I went in: for I could see that she was as shocked as McCall.

Then I got in front of a glass. How is it that in all the times I've looked at myself in these months I've never seen what they see in a second?

Good God! it's too awful to talk about. My face is drawn and haggard and pale and wrinkled. I might be sixty. Well, what do I care? I've had three beautiful sniffs!

Madame dolled me up as well as she could. Already I looked much better, and I felt superb.

Peter was out when I got to Greek Street; so I opened my dressing case and wrote this up, and had a few more sniffs. The only trouble before was simply our own foolishness. We didn't take ordinary precautions. This time we're going to watch out. . . .

Peter is back, furious. His pedlar has been pinched. So I came to the rescue.

"We'll go out to dinner and make a night of it."

We've arranged for a regular supply; but the hellish thing is that the stuff doesn't work any more. We get the insomnia and those things all right, but we can't get any fun out of it. We've tried all sorts of dodges. It's no good. Being with it simply dulls the pain of being without. That's the best I can say. What are we to do?

(There are three more entries in this diary; but they are illegible, quite beyond conjecture. The only words decipherable are "sleep" near the beginning of the first; the name "Basil" in the second; and the word "poison" in the third.)

BOOK III
PURGATORIO

[NOTE.-The Abbey of Thelema at "Telepylus" is a real place. It and its customs and members, with the surrounding scenery, are accurately described. The training there given is suited to all conditions of spiritual distress, and for the discovery and development of the "True Will" of any person. Those interested are invited to communicate with the author of this book.]

CHAPTER I
KING LAMUS INTERVENES

It is only three months ago; but it seems a lifetime. My memory is now very good, and I remember more details of the past every day. I am writing this account of the past three months, partly because my best friend tells me that it will strengthen it if I exercise it by putting down what has occurred in sequence. And you know, even a month ago, I couldn't have recalled anything at all with regard to certain periods.

My friend tells me that memory fails me in part because nature mercifully wishes to hide from us things which are painful. The spider-web of protective forgetfulness is woven over the mouth of the cave which conceals the raw head and bloody bones of our misfortunes.

"But the greatest men," says King Lamus, "are those that refuse to be treated like squalling children, who insist on facing reality in every form, and tear off ruthlessly the bandages from their own wounds."

But I have to think very hard to write down the incidents of the dinner at the Wisteria when Lou and I had made up our minds to end our lives.

I had got some prussic acid from the chemist's more than a week before. It took us that time to make up our minds to get up and to acquire Dutch courage enough to take the plunge.

Some instinct prevented us dropping out of existence in a place like those lodgings in Greek Street. When all one's moral sense is gone, there remains a racial instinct in men and women of good blood which tells them, like Macbeth and Brutus, to die positively and not negatively.

I believe it was this alone that dragged us up from the dirty bed from which we had not moved for weeks, sunk in a state which was neither sleep nor waking.

It was by a gigantic effort that I got up and put some clothes on, and went out and got shaved. Nothing but excitement and the idea of death enabled me to do it. I found the same thing in the war; and so did lots of men.

It seems as if the soul is tired of the body, and welcomes the chance to be done with it once and for all. But it wants to offer itself gallantly in a flight or a charge. It objects to dying in a ditch passively. I am sure that nothing less would have got us up from that foetid stupor.

We had some champagne before starting, and then tottered giddily over the unfamiliar streets. There was something faintly attractive about the bustle of humanity. There was a momentary regret about leaving it. Yet we had already left it so long, so long ago, in every intelligible sense of the word. We should, I suppose, have been classed as human beings by statisticians, but surely by nobody else. We could never return to their midst. And even in the midst of our wretchedness, we felt a repulsion of contempt for the ruck of humanity which made us content to widen the gap between them and ourselves. Why preserve the outward semblance of these futile insects? Even their happiness disgusted us; it was so stupidly shallow.

We could see that the people of the Wisteria were shocked at our appearance. The *maitre d'hotel* bustled over and made some sympathetic remarks about our not having been there for a long time. I told him that we had both been very ill; and then Lou put in, in a hollow voice:

"We shall be better tonight."

Her intonation was so sinister that the man almost jumped. I was

afraid for the moment that everything would be spoilt, but I saved the situation by some silly joking remark. However, I could see that he was very uncomfortable and glad to get away from our table.

We had ordered a wonderful dinner; but, of course, we couldn't eat anything. The mockery of having all those expensive dishes brought, one after the other, and taken away again untouched, was irritating at first, and then it began to be amusing. I vaguely remember something in history about funeral feasts. It seemed singularly appropriate to start west in such conditions.

Yes, we were participating in some weird ceremony such as delighted the ancient Egyptians. The thought even came to my mind that we had already died, that this was our mocking welcome to Hades, the offering of dishes of which we were unable to partake. And yet, between us and the unknown was the act of drinking the contents of the little bottle in my waistcoat pocket.

It was nearly an hour and a half since we had some heroin, and already the loathsome fumes of abstention were suffocating us. We had as much as our bodies could tolerate. We didn't want any more actively. It would do us no good to take more, but nature had already begun her process of eliminating the poison.

In the body, morphine and heroin become oxydised, and it is the resulting poisons, not the drugs themselves, that are responsible for the appalling effects. Thus the body begins to give off these products through the secretions; therefore the nose begins to run; there are prolonged foul sweats; there is a smell and a taste which cannot be called unpleasant even, it can only be called abominable in the proper sense of that word: that which is repugnant to man. It is so detestable as to be unendurable. One might get relief by cleaning one's teeth or by having a Turkish bath, but the energy to do such things is lacking.

But if you take a fresh dose of the drug, it puts a temporary stop to the efforts of nature to eliminate it. That is why it is such a vicious circle; and these premonitory symptoms of abstinence are merely the foetor of the foul breath of the dragon who is on his way to crunch you.

If you make up your mind to endure the disgusting symptoms, the demon soon proceeds to more serious measures.

Lou has explained in her diary more or less what these are. But even with the help of the poet, one cannot give any idea of what it is like. For example, the question of cold. The reader thinks at once of the cold of winter. If he has travelled a little and has some imagination, he may think of the chill spells of fever. But neither of these give much idea of the nature of the cold produced by abstinence.

Our poet, whoever he is (his name is not given in the magazine) certainly succeeds in conveying to his reader the truth, that is, provided his reader already knows it. I can't imagine how it would strike any one who had not experienced it. For he conveys his meaning, so to speak, in spite of the words. This business of expression is very curious.

How could one describe, say, a love affair to a person who had never had one or imagined one? All expression does is to wake up in the reader the impressions in his own experience which are otherwise dormant. And he will interpret what is said or written only in terms of that experience.

Lamus said the other day that he had given up trying to communicate the results of his researches to people. They couldn't even be trusted to read words of one syllable, though they might have taken the best degrees in Humane Letters at Oxford. For example, he would write, "Do what thou wilt" to somebody, and would be attacked by return of post for having written "Do as thou wilt."

Every one interprets everything in terms of his own experience. If you say anything which does not touch a precisely similar spot in another man's brain, he either misunderstands you, or doesn't understand you at all.

I am therefore extremely depressed by the obligation under which King Lamus has put me to write this section, with the avowed object of instructing the world in the methods of overcoming the craving for drugs.

He admits frankly that he feels it quite useless to do it himself, for the very reason that he is so abnormal a man. He even distrusts me, on the ground that he has had so much influence on my life and thought.

"Even a mediocrity like yourself, Sir Peter," he said to me the other day, "dull as you are, cannot be trusted in my neighbourhood. Your brain unconsciously soaks up the highly charged particles of my atmosphere.

And before you know where you are, instead of expressing yourself – what little self you have to express – you will be repeating, in a debased currency, the words of wisdom that from time to time have dropped from my refined lips."

There was a time when I should have resented a remark like that. If I don't do so now, it isn't because I've lost my manhood, it isn't because I feel such gratitude to the man who pulled me through; the reason is that I have learned what he means when he talks like that. He has completely killed out in himself the idea of himself. He takes no credit for his marvellous qualities, and has even got over kicking himself for his weaknesses. And so he says the most serious things in the language of absurdity and irony. And when he talks in a serious strain, his language merely accentuates the prodigious sense of humour which, as he says himself, saves him from going insane with horror at the mess into which humanity has got itself. Just as the Roman Empire began to break down when it became universal, when it was so large that no individual mind could grasp the problems which it postulated, so today, the spread of vulgar education and the development of facilities for transport have got ahead of the possibilities of the best minds. The increase of knowledge has forced the thinker to specialise, with the result that there is nobody capable to deal with civilisation as a whole.

We are playing a game of chess in which nobody can see more than two or three squares at once, and so it has become impossible to form a coherent plan.

King Lamus is trying to train a number of selected people to act as a sort of brain for the world in its present state of cerebral collapse. He is teaching them to co-ordinate the facts in a higher synthesis. The suggestion is that of his old teacher, Prof. Henry Maudsley, with whom he studied insanity. Herbert Spencer, too, had a similar idea. But King Lamus is the first to endeavour to make a practical effort to embody this conception in a practical way.

I seem to have wandered a long way from our farewell dinner party; but my mind is still unable to concentrate as it should. Heroin and cocaine enable one to attain a high degree of concentration artificially, and this has to be paid for by a long period of reaction in which one cannot fix

one's mind on a subject at all. I am very much better than I was, but I get impatient at times. It is so tedious to build oneself up on biological lines, especially when one knows that a single dose of heroin or even morphine would make one instantly the equal of the greatest minds in the world.

We had decided to take the prussic acid in our coffee. I do not think we were afraid of death; life had become such an infinitely boring alternation between a period of stimulation which failed to stimulate and of depression which hardly even depressed.

There was no object in going on. It was simply not worthwhile. On the other hand, there was a certain hesitation about stopping because of the effort required. We felt that even to die required energy. We tried to supply this with Dutch courage, and we even succeeded in producing a sort of hilarity. We never had a moment's doubt about carrying out our programme.

The waiter brought two Pêches Melba; and as he retired we found that King Lamus, was standing at our table.

"Do what thou wilt shall be the whole of the Law," came his calm voice.

A sudden flush of hostility suffused my face.

"We've been doing it," I answered with a sort of surly anger, "and I suppose the great psychologist can see what's come of it."

He shook his head very sadly; and sat down without being invited on the chair opposite to us.

"I'm afraid not," he said. "I'll explain what I mean on a more convenient occasion. I can see you want to get rid of me; but I know you won't refuse to help a man out when he's in trouble like I am."

Lou was all sympathy and tenderness at once; and even in the state in which I was, I was aware of a feeble movement of hate both towards her and him. The fact is that the man's mere presence acted as a powerful stimulant.

"It's only a trifle," he said, with a curious smile, "just a little literary difficulty in which I find myself. I was hoping you might remember my giving you a poem to read a little while ago."

His tone was airy and supercilious; but yet there was an undercurrent of earnestness in his voice which compelled the attention.

Lou nodded easily enough; but I could see that in her heart, no less than in mine, an arrow had struck, charged with acid venom. The reference recalled the dreadful days at Barley Grange; and even the Bottomless Pit of Nothingness into which we had since fallen seemed less outrageous than the lake of fire through which we had passed.

The poem rang through my brain, snatches of the anthem of the damned.

His elbows were upon the table, his head between his hands; he watched us intently for a few moments.

"I want to quote that poem in something I'm writing," he explained, "and can you tell me the last line of it?"

Lou answered mechanically, as if he had pressed a button:

"Death is not a way out of it!"

"Thank you," he said. "It's a great help to me that you should have been able to remember."

Something in his tone caught my imagination vividly. His eyes burnt through me. I began to wonder whether there were any truth in what was said about the diabolical powers of the man.

Could he have divined the reason for our coming to the cafe? I had the absolute certainty that he knew all about it, though it was humanly impossible that he should.

"A very strange theory, that about death," he said. "I wonder if there's anything in it. It would really be too easy if we could get out of our troubles in so simple a fashion. It has always seemed to me that nothing can ever be destroyed. The problems of life are really put together ingeniously in order to baffle one, like a chess problem. We can't untie a real knot in a closed piece of string without the aid of the fourth dimension; but we can disentangle the complexities caused by dipping the string in water – and such things," he added, with an almost malicious gravity in his tone.

I knew what he meant.

"It might very well be," he continued, "that when we fail to solve the puzzles of life, they remain with us. We have to do them sooner or later; and it seems reasonable to suppose that the problems of life

ought to be solved during life, while we have to our hands the apparatus in which they arose. We might find that after death the problems were unaltered, but that we were impotent to deal with them. Did you ever meet any one that had been indiscreet about taking drugs? Presumably not. Well, take my word for it, those people get into a state which is in many ways very like death. And the tragic thing about the situation is this; that they started taking the drugs because life, in one way or another, was one too many for them. And what is the result? The drugs have not in the least relieved the monotony of life or whatever their trouble was, and yet they have got into a state very like that of death, in which they are impotent to struggle. No, we must conquer life by living it to the full, and then we can go to meet death with a certain prestige. We can face that adventure as we've faced the others."

The personality of the man radiated energy. The momentary contact with his mind had destroyed the current of thought which had been obsessing ours. Yet it was a fearful pang to be torn away from the fixed idea which had imposed itself as the necessary conclusion of a course of thought and action extending over so long a period.

I can imagine a man reprieved at the foot of a scaffold experiencing an acute annoyance at being wrenched away from the logical outcome of his tendencies.

"Cowards die many times before their death." And those who have decided whether with their will or against it, to put an end to their lives, must resent interference. As Schopenhauer says, the will to die is inherent in all of us, as much as the will to live.

I remember a lot of fellows in the trenches saying that they dreaded being sent to the base; they would rather have it over than take a temporary respite. Life had ceased to be precious. They had become accustomed to face death, and had acquired a fear of life of just the same quality as the fear of death that they had had at first. Life had become the unknown, the uncertain, the dreadful.

A hot, fierce wave of annoyance went through me like a flush of fever.

"Damn the fellow," I muttered, "why must he always butt in like this?"

And then I noticed that Lou had taken the little bottle from my waistcoat pocket, and handed it to King Lamus.

"I believe you're right, Basil," she said. "But if you take that bottle away from us, the responsibility lies with YOU."

"Is that calculated to frighten me?" he answered smiling, and rose to his feet. He dropped the bottle to the ground, and stamped his heel deliberately on it.

"Now," he said, "let's get down to business," resuming his seat.

The fumes of the acid enveloped the table.

"Hydrocyanic acid," he remarked, "is an excellent pick-me-up when absorbed into the system in this diluted form, but to take it in large doses is an indiscretion."

There is no doubt that the man had a tendency to what in a woman is called nagging. He constantly used the word "indiscretion" as if it were a weapon.

We both winced.

"You accept me," he went on, "as responsible for getting you out of this mess?"

There was nothing else to do. It went against the grain. However, I blurted out something about being grateful.

"You needn't talk that nonsense," he retorted severely. "It's my business to help people to do their wills. The gratitude is on my side. I want you to understand from the beginning that you are helping me to justify my existence by allowing me to do what I can to straighten out this tangle. But my conditions are that you give me a fair chance by doing what I say."

He did not even wait for acquiescence.

"You are a bit excited nervously," he went on. "Depression is only another form of excitement. It means a variation from normal tone. So when you have had your coffee, I will join you in a cup, we will go around to my studio and try what some of those tablets will do. Then, where are you living?"

We told him we had gone back to our old place in Greek Street.

"Hardly a salubrious neighbourhood," he remarked. "I think we ought to celebrate the occasion by making a night of it in my studio, and tomorrow morning we must see about getting you some decent rooms."

I remembered that our supply of heroin was in Greek Street.

"You know, Lamus," I stammered, "I'm ashamed to admit it, but we

really can't get on without H. We tried – in fact, once we got clean away – but we couldn't possibly go through that again."

"Nothing to be ashamed of, my dear man," returned our physician. "You can't get on without eating. That's no reason for stopping. All I ask you to do is to do it sensibly."

"Then you won't cut us off?" put in Lou.

"Certainly not, why should I? You take as much as you want, and when you want, and how you want. That's no business of mine. My business is to remove the want. You say you cured yourselves, but you didn't. You only cut off the drug; the want remained. And as soon as the opportunity for starting again arrived, you started again. Perhaps, in fact, you made the opportunity."

The man was really uncanny. I must confess it put me off, being hit every time like that when I wasn't expecting it. But Lou took it in quite a different way. She was glad to be so thoroughly understood. She clapped her hands. I was amazed. It was the first time in months that I had ever seen her make the slightest movement that wasn't absolutely necessary.

"You're quite right," she said. "We said nothing to each other about it, and I hadn't the slightest conscious intention of doing what I did. But the moment I got to London I drove to the place where I knew I could get heroin. And when I got back, I found that Peter had been out trying to find the man who had sold him the cocaine before. I assure you it wasn't deliberate."

"That's exactly the trouble," retorted Lamus. "It leads you by the nose, and prevents your doing your will. I remember once when I was making experiments with it myself, how I would go out with the intention of keeping away from the stuff all day, and how, without my knowing it, I took advantage of all sorts of little incidents that cropped up to get back to the studio some hours before I had intended. I found myself out at once, of course, having learnt some of the tricks of the mind. And I sat and watched myself finding excuses for starting in. One gets into an absolutely morbid state, in which everything that happens has some bearing on the question, 'Shall I or shall I not take it?'; and one gets so pleased with oneself for saying 'no' so often that one is emptied to reward oneself by saying 'yes' just once. I can promise

you a very interesting time watching your minds and spotting all the little dodges. The great thing I want you to remember is that you have to learn to take pleasure in what is really the most pleasurable thing in the world – introspection. You have got to find amusement in observing the details of the discomfort of being without the drug. And I don't want you to overdo it, either. When the discomfort becomes so acute that you can't enjoy it properly, then is the time to take a small dose and notice the effects. I hope, by the way, you've been a good little girl and kept that magical diary."

Lou was astonishingly pleased to be able to say it, "Yes."

"Some of it's done very fully," she said, "but you know there were days and weeks when I couldn't think, I couldn't move. Life was a perpetual struggle to get back to –" she hesitated for a word, and then ended with a pained little laugh, "oh, to anywhere."

King Lamus nodded gravely. We had finished our coffee.

"Now," said he, "to business," and led the way to the door.

I stayed behind for a moment to pay the bill. There was still a faint smell of bitter almond in the air. It reminded me of how the dinner might have ended, and I trembled all over like a man in an ague fit.

What was happening in me? Had I suddenly fallen in love with life, or had I simply become aware of the fear of death?

When we reached the fresh air, I knew it was the former. Lamus had made me feel. The effect of the drug had been to kill all feeling in me. My impulse to kill myself had not been so wholly negative as I had thought. It was a positive craving for what I supposed to be the anaesthesia of death. The pain of life had been too much to endure, and the influence of King Lamus had been to brace me to meet life face to face, whatever it might have in store, and conquer it.

I did not fear death any more than I had done in the old days, flying over the lines. I didn't mind dying at all; but I wanted to die fighting.

Lou was talking quite briskly to King Lamus on the steps of the restaurant while the commissionaire called a taxi. And I realised too that I loved her, that she was worth fighting to recover, that I had been a cad to drag her down with me. I understood my jealousy of King Lamus. His colossal strength, even his callousness about women,

253

attracted them. The man himself had made me sit up and match myself against him.

I wasn't going to have Lou see me constantly at a disadvantage.

We drove around to the studio.

The atmosphere invigorated us. I got an entirely new point of view about Lala. Before, she had seemed to me little more than part of the furniture, but tonight she was the resident spirit of the place. She informed it, gave it a meaning. The intimacy between her and her master was not in any way personal. She was the medium by which his thoughts became perceptible.

The fantastic appointments of the studio were projections in terms of material substances of his mind interpreted through her consciousness. I had an uncanny feeling that if it were not for her, King Lamus would be invisible.

In his mind, there was no difference between any two things, but through her mediation he was able to pretend that there was.

The studio was divided into several parts by arrangements of curtains. There was a perpetual soft noise of laughter, singing, and dancing; interrupted only by periods of intense silence which was somehow more significant than the sound. The firelight threw doubtful shadow pictures upon the glass roof; and from time to time figures moved with intimate softness through the dark corners and out into the courtyard. These swathed and muffled forms possessed an uncanny quality of unreality.

The studio was full of subtle incense. No smoke was visible; it was as if the atmosphere had somehow been impregnated with it.

Our little party fell very silent. He had given Lou and myself some tablets which had the effect of silencing the nervous restlessness which had begun to seize us after even so short an abstinence from heroin.

"I want you to hang on a little," explained our host. "The sting of abstinence will make the indulgence worth while. You have noticed, I am sure, that the vast majority of doses fail to produce any definite active effect."

It was quite true. We had been cursing the drug for its failure to reproduce the original sensations. We had tried to overcome the difficulty by increasing the quantity. But a time had come when we were immune

to its action; horridly aware of its absence, without obtaining any satisfaction from its presence.

"That stuff I have given you," Lamus explained, "dilutes your symptoms, and enables you to some extent to bear the discomfort. I want you to take advantage of the fact to watch your discomfort as if it were somebody else. When you find that you can enjoy this instead of blindly rushing to heroin for relief, you will already have gone a long way in the direction of acquiring mental control."

Several times during the night Lala intervened vigorously in such a way that it was impossible for us not to give her our attention. We found out later that this was part of the plan, that we were being watched for symptoms of acute disquietude, and that whenever these appeared, she interfered to prevent our dwelling on the subject.

I was astonished to find it about four o'clock in the morning, when King Lamus said:

"I've just been thinking that we should all be the better for a little heroin," and proceeded to hand it around.

The effect was extraordinary. I was aware of an infinite sense of relief; but it was evanescent. It could only have been a few instants before I sank into a dreamless slumber.

CHAPTER II
FIRST AID

When I woke, the winter sun was already high. It streamed upon my face through the glass skylight of the studio. The sensation of waking was itself a revelation. For months past I had been neither awake nor asleep; simply passing from the state of greater to one of less unconsciousness. But this was a definite act.

King Lamus had gone out, and Lala had only just returned, for she was taking off her furs as I woke.

I had been covered with blankets. She came and took them off, and told me it was time to go and get my things from Greek Street and take them to the new rooms which she had engaged for us that morning.

Lou, it seemed, was already there; and had fallen asleep again, said Lala, only a few minutes before she left.

I could not help feeling a dislike for the way in which everything was being managed for me. I must have shown something of this in my manner. Lala, after bundling me into the automobile which I had driven to Barley Grange on that first tremendous night, began to turn the conversation so as to answer my unspoken resentment.

She made a pleasant little excuse for not offering me the steering-wheel. I knew too well that I couldn't have driven that car a hundred yards through traffic. I had abdicated my manhood. I must resign myself to be driven where any one was willing to take me. I might count myself lucky if I had fallen into reasonably good hands.

At Greek Street we met with a surprise. It appeared that a few minutes before our arrival, a lady and gentleman had called and were very anxious to see me. They would come back in half an hour. I couldn't imagine who on earth it could be, and the matter slipped from my mind. I was hot and eager to get out of the disgusting atmosphere of those rooms. I wouldn't let Lala come in; but I found that I wasn't strong enough to pack my stuff. The smell of the den was foul beyond all belief.

Lou has not described a hundredth part of the dark abominations which had become habitual.

In fact, I was overcome by the foetor. I had no strength left. I sunk helplessly into a chair, and began to look feebly about me for the heroin to buck me up.

I must have gone off into a sort of swoon; for I don't know how it happened, but the fresh, cold air was blowing on my face. Our things had been packed as if by magic, and had been taken out to the motor. The bill had been paid.

As I set foot in the car, I heard the landlady asking what she should do if the lady and gentleman came back. I gave the address of my new rooms. As I stumbled into the seat the clear incisive tones of Lala rang across.

"You'd better tell them that Sir Peter's far from well. He will probably not be able to see any one this week."

I sat limply, shaken by the vibrations of the car.

I was an empty vessel; but I felt that, as we got out of the twisted network of streets, and the automobile bounded forward, I was escaping from some infernal labyrinth.

I found Lou at the new rooms. She was sitting in a big lounge chair holding tight to the arms. Her face told the same tale as my own. We felt that we had come through a great illness by a miracle. It struck me as dreadfully unfair that instead of being gently nursed back to health, a

demand was to be made upon us for the exercise of the utmost moral and physical strength and courage.

It was impossible for either of us to put forth the slightest effort without the help of the drug. It seemed logically impossible that we should be able to stop drugs by our own efforts; and we knew only too well from experience that we had got to a state where even a few moments delay in taking a dose might result in complete collapse and death.

"I shall leave you children alone for an hour to get settled in, and then we might drive down and have lunch in the country, don't you think? But of course you'll be needing heroin all the time, and I notice that you have a plentiful supply, so there's nothing to worry about there. It's not taking the drug that does the harm, it's the not knowing what you take. So I brought you a couple of charts marked off into hours; and what I want you to do is to promise to make a cross in the proper space every time you take it."

The condition was easy enough. What we had been dreading, in spite of what Lamus had said, was the forcible suppression which we had experienced at Barley Grange, and which had brought us to such extremities.

But Lala's last remark removed all our apprehensions. The matter was left entirely in our own hands. All we were asked was to keep a record of what we were doing.

I couldn't see how the fact of putting a thing down could make any difference to the act itself.

At that moment King Lamus came in, and kept us amused for half an hour with a perfectly absurd story of some trifling adventure that had happened to him that morning. But despite his vivacity and the interest which he excited, I found my hands instinctively going to the little wooden box in which I kept my heroin.

I took a dose. Lamus immediately broke off his remarks.

"Go on," I said feebly. "I didn't mean to interrupt."

"That's all right," said Lamus. "I'm only waiting for you to put it down."

Lala had pinned my chart to the wall. I looked at my watch, and went over and scrawled a cross in the proper section.

As I returned, I noticed that Lamus was watching with a smile of singular amusement. I know now that it was due to his recognising the nature of my annoyance.

He finished his story in a few words, and then asked me point-blank how the cure was going.

I said I didn't see how I could even begin to be cured, and pointed out the nature of the deadlock.

"Well," he said, "you aren't making any allowance for something that the doctors all talk about and forget nine-tenths of the time, which is yet the only thing that saves them from being found out as the ignorant meddlers they are. Do you know that the post-mortems on people who die in New York hospitals show that about fifty per cent of the cases have been wrongly diagnosed? No, Sir Peter, while you and I are wasting our time discussing our troubles, there's one thing working for us, never stops day or night, and that is *Vis medicatyix nalurx*."

Lala nodded emphatically.

"Didn't you notice that even in the Red-Cross?" she said to Lou. "The cases that got well were those that were left alone. All the surgeons did was to repair, as well as possible, the interference with nature caused by the wound. Anything beyond that was a mistake."

"We'll be back in about an hour," said Lamus, "and take you to lunch at Hindhead. Have you a pocket-knife, by the way?"

"Why, yes," I said with surprise. "Why?"

"Otherwise I would have left you mine. You may need one to sharpen your pencil."

Lou and I fell to talking as soon as they were gone. We were already better in this respect, that we had begun to take an interest in ourselves once more. We resorted once or twice to heroin during the absence of our friend; and we made a kind of little family joke of keeping each other up to the mark in the matter of recording the facts.

I discovered what had amused King Lamus on the first occasion. I was conscious of a distinct shade of annoyance at having to get up and make a little cross. It had never occurred to me to break my word. There was a fascination in watching the record.

The drive was a revelation. It was like coming out of a charnel house into the fresh air. A keen cold wind beat against our faces, almost blinding us.

It was not until we reached the inn that we remembered that we had

come out without any heroin. Lamus was immediately all sympathy when he heard of our plight. He offered to go out and get some immediately; but Lala protested that she was dying of hunger, and she was sure that lunch would restore our strength just as well, and King Lamus could go out immediately we were finished eating.

We agreed. We could hardly do anything else. As a matter of fact, the fresh air had excited in us both a very keen appetite. The meal did us a lot of good, and at its conclusion our host slipped out unostentatiously and returned in ten minutes with a little packet of powder.

It struck me as very extraordinary that he should have been able to procure it at so remote a place without a prescription. But Lou's eyes were fixed on him with an expression of delighted curiosity. I felt as though somehow or other she had divined the secret.

She seemed intensely amused at my perplexity, and stroked my hair in her most patronising manner. "You poor brainless creature," she seemed to be saying with her finger-tips.

Well, we all had heroin with our second cup of coffee, and my spirits rose immediately.

Lamus produced two little note books which he had bought in the village, so that we might record our doses while we were out and copy them on our charts when we got back.

We drove back to London, and had tea on the way in a cottage where the people seemed to know our friends very well. It was kept by a little old man and his wife who had the air of being family retainers. The cottage stood well away from the road in grounds of its own. Two mighty yew trees stood one on either side of the gate. Lala told us that the place belonged to the Order of which King Lamus was the head, and that he occasionally sent people down here for certain parts of his training which could only be carried out in solitude and silence.

A great longing came upon me to experience the subtle peace which dwelt in this simple habitation. For some reason or other I felt a natural disinclination to take the dose of heroin which was offered to me. It seemed out of keeping with the spirit of the surroundings. I took it and enjoyed it; but the act was mechanical, and the effect in some obscure fashion unsatisfactory.

We drove back to town, and had dinner in my new apartment, where they had an excellent restaurant service.

I found that during the day I had had fifteen sniffs of heroin. Lou had only had eleven. The reaction in my mind was this: If she can get on with eleven, why shouldn't I? – though I hadn't sufficient logic to carry on the argument to the people, millions of them, who hadn't had any at all, and seemed to be thriving!

We were both pretty tired. just as Lamus and Lala rose to leave I took a final sniff.

"What did you do that for?" he said, "if you don't mind my asking."

"Well, I think it was to go to sleep."

"But this morning you told me you took it to wake up," he retorted.

That was true, and it annoyed me; especially as Lou, instead of being sympathetic, gave one of her absurd little laughs. She actually seemed to take a perverse pleasure in seeing me caught out in a stupidity.

But Lamus took the matter very seriously.

"Well," he said, "it certainly is extraordinary stuff if it does two precisely opposite things at the will of the taker."

He spoke sarcastically. He refrained from telling me what he told me long afterwards, that the apparently contradictory properties that I was ascribing to it were really there, that it can be used by the expert to produce a number of effects, some of which seem at first sight mutually exclusive.

"Well, look here, Sir Peter," went on Lamus. "You can't have it both ways. You really ought to make up your mind as to the purpose of taking a dose."

I replied rather piteously that we had found out long ago that we couldn't sleep without it. Mabel Black had told us that.

"And the result of that delusion," returned Lamus "is that she's dead. I think your experience has been influenced by her foolish remark. You have told me yourself that the delightful result, in the first instance, was to keep you lying awake all night in a state of suspended animation, with a most fascinating flow of fancies filling your brain."

I had to admit the truth of what he said.

"Heroin," he explained, "is a modification of morphine, and morphine

is the most active of the principles of opium. Now surely you remember what Wilkie Collins says in *The Moonstone* about opium and its preparations, that they have a stimulating effect followed by a sedative effect. Heroin is much more positive in its action than opium; and the reasonable thing to do, as it seems to me, would be to go ahead with it pretty hard in the morning and keep yourself going by that means, but to leave it entirely alone for some hours before you go to bed, so that the sedative effect may send you nicely to sleep at the proper time. I know the objection to that. The abuse of the drug has left you full of nervous irritability. The reason why you want heroin at night is to deaden yourself to that. When you take it in the morning after a night's rest, you are giving it to a more or less healthy person refreshed by sleep; it is able to stimulate you because your sleep has given you some reserves of force on which it can work. When you take it at night, you are administering it to a sick person, which is a very different thing. However, what you should do is to replace it at night by these tablets, with a nice warm drink of whisky or rum and water, and you will find yourself asleep before you know it. Then in the morning, you awake much fresher than usual, and the heroin will have something more to catch hold of. The result of this will be that you will find quite a small quantity will do you as much good as a big one did last week, and more."

Well, all that seemed pretty sensible to me. We took his advice. We did not go to sleep at once. I felt my thoughts too varied. They wandered from one thing to another without reasonable sequence. There seemed to be gaps of unconsciousness between two sets of thoughts; but eventually the irritation subsided, and I knew no more till the morning.

We woke very late, completely exhausted. But as Lamus had prophesied, the heroin took hold immediately; the first two doses made us lively, and with the third we were out of bed and having a bath for the first time in – I'm ashamed to say how long.

Lou fell into a rage at the condition of our underwear, and of our outer clothes, too, for the matter of that. It was all soiled and dirty and stained. We must literally have stunk. And with the realisation of this came an acute feeling of disgrace that we should have been going about with Lamus and Lala in such a condition. If they had said anything about

it to us, we might have worked up an artificial indignation about it. But that they should have said nothing was absolutely damnable.

We could not tolerate the idea of ourselves. And yet, only forty-eight hours before, nothing mattered at all.

Lou, in a state of almost insane excitement, was calling up Barley Grange on long distance. The housekeeper was to send up something to wear that morning.

While she shouted the order, I suddenly recollected that Lamus and Lala were coming in after lunch; the clothes couldn't possibly reach us till after three o'clock. The best thing to do was to have some dressing-gowns sent up from Piccadilly.

They sent people round with a selection at once, and what with that and sending out for some toilet things, and having in the hairdresser, we made ourselves fairly presentable by half-past one.

That morning gave me the impression of a vaudeville turn or a farce. We had to dodge about from one room to another according as male or female angels ministered unto us.

The excitement kept our minds off heroin very successfully; but it obtruded itself constantly on our notice none the less by insistent physical attacks. Of course, we warded them off at once by taking suitable doses. I cannot say that there was any real diminution. For one thing, taking the stuff by the nose, you can't tell exactly how much you are getting, and a good deal of what you take is wasted.

But the whole atmosphere had changed. We had been taking it till now in a steady, regular manner. It had become a continuous performance. But this morning each patch of craving and each dose were definite incidents. The homogeneity of the vice had been broken up into sections. The dull monotony of the drug had developed dramatic qualities. We were reminded of our early experiences with it. We had, to a certain extent, recovered what addicts call "drug virginity". That alone was sufficient to fill us with a keen sense of exhilaration. We had regained the possibility of hope.

On the other hand, we were brought very sharply up against ourselves by the efforts of the hairdresser and the haberdasher. The smart new dressing-gowns contrasted so strikingly with the deadly illness of our appearance!

However, we could see the daylight afar off, and we sat down to lunch with a certain pleasure. Our appetites had not returned, of course, and we ate very little of the light and exquisite food we had ordered. But at least the idea of food did not disgust us, as had been too long the case.

Lamus came in in time to join us at coffee. It was easy to see that he was pleased at the result so far obtained. Lala was not with him. Instead, he had brought Maisie Jacobs.

I found myself wondering acutely whether there was any serious reason for the change. I had got to the state where I suspected the man's slightest action of having some occult significance, especially as he gave no explanation. Decidedly his manners were not calculated to reassure the unwary. It was easy to understand why his name had become the focus for a host of ridiculous inventions.

After all, it is not pleasant to feel oneself in the presence of an intelligence capable of out-manoeuvring one's own at every point without even taking the trouble to do so. The way he took everything for granted was in itself annoying.

He strolled over to the charts, and stood studying them for a long time while he puffed at a cigar. Even the cigar was offensive. It was the kind that millionaires have specially made for themselves. Lamus smoked no other kind; and yet he was a comparatively poor man.

Of course, the explanation was perfectly simple. He really understood and really appreciated good tobacco, and preferred to indulge in cigars disproportionately.

It was the man's own business what he smoked; and yet he had managed to get himself an absolutely bad name in London on that one trait alone. People felt that it was monstrous for him to dine on a mutton chop and a piece of Stilton, and then pull out a cigar that cost half as much again as his dinner.

He studied our charts as if they had been maps and he was trying to work out his overland route from Bokhara to Khatmandu!

Ultimately he said, "There seems a very long gap here – fifteen hours – 9 to 12, that's right, isn't it?"

He turned to Maisie for confirmation. He was, so he said, quite unable to trust himself to calculate.

Maisie entered into the spirit of the absurdity and counted it solemnly out on her fingers.

The tone of his voice had been mournful, as if his plans had been seriously disconcerted. That was another trick of his that put people off. It was Lou's sparkling eyes that told me what he meant.

And then I was brought up with a tremendous shock to realise what it meant to me. I went to the chart myself with excited curiosity, quite as if I had never seen it before.

It did not need a mathematician to put the situation into English. The crosses for the last thirty-six hours were crowded into a few spaces, leaving large empty gaps. In other words, the indulgence had become irregular. I stared at the chart as if it had been a ghost.

Lamus turned his head and looked down at me over his shoulder with a queer grin. Then he uttered the extraordinary word: "*Kriegspiel*".

I was completely taken aback. What in the name of thunder was the man talking about? And then it slowly dawned upon me that there was an analogy between the chart and the distribution of the troops in the war. It was obvious as soon as the idea struck one.

As long as the armies were evenly distributed along the line, it was a matter of trench warfare. Great victories and defeats were impossible in the nature of things. But once the troops were massed at points of vantage, aggregated in huge mobile units, it became possible to destroy them on the large scale.

When a British square is broken, the annihilation of its defenders does not come from any diminution in the fighting power of the individual soldiers; its military value is not sensibly diminished by the loss of the few men at the point of attack. It has become worthless because their regular arrangement has been thrown into disorder.

"At the Battle of Waterloo," said King Lamus, turning from the wall and going back to his coffee, "Napoleon sent forward the Old Guard. A few minutes later he cried, 'They are mixed,' and drove in despair from the field. He did not have to wait to see them destroyed."

Lou's breath was coming in great gasps. She had understood the essence of our friend's tactics.

We looked abominably ill; we were actually suffering at the moment

from the craving, and embarrassed by the presence of Maisie Jacobs. We did not want to take it in front of her. And yet we knew that we had won the victory. It might be a matter of weeks or months; we didn't even care. We were content to have mastered the principle of the thing. It would be easy to attack those clusters of crosses, and eliminate them little by little.

King Lamus asked Maisie to sing. Luckily there was a baby grand in the room. He sat down and began to accompany her. I found myself enthralled by watching the man's mind work. It taught me something constantly.

This last act, for example. We couldn't go out as we were, and the singing would be an alternative distraction. At the same time, he wanted Maisie's back turned so that we could take our heroin.

We wanted it very badly indeed; and yet – so strange is nature! – we were just as ashamed to take it secretly as a moment before we had been to take it openly.

The thought hit me between the eyes.

It has already been mentioned that Lou and I both had the impulse to conceal the act from each other even while we were taking it openly together. We wanted to pretend that we were taking less than we were. The use of drugs develops every morbid kink in the mind.

Meanwhile, Maisie was singing in her rich contralto voice an English translation of one of Verlaine's most exquisite lyrics: "With muted strings".

"Calm in the twilight of the lofty boughs
Pierce we our love with silence as we drowse"

"Melt we our souls, hearts, senses in this shrine,
Vague languor of arbutus and of pine!"

"Half-close your eyes, your arms upon your breast
Banish for ever every interest!"

"The cradling breeze shall woo us, soft and sweet,
Ruffling the waves of velvet at your feet."

"When solemn night of swart oaks shall prevail
  Voice our despair, musical nightingale!"

The exquisite images, so subtle and yet so concrete, filled my mind with memories of all my boyhood's dreams. They reminded me of the possibilities of love and peace. All this was familiar to me, familiar in the most intense and alluring form. That was what nature had to offer; this pure and ecstatic rapture was the birthright of mankind. But I, instead of being content with it as it was, had sought an artificial Paradise and bartered the reality of heaven for it. In nature, even melancholy is subtly enthralling. I thought of Keats' ode to her, and even of James Thomson's "Melancholia that transcends all wit", whom he adored, and on whose altar lay his bleeding heart. Well might Verlaine say: "Voice our despair, musical nightingale!"

But in our chemical substitute for natural stimulus, our despair could be sung by no nightingale. Could even the carrion buzzard give any idea of the hoarse and horrible discord of our disenchantment? The shreds of our souls were torn by filthy fish-hooks, and their shrieks were outside the gamut of merely human anguish.

Was it still possible to return? Had we forfeited for ever our inheritance "for a mess of beastlier pottage than ever Esau guzzled"?

Lamus had been watching us intently while Maisie sang. Lou's eyes were full of tears. They ran down her thin, worn face. She made no effort to wipe them away. I do not know whether she felt them. Heroin dulls all physical sensation, leaving only the dull intolerable craving, the acrid irritation, to break in upon the formless stupor which represents the height of well-being.

But I had no inclination to weep; mine was the bitter black remorse of Judas. I had sold my master, my True Will, for thirty pieces of poisonous copper, smeared with the slime of quicksilver. And all I had bought was a field of blood in which I might hang myself and – all my bowels gushed out.

King Lamus rose from the piano with a heavy sigh.

"Forgive me for nagging," he said slowly, "but you spoilt your enjoyment of the song by being ashamed to put yourself in the proper

condition to do so by taking the heroin that you need. How often must I tell you that there is nothing to be ashamed of, and everything to be proud of? You know yourself that you are running a greater risk than you ever did when you flew over the Boche lines. I don't want you to swank about it, of course; but you certainly don't want to act like a schoolboy puffing his first cigarette behind a hedge. For God's sake, man, can't you see that half the danger of this business lies in the secrecy and duplicity which go with it?

"Suppose we made all the fuss about eating that we do about drinking and loving, can't you see what evils would immediately arise? Remember the food restrictions during the war."

"By Jove, I never thought of that," I said, as a hundred half-forgotten incidents bounced into my mind. There were all sorts of stratagems for dodging the regulations, on the part of people who in the ordinary way were plain straightforward law-abiding citizens.

"Of course, we must have restrictions about love and drink and drugs. It is quite obvious how frightfully people would abuse their liberty if they had it."

"I'm sorry to have to disagree," said Lamus. "And as you know, I've got into endless trouble of one sort or another for holding the views I do. But I'm afraid I do honestly think that most of the troubles spring directly from the unnatural conditions set up by the attempts to regulate the business. And in any case, the state of mind brought about by them is so harmful indirectly to the sense of moral respon- sibility that I am really not sure whether it would not be wiser in the long run to do away with the Blue laws and the Lizzie laws altogether. Legislative interference with the habits of the people produces the sneak, the spy, the fanatic, and the artful dodger. Take finance! Swindling has become a fine art, and is practised on a gigantic scale in ways which would have been impossible when there were no laws intended to protect the public."

It was a very strange view to take. I could hardly believe that Lamus was serious; and yet it did seem to me that the modern criminal millionaire was actually assisted by the complexity of the Company laws. It is impossible for the plain man to understand them, so that an

unscrupulous man armed with expert knowledge is much more likely to get the better of his unwary fellows than in the old days when his activities were confined to thimble-rigging and pulling favourites.

"Oh, Basil," put in Maisie, "do tell our friends what you were saying the other day about the South Sea Islands."

Lamus laughed merrily.

"Good for you, kid, very much to the point!

"I've wandered a good deal through queer parts of the world, as you know, and in some of those places there are still taboos about eating and hunting and fishing – all sorts of things which we in England take quite simply, in consequence of which they give no trouble.

"But where a man has to think of a thousand things before he has his dinner: what he eats, and how it was killed, and who cooked it, and so on for ever and ever, he gets no chance to develop his mind in more important ways. Taboo is responsible for the low mental and moral development of the peoples whom it afflicts, more than anything else. An appetite should be satisfied in the simplest and easiest way. Once you begin to worry about the right and wrong of it, you disturb the mind unnaturally, and begin to think awry in all sorts of ways that have apparently nothing to do with it.

"Think of the Queen of Spain who was being dragged by her horse, and lost her life because of the absence of the official appointed by etiquette to assist her to dismount!"

We all laughed; the girls frankly, but I with an ill-defined, uncomfortable feeling that Lamus was getting on to dangerous ground.

"What is modern fiction?" he asked, "from Hardy and Dostoevski to the purveyors of garbage to servant girls, but an account of the complications set up by the exaggerated importance attached by themselves or their neighbours to the sexual appetites of two or more bimanous monkeys.

"Most sexual troubles and offences so-called would do very little harm if nobody attached any importance to what was or was not going on."

Of course, there is an answer to this type of argument but I don't know what it is. I felt very uneasy. He was laying his axe to the root of the tree of civilisation. That was evident.

Lou must have caught my thought. She quoted sarcastically:

"O woodman, spare that tree,
Touch not a single bough,
In youth it sheltered me
And I'll protect it n-yow!"

Since the war, women are taking a very peculiar attitude. I didn't like the tone of the conversation. I instinctively looked to Maisie Jacobs for support.

The Jewish tradition, which is, after all, the foundation of the so-called Christian point of view, could surely be trusted. But Maisie merely retorted with some verses from Heine which showed that she was entirely on the enemy's side.

Lamus noticed my annoyance, and hastily changed the conversation.

"I'm afraid the only thing you can do," he said to me, "is to chain yourself to Buckingham Palace and then go on hunger-strike, until they give you permission to vote more early and often than ever, after which you won't care to go to the polls at all. That's another example of the same old story. However little we want a thing, we howl if we discover that we can't get it; and the moment we've got it the whole business drops out of sight.

"You'll find it's the same with your drugs. You've practically hypnotised yourself into thinking you can't do without them. It's not a real need, as you know. It's a false and perverse appetite; and as soon as you get out of the way of thinking that it's vitally important, you'll begin to forget how much you depend on it."

Well, of course, I could see the sense of that; and I was glad to see how gay and light-hearted Lou had become under the influence of the idea.

Maisie called Lamus away to the piano to sing another song.

"I love you because you're as crazy as I,
Because all the shadows and lights of the sky
Of existence are centred in you;

The cross-jagged lightning, the roar of typhoon
Are as good as the slumber of time as we swoon
With the sun half asleep in the blue.

You're a dream, you're a mystery, empress and slave,
You're like life, the inscrutable beat of its wave,
You are always the all – unexpected!
When you've promised yourself, then you push me away;
When you scorn me, you suddenly kindle and slay;
You hate truth as the lies She rejected!

I love you because you are gallant and proud,
(Your soul is a sun and your body a cloud)
And you leap from my arms when I woo you;
Because you love earth and its worms, you caress
The stars and the seas, and you mock my distress
While the sorrows of others thrill through you!

I love you because my life's lost in your being;
You burn for me all the night long, and on seeing
Me, jest at your tears – and allot mine!
Because you elude me, a wave of the lake,
Because you are danger and poison, my snake,
Because you are mine, and are not mine!"

Just as she had finished, Elsie arrived from Barley Grange with our trunks. Maisie and Lamus said they would leave us to unpack, and went off.

She and Lala dropped in from time to time in the course of the next five days to take us motoring, or to dinner, or the theatre, or to parties.

I thought they made rather a point of keeping off the subject which was the real reason of their visits.

CHAPTER III
THE VOICE
OF VIRTUE

Basil had gone out of town; but he turned up on the fifth day at eleven o'clock in the morning, and he came in his most serious professional manner. After a very brief greeting, he went straight to the charts and inspected them attentively.

Lou and I both felt very uncomfortable. He noticed it at once.

"You've still got heroin on the brain, I see," he remarked severely. "You insist on considering yourselves as naughty children instead of as pioneers of humanity undertaking a desperate adventure for the good of the race."

I began a sort of apology; I don't quite know for what.

"Nonsense," he interrupted. "I know perfectly well why you're ashamed of yourself. You've had what you call a relapse. After getting down to five, six and seven doses, you've suddenly gone back. Yesterday, I see, Lou had fourteen and you sixteen – more than you were taking ever since you have been in this place. You think that's a bad sign. I don't."

"To begin with, you've been honest with yourselves; and that's the thing that matters most. Then it's a good sign again that the daily variation is as large as it is. I'd much rather see "two eighteen" than "eight eight" in spite of the four extra doses. And that for exactly the same reason as applies to the hourly distribution.

"It's the same with drink. The man who goes on the bust occasionally is very much easier to manage than the steady soaker. Every child in the Fourth Standard knows that. I believe it's written in golden letters round the chancel in Westminster Abbey. If it isn't, it ought to be.

"Now don't worry. And above all things, don't get a fit of repentance and take too little today and tomorrow. If you do, you'll have another relapse. I know it sounds as though I were contradicting myself. Make the most of it, I don't care. I'm going to do it again in the following elegant manner.

"I want you to get the whole subject of heroin out of your mind; and that is the reason why I insist so strongly on your keeping a record of every time you take it. It's a psychological paradox that the best way to forget about a thing is to make a memorandum of it.

"Now, goodbye, and come to dinner tonight at the studio. Perhaps you'll feel like dancing."

He went off with an airy wave of the hand.

When we came back from the dance the porter told us that a lady and gentleman had called to see us. They hadn't left their names. They would call again in the morning.

It struck me as curious; but I gave the matter little enough thought. The fact is that I was in rather a bad temper. I had used a good deal of heroin off and on during the last few days, and it had certainly not cost me anything to cut off the cocaine. Morphine and heroin give one a physical craving; but the pull of cocaine is principally moral and when one is taking H. one doesn't care such a lot about taking it.

But that night, raw as it was, I almost made up my mind to drive back and try to get a little snow for a change.

We were getting over the heroin, the first stage of diminution, without too much suffering. But there was something exceedingly tedious about the process.

We had had a very pleasant evening; but I couldn't help comparing it with the same sort of thing in honeymoon days. The sparkle had gone out of the champagne of life.

It was our fault of course, for trying to outwit nature. But at the same time, one couldn't shut one's eyes to the facts, and I knew Lamus would have had no hesitation in giving us a little snow, feeling the way I was.

I don't know why I felt such a disinclination to go back and ask him. It may have been the instinctive dislike of bothering him; and besides, it was rather humiliating to have to admit. There was also a trace of sturdy British feeling that the thing to do was to stick it out and trust a night's rest to tone up my nerves.

Lamus had advised us to take Turkish baths if we felt unduly depressed. We had found them very useful.

We had got down to three goes a day two days running, chiefly by following his advice to take one of the white tablets instead of the heroin whenever the craving became irresistible. He made rather a point of that, by the way.

It was a bad thing, he said, to yield to stress. It wasn't nearly so harmful to take the heroin when one didn't feel so badly in need of it.

Even after all this time I hadn't quite got onto the peculiarities of the man's mind. I had never reached the stage where I could be sure what he could say next.

One day we were talking about Lou's Chinese appearance; and he said quite seriously that he must have some Chinese blood in him or was the reincarnation of a Chinese philosopher. Ko Yuen, I think he said the name was. He said that he owed it to his European reason to explain categorically why his thoughts had such an Asiatic cast.

They certainly had. From our point of view it was simply perversity. And yet, as a rule, it seemed to work out all right in the end. But it gives one a pain in the neck to try to follow the way his mind works. And he takes a Satanic pleasure in taking hold of one's most obviously reasonable ideas and putting up a series of paradoxes which bewilder one with their strangeness, yet to which there seems to be no answer.

Yet in spite of all this subtlety he had a downright British doggedness; the most perverse train of reasoning would suddenly pull out into a

bulldog kind of conclusion that would leave one wondering whether he had been really thinking at all on the lines he pretended.

The upshot in my own case was to keep me up to the mark. So I went to bed, meaning to get up early and go to the Turker in the morning. But as it happened, we both slept late. By the time we were dressed we were getting hungry for lunch.

I was annoyed at this. I had wanted to get out of the house and change my ideas as completely as possible. The Hot Room is an excellent place for the purpose. While I'm there, I find I can't think of anything at all but the immediate effects of the temperature.

I was annoyed, too, to find Lou comparatively cheerful. I decided I would go out after all and have lunch in the Cooling Room, when the porter called up to ask if we could see a lady and gentleman.

These people had begun to obsess me. I demanded their names. There was a pause as if a discussion were taking place at the other end of the wire; and then he announced that it was Mrs. Webster and a friend.

Why the mystery? I didn't want to see her. What did she want with me? I had taken a strong dislike to the woman. I had come to blame her for putting us on to the drug business. It was so much easier than blaming myself.

However, we couldn't exactly refuse to see her, so I told the porter to show them up.

"So it was you," we both said in a breath as we advanced to meet each other. We were referring to the night of the suicide dinner at the Wisteria. As I was going out of the room I had thought I recognised her; but I had supposed she was out of London. She had been a couple of months before; but my mind had gotten into such a state that it never occurred to me that she might have come back.

That's the sort of thing that heroin does to one. One gets an idea about something, and it's too much trouble to change it.

She, on her side, had only half recognised me; and goodness knows she needed no excuse for that.

"We heard you were in London," she began volubly, in a tone which somehow rang false, "and of course I couldn't rest till I had come and welcomed you and Lou in person. We heard you were in a little place in

Greek Street from one of the crowd; but you had gone the very morning I called, and they told us you were ill and couldn't see any one for a week. But Billy Bray and Lady Rhoda came in last night and said they'd seen you at a dance. So I wouldn't waste a minute in coming to see you."

She rattled off all this as if she was in a violent hurry, punctuating her remarks by kissing Lou extravagantly.

I could see that Lou resented the woman even more than I did, but she naturally took care not to show it.

Hanging fatuously on the outskirts of the group was no less a person than the famous philanthropist, Jabez Platt. But he, too, had changed since we had seen him at the time of our marriage. Then he had been the very type of a smug, prosperous, contented Chadband; a placid patriarch with an air of disinterested benevolence and unassuming sanctity. If ever a man was at peace with himself and the world, it was Mr. Jabez Platt on the occasion of our first meeting.

But today, he was a very different individual indeed. He seemed to have shrunk. His black clothes had fitted him like the skin of a well-conditioned porpoise. Now they hung loosely like a toad's. He resembled that animal in several other respects. The virtue had somehow gone out of him. There was a hungry, hunted look in his eyes. Of course, I could see instantly what was the matter with him; he had been taking heroin.

"Dear me," thought I, for my dislike for the creature was instinctive, "how are the mighty fallen!"

Excuse a digression. There is a great deal of discussion about various pleasures – whether they are natural or unnatural. Lamus has since told me that the true test of the perversity of a pleasure is that it occupies a disproportionate amount of the attention.

According to him, we have no right to decide off-hand that it is an unnatural pleasure to eat sawdust. A man might be constituted so that he liked it. And as long as his peculiarity doesn't damage or interfere with other people, there's no reason why he shouldn't be left alone.

But if it is the man's fixed belief that sawdust eating is essential to human happiness; if he attributes almost everything that happens either to the effects of eating it or not eating it; if he imagines that most of the people he meets are also sawdust-eaters, and above all, if he thinks that

the salvation of the world depends entirely upon making laws to compel people to eat sawdust, whether they like it or not, then it is fair to say that his mind is unbalanced on the subject; and that, further, the practice itself, however innocent it may appear, is in that particular case perverse. Sanity consists in the proper equilibrium of ideas in general. That is the only sense in which it is true that genius is connected with insanity.

The conviction of Michael Angelo that his work was the most important thing in the Renaissance was not quite sane, even although in a way time has justified his belief.

That is what is wrong with the majority of vaccinationists and anti-vaccinationists and vegetarians and anarchists and the "irascible race of seers" in general, that they over-play their hands. However right they are in their belief, and in thinking that belief important, they are wrong in forgetting the equal or greater importance of other things. The really important things in the world are the huge silent inexorable things.

"What are the wild waves saying?" – that the pull of the tides is gradually slowing down the earth's rate of rotation. And that was what was wrong with me. I had a tendency to see heroin everywhere.

That was not what was wrong with Mr. Jabez Platt!

Gretel Webster was a mistress of the social arts, yet all her skill in small talk could not camouflage the artificial character of the visit. She saw it herself, and took advantage of the fact to ask Lou to take her in her bedroom and "talk clothes and leave dear Sir Peter and Mr. Platt to get better acquainted with each other".

But the process did not promise to be rapid. Dear Sir Peter and Mr. Platt seemed to have nothing to say to each other; dear Sir Peter did his best to offer cigars, cigarettes, and various drinks to relieve the tension, but Mr. Platt's Roman virtue did not permit him to indulge in such things.

Mr. Platt, however, was so sensible of the hospitality of dear Sir Peter that he felt obliged to ask dear Sir Peter's opinion of – and he suddenly whipped a ten-gramme bottle of cocaine out of his coat-tail pocket.

"We believe," he said, "that this is a particularly pure sample. There is strong scientific reason to believe," he explained, and the atmosphere of the pulpit positively radiated from him, "that it is not the drug itself but the impurities so often associated with it by careless manufacture that

are responsible for the deplorable effects occasionally observed in persons who take it, whether for legitimate or other reasons."

To say that I sat stupefied is a gross understatement of the case. My astonishment prevented me recognising for a moment that my heart was bounding and leaping within me at the sight of the drug.

"I should really value your opinion as a connoisseur," continued Platt.

There was something tremulous in his voice, as if he were keeping hold on himself by some incredible effort of will.

I positively stammered.

"Why, Mr. Platt," I said, "I thought you were so anxious to stop the use of the drug altogether. I thought it was you who were chiefly responsible for putting through the Diabolical Dope Act."

"Ignorance, pure ignorance, my dear Sir Peter," he cried. "We live and learn, we live and learn. Used in moderation, we find it to be positively wholesome. A stimulant no doubt, you will say. And all stimulants may undoubtedly be dangerous. But I'm afraid people will have them, and surely the wisest course is to see that what they have is as little deleterious as possible."

While he spoke he kept on nervously jerking the bottle in my direction as if afraid to put it into my hands outright. And then I realised how very badly I wanted it.

"Well, certainly, Mr. Platt," I replied, entering into the spirit of the thing, "I shall be only too glad to give you my opinion for what it may be worth."

I could not conceal the feverish eagerness with which I shook out a dose. My pretence at sniffing with a critical air was ludicrously feeble. A child could have seen that I was shaken, body and soul, by the feverish lust to get it into my system after so long an abstinence.

Time had purged my system of the poison. It found the house "empty and swept and garnished"; and seven devils entered into me instead of the ejected one. My malaise passed like a cloud swept by the wind from the face of the sun. I became physically buoyant as I had not been for months. I was filled with superb self-confidence. My hesitation vanished. I played the game with all the sublime intoxication of recovered divinity.

"I must admit that it seems to me excellent," I pronounced with lofty calm, though my blood was singing in my ear.

I handed back the bottle.

"Keep it, I beg of you, my dear Sir Peter," protested Platt enthusiastically. "One never knows when a little household medicine may not come in handy."

Something set me off into roars of internal laughter. I couldn't see the joke, but it was the biggest joke in the world.

"It's really awfully kind of you, my dear Mr. Platt," I said with unction, feeling that I was cast for the star part in some stupendous comedy.

"The obligation is entirely on my side," returned my guest. "You have no idea how your kind approval has set my mind at ease."

I took another sniff. I was fainting away into an inexpressible ecstasy. I re-corked the bottle and put it in my pocket, thanking Platt profusely.

"I can't imagine your mind being ill at ease," I went on with a note of irony, which was, however, absolutely genial. I was friends with every one in the world. "If there was ever a man with a conscience void of offence toward God and man, that man is surely Jabez Platt."

"Ah, conscience, conscience," he sighed. "You have no idea, Sir Peter, how it has tormented me of late. The moral responsibility, the appalling moral responsibility."

"Whatever it is," I answered, "you are certainly the right man to shoulder it."

"Well," he said, "I think I may say without boasting that I trust I have never tried to shirk it. Your approval has absolved me of the last shred of hesitation. I must explain, my dear Sir Peter, that I have always been a poor man. The service of humanity demands many sacrifices from its devotees, and I assure you that in that bottle there lies not only, as I now feel assured, the salvation of mankind from one of its direst dangers, but an enormous fortune."

He leant forward and tapped my knee with his forefinger.

"An enormous fortune," he repeated in awed tones. And then lowering his voice still further, "Enough, more than enough, for both of us."

"Why, how do I come in?" I asked in surprise, while a little thrill of avarice tickled my heart-strings.

I reflected that what with one thing or another, I had made a disagreeably large hole in my capital. Only two mornings ago I had had

a rather irritating letter from Mr. Wolfe on the subject. It would suit me perfectly well to make an enormous fortune.

He drew his chair closer to mine, and began to talk in a quiet, persuasive voice. "It's this way, my dear Sir Peter. The workings of Providence are indeed strange. just before the passing of my Act, I had invested what little fortune I possessed in the purchase of a Cocaine Factory in Switzerland, with the intention of putting an end to its nefarious activities. Now here is an instance of what I can only refer to with reverent gratitude as the Moving of the Divine Finger. On the one hand, my chemical manager informed me of the marvellous scientific discovery which I have already mentioned – I am sure you feel no ill effects from what you have taken?" His voice took on a tone of grave concern, almost paternal.

"Not much," I countered cheerfully, "It's splendid. I can do with another sniff right now!" I suited the action to the words, like Hamlet's ideal mummer.

"Won't you be persuaded?" I queried maliciously.

"Ah, no, I thank you, dear Sir Peter! Your remarks have raised me to the highest pinnacle of happiness."

I took a fourth dose, just for luck.

"Well, on the other hand, I discovered that, thanks to the very Act which I had so arduously laboured to put upon the Statute Book, that little bottle of yours which costs me less than five shillings to manufacture, and was sold retail for a matter of fifteen shillings, can now be sold – discreetly, you understand – in the West End for almost anything one cares to ask – ten, twenty, even fifty pounds to the right customer. Eh? What do you say to that?" He laughed gleefully. "Why, ill-natured people might say I had put through the Act for the very purpose of making a bull market for my produce!"

"And you save humanity from its follies and vices at the same stroke!" The cocaine had cleared my mind – it was like one of those transparent golden sunsets after a thunderstorm in the Mediterranean. I revelled in the ingenuity of Mr. Platt's proceedings. I gloated with devilish intensity upon the jest of carrying out so magnificent a scheme beneath so complete a camouflage. It was the vision of Satan disguised as an angel of light.

"Yes, indeed, the whole affair is eminently gratifying from every point of view," answered Platt. "Never in all my life have I been permitted to see with such luminous clarity the designs of providential loving-kindness."

"Alas I, my dear Mr. Platt," I replied gloomily, as the stage directions seemed to indicate, "I am a very young and ignorant man, and I am unable at present to see any part for me in the design. My mere approval of your product – " I took it out and treated myself to a long, languishing kiss – yes, kiss, there is no other word for it! "My long-lost love, home to my heart once more!"

Platt in his turn assumed an air of Stygian melancholy. "My dear Sir Peter," he pursued, with a heavy sigh, "you can easily understand that, huge as my fortune, thanks to the inscrutable ways of Destiny, now is, time is necessary to realise it fully – and, by a singular and most unfortunate conjunction of circumstances, not only time is required, but – Capital."

"Unfortunate conjuncture of circumstances?" I echoed dreamily – my mind was royally racing in the Circus of Infinity, a billion leagues from where anybody sat.

"Unfortunate, that is, for me," corrected Platt, "no, no, I won't say that, since it is fortunate for my friend – for you!"

"For me?"

"For you, my dear Sir Peter! I told Mrs. Webster of the state of the case – and she immediately suggested your name. She has come to the rescue splendidly herself, I need hardly tell you – took all the shares she could – but there is still a matter of three thousand pounds to find. And remember, after insuring against all risks, and so forth, we shall be paying at the very least four thousand per cent."

I have never been any sort of a business man; but a child of twelve could grasp the gigantic nature of the proposition.

"I have brought the papers for your inspection, my dear Sir Peter. You will see that the capital is only £20,000 in shares of £1 fully paid up – and I am offering you £3,000 at par."

"It's princely, my dear sir," I exclaimed. "You overwhelm me. But – excuse me – I don't see why you need the money at all, or why you don't sell the shares through a broker."

At this moment Lou popped into the room. It annoyed me. Did I show it? Her face went suddenly white as marble. She stood in the doorway of the bedroom for a moment, swaying; and then went swiftly and softly through the room to the hallway. The portiere swung to behind her – and I instantly forgot her existence, after vaguely supposing that she had gone to get her furs to show to Gretel, returning to the bedroom by the other door so as not to disturb us.

Platt was explaining the situation. "A most unfortunate affair, Sir Peter! I fear I am overmuch preoccupied with the welfare of my fellows – and in consequence neglect my own. I certainly was surprised, when I went to my bank to see if I had enough money to purchase these chemical works, to find my balance so large – I am only too accustomed, alas! to find that my impulsive charity has denuded my little savings. But I only discovered last month that £3,000 of the amount did not belong to me at all; it was part of a fund of which I am trustee. I am not allowed by our foolish laws to invest trust funds in such securities as this *Schneezugchemischerwerke* of ours; and I must replace the £3,000 by the end of the month, or the consequences may be really most disastrous." He broke off short, trembling with fear. He was not playing a part about this. He undoubtedly felt that it might be difficult to explain to an unsympathetic jury how a Trust Fund had lost its way to the extent of wandering into the Trustee's private account without his suspecting it had behaved in so erratic a manner.

"You are a man of the world, Sir Peter," he declared, almost blubbering, "and I feel sure you understand."

I am not altogether a man of the world, as a matter of fact; but, whether helped by the cocaine or not, I really did think I understood fairly well what had happened.

"But why not go to the City?" I repeated, "they ought to fight like wolves over such a plump little doe as the *Schneezug!*"

"My dear Sir Peter!" He raised his hands in horrified surprise. "Surely, surely you realise that it may take years and years to educate the public to appreciate the difference between our Pure Cocaine, a wholesome household tonic, and the Impure Cocaine, which is a Deadly and Deleterious Habit-forming Drug! I felt I could approach you, because

you are a man of the world, and a connoisseur, and – to be frank with you – because I took a liking for you the first time I saw you, so handsome and splendid with your beautiful young bride! But what, oh what, would people say if it became known that Jabez Platt had the majority of the shares in a Cocaine Factory? My dear Sir Peter, we are in England, remember!"

I wasn't deceived by any of the nauseating humbug of the scoundrel, but it was evident that his proposal was a genuine good thing.

The *Schneezugchemischewerke* had been paying well enough in the ordinary way when he bought them.

I determined to sell the necessary securities and take over the shares. My state of mind was exceedingly complex. My reasons for the purchase were not merely various but mutually exclusive. For one thing, the Satanistic idea of working evil for its own sake; for another, the schoolboy delight in doing things on the sly; then there was the simple and straight-forward money lust. Again, my hatred of hypocrisy had turned into a fascination. I wanted to enjoy a taste of so subtle and refined a vice.

On the top of this there was a motive which really encroached on the category of insanity. On the one side I was exuberantly delighted to find myself in possession of boundless supplies of cocaine; on the other I was enraged with mankind for having invented the substance that had ruined my life, and I wanted to take my revenge on it by poisoning as many people as I could.

These ideas were tossed about in my mind like pieces of meat in boiling soup. The fumes intoxicated me. I shook Platt's hand and promised to go down to my bank at once and make the necessary arrangements.

I swelled with the delirious pride of the great man of affairs who sees the golden opportunity and grasps it. More crazily still, I enjoyed the sensation of being the generous benefactor to a brother man in misfortune.

Platt pulled out his watch. "We could drive down at once and have our lunch in the city. Bless my soul," he interrupted himself, "I shall never forgive myself for being so rude. I had quite forgotten Lady Pendragon and Mrs. Webster."

"Oh, they'll be delighted," I tittered. "They'll have a horrible lunch on cream buns and watercress and mince pies and champagne and

go shopping afterwards like good little millionairesses."

"Yes, indeed," said Platt heartily and quite genuinely, "they're that all right. As for us, we'll lunch at Sweeting's on oysters and stout and drink to the prosperity of Parliamentary Institutions."

I laughed at the little joke, like a madman, and shouted wildly:

"Come in, girls, and hear the news. We're all going to be elected to the Diamond Dog-collar Club."

Gretel appeared in the doorway. She was wearing a worried look which was perfectly incomprehensible.

"Where is Lou?" she said at once, her shrill voice off pitch with agitation.

"Isn't she with you?" I snapped back idiotically.

A sudden spasm of alarm set me shivering. What the devil could have happened?

Platt was more upset than any of us, of course. He had pulled off a delicate and dangerous intrigue; and at the moment of success he saw that his plan was in some incomprehensible danger. His mind's spy-glass showed him a bird's-eye view of the Old Bailey. The fact that there was no tangible reason for alarm only intensified the feeling of uneasiness.

"She must be hiding for a joke," said Gretel in a hard, cold voice, mastering her anxiety by deliberate violence.

We hunted over the apartment. There was no sign of her; and her fur coat and cap were missing from the hall. I turned to Mrs. Webster.

"What happened?" I asked curtly.

The woman had resumed her mask. She threw a defiant glance at Platt, whose eyes shot a venomous question.

"I can't understand it at all," she said slowly. "She seemed very uneasy all the time she was in the bedroom. I thought she was missing her dope. If I had had any on me, I'd have given her a big jolt. *Dummer Esel!* I'll never go out without it again so long as I live. I forget what excuse she made. I thought it was just camouflage to go and get her heroin."

Silence fell between us. Platt was afraid to say what he wanted to say. I was honestly puzzled. The incident had destroyed the effect of the cocaine I had taken. (It's extraordinary how easy it is to break the spell.)

I went to the Tantalus and poured out three brandies, dropping a pinch of snow into mine to make sure of getting back to where I was.

Mrs. Webster had recovered her equipoise.

"We're really very foolish children," she said gaily, as she sipped her brandy, "making all this fuss about nothing at all. There are a thousand and one reasons why she may have taken it into her head to go out. Why, of course – it's awfully hot in here, she probably thought she'd take a turn in the fresh air. Anyhow, you don't have to bother about me. You boys had better get down to the city and do your business. I'll wait here for her until she turns up, and spank her hard for frightening us all like this."

Platt and I put on our hats and coats. We were just shaking hands with Gretel, telling her to order herself a good lunch from downstairs, when we heard the latch-key put into the lock.

"There she is," cried Gretel gaily. "What babies we have been!"

The door opened; but it was not Lou who came in. It was Maisie Jacobs, and her face was stern and set. She gave two quick formal bows to the others, took my hand, and said in a deep, tense voice: "You must come with me at once, Sir Peter. Lady Pendragon needs you."

I went white. Once again I had been brought back from a complex chaos of conflicting emotions to the bed-rock truth which had been buried so elaborately and so often.

The deepest thing in myself was my love for my wife. I resented the realisation, and yet I could not bring myself to admit it. I asked, stupidly enough: "Is anything wrong?" as if Maisie's face, to say nothing of her appearance, were not sufficient guarantee of the seriousness of the situation.

"Come with me," she repeated.

Gretel had been watching the dialogue like a cat. She flashed forked lightning at Platt, thinking that his fears might betray him into saying something irrevocably stupid.

"Of course, there's only one thing to be done," she said hurriedly, summing the psychology of the situation in a brilliant synthesis. "You must go at once with Miss Jacobs, Sir Peter. I needn't say how terribly anxious I feel; but I hope there is nothing really wrong. I'll look in late

this afternoon with Mr. Platt for news; and if everything is all right – I won't allow myself to think that it can be otherwise – we can make an appointment for the morning over our business affairs. Don't let's lose any time."

I shook hands hastily and slipped my hand into Maisie's arm. She ran downstairs with me, leaving the others to wait for the lift.

CHAPTER IV
OUT OF HARM'S WAY

Lamus's motor was at the door. Maisie sprang to the wheel and drove off without saying a word. I shivered at her side, filled with inexplicable qualms. The exaltation of the cocaine had completely left me. It seemed to increase my nervousness; and yet I resorted to it again and again during the short drive.

When we got to the studio, Lala was sitting as usual at the desk, but Lamus was walking up and down the room with his hands behind his back; his head bowed in thought so deep that he seemed not to notice our arrival. Lou had not removed her furs. She was standing like a statue in the middle of the room. The only sign of life was that her face continually flushed from white to red and back again. Her eyes were closed. For some reason or other she reminded me of a criminal awaiting sentence.

Lamus stopped short in his stride and shook hands with me.

"Take your things off, and sit down, Sir Peter," he said brusquely. His

manner was completely different from anything I'd ever seen in him. He turned away and flung himself into a chair, searched in his pockets for an old black pipe, filled it and lit it. He seemed the prey of a peculiar agitation. That again was utterly unlike him. He cleared his throat and got up, with an entire change of behaviour. He offered me one of his millionaire cigars and motioned to Lala to get me a drink.

"This is the latest fashion in the studio," said Lala gaily. She was obviously trying to relieve the tension. "Basil invented it last night. We call it Kubla Khan No. 2. As you see, it's half gin and half Calvados, with half a teaspoonful of crème de menthe and about twenty drops of laudanum. You filter it through cracked ice. It's really the most refreshing thing I know."

I accepted the luxuries automatically, but I couldn't help fidgeting. I wanted to get down to business. I could feel that something urgent was on hand. I didn't like the way Lou was acting. She stayed so absolutely still and silent, it was uncanny.

Lamus had taken three matches to light his pipe and it kept on going out between almost every puff. By-and-by he threw it angrily on the carpet and lighted a cigar. There was a club fender round the grate. Maisie was sitting on it swinging her legs impatiently. We all seemed to be waiting for something to happen and it was as if nobody knew where to begin.

"Tell him, Lou," said Lamus suddenly.

She started as if he had struck her. Then she turned and faced me. For the first time in my life I realised how tall she was.

"Cockie," she said, "I've come to the cross-roads." She made a movement of swallowing, tried to go on, and failed.

King Lamus sat up in his chair. He had completely recovered himself; and was watching the scene with impersonal, professional interest. Lala bent over his chair, and whispered long and earnestly in his ear. He nodded.

Again he cleared his throat, and then began to speak in a strained voice.

"I think the simplest way in the long run is for Lady Pendragon to tell Sir Peter, as she has already told us, exactly what has happened, as if she were in the witness-box."

Lou began to twist herself about uneasily.

"I'm fed up," she burst out at last.

"The witness will kindly control herself," remarked Lamus, judicially.

The callousness of his tone restored Lou not merely to herself, but to herself as she might have been before I ever knew her.

"When those people arrived this afternoon," she said quite calmly, "I saw at once that they were up to some game. I knew why Gretel wanted to get me out of the room, and I tackled her about it point-blank. She told me the truth, I think, as nearly as a woman of that sort can ever get to it. Something about buying shares in a chemical works?"

"Yes, certainly," I returned, and I could feel the hostility creeping into my voice. "And why not? It's a wonderful investment and the chance of my life financially, and I don't see why women have to poke their noses into men's business which they don't understand and never will. Between you, you may have made me miss my chance. Confound you! If I knew where to find Platt, I'd go around and sign the contract this moment. As it is, I can go down to the bank and arrange to get the money."

I pulled out my watch.

"I can't even have my lunch, I suppose," I went on, working myself up deliberately into a fury.

Lou walked a few steps away and then turned back and faced me.

"Accept my apologies, Sir Peter," she said, in icy, deliberate tones. "I have no right whatever to interfere with your plans. After all, they don't concern me any more."

I rose to my feet and flung away the half-smoked cigar into the fireplace.

"What do you mean by that?" I said passionately. I had something else in mind to say, but all of a sudden my whole being seemed to falter. I sat down weakly in the chair, gasping for breath. Through my half-shut eyes I could see Lou take an impulsive step towards me; and then, controlling herself, she recoiled as a man might who had approached what he thought was a beautifully marked piece of fallen timber and recognised it for a rattlesnake.

The pulse of my brain was beating feebly and slowly; but she went on with pitiless passion, and swept me away with the tempestuous rush of her contempt.

"I made an excuse, and came to see what was going on. I found you had utterly forgotten the facts. You were sniffing cocaine, not as an experiment, not because of any physical need, but as a vice pure and simple. You were already insane with it. I might have stood that, for I loved you. But that you should plan to become the partner of that murderous villain with his hypocritical piety, that was another matter. That was a matter of honour. I don't know how long I stood there. I lived a lifetime in a second, and I made up my mind once for all to be done with such dirt. I slipped out and came here. I'm half insane myself at this moment with craving for H.; but I won't take it till I've seen this thing through. The pain of my body helps me to bear up against the mortal anguish of my soul. Oh, I know it's heroics and hysterics – you can call me what you like – what you say doesn't count any more. But I want to live; and I have asked Basil to take me away as once he promised to do long before I met you. He has promised to cure me, and I hold him to that. He has promised to take me away, and I hold him to that. You can get a divorce. You'd better. For I never want to look upon your face again."

The other three people in the room did not exist for me. I had to brace myself to meet Lou's attack. There was absolute silence except for the sound of my sniffing. I became my own master again, and broke out into a fit of yelling laughter.

"So that's the game, is it?" I answered at last.

"You are selling me out to buy a third share in that cad!"

I stopped to try to think of some viler insults; but my brain refused to work. It merely prompted me to abuse of the type usually associated with bargees. I spluttered out a torrent of foul language; but I felt even at the time that I was not doing myself justice.

My remarks were received with complete indifference. Even Lou merely shrugged her shoulders, and looked at Lamus as much as to say, "You see, I was right."

Lamus slowly shook his head. As a matter of fact, I could hardly see. My eyesight was disturbed in some peculiar way which frightened me, and my heart began to protest. I took out the cocaine once more. To my astonishment, Lamus bounded from his chair and took the bottle from my hands. I wanted to get up and kill him; but a deathly faintness seized

me. The room swam. Lamus returned to his chair, and once again silence fell on the studio.

I think I must have lost consciousness for a while for I do not remember who put an ice-cold towel round my head or how it came about that the freezing moisture dripped down my spine.

I came to myself with a heavily heaved sigh. Every one was in the same position as before, except that Lou had taken off her furs and curled herself up on the settee.

"If you feel well enough, Sir Peter," said Lamus, "you may as well hear the end of the story."

Lou suddenly choked with sobs and buried her head in the cushions. Lamus gave a gesture which Lala apparently understood. She came forward and stood in front of me with her hands behind her back like a child repeating a lesson.

"Sir Peter," she said in a gentle voice, "Basil explained to Lady Pendragon that she was taking a very wrong view of the matter. He told her that when people are getting over drug-habits they were liable to say and do things entirely foreign to their characters. We all know how abundantly you have shown your courage and your sense of honour. We know your race, and we know your exploits. What happened at the interview with Mr. Platt didn't count. You were a sick man. That was all. Maisie suggested that she should go round and fetch you; and thank heaven she got there in time!"

Lou twisted herself round, and turned savagely on King Lamus.

"I hold you to your promise," she cried violently. "I hold you to your promise."

"That, once more," he said calmly, "is simply because you are a sick woman as much as he is a sick man."

"So it's honourable to break your word to a sick woman, is it?" she flashed back like a tigress.

A curious smile curled his lips.

"Well, what does Sir Peter say?" he asked with a kind of lazy humour.

I suddenly became acutely conscious of what a ridiculous figure I was cutting, sitting there like a sick monkey with a towel round my head. I tore it off – and dashed it to the ground.

Lala came forward immediately and picked it up. I felt the action as an insult. I was being treated as a person who is a nuisance making a mess in another man's studio. The effect was to induce a surly mood.

"What I say doesn't seem to matter," I answered gruffly. "But since you ask, I say this. Take her and keep her and let me hear no more of her. And I'll say thank you."

My own voice made me wince. Could it really be I who was indulging in this vulgar repartee? It was an extraordinary thing the way everything that happened seemed to make my position less and less dignified.

The thought was interrupted by Lou's gleaming tones.

"There, Basil, he sets me free. I come to you without a stain. You can keep your promise without breaking your faith."

She got up from the sofa and went across to his chair. She threw herself at his feet, and buried her face in his knees; while her long arms reached up and groped for his face to stroke it.

He patted her head affectionately.

"Yes," he said, "we're free, and I'll keep my promise. I'll cure you, and I'll take you away with me. But will you let me make one condition?"

She lifted her face to his. In spite of the physical wreckage of the last few months, love was able to transform her bodily. She was radiantly beautiful. She only waited for him to take her in his arms. She was trembling all over with ecstatic passion.

I gripped the arms of my chair in futile rage. Before my very face the only woman I had ever loved had disowned me, cast me off with contempt, and was offering herself to another man with the same impulsive ardour that she had once shown toward me. No, by all the powers of hell, it was worse! For I had wooed her rapturously; and he had made no effort.

"One condition?" her voice rang high and clear through the studio. "I'm giving you myself, my Lord and lover; body and soul to have and to hold. What do conditions matter to me?"

"Well," said King Lamus, "it's really only a small condition; and to prove that I keep my promises, I must keep them all round. You see, I promised to cure Sir Peter, too, and so my condition is that he comes with us."

She sprang to her feet as if a cobra had struck her. Her long arms wrestled against the unresisting air. The humiliation was unspeakable.

Lamus put his pipe away in his pocket, rose to his feet, and stretched himself like some great lazy lion. He took her in his arms and held her firmly, fixing his eyes upon her tortured face; the long jagged scarlet mouth stretched to a tragic square through which the scream refused to come.

He shook her shoulders gently. Her rigid muscles began to relax.

"It's a deal, then, little girl," he said.

Her mouth closed, and then curled itself into a smile of exquisite happiness. The sombre fire of lust died out of her eyes. They kindled with the light of understanding.

He put his arm around her waist, and brought her over to me, his right hand fastened under my armpit. And he lifted me bodily out of my chair as if he had reached down like Hercules into the darkest depths of hell, and dragged forth a damned soul into the light of heaven.

He put her hands in mine and closed his own over them.

"Whom God hath joined together," he said solemnly, "let no man put asunder."

He turned on his heel and became a man of quick decisive action.

"Maisie," he said, "you have the key. Go over and have their things packed and leave them in the cloak room at Victoria. Lala, 'phone for reserve places and a cabin for these good people on the boat. London's no place for us – too many philanthropists about seeking whom they may devour. Ring up Dupont and have him send in dinner for five for seven o'clock. We'll catch the ten o'clock and be in Telepylus *sabse jeldi*."

Maisie was already out of the studio and Lala at the telephone before he had finished talking. He turned to us with the same affectation of hustle.

"Here, young people," he said breezily. "Your nerves are all shot to pieces, and no wonder. White tablets for two and a little H. to sweeten them. And you've missed your lunch! That's too bad. We'll have an old-fashioned high tea. I know there's something to eat in the coal scuttle or somewhere, and Lala can cook something while I make the buttered toast.

"You sit down and talk and make your plans for honeymoon number eight, or whichever it is. And don't get in my way, because I'm going to

be a very busy man. In fact, it's rather lucky that I've acquired the habit of starting for three years' trips around the world at three minutes notice."

It was half an hour before tea was ready. Lou and I sat on the sofa, shaken and sore by what we had gone through. Morally, mentally, physically – we were both aching with the most cruel fatigue. And yet its waves surged vainly against the silent and immovable rock of our sublime felicity. It did not find expression. We were far too weary. And yet we were aware in some deepest part of our consciousness, laid bare for the first time by the remorseless stripping off of all its upper layers, that it existed. It always had existed "before the beginning of years," and always would exist. It had nothing to do with conditions of time and space. It was an ineffable union, in infinity, of our individualities.

I must not describe our journey to Telepylus in any detail. If once the beauty of the place were discovered, it would soon be spoilt. There is no harm, however, in indicating what the place itself is like, especially as not less than three thousand years ago it became one of the most famous places in the world. And one of its chief claims was that even then it was famous for the ruins of forgotten civilisations. Today, the hand of man has left ephemeral scribbles all over the great rock which dominates the city.

Approaching Telepylus from the west, we were astounded when that mighty crag burst into view as the train rounded a corner. Like another Gibraltar, it stood out against a background of sky twelve hundred feet above the sea. It stretched out two great paws over the city like a crouching lion playing with its prey which it was about to devour – as indeed it is.

The biggest morsel there is a magnificent cathedral dating from the Normans. It stands on an eminence below the edge of the overhung cliff, and beneath it the town is spread like a fan. It is reduced to insignificance by the cathedral as the cathedral is by the rock; and yet one's familiarity with the size of an ordinary house makes one run up the scale instead of down it.

The town is witness to the stupendous size of the cathedral; and as soon as one has realised the cathedral, it, in its turn, becomes a measure of the grandeur of the rock.

We walked up from the station to the residence of King Lamus, high on the hillside above the neck of land which joins it to the rock. The cliffs towered above us. They were torn into huge pinnacles and gullies; but above the terrific precipices we could see the remains of successive civilisations; Greek temples, Roman walls, Saracen cisterns, Norman gateways, and houses of all periods were perishing slowly on the gaunt, parched crags.

It was very hard work for Lou and myself to climb the hill in the wretched condition of our health. We had to sit down repeatedly on the huge boulders which lined the paths that wound among the well-tilled fields dotted with gnarled grey olives.

The air of the place was a sublime intoxication, and yet its enchantment merely rubbed into our souls the shame of our wretched physical condition. We had to take several goes of heroin on the way. We didn't see why we couldn't have had a carriage part of the way. But it was part of King Lamus's plan, no doubt that we should be stung with the realisation of our impotence in so divine a spot, where every voice of nature swelled the chorus that spurred us to physical activity. Our invalidism had not seemed so horribly unnatural in London as it did in this consecrated temple of beauty.

Lamus himself seemed invigorated to an extraordinary degree by his home-coming. He gambolled like a young goat while we plodded gaspingly up the slope. And while we rested he told us the history of the monuments that crumbled on the crags.

"This place will help you to correct your ideas," he said, "of what is permanent, so far as anything is permanent."

We were indeed filled with a feeling of the futility of human effort as we contemplated the layers of civilisations, and looked down upon that last of them which was still flourishing, although the signs of decay were only too obvious. The modern town was not even built with the idea of defying the centuries. It was essentially flimsy and ramshackle, and the events of the last few hours had given repeated evidence not only of the state of social unrest which was likely at any moment to lay the modern structure in ruins, but of general lassitude and lack of energy on the part of everybody with whom we came into contact.

Our little party obviously represented undreamed-of possibilities of doing good business. But no one seemed to want to fulfil even that last of human ambitions: the acquiring of the good will of prosperous travellers.

"Don't be downhearted," laughed Lamus. "Your trouble is that you are looking for permanence in the wrong place. Do you see those two men?"

On the road below us were two goatherds, one driving his flock up from the town after having been milked, the other driving them down for that purpose.

Lamus quoted two lines of Greek poetry. I did not remember enough to be able to translate them, but the words had an extraordinarily familiar ring. Lamus translated.

"'The city Telepylus, where the shepherd who drives his flock into the town salutes another who is driving them out, and the other returns his salute. A man in that country could earn double wages if he could do without sleep, for they work much the same by night as they do by day.'

"That was written three thousand years ago, and even the name of the woman who wrote that poem, albeit it is one of the most famous poems in the world, is lost. But there are the shepherds saluting each other today as they did then. ΠΑΝΤΑ ΡΕΙ said Heracleitus, 'all things flow.' And everything that tries to escape that law, that relies on its strength, that becomes rigid, that endeavours to call a halt, is broken up by the irresistible waves of time. We think steel stronger than water; but we cannot build a ship to resist its action. Compare the soft-flowing winds with the inflexible rock. We breathe those winds into our lungs today – the air is as fresh as ever. But see how those temples and strongholds, nay, the very crags themselves, have been worn down by the languorous caresses of this invigorating breeze. That is one of the reasons why I came to live here, though one hardly needs support after one glance at the incomparable beauty of the place; a beauty which varies every day and never tires. Look at the sunset every night. It is good for two hours of grand opera. It is almost stupefying to sit on the terrace of the villa and watch the ever-changing glories of night-fall. And night itself! There stands the Pole Star over the rock.

As the months move the Great Bear wheels about its stable splendour, and one's mind begins to work on a totally different scale of time. Each revolution of the heavens about the Pole is like the second hand of one's spiritual watch."

We listened with enthralled attention. The beauty of the place beat hard upon our brains. It was unbelievable. Patches of cancer like London and Paris were cut ruthlessly out of our consciousness. We had come from the ephemeral pretentiousness of cities to a land of eternal actuality. We were re-born into a world whose every condition was on a totally different scale to anything in our experience. A sense of innocence pervaded us. It was as if we had awakened from a nightmare; our sense of time and space had been destroyed; but we knew that our old standards of reality had been delusions, clocks and watches were mechanical toys. In Telepylus, our time-keeper was the Nature of which we were part.

We walked on for another five minutes; but again weakness overcame us. The scenery was blotted out by the persistent ache for heroin. We satisfied the craving, but the act now seemed abominable. There was no one to see us; and yet we felt as if Nature herself were offended by the presence of a monstrosity.

"I'll go on to the Abbey," said Lamus. "You'd better take it easy. I'll tell them to get some refreshments ready and send some one down to bring you along."

He waved his hand and strode up the hill with the steady swinging step of the practised mountaineer.

Lou's hand crept into mine. We were alone with nature. A new feeling had been born in us. The sense of personality had somehow faded out. I drew her gently into my arms; and we exchanged a long kiss such as we had never done before. We were not kissing each other. We were parts of the picture, whose natural expression it was to kiss.

"Hadn't we better go on?" said Lou after a while, releasing herself.

But at this moment we found ourselves confronted by a very extraordinary person indeed. It was a fair-haired boy of five years old, bare-footed but dressed in a short robe of rich blue with wide sleeves and a hood; the lining was of scarlet. He had a very serious face, and accosted us with a military salute –

"Do what thou wilt shall be the whole of the Law," said the little fellow stoutly, and held out his hand. "I've come to take you up to the Abbey."

Even Lou realised that it was quite impossible to pick up such an important little person and kiss him. We entered into the solemnity of the occasion with proper dignity, and got up and shook hands.

Then, running down behind him, came an even smaller boy.

"Love law, love will," he said. It was obviously a point of politeness.

"They don't know what to say," explained the elder boy in a lenient tone. "My name is Hermes," he said to Lou, "and this is my friend Dionysus."

We broke into a fit of uncontrollable laughter which Hermes evidently thought highly improper. But Dionysus said to Lou, "I'll dive you a bid tiss."

She caught up the astonishing brat, and returned his salute with interest. When she put him down, he gave each of us one of his hands while Hermes led the way up the hill in an extremely business-like manner, looking back from time to time to make sure that we were all right.

Dionysus seemed to think it his business to entertain us with an account of the various objects along the road.

"That's the nice man's house down there," he said,

"I'll take you to lunch with him if you promise to behave properly. And that's where the goat-woman lives," he went on, apparently assured by our guarantees of proper conduct.

The solemnity of the elder boy and the rollicking disposition of the other carried us from spasm to spasm of suppressed laughter.

"We seem to have walked straight into a fairy tale," said Lou.

"The Big Lion says that that's the only true kind of tale," replied Hermes, evidently prepared to argue the subject at great length if necessary. But I admitted the truth of his statement without difficulty.

"That's the Abbey," he went on, as we turned the corner of the hillside. And a long, low, white building came into sight.

"But that isn't an Abbey," I protested. "That's a villa."

"That's because you're looking with the wrong kind of eyes," objected Hermes. "I used to think the same myself before I was educated."

"Do you think Mr. Lamus will be able to educate us?" I asked, overpowered by a sense of the comicality of the situation.

298

"Oh, he isn't Mr. Lamus here," retorted Hermes loftily. "Here he's the Big Lion, and of course he can train anybody that isn't too old or too stupid. I was very stupid myself when I first came here," he continued in an apologetic tone. "It was the turning point of my career."

The child was certainly not more than five years old, and his conversation was absolutely incredible. The feeling grew that we had somehow strayed into an enchanted country. At the same time the country was enchanting.

Dionysus was all on fire to get us up to the Abbey, and tugged at our arms.

"Now, Di," said Hermes, "you know it's wrong to pull at people like that. It's one of the rules," he explained to Lou, "not to interfere with people. The Big Lion says that every one would get on all right if only he were left alone."

He seemed to think the statement required explanation.

"Cypris is reading Gibbon to us this week; and she shows us how all the trouble came from people meddling with other people's business."

I shouted with laughter. "Gibbon?" I cried,

"What next, I wonder?"

"Well, one must know Roman history," explained Hermes, in the tone of a headmaster addressing an educational conference.

"And what did you read last week?" said Lou, though she was rocking with laughter as much as I was.

"Shelley was being read to us," he corrected. "We don't read ourselves."

"The Tenth don't dance," I quoted.

"Don't be an ass, Cockie," said Lou.

"Well, Hermes, but why don't you read?"

"The Big Lion doesn't want us to learn," he said.

"We have to learn to use our eyes, and reading spoils them."

"But why?" asked Lou, in surprise. "I don't understand. I thought reading was the best way to get knowledge."

Dionysus put his foot down.

"Enough of Betause, be he damned for a dod."

It wasn't physical fatigue this time. These amazing children had made us forget all physical sensation. But when one is walking uphill it is

impossible to laugh as we wanted to laugh. We sat down on a patch of grass ablaze with flowers and rolled over and over, tearing up tufts of grass and biting them to overcome our emotions.

Dionysus evidently thought it was a game and began to romp; but Hermes, though evidently eager to join in the fun, was held back by his sense of responsibility.

"Where on earth did you learn such extraordinary language?" cried Lou at last, the tears running down her cheeks.

Hermes became more serious than ever.

"It's from the *Book of the Law*. Change not so much as the style of a letter," he said.

We began quite seriously to wonder whether we had not got into one of those fantastic waking dreams with which heroin had made us familiar. But this was a dream of a totally different quality. It had a strain of wholesomeness and actuality running through its incredible tissue of marvels.

At last we sat up and drew a long breath. Hermes hastened to assist Lou to her feet, and the action, natural as it was, coming from such an extraordinary quarter, set us off laughing again.

Dionysus was regarding us with big serious eyes.

"You'll do," he suddenly decided; and began to execute a little step-dance of his own.

But we could see that Hermes, with all his unwillingness to interfere with other people, was impatient; and we scrambled to our feet. This time, Lou took his hand, and left me to bring up the rear with Dionysus, who poured forth an unending stream of prattle. I could not even hear it; the whole thing was too much for me.

We came out on to the terrace of the villa; King Lamus was standing in the open doorway. He had changed his travelling clothes for a silken robe of the brightest blue, with scarlet linings to the hood and sleeves like that of the boys. But on the breast in golden embroidery was an Egyptian eye within an equilateral triangle which was surrounded by a sun-blaze of rays.

Behind him stood two women in robes similar to those of the boys. One was about twenty-five years old, and the other nearer forty. Both

had bobbed hair; the younger woman's of flaming chestnut, the elder's a rich silvery grey.

"That's the Bid Lion," said Dionysus, "with Athena and Cypris."

Hermes drew back and told us confidentially: "Now you be the first to say 'Do what thou wilt' to show you're more awake than they are."

We nodded encouragingly, and carried out the programme with success.

"Love is the law, love under will," answered the three people in the doorway. "Welcome to the Abbey of Thelema!"

In a moment, as by the breaking of a spell, the seriousness broke up. We were introduced warmly to the women, and began jabbering as if we had known each other all our lives. Basil had taken the two gods on his knees, and was listening happily to Hermes' story of how he had acquitted himself of his responsibility.

A table had been brought out on to the terrace, and we sat down to a meal. Athena put us in our places, and then explained "that it was the custom at the Abbey to eat in silence as soon," she said, "as we have said Will."

"What did she mean by saying Will?" We had heard of saying grace before meat, but it was a long while since either of us had said it. However, the little mystery was soon explained.

She knocked on the table with the handle of a Tunisian dagger, its steel blade inlaid with silver. She knocked three times, then five, then three times more. Some significance was apparently attached to this peculiar method. She then said "Do what thou wilt shall be the whole of the Law."

Dionysus showed signs of strong agitation. It was his turn to answer, and he was terribly afraid of forgetting his words in the presence of strangers. He looked up to Cypris pleadingly, and she whispered into his ear.

"What is thy will?" with a sudden burst of confidence and pride.

"It is my will to eat and drink," replied Athena gravely.

"To what end?" inquired Dionysus doubtfully.

"That my body may be fortified thereby."

The brat looked about him uneasily, as if the answer had taken

the wind out of his sails. Cypris pressed his hand, and he brightened up again.

"To what end?" he repeated boldly.

"That I may accomplish the Great Work," replied Athena.

Dionysus seemed to have got on to his game. He retorted without the slightest hesitation.

"Love is the law, under will."

"Love is the law, love under will," corrected Cypris and the baby repeated it solemnly.

"Fall to," cried Athena cheerfully, and sat down.

CHAPTER V
AT TELEPYLUS

Lunch consisted of fish of a kind that we had never seen before; long, thin bodies with beaks like sword-fish. We were very hungry; but they would have tasted exquisite under any circumstances. The meal continued with cheese, honey, and medlars; and ended gloriously with real Turkish coffee; not one cup but as many as we wanted; and Benedictine.

We had drunk the rough, strong wine of the country with the meal; and to us it tasted as if it had been the best red wine ever made. It had not been submitted to any chemical process. There was a sort of vitality inherent in it. It was primitive like all the arrangements of the Abbey, but the freshness and naturalness of everything made more than amends even to our cultivated palates. We were apparently sitting down to lunch with a choice selection of Olympian Deities and the food seemed to be in keeping!

Besides that, we had no time to be critical; we were overwhelmed by the beauty of our surroundings.

Far away to the west, a line of hills ran out into the sea, the farther peaks were over fifty miles away, yet in that translucent atmosphere of

spring they stood out sharply. We could even see in front of the range a small, dark line of crags which jutted out parallel with them and about ten miles nearer. Thence the coast line swept towards us in a complex curve of indescribable beauty and majesty. Telepylus being itself on a promontory, there was nothing to break the mighty stretch of sea between us and the distant range with its twin cones which overhang the principal city of the country; the city from which we had started that morning.

To the left of the coast line, a range of tumbled mountains, fantastically shaped and coloured, reached thence to the very hillside on which we were sitting. In front the ocean reached to the horizon. The light played upon its waves like some mysterious melody of Debussy's. It varied in hue from the most delicate canary yellow and glaucous green through infinite changing shades of peacockry to lilacs and deep purples. Ever-changing patches of colour wandered about the surface in kaleidoscopic fantasy.

A little to the right again, the limitless prospect of water was cut off by a precipitous cliff crowned by the ruins of a church, and up again to the right, the sheer crag reared its perpendicular terror to the skyline; a jagged line of quaintly carven pinnacle. Beyond these the slope suddenly eased off, and thence the rock took a final leap to its summit on which stood the remains of ancient Grecian temples.

With even greater suddenness the right hand precipice plunged clear into the sea. But on this side the view was closed in by groves of olive, cactus, and oak. The terrace before us was edged by a rock garden where flowered enormous geraniums, bushes of huge daisies, tall stems of purple iris, and a clump of reeds twice a man's height that swayed like dancers to the music of the gentle breeze that streamed up from the slopes of the sea.

Below the terrace were mulberry, cherry, and apple trees in blossom, together with a number of many-coloured trees whose names I did not know.

Between the house and the hill that overhung it on the south was a grassy garden shadowed by a gigantic tree of unfamiliar leaves, and behind this stood two Persian nuts, like cyclopean telegraph poles tufted with dark green leaves which reminded one of a guardsman's busby.

With the arrival of the coffee the rule of silence was broken. But Lamus had already left the table. Athena explained that the theory of meals in the Abbey was that they were deplorable interruptions to work, and that

"Will" was said before beginning to eat in order to emphasise the fact that the only excuse for eating was that it was necessary to keep one's body in condition to assist one in the performance of the Great Work, whatever that might be in any particular case. When any one had finished he or she got up and went away without ceremony, the interruption being over. Lamus now came out of the house in a flannel shirt and buckskin riding breeches. He sat down and began to drink his coffee and Benedictine. He was smoking a thin, black cigar, so strong that its very appearance was alarming.

"I hope you'll excuse me this afternoon," he said, "I have to go and inspect the other houses. This house is the antechamber, so to speak, where we receive strangers. In the other houses, various courses of training are carried on according to the Wills of their inhabitants. You will sleep here, of course, and considering the reason for which you have come – No, Dionysus, this isn't the time to say 'He shall fall down into the pit called Because, and there he shall perish with the dogs of Reason' – I will sleep down here for the present instead of in my lonely little tower, as I usually do."

We noticed that Cypris and the boys had slipped away quietly; but Athena sat engrossed in studying us "In the absence of Lala," he said, "Sister Athena is our chief psychologist. You will find her knowledge very useful to you and your work. I will leave her to talk things over with you for the next couple of hours. But, of course, the first thing is to get you rested from your journey."

He got up and walked off round the corner of the house. We didn't feel that we needed rest, we were much too interested by the atmosphere of the place. It was not merely the curious customs that stimulated our imaginations; there was an indefinable atmosphere about the place and the people which left us at a loss. The mixture of simplicity and elegance was in itself bizarre but still more so was the combination of absolute personal liberty with what was evidently in some ways a rather severe discipline. The automatic regularity with which everything was done seemed to imply an almost Prussian routine.

Lou saw the point at once, and with her usual frankness asked Sister Athena outright to explain it.

"Thank you for reminding me," said Sister Athena. "The Big Lion said you had better rest. Suppose you lie down in the studio. I know you don't want to go to sleep, but we can talk there just as well as we can here. So you'd better make yourselves comfortable while I explain our funny little ways."

The arrangements for repose were as primitive as everything else. The studio was furnished with narrow mattresses on steel springs on the floor. They were covered with comfortable cushions. We threw ourselves down with a certain hesitation; but immediately discovered that we were much more at home than if we had been at a higher elevation. It made the room seem larger, and the sensation of rest was more in evidence. There was a sort of finality about being so low, and it was certainly much more convenient to have our drinks and cigarettes on the floor than on a table. We found out that we had always gone about the world with a subconscious fear of knocking things over. I began to understand why a picnic on the grass gives such a sense of freedom. It was the absence of a worry which had annoyed us none the less because we had not been aware of it.

Sister Athena stretched herself out on a folding chair, also very low. It was no trouble for her to pick up her glass from the ground.

"About what you asked," she began, "it's perfectly true that we have vanadium steel discipline in this place; but we are made to think out everything for ourselves and the regulations don't bother us, as soon as we see their object."

In civilised life, so-called, at least two-thirds of every one's time is wasted on things that don't matter. The idea of this place is to give every one the maximum time for doing his own Will. Of course, if you come here with the fixed determination to resent everything that is different to what you are accustomed to, you can work yourself up into a constant irritation, which is all the worse because there is nothing to interfere with your indulgence. When I came here two years ago, every detail was an annoyance and an insult. But I came around gradually, through seeing that everything had been thought out. These people were enormously more efficient than I was, through economising the time and trouble which I had been accustomed to waste on trifles. I could no more fight them than Dionysus could fight Jack Dempsey. There is absolutely nothing

to do here in the way of amusement except walking and climbing and reading, and playing Thelema; and, of course, bathing in the summer. The housework occupies practically no time at all because of the simplification of life. There is nowhere to go and nothing to do. The result is that with eating and everything else thrown in there is not much more than an hour of our waking time which is occupied by what one may call necessary work. Compare that with London! Mere dressing accounts for more than that. These robes are decorative enough for a royal banquet and yet they're absolutely practical for anything but rock climbing. To dress or undress is a matter of thirty seconds. Even our climbing clothes – it's merely a shirt and a pair of breeches, stockings and tennis shoes instead of these sandals – and off we go."

Lou and I listened sleepily to this disquisition. We were so interested that we simply had to keep awake. We each took a big sniff of heroin for the purpose. Sister Athena jumped up from her chair.

"That reminds me," she said, "I must get you your charts."

She went to a cabinet and produced two forms. We languidly marked our little crosses in the proper section.

"Excuse the interruption," she said, "but the Magical Record is always the first consideration in the Abbey."

The heroin woke me completely.

"I see the point, I think. All your rules are intended to reduce the part of life that has to be run by rules, as much as possible."

"That's it," she nodded emphatically.

"But I say," said Lou, "it's all very well; but I don't know whatever I'm to do with myself. The time must hang frightfully heavy on your hands."

"God forgive you," cried Athena. "One never has a minute one can call one's own!"

We laughed outright.

"It's easy to see you're a pupil of King Lamus. You have acquired his talent for paradox in a very complete manner."

"I know what you mean," she said, smiling. "If you're a lazy person, this is the worst place in the world for getting bored, and the lazier you determine to be the more bored you get. We had two people last year, absolutely hopeless rotters. They called themselves writers, and imagined

they were working if they retired solemnly after breakfast and produced half a page of piffle by lunch. But they didn't know the meaning of work; and the place nearly drove them insane. They were bored with the Abbey, and bored with each other, and were very insulted because everybody laughed at them. But they couldn't see the way out, and wouldn't take it when it was shown them. It made them physically ill, and they went away at last to every one's relief to an environment where they could potter about indefinitely and pose as great geniuses. The Big Lion does more in a day than they will ever do in their lives if they live into the next century. I'm sorry, too, as sorry as sorry can be. They were delightful personally, when they weren't pinned to a cork by their fixed ideals of what we ought to be doing. They had come one thousand miles to be trained, and then wouldn't give us a chance to train them. But they have good brains, and the stamp of this Abbey never wears off. They're better and wiser for their stay here, and they'll be better and wiser still as soon as they allow themselves to admit it!"

"You don't encourage us much," said Lou in a really alarmed tone. "I haven't got even the consolation of these people. I can't fool myself that I am a *Wunderkind*. You probably know without my telling you that I've done nothing all my life but potter. And if I've nothing to potter about, I go off into the blackest boredom."

Sister Athena acquiesced.

"Yes, this place is kill or cure," she admitted, with a laugh. "But I'm glad to say that it's cure for most people. The two I was telling you about only failed because their vanity and selfishness was so extreme. They interpreted everything wrong, and expected the world to fall down and worship them for being wastrels. And at every turn they found the Big Lion in the way, to bring them back to reality. But the truth was too bitter medicine for them. If they had accepted the facts, they could have altered the facts; and learnt to do something worthwhile. But they preferred to cherish delusions of persecution. They persuaded themselves that they were being crucified when they were only having their faces washed. But the paint of self-esteem had been put on too thick; so away they went, and said how badly they'd been treated. Well, they had asked for the treatment themselves; and it will do them some good yet when they see

the thing in perspective and discover that the adulation of their silly little clique of cranks in Soho is not really so good for their souls as the accurate abuse of their friends in this Abbey."

"Yes, I see that all right," said Lou, "and I know Basil too well to make that kind of fool of myself. But I'm still a little worried about this horrid efficiency of yours. Whatever am I to do with myself? Don't you understand that it was really boredom or the dread of it that drove me to heroin to pass away the time?"

"That's just it," said Athena very seriously, "This is all kinds of a place for driving a fellow to drink. And that's why the Big Lion insists on our going through the mill. But it takes us a very short time to realise that there is not enough heroin in the world to tide us over a single day in such a ghastly place, so we quit."

Here was another of Basil's paradoxes in full working order. But they came quite differently from the lips of a steady-going serious-minded person of this kind. The personality of the Big Lion is his greatest asset in one way, but in another it handicaps him frightfully. His cynical manner, his habitual irony, the sensation he produces that he is making fun of one; all these make one inclined to dismiss everything that he says as "mere paradox" without investigation. Lamus is too clever by half; but Sister Athena spoke with such simple earnestness and directness that although she too had a sense of humour of her own, Basil's ideas were very much more effective when they had passed through the machinery of her mind than when they frothed fresh from his. I had always been inclined to distrust King Lamus. It was impossible to distrust this woman who trusted him, or to doubt that she was right to trust him.

He never seemed able even to take himself seriously, perhaps because he was afraid of appearing pompous or a prig; but she had taken him seriously and got the best out of him.

"Well, Sister Athena," said Lou, "if even heroin's no good, what is?"

"I'm afraid I'll have to treat you to another paradox," she said, lighting a cigarette. "I'm afraid that at first sight you'll think there must be something wrong. It's really such a revolutionary reversal of what seems obvious. But I've been through it myself, and the plain fact is this: finding ourselves here with so much more time on our hands than we ever had in our

lives, we get desperate. In a big city, if we're bored, we simply look around for some diversion, and there are plenty of them. But here, there's no alleviation or the possibility of it. We must either go under completely or decide to swim. Here's another case where the Big Lion, who must certainly be Satan himself, economises time. One has to be very stupid not to discover within forty-eight hours that there is no possibility of amusing oneself in any of the ordinary ways. In London one could waste one's life before bringing one's mind to the point where Big Lion wants it. So one finds oneself immediately up against the fact that one has got to find something to do. Well, we go and ask Big Lion; and Big Lion says: 'Do what thou wilt.' 'But, yes,' we say, 'what is that?' He replies rudely, 'Find out.' We ask how to find out; and he says, 'How do you know what is the good of a motorcar?' Well, we think a bit; and then we tell him that we find out the use of a motorcar by examining it, looking at its various parts, comparing it and them with similar machines whose use we already know, such as the bullock wagon and the steam engine. We make up our minds that an automobile is constructed in order to travel along the high road. 'Very good,' says Big Lion, 'go up top. Examine yourself, your faculties and tendencies, the trend of your mind, and the aspirations of your soul. Allow me to assure you that you will find this investigation leaves you very little time to wonder what in the devil to do with yourself.' 'Thank you very much,' we say, 'but suppose our judgment is wrong, suppose that what we have decided is an automobile intended to go, is in reality a coffin intended to contain a corpse?' 'Quite so,' says Big Lion, 'you have to test your judgment; and you don't do that by asking the opinion of people who are probably more ignorant than yourself; you get into the beastly thing and press the proper button, and if it goes it's an automobile, and you've made no mistake. Didn't you read what it says in the *Book of the Law*: "Success is your proof"? And allow me again to assure you that when you've got yourself going, doing your True Will, you won't find you have any time to get bored."

She threw away her cigarette after lighting another from the butt. She seemed to be brooding, as if much deeper thoughts were passing through her mind than even those to which she was giving such airy expression.

We watched her intently. The heroin had calmed and intensified our

thought, which was intensely stimulated by her explanation. We had no wish to interrupt. We wished she could have gone on talking for ever.

Her self-absorption became still more marked. After a very long pause she went on slowly talking, so it seemed, to herself more than to us and with the intention to giving form to her own idea, that of instructing us.

"I suppose that must be the idea," she said.

She had a curious mouth, with square-cut lips like one sees in some old Egyptian statues, and a twist at the corners in which lurked incalculable possibilities of self-expression. Her eyes were deep-set and calm. It was a square face with a very peculiar jaw expressing terrific determination. I have never seen a face in which courage was so strongly marked.

"Yes, I think I see it now. He forces one to come to what I might call the point of death. The whole of life is reviewed in perspective, and its meaning seized. But instead of being snatched away to face the unknown, as in the case of death, one has the opportunity and the necessity to take up the old life from the point at which one left off, with a clear apprehension of the past which determines the future. That is the meaning of what he calls initiation. I understand 'Thou hast no right but to do thy will.' That is why the old hierophants shut up the candidate in silence and darkness. He had the choice between going mad or knowing himself. And when he was brought out into light and life, restored to love and liberty, he was in very truth a Neophyte, a man new-born. Big Lion puts us through it without our knowing what he's doing. Though I've been through it myself, I didn't know in this clear way what had really happened until I tried to explain it to you."

The sense of being enchanted came over me again very strongly. I looked across at Lou, and I could see in her eyes that she felt the same. But she was trembling with excitement and eagerness. Her eyes were fixed on the face of Sister Athena with devouring ardour. She was looking forward to undergoing this terrific experience. My own mood was slightly different.

Already my past life surged up before me in a series of pulsating pictures. I was revolted by the incoherence and fatuity of the past. The achievements of which I was proudest had lost their savour because they pointed to nowhere in particular. The words of Lewis Carroll came into my mind:

"A wise fish never goes anywhere without a porpoise." And quite inconsequentially my brain took up the tune:

"Will you, won't you, will you, won't you,
Won't you join the dance?"

When I woke it was, I suppose, about midnight. Rugs had been thrown over me where I lay. I was quite warm, despite the breeze that came in through the open door. It struck me as very strange that it should be open. The country was notoriously infested with brigands.

King Lamus was sitting at his desk writing by the light of a lamp. I watched him idly, feeling very comfortable and disinclined to move.

Presently I heard the deep booming of a bell in the far-off cathedral. It was twelve o'clock.

He immediately rose and went to the doorway, down the steps and on to the moonlit terrace. He faced the north. In a deep solemn voice he recited what was apparently an invocation.

"Hail unto thee who art Ra in thy silence, even unto thee who art Kephra the beetle, that travellest under the heavens in thy bark in the midnight hour of the sun. Tahuti standeth in his splendour at the prow, and Ra-Hoor abideth at the helm. Hail unto thee from the abodes of evening!"

He accompanied the speech with a complicated series of gestures. When he had finished he returned and noticed that I was awake.

"Well, did you have a good sleep?" he said softly, standing over my mattress.

"I never had a better one."

It would be impossible to give the details of even one day at Telepylus. Life there has all the fullness of the heroin life with none of its disillusions. I must simply select such incidents as bear directly on our Purgatorio. I dropped off to sleep again after a short chat with Basil about indifferent affairs, and woke in the morning very much refreshed, and yet overpowered by the conviction that it was impossible to get up without heroin.

But the bright spring sun, his rays falling so freshly on the crags green-grey and dun opposite, reminded me that I had come to Telepylus

to renew my youth. I held back my hand. Little by little, strength came back to me; but as it did so the feeling of helplessness in the absence of heroin was replaced by the presence of craving for it.

I dragged myself from the mattress and got unsteadily to my feet. Lou was still sleeping, and she looked so lovely in the pure pale light that filtered into the room that I took a firmer resolve to break off the habit that had destroyed our love. It was only in sleep that she was beautiful at all in these last months. Waking, the expression of tenseness and wretchedness, the nervous twitching of her face and the destruction of her complexion by the inability of the liver to throw off the toxic effects of the drug, made her look not only twice her age but ugly, with that ugliness of vice and illness which is so much more repulsive than any merely aesthetic errors of nature.

Lou, more than any girl I ever knew, depended for her beauty upon her spiritual state. The influence of an idea would transform her in a moment from Venus to Echidna or the reverse.

It was deep spiritual satisfaction that made her so lovely this morning. But even as I stood and looked, the horrible restlessness of the heroin craving nearly drove me to take the stuff without my body telling me what it was doing. But I detected the movement in time.

I thought a brisk walk might help me to pass through the critical moment. Just as I got out of the house, I was met by Sister Athena.

"Do what thou wilt shall be the whole of the Law," she said.

It was the regular morning greeting at the Abbey. Accustomed as I was to the phrase, it still took me rather aback.

"Good morning," I said in a rather embarrassed way.

"The answer is 'Love is the law, love under will,'" she smiled. "We exchange this greeting so as to make sure that the sight of our friends doesn't distract us from the Great Work. Now we can talk about whatever we like. Oh, no, we can't, I must first inspect your yesterday's chart."

I brought it out, and we sat down at the table together. Of course, there was only the one cross. She assumed a very severe look.

"This is extremely irregular, brother," she said. "You haven't filled in column two."

I discovered later that it was part of the system of the Abbey to pretend to be very severe about any infraction of the rules, and then to show by some pleasant remark that it wasn't meant in anger. The object was to fix in one's mind that the offence was really grave, so that the pretended scolding had all the effect of the genuine article.

Not knowing this, I was surprised when she continued: "That's all right, Cockie, we know you're a new chum."

But her finger pointed sternly to column two. It was headed "Reason for taking the dose."

Well, Dionysus had shown me the way out of that, so I turned impudently around and said:

"Enough of Because, be he damned for a dog!"

The effect was electric. We both broke into a duet of low musical laughter that seemed to me in exquisite harmony with the beauty of the April morning.

"The devil can quote scripture," she retorted, "that business about Because refers to something entirely different. The point about this (she was very serious now) is that we want you to know what is going on in your own mind. We all do so many stupid things, for bad reason or no reason at all. 'Forgive them, Father, they know not what they do' applies to nine-tenths of our actions. We get so much work done in this Abbey because we have learnt to watch our minds and prevent ourselves wasting a moment on what is worthless, or cancelling out one course of action by another, and so getting nowhere. In the case of this experiment of yours, in learning to master a drug so powerful that hardly one man in ten thousand stands a dog's chance of coming out, it's especially important because, as I'm afraid you will find out, I mean, as I hope you will find out very soon, your brain has developed certain morbid tendencies. You are liable to think crooked. Big Lion has told me already how you got to the stage where you took one dose to sleep and another to wake up again, and where you would try to conceal the amount you were taking from the very person with whom you were taking it openly. Another point is that privation always upsets the mental balance. A man who lacks food or money finds very queer thoughts come into his mind, and does things, not necessarily connected with

his necessity, obsessing though that be, which are entirely out of keeping with his character."

I took a pencil, and wrote at once against the cross in column two "In order to make the most of Sister Athena's illuminating discourse."

She laughed, merrily.

"You see, it's Adam and Eve all over again! You're trying to shift the blame on to me. By the way, I see your body is nervous at this moment. If you don't want to take heroin, as you don't, else you wouldn't have let yourself get as shaky as you are, you'd better take a white tablet. It won't put you to sleep, as you've had a night's rest, and the poor little thing won't have anything to do but run around your solar plexus and stroke all your little pussycat nerves the right way."

I took the advice and felt much better. At that moment King Lamus appeared, and challenged Sister Athena to a set of Thelema. I brought Lou out; and we sat in the courtyard and watched them play.

Thelema is so called because of the variety of strokes.

It is a sort of Fives played with an association football, but there are no side walls, only a low wall at the back over which, if the ball goes, it is out of play, as also if it strikes outside the vertical lines painted on the wall or below a ledge about a foot from the ground. The ball may be struck with any part of the body so long as it is struck clean, and the game is bewilderingly fast to watch.

After two games, the players were perspiring violently. The score was kept somewhat as in tennis, but each point had a monosyllabic name to economise time. It also had a certain startling implication – with the object of familiarising the mind with ideas which normally excited.

The whole system of King Lamus was to enable people to take no notice, that is, no emotional notice, of anything soever in life. A great deal of the fascination of drugs arises from the fuss that is made about them; the focusing of the attention upon them. Absinthe, forbidden in France, Switzerland, and Italy, is still sold freely in England, and no one ever met an English absinthe fiend. If any one took it into his head to start a newspaper campaign against absinthe, it would become a public danger in very short order.

King Lamus emancipated people's minds by adopting the contrary formula. He had all sorts of dodges for compelling people to accept the most startling sights and sounds as commonplace. The very children were confronted with the most terrifying ideas while they were still too young to have acquired settled phobias.

Hermes, at the age of five, was already accustomed to witness surgical operations and such things, to face the dangers of drowning and falling from cliffs, with the results that he had completely lost his fear of such things.

The intense activity and lightheartedness of everybody amazed us. We were asked to join in the game and our incompetence was a keen source of annoyance. We were too enfeebled by our indulgence in drugs to hold our own; and the result was to inspire us with a passionate determination to emancipate ourselves from the thraldom.

But the tribulations of the morning had only begun. It was the custom of the Abbey to celebrate the arrival of newcomers by a picnic at the top of the rock. From the Abbey, a path leads through a patch of trees to a rough narrow track between two walls. At the end of this is an aqueduct across the road, and both Lou and I were too nervous to walk along the narrow causeway. We had to go around, feeling more and more ashamed of ourselves with every incident.

On the other side, the hill rises steeply. A tongue of grass leads to a gully which is filled by the wall of the old city which crowned the rock two thousand years or more ago, when the world was less arid and the population could depend on rainfall instead of having to cluster in the neighbourhood of springs and streams for its water.

King Lamus made Hermes lead up the most astonishingly precipitous crags, with little advice and no assistance. But his hand was always within reach of the boy; so that if he made a mistake and fell he could immediately be caught without hurting himself.

But the child himself did not know how carefully he was being watched and guarded. Basil treated him in every way as a responsible leader.

Their progress was necessarily slow; but so was ours. Both Lou and I found it impossible to go more than twenty paces or so without a rest. We had plenty of time to watch them, and it was amazing to see the working

of the mind of Hermes as problem after problem presented itself to him.

There were many occasions on which it would have been easy for him to go around an obstacle, but he never attempted to do so. King Lamus had already implanted in his mind the idea that the fun of rock climbing consisted in attacking the most difficult passages.

The child would occasionally stop at the foot of a pitch, and contemplate it as if it were a mathematical problem. Once or twice he decided that it was too hard for him. On these occasions, King Lamus would go up first, calling out instructions to note the exact places where he put his hands and feet; and when it was the turn of Hermes to follow, as often as not he did so on a slack rope. His leader's example had taught him how to negotiate the difficulty.

As for Dionysus, his methods were entirely different. He had neither the intellectual power of the elder boy nor his prudence, and he climbed with a sort of tempestuous genius.

At the top of the tongue, the goat track bends suddenly to the right, under the wall, to a point where there is a breach where one can crawl through very comfortably. Here we rejoined the climbers.

"Tomorrow," said Hermes, "I shall take you up the Great Gully," with the air of a full-fledged alpine guide.

Dionysus shook his little head. "I don't know if he tan det through the hole," he lamented.

King Lamus had taken off the rope and made it into a coil by winding it around his knee and foot. We plodded painfully over very rough ground to the top of the rock. It was both exhilarating and disheartening to see the way the two boys scrambled from boulder to boulder.

At last we reached the top. The two brethren who had carried up the provisions in knapsacks had already begun to spread them out on a level patch of grass.

CHAPTER VI
THE TRUE WILL

Lou and I were both utterly exhausted by the climb; and King Lamus reminded us that this was the formula of the Abbey of Thelema at Telepylus, that every one had to reach the top, step by step, through his own exertions. There was no question of soaring into the air by alien aid; and in all probability coming to earth with a bump.

We had found ourselves repeatedly out of breath during the ascent, though it had only occupied three-quarters of an hour, and we should certainly never have reached the top without recourse to heroin.

But all the time we were lost in amazement at the behaviour of the boys; their independence, their fearlessness, and their instinctive economy of force. We had no idea that it was possible for children of that age to achieve, even physically, what they had done, apparently without effort.

And as for their moral attitude, it was entirely outside our experience. I said something of the sort; and King Lamus retorted at once that it was the moral attitude which made possible the physical attainment.

"You will find that out for yourself in the case of your own experiment. It will do you very little good to break off your present practice. When

you begin to tackle a subject, you must endure to the end, and the end never comes until you can say either yes or no, indifferently, to physical considerations."

But for all that, both Lou and I were exalted by our physical triumph over the rock, trifling as it was; and our situation on the summit reminded us of some of the sensations of flying. There was the same detachment from the affairs of the world, the same visions of normal life in perspective; the ruddy brown roofs of the houses, the patches of tilled land, the distant hillsides with their fairy-like remoteness, the level plain of the sea, the receding coast line; all these things were so many witnesses of one great truth – that only by climbing painfully to a spot beyond human intervention, could one obtain a stable point of view from which to regard the Universe in due proportion.

At once we drew the moral analogy to our physical situation, and applied it to our immediate problem. Yet, in spite of what Lamus had said, we were both obsessed by the idea that we must stop taking heroin.

The next few days passed in strenuous efforts to reduce the number of the doses, and it was then that we began to discover the animal cunning of our bodies. Do what we might, there was always a reason, an imperative reason, for taking a dose at any given moment.

Our minds, too, began to play us false. We found ourselves arguing as to what a dose was. As the doses became fewer, they became larger. Presently, we arrived at the stage where what we considered a fair dose could not be conveniently taken at a single sniff. And then, worst of all, it broke on me one day, when I was struggling hard against the temptation to indulge, that the period between doses, however prolonged it might be, was being regarded merely in that light. In other words, it was a negative thing.

Life consisted in taking heroin. The intervals between the doses did not count. It was like the attitude of the normal man with regard to sleep.

It suddenly dawned upon me that this painful process of gradually learning to abstain, was not a cure at all in any right sense of the word.

Basil was perfectly right. I must reverse the entire process and reckon my life in positive terms. That's what he means by "Do what thou wilt." I wonder what my true will is? Is there really such a thing at all? My

mathematics tells me that there must be. However many forces there may be at work, one can always find their resultant.

But this was all terribly vague. The desire to take heroin was clear-cut. It no longer produced any particular effect to take it. Now that I was getting down to two or three doses a day, at the most, it seemed as though there were no particular object in taking it, even as dulling the craving for it. I found it increasingly difficult to fill column two.

King Lamus descended on me one morning, just after I had taken a dose, and was raking my brain for a reason for my action. I was alternately chewing the end of my pencil and making meaningless marks on the paper. I told him my difficulty.

"Always glad to help," he said airily; went to a filing cabinet and produced a docket of typed manuscripts. He put it in my hand. It was headed, "Reasons for taking it."

1. My cough is very bad this morning. (Note: (a) Is cough really bad? (b) If so, is the body coughing because it is sick or because it wants to persuade you to give it some heroin?)
2. To buck me up.
3. I can't sleep without it.
4. I can't keep awake without it.
5. I must be at my best to do what I have to do. If I can only bring that off, I need never take it again.
6. I must show I am master of it – free to say either "yes" or "no". And I must be perfectly sure by saying "yes "at the moment. My refusal to take it at the moment shows weakness. Therefore I take it.
7. In spite of the knowledge of the disadvantages of the heroin life, I am really not sure whether it isn't better than the other life. After all, I get extraordinary things out of heroin which I should never have got otherwise.
8. It is dangerous to stop too suddenly.
9. I'd better take a small dose now rather than put it off till later; because if I do so, it will disturb my sleep.
10. It is really very bad for the mind to be constantly

preoccupied with the question of the drug. It is better to take a small dose to rid myself of the obsession.

11. I am worried about the drug because of my not having any. If I were to take some, my mind would clear up immediately, and I should be able to think out good plans for stopping it.

12. The gods may be leading me to some new experience through taking it.

13. It is quite certainly a mistake putting down all little discomforts as results of taking it. Very likely, nearly all of them are illusions; the rest, due to the unwise use of it. I am simply scaring myself into saying "no".

14. It is bad form morally to say "no". I must not be a coward about it.

15. There is no evidence at all that the reasonable use of heroin does not lengthen life. The Chinese claim, and English physicians agree, that opium smoking, within limits, is a practice conducive to longevity. Why should it not be the same with heroin? It has been observed actually that addicts seem to be immune to most diseases which afflict ordinary people.

16. I take it because of its being prohibited. I decline being treated like a silly schoolboy when I'm a responsible man. (Note: Then don't behave like a silly schoolboy. Why let the stupidity of governments drive you into taking the drug against your will? – K. L.)

17. My friend likes me to take it with her.

18. My ability to take it shows my superiority over other people.

19. Most of us dig our graves with our teeth. Heroin has destroyed my appetite, therefore it is good for me.

20. I have got into all sorts of messes with women in the past. Heroin has destroyed my interest in them.

21. Heroin has removed my desire for liquor. If I must choose, I really think heroin is the better.

22. Man has a right to spiritual ambition. He has evolved to what he is, through making dangerous experiments. Heroin certainly helps me to obtain a new spiritual outlook on the world. I have no right to assume that the ruin of bodily health is injurious; and "whosoever will save his life shall lose it, but whoever loseth his life for My sake shall find it."

23. So-and-so has taken it for years, and is all right.

24. So-and-so has taken it for years, and is still taking it, and he is the most remarkable man of his century.

25. I'm feeling so very, very rotten, and a very, very little would make me feel so very, very good.

26. We can't stop while we have it – the temptation is too strong. The best way is to finish it. We probably won't be able to get any more, so we take it in order to stop taking it.

27. Claude Farrere's story of Rodolphe Hafner. Suppose I take all these pains to stop drugs and then get cancer or something right away, what a fool I shall feel!

"Help you at all?" asked Lamus.

Well, honestly, it did not. I had thought out most of those things for myself at one time or another; and I seemed to have got past them. It's a curious thing that once you've written down a reason you diminish its value. You can't go on using the same reason indefinitely. That fact tends to prove that the alleged reason is artificial and false, that it has simply been invented on the spur of the moment by oneself to excuse one's indulgences.

Basil saw my perplexity.

"The fact is," he said, "that you're taking this stuff as the majority of people go to church. It's a meaningless habit."

I hated to put that down on my paper. It was confessing that I was an automaton. But something in his eye compelled me. I wrote the word, and broke out as I did so into a spasm of internal fury. I recollected a story from my hospital days, of a man who had committed suicide when it was proved to him that he couldn't move his upper jaw.

Meanwhile Lamus was looking at my average. I had got down to less than two doses daily. But the rest of the twenty-four hours was spent in waiting for the time when I could indulge.

I knew that Lou was ahead of me. She had gone on what Basil called his third class. She was taking one dose a day; but every day she was taking it later and later. She had about an hour of real craving to get through, and Sister Athena or Sister Cypris, or Sister some one would always intervene, as if by accident, and take some active steps to keep her mind off the subject during those critical minutes.

As soon as one had reached an interval of forty-eight hours between doses, one entered class four and stopped altogether unless some particular occasion arose for taking a dose.

I was very annoyed that Lou should have got on faster than myself. Basil told me he thought I needed more active exercise, though already I had begun to take some interest in the sports of the place. I had even got through a whole game of Thelema without having to sit down and gasp.

But there was still an obscure hankering after the drug life. It had been burnt into me that normal interests were not worthwhile.

King Lamus had taken me out climbing several times; but while I experienced profound physical satisfaction, I could not overcome the moral attitude which is really, after all, expressed in Ecclesiastes, "Vanity, vanity, all is vanity!"

My relations with Lou herself were poisoned by the same feeling. The improvement in our physical health, and the intoxicating effect of the climate and the surroundings urged us to take part in the pageant of nature. Yet against all such ideas we could not help but hear the insistent voice of Haidé Lamoureux, that the end of all these things is death. She had deliberately renounced existence as futile, and there was no answer to her pleadings.

Besides this, my mind had eaten up its pabulum. I had literally nothing to think of except heroin, and I discovered that heroin appealed to me behind all veils, as being an escape from life.

A man who has once experienced the drug-life finds it difficult to put up with the inanity of normal existence. He has become wise with the wisdom of despair.

The Big Lion and Sister Athena exhausted their ingenuity in finding things with which I might occupy my weary aimless hours. But nothing seemed to get me out of the fixed idea that life was heroin with intervals that did not count.

For about a week King Lamus tried to get me out of my groove by giving me cocaine, and asking me to employ my time by writing an account of my adventures from the time when I began to take it. The drug stimulated me immensely; and I was quite enthusiastic for the time. I wrote the story of my adventures from the night of my meeting Lou to our return to England from Naples.

But when the episode was over, I found the old despair of life as strong as ever. The will to live was really dead in me.

But two evenings later King Lamus came to smoke a pipe with me on the terrace at sunset. In his hand was the Paradiso record which I had written. Sister Athena had typed it.

"My dear man," he said, "what I can't see is why you should be so blind about yourself. The meaning of all this ought to be perfectly obvious. I'm afraid you haven't grasped the meaning of 'Do what thou wilt'. Do you see how the application of the Law has helped you so far?"

"Well, of course," I said, "it's pretty clear I didn't come to this planet to drug myself into my grave before my powers have had a chance to ripen. I've thought it necessary to keep off heroin in order to give myself a show. But I'm left flat. Life becomes more tedious every day, and the one way of escape is barred by flaming swords."

"Exactly," he replied. "You've only discovered one thing that you don't will; you have still to find the one thing that you do will. And yet there are quite a number of clues in this manuscript of yours. I note you say that your squad commander, who didn't become that without some power of dealing with men, told you that you were not a great flyer. How was it exactly that you came to take up flying?"

That simple question induced a very surprising reaction. There was no reason why it should produce the intense irritation that it did.

Basil noticed it, rubbed his hands together gleefully, and began to hum "Tipperary". His meaning was evident. He had drawn a bow in a venture; and it had pierced the King of Israel between the joints

of his harness. He got up with alacrity, and went off with a wave of the hand.

"Think it over, dear boy," said he, "and tell me your sad story in the morning."

I was in a very disturbed state of mind. I went to look for Lou, but she had gone for a walk with Cypris, and when she came back, she wore an air of wisdom which I found insupportable. However, I told her my story. To my disgust, she simply nodded as if highly appreciative of some very obscure joke. There was no getting any sense out of her. I went to bed in a thoroughly bad temper.

Almost immediately, the usual struggle began, as to whether I should or should not take a dose of heroin. On this occasion, the controversy was short. I was so annoyed with myself that I took a specially large sniff, apparently less to soothe myself than to annoy somebody else indirectly. It was the first I had had for a week. I had been supplying its place with codeine.

Partly from this and partly from the psychological crisis, its effects were such as I had never before experienced. I remained all night in a state between sleep and waking, unable to call for assistance, unable to control my thoughts; and I was transported into a totally unfamiliar world. I did not exist at all, in any ordinary sense of the word. I was a mathematical expression in a complex scheme of geometry. My equilibrium was maintained by innumerable other forces in the same system, and what I called myself was in some mysterious way charged with a duty of manipulating the other forces, and these evaded me. When I strove to grasp them, they disappeared. My functions seemed to be to simplify complex expressions, and then to build up new complexes from the elements so isolated as to create simulacra of my own expression in other forms.

This process continued, repeating itself with delirious intensity through endless aeons. I suffered the intolerable pang of losing my individuality altogether by confusing it, so to speak, with some of the expressions that I had formulated. The distress became so acute that I felt the necessity of getting Lou to assist me. But I could not discover her anywhere in the system.

And yet, there was something in the nature of the curves themselves which I identified with her. It was as if their ultimate form in some way depended upon her. She was concealed, so to speak, in the expression of the ideas. She was implicit in their structure; and as the worst of the excitement and the anxiety subsided, I found a curious consolation in the fact that she was not an independent and conflicting unit in this complicated chaos of machinery, but was, as it were, the reason for its assuming its actual appearance in preference to any other. And as the night went on, the enormous complexity of the vision co-ordinated itself. There was a sensation of whirling and rising communicated to the entire universe of my thought. A sort of dizziness seized upon my spirit. It was as if a wheel had been set in motion and gradually increased its pace so that one could no longer distinguish the spokes. It became an indefinite whirr. This feeling invaded my entire consciousness little by little, so that it was reduced to an unchanging unity; but a unity composed of diverse forces in regular motion. The monotony devoured consciousness so that my waking sleep merged into true sleep.

The strangest part of the whole experience was that I woke up an entirely new man. I found myself engrossed in abstruse calculations, loosely knit together, it is true, but very intense, with regard to an idea which had not entered my mind for months. I was working out in my mind a plan for constructing a helicopter, the invention of which had occupied me deeply when I was out of a job. It had been driven completely out of my mind by my becoming heir to Uncle Mortimer's estate.

As I regained full wakefulness, I found myself extremely puzzled by my surroundings. In fact, I could not remember who I was. The question seemed in some extraordinary way to lack meaning. The more I regained consciousness of myself, of Telepylus, and of the immediate past, the more these things became unreal. The true "I" was the mathematician and engineer working on the helicopter, and the interval had been an elaborate nightmare.

I threw it all off like a retriever coming out of a pond with a stick in his mouth, and bent myself to my work. I was disturbed by some person or persons unknown kissing me on the back of my neck, and putting a

tray with my breakfast at my side. I was aware of a vague subconscious annoyance that the food was cold.

When the tom-tom sounded for the noonday Adoration, I got up and stretched myself; my brain was completely fagged out. I joined the little party on the terrace at the salutation to the sun.

"Hail unto thee who art Ahathor in thy triumphing, even unto thee who art Ahathor in thy beauty; that travellest over the heavens in thy bark at the mid-career of the Sun. Tahuti standeth in his splendour at the prow, and Ra-Hoor abideth at the helm. Hail unto thee from the abodes of morning!"

One of the party made a very singular impression on me. There was something indefinably Mongolian about her face. The planes were flat; the cheek-bones high; the eyes oblique; the nose wide, short, and vital; the mouth a long, thin, rippling curve like a mad sunset. The eyes were tiny and green with a piquant elfin expression. Her hair was curiously colourless; it was very abundant; she had wound great ropes about her head. It reminded me of the armature of a dynamo. It produced a weird effect – this mingling of the savage Mongol with the savage Norseman type. Her strange hair fascinated me. It was that delicate flaxen hue – so fine. The face was extraordinarily young and fresh, all radiant with smiles and blushes.

"Peter, my boy," I said to myself, "you'd better get busy and finish that helicopter and make some money, because that's the girl you're going to marry –"

This conviction seized me with the force of a revelation; for the girl was mysteriously familiar. It seemed as if I had seen her in a dream or something like that. I was very annoyed to find an arm familiarly slipped through mine, while a voice said in my ear:

"We may as well walk over to the refectory for lunch. You haven't answered my question about how you came to take up flying."

"When you asked me, I wasn't at all clear in my mind, but the chain of causes is sufficiently obvious now."

I had never taken kindly to medicine. Its unscientific procedure, its arrogance, its snobbishness, and its empiricism all combined to disgust me. I had simply gone to the hospital because my father was bent on it,

and wouldn't put up the money for anything else. I wanted to be an engineer. I was keen as mustard on bicycles and automobiles. Even as a boy I had had a sort of workshop of my own. The greatest pleasure of my childhood had been the rare visits to my mother's father, who in his time had been a great inventor and done an immense amount of work relative to the mechanical perfection of railway travelling.

When the war broke out I had gone straight to the engineering shops; and I became a flying man rather against my will, on account of my weight and the dearth of pilots.

I broke off in my enthusiastic harangue, because King Lamus had stopped on the crest of the ridge which divided the strangers' house at the Abbey from the main buildings.

"The climb has put you out of breath," he said.

"Take a sniff of this; it will put you all right in a second."

I pushed the man's hand away impatiently, and the little heap of powder fell to the ground.

"Oh, it's like that, is it?" said Basil laughing.

I realised how rude I had been, and began to apologise.

"That's all right," he said. "But, of course, you aren't going to get out of it as easily as that. You don't give up eating mutton because you ate too much one day and got indigestion. You'll find heroin pretty useful when you know how to use it. However, your gesture just now was automatic. It was evidence that your unconscious or true will objects to your taking heroin. So far so good for the negative side. But the question is, what does your true will actually want you to do in a positive way?"

"Confound the fellow and his eternal metaphysics," I thought.

"I haven't the least idea," I answered sharply, "and what's more, I've no time to waste on this occult stuff of yours. Don't think I'm rude. I'm very grateful for all you've done for me."

Strangely enough, the memory of the last few months had just returned to my mind. Yet it was merely the background of the burning flame of thought that filled my consciousness.

Basil did not answer, and as we walked down the hill together I began to explain my ideas about the new helicopter. Almost without knowing it, we had reached the door of the large house which the Abbey used for

a refectory, and we sat down on the stone seats which lined its north-eastern wall, and gazed over the marvellous prospect.

The refectory was set on a steep slope. The ground fell sharply away from below our feet. On the left, the great rock towered even more tremendously than on the other side; and on the right, the hills above the coast-line danced away into dim purple. In front was a strange jagged headland crowned with a fantastic cluster of rocks, and beyond this the great sea stretched away, in masses of greens and blues and violets, to where a number of volcanic islands slumbered dimly on the horizon.

Basil annoyed me intensely by interpolating remarks about the beauty of the scenery. I couldn't seem to interest him in the helicopter at all. Was I really talking such rubbish?

"I'm too old to be snubbed, Sir Peter," (Oh, yes, I was Sir Peter now! Of course I was.) he interjected, shaking me gently by the shoulder.

I had paused to clear up a point in my mind about one of the gauges.

"And I must remind you that you are a gentleman; and that when you came to this Abbey the first thing you did was to sign a pledge-form."

He repeated the words:

"I do solemnly declare that I accept the Law of Thelema, that I will devote myself to discover my True Will, and to do it."

"Yes, yes, of course," I said hurriedly. "I'm not trying to get out of it; but really, I am at the moment most frightfully preoccupied with this idea about the helicopter."

"Thank you, that will do," said King Lamus briskly. "The meeting will now adjourn."

I felt a little irritation at his offhand manner, but I followed him in to lunch. He stood at the end of the table, facing Sister Athena at the other.

"There will be champagne," he said, "for lunch today."

The remark was received with a hilarity which seemed positively indecent, and altogether out of proportion to the good news announced. The whole Abbey seemed to have gone wild with delight.

Following the example of the Big Lion, every one pointed a forefinger downwards to the left, swung it sharply across to the right. This gesture was repeated three times and accompanied by the words:

"Evoe Ho! Evoe Ho! Evoe Ho!"

They began to clap hands but checked the movement before contact and only allowed the clash to take place on the third syllable of the great cry:

I A O

This was followed by very rapid clapping three times three, in silence.

I was entirely bewildered by this demonstration, but had no opportunity to make inquiries, for Sister Cypris immediately said "Will" with Hermes, and lunch began in the invariable silence, a silence somewhat modified by the exuberant hilarity of the entire assembly.

The champagne would not account for it all. The unrestrained glee reminded me of my early days with cocaine. However, I had something better to think about. The question was how to reduce W to an indefinitely small quantity in the formula

$$S^{-1} = \sqrt{\dfrac{tm^2}{1 - \dfrac{t + w}{t}}}$$

Confound it, what was the use of making a rule of silence at meals when everybody was breaking it in the spirit if not in the letter? I got hot and red behind the ears. Everybody from Big Lion with his tumbler full of champagne to Dionysus with his liqueur glass of the same was holding it out to me as if drinking to my health. I availed myself of the rule which permits us to leave the table without ceremony. I would go back to the other house and work.

But a sudden thought struck me just as I got outside the door. I sat down again on the stone seats, whipped out a note-book and began my calculations. I saw my way to a solution, jotted down my idea, and snapped the book to in triumph.

It was then that I became aware that Big Lion was putting a cigar in my mouth, and that everybody was crowding around me and

shaking hands. Was this another of the buffoon's stupid jokes?

"To what end?" said Big Lion, as he lighted my cigar.

I had sunk back in the bench in a sort of lazy triumph. Nothing bothered me now. I could see my way to solve my problem.

"You must say 'attomplish great wort.'" said Dionysus, in a tone of dignified reproach.

"Confound the Great Work!" I replied pettishly, and then became sorry for myself.

I picked up my Pagan friend, took him on my knee, and began to stroke his head. He snuggled up to me delightfully.

"You must excuse us," said Hermes very seriously, "but we're all so glad."

CHAPTER VII
LOVE UNDER WILL

I began to laugh despite myself.

"Well," I said, puffing at my cigar, "I do really wish you'd let me know what this is all about. Has Lloyd George resigned?"

"No," said Big Lion, "it's just you!"

"What about me?" I retorted.

"Why, your success, of course," said Sister Cypris.

Something, of course, quite obvious to them was hidden from my dull understanding.

I turned on Basil point-blank.

"What success?" I said. "It's true I do see my way through a formula that's been bothering me. But I don't see how you know about it. Do Hermes and Dionysus comprise a knowledge of the differential calculus in their attainments?"

"It's very simple," said the Big Lion. "It involves a knowledge of nothing but the Law; and the Law, after all, is nothing but the plainest

common sense. Do you remember my asking you before tiffin what was your true will?"

"Yes," I said, "I do. And I told you then, and I tell you again now, that I haven't the time to think about things like that."

"That fact," he retorted, "was quite enough to assure me that you had discovered it."

"Look here," I said, "you're a good sort and all that, but you are really a bit queer, and half the time I don't know what you are driving at. Can't you put it in plain English?"

"With all the pleasure in life," he returned. "Just look at the facts for a moment. Fact one: Your maternal grandfather is a mechanical genius. Fact two: From your earliest childhood, subjects of this sort have exercised the strongest fascination for you. Fact three: Whenever you get off those subjects, you are unhappy, unsuccessful, and get into various kinds of mess. Fact four: The moment the war gives you your opportunity, you throw up medicine and go back to engineering. Fact five: You graduate reluctantly from the bench to the pilot's seat, and your squad commander himself sees that it's a case of a square peg in a round hole. Fact six: As soon as the Armistice throws you on your beam ends, you get busy again with the idea of the helicopter. Fact seven: You are swept off your feet by coming into a fortune and immediately go astray with drugs – clear evidence that you have missed your road. Fact eight: As soon as your mind is cleansed by the boredom of Telepylus of all its artificial ideas, it returns to its natural bent. The idea of the helicopter comes back with such a rush that you let your breakfast get cold, you don't know your wife when she brings it, and you can talk about nothing else. For the first time in your life your self-consciousness is obliterated. You even start to explain your ideas to me, though I know nothing whatever of the subject. It doesn't require any particular genius to see that you have discovered your true will. And that accounts for the champagne and applause at lunch."

I scratched my head, still hardly comprehending. But one clause in the Big Lion's roar had struck me with appalling force. I looked round the circle of faces.

"Yes, I've discovered my will, all right," I said, "I know now what I'm good for. I understand why I came to this silly planet. I'm an engineer. But you said 'my wife.' That doesn't fit in at all. Where is she?"

"Well, you know," returned Big Lion, with a grin, "you mustn't imagine me to be a cold storage warehouse for other people's wives. If I might hazard a guess, however, your wife's discovered what her own will is, and has gone off to do it."

"Oh, damnation," said I. "Here, you know, I say I can't allow that sort of thing!"

The Big Lion turned his sternest gaze upon me. "Now, Sir Peter," he said incisively, "pull yourself together. You've only just discovered your own will, and you naturally want to be let alone to do it. And yet, at the very first opportunity, you butt in and want to interfere with your own wife doing hers. Let me tell you point-blank that it's none of your business what she chooses to do. Haven't you seen enough harm come from people meddling with other people's business? Why, hang it, man, your first duty to your wife is to protect her."

"Another of your paradoxes," I growled.

As a matter of fact, I was torn between two attitudes. Lou had been an ideal companion in debauchery of all sorts. A woman like that was bound to be the ruin of a hard-working engineer. At the same time I was madly in love with her, especially after seeing her for the first time that morning; and she belonged to me.

It was only too clear to me what he meant by saying she had discovered her true will. She had shown that plainly enough when she had begged him to take her away. He had simply worked one of his devilish tricks on me, and got rid of me, as he thought, by getting me absorbed in my helicopter.

I was to be the complacent husband, and allow my wife to go off with another man right under my nose, while I was busy with my calculations. I was to be the *mari complaisant*, was I?

Well, the fiend was ingenious, but he had calculated wrong for once. I got up and deliberately slapped him in the face.

"Before breakfast," he said to Sister Athena, "we shall require pistols for two and coffee for one. But while we are waiting for the fatal rendezvous,"

he added, turning to me with one of his inscrutable grins, "I must continue to keep my oath, As it happens, one of the brethren here is himself a mechanic. That little house on the headland (he pointed as he spoke) is fitted up as a fairly complete workshop. We might stroll down together and see you started. There will probably be a lot of things that you need which we haven't got and you can make a list of them, and we'll telegraph Lala to buy them in London and bring them down here. She is coming in three days' time. I will also ask her to stop in Paris for one of those nice iron wreaths with enamelled flowers to put on my nameless grave."

The man's nonchalance made me suddenly furiously ashamed of myself. I had to spit out between my teeth that he was an unutterable scoundrel.

"That's right, Sir Peter," retorted the Big Lion, "reassure yourself, by all means. 'The unspeakable Lamus' is the classical expression, and it is customary to give a slight shudder; but perhaps a genius like yourself is justified in inventing new terms of abuse."

I was disconcerted abominably by the attitude of the audience, whose faces were fixed in broad grins, with the exception of Dionysus, who came straight up to me and said:

"Sonna mabitch," and hit me in the eye. "If you shoot my Bid Lion," he added, "I'll shoot you."

The entire company broke into screams of uncontrollable laughter. Lamus rose with assumed indignation, and observed ferociously –

"Is this your idea of doing your wills, you wasters? Did you come to this planet to turn the most serious subjects into mockery? You ought all to be weeping, considering that within twenty-four hours you will have to bury your beloved Big Lion or our esteemed guest, who has endeared himself to all of us by his unconscious humour. Come along, Sir Peter," and he slipped his arm through mine. "We have no time to waste with these footlers. As to Unlimited Lou. . . ."(he began to sing):

> "Has any one seen my Mary?
> Has any one seen my Jane?
> She went right out in her stocking feet
> In the pelting pouring rain.

If any one sees my Mary,
He'll oblige me, I declare,
If he'll send her back in a packing case,
'This side up, with care.'"

We were already far down the slope, striding like giants. From above came a confused chorus of shouts and laughter.

One has to be an athlete to run downhill arm in arm with Big Lion. He didn't seem to mind the cactus, and when we came to a ditch, it had to be jumped. And when the path took a little turn uphill, he used our momentum to take us over the crest like a switch-back. It made me positively drunk. Physical alarm was combined with physical exhilaration. I was sweating like a pig; my sandals slipped on the hard dry grass; my bare legs were torn by brambles, gorse, and cactus.

I kept on slipping; but he always turned the slip into a leap. We never checked our career till we pulled up at the door of the house on the headland.

He let go of me suddenly. I flopped, and lay on my back panting for breath. He was absolutely cool; he had not turned a hair. He stood watching me while he pulled out his pipe, filled it and lit it.

"Never waste time on the way to work," he observed, in a tone which I can only describe as pseudo-sanctimonious. "Do you find yourself sufficiently recovered," he added in mock anxiety, "to resume the vertical position which distinguishes the human species from other mammals? I believe the observation is due to Vergil," he continued.

There was a twinkle in his eye which warned me that he had another surprise in store for me; I had begun to realise that he took a school-boyish delight in pulling people's legs. He seemed to enjoy leading one on, putting one in a false position, and making a mystery out of the most commonplace circumstances. It was extremely idiotic and extremely annoying; but at the same time one had to admit that the result of his method was to add a sort of spice to life.

I remembered a remark of Maisie Jacobs: "Never dull where Lamus is."

The events had been of an ordinary and insignificant character, and yet he had given a value to each one. He made life taste like it does when

one is using heroin and cocaine, yet he did it without actual extravagance. I could understand how it was that he had his unique reputation for leading a fantastic life, and yet how no one could put a finger on any particular exploit as extraordinary in itself.

I picked myself slowly together, and, after removing a few thorns from my bare legs, was sufficiently master of myself to say:

"So this is the workshop?"

"Once again, Sir Peter," replied Lamus, "your intuition has proved itself infallible. And once again your incomparable gift of expression has couched the facts in a tersely epigrammatic form, which Julius Caesar and Martial might despair of editing."

He opened the door of the house, repeating his old formula:

"Do what thou wilt shall be the whole of the Law."

Till that moment I had found the phrase by turns ridiculous, annoying, or tedious. It had completely lost these attributes. The dry bones lived. I thrilled to the marrow as he uttered it. A soft, sweet voice, strangely familiar, answered him out of the vast, dim room. Dim, for the blinding sunlight of the open air was unable wholly to illuminate the interior to my contracted pupils.

"Love is the law, love under will."

I thrilled again, this time with a combination of surprise and exultation which was curiously unintelligible.

Then I saw, in one corner of the room, behind the array of benches and tables crowded with neatly disposed apparatus, a glimmering form. The back was turned to us; it was on the floor busily occupied in cleaning up.

"This is Sir Peter Pendragon," said Big Lion, "who is coming to take charge of the laboratory."

My eyes were still unaccustomed to the gloom, but I could see the figure scramble to its feet, curtsey, and advance to me, where I stood in the shaft of sunlight that came through the half-open doorway.

It was dressed in a knickerbocker suit of black silk. It wore sandals and black stockings.

I recognised Lou.

"Big Lion said you might want to begin work this afternoon, Sir Peter,"

she said with dignity, "so I have been trying to put the place in some sort of order."

I stood absolutely aghast. It was Lou, but a Lou that I had never seen or known. I turned to King Lamus for an explanation, but he was not there.

A ripple of laughter ran over her face; the sunlight blazed in her magnetic eyes. I trembled with indescribable emotion. Here was an undecipherable puzzle. Or was it by any chance the answer to a puzzle – to all my puzzles – the puzzle of life?

I could think of nothing to say but the most lame and awkward banality.

"What are you doing here?" I inquired.

"My will, of course," came the answer, and her eyes twinkled in the sunshine as unfathomably as the sea itself.

"Thou hast no right but to do thy will," she quoted.

"Do that and no other shall say nay."

"Oh, yes," I retorted, with a trace of annoyance.

I had still a feeling of reaction against the *Book of the Law*. I hated to submit to a formula, however much my good sense, confirmed by my experience, urged me to surrender.

"But how did you find out what your will was?"

"How did you find out?" she flashed back.

"Why," I stammered, "Big Lion showed me how my heredity, my natural inclination, and the solution of my crisis, all pointed to the same thing."

"You said it," she answered softly, and fired another quotation. "The Law is for all."

"Tell me about it," I said.

My stupefaction and my annoyance were melting away. I began to perceive dimly that the Big Lion had worked out the whole situation in a masterly fashion. He had done with his material – us, what I was doing with my material, the laws of mechanics.

"I discovered my will four days ago," she said very seriously. "It was the night that you and Big Lion climbed Deep Ghyll and took so long over Professor's Chimney, that you missed the champagne dinner."

"Yes, yes," I said impatiently, "and what was it?"

She put her hands behind her back and bent her head. Her eyelids closed over her long slanting eyes, and her red, snaky mouth began to work tremulously.

"While you were asleep after tiffin," she said, "Big Lion took me up to the semicircular seat on the hill above the Strangers' House, and put me through my paces. He made me tell him all my early life and especially the part just before I met you, when I thought I loved him. And he made me see that all I had done was to try to please myself, and that I had failed. My love for him was only that of a daughter for her father. I looked to him to lead me into life, but nothing meant anything to me till the night I met you. At that moment I began to live. It was you, and not Gretel's beastly cocaine, that filled my soul with that Litany of Fuller's. I had chanted it often enough, but it had never touched the spot. That night I used it to get you. I had only lived that I might one day find you. And all my life curled itself, from that moment, round you. I was ready to go to hell for you. I did go to hell for you. I came out of hell for you. I stopped taking heroin only because I had to fit myself to help you to do your will. That is my will. And when we found out this morning what your will was, I came down here to get the place ready for you to do it. I'm going to keep this place in order for you and assist you as best I can in your work, just as I danced for you, and went to McCall for you, in the days when you were blind. I was blind too about your will, but I always followed my instinct to do what you needed me for, even when we were poisoned and insane."

She spoke in low, calm tones, but she was trembling like a leaf. I didn't know what to answer. The greatness of her attitude abashed me. I felt with utmost bitterness the shame of having wronged so sublime a love, of having brought her into such infamy.

"My God!" I said at last. "What we owe to Big Lion!"

She shook her head.

"No," she said, with a strange smile, "we've helped him as much as he's helped us – helped him to do his will. The secret of his power is that he doesn't exist for himself. His force flows through him unhindered. You have not been yourself till this morning when you forgot yourself, forgot who you were, didn't know who kissed you and brought you your breakfast."

She looked up with a slow half-shamefaced smile into my eyes.

"And I lost you," said I, "after tiffin, when I remembered myself and forgot my work. And all the time you were here helping me to do my work. And I didn't understand."

We stood awhile in silence. Both our hearts were seething with suppressed necessity to speak. It was a long, long while before I found a word; and when it came, it was intense and calm and confident.

"I love you."

Not all the concentration given by heroin, or the exaltation of cocaine, could match that moment. The words were old; but their meaning was marvellously new. There had never been any "I" before, when I thought "I" was I, there had never been any "you" before when I thought of Lou as an independent being, and had not realised that she was the necessary complement of the human instrument which was doing "my" work. Nor had there been any love before, while love meant nothing but the manifold stupid things that people ordinarily mean by it. Love, as I meant it now, was an affirmation of the inevitable unity between the two impersonal halves of the work. It was the physical embodiment of our spiritual truth.

My wife did not answer. There was no need. Her understanding was perfect. We united with the unconscious ecstasy of nature. Articulate human language was an offence to our spiritual rapture. Our union destroyed our sense of separateness from the universe of which we were part; the sun, the sky, the sea, the earth, partook with us of that ineffable sacrament. There was no discontinuity between that first embrace of our true marriage, and the occupation of the afternoon in taking stock of the effects of the laboratory, and making notes of the things we should ask Lala to bring us from London. The sun sank behind the ridge, and far above us from the Refectory came the sonorous beat of the tom-tom which told us that the evening meal was ready. We shut up the house, and ran laughing up the slopes. They no longer tired and daunted us. Halfway to the house, we met the tiny Dionysus, full of importance. He had been deputed to remind us of dinner. Sister Athena (we laughed to think) must have realised that our honeymoon had begun; and – this time – it was no spasmodic exaltation depending on the transitory

excitement of passion, or stimulants, but on the fact of our true spiritual marriage, in which we were essentially united to each other not for the sake of either, but to form one bride whose bridegroom was the Work which could never be satiated so long as we lived, and so could never lead to weariness and boredom. This honeymoon would blossom and bear fruit perennially, season by season, like the earth our mother and the sun our father themselves, an inexhaustible, frictionless enthusiasm. We were partakers of the eternal sacrament; whatever happened was equally essential to the ritual. Death itself made no difference to anything; our calm continuous candescence burst through the chains of circumstance, and left us free for ever to do our wills, which were one will, the will of Him that sent us.

The walk up to the Refectory was one long romp with Dionysus. Oh, wise dear Sister Athena! Was it by chance that you chose that sturdy sunlight imp to lead us up the hill that night? Did you suspect that our hearts would see in him a symbol of our own serene and splendid hope? We looked into each other's eyes as we held his hands on the last steep winding path among the olives, and we did not speak. But an electric flame ran through his tiny body from one to the other, and we knew for the first time what huge happiness lay in ambush for our love.

The silence of dinner shone with silken lustre. It lasted long – so long – each moment charged with litanies of love.

When coffee came, Big Lion himself broke the spell. "I am going to the tower to sleep tonight; so you will be in charge of the Strangers' House, Sir Peter! The duties are simple; if any wanderer should ask our hospitality, it is for you to extend it on behalf of the Order."

We knew one wanderer who would come, and we would make him welcome.

"A bright torch and a casement open at Night To let the warm Love in."

"But before you go across, you will do well to join us, now that you have discovered your true wills, in the Vesper Ceremony of the Abbey, which we perform every night in the Temple of my tower. Let us be going!"

We followed, hand in hand, along the smooth, broad, curving path that bordered the stream, cunningly bended to run along the crest of the

ridge so that its power might be used to turn various mill-wheels. The gathering shadows whispered subtle lyrics in our ears; the scents of spring conveyed superb imaginations to our senses; the sunset squandered its last scarlet on the sea, and the empurpled night began to burst into blossom of starlight. Over the hilltop before us hung the golden scimitar of the moon, and in the stillness the faint heart-beat of the sea was heard, as if the organ in some enchanted cathedral were throbbing under the fingers of Merlin, and transmuting the monotonous sadness of existence into a peaceful paean of inexpressible jubilance of triumph, the Te Deum of mankind celebrating its final victory over the heathen hordes of despair.

A turn in the path, and we came suddenly upon a cauldron-shaped depression in the hillside; at the bottom a silver streak of foam darted among huge boulders piled bombastically along the bed of the valley. Opposite, jutting from the grassy slopes, there stood three stark needles of red rock, glowing still redder with some splash of crimson stolen from the storehouse of the sunset; and above the highest of these there sprang a sudden shaft of stone against the skyline. A blind dome of marble rimmed with a balcony at the base crowned the tower, circular, with many tall windows Gothic in design, but capped with fleurs-de-lys; and this was set upon eight noble pillars joined by arches which carried out the idea of the windows on a larger scale. When we reached the tower, by a serpentine series of steps, megalithic stones laid into the mountain side, we saw that the floor of the vault was an elaborate mosaic. At the four quarters were four thrones of stone, and in the centre a hexagonal altar of marble.

Four of the principals of the Abbey were already robed for the ceremony; but they furnished themselves with four weapons – a lance, a chalice, a sword, and a disk – from a pillar which had a door and a staircase which formed the only means of access to the upper rooms.

Basil seated himself in one of the thrones, Sister Athena in another; while a very old man with a white beard, and a young woman whom we had not yet seen, took their places in the other two. Without formality of any sort beyond a series of knocks, the ceremony began. The impression was overwhelming. On the one hand, the vastness of the amphitheatre, the sublimity of the scene, and the utter naturalness of the celebrants; on

the other, the amazing distinction of the prose, and the sharp clarity and inevitability of the ideas.

I can only remember one or two clauses of the Credo: they ran thus:

"And I believe in one Gnostic and Catholic Church of Light, Life, Love and Liberty, the Word of whose Law is THELEMA."

"And I believe in the communion of Saints."

"And, forasmuch as meat and drink are transmuted in us daily into spiritual substance, I believe in the Miracle of the Mass."

"And I confess one Baptism of Wisdom, whereby we accomplish the Miracle of Incarnation."

"And I confess my life one, individual, and eternal, that was, and is, and is to come."

I have always told myself that I had not a spark of religious feeling, yet Basil once told me that the text, "The fear of the Lord is the beginning of wisdom", ought to be translated "The wonderment at the forces of nature is the beginning of wisdom."

He claims that every one who is interested in science is necessarily religious, and that those who despise it and detest it are the real blasphemers.

But I have certainly always been put off by the idea of ceremonial or ritual of any kind. There again, Basil's ideas are fantastically different to other people's. He says; what about the forms and ceremonies used in an electric light plant?

I gave a little jump when he made the remark. It was so destructive of all my ideas.

"Most ritual," he agreed, "is vain observance, but if there is such a thing as the so-called spiritual force in man, it requires to be generated, collected, controlled, and applied, by using the appropriate measures, and these form true ritual."

And, in fact, the weird ceremony in progress in his Titan tower produced a definite effect upon me, unintelligible as it was to me for the most part, on one hand, and repellent as it was to my Protestant instincts on the other.

I could not help being struck by the first of the collects.

"Lord visible and sensible, of whom this earth is but a frozen spark

turning about thee with annual and diurnal motion, source of light, source of life, source of liberty, let thy perpetual radiance hearten us to continual labour and enjoyment; so that as we are constant partakers of thy bounty we may in our particular orbit give out light and life, sustenance and joy to them that revolve about us without diminution of substance or effulgence for ever."

The words were full of the deepest religious feeling and vibrated with a mysterious exultation, and yet the most hardened materialist could not have objected to a single idea.

Again, after an invocation of the forces of birth and reproduction, all rose to their feet and addressed Death with sublime simplicity, masking nothing, evading nothing, but facing the huge fact with serene dignity. The gesture of standing to meet Death was nobly impressive.

"Term of all that liveth, whose name is inscrutable, be favourable unto us in thine hour."

The service ended with an anthem which rolled like thunder among the hills and was re-echoed from the wall of the great rock of Telepylus.

It was a very curious detail of life at the Abbey, that one act merged into the next insensibly. There were no abrupt changes. Life had been assimilated to the principle of the turbine, as opposed to the reverberatory engine. Every act was equally a sacrament. The discontinuity and abruptness of ordinary life had been eliminated. A just proportion was consequently kept between the various interests. It was this as much as anything else that had helped me to recover from the obsession of drugs. I had been kept back from emancipation by my reaction against the atmosphere, in general, and my latent jealousy of Basil, in particular. Lou, not having been troubled by either of these, had slid out of her habit as insidiously, if I may use the word, as she had slid into it.

But the culminating joy of my heart was the completeness of the solution of all my problems. There was no possibility of a relapse, because the cause of my downfall had been permanently removed. I could understand perfectly how it was that Basil could take a dose of heroin or cocaine, could indulge in hashish, ether, or opium as simply and usefully as the ordinary man can order a cup of strong black coffee when he happens to want to work late at night. He had become completely

master of himself, because he had ceased to oppose himself to the current of spiritual willpower of which he was the vehicle. He had no fear or fascination with regard to any of these drugs. He knew that these two qualities were aspects of a single reaction; that of emotion to ignorance. He could use cocaine as a fencing-master uses a rapier, as an expert, without danger of wounding himself.

About a fortnight after our first visit to the tower, a group of us was sitting on the terrace of the Strangers' House. It was bright moonlight, and the peasants from the neighbouring cottages had come in to enjoy the hospitality of the Abbey. Song and dance were in full swing. Basil and I fell into a quiet chat.

"How long is it, by the way," he said, "since you last took a dose of anything?"

"I'm not quite sure," I answered, dreamily watching Lou and Lala, who had arrived a week since with the apparatus I required for my experiments, as they waltzed together on the court. They were both radiant. It seemed as if the moon had endowed them with her pure subtlety and splendour.

"I asked you," continued Big Lion, pulling at a big meerschaum and amber pipe of the Boer pattern, which he reserved for late at night, "because I want you to take the fullest advantage of your situation. You have been tried in the crucible and come out pure gold. But it won't do for you to forget the privileges you have won by your ordeal. Do you remember what it says in the *Book of the Law*?

"'I am the Snake that giveth Knowledge and Delight and bright glory, and stir the hearts of men with drunkenness. To worship me take wine and strange drugs whereof I will tell my prophet, and be drunk thereof! They shall not harm ye at all.'"

"Yes," I said slowly, "and I thought it a bit daring; might tempt people to be foolhardy, don't you think?"

"Of course," agreed Basil, "if you read it carelessly, and act on it rashly, with the blind faith of a fanatic; it might very well lead to trouble. But nature is full of devices for eliminating anything that cannot master its environment. The words 'to worship me' are all-important. The only excuse for using a drug of any sort, whether it's quinine or Epsom-salt,

is to assist nature to overcome some obstacle to her proper functions. The danger of the so-called habit-forming drugs is that they fool you into trying to dodge the toil essential to spiritual and intellectual development. But they are not simply man-traps. There is nothing in nature which cannot be used for our benefit, and it is up to us to use it wisely. Now, in the work you have been doing in the last week, heroin might have helped you to concentrate your mind, and cocaine to overcome the effects of fatigue. And the reason you did not use them was that a burnt child dreads fire. We had the same trouble with teaching Hermes and Dionysus to swim. They found themselves in danger of being drowned and thought the best way was to avoid going near the water. But that didn't help them to use their natural faculties to the best advantage, so I made them face the sea again and again, until they decided that the best way to avoid drowning was to learn how to deal with oceans in every detail. It sounds pretty obvious when you put it like that, yet while every one agrees with me about the swimming, I am howled down on all sides when I apply the same principles to the use of drugs."

At this moment, Lala claimed me for a waltz, and Lou took Basil under her protection. After the dance, we all four sat down on the wall of the court and I took up the thread of the conversation.

"You're quite right, of course, and I imagine you expected to be shouted at."

"No," laughed Lamus, "my love for humanity makes me an incurably optimistic ass on all such points. I can't see the defects in my inamorata. I expect men to be rational, courageous, and to applaud initiative, though an elementary reading of history tells one, with appalling reiteration, how every pioneer has been persecuted, whether it's Galileo, Harvey, Gauguin, or Shelley; there is a universal outcry against any attempt to destroy the superstitions which hamper or foster the progress which helps the development of the race. Why should I escape the excommunication of Darwin or the ostracism of Swinburne? As a matter of fact, I am consoled in my moments of weakness and depression by the knowledge that I am so bitterly abused and hated. It proves to me that my work, whether mistaken or not, is at least worthwhile. But that's a digression. Let's get back to the words 'to worship me'. They mean that things like heroin and

alcohol may be and should be used for the purpose of worshipping, that is, entering into communion with, the 'Snake that giveth Knowledge and Delight and bright glory' which is the genius which lies 'in the core of every star'. And, 'Every man and every woman is a star.' The taking of a drug should be a carefully thought out and purposeful religious act. Experience alone can teach you the right conditions in which the act is legitimate, that is, when it assists you to do your will. If a billiard player slams the balls around indiscriminately, he soon takes the edge off his game. But a golfer would be very foolish to leave his mashie out of his bag because at one time he got too fond of it and used it improperly, and lost important matches in consequence. Now with regard to you and Lou, I can't see that she has any particular occasion for using any of these drugs. She can do her will perfectly well without them, and her natural spirituality enables her to keep in continual communion with her inmost self, as her magical diary shows clearly enough. Even when she had poisoned herself to the point of insanity, her true instincts always asserted themselves at a crisis; that is, at any moment when you, the being whom it is her function to protect, was in danger. But there must be occasions in your work when 'the little more and how much it is' could be added to your energy by a judicious dose of cocaine, and enable you to overcome the cumulative forces of inertia, or when the effort of concentration is so severe that the mind insists on relieving itself by distracting your thoughts from the object of your calculations, a little heroin would calm their clamour sufficiently long to enable you to get the thing done.

"Now, it's utterly wrong to force yourself to work from a sense of duty. The more thoroughly you succeed in analysing your mind, the more surely you become able to recognise the moment when a supreme effort is likely to result in definite achievement. Nature is very quick to warn one when one makes an error. A drug should act instantaneously and brilliantly. When it fails to do so, you know that you shouldn't have taken it, and you should then call a halt, and analyse the circumstances of the failure. We learn more from our failures than from our successes, and your magical record will tell you by the end of the year so accurately what precise circumstances indicate the propriety of resorting to any drug, that in your second year you must be a great fool if you make even

half a dozen mistakes. But, as the *Book of the Law* says, 'Success is your proof.' When you resort to such potent and dangerous expedients for increasing your natural powers, you must make sure that the end justifies the means. You're a scientific man; stick to the methods of science. Wisdom is justified of her children; and I shall be surprised if you do not discover within the next twelve months that your Great Experiment, despite the unnecessary disasters which arose from your neglecting those words, 'to worship me,' has been the means of developing your highest qualities and putting you among the first thinkers of our generation."

The mandolin of Sister Cypris broke into gay triumphant twitterings. It was like a musical comment upon his summary of the situation. The moon sank behind the hill, the peasants finished their wine and went off singing to their cottages; Lou and I found ourselves alone under the stars. The breeze bore the murmur of the sea up the scented slopes. The lights in the town went out. The Pole Star stood above the summit of the rock. Our eyes were fixed on it. We could imagine the precession of the Equinoxes as identical with our own perpetual travelling through time.

Lou pressed my hand. I found myself repeating the words of the creed.

"'I confess my life, one, individual, and eternal, that was, and is, and is to come.'"

Her voice murmured in my ear, "I believe in the communion of Saints."

I made the discovery that I was after all a profoundly religious man. All my life I had been looking for a creed which did not offend my moral or intellectual sense. And now I had come to understand the mysterious language of the people of the Abbey of Thelema.

"Be the Priest pure of body and soul!"

The love of Lou had consecrated me to do my will, to accomplish the Great Work.

"Be the Priest fervent of body and soul!"

The love of Lou not only kept me from the contamination of ideas and desires alien to my essential function in the universe, but inspired me to dynamic ecstasy.

I do not know how long we sat under the stars.

A deep eternal peace sat like a dove, a triple tongue of flame upon our souls, which were one soul for ever.

Each of our lives was one, individual, and eternal, but each possessed its necessary and intimate relation with the other, and both with the whole universe. I was moreover aware that our terrific tragedy had been necessary, after all, to our attainment.

"Except a corn of wheat fall into the ground and die, it abideth alone. But if it die, it bringeth forth much fruit."

Every step in evolution is accompanied by colossal catastrophe, as it seems when regarded as an isolated event, out of its context, as one may say.

How fearful had been the price which man had paid for the conquest of the air! How much greater must be the indemnity demanded by inertia for the conquest of the spirit! For we are of more value than many sparrows.

How blind we had been! Through what appalling abysses of agony had we not been led in order that we might say that we had conquered the moral problem posed by the discoveries of organic chemistry.

"The master of tide and thunder against the juice of a flower?"

We had given the lie to the poet.

"This is the only battle he never was known to win."

We no longer looked back with remorse on our folly. We could see the events of the past year in perspective, and we saw that we had been led through that ghoulish ghastliness. We had followed the devil through the dance of death, but there could be no doubt in our minds that the power of evil was permitted for a purpose. We obtained the ineffable assurance of the existence of a spiritual energy that worked its wondrous will in ways too strange for the heart of man to understand until the time should be ripe.

The pestilence of the past had immunised us against its poison. The devil had defeated himself. We had attained a higher stage of evolution. And this understanding of the past filled us with absolute faith in the future.

The chaos of crumbled civilisations whose monuments were on the rock before us, had left that rock un-marred. Our experience had fortified

us. We had reached one more pinnacle on the serrated ridge that rises from the first screes of self-consciousness to a summit so sublime that we did not even dare to dream how far it soared above us. Our business was to climb from crag to crag, with caution and courage, day after day, life after life. Not ours to speculate about the goal of our Going. Enough for us to Go. We knew our way, having found our will, and for the means, had we not love?

"Love is the law, love under will."

The words were neither on our lips nor in our hearts. They were implicit in every idea, and in every impression. We went from the court up the steps, through the open glass doors, into the vaulted room with its fantastic frescoes that was the strangers' room of the Abbey of Thelema; and we laughed softly, as we thought that we should never more be strangers.

MOONCHILD

A PROLOGUE

AUTHOR'S NOTE

THIS book was written in 1917, during such leisure as my efforts to bring America into the War on our side allowed me. Hence my illusions on the subject, and the sad showing of Simon Iff at the end. Need I add that, as the book itself demonstrates beyond all doubt, all persons and incidents are purely the figment of a disordered imagination?

London, 1929. A.C.

—Aleister Crowley

CONTENTS

CHAPTER I
A CHINESE GOD

LONDON, in England, the capital city of the British Empire, is situated upon the banks of the Thames. It is not likely that these facts were unfamiliar to James Abbott McNeill Whistler, a Scottish gentleman born in America and resident in Paris but it is certain that he did not appreciate them. For he settled quietly down to discover a fact which no one had previously observed; namely, that it was very beautiful at night. The man was steeped in Highland fantasy, and he revealed London as Wrapt in a soft haze of mystic beauty, a fairy tale of delicacy and wistfulness.

It is here that the Fates showed partiality; for London should rather have been painted by Goya. The city is monstrous and misshapen; its mystery is not a brooding, but a conspiracy. And these truths are evident above all to one who recognises that London's heart is Charing Cross.

For the old Cross, which is, even technically, the centre of the city, is so in sober moral geography. The Strand roars toward Fleet Street, and so to Ludgate Hill, crowned by St. Paul's Cathedral; Whitehall sweeps down to Westminster Abbey and the Houses of Parliament. Trafalgar Square, which guards it at the third angle, saves it to some extent from the modern banalities of Piccadilly and Pall Mall, mere Georgian sham stucco, not even rivals to the historic grandeur of the great religious monuments, for Trafalgar

really did make history; but it is to be observed that Nelson, on his monument, is careful to turn his gaze upon the Thames. For here is the true life of the city, the aorta of that great heart of which London and Westminster are the ventricles. Charing Cross Station, moreover, is the only true Metropolitan terminus. Euston, St. Pancras, and King's Cross merely convey one to the provinces, even, perhaps, to savage Scotland, as nude and barren today as in the time of Dr. Johnson; Victoria and Paddington seem to serve the vices of Brighton and Bournemouth in winter, Maidenhead and Henley in summer. Liverpool Street and Fenchurch Street are mere suburban sewers; Waterloo is the funereal antechamber to Woking; Great Central is a "notion" imported, name and all, from Broadway, by an enterprising kind of railway Barnum, named Yerkes; nobody ever goes there, except to golf at Sandy Lodge. If there are any other terminals in London, I forget them; clear proof of their insignificance.

But Charing Cross dates from before the Norman Conquest. Here Caesar scorned the advances of Boadicea, who had come to the station to meet him; and here St. Augustin uttered his famous mot, "*Non Angli, sed angeli*".

Stay: there is no need to exaggerate. Honestly, Charing Cross is the true link with Europe, and therefore with history. It understands its dignity and its destiny; the station officials never forget the story of King Alfred and the cakes, and are too wrapped in the cares of – who knows what? – to pay any attention to the necessities of would-be travellers. The speed of the trains is adjusted to that of the Roman Legions: three miles per hour. And they are always late, in honour of the immortal Fabius, "*qui cunctando restituit rem*".

This terminus is swathed in immemorial gloom; it was in one of the waiting-rooms that James Thomson conceived the idea for his City of Dreadful Night; but it is still the heart of London, throbbing with a clear longing towards Paris. A man who goes to Paris from Victoria will never reach Paris! He will find only the city of the *demi-mondaine* and the tourist.

It was not by appreciation of these facts, it was not even by instinct, that Lavinia King chose to arrive at Charing Cross. She was, in her peculiar, esoteric style, the most famous dancer in the world; and she was about to poise upon one exquisite toe in London, execute one blithe pirouette, and leap to Petersburg. No: her reason for alighting at Charing Cross was utterly unconnected with any one of the facts hitherto discussed; had you asked her, she would have replied with her unusual smile, insured for seventy-five thousand dollars, that it was convenient for the Savoy Hotel.

So, on that October night, when London almost shouted its pity and terror at the poet, she only opened the windows of her suite because it was unseasonably hot. It was nothing to her that they gave on to the historic Temple Gardens; nothing that London's favourite bridge for suicides loomed dark beside the lighted span of the railway.

She was merely bored with her friend and constant companion, Lisa la Giuffria, who had been celebrating her birthday for twenty-three hours without cessation as Big Ben tolled eleven.

Lisa was having her fortune told for the eighth time that day by a lady so stout and so iron-clad in corsets that any reliable authority on high explosives might have been tempted to hurl her into Temple Gardens, lest a worse thing come unto him, and so intoxicated that she was certainly worth her weight in grape-juice to any Temperance lecturer.

The name of this lady was Amy Brough, and she told the cards with resistless reiteration. "You'll certainly have thirteen birthday presents," she said, for the hundred and thirteenth time, "and that means a death in the family. Then there's a letter about a journey; and there's something about a dark man connected with a large building. He is very tall, and I think there's a journey coming to you – something about a letter. Yes; nine and three's twelve, and one's thirteen; you'll certainly have thirteen presents." "I've only had twelve," complained Lisa, who was tired, bored, and peevish. "Oh, forget it!" snapped Lavinia King from the window, "you've got an hour to go, anyhow!" "I see something about a large building," insisted Amy Brough, "I think it means Hasty News." "That's extraordinary!" cried Lisa, suddenly awake. "That's what Bunyip said my dream last night meant! That's absolutely wonderful! And to think there are people who don't believe in clairvoyance!"

From the depths of an armchair came a sigh of infinite sadness "Gimme a peach!" Harsh and hollow, the voice issued cavernously from a lantern-jawed American with blue cheeks. He was incongruously clad in a Greek dress, with sandals. It is difficult to find a philosophical reason for disliking the combination of this costume with a pronounced Chicago accent. But one does. He was Lavinia's brother; he wore the costume as an advertisement; it was part of the family game. As he himself would explain in confidence, it made people think he was a fool, which enabled him to pick their pockets while they were preoccupied with this amiable delusion.

"Who said peaches?" observed a second sleeper, a young Jewish artist of uncannily clever powers of observation.

Lavinia King went from the window to the table. Four enormous silver bowls occupied it. Three contained the finest flowers to be bought in London, the tribute of the natives to her talent; the fourth was brimmed with peaches at four shillings a peach. She threw one apiece to her brother and the Knight of the Silver Point.

"I can't make out this Jack of Clubs," went on Amy Brough, "it's something about a large building!"

Blaustein, the artist, buried his face and his heavy curved spectacles in his peach.

"Yes, dearie," went on Amy, with a hiccough, "there's a journey about a letter. And nine and one's ten, and three's thirteen. You'll get another present, dearie, as sure as I'm sitting here."

"I really will?" asked Lisa, yawning.

"If I never take my hand off this table again!"

"Oh, cut it out!" cried Lavinia. "I'm going to bed!"

"If you go to bed on my birthday I'll never speak to you again!"

"Oh, can't we do something?" said Blaustein, who never did anything, anyhow, but draw.

"Sing something!" said Lavinia's brother, throwing away the peach-stone, and settling himself again to sleep. Big Ben struck the half hour. Big Ben is far too big to take any notice of anything terrestrial. A change of dynasty is nothing in his young life!

"Come in, for the land's sake!" cried Lavinia King. Her quick ear had caught a light knock upon the door.

She had hoped for something exciting, but it was only her private tame pianist, a cadaverous individual with the manners of an undertaker gone mad, the morals of a stool-pigeon, and imagining himself a bishop.

"I had to wish you many happy returns," he said to Lisa, when he had greeted the company in general, "and I wanted to introduce my friend, Cyril Grey."

Every one was amazed. They only then perceived that a second man had entered the room without being heard or seen. This individual was tall and thin, almost, as the pianist; but he had the peculiar quality of failing to attract attention. When they saw him, he acted in the most conventional way possible; a smile, and a bow, and a formal handshake, and the right word of greeting. But the moment that introductions were over, he apparently vanished! The conversation became general; Amy Brough went to sleep; Blaustein took his

leave; Arnold King followed; the pianist rose for the same purpose and looked round for his friend. Only then did anyone observe that he was seated on the floor with crossed legs, perfectly indifferent to the company.

The effect of the discovery was hypnotic. From being nothing in the room, he became everything. Even Lavinia King, who had wearied of the world at thirty, and was now forty-three, saw that here was something new to her. She looked at that impassive face. The jaw was square, the planes of the face curiously flat. The mouth was small, a poppy-petal of vermilion, intensely sensuous. The nose was small and rounded, but fine, and the life of the face seemed concentrated in the nostrils. The eyes were tiny and oblique, with strange brows of defiance. A small tuft of irrepressible hair upon the forehead started up like a lone pine-tree on the slope of a mountain; for with this exception, the man was entirely bald; or, rather, clean-shaven, for the scalp was grey. The skull was extraordinarily narrow and long.

Again she looked at the eyes. They were parallel, focussed on infinity. The pupils were pin-points. It was clear to her that he saw nothing in the room. Her dancer's vanity came to her rescue; she moved in front of the still figure, and made a mock obeisance. She might have done the same to a stone image.

To her astonishment, she found the hand of Lisa on her shoulder. A look, half shocked, half pious, was in her friend's eyes. She found herself rudely pushed aside. Turning, she saw Lisa squatting on the floor opposite the visitor, with her eyes fixed upon his. He remained apparently quite unconscious of what was going on.

Lavinia King was flooded with a sudden causeless anger. She plucked her pianist by the arm, and drew him to the window-seat.

Rumour accused Lavinia of too close intimacy with the musician: and rumour does not always lie. She took advantage of the situation to caress him. Monet-Knott, for that was his name, took her action as a matter of course. Her passion satisfied alike his purse and his vanity; and, being without temperament – he was the curate type of ladies' man – he suited the dancer, who would have found a more masterful lover in her way. This creature could not even excite the jealousy of the wealthy automobile manufacturer who financed her.

But this night she could not concentrate her thoughts upon him; they wandered continually to the man on the floor. "Who is he?" she whispered, rather fiercely, "what did you say his name was?" "Cyril Grey," answered

Monet-Knott, indifferently; "he's probably the greatest man in England, in his art." "And what's his art?" "Nobody knows," was the surprising reply, "he won't show anything. He's the one big mystery of London." "I never heard such nonsense," retorted the dancer, angrily; "anyhow, I'm from Missouri!" The pianist stared. "I mean you've got to show me," she explained; "he looks to me like One Big Bluff!" Monet-Knott shrugged his shoulders; he did not care to pursue that topic.

Suddenly Big Ben struck midnight. It woke the room to normality. Cyril Grey unwound himself, like a snake after six months' sleep; but in a moment he was a normal suave gentleman, all smiles and bows again. He thanked Miss King for a very pleasant evening; he only tore himself away from a consideration of the lateness of the hour –

"Do come again!" said Lavinia sarcastically, "one doesn't often enjoy so delightful a conversation."

"My birthday's over," moaned Lisa from the floor, "and I haven't got my thirteenth present."

Amy Brough half woke up. "It's something to do with a large building," she began and broke off suddenly, abashed, she knew not why.

"I'm always in at tea-time," said Lisa suddenly to Cyril. He simpered over her hand. Before they realised it, he had bowed himself out of the room.

The three women looked at each other. Suddenly Lavinia King began to laugh. It was a harsh, unnatural performance: and for some reason her friend took it amiss. She went tempestuously into her bedroom, and banged the door behind her.

Lavinia, almost equally cross, went into the opposite room and called her maid. In half-an-hour she was asleep. In the morning she went in to see her friend. She found her lying on the bed, still dressed, her eyes red and haggard. She had not slept all night. Amy Brough on the contrary, was still asleep in the armchair. When she was roused, she only muttered: "something about a journey in a letter." Then she suddenly shook herself and went off without a word to her place of business in Bond Street. For she was the representative of one of the great Paris dressmaking houses.

Lavinia King never knew how it was managed; she never realised even that it had been managed; but that afternoon she found herself inextricably bound to her motor millionaire.

So Lisa was alone in the apartment. She sat upon the couch, with great eyes, black and lively, staring into eternity. Her black hair coiled upon her

head, plait over plait; her dark skin glowed; her full mouth moved continually.

She was not surprised when the door opened without warning. Cyril Grey closed it behind him, with swift stealth. She was fascinated; she could not rise to greet him. He came over to her, caught her throat in both his hands, bent back her head, and, taking her lips in his teeth, bit them, bit them almost through. It was a single deliberate act: instantly he released her, sat down upon the couch by her, and made some trivial remark about the weather. She gazed at him in horror and amazement. He took no notice; he poured out a flood of small-talk – theatres, politics, literature, the latest news of art –

Ultimately she recovered herself enough to order tea when the maid knocked.

After tea – another ordeal of small-talk – she had made up her mind. Or, more accurately, she had become conscious of herself. She knew that she belonged to this man, body and soul. Every trace of shame departed; it was burnt out by the fire that consumed her. She gave him a thousand opportunities; she fought to turn his words to serious things. He baffled her with his shallow smile and ready tongue, that twisted all topics to triviality. By six o'clock she was morally on her knees before him; she was imploring him to stay to dinner with her. He refused. He was engaged to dine with a Miss Badger in Cheyne Walk; possibly he might telephone later, if he got away early. She begged him to excuse himself; he answered – serious for the first time – that he never broke his word.

At last he rose to go. She clung to him. He pretended mere embarrassment. She became a tigress; he pretended innocence, with that silly shallow smile.

He looked at his watch. Suddenly his manner changed, like a flash. "I'll telephone later, if I can," he said, with a sort of silky ferocity, and flung her from him violently on to the sofa.

He was gone. She lay upon the cushions, and sobbed her heart out.

The whole evening was a nightmare for her – and also for Lavinia King.

The pianist, who had looked in with the idea of dinner, was thrown out with objurgations. Why had he brought that cad, that brute, that fool? Amy Brough was caught by her fat wrists, and sat down to the cards; but the first time that she said "large building", was bundled bodily out of the apartment. Finally, Lavinia was astounded to have Lisa tell her that she would not come to see her dance – her only appearance that season in London! It was incredible. But when she had gone, thoroughly huffed, Lisa threw on her wraps to follow

her; then changed her mind before she had gone halfway down the corridor.

Her evening was a tempest of indecisions. When Big Ben sounded eleven she was lying on the floor, collapsed. A moment later the telephone rang. It was Cyril Grey – of course – of course – how could it be any other?

"When are you likely to be in?" he was asking. She could imagine the faint hateful smile, as if she had known it all her life. "Never!" she answered, "I'm going to Paris the first train tomorrow." "Then I'd better come up now." The voice was nonchalant as death – or she would have hung up the receiver. "You can't come now; I'm undressed!" "Then when may I come?" It was terrible, this antimony of persistence with a stifled yawn! Her soul failed her. "When you will," she murmured. The receiver dropped from her hand; but she caught one word – the word "taxi".

In the morning, she awoke, almost a corpse. He had come, and he had gone – he had not spoken a single word, not even given a token that he would come again. She told her maid to pack for Paris: but she could not go. Instead, she fell ill. Hysteria became neurasthenia; yet she knew that a single word would cure her.

But no word came. Incidentally she heard that Cyril Grey was playing golf at Hoylake; she had a mad impulse to go to find him; another to kill herself.

But Lavinia King, perceiving after many days that something was wrong – after many days, for her thoughts rarely strayed beyond the contemplation of her own talents and amusements – carried her off to Paris. She needed her, anyhow, to play hostess.

But three days after their arrival Lisa received a postcard. It bore nothing but an address and a question-mark. No signature; she had never seen the handwriting; but she knew. She snatched up her hat, and her furs, and ran downstairs. Her car was at the door; in ten minutes she was knocking at the door of Cyril's studio.

He opened.

His arms were ready to receive her; but she was on the floor, kissing his feet.

"My Chinese God! My Chinese God!" she cried. "May I be permitted," observed Cyril, earnestly, "to present my friend and master, Mr. Simon Iff?"

Lisa looked up. She was in the presence of a man, very old, but very alert and active. She scrambled to her feet in confusion.

"I am not really the master," said the old man, cordially, "for our host is a Chinese God, as it appears. I am merely a student of Chinese Philosophy."

CHAPTER II
A PHILOSOPHICAL DISQUISITION
UPON THE NATURE OF THE SOUL.

"THERE is little difference – barring our Occidental subtlety – between Chinese philosophy and English," observed Cyril Grey. "The Chinese bury a man alive in an ant heap; the English introduce him to a woman."

Lisa la Giuffria was startled into normality by the words. They were not spoken in jest.

And she began to take stock of her surroundings. Cyril Grey himself was radically changed. In fashionable London he had worn a claret-coloured suit, an enormous grey butterfly tie hiding a soft silk collar. In bohemian Paris his costume was diabolically clerical in its formality. A frock coat, tightly buttoned to the body, fell to the knees; its cut was as severe as it was distinguished; the trousers were of sober grey. A big black four-in-hand tie was fastened about a tall uncompromising collar by a cabochon sapphire so dark as to be hardly noticeable. A rimless monocle was fixed in his right eye. His manner had changed to parallel his dress. The supercilious air was

gone; the smile was gone. He might have been a diplomatist at the crisis of an empire: he looked even more like a duellist.

The studio in which she stood was situated on the Boulevard Arago, below the Santé prison. It was reached from the road through an archway, which opened upon an oblong patch of garden. Across this, a row of studios nestled; and behind these again were other gardens, one to each studio, whose gates gave on to a tiny pathway. It was not only private – it was rural. One might have been ten miles from the city limits.

The studio itself was severely elegant – *simplex munditiis*; its walls were concealed by dull tapestries. In the centre of the room stood a square carved ebony table, matched by a sideboard in the west and a writing-desk in the east.

Four chairs with high Gothic backs stood about the table; in the north was a divan, covered with the pelt of a Polar bear. The floor was also furred, but with black bears from the Himalayas. On the table stood a Burmese dragon of dark green bronze. The smoke of incense issued from its mouth.

But Simon Iff was the strangest object in that strange room. She had heard of him, of course; he was known for his writings on mysticism and had long borne the reputation of a crank. But in the last few years he had chosen to use his abilities in ways intelligible to the average man; it was he who had saved Professor Briggs, and, incidentally, England when that genius had been accused of and condemned to death for murder, but was too preoccupied with the theory of his new flying-machine to notice that his fellows were about to hang him. And it was he who had solved a dozen other mysteries of crime, with apparently no other resource than pure capacity to analyse the minds of men. People had consequently begun to revise their opinions of him; they even began to read his books. But the man himself remained unspeakably mysterious. He had a habit of disappearing for long periods, and it was rumoured that he had the secret of the Elixir of Life. For although he was known to be over eighty years of age, his brightness and activity would have done credit to a man of forty; and the vitality of his whole being, the fire of his eyes, the quick conciseness of his mind, bore witness to an interior energy almost more than human.

He was a small man, dressed carelessly in a blue serge suit with a narrow dark red tie. His iron-grey hair was curly and irrepressible; his complexion, although wrinkled, was clear and healthy; his small mouth was a moving wreath of smiles; and his whole being radiated an intense and contagious happiness.

His greeting to Lisa had been more than cordial; at Cyril's remark he took her friendlily by the arm, and sat her down on the divan. "I'm sure you smoke," he said, "never mind Cyril! Try one of these; they come from the Khedive's own man."

He extracted an immense cigar-case from his pocket. One side was full of long Partagas, the other of cigarettes. "These are musk-scented the dark ones; the yellowish kind are ambergris; and the thin white ones are scented with attar of roses." Lisa hesitated; then she chose the ambergris. The old man laughed happily. "Just the right choice: the Middle Way! Now I know we are going to be friends." He lit her cigarette, and his own cigar. "I know what is in your mind, my dear young lady: you are thinking that two's company and three's none; and I agree; but we are going to put that right by asking Brother Cyril to study his Qabalah for a little; for before leaving him in the ant-heap – he has really a shocking turn of mind – I want a little chat with you. You see, you are one of Us now, my dear."

"I don't understand," uttered the girl, rather angrily, as Cyril obediently went to his desk, pulled a large square volume out of it, and became immediately engrossed.

"Brother Cyril has told me of your three interviews with him, and I am perfectly prepared to give a description of your mind. You are in rude health, and yet you are hysterical; you are fascinated and subdued by all things weird and unusual, though to the world you hold yourself so high, proud, and passionate. You need love, it is true; so much you know yourself; and you know also that no common love attracts you; you need the sensational, the bizarre, the unique. But perhaps you do not understand what is at the root of that passion. I will tell you. You have an inexpressible hunger of the soul; you despise earth and its delusions; and you aspire unconsciously to a higher life than anything this planet can offer.

"I will tell you something that may convince you of my right to speak. You were born on October the eleventh; so Brother Cyril told me. But he did not tell me the hour; you never told him; it was a little before sunrise."

Lisa was taken aback; the mystic had guessed right.

"The Order to which I belong," pursued Simon Iff, "does not believe anything; it knows, or it doubts, as the case may be; and it seeks ever to increase human knowledge by the method of science, that is to say by observation and experiment. Therefore you must not expect me to satisfy your real craving by answering your questions as to the existence of the Soul;

but I will tell you what I know, and can prove; further, what hypotheses seem worthy of consideration; lastly what experiments ought to be tried. For it is in this last matter that you can aid us; and with this in mind I have come up from St. Jean de Luz to see you."

Lisa's eyes danced with pleasure. "Do you know," she cried, "you are the first man that ever understood me?"

"Let me see whether I do understand you fully. I know very little of your life. You are half Italian, evidently; the other half probably Irish."

"Quite right."

"You come of peasant stock, but you were brought up in refined surroundings, and your nature developed on the best lines possible without check. You married early."

"Yes; but there was trouble. I divorced my husband, and married again two years later."

"That was the Marquis la Giuffria?"

"Yes."

"Well, then, you left him, although he was a good husband, and devoted to you, to throw in your lot with Lavinia King."

"I have lived with her for five years, almost to a month."

"Then why? I used to know her pretty well myself. She was, even in those days, heartless, and mercenary; she was a sponger, the worst type of courtesan; and she was an intolerable poseuse. Every word of hers must have disgusted you. Yet you stick to her closer than a brother."

"That's all true! But she's a sublime genius, the greatest artist the world has ever seen."

"She has a genius," distinguished Simon Iff. "Her dancing is a species of angelic possession, if I may coin a phrase. She comes off the stage from an interpretation of the subtlest and most spiritual music of Chopin or Tschaikowsky; and forthwith proceeds to scold, to wheedle, or to blackmail. Can you explain that reasonably by talking of 'two sides to her character'? It is nonsense to do so. The only analogy is that of a noble thinker and his stupid, dishonest, and immoral secretary. The dictation is taken down correctly, and given to the world. The last person to be enlightened by it is the secretary himself! So, I take it, is the case with all genius; only in many cases the man is in more or less conscious harmony with his genius, and strives eternally to make himself a worthier instrument for his master's touch. The clever man, so-called, the man of talent, shuts out his genius by setting

up his conscious will as a positive entity. The true man of genius deliberately subordinates himself, reduces himself to a negative, and allows his genius to play through him as It will. We all know how stupid we are when we try to do things. Seek to make any other muscle work as consistently as your heart does without your silly interference – you cannot keep it up for forty-eight hours. (I forget what the record is, but it's not much over twenty-four.) All this, which is truth ascertained and certain, lies at the base of the Taoistic doctrine of non-action; the plan of a doing everything by seeming to do nothing. Yield yourself utterly to the Will of Heaven, and you become the omnipotent instrument of that Will. Most systems of mysticism have a similar doctrine; but that it is true in action is only properly expressed by the Chinese. Nothing that any man can do will improve that genius; but the genius needs his mind, and he can broaden that mind, fertilise it with knowledge of all kinds, improve its powers of expression; supply the genius, in short, with an orchestra instead of a tin whistle. All our little great men, our one-poem poets, our one-picture painters, have merely failed to perfect themselves as instruments. The Genius who wrote *The Ancient Mariner* is no less sublime than he who wrote *The Tempest* ; but Coleridge had some incapacity to catch and express the thoughts of his genius – was ever such wooden stuff as his conscious work? – while Shakespeare had the knack of acquiring the knowledge necessary to the expression of every conceivable harmony, and his technique was sufficiently fluent to transcribe with ease. Thus we have two equal angels, one with a good secretary, the other with a bad one. I think this is the only explanation of genius – in the extreme case of Lavinia King it stands out as the one thing thinkable."

Lisa la Giuffria listened with constantly growing surprise and enthusiasm.

"I don't say," went on the mystic, "that the genius and his artist are not inseparably connected. It may be a little more closely than the horse and his rider. But there is at least a distinction to be drawn. And here is a point for you to consider: the genius appears to have all knowledge, all illumination, and to be limited merely by the powers of his medium's mind. Even this is not always a bar: how often do we see a writer gasp at his own work? 'I never knew that,' he cries, amazed, although only a minute previously he has written it down in plain English. In short, the genius appears to be a being of another plane, a soul of light and immortality! I know that much of this may be explained by supposing what I have called the genius to be a bodily substance in which the consciousness of the whole race (in his particular time) may

become active under certain stimuli. There is much to be said for this view; language itself confirms it; for the words 'to know', 'gnosis', are merely sub-echoes of the first cries implying generation in the physical sense; for the root GAN means 'to know' only in the second place; its original sense is 'to beget.' Similarly 'spirit' only means 'breath'; 'divine' and most other words of identical purport imply no more than 'shining'. So it is one of the limitations of our minds that we are fettered by language to the crude ideas of our savage ancestors; and we ought to be free to investigate whether there may not be something in the evolution of language besides a monkey-trick of metaphysical abstractions; whether, in short, men have not been right to sophisticate primitive ideas; whether the growth of language is not evidence of a true growth of knowledge; whether, when all is said and done, there may not be some valid evidence for the existence of a soul."

"The soul!" exclaimed Lisa, joyfully. "Oh, I believe in the soul!"

"Very improper!" rejoined the mystic; "Belief is the enemy of knowledge. Skeat tells us that Soul probably comes from SU, to beget."

"I wish you would speak simply to me, you lift me up, and throw me down again all the time."

"Only because you try to build without foundations. Now I am going to try to show you some good reasons for thinking that the soul exists, and is omniscient and immortal, other than that about genius which we have discussed already. I am not going to bore you with the arguments of Socrates, for, although, as a member of the Hemlock Club, which he founded, I perhaps ought not to say so, the Phaedo is a tissue of the silliest sophistry.

"But I am going to tell you one curious fact in medicine. In certain cases of dementia, where the mind has long been gone, and where subsequent examination has shown the brain to be definitely degenerated, there sometimes occur moments of complete lucidity, where the man is in possession of his full powers. If the mind depended absolutely on the physical condition of the brain, this would be difficult to explain.

"Science, too, is beginning to discover that in various abnormal circumstances, totally different personalities may chase each other through a single body. Do you know what is the great difficulty with regard to spiritualism? It is that of proving the identity of the dead man. In practice, since we have lost the sense of smell on which dogs, for instance, principally rely, we judge that a man is himself either by anthropometric methods, which have nothing to do with the mind or the personality, or by the sound of the

voice, or by the handwriting, or by the contents of the mind. In the case of a dead man, only the last method is available. And here we are tossed on a dilemma. Either the 'spirit' says something which he is known to have known during his life, or something else. In the first case, somebody else must have known it, and may conceivably have informed the medium; in the second case, it is rather disproof than proof of the identity!

"Various plans have been proposed to avoid this difficulty; notably the device of the sealed letter to be opened a year after death. Any medium divulging the contents before that date receives the felicitations of her critics. So far no one has succeeded, though success would mean many thousands of pounds in the medium's pocket; but even if it happened, proof of survival would still be lacking. Clairvoyance, telepathy, guesswork – there are plenty of alternative explanations.

"Then there is the elaborate method of cross-correspondences: I won't bore you with that; Brother Cyril will have plenty of time to talk to you at Naples."

Lisa sat up with a shock. Despite her interest in the subject, her brain had tired. The last words galvanised her.

"I shall explain after lunch," continued the mystic, lighting a third Partaga; "meanwhile, I have wandered slightly from the subject, as you were too polite to remark. I was going to show you how a soul with a weak hold on its tenant could be expelled by another; how, indeed, half-a-dozen personalities could take turns to live in one body. That they are real, independent souls is shown by the fact that not only do the contents of the mind differ – which might conceivably be a fake but their handwritings, their voices, and that in ways which are quite beyond anything we know in the way of conscious simulation, or even possible simulation.

"These personalities are constant quantities; they depart and return unchanged. It is then sure that they do not exist merely by manifestation; they need no body for existence."

"You are coming back to the theory of possession, like the Gadarene swine," cried Lisa, delighted, she could hardly say why. Cyril Grey interrupted the conversation for the first time. He swung round in his armchair, and deliberately cleared his throat while he refixed his eyeglass.

"In these days," he observed, "when devils enter into swine, they do not rush violently down a steep place. They call themselves moral reformers, and vote the Prohibition ticket." He shut up with a snap, swung his chair round again, and returned to the study of his big square book.

"I hope you realise," remarked Simon Iff, "what you have let yourself in for."

Lisa blushed laughingly. "You have set me at my ease. I should certainly never know how to talk to him."

"Always talk," observed Cyril Grey, without looking up. "Words! Words! Words! It's an awful thing to be Hamlet when Ophelia takes after Polonius. She wants to know how to talk to me! And I want to teach her to be silent – even as the friend of Catullus turned his uncle into a statue of Harpocrates."

"Oh yes! I know Harpocrates, the Egyptian God of Silence," gushed the Irish-Italian girl.

Simon Iff gave her a significant glance, and she was wise enough to take it. There are subjects which it is better to drop.

"You know, Mr. Iff," said Lisa, to lighten the sudden tension, "I've been most fearfully interested in all you have said, and I think I have understood quite a part of it; but I don't see the practical application. Do you want me to get messages from the Mighty Dead?"

"Just at present," said the mystic, "I want you to digest what you have heard, and the *dejeuner* which Brother Cyril is about to offer us. After that we shall feel better able to cope with the problems of the Fourth Dimension."

"Dear me! And poor little Lisa has to do all that before she learns the reason of your leaving St. Jean de Luz?"

"All that, and the whole story of the Homunculus!"

"Whatever is that?"

"After lunch."

But as it turned out, it was a very long while before lunch. The bell of the studio rang brusquely.

Cyril Grey went to the door; and once again Lisa had the impression of a duellist. No: it was a sentinel that stood there. Her vivid power of visualization put a spear in his hand.

It was his own studio, but he announced his visitors as if he had been a butler. "Akbar Pasha and Countess Helena Mottich." Simon Iff sprang to the door. It was not his studio, but he welcomed the visitors with both hands outstretched.

"Since you have crossed our threshold," he cried, "I am sure you will stay to *dejeuner*." The visitors murmured a polite acceptance. Cyril Grey was frowning formidably. It was evident that he knew and detested his guests; that he feared their coming; that he suspected – who could say what? He

acquiesced instantly in his master's words; yet if silence ever spoke, this was the moment when it beggared curses.

He had not given his hand to his guests. Simon Iff did so: but he did it in such a way that each of them was obliged to take a hand at the same moment as the other.

Lisa had risen from the divan. She could see that some intricacy was on foot, but could form no notion of its nature.

When the newcomers were seated, Lisa found that she was expected to regale them with the news of Paris. It was rather a relief to her to get away from the mystic's theories. The others left everything to her. She rattled off some details of Lavinia King's latest success. Then suddenly noticed that Cyril Grey had laid the table. For his eager cynical voice broke into the conversation. "I was there," he said, "I liked the first number: the Dying Grampus Phantasy in B flat was extraordinarily realistic. I didn't care so much for the 'Misadventures of a pat of butter' Sonata. But the Tschaikowsky symphony was best: that was Atmosphere; it put me right back among the old familiar scenes; I thought I was somewhere on the South-Eastern Railway waiting for a train."

Lisa flamed indignation. "She's the most wonderful dancer in the world." "Yes, she is that," said her lover, with affected heavy sadness. "Wonderful! My father used to say, too, that she used even to dance well when she was forty."

The nostrils of la Giuffria dilated. She understood that it was a monster that had carried her away; and she made ready for a last battle.

But Simon Iff announced the meal. "Pray you, be seated!" he said. "Unfortunately, today is a fast-day with us; we have but some salt fish with our bread and wine."

Lisa wondered what kind of a fast-day it might be: it was certainly not Friday. The Pasha made a wry face. "Ah!" said Iff, as if he had just remembered it, "but we have some Caviar." The Pasha refused coldly. "I do not really want *dejeuner*," he said. "I only came to ask whether you would care for a seance with the Countess."

"Delighted! Delighted!" cried Iff, and again Lisa understood that he was on the alert; that he sensed some deadly yet invisible peril; that he loathed the visitors, and yet would be careful to do every thing that they suggested. Already she had a sort of intuition of the nature of "the way of the Tao".

CHAPTER III

TELEKINESIS:

BEING THE ART OF MOVING OBJECTS AT A DISTANCE

THE Countess Mottich was far more famous than most Prime Ministers or Imperial Chancellors. For, to the great bewilderment of many alleged men of science, she had the power of small objects to move without apparent physical contact. Her first experiments had been with a purblind old person named Oudouwitz, who was in love with her in his senile way. Few people swallowed the published results of his experiments with her. If convinced they would have been very much startled. For she was supposed to be able to stop clocks at will, to open and close doors without approaching them – and other feats of the same general type. But she had sobered down since leaving the Professor – which she had done, just as soon as she had acquired enough money to get married to the man she wanted. Her power had left her instantly, strange to say; and many were the theories propounded connecting these circumstances. But her husband had displeased her; she had flown off in a rage – and her power had returned! But most of her sensational feats were relegated to the bad mad old days of wild and

headstrong youth; at present she merely undertook to raise light small objects, such as tiny celluloid spheres, from the table, without touching them.

So Cyril explained, when Lisa asked "What does she do?"

(The Countess was supposed to know no English. She spoke it as well as anyone in the room, of course.)

"She moves things," he said; "manages to get hold of a couple of hairs when we're tired of looking at foolishness for hours together, twists them in her fingers, and, miracle of miracles! the ball rises in the air. This is everywhere considered by all rightly-disposed people to be certain proof of the immortality of the soul."

"But doesn't she challenge you? Ask you to search her, and all that?"

"Oh yes! You've got the same chance as a deaf man has to detect a mistake in a Casals recital. If she can't get a hair, she'll pull a thread from her silk stockings or her dress; if you get people that are really too clever for her, then 'the force is very weak this afternoon,' though she keeps you longer than ever in the hope of tiring your attention, and perhaps to pay you out for baffling her!"

Grey said all this with an air of the most hideous boredom. It was evident that he hated the whole business. He was restless and anxious, too, with another part of his brain; Lisa could see that, but she dared not question him. So she went on the old track.

"Doesn't she get messages from the dead?"

"It's not done much now. It's too easy to fake, and the monied fools lost interest, as a class. This new game tickles the vanity of some of the sham scientific people, like Lombroso; they think they'll make a reputation like Newton out of it. They don't know enough science to criticise the business on sensible lines. Oh, really, I prefer your fat friend with the large building and the letter about a journey!"

"You mean that the whole thing is absolute fraud?"

"Can't say. Hard to prove a negative, or to affirm a universal proposition. But the onus of proof is on the spiritualists, and there are only two cases worth considering, Mrs. Piper, who never did anything very striking, anyhow, and Eusapia Palladino."

"She was exposed in America some time ago," said the girl, "but I think it was only in the Hearst newspapers."

"Hearst is the American Northcliffe," explained Cyril for the benefit of the Pasha. "And so is Northcliffe," he added musingly and unblushingly!

"I'm afraid I don't know who Northcliffe is," said Akbar. "Northcliffe was Harmsworth." Cyril's voice was caressing, like one soothing a fractious child.

"But who was Harmsworth?" asked the Turk.

The young magician spoke in a hollow tone: "Nobody."

"Nobody?" cried Akbar. "I don't understand!"

Cyril shook his head solemnly and sadly. "There ain't no such person."

Akbar Pasha looked at Grey as if he were a ghost. It was a horrible trick of the boy's. He would invite confidence by a sensible, even possibly a bright, remark; then, in an explanatory way, he would lead his interlocutor, with exquisite skill, through quaking sands of various forms of insanity, only to drop them at the end into the bog of dementia. The dialogue suddenly realised itself as a nightmare. To Cyril it was probably the one genuine pleasure of conversation. He went on, in a brisk professional manner, with a suave persuasive smile: "I am trying to affirm the metaphysical dogma enunciated by Schelling in his philosophy of the relative, emphasizing in particular the lemma that the acceptation of the objective as real involves the conception of the individual as a tabula rasa, thus correlating Occidental theories of the Absolute with the Buddhist doctrine of Sakyaditthi! But confer in rebuttal the Vagasaneyi-Samhita-Upanishad!" He turned brusquely to Lisa with the finality of one who has explained everything to the satisfaction of everybody. "Yes, you do right to speak in defence of Eusapia Palladino; we will investigate her when we reach Naples."

"You seem determined that I should go to Naples."

"Nothing to do with me: the master's orders. He'll explain, by-and-by. Now let's prove that this lady, whose locks are bushy and black as a raven's, has no hairs concealed upon her person!"

"I hate you when you're cynical and sarcastic."

"Love me, love my dog!" –

Simon Iff arrested his attention with an imperious gesture.

"Come into the garden, Maud," said Cyril suddenly; "For the black bat, Night, hath flown." He took her by the arm.

"Girl," he said, when they were among the flowers with his long arms about her, and a passionate kiss still flaming through every nerve of both their bodies, "I can't explain now, but you're in the most deadly danger from these people. And we simply can't get rid of them. Trust us, and wait! Till they're gone, keep away from them: make any excuse you like, if it's necessary; sham a hysterical attack and bolt if the worst comes to

the worst – but don't let either of them manage to scratch you! It might be your death."

His evident earnestness did more than convince her. It reassured her on her whole position. She realised that he loved her, that his manner was merely an ornament, an affectation like his shaved head and his strange dress. And her own love for him, freed from all doubt, rushed out as does the sun from behind the crest of some cold pyramid of rock and ice, in mountain lands.

When they returned to the studio, they found that the simple preparations for the seance had been completed. The medium was already seated at the table, with the two men one on either side of her. Before her, between her hands, were some small spheres of celluloid, a couple of pencil-ends, and various other small objects. These had been "examined" with the utmost care, as who should examine the tail of a dog to find out whether he would bite. The history of spiritualism is that of blocking up every crack in a room with putty, and then leaving the door wide open.

It may well be doubted whether even the most tedious writer could describe a seance with success. People generally have an idea that there is something exciting and mysterious about it. In reality, people who boast of their ability to enjoy their third consecutive sleepless night have been known to pray to their Maker for sudden death at least two hours before the occurrence of the first "phenomenon". To be asked to keep the attention unceasingly on things of not the slightest intrinsic interest or importance is absolutely maddening to anyone above the mental level of a limpet.

"Observe how advantageously we are placed," whispered Cyril to Lisa as they took seats on the divan, toward which the table had been drawn. "For all we know, one or both those men are in collusion with Mottich. I'd stake my life Simple Simon isn't; but I wouldn't expect my own twin brother to take my word for it, in a matter like this. Then the curtains have been drawn; why? To help the force along. Yet it is supposed to be kinetic force; and we cannot even imagine how light could interfere with it. Otherwise, it is that the light 'distresses the medium in her peculiar state'. Just as the policeman's bull's-eye distresses the burglar in his peculiar state! Now look here! These arguments about 'evidential' phenomena always resolve themselves into questions of the conditions prevailing at the time; but the jest is that it always turns out that the argument is about conjuring tricks, not about 'forces' at all."

"Won't she mind us talking?"

"Mediums alway's encourage the sitters to talk. The moment she sees us getting interested in what we are saying, she takes the opportunity to do the dangerous, delicate part of the trick; then she calls our attention, says we must watch her very carefully to see that the control is good and no cheating possible, because she feels the force coming very strong. Everybody disguises himself as a cat at a mousehole – which you can keep up, after long training, for about three minutes; then the attention slackens slightly again, and she pulls off the dear old miracle. Listen!"

Simon Iff was engaged in a violent controversy with the Pasha as to the disposition of the six legs at their end of the table. On the accurate solution of this problem, knotty in more than one sense, depended the question as to whether the medium could have kicked the table and made one of the balls jump. If it were proved that it was impossible, the question would properly arise as to whether a ball had jumped, anyhow.

"Isn't it the dullest thing on earth?" droned Cyril. But, even without what he had said in the garden, she would have known that he was lying. For all his nonchalance, he was watching very acutely; for all his bored, faded voice, she could feel every tone tingling with suppressed excitement. It was certainly not the seance that interested him; but what was it?

The medium began to moan. She complained of cold; she began to twist her body about; she dropped her head suddenly on the table in collapse. Nobody took any particular notice; it was all part of the performance. "Give me your hands!" she said to Lisa, "I feel you are so sympathetic." As a matter of fact, the girl's natural warmth of heart had stirred her for a moment. She reached her hands out. But Simon Iff rose from the table and caught them. "You may have a hair or a loose thread," he said sharply. "Lights up, please, Cyril!"

The old mystic proceeded to make a careful examination of Lisa's hands. But Cyril watching him, divined an ulterior purpose. "I say," he drawled, "I'm afraid I was in the garden when you examined the Countess. Oughtn't I to look at her hands if this is to be evidential?" Simon Iff's smile showed him that he was on the right track. He took the medium's hands, and inspected them minutely. Of course he found no hairs; he was not looking for them. "Do you know," he said, "I think we ought to file off these nails. There's such a lot of room for hairs and things."

The Pasha immediately protested. "I don't think we ought to interfere with a lady's manicuring," he said indignantly. "Surely we can trust our eyes!"

Cyril Grey had beaten links in the Open Championship; but he only murmured: "I'm so sorry, Pasha; I can't trust mine. I'm threatened with tobacco amblyopia."

The imbecility of the remark, as intended, came near to upset the Turk's temper.

"I've always agreed with Berkeley," he went on, completely changing the plane of the conversation, while maintaining its original subject, "that our eyes bear no witness to anything external. I am afraid I'm only wasting your time, because I don't believe anything I see, in any case."

The Turk was intensely irritated at the magician's insolence. Whenever Cyril was among strangers, or in any danger, he invariably donned the bomb-proof armour of British aristocracy. He had been on the *Titanic*; a second and a half before she took the last plunge, he had turned to his neighbour, and asked casually, "Do you think there is any danger?"

Half an hour later he had been dragged into a boat, and, on recovering consciousness, took occasion to remark that the last time he had been spilt out of a boat was in Byron's Pool – "above Cambridge, England, you know" – and proceeded to relate the entire story of his adventure. He passed from one story to another, quite indifferent to the tumult on the boat, and ended by transporting the minds of the others far from the ice of the Atlantic to the sunny joys of the May Week at Cambridge. He had got everybody worked up as to what would happen after "First shot just before Ditton, and missed by half a blade; Jesus washed us off, and went away like the devil! Third were coming up like steam, with Hall behind them, and old T. J. cursing them to blazes from his gee; it was L for leather all up the Long Reach; then, thank goodness, Hall bumped Third just under the Railway Bridge: Cox yelled, and there was Jesus – " But they never heard what happened to the first boat of that excellent college, for Grey suddenly fainted, and they found that he was bleeding slowly to death from a deep wound over the heart.

This was the man who was frightened out of his life at the possibility of a chance scratch from an exquisitely clean and polished finger-nail.

The Turk could do nothing but bow. "Well, if you insist, Mr. Grey, we can only ask the lady."

He did so, and she professed most willing eagerness. The operation was a short one, and the seance recommenced.

But in a few minutes the Countess herself wearied. "I know I shall get

nothing; it's no use; I do wish Baby were here; she could do what you want in a minute."

The Pasha nodded gleefully. "That's always the way we begin," he explained to Simple Simon. "Now I'll have to hypnotise her and she'll wake up in her other personality."

"Very, very interesting," agreed Simon; "curiously enough, we were just discussing double personalities with Madame la Giuffria when you honoured us with your visit. She has never seen anything of the kind."

"You'll be charmed, Marquise," the old Turk assured Lisa; "it's the most wonderful thing you ever saw." He began to make passes over the medium's forehead; she made a series of convulsive movements, which gradually died away, and were succeeded by deep sleep. Cyril took Lisa to one side. "This is really great magic! This is the old original confidence trick. Pretend to be asleep yourself, so that all the others may go to sleep in reality. It is described at no length whatever by Frazer in his book on sympathetic magic. For that most learned doctor, *vir praeclarus et optimus*, omits the single essential of his subject. It is not enough to pretend that your wax image is the person you want to bewitch; you must make a real connexion. That is the whole art of magic, to be able to do that; and it is the one point that Frazer omits."

The Countess was now heaving horribly, and emitting a series of complicated snorts. The Pasha explained that this was "normal", that she was "waking up into the new personality". Almost before he finished, she had slid off her chair on to the floor, where she uttered an intense and prolonged wail. The men removed the table, that her extrication might become more simple. They found her on her back, smiling and crowing, opening and closing her hands. When she saw the men she began to cry with fright. Then her first articulation was "Mum – Mum – Mum – Mum – Mum."

"She wants her mother," explained Akbar. "I didn't know a lady was to be present; but as we are so happy, would you mind pretending to be her mother? It would help immensely."

Lisa had quite forgotten Cyril's warning, and would have accepted. She was quite willing to enter into the spirit of the performance, whether it was a serious affair, a swindle, or merely an idiotic game; but Simon Iff interfered.

"Madame is not accustomed to seances," he said; and Cyril darted a look at her which compelled her obedience, though she had no idea in the world why she should, or why she shouldn't, do any given thing. She was like one

in a strange country; the only thing to do is to conform to the customs as well as one can; and to trust one's guide.

"Baby" continued to yell. The Pasha, prepared for the event, whipped a bottle of milk out of his pocket, and she began to suck at it contentedly.

"What ridiculous fellows those old alchemists were!" said Cyril to his beloved. "How could they have gone on fooling with their athanors and cucurbites and alembics, and their Red Dragon, and their Caput Mortuum, and their Lunar Water? They really had no notion of the Dignity of Scientific Research."

There was no need to press home the bitterness of his speech; Lisa was already conscious of a sense of shame at assisting at such degrading imbecilities.

"Baby" relinquished the bottle, and began to crawl after one of the celluloid balls, which had rolled off the table when they moved it. She found it in a corner, sat up, and began to play with it.

All of a sudden something happened which shocked Lisa into a disgusted exclamation.

"It is all part of the assumption of baby-hood," said Cyril, coldly "and a bad one; for there is no reason why obsession by a baby's soul or mind should interfere with adult reflexes. The real reason is that this woman comes from the lowest sewers of Buda-Pesth. She was a common prostitute at the age of nine, and only took up this game as a better speculation. It is part of her pleasure to abuse the licence we allow her by such bestialities: it is a mark of her black envy; she does not understand that her foulness does not so much as soil our shoe-leather."

Despite her years of practice in the art of not understanding English, "Baby" winced momentarily. For her dearest thought was the social prestige which she enjoyed. It was terrible to see that the Real Thing was not under the slightest illusion. She did not mind a thousand "exposures" as a fraud; but she did want to keep up the bluff of being a Countess. She was past thirty-five; it was high time she found an old fool to marry her. She had designs on the Pasha; she had agreed to certain proposals in respect of this very seance with a view to getting him into her power.

He was apologising for her in the conventional way to Simon Iff. She had no consciousness or memory of this state at all, it appeared. "She will grow up in a little while; wait a few moments only."

And so it happened; soon she was prattling to the Pasha, who thoughtfully produced a doll for her to play with. Finally, she came over on her knees to

Lisa, and began to cry, and simulate fear, and stammer out a confession of some kind. But Lisa did not wait to hear it; she was hot-tempered, and constitutionally unable to conceal her feelings beyond a certain point. She dragged her skirts away roughly, and went to the other end of the room. The Pasha deprecated the action, with oriental aplomb; but the medium had already reached the next and final stage. She went to the Pasha, sat on his knee, and began to make the most violent love to him, with wanton kisses and caresses.

"That's the best trick of the lot," explained Cyril; "It goes wonderfully with a great many men. It gets their powers of observation rattled; she can pull off the most obvious 'miracles', and get them to swear that the control was perfect. That's how she fooled Oudouwitz; he was a very old man, and she proved to him that he was not as old as he thought he was. Great Harry Lauder! apart from any deception, a man in such circumstances might be willing to swear away his own reputation in order to assure her a career!"

"It's rather embarrassing," said the Pasha, "especially to a Mohammedan like myself; but one must endure everything in the cause of Science. In a moment now she'll be ready for the sitting."

Indeed, she changed suddenly into Personality Number Three, a very decorous young Frenchwoman named Annette, maid to the wife of a Jewish Banker. She went with rather stiff decorum to the table – she had to lay breakfast for her mistress, it appeared – but the moment she got there, she began to tremble violently all over, sank into the chair, and resumed the "Baby" personality, after a struggle. "Det away, bad Annette – naughty, naughty!" was the burden of her inspiring monologue for a few minutes. Then she suddenly became absorbed in the small objects before her – the Pasha had replaced them – and began to play with them, as intently as many children do with toys.

"Now we must have the lights down!" said the Pasha. Cyril complied. "Light is terribly painful and dangerous to her in this state. Once she lost her reason for a month through some one switching on the current unexpectedly. But we shall make a close examination, for all that." He took a thick silk scarf, and bound it over her eyes. Then, with an electric torch, he swept the table. He pulled back her sleeves to the shoulder and fastened them there; and he went over her hands inch by inch, opening the fingers and separating them, searching the nails, proving, in short, to demonstration, that there was no deception.

"You see," whispered Cyril, "we're not preparing for a scientific experiment; we're preparing for a conjuring trick. It's the psychology of trickery. Not my idea; the master's."

However, the attention of Lisa la Giuffria, almost despite herself, was drawn to the restless fingers on the table. They moved and twisted into such uncanny shapes; and there was something in the play of them, their intention towards the frail globe on which they converged, that fascinated her.

The medium drew her fingers swiftly away from the ball; at the same instant it jumped three or four inches into the air. The Turk purred delight. "Quite evidential, don't you think, sir?" he observed to Simon.

"Oh, quite," returned the old man, but in a tone that would have made any one who knew him well continue the conversation with these words "Evidential of WHAT?" But Akbar was fully satisfied. As a matter of form, he turned the torch on again, and made a new examination of the medium's fingers; but no hairs were to be discovered.

From this moment the phenomena became continuous. The articles upon the table hopped, skipped and danced like autumn leaves in a whirlwind. For ten minutes this went on, with constantly increasing energy.

"The fun is fast and furious," cried Lisa.

Cyril adjusted his monocle with immense deliberation. "The epithet of which you appear to be in search," he remarked, "is, possibly, 'chronic.'"

Lisa stared at him, while the pencils and balls still pattered on the table like dancing hail.

"Doctor Johnson once remarked that we need not criticise too closely the performance of a whistling cabbage, or whatever it was," he explained wearily, "the wonder being in the fact of the animal being able to do it at all. But I would venture to add that for my part I find wonder amply satisfied by a single exhibition of this kind; to fall into a habit appears to me utterly out of accord with the views of the late John Stuart Mill on Liberty."

Lisa always found herself whirled about like a Dervish by the strange twists which her lover continued to give to his conversation.

Monet-Knott had told her in London of his famous faux pas at Cannon Street Station, when the railway official had passed along the train, shouting "All change! All change!" only to be publicly embraced by Cyril, who pretended to believe that he was a Buddhist Missionary, on the ground that one of the chief doctrines of Buddhism is that change is a principle inherent in all component things!

And unless you knew beforehand what Cyril was thinking, his words gave you no clue. You could never tell whether he were serious or joking. He had fashioned his irony on the model of that hard, cold, cruel, smooth glittering black ice that one finds only in deep gullies of the loftiest mountains; it was said in the clubs that he had found seventy-seven distinct ways of calling a man, to his face, something which only the most brazen fish-wives of Billingsgate care to call by its name, without his suspecting anything beyond a well-turned compliment.

Fortunately his lighter side was equally prominent. It was he who had gone into Lincoln Bennett's – Hatters to his Majesty since helmets ceased to be the wear – had asked with diffidence and embarrassment to see the proprietor on a matter of the utmost importance; and, on being deferentially conducted to a private room, had enquired earnestly: "Do you sell hats?"

The mystery of the man was an endless inquietude to her. She wished to save herself from loving, him, but only because she felt that she could never be sure that she had got him. And that intensified her determination to make him wholly and forever hers.

Another story of Monet-Knott's had frightened her terribly. He had once put himself to a great deal of trouble to obtain a walking-stick to his liking. Ultimately he had found it, with such joy that he had called his friends and neighbours together, and bidden them to a lunch at the Carlton. After the meal, he had walked down Pall Mall with two of his guests – and discovered that he had forgotten the walking-stick. "Careless of me!" had been his only remark; and nothing would persuade him to stir a step towards its recovery.

She preferred to think of that other side of his character which she knew from the *Titanic* episode, and that other of how his men had feared to follow him across a certain snow-slope that hung above a Himalayan precipice – when he had glissaded on his back, head foremost, to within a yard of the brink. The men had followed him then; and she knew that she too would follow him to the end of the world.

Lost in these meditations, she hardly noticed that the seance was over. The medium had gradually fallen "asleep" again, to wake up in her Number One personality. But as the others rose from the table, Lisa too rose, more or less automatically, with them.

The foot of Akbar Pasha caught in the edge of a bearskin; and he stumbled violently. She shot out an arm to save him; but the young magician was quicker. He caught the Turk's shoulder with his left hand,

and steadied him; at the same moment she felt his other hand crushing her wrist, and her arm bent back with such suddenness that she wondered that it did not snap.

The next moment she saw that Cyril, with his hand on the Pasha's arm, was begging permission in his silkiest tones to examine a signet-ring of very beautiful design. "Admirable!" he was saying, "but isn't the edge too sharp, Pasha? One could cut oneself if one drew one's hand across it sharply, like this." He made a swift gesture. "You see?" he remarked. A stream of blood was already trickling from his hand. The Turk looked at him with sudden black rage, of which she could not guess the cause. Cyril had expressly told her that a scratch might be death. Yet he had courted it; and now he stood exchanging commonplaces, with his blood dripping upon the floor. Impulsively she seized his hand and bound it with her handkerchief.

The Countess had wrapped her furs about her; but suddenly she felt faint. "I can't bear the sight of blood," she said, and collapsed upon the divan. Simon Iff appeared at her side with a glass of brandy. "I feel better now; do give me my hat, Marquise!" Again Cyril intervened. "Over my dead body!" he cried, feigning to be a jealous lover; and adjusted it with his own hands.

Presently the visitors were at the door. The Turk became voluble over the seance. "Wonderful!" he cried; "one of the most remarkable I was ever present at!"

"So glad, Pasha!" replied Grey, with his hand on the door, "one can't pick a winner every time at this game, can one?"

Lisa La Giuffria saw that (somehow) the courteous phrase cut like a whip of whalebone.

She turned as the door closed. To her surprise she saw that Simon Iff had sunk on the divan, and that he was wiping the sweat from his brows.

Behind her, her lover took a great breath, as one who comes out of deep water.

And then she realised that she had been present not at a seance, but at a battle. She became conscious of the strain upon herself, and she broke into a flood of tears.

Cyril Grey, with a pale smile, was bending upon her face, kissing away the drops even as they issued; and, beneath her, his strong arm bore her whole weight without a tremor.

CHAPTER IV

LUNCH, AFTER ALL;

AND A LUMINOUS ACCOUNT
OF THE FOURTH DIMENSION

"I CONFESS to hunger," said Simon Iff, after a few moments. Cyril kissed Lisa on the mouth, and walked with his arm still circling her, to the sideboard. "You are hostess here now you know," he said quite simply. All his affectations dropped from him at that moment, and Lisa understood that he was just a simple-minded, brave, and honest man, who, walking in the midst of perils, had devised a formidable armament both for attack and defence.

She felt a curious pang of pain simultaneously with a sense of exaltation. For she was no longer merely his mistress; he had accepted her as a friend. It was no longer a purely sexual relation, which is always in the nature of a duel; he might cease to love her, in the crude savage sense; but he would always be a pal – just as if she were a man. And here was the pang: was he sure to return to the mood that her whole body and soul were even at that moment crying out for?

The story of his "Judgment of Paris", as they called it, came into her mind. Some years before, he had had three women in love with him at once. It

seemed to each that she was the only one. But they discovered the arrangement – he never took pains to hide such things – and they agreed to confront him. They called at his studio together, and told him that he must choose one of them. He smoked a full pipe before replying; then went to his bedroom and returned with a pair of socks – in need of attention. "Simon, Son of Jonas, lovest thou me? – Yea, Lord, thou knowest that I love thee. Mend my socks," he misquoted somewhat blasphemously, and threw the socks to the one he really loved.

Lisa meant to lay the table in that sense of the word, so to speak. She remembered that the only words spoken by Kundry after her redemption were "*Dienen! Dienen!*"

"Is this your fast?" she cried gaily, discovering the contents of the sideboard. For her gaze fell upon a lobster salad of surprising glory flanked by a bowl of caviar in ice on one side, and one of those *foie gras* pies – the only kind really worth eating which you have to cut with a spoon dipped in hot water. On an upper shelf was a pyramid of woodcock, prepared for the chafing dish which stood beside them; there was a basket of pears and grapes of more value than a virtuous woman – and we know that her price is above rubies! In the background stood the wines in cohorts. There was hock from the cellars of Prince Metternich; there was Burgundy – a Chambertin that could have given body to a ghost, and hardly lost its potency; there was a Tokay that really was Imperial; there was 1865 brandy made in 1865 – which is as rare as radium in pitchblende.

Simon Iff took it upon himself to explain his apparent lack of hospitality toward the visitors.

"Akbar Pasha came here for blood: a drop of your blood, my dear; Cyril's and mine are not in his power – you saw how contemptuously the boy played up to his trick! So I persisted in offering him salt, and nothing but salt."

"But why should he want my blood? And why should you give him salt?"

"If he accepts salt it limits his powers to injure the house where he accepts it, or its inmates; and it exposes him to a terrible riposte. Why he should want your blood – that is another question, and a very serious one. Unfortunately, it implies that he knows who you are, and what we purpose for you. If he had it, he could influence you to do his will; we only wish that you should be free to do your own. I won't insult you by telling you that you can go scatheless by the simple process of returning to your ordinary life. I've been watching you, and I know you would

385

despise me for suggesting it. I know that you are ignorant of what may lie before you, but that you judge it to be formidable; and that you embrace the adventure with both hands."

"I mustn't contradict the famous expert in psychology!" she laughed back at him. "I ought to deny it indignantly. And I surely am crazy to leap in the dark – only it isn't dark when Love is the lamp."

"Be careful of love!" the old magician warned her. "Love is a Jack o' Lantern, and hovers over bogs and graves; it's but a luminous bubble of poisonous gas. In our Order we say, 'Love is the law, love under will.' Will is the iron signal staff. Fix love on that, and you have a lighthouse, and your ship comes safe to harbour!"

"I may now apologise," remarked Cyril, as they seated themselves at the table, "for leaving you the other night to dine at Miss Badger's. I had given my word to her, and nothing but physical inability would have stopped me from going. I didn't want to go, any more than I wanted to drown myself; and that is a great compliment to you, for she is one of the two nicest women in London; but I would have faced a thousand deaths to get there."

"It is right to be so stern about a trifle?"

"Keeping one's word is no trifle. False in one, false in all. Can't you see how simple it makes life for me, never to have to worry about a decision, always to be able to refer everything to a simple standard, my Will? And can't you see how simple it makes life for you, to know that if I once say a thing, I'll do it?"

"Yes. I do see. But, oh, Cyril, what agony I passed through that evening!"

"That was ignorance," said Simon Iff, "the cause of all suffering. You failed to read him, to be assured that, just as he was keeping his word to Miss Badger about the dinner, he would keep his to you about the telephone."

"Now, tell me about the Battle. I see that I am in the thick of the fight; but I haven't got a ghost of a notion why!"

"I'm sorry, dear child, but this Knowledge is unsuited to your exalted grade," he answered playfully. "We must get up to it slowly by telling you exactly what we want to do, and why. Then you will see why others should try to thwart us. And I deeply regret to have to inform you that our road lies through somewhat hilly country. You will have to listen to a lecture on the Fourth Dimension."

"Whatever in the world is that?"

"I think we had better talk of simpler matters until lunch is over."

They began to discuss their private affairs. There was no reason at all why Lisa should not take up her residence with Cyril from that moment. She had merely to telephone her maid to pack, and come along. She offered to do so when Simon Iff said that he thought they ought to leave Paris without a day's delay. But he said: "I don't think it quite fair on the girl. It's a battle, and no call for her to fight. Besides" – he turned to Cyril – "she would probably be obsessed in twenty-four hours."

"I shouldn't be surprised to learn that they were after her already. Let's try! Call her, Lisa, and say you'll not be back tonight; tell her to await further instructions."

Lisa went to the telephone. Instead of getting her room, she was connected with the manager of the hotel. "I much regret to have to tell you, madame, that your maid was seized with epileptic fits shortly after you left this morning."

Lisa was too stunned to reply. She dropped the receiver. Cyril crossed to her instantly, and told the man that his news had upset Madame; she would telephone again later.

Lisa repeated what the manager had said.

"I thought as much," said Cyril.

"I didn't," said Iff frankly, "and it worries me. I'm not guessing, like you are – and it's no credit to guess right, my young friend, but a deceit of the devil, like winning at roulette. I'm deducing from what I know. Therefore, the fact that I'm wrong proves that there is something I don't know – and it worries me. But, clearly, we must get into a properly protected area without a moment wasted. That is, you must. I'll watch at the front. There must be somebody big behind that clumsy fool Akbar Pasha."

"Yes; I've been guessing," admitted Cyril, with some shame. "Or, perhaps worse, I've let my ego expand, and taken the largest possible view of the importance of our project."

"Well, tell me the project!" said Lisa. "Can't you see I can hardly bear this any more?"

"You're safe within these walls," said Simon, "now that there is no enemy within the gates; and tonight we shall take you under guard to a protected area. Tomorrow the fun will begin in good earnest. Meanwhile, here is the preliminary knowledge with regard to the project. Before you start, you have to take a certain vow; and we cannot allow you to do that in ignorance of all that it implies, down to the tiniest iota."

"I am ready."

"I am going to make everything as simple as I possibly can. You have a good imagination, and I think you should be able to follow.

"See here: I take a pencil and a piece of paper. I make a point. It stays there. It doesn't go in any direction. In mathematics we say: 'It is extended in no dimension.' Now I draw a straight line. That goes in one direction. We say, it is extended in one dimension.

"Now I make another line to cross it at right angles. That is one extension in a second dimension."

"I see, and another line would make a third dimension."

"Don't go too fast. Your third line is no use. If I want to show the position of any point on the paper, I can do it by reference to these two lines only. Make a point, and I'll show you."

She obeyed.

"Now, I draw lines from your point to make right angles with my lines. I say your point is so far east of the central point, and so far north. You see? I determine the position by only two measurements."

"But if I made my point right in the air here?"

"Exactly. We need a third line, but it must be at right angles to the other two; sticking straight up, as you might say. Then we can measure in three directions, and determine the point. It is so far east, so far south, and so high."

"Yes."

"Now I'll go over that again in another way.

"Here is a point, not long nor broad nor thick: no dimension.

"Here is a line, long but neither broad nor thick: one dimension. Here is a surface, long and broad, but not thick: two dimensions.

"Here is a solid, long and broad and thick: three dimensions."

"Now I quite understand. But you said: four dimensions."

"I will say it presently. But just now I am going to hammer at two.

"Observe: I make a triangle. All the sides are equal. Now I draw a line through it from one angle to the middle of the other side. I have two triangles. They are exactly alike, as you see; same size, same shape. But – they point in opposite directions. Now we will cut them out with scissors."

He did so.

"Slide them about, so that one lies exactly to cover the other!"

She tried and failed: then, with a laugh, turned one over, when it easily fitted.

"Ah, you cheated. I said, 'slide them.'"

"I'm sorry."

"On the contrary, you have acted divinely, in the best sense! You took the thing that wouldn't fit out of its world of two into the world of three, put it back, and they all lived happy ever after!

"The next thing is this. Everything that exists – everything material – has these three dimensions. These points and lines and surfaces have all a minute extension in some other dimension, or they would be merely things in our imagination. The surface of water, for instance, is merely the boundary between it and the air.

"Now I am going to tell you why some people have thought that another dimension might exist. Those triangles, so like, yet so unlike, have analogies in the world of what we call real things. For example there are two kinds of sugar, exactly alike in every way but one. You know how a prism bends a ray of light? Well if you take a hollow prism, and fill it with a solution of one of these kinds of sugar, the ray bends to the right; use the other kind, and it bends to the left. Chemistry is full of these examples.

"Then we have our hands and feet; however we move about, we can never make them fill exactly the same place. A right hand is always a right hand, however you move it. It only becomes a left hand in a looking-glass – so your mirror should in future afford you a superior sort of reflection! It should remind you that there is a looking-glass world, if you could only get through!"

"Yes, but we can't get through!"

"Don't let us lose our way! Enough to say that there might be such a world. But we must try to find a reason for thinking that there is one. Now the best reason of all is a very deep one; but try to understand it."

Lisa nodded.

"We know that the planets move at certain rates in certain paths, and we know that the laws which govern them are the same as those which made Newton's apple fall. But Newton couldn't explain the law, and he said that he found himself quite unable to imagine a force acting at a distance, as gravitation (so called) appears to do. Science was hard put to it, and had finally to invent a substance called the ether, of which there was no evidence, only it must be there! But this ether had so many contradictory and impossible qualities, that people began to cast about for some other explanation. And it was found that by supposing an extension of the universe (thin but uniform) in a fourth dimension, that the law would hold good.

"I know it's hard to grasp the idea; let me put it to you this way. Take this cube. Here is a point, a corner, where the three bounding lines join. The point is nothing, yet it is part of the lines. To imagine it at all as a reality, we must say that it has a minute extension in these lines.

"Now take a line. It has a similar minute uniform extension in the two surfaces which it bounds. Take the surface; it is similarly part of the one cube.

"Go one step further; imagine that the cube is related to some unknown thing as the surface is to the cube. You can't? True; you can't make a definite image of it; but you can form an idea – and if you train yourself to think of this very hard, presently you will get a little closer to it. I'm not going to bother you much longer with this dry theoretical part; I'll only just tell you that a fourth dimension, besides explaining the difficulties of gravitation, and some others, gives us an idea of how it is that there is only a definite fixed number of kinds of things, from which all others are combined.

"And now we can get down to business. Brother Cyril, who obliged with the cube, will be so good as to produce a wooden cone and a basin of water."

Brother Cyril complied.

"I want you to realise," went on the old man, "that all the talk about the Progress of Science is cheap journalism. Most of the boasted progress is mere commercial adaptation of science, as who should say that he is Experimenting with Electricity when he rides in an electric train. One hears of Edison and Marconi as 'men of science'; neither of them ever discovered a single fact; they merely exploited facts already known. The real men of Science are in absolute agreement that the advance in our knowledge, great as it has been, leaves us as ignorant of ultimate truth and reality as we were ten thousand years ago. The universe guards its secret: Isis can still boast that no man hath lifted her veil!

"But, suppose our trouble were due to the fact that we only received our impressions in disconnected pieces. A very simple thing might seem the maddest jumble. Ready, Cyril?"

"Quite ready."

"I. A. A. I. U. I. A."

"R. F. G. L. S. L."

"What were we saying?"

Lisa laughed rather excitedly. Her vivid mind told her that these instructions were going to take sudden shape.

"Only your very pretty name, my dear! Now, Cyril, the cone." He took it in his hand, and poised it over a bowl of water.

"We are now going to suppose that this very simple object is going to try its best to explain its nature to the surface of the water, which we will imagine as endowed with powers of observation and reasoning equal to our own. All that the cone can do is to show itself to the water, and it can only impress the water by touching it.

"So it dips its point, thus. The water perceives a point. The cone goes on dipping. The water sees a circle round where the point was. The cone goes on. The circle gets bigger and bigger. Suddenly, as the cone goes completely through, snap!

"Now, what does the water know?

"Nothing about any cone. If it got any idea that the various commotions were caused by a single object, which it would only do if it compared them carefully, noted a regularity of rate of increase in the size of the circle, and so on – in other words, used the scientific method – it would not evolve a theory of a cone, for we must remember that any solid body is to it a thing as wildly inconceivable as a fourth-dimensional body is to us.

"The cone would try again. This time, we dip it obliquely. The water now perceives a totally different set of phenomena; there are no circles, but ellipses. Dip again, first at this angle, then at that. One way we get curious curves called parabolas, the other way equally curious curves called hyperbolas.

"By this time the water would be nearly out of its mind, if it insisted on trying to refer all these absolutely different phenomena to a single cause!

"It might work out a geometry – our own plane geometry, in fact – and it would perhaps get some extraordinary poetic conception of a Creator who manifested in his universe such marvellous and beautiful relations. It would get all sorts of fantastic theories of this Creator's power; what it would never get – until it produced a James Hinton – would be the idea that all this diversity was caused by seeing, disjointedly, different aspects of one single simple thing.

"I purposely took the easiest case. Suppose that instead of a cone we used an irregular body – the series of impressions would seem to the water like absolute madness!

"Now slide your imagination up one dimension! Do you not see at once how parallel is our situation to that of the surface of the water?

"The first impression of the savage about the universe is of a great

mysterious jumble of things which come upon him without rhyme or reason, usually to smite him down.

"Long later, man developed the idea of connecting phenomena, at least a few at a time.

"Centuries elapse; he begins to perceive law, at first operating only in a very few matters.

"More centuries; some bold thinker invents a single cause for all these diverse effects, and calls it God. This hypothesis leads to interminable disputes about the nature of God; in fact, they have never been settled. The problem of the origin of evil, alone, has quite baffled Theology.

"Science advances; we now find that all things are subject to law. There is no need of any mysterious creator, in the old sense; we look for causes in the same order of nature as the effects they produce. We no longer propitiate ghosts to keep our fires alight.

"Now, at last, I and a few others are asking whether the whole universe be not illusion, in exactly the same way as a true surface is an illusion.

"Perhaps the universe is a four-dimensional object, or collection of objects, quite sane, and simple, and intelligible, manifesting itself in diversity, regular or irregular, just as the cone did to the water."

"Of course I can't grasp all this; I will ask Cyril to tell me again and again till I do. But what is this fourth-dimensional universe? Can't you give me something to cling to?"

"Just so. Here this long lecture links up with that little chat about the soul!"

"0– o – oh!"

"And the double personality, and all the rest of it!

"It's perfectly simple. I, the fourth-dimensional reality, am going about my business in a perfectly legitimate way. I find myself pushing through to my surface, or let us say, I become conscious of my surface, the material universe, much as the cone did as it went through the water. I make my appearance with a yell. I grow. I die. There are the same phenomena of change which we all perceive around us. My three-dimensional mind thinks all this 'real,' a history; where at most it is a geography, a partial set of infinite aspects. I say infinite, for the cone contains an infinite number of curves. Yet this three-dimensional being is actually a part of me, though such a minute one; and it rather amuses me, now I have discovered a little bit more of myself, to find that mind think that he, or even his yet baser body, is the one and only."

"I'm understanding you with a part of me that I didn't know was there."

"That's the way, child. But I'm going on a little. I want you to consider how nicely this explains the psychology of crowds, for example. We may suppose an Idea to be a real four-dimensional thing. I, when I know myself more fully, shall probably turn out to be a pretty simple kind of a thing, manifesting in perhaps one person only. But we can imagine abstract 'Individuals' who come to the surface in hundreds or thousands of minds at the same time. Liberty, for example. It begins to push through. It is noticed by one or two men only at first; that is like the point of the cone. Then it spreads gradually – or it breaks out suddenly, just as the circle would, if, instead of a cone, you dropped a spiked shield upon the water. And that is all the lesson for this afternoon, child. Think it over, and see if you have it all clear, and if you can find any other little problems to straighten out. The next lesson will be of a more desperate sort – the kind that leads directly to action."

Cyril broke in on the word. "We have a great deal to do," he said sharply, "even before we leave this house. It's pretty dark – and there's a Thing in the garden."

393

CHAPTER V
OF THE THING IN THE GARDEN;
AND OF THE WAY OF THE TAO

"OH, little Brother!" said the old mystic sadly.

"How long will it take you to work through this wretched business?"

"I have omnipotence at my command, and eternity at my disposal," smiled the boy, using Eliphaz Levi's well-known formula.

"I ought to explain," said Simple Simon, turning to Lisa. "This boy is a desperate magician confined within the circle of this forest. His plan is Action; he is all for Magick; give him a Wand and a host of Demons to control, and he is happy. For my part, I prefer the Way of the Tao, and to do everything by doing nothing. I know it sounds difficult; one day I will explain. But the practical result is that I lead a placid and contented life, and nothing ever happens; he, on the contrary, makes trouble everywhere, excites the wrath of Turks, and worse, if I am right; he thereby brings about a situation where perfectly competent ladies' maids have epileptic fits, mediums endeavour to procure blood from bewitching damozels – and now there's a Thing in the Garden." His voice had a wail of comic disgust.

"However, this is Cyril's funeral, not mine. He called me in; I must say I approve of his general plan, on the whole, and I dare say much of the opposition is unavoidable. In any case he is the magician; Principal Boy in a Pantomime. I merely hold the sponge; and we have to use his formula throughout, not mine. If it ends in disaster," he added as a cheerful afterthought, "perhaps it will teach him a lesson! A Chinese God, indeed! He would be better as a Chinese coolie, smoking opium at the feet of Chwangtze!"

"He tells me that I stand in my own way, that I love struggle and adventure, and that this is weakness and not strength."

"This girl is in danger: quite unnecessary danger."

"I am going to ask my master to show you his method; you will see plenty of mine in the next few weeks; and I should like you to have a standard of comparison. Maybe you'll want to choose one day!"

"I'm afraid I, too, like danger and excitement!" cried Lisa.

"I'm afraid you do! However, since Brother Cyril asks it, the Way of the Tao shall be trodden so far as this is possible: What would Brother Cyril do?"

"I should take the Magic Sword, make the appropriate symbols, and invoke the Names Divine appurtenant thereto: the Thing, shrivelled and blasted, would go back to those that sent it, screaming in agony, cursing at the gods, ready to turn even on its employers, that they might wail with it in torment."

"One of the best numbers on the programme," said Simon Iff. "Now see the other way!"

"Yes: if your way is better than that!" cried the girl, her eyes gleaming. "It isn't my way," said the mystic, with a sudden inflection of solemnity. His voice rose in a low monotonous chant as he quoted from "The Book of the Heart girt with the Serpent."

"I, and Me, and Mine were sitting with lutes in the market-place of the great city, the city of the violets and the roses.

"The night fell, and the music of the lutes was stilled.

"The tempest arose, and the music of the lutes was stilled.

"The hour passed, and the music of the lutes was stilled.

"But Thou art Eternity and Space; Thou art Matter and Motion; and Thou art the Negation of all these things. For there is no symbol of Thee."

The listeners were thrilled to the marrow of their bones. But the old man merely gathered a handful of dittany leaves from the chased golden box where they were kept, and led the way to the garden.

It was very dark; nothing could be distinguished but the outlines of the shrubs and the line of the fence beyond.

"Do you see the Thing?" said Iff.

Lisa strained her eyes.

"You mustn't look for anything very definite," said the mystic.

"It seems as if the darkness were somehow different in that corner," said Lisa at last, pointing. "A sort of reddish tinge to the murk."

"Oh dear me! if you will use words hike 'murk'! I'm afraid you're all on Cyril's side! Look now!" And he put his hand on her head. With the other he offered her the dittany. "Chew one of these leaves!" he said.

She took one of the silver-grey heaves, with its delicate snow-bloom, between her teeth.

"I can see a sort of shapeless mass, dark-red," she said after a pause.

"Now watch!" cried Iff. He took several steps into the garden, and raised his right hand. "Do what thou wilt shall be the whole of the Law!" he proclaimed in such a voice as once shook Sinai.

Then he threw the rest of the dittany in the direction of the Thing.

"By all the powers of the Pentagram!" shouted Cyril Grey; "he's deliberately making a magical link between it and Lisa." He bit his lip, and cursed himself in silence; he knew he had been startled out of prudence.

Simon Iff had not noticed the outburst. He quoted *The Book of the Law*, "Be strong!" he cried. "Enjoy all things of sense and rapture! There is no god that shall deny thee for this!"

The Thing became coherent. It contracted slightly. Lisa could now see that it was an animal of the wolf type, couchant. The body was as big as that of a small elephant. It became quite clearly visible. It was a dull fiery red. The head was turned toward her, and she was suddenly shocked to see that it had no eyes.

The old man advanced towards it. He had abandoned his prophetic attitude. His whole gait expressed indifference – no, forgetfulness. He was merely a quiet old gentleman taking an evening stroll.

He walked right into the Thing. Suddenly, as it enveloped him, Lisa saw that a faint light was issuing from his body, a pale phosphorescence which kindled warmly as he went. She saw the edges of the Thing contract, as if they were sucked inwards. This proceeded, and the light became intense. About a burning ovoid core dawned and vibrated the flashing colours of the rainbow. The Thing disappeared completely; at the same moment the light

went out. Simon Iff was once again merely an old gentleman taking an evening stroll. But she heard a soft voice, almost as faint as an echo; it murmured: "Love is the law, love under will."

"Let us go in," said he as he rejoined them. "You must not catch a chill."

Lisa went to the divan. She said nothing; she was stupefied by what she had seen. Perhaps she even lost full consciousness for a moment; for her next impression was of the two men arguing.

"I agree," Cyril was saying, "it is very neat, and shows the restraint of the great artist; but I am thinking of the Man behind the gun. I should have struck terror into him."

"But fear is failure!" protested Iff mildly, as if surprised.

"But we want them to fail!"

"Oh no! I want them to succeed."

Cyril turned rather angrily to Lisa. "He's impossible! I fancy myself at paradox, you know; but he goes beyond my understanding every time. I'm an amateur, and a rotten amateur at that."

"Let me explain!" said Simple Simon. "If everybody did his Will, there would be no collision. Every man and every woman is a star. It is when we get off our orbits that the clashes come. Now if a Thing gets off its orbit, and comes into my sphere of attraction, I absorb it as quietly as possible, and the stars sing together again."

"Whew!" said Cyril, and pretended to wipe the sweat from his brow.

"But weren't you in danger from that devilish Thing?" asked Lisa, with the memory of a great anxiety. She had trembled like an aspen during the scene in the garden.

"The rhinoceros," quoted Simon Iff, "finds no place in him into which to thrust its horn, nor the tiger a place in which to fix its claws, nor the weapon a place to admit its point. And for what reason? Because there is in him no place of death."

"But you did nothing. You were just acting like an ordinary man. But I think it would have been death for any one but you."

"An ordinary man would not have touched the Thing. It was on a different plane, and would no more have interfered with him than sound interferes with light. A young magician, one who had opened a gate on to that plane, but had not yet become master of that plane, might have been overcome. The Thing might even have dispossessed his ego, and used his body as its own. That is the beginner's danger in magick."

"And what is your secret?"

"To have assimilated all things so perfectly that there is no longer any possibility of struggle. To have destroyed the idea of duality. To have achieved Love and Will so that there is no longer any object to Love, or any aim for Will. To have killed desire at the root; to be one with every thing and with Nothing.

"Look!" he went on, with a change of tone, "why does a man die when he is struck by lightning? Because he has a gate open to lightning; he insists on being an electrical substance by possessing the quality of resistance to the passage of the electric current. If we could diminish that resistance to zero, lightning would no longer take notice of him.

"There are two ways of preventing a rise of temperature from the sun's heat. One is to oppose a shield of non-conducting and opaque material: that is Cyril's way, and at the best it is imperfect; some heat always gets through. The other is to remove every particle of matter from the space which you wish to be cold; then there is nothing there to become hot; and that is the Way of the Tao."

Lisa put an arm round Cyril's neck, and rested her head on his shoulder. "I shouldn't know how to begin!" she said: "and – I know it would mean giving up Cyril."

"It would mean giving up yourself," retorted the mystic, "and you'll have to do it one day: But be reassured! Everybody has to go through your stage – and unless I'm mistaken, you are about to go through it in a particularly acute form."

"I've tried the Tao," said Cyril, half regretful, "but I can't manage it."

The old man laughed. "You're like the old man in the storm who realised that he would be warmer elsewhere. So he decided to diminish the amount of himself by removing his clothes, and only found it colder. It gets worse and worse till the moment when you vanish utterly and for ever. But you have only tried half-measures. Naturally, you have found your will divided against itself – the will to live against the will to Nirvana, if I may call it so – and that is not even good magick."

The boy groaned inwardly. He could understand just enough to realise how far the heights reached above him. His heart almost failed him at the thought – which was instinctive knowledge – that he must scale them, whether he would or no.

"Take care!" suddenly cried Simon Iff.

At almost the same instant a terrible scream shrilled out from a neighbouring studio. "It is my fault," murmured the old man, humbly. "I divided his will. I have been talking like an old fool. I must have been identified with Simon Iff for a moment. Oh, pride! Oh, pride!"

But Cyril Grey had understood the warning. He rose to his full height, and made a curious gesture. Then, with a grim face, he ran out of the studio. In a moment he was battering at the door of his neighbour. It burst open under the momentum of his shoulder.

A woman lay upon the floor. Over her stood the sculptor, a blood-stained hammer in his hand. He seemed absolutely dazed. Grey shook him. He looked round stupidly. "What have I done?" he said. "Nothing!" snarled Cyril. "I did it, I. Quick! can't we save her?" But the sculptor burst into lamentation: he was incapable of anything but tears. He flung himself upon the body of his model, and wept passionately. Cyril gritted his teeth; the girl was on the borderland. "Master!" he cried, in a terrible voice.

"In a case of this kind," said Simple Simon, who was standing unperceived within a foot of him, "where Nature has been outraged, an attempt made to interfere violently with her laws, it is permissible to act – or rather, to counteract just so much as is necessary to restore equilibrium. There was a seed of quarrel in the hearts of these young people; the blow aimed at you, when your own will became divided, struck aslant; their own division attracted the murder-force to them.

"I will administer The Medicine." He took a flask from his pocket, put a drop of the contents on the lips of the girl, and one in each nostril. He then sprinkled a little upon a handkerchief, and put it to the wound on her head.

Suddenly the sculptor rose to his feet with a great cry. His hands were covered in blood, which streamed from his own scalp.

"Quick! back to the studio!" said Simon. "We don't want to make explanations. They'll both be all right in five minutes, and they'll think it all a dream. As, indeed, like the rest of things, it is!"

But Cyril had to carry la Giuffria. The rapid successions of these mysterious events had ended by throwing her consciousness completely out of gear. She lay in a deep trance.

"A very fortunate circumstance!" remarked Simon, when he observed it. "This is the time to take her over to the Profess-House." Cyril wrapped her in her furs; between them they carried her to the boulevard, where Simon Iff's automobile was in waiting.

The old mystic held up his left hand, with two of the fingers crossed. It was a signal to the chauffeur. In another moment they were running on easy speed up the Boulevard Arago.

Lisa came to herself as the car, crossing the Seine, pointed at the heights of Montmartre; and she was perfectly recovered as it stopped before a modest house of quite modern type, which was set against the steepest part of the hill.

The door opened, without alarm being given. Lisa learnt later that in this house no orders needed to be issued, that simplicity had reached so serene a level that all things operated together without question. Only when unusual accidents took place was there need for speech; and little, even then.

The door stood open, and a quite ordinary butler presented himself, bowing. Simon Iff returned the salute, and walked on, when a second door opened, also spontaneously. Lisa found herself in a small lobby. The man who had opened the inner door was clad from neck to knee in a single black robe, without sleeves. From his belt hung a heavy sword with a cross-hilt. This man held up three fingers. Simon Iff again nodded, and led his guests to the room on the left.

Here were the three guests indicated by the gesture of the guard. Lord Antony Bowling was a familiar friend of the old mystic. He was a stout and strong man of nearly fifty years of age, with a gaze both intrepid and acute: His nose was of the extreme aristocratic type, his mouth sensual and strong.

Cyril Grey had nicknamed him "The Merman of Mayfair" and claimed that Rodin got the idea for his "Centaur" the day that he met him.

He was the younger brother of the Duke of Flint, his race probably Norman in the main: but he gave the impression of a Roman Emperor. Haughtiness was here, and great good-nature; the intellect was evidently developed to the highest possible pitch of which man as man is capable; and one could read the judicial habit on his deep wide brows. Against this one could see the huge force of the man's soul, the passionate desire for knowledge which burnt in that great brain. One could conceive him capable of monstrous deeds, for he would let no man, no prejudice of men, stand in his way. He would certainly have fiddled while Rome was burning if it had been his hobby to play the violin.

This man was the mainstay of the Society for Psychical Research. He was the only absolutely competent man in it, perhaps; at least, he stood well above all others. He had the capacity for measuring the limits of error in any investigation with great accuracy. Just as the skilful climber can make

his way on rotten chalk by trusting each crumbling fragment with just that fraction of his weight which will not quite dislodge it, so Lord Antony could prepare a sound case from worthless testimony. He knew the limits of fraud. He might catch a medium in the act of cheating a dozen times in a seance, and yet record some of the phenomena of that seance as evidential. He used to say that the fact of a medium having his hands free did not explain the earthquake at Messina.

If this man had ever caused people to distrust his judgment – nobody but an imbecile could have doubted his sincerity – the cause lay in his power to fool the mediums he was investigating to the top of their bent. He would enter into every phase of their strange moods as if he had been absolutely one with them in spirit; then, when they were gone, he would withdraw and look at the whole course of events from without, as if he had had no share in them.

But people who saw him only in the first phase thought him easily hoodwinked.

The second of the guests of Simon Iff, or, rather, of the Order to which he belonged, was a tall man bowed with ill-health. A shock of heavy black hair crowned a face pallid as death itself; but his eyes blazed formidably beneath their bushy brows. He had just returned from Burma, where he had lived for many years as a Buddhist monk. The indomitable moral valour of the man shone from him; one could see in every gesture the marks of his fierce fight against a dozen deadly sicknesses. With hardly a week of even tolerable health in any year, he had done work that might have frightened the staff of a great University. Almost single-handed, he had explored the inmost doctrine of the Buddha, and thrown light on many a tangled grove of thought. He had reorganised Buddhism as a missionary religion, and founded societies everywhere to study and practise it. He had even found time and strength, amid these labours, to pursue his own hobby of electrical research. Misunderstood, thwarted, hampered in every way, he had won through; and he had never violated the precepts of his Teacher by raising his voice to denounce error. Even his enemies had been compelled to recognise him as a saint. Simon Iff had never met him, but he went to greet Cyril with the affection of a brother. The boy had been the greatest of his pupils, but the Mahathera Phang, as he was now called in his monastery, had long ago abandoned magick for a path not very different from that of Simon Iff.

The third man was of very inferior calibre to either of the others. He was of medium height and good build, though somewhat frail. But in him was no great development. One divined a restless intelligence fettered to mere cleverness, a failure to grasp the distinction between genius and talent. He was an expert conjurer, had all the facts of psychic research at his finger's end, was up in all the modern theories of psychology, but was little more than a machine. He was incapable of refuting his own logic by an appeal to his common sense. Some one having once remarked that we all dig our graves with our teeth, Wake Morningside had started to prove scientifically that eating was the direct cause of death; and that, consequently, absolute fasting would confer immortality. This was of course easy to prove – in America.

He had continued with experiments in weighing souls, photographing thoughts, and would probably have gone fishing for the Absolute if he had only thought of it! He was a prop to the editors of the New York Sunday Newspapers, and was at present engaged on writing a scenario for moving pictures in which he was to incorporate the facts of psychical research. Nobody in the world was better aware than he that everything reliable could be packed into a single reel, and rattle, but he had undauntedly contracted for a series of fifty five-part pictures. He chewed his chocolate his latest specific for averting the perils of more complex nutrition – with no idea that these activities might damage his reputation as a research student. And he was really a very clever man, with a quick eye and brain. If he had possessed moral force, he might have been saved from many of his follies. But his belief in his own fads had impaired his health and made him somewhat hysterical; as a result of this, and of his tendency to exploit his knowledge in second-rate ways, people had begun to doubt the value of his testimony even in serious matters. For instance. Some years before, he had been one of the signatories to a favourable report on a medium named Jansen; the following year he had brought the man over to America, and made a great deal of money out of the tour. The action destroyed both Jansen and the earlier report. In New York the Scandinavian medium had been exposed, and when Morningside had objected that this did not invalidate the earlier report, his opponent retorted: "No! Your presence there does that!"

But Bowling, with whom he had just crossed from England, knew him better than to think venality of him, and still valued his co-operation in the investigations of alleged spiritualistic phenomena for his extraordinary skill in conjuring, and his practically complete knowledge of every trick that ever

had been played, or could be played. In fact, he was Bowling's expert witness on the question of the limits of possible fraud.

Until Simon Iff and his party entered, these three men had been entertained by a woman. She was dressed in a plain purple robe, made in a single piece. It fell to her feet. The sleeves were long and widening towards the wrist. A red rose, upon a cross of gold, was embroidered on the breast. Her rich brown hair was coiled over her ears.

The face of this woman was of extreme beauty, in a certain esoteric fancy. Like her whole body, it was sturdy and vigorous, but there was infinite delicacy, surprising in so strong a model. Her eyes were clear and fearless and true; but one could see that they must have served her ill indeed often enough, for they were evidently incapable of understanding falsity, and evil. The nose was straight and broad, full of energy; and the mouth passionate and firm. The lips were somewhat thick, but they were mobile and the whole expression of the face redeemed any defect of any feature. For while its general physical aspect was severe, even savage – she might have been a Tartar beauty, the bride of a Gengis Khan, or a South Sea Island Queen, tossing her lovers into the crater of Mauna Loa after killing them in the excess and fantasy of her passion – yet the soul within shone out and turned the swords to ploughshares. There was pride, indeed, but only of that kind which is (as it were) the buckler on the arm of nobility; the woman was incapable of meanness, of treachery, or even of unkindness.

There were terrible fires in the depths of that volcano; but they had been turned to human service; they had been used to heat the forge of art. For this woman was a great singer; and no one outside the Order knew of her secret aspirations, or that she retired from time to time to one or the other of the Profess-Houses of the Order, there to pursue a mightier transmutation of her being.

She greeted Cyril with peculiar warmth – indeed, it had been she to whom he had once thrown a pair of socks. In a way, it was he that had made her a great artist; for his personality had broken down her dykes; not till she met him had she ever let herself go. And it was by a magical trick that he had shown her how to use her art as a vehicle for her soul.

Later, he had brought her into the Order, realizing the inestimable value of her virtue; and if she was not its most advanced member she was its most beloved.

They called her Sister Cybele.

CHAPTER VI

OF A DINNER,

WITH THE TALK OF DIVERS GUESTS

SIMON IFF and Cyril Grey had slipped out of the reception-room to clothe themselves according to their dignity in the Order.

They returned in a few moments. The old man was in a robe of the same pattern as Sister Cybele's – all the robes of the Order were thus fashioned – but it was of black silk, and on the breast was embroidered a golden eye within a radiant triangle.

Cyril Grey was in a similar robe, but the eye was enclosed in a six-pointed star, and swords with undulating blades issued from each re-entrant angle.

Their return broke up the conversation, and Sister Cybele led the way, with Lisa on her arm, to the lobby.

There the wonder of the house began. The wall facing the front door was masked by a group of statuary of heroic size.

It was a bronze, and represented Mercury leading Hercules into Hades. In the background stood Charon in his boat, one hand upon his oar, the other stretched to receive his obolus.

Sister Cybele waited until all the guests were in the boat. Then she made pretence to place the coin in Charon's hand.

In reality she touched a spring. The wall parted; the boat moved slowly through; it took its place beside another wharf.

They were in a vast hall; and Lisa realised that the hill behind the house must have been profoundly hollowed out. This hall was lofty, narrow and long. In the midst, a circular table awaited the guests. Behind each chair stood one of the Probationers of the Order in a white robe, on whose breast was a scarlet Pentagram. Neck, sleeves, and hem were trimmed with gold. Beyond this table, at which a number of other members, in variously coloured robes, were already seated, though they rose to salute the newcomers briefly and in silence, was a triangular slab of black marble, the points truncated for convenience. Around this there were six seats, made of ebony inlaid with silver discs.

Sister Cybele left the others to take her seat as president of the circular table. Simon Iff himself sat at the head of the triangle, placing Cyril Grey and the Mahathera Phang at the other corners. Lord Antony Bowling was at his left, Lisa at his right; Morningside faced him from the base.

When all were seated, Sister Cybele rose, struck a bell that stood at her hand, and said: "Do what thou wilt shall be the whole of the Law. O Master of the Temple, what is thy will?"

Simon Iff rose in his place. "It is my will to eat and drink," said he.

"Why shouldst thou eat and drink?"

"To sustain my body in strength."

"Why is it thy will that thy body may be sustained in strength?"

"That it may aid me in the accomplishment of the Great Work."

At this word all rose, and chanted solemnly in chorus, "So mote it be."

"Love is the law, love under will," said Sister Cybele softly, and sat down.

"Of course it's a most absurd superstition," remarked Morningside to Simon Iff, "to think that Food sustains the body. It is sleep that does that. Food merely renews the tissues."

"I agree entirely," said Cyril, before Iff could answer, "and I am about to renew my tissues to the extent of a dozen of these excellent Cherbourg prawns – to begin with!"

"My dear man," said Lord Antony, "prawns are much better at the end of a dinner – as you'd know if you had been to Armenia lately."

When Morningside said something absurd, it merely meant that he was airing his fads; when Lord Antony did so, it meant a story. And all his stories were good ones. Simon Iff jumped at the opening. He turned immediately, and asked for the yarn.

"It's rather long," said Bowling, a little dubiously. "But it's very, very beautiful."

Unacknowledged quotations gave a curious fascination to his narrative style. People became interested through the psychological trick involved. They recognised, yet could not place, the remark, and they were stirred by the magick of association, just as one becomes interested in a stranger who reminds one of one can't quite think who.

"At the close of a dark afternoon," pursued Lord Antony, "a huntsman of sinister appearance might have been seen approaching the hamlet of Sitkab in Armenia. This was myself – or I should hardly think it worth while to tell the story. Why detain you with a lesser potentate? I was in pursuit of the most savage, elusive, and dangerous wild beast, with the exception of woman," (he smiled at Lisa so delightfully that she could only take it as a compliment) "that infests this globe. Need I say that I refer to the Poltergeist?"

"You must do more," laughed Lisa. "You must tell me what my rival is!"

"A Poltergeist is a variety of spook distinguished by its playful habit of throwing furniture about, and otherwise playing practical jokes of the clown-in-the-pantomime order. The particular specimen, whose hide – if they have hides – I was anxious to add to my collection of theosophical tea-cups, spirit cigarettes, and other articles of vertu, was an artist of singular refinement, for he performed upon only one instrument, as a rule; but of that instrument he had acquired the most admirable mastery. It was a common broomstick. This genial spectre – or rather non-spectre, for they are but rarely seen, only heard, conditions precisely opposed, I beg you to note, to those that we require in little boys – this Poltergeist, then, was alleged to be the guest of the local lawyer in the aforesaid hamlet. It had annoyed him considerably for some two years; for while claiming, through an excellent medium in the locality, to be the spirit of a deceased Adept, it had merely thrown broomsticks at him as he went about his daily task of making mischief between the citizens of that deplorably peaceful corner of the earth, or misappropriating funds intrusted to him for investment. He was an honest lawyer, as lawyers go – I was called to the Bar myself in my unregenerate days – and he resented the interference, the more so as no writ of habeas broomstick seemed to abate the nuisance.

"The amiable creature, however, had recently taken pity upon his host, and sought to establish a claim upon his gratitude by saving him from death. For one day, as the lawyer was about to drive across the village bridge he

saw the broomstick fall from the sky and stand erect, precisely in his path. His horse reared; a moment later the bridge was swept away by the torrent. (This is really excellent Bortsch, Mr. Iff.) Well, I had been called in to investigate this matter, and there I was, installed in the house of my brother brigand. The results of my stay of six weeks or so were inconclusive. I was convinced of the man's entire belief in his story, and the broomstick certainly moved in various ways for which I could not account; but I was not fortunate enough to observe anything of the kind when he was not somewhere in the offing. And one is bound to strain one's theories of the limits of fraud as far as it is humanly possible – especially when one is dealing with a lawyer or a broomstick. So I returned from the parts of the tribes even unto the modern Babylon, where I abode for a season. A little while later I received a card announcing my friend's marriage to the heiress of Sitkab, and, a year later again, in response to kind enquiries, he had the honour to announce that the manifestations of the Poltergeist had totally ceased since the day of the wedding. Some of these Adepts are of course fearfully particular on the sex-question, as we all know. Fall for an hour from the austerities of a Galahad, and devil a cigar will precipitate itself into your soup, nor will you be interrupted at billiards by the arrival of an urgent message from Tibet, written on notepaper of the kind you purchase in Walham Green if you are a real lady, to the effect that the secret Wisdom is beyond the Veil, or some other remark evidential of Supreme Enlightenment in too much of a hurry to use the regular post.

"No, the story does not end here; in fact, the above has been but the prelude to a mightier theme. Once more a year passed by. By a singular, and, in view of what happened later, I think an ominous, train of circumstance, it occupied exactly twelve calendar months in the process.

"I now received another letter from the lawyer. Whether love's moon had waned or no he did not say; but he announced the resumption of the phenomena, with additions and improvements. One encouraging point was that in the previous series nothing had ever happened outside his house, except in the case of the bridge incident; now the broomstick was ubiquitous indeed, and followed him about like Mary's lamb. His wife, too, had developed the most surprising powers of mediumship and was obtaining messages from Herr P. Geist, which seemed of unusual importance. A new world was open to our view. I have always fancied myself as a Columbus; and, as I had recently made a considerable sum of money by a fortunate

speculation in oil, I did not hesitate to go to the expense of a telegram. I have always fancied myself as a Caesar, and I endeavoured to emulate his conciseness. 'Come stay winter' was the expression employed. A week later those simple and pious souls, escaping the perils of the journey to Constantinople, were safely cloistered, if I may use the term, in the Orient Express. They were extricated from Paris by a friend whom I had thoughtfully sent to meet them; and the following day my heart was gladdened by the realization of my dreams – the actual physical presence of my loved ones in my ancestral halls in Curzon Street – those which I rented two years ago from Barney Isaacs; or rather from his heirs, for the poor fellow was hanged, as you remember.

"Well, the conclusions of science appear to indicate that a Poltergeist of the better classes takes a fortnight or more to accustom himself to a new domicile; from which circumstance learned men have written many treatises to suggest that it may be of the cat tribe; though others equally learned have contended with great plausibility that its touching attachment to this lawyer shows its nature to conform rather with that of the dog.

"To me it has seemed possible that the light is not altogether withheld from either party to the discussion; I have in fact diffidently put forward the theory that the Poltergeist, for all its German name, is of an ambiguous nature, like the animals of Australia; and I have ventured to rely upon the analogy between the broomstick employed in this case and the throwing-stick of the aborigines of that continent. However this may be, friend Poltergeist began to rehearse exactly fourteen days after the arrival of the lawyer and his wife, and was so kind as to oblige with a full recital – Scherzo in A flat, or more accurately A house – three days later. I never really valued the Sevres vase which was offered on this occasion to the infernal gods.

"The mediumistic powers of the lady began to develop at the same time. The spirit had devised an ingenious method of communication, known to science as Planchette. This instrument is probably familiar to you all; it is an inconvenient way of writing, but otherwise exhibits no marked peculiarity. Now that we have accepted 'automatic wrriting' as automatic, there is really no reason why mediums should pretend that a planchette is not under control.

"This planchette gave us much invaluable information as to the habits, mode of life, social and other pleasures, of various parties deceased; and added, free of all charge, advice which, followed out, would undoubtedly tend to make me an even better man than I am. It is, however, with regret that I find myself obliged to confess that scientific truth is an even dearer

object of my heart than moral beauty, and at the moment I was wholly absorbed in the desire to verify the latest facts about the Poltergeist, for these lent great weight to the theory that it was some kind of dog. Under the inspiring intuition of its charming mistress, it had developed those qualities which we associate with the spaniel or the retriever.

"Even in Armenia it had been wont, when weary of its solos upon the broomstick, to gladden and instruct humanity by putting small articles in places where they should not be. I would occasionally find my socks stuffed tightly into my trousers' pockets, or my razor poised upon a mirror, when I realised that morning in the bowl of night had flung the stone that puts the stars to flight, and that the Hunter of the East had caught the Sultan's Turret in a noose of light. But in the second series of phenomena the faithful and intelligent animal had done far more than this, bringing into the house various objects from afar. It was evidently appreciated in the Beyond that a Poltergeist's reach should exceed his grasp.

"One day, in the wonderful month of May with all its flowers a-blossom, the planchette produced an exceedingly mysterious message. So far as we could understand him, he would bring more evidence of his presence. 'Proof' was one of the words used, I remember; yes, I remember that very distinctly.' And the message ended, with a sudden transition, 'Look out for game!' There could hardly have been a more superfluous injunction so far as I was concerned!

"I must now describe my dining-room. It is very like any other room of the sort, I dare say; the point is that there is a big table, over which is suspended a cluster of electric lamps, a flat shade covering these from above. The top of this shade is just about on the level of the eyes of a fairly tall man, standing. I can see clear over it from the edge of the table without straining.

"Well, we went down to dinner, and the Poltergeist was exceptionally active all through the meal. The medium was exceedingly distressed by his insistence on the mysterious injunction to look out for game. It was only at dessert that the problem was solved. The medium screamed out suddenly, 'Oh! he's pinching my neck!' – and a second later – lightning in a clear sky – a large quail fell from the empyrean upon my humble mahogany.

"I only wished I could have had Rear Admiral Moore, Sir Oliver Lodge, Colonel Olcott, Sir Alfred Turner, Mr. A. P. Sinnett, and Sir Arthur Conan Doyle present on that sublime occasion. There could have been no dissentient

voice to say that this was not 'evidential' – save, possibly, what is negligible, my own. A poor thing, but mine own!

"I wonder if you have ever reflected upon the halo of excitement and romance which must gild the lives of the members of the worshipful Company of Poulterers. They are the true sportsmen of our times; theirs to beard the turkey in his den, theirs to grapple the lordly pheasant, to close in deadly combat with the grouse, to wrest the plover's egg from its lonely nest upon the moors, to dare a thousand deaths in their grim heroism, the fulfilment of their oaths to supply us with sparrow, cat or rabbit. Think, too, of their relations with the mysterious bazaars of Baghdad; their traffickings with wily orientals, the counting-out of secret gold by moonlight in the shadow of the mosques; think of Mason, as he painfully deciphers the code cablegram from Fortnum, burns the message, and armed with a dagger and a bag of uncut rubies, plunges from the Ghezireh Palace Hotel to his rendezvous with Achmet Abdullah in the Fishmarket, where, with no eye to see, the hideous bargain is concluded, and, handing over his rubies, Mason sallies from that dreadful alley, clutching beneath his gaberdine – a quail.

"You have not thought such thoughts? Nor, until now, had I. But I knew that quails were cold storage products of the burning East, and I knew that the number of poulterers in my vicinity was limited. Early the next morning I visited in turn these respectable tradesmen, the third of whom remembered the sale of a quail to a lady on the previous day. Both quail and lady answered to the descriptions I had in mind.

"It had been the custom of my guests to walk abroad in the afternoons, now singly, now together, now with one or another of the members of my household.

"On this particular day, I begged the medium to permit me the honour of escorting her. She agreed with characteristic amiability; and, once in the street, I pleaded with her, like a child, to tell me a story. I said that I was sure she had a nice story to tell me. But no; it appeared not.

"In the course of our ambulation, we came – surely led by some mysterious Providence – to the very poulterer whom I had seen in the morning. I led her to that worthy man. 'Yes, my lord,' he replied to my urbane question with affable obsequience, 'this is the lady to whom I sold the quail.' She contradicted the statement brusquely; she had never been in the shop in her life. We proceeded on our walk. 'Tell me,' I said, 'exactly what you did do when you were out yesterday.' 'Nothing at all,' she answered. 'I went and

sat in the park for a little. Presently my sister came and sat down with me, and we talked for a little. Then she went away, and came back in about half-an-hour. We talked some more, and them I came away back to Curzon Street.'

"On our return I questioned her husband. 'Sister!' he exclaimed, 'she never had a sister!'

"The mystery was cleared up. It was a case of Double Personality! There was, however, still one small point. How did that Spirit Quail get on to the table? It had fallen very straight, or so it seemed to us; and the butler said that he could hardly believe that a quail could have been concealed on the lamp-shade; he would have noticed it, he thought, while laying the table.

"The experiments continued. Some time later Brother Poltergeist permitted himself some allusions to fish – in the best possible taste – and I took my precautions accordingly. Before dinner I slipped downstairs and made a thorough search of the dining room. Alas! to what treacheries are the most virtuous of us liable to be subjected? That medium's saucy Sister Second Personality had again betrayed her to a most unjustifiable suspicion! For one dozen prawns, of the best quality, were distributed in most excellent symmetry about the lamp-shade.

"A hasty reference to the dictionary not yet published by the Society for Psychical Research assured me that this sort of thing was a 'prepared phenomenon'.

"Now, if you are going to prepare a phenomenon, you may as well prepare it properly; and I attended – you shall soon learn how – alike to decency and to asthetics.

"Dinner was served; the Poltergeist supplied the conversation. Never before had he been so light, so genial, so anxious to assure us of our future in Summerland; but ever and anon he touched the minor chord, spoke darkly of 'proof', and of fish! (I beg you all to bear witness that I have not degraded myself by the evident pun). The dessert arrived. And now the Poltergeist was imminent. The lawyer thought to touch him and to hold him; he saw signs of him all over the room; he ran about after him, like a boy with a butterfly-net. But of all this I took no heed; I was watching the lady's face.

"Professor Freud would perhaps explain my motive as 'infantile psycho-sexual pre-sexuality'; but no matter: I watched her face.

"The lawyer, like what's his name pursuing Priam, was close on the heels of the Poltergeist – 'jam, jam' as used by Vergil in the sense of prolonging the suspense – at last he made one grab in empty air. He overbalanced; must

411

have touched the lamp-shade, I suppose – for a shower of prawns fell upon us like the gentle rain from heaven, blessing both him that gives and him that takes.

"And oh! those spirit prawns were beautiful upon the table-cloth; for each had a bunch of blue ribbon, blue ribbon, to tie up its bonny red hair. I had not moved my eyes from that fair lady's face; and I am sorry to conclude this abstract and brief chronicle of the prawn by saying that I cannot swear that she betrayed any guilty knowledge!"

Lord Antony stopped with a jerk; and lifting his liqueur glass, drained it suddenly.

Sister Cybele rose and bowed to Simon Iff.

But Cyril Grey's voice rose in a high-pitched drawl: "Better a dinner of herbs where love is, than a stalled prawn, and discontentment therewith!"

The Master frowned him down. "Gentlemen!" he said, "It is the custom of this House that its guests pay for their entertainment. Lord Antony Bowling has done so by his delightful story; Mr. Morningside by his brilliant theory upon the function of food; and the Mahathera Phang by his silence. I may say that I expected no less, and no different, from any one of you; we are overpaid; and the debt of gratitude is ours."

Morningside was pleased; he thought the compliment sincere; Bowling understood something of the soul which had escaped him until that moment; the Mahathera Phang remained in his superb indifference.

Lisa addressed the Master: "I'm afraid I haven't paid; and I've had a perfectly wonderful dinner!"

Simon Iff replied with weight: "My dear young lady, you are not a guest – you are a candidate."

Suddenly conscious of herself, she blanched, and became rigid in her chair.

Simon Iff bade farewell to the three guests; Cyril and Sister Cybele conducted them to the boat, and bade them God-speed. The other brethren of the Order dispersed, one to one task, one to another.

Presently Simon and Cyril, Cybele and Lisa were together alone. The old man led the way to a cell cunningly hidden in the wall. There they took seats.

Lisa la Giuffria recognised that the critical moment of her life was come upon her.

CHAPTER VII

OF THE OATH OF LISA LA GIUFFRIA;

AND OF HER VIGIL IN THE CHAPEL OF ABOMINATIONS

"BEFORE we go further," began Cyril Grey, "I think it right to express a doubt as to the advisability of our procedure. We have already seen the most determined opposition to our plans; and for my part, I would say frankly that it might be wiser, certainly safer, to abandon them."

Lisa turned on him like a tigress. "I don't know what your plans are, and don't care. But I didn't think you'd go back on them."

"Impulsive ladies," returned Cyril, "rush in where angels fear to tread."

"I'll go," said she. "I'm sorry for all that has happened – all!" and she fixed her lover with a look of infinite contempt.

Cyril shrugged his shoulders. "If you feel like that, of course, we can continue. But when the pinch comes, don't squeal! I have warned you."

"Brother Cyril could not draw back if he wished," put in Sister Cybele. "He is bound by his oath – as, in a little while, you will be."

Lisa read upon the woman's face a smile, as of triumphant malice. It disturbed her far more than Cyril's protest. Was she indeed in a trap? It might be so; then, Cyril, who had tried to save her, was in the trap too. She must go on, if only to be able to save him when opportunity occurred. At present she was wholly in the dark. She could feel the atmosphere of constraint, of subtle and terrible forces in the abyss which she was treading blindfold upon some razor-edge whose supports she could not even imagine; the adventure was to her a supreme excitement, and she lived first and last for that. Had she known herself better, she would have understood that her love for Cyril was little more than a passion for the bizarre. But at the moment she was Joan of Arc and Juliet in one.

Moreover, she had the instinctive feeling that wherever these people might be going it was certainly somewhere. They were engineers building a bridge to an unknown land, just as methodically and purposefully as the builders of an earthly bridge. There was no doubt as to the validity of their knowledge or their powers. She perceived that Lord Antony Bowling had spent his life in the investigation of disjointed, purposeless items of mostly plain fraud; while under his very nose the Brethren of this Order were proceeding calmly with some stupendous task, not troubling even to acquaint the world with their results. And she could dimly guess why this was so, and must be so. They did not wish to be dragged into foolish controversies with the ignorant.

And just then Simon Iff took up the conversation with a remark in tune with that thought.

"We shall not ask you for any pledge of secrecy," he said, "for you have only to say what you see and hear to be laughed at for a liar. If this be our last meeting, we are quits. You will be taken to a little chapel leading from this room. There you will find a circle, which you must enter, being careful not to touch it, even with your dress; for that would be dangerous. Within that circle you must remain until we send for you, unless you wish to leave, in which case you have only to pass through the white curtains in the north. You will find yourself in a lighted passage; open the door at the end, you will be in the street, where my automobile awaits your orders. Your use of this exit will, however, close your career in magick; in any future relations we should merely be good friends – or I hope so – but we should not consider any proposal to reconstruct the present situation."

"I will wait until you send for me," cried Lisa. "I swear it."

Simon Iff placed his hand upon her brow; in another instant he was gone from the room.

Sister Cybele rose and took her by the hand. "Come!" said she; "but you had better bid farewell to your lover." The girl once again thrilled to the undertone of malice in the voice. But Cyril took her fondly in his arms, and crushed her to him.

"Tomorrow," he said, "brave heart, true heart! Tomorrow we shall be alone together!"

Trembling, la Giuffria returned to Sister Cybele, and followed her to the door of the chapel. She threw a last look over her shoulder: to her amazement Cyril was regarding her with a cynical smile of amusement. Her heart went deadly cold; she felt the pull of Sister Cybele's hand, suddenly grown iron and inexorable. The door shut behind her with a monstrous clang; and she found herself in a room at once obscure and menacing.

She wondered why they called it a chapel. It was a bell-shaped cave. She dimly saw the white curtains of which Iff had spoken; there was nothing else in the room but a square thin altar whose surface was of polished silver, around whose base ran a broad copper band, evidently the circle referred to, and ten lamps, set in little stars of iron, which gave a faint blue light. The entire chamber was cut out of the solid rock. Only that part of it which lay within the circle had been dressed; the rest of the floor, and the walls, which bent over to meet in a point, were rough.

She stepped carefully into the circle, raising her dress. Sister Cybele faced her squarely. In the woman's face Lisa read a thousand evil purposes, a cruelty devilishly hot as Cyril's was devilishly cold, and the assurance in those grey eyes that she had fallen into the power of creatures utterly abominable. Sister Cybele suddenly broke into a short harsh laugh, then stepped aside, and Lisa, turning quickly, only saw the door close behind her. Heedless of caution, she leapt after her in the impulse of self-preservation – but the door was entirely smooth on the inside. She beat against it, uttering a horrible, fierce cry: but only silence answered her.

The impulse passed as quickly as it had come. Mechanically she stepped back into the circle. And as she did so the thought of Simon Iff came to calm her. The other two might puzzle her, but she felt that Iff would neither do nor suffer wrong.

During dinner, too, she had fixed her gaze, fascinated, upon the Mahathera Phang. She knew that he was more than friendly to the Order, though not

a member of it; and his face, coupled with the fact that he had not spoken even once in her presence, redoubled that confidence.

In front of the little altar, she discovered, as her eyes accommodated themselves to the dimness, a curiously-shapen stool covered with leather. She squatted on it, and found it a very Paradise of ease. And then it dawned upon her that she had to wait. To wait!

There was no sound or movement to fix her attention; presently she began to amuse herself by making faces at herself in the polished silver of the altar. It was not long before she tired of that; and once again she found herself waiting.

Her imagination soon began to people the little room with phantoms; the memory of the Thing in the Garden began to obsess her. Once again Simon Iff came to the rescue. She knew that her imagination was at work, and that, even had the shapes about her been real, they could not harm her. She heard herself repeating the old mystic's words: "Because there is in him no place of death."

She became perfectly calm; for a little while her thoughts occupied her. Suddenly they fled, and she found herself (so to speak) in a small open boat, without provisions, in the midst of a limitless ocean of unutterable boredom.

She had a period of fidgets; that over, she became listless, and merely prayed for sleep.

Then she noticed that a square pencil of light had entered from the apex of the chapel, and was casting glory upon the top of the altar. She rose instantly – and gasped in amazement, for figures were moving on the silver.

Three men, with strange musical instruments, species respectively of flute, viol, and drum, were walking across a room. This room was hung with rose-coloured curtains, and lit with silver candelabra. At one end was a dais, and on this the men took their seats. They began to tune their instruments, and so strong was her fancy, that she thought she heard them. It was a fantastic Oriental dance-music. Presently a small boy, a negro, dressed in a yellow tunic and baggy breeches of pale blue, entered the room. He carried a salver, on which were a great flask of wine and two goblets of gold.

Then, to her utter amazement, Cyril Grey stepped into the room with Sister Cybele. They took the wine from the boy, and, each placing the left hand on the left shoulder of the other, they touched their goblets, and, throwing their heads back, drained them. The boy took the empty cups and disappeared.

She saw Cyril and Cybele draw together; they gave a laugh which (once again) she fancied she could hear. It rang demoniac in her very inmost soul. An instant more, and their mouths met in a kiss.

Lisa felt her knees give way. She caught the altar, and saved herself from falling; but she must have lost consciousness for a second or two, for when her eyes opened she saw that they had discarded their robes, and were dancing together. It was wild and horrible beyond all imagination; the dancers were locked so closely that they appeared like a single monster of fable, a thing with two heads and four legs which writhed or leapt in hideous ecstasy.

She was so shaken that she did not even ask herself the nature of the vision, whether it was a dream, an hallucination, a picture of the past, or an actual happening. The bacchanal obscenity of it was overwhelming. Again and again she turned her eyes away; but they always returned to the gaze, and every gesture shot a pang of agony to her soul. She understood the ambiguities of her lover; his strange behaviour seemed like an open book to her; and the malice of Sister Cybele, her elfin laughter, her satanic sneer, sank into her bleeding heart like acid, burning, fuming.

The revel did not diminish; instead, it took novel and more atrocious forms. All that she had ever conceived of sensuality of bestiality, was a thousandfold surpassed. It was an infinite refinement of abomination joined with an exaggeration of grossness that might have turned Georges Sand to stone. The light went out.

The thought of flight from that abominable chapel never came to her. It was Cyril – the man to whom she had given herself utterly at the first touch – who was plunging this poisoned dagger into her soul. And she could not even die; it was ferocity and madness that awoke in her. She would wait until the morning – and she would find a way to be avenged. Yet she felt that she was slowly bleeding to death; it did not seem that any morning could ever come to her. She would not be able to face Cyril; it seemed somehow as if the shame were hers.

And then she screamed aloud – a soft hand was on her shoulder. "Hush! Hush!" came a gentle voice in her ear. It was the girl who had waited on her at dinner. Even at the time Lisa had noticed that she was very different to the others; for they were of most cheerful countenance, and this girl's eyes were red with weeping. "Come away!" said the girl, "come away while it is time. This is the first chance I have ever had to escape; I was set to watch the chapel door tonight; and I found the spring. Oh, come away quickly!

They're criminals; they corrupt you and they torture you. Oh do come, sister! I can't escape without you; the man in the automobile would stop me. But if you come, I can slip away. It's only a step through the passage. Oh God! Oh God! if I had only gone when I was as you are!" Lisa's whole soul went out in sympathy to the gentle creature. "Look what they've done to me!" "Feel all down my back!" The girl winced with pain even at Lisa's gentle fingertips. Her back was a mass of knotted weals; she must have been beaten savagely with a sjambok or a knout.

"And see my arms!" The girl lifted her hands, and the loose sleeves of her robe fell back. From wrist to elbow she was a mass of parallel cuts. "I wouldn't do what they wanted," she moaned, "it was too horrible. You'd think no woman would; but they do. Sister Cybele's the worst. O come! Do come from this abominable house!"

Lisa had touched the summit of the mountain of hysteria. Her feelings were far beyond all expression; she was living in a world deeper than feeling. She gained the consciousness of her own nature, something far deeper than anything she had ever known, and she expressed its will in words of absolute despair. "I can't leave Cyril Grey."

"I'm afraid of him more than all the others," whispered the girl. "I loved him too. And when I came to him two days ago, thinking that he still loved me – he laughed and he had me whipped. Oh come away!"

"I can't," said Lisa, brokenly. "But you shall go. Here, take my dress; give me your robe. The chauffeur won't know the difference. Tell him to drive to the Grand Hotel; ask for Lavinia King; I'll get word to you tomorrow, and money if you need it. But – I – can't – go."

The last words dripped out icily from the frozen waters of her soul. Quickly the girl dressed herself in Lisa's clothes: then she threw the white robe over her – La Giuffria never thought of the symbolism of the action; she would have rather stood naked before a thousand men than appear in that garment of infamy –

The girl pressed one soft kiss upon her forehead: then was gone headlong through the curtains. Lisa heard the clang of the outer door, and a breath of cold air swept round the room.

It dizzied her, as if she had been drunk; she remembered no more; probably she slept.

At last, she came to consciousness again in a most strange state of being. A peculiar smell was in the air, something as of the sea; she felt a physical

exhilaration incomparable. Her mind was still quite blank as to the past; she was not even surprised at her surroundings. She rose and began to stretch her arms in a dozen physical exercises. Just as she touched her toes for the tenth time the door behind her opened. Sister Cybele was standing there. "Come, Sister!" she cried, "it will be dawn in three minutes; first we must make the Adoration of the Sun, and then comes breakfast!"

The horror of the night returned to Lisa in a flash. But somehow it had receded into a deeper stratum of her being; when it came to a question of any possible action, she seemed remote. She had the horrible fancy that she had died in the night. She followed Sister Cybele as she would have followed her executioner to the block.

Together they went up a spiral staircase. They came to a large room, circular in shape; it was full of the members of the Order, in their robes. At the East, where an oriel opened toward the dawn, she could see the figure of Simon Iff, his eyes fixed, awaiting the rising of the Sun.

A beam touched his face; and he began:

"Hail unto thee that art Ra in thy rising; even unto thee that art Ra in thy strength, that travellest over the Heavens in thy Bark in the uprising of the Sun! Tahuti standeth in his splendour at the prow, and Ra-Hoor abideth at the helm; hail unto thee from the abodes of night!"

It seemed to her that the whole assembly, uniting in the singular gesture with which Simon Iff accompanied his words, was uplifted in some subtle way beyond her understanding. The crowd-psychology assailed her; and she gritted her teeth to curse this hypocrisy of devilry.

But at that moment the crowd broke like a wave upon the beach; and she saw a girl running upon her.

"Oh, you were splendid, sister!" cried a voice, and two scarred arms were thrown about her neck. It was the girl of the night before!

"Didn't you escape?" babbled Lisa, incoherent.

But the child's ringing laughter silenced her. "I forgive you for spoiling my record," she bubbled over. "You know, I'm supposed to get them five times in six."

Lisa stood bewildered. But Sister Cybele was wringing her hands and kissing her, and Cyril Grey was telling the child that he had first claim on the strangle-hold –

And then they all suddenly melted from her. Simon Iff was walking toward her, and his hand was open.

"I congratulate you, sister," he said solemnly, "upon your initiation to our holy Order. You have well earned the robe in which you stand, for you have paid its price – service to others without thought of the consequence to yourself. Let us break our fast!"

And he took Lisa's arm; presently they came to the refectory. As in a well-rehearsed play, every one fell into his place; and before Lisa realised the utter subversion that had taken place in her being, Sister Cybele was on her feet, proclaiming:

"Do what thou wilt shall be the whole of the Law."

Lisa thought that breakfast the most delicious she had ever tasted in her life.

A great reaction from the strain of the previous twenty-four hours was upon her. She had lived a lifetime in that period; and in a sense she had most surely died and been reborn. She felt like a little child. She wanted to climb on to everybody's knee, and be hugged! She had regained at a single stroke the infant's faith in human nature; she looked at the universe as simply as a great artist does. (For in him too lives and rejoices the Eternal Babe.)

But her greatest surprise was in her physical health and energy. She had passed through a fierce and furious day, a night of infernal torture; yet she was unaccountably buoyant, eager, assiduous in every act, from her smiled word of pleasure to the drinking of her coffee.

Everything at that meal seemed matter of intoxication. She had not previously realised that toast, properly understood, was a superior stimulant to brandy.

When breakfast ended, she could not have walked across the room. It was dancing or nothing, so she said to herself.

Somehow she found herself once more in the Chapel of Abominations. On the altar was laid a sprig of gorse, and the sunlight, streaming through the apex of the vault, made its thorny bloom of the very fire and colour of day.

Simon Iff stood behind the altar; Cyril Grey was on her right hand, Sister Cybele on her left. They joined their hands about her.

"I will now complete the formality of your reception," said the old man. "Say after me: 'I (your name).'"

"I, Lisa la Giuffria –

"Solemnly promise to devote myself – " She repeated the phrase.

"To the discovery of my true purpose in this life." She echoed in a lower tone. All three concluded "So mote it be."

"I receive you into this Order," which Simon Iff added, "I confirm you in the robe which you have won; I greet you with the right hand of fellowship; and I induct you to the Gate of the Great Work." Still holding the hand which he had grasped, he led her from the chapel.

They passed through the refectory, and entered a room on its other side. This room was furnished as a library; there was nothing in it to suggest magick.

"This is the Hall of Learning," said Simon Iff. "Here must your work begin. And, innocent as it seems, it is a thousandfold more dangerous than the chapel from which you have come forth with so much credit."

Lisa seated herself, and prepared to listen to the exposition of her task in life which she expected to follow.

But she could not know why the old mystic was at such great pains (as he afterwards proved) to make every syllable of his discourse intelligible; for she had not heard his conference with Cyril Grey at the moment when Sister Cybele had called her.

"Brother Cyril!" the old mystic had said, "I shall go on – I shall even put more than the necessary care into the work – as if this were victory and not defeat.

"I tell you that you will never do anything yourself, still less anything for others, so long as you rely on women. This victory of the woman's is only the chance resultant of a chaos of emotional states. She's in it for the fun of the thing; she's not even an artist; she's merely the female of the species; and I do not alleviate the situation by one further precision – your species!"

"Are women no use? Why were they made?" asked Cyril, angry. He did not know that his question was prompted by a desire yet unconquered in himself. But Simon Iff answered him with mock humility.

"I am unskilled to unravel the mysteries of the Universe. Like Sir Isaac Newton, I am." But seeing the muffled rage in the boy's eyes, he spared him the conclusion.

CHAPTER VIII

OF THE HOMUNCULUS;

CONCLUSION OF THE FORMER ARGUMENT CONCERNING THE NATURE OF THE SOUL

"I AM going to be perfectly horrid," said Simon Iff, leaning over to Lisa, and measuring his words with the minutest care. "I am going to do everything possible to damp your enthusiasm. I would rather have you start from cold and spark up well as you go, than have you go off with a spurt, and find yourself without petrol in the middle of the big rise.

"I want you to take up this research because of your real love of knowledge, not because of your passion for Brother Cyril. And I tell you honestly that I am mortally afraid for you, because you live in extremes. It is good for a swift push to have that sudden energy of yours; but no research in science is to be taken by storm. You need infinite patience, nay, even infinite indifference to the very thing on which your heart is set:

"Well, I have prated. The old man must utter his distrust of fiery youth. So we'll go on.

"I'm going to talk to you about the soul again. Remember our conception

of it, the idea that seemed to do away with all the difficulties at a blow. We had the idea of a soul, of a real physical substance, one of whose surfaces, or rather boundary-solids, was what we call body and mind. Body and mind are real, too, and truly belong to the soul, but are only minute aspects of it, just as any ellipse or hyperbola is an aspect of the section of a cone.

"We'll take just one more analogy in the lower dimensions as we pass.

"How do solids know one another? Almost entirely by their surfaces! Except in chemistry, which we have reason to believe to be a fourth-dimensional science, witness the phenomena of polarization and geometrical isomerism, solids only make contact superficially.

"Then, shifting the analogy as we did before, how do fourth-dimensional beings know one another? By their bounding solids. In other words, my soul speaks to yours through the medium of our minds and bodies.

"That is the common phrase? Quite so; but I am using it in an absolute physical sense. A line can only be aware of another line at a point of contact; a plane of another plane at the line where they cut; a cube of another cube at the surface common to both; and a soul of another soul where their ideas are in conjunction.

"I do want you to grasp this with every fibre in your being; I believe it to be the most important thesis ever enunciated, and you will be proud to learn that it is wholly Brother Cyril's, with no help from me. Hinton, Rouse Ball, and others, laid the foundations; but it was he that put it in such a clear light, and correlated it with occult science."

"You must give the honour to the Mahathera Phang!" interjected Cyril. "I was proving to him the metaphysical nature of the soul – and he regarded me with so amused a smile that I perceived my asininity. Of course there can be but one order of Nature!"

"In any case," continued Iff, "this theory of Cyril's wipes the slate clean of every metaphysical speculation. Good and evil vanish instantly, with Realism and Nominalism, and Free will and Determinism – and all the 'isms' and all the 'ologies'! Life is reduced to mathematical formulae, indeed, as the Victorian scientists rightly wished to do; but at the same time mathematics is restored to her royal pre-eminence as not only the most exact, but the most exalted of the sciences. The intelligible order of things, moreover, becomes natural and inevitable; and such moral problems as the cruelty of organic life return to their real insignificance. The almost comic antinomy between man's size and his intelligence is reduced; and although the mystery

of the Universe remains unsolved, at least it is a rational mystery, and neither senseless nor intolerable.

"Let us now come down to a simple practical point. Here is a soul anxious to communicate with other souls. He can only do it by obtaining a mind and body. Now you'll notice, taking that cone image of ours again, that any section of it is always one of three regular curves. It would not fit into a square, for example, however you turned it. And so our soul has to look about for some mind which will fit one of his sections. There is a great deal of latitude, no doubt; for the mind grows, and is at first very plastic. But there must be some sort of relation. If I am a wandering soul, and wish to communicate with the soul now manifesting a section of itself as Professor of Electricity at Oxford, it is useless for me to take the mind of a Hottentot. (Cyril sighed a doubt.)

"I'm going to digress for a moment. Look at the finished product, the soul 'incarnated,' as we may call it. There are three forces at work upon it; the soul itself, the heredity and the environment. A clever soul will therefore be careful to choose the embryo which seems most likely to be fairly free in the two latter respects. It will look for a healthy stock, for parents who will, and can, give the child every chance in life. You must remember that every soul is, from our point of view, a 'genius', for its world is so incalculably greater than ours that one spark of its knowledge is enough to kindle a new epoch in mankind.

"But heredity and environment usually manage to prevent any of this coming to light. No matter how full of whisky a flask may be, you will never make it drunk!

"So we may perhaps conceive of some competition between souls for possession of different minds and bodies; or, let us say, to combine the ideas, different embryos. I hope you notice how this theory removes the objection to reincarnation, that one's mind does not remember 'the last time'. Why should our cone make connexion between its different curves? Each is so unimportant to it that it would hardly think of doing so. Yet there might be some similarity between successive curves (in our case, lives) that might make an historian suspect that they were connected; just as a poet's style would be constant in some respects, whether he wrote a war-story or a love-lyric.

"You see, of course, by the way, how this theory does away with all the nonsense about 'Are the planets inhabited?' with its implication of idiotic

waste if they be not. To us every grain of dust, every jet of hydrogen on the sun's envelope, is the manifestation of a section of some soul:

"And here we find ourselves quite suddenly and unexpectedly in line with some of the old Rosicrucian doctrines.

"This brings us to the consideration of certain experiments made by our predecessors. They had quite another theory of souls; at least, their language was very different to ours; but they wanted very much to produce a man who should not be bound up in his heredity, and should have the environment which they desired for him.

"They started in paraphysical ways; that is, they repudiated natural generation altogether. They made figures of brass, and tried to induce souls to indwell them. In some accounts we read that they succeeded; Friar Bacon was credited with one such Homunculus; so was Albertus Magnus, and, I think, Paracelsus.

"He had, at least, a devil in his long sword 'which taught him all the cunning pranks of past and future mountebanks', or Samuel Butler, first of that dynasty, has lied.

"But other magicians sought to make this Homunculus in a way closer to nature. In all these cases they had held that environment could be modified at will by the application of telesmata or sympathetic figures. For example, a nine-pointed star would attract the influence which they called Luna – not meaning the actual moon, but an idea similar to the poets' ideas of her. By surrounding an object with such stars, with similarly-disposed herbs, perfumes, metals, talismans, and so on, and by carefully keeping off all other influences by parallel methods, they hoped to invest the original object so treated with the Lunar qualities, and no others. (I am giving the briefest outline of an immense subject.) Now then they proceeded to try to make the Homunculus on very curious lines.

"Man, said they, is merely a fertilised ovum properly incubated. Heredity is there even at first, of course, but in a feeble degree. Anyhow, they could arrange any desired environment from the beginning, if they could only manage to nourish the embryo in some artificial way – incubate it, in fact, as is done with chickens today. Furthermore, and this is the crucial point, they thought that by performing this experiment in a specially prepared place, a place protected magically against all incompatible forces, and by invoking into that place some one force which they desired, some tremendously powerful being, angel or archangel – and they had conjurations

which they thought capable of doing this – that they would be able to cause the incarnation of beings of infinite knowledge and power, who would be able to bring the whole world into Light and Truth.

"I may conclude this little sketch by saying that the idea has been almost universal in one form or another; the wish has always been for a Messiah or Superman, and the method some attempt to produce man by artificial or at least abnormal means. Greek and Roman legend is full of stories in which this mystery is thinly veiled; they seem mostly to derive from Asia Minor and Syria. Here exogamic principles have been pushed to an amusing extreme. I need not remind you of the Persian formula for producing a magician, or of the Egyptian routine in the matter of Pharaoh, or of the Mohammedan device for inaugurating the Millenium. I did remind Brother Cyril, by the way, of this last point, and he did need it; but it did him no good, for here we are at the threshold of a Great Experiment on yet another false track!"

"He is only taunting me to put me on my mettle," laughed Cyril.

"Now I'm going to bring all this to a point," went on the old mystic. "The Greeks, as you know, practised a kind of eugenics. (Of course, all tribal marriage laws are primarily eugenic in intention.) But like the mediaeval magicians we were speaking of, with their Homunculus, the Greeks attached the greatest possible importance to the condition of the mother during gestation. She was encouraged to look only on beautiful statues, to read only beautiful books. The Mohammedans, again, whose marriage system makes Christian marriage by comparison a thing for cattle, shut up a woman during that period, keep her perfectly quiet and free from the interference of her husband.

"This is all very good, but it falls short of Brother Cyril's latest lunacy. As I understand him, he wishes indeed to proceed normally in a physical sense, but to prepare the way by making the heredity, and environment as attractive as possible to one special type of soul, and then – to go soul-fishing in the Fourth Dimension!

"Thus he will have a perfectly normal child, which yet is also a Homunculus in the mediaeval sense of the word!

"And he has asked me to lend you the villa of the Order at Naples for the purpose."

Lisa had lent forward; her face, between her hands was burning.

Slowly she spoke: "You know that you are asking me to sacrifice my humanity?" She was not silly enough to pretend to misunderstand the proposal and Simon liked her better for the way she took it.

He thought a moment. "I see now; I never thought of it before, and I am foolish, The conservatism of woman calls this sort of thing a 'heartless experiment.' Yet nothing is farther from our thoughts. There will be no action to annoy or offend you on the contrary. But I understand the feeling – it is the swift natural repugnance to discuss what is sacred."

"Tut – tut – my memory is always failing me these days," muttered Cyril; "I've quite forgotten the percentage of children that were born blind in 1861."

Lisa started to her feet. She did not know what he meant, but in some way it stung her like a serpent.

Simon Iff intervened. "Brother Cyril, you always use strong medicine!" he said, shaking his head; "I sometimes think you're too keen to see your results."

"I hate to beat about the bush. I say the thing that can never be forgotten."

"Or forgiven, sometimes," said the old man in gentle reproof.

"But come, my dear, sit down; he meant truth, after all, and truth cuts only to cure. It's a brutal fact that children used to be born blind, literally by the thousand, because it wasn't quite nice to publish the facts about certain diseases; and precautions against them were called 'heartless experiments'. What Cyril is asking you to do is no more than what your whole heart craves for; only he wants to crown that with a gift to humanity such as has never yet been given. Suppose that you succeed, that you can attract a soul to you who will find a way to abolish poverty, or to cure cancer, or to – oh! surely you glow with vision, a thousand heights of human progress thrusting their sunlit snows through the clouds of doubt!"

Lisa rose again to her feet, but her mood was no longer the same. She put her hands in Simon Iff's. "I think you're a very noble man," she said, "and it's an honour to work in such a cause." Cyril took her in his arms. "Then you will come with me to Naples? To the Master's own villa?"

She looked at Iff with a queer smile. "May I make a joke?" she said. "I should like to rechristen the villa – The Butterfly-Net!"

Simple Simon laughed with her like a child. It was just the delicate humour that appealed to him; and the classical allusion to the Butterfly as allegorical of the Soul showed him a side of the girl that he had hardly suspected.

But Cyril Grey swerved instantly to the serious aspect of the problem. "We have merely been discussing an A. B. case," he said; "we have forgotten where we stand. Somewhere or other I have made a blunder already, mark you! – and we have the Black Lodge on our trail. You may possibly recall

some of the events of yesterday?" he concluded, with a touch of his old airy manner.

"Yes," said Simon, "I think you had better get to business."

"We discussed the thing on general lines during your vigil last night," said Cyril. "Our first need is defence. The strongest form of defence is counter-attack; but you should arrange for that to take shape as far as possible from the place you are defending, In this game you are keeping goal, Lisa; I am full back; Simple Simon is the captain playing at half-back; and I think we have a fairly fit eleven! So that's all right. There is reason to believe that the enemy's goal is in Paris itself. And if we can keep the ball in their half all through the game, you and I can spend a very quiet year in Italy."

"I can't follow all that football slang; but do explain why anyone should want to interfere with us. It's too silly."

"It's only silly when you get to the very distant end of a most abstruse philosophy. On the surface it's obvious. It's the objection of the burglar to electric lights and bells. You can imagine him having enough foresight to vote against a town councillor who proposed an appropriation for the study of science in general. Something might turn up which would put him out of business."

"But what is their business?"

"Ultimately, you may call it selfishness – only that's a dreadful word, and will mislead you. We're just as selfish; only we realise that other things beyond our own consciousnesses are equally ourselves. For instance, I try to unite myself as intimately as I can with every other mind, or body, or idea, that comes in my way. To take that cone simile, I want to be all the different curves I can, so as to have a better chance of realizing the cone. The Black Lodge magician clings to his one curve, tries to make it permanent, to exalt it above all other curves. And of course the moment the cone shifts, out he goes: pop!"

"Observe the poet!" remarked Simon Iff. "He values himself enormously; but his idea of perpetuating himself is to make the beauty that is inherent in his own soul radiate beyond him so as to illumine every other mind in the world. But your Black Magician is secret, and difficult of access; he isn't going to tell anyone anything, not he! So even his knowledge tends to extinction, in the long run."

"But you are yourselves a secret society!" exclaimed Lisa.

"Only to secure freedom from interruption. It is merely the same idea as

that which makes every householder close his doors at night; or, better, as public libraries are guarded by certain regulations. We can't allow lunatics to scrawl over our unique manuscripts, and tear the pages out of all our books. Shallow people are always chattering about science being free to all; the truth is that it is guarded as no other secret ever was in all history, by the simple fact that, with all the help in the world, it takes half a lifetime to begin to master even one small section of it. We guard our magick just as much and as little as our other branches of physics; but people are so stupid that, though they know it requires years of training to use so simple an instrument as a microscope, they are indignant that we cannot teach them to use the Verendum in an hour."

"Ah, but they complain that you have never proved the use of the Verendum at all."

"Only those who have not learnt its use. I can read Homer, but I can only prove the fact to another man by teaching him Greek; and he is then obliged to do the same to a third party, and so on. People generally acquiesce that some men can read Homer because – well, it's their intellectual laziness. A really stout intelligence would doubt it.

"Spiritualism and Christian Science, which are either fraud or bluff or misinterpretation of facts, have spread all over the Anglo-Saxon world because there is no true critical spirit among the half-educated. But we are not willing to have our laboratories invaded by reporters and curiosity-mongers; we are dealing with delicate forces; we have to train our minds with an intensity which no other study in the world demands. Public indifference and incredulity suit us perfectly. The only object of advertisement would be to get suitable members; but we have methods of finding them without publicity. We make no secret of our methods and results, on the other hand; but only the right man knows how to discover them.

"It is not as if we were working in an old field where all the terms were defined, and the main laws ascertained. In Magick, even more than in any other science, the student must keep his practice level with his theory."

"Don't you ever do magick under test conditions?"

"Unfortunately, my child, creative magick, which is the thaumaturgic side of the business, depends on a peculiar excitation which objects to 'test conditions' very strongly. You might as well ask Cyril to prove his poetic gift, or even his manhood, before a set of fools. He will produce you poems, and infants, and events, as the case may be; but you have more or less to

take his word for it that he did the acts responsible primarily for them. Another difficulty about true magick is that it is so perfectly a natural process that its phenomena never excite surprise except by their timeliness – so that one has to record hundreds of experiments to set up a case which will even begin to exclude coincidence. For instance, I want a certain book. I use my book-producing talisman. The following day, a bookseller offers me the volume. One experiment proves nothing. My ability to do it every time is the proof. And I can't even do that under 'test conditions'; for it is necessary that I should really want the book, in my subconsciousness, whose will works the miracle. It is useless for me to think, or pretend, that I want it. Any man may fluke a ten-shot at billiards, but you call him a player only when he can average a break of thirty or so every time he goes to the table.

"But in some branches of magick we can give proof on the spot; in any branch, that is, where the female, and not the male, part of us is concerned. The analogy is quite perfect. Thus, in my guess at your birth-hour – was not that a test? I will do it all day, and be right five times in six. Further, in the event of error, I will show exactly why I was wrong. It's a case where one is sometimes right to be wrong, as I'll explain one day. Then again, your own clairvoyance; I did not tell you that sort of a Thing to look for; yet you saw it under the same form as I did. You shall practise these things daily with Cyril if you like, always checking your results in a way which he will show you; and in a month you will be an expert. Then, if you feel you want to advertise, do. But you won't.

"Besides, the real trouble is that not one person in a thousand cares for any form of science whatever; even such base applications of science as the steam-engine and all its family, from the telegraph to the automobile, were only thrust upon the unwilling people by bullies who knew that there was money in them. Who are your 'men of science' in the popular notion of today? Edison and Marconi, neither of whom ever invented anything, but were smart businessmen, with the capacity to exploit the brains of others, and turn science to commercially useful and profitable ends. Heigho!"

"We're a long way from our subject," said Cyril. "I have had a delightful morning – I have felt like Plato with the Good, the True, and the Beautiful in contemplating you three – but we have work before us. I propose in this emergency to copy the tactics of Washington at Valley Forge. We will make a direct and vehement attack on the Black Lodge: they will expect me to be

in my usual position in the van – I will slip away with Lisa while the fires blaze brightest."

"A sound plan," said Simon. "Let us break up this conference, and put it immediately into execution. You had better not attract attention by collecting luggage, and you must certainly take no person outside the Order into your circle. So after dinner you will put on your other clothes, walk down to the Metro, cross to the Gare de Lyon, and jump into the Rome rapide. Wire me when you arrive at The Butterfly-Net!"

CHAPTER IX

HOW THEY BROUGHT THE BAD NEWS FROM ARAGO TO QUINCAMPOIX:

AND WHAT ACTION WAS TAKEN THEREUPON

JUST as Lord Antony Bowling turned into the Grands Boulevards from the Faubourg Montmartre, Akbar Pasha was leaving them. The Turk did not see the genially flourished cane; he was preoccupied – and perhaps he did not wish to be recognised. For he dodged among the obscure and dangerous streets of "The Belly of Paris" with many a look behind him. To be sure, this is but a reasonable precaution in a district so favourable to Apache activities. At last he came out into the great open square of the markets; and, crossing obliquely, came to a drinking den of the type which seeks to attract foreigners, preferably Americans. It bore the quite incongruous name "*Au Père Tranquille*". Akbar mounted the stairs. It was too early for revellers; even the musicians had not arrived; but an old man sat in one corner of the room, sipping a

concoction of gin, whisky and rum which goes in certain circles by the name of a Nantucket Cocktail.

This individual was of some sixty years of age; his hair and beard were white; his dress was that of a professional man, and he endeavoured to give dignity to his appearance by the assumption of a certain paternal or even patriarchal manner. But his eye was pale and cold as a murderer's, shifty and furtive as a thief's. His hands trembled continually with a kind of palsy; and the white knuckles told a tale of gout. Self-indulgence had bloated his body; unhealthy fat was everywhere upon him.

The trembling of his hands seemed in sympathy with that of his mind; one would have said that he was in deadly fear, or the prey to a consuming anxiety.

At the Turk's entrance he rose clumsily, then fell back into his chair. He was more than half intoxicated.

Akbar took the chair opposite to him. "We couldn't get it," he said; in a whisper, though there was nobody within earshot. "Oh, Dr. Balloch, Dr. Balloch! do try to understand! It was impossible. We tried all sorts of ways."

The doctor's voice had a soft suavity. Though a licensed physician, he had long since abandoned legitimate practice, and under the guise of homeopathy pursued various courses which would have been but ill regarded by more regular practitioners.

His reply was horrible, uttered as it was in feline falseness, like a caress. "You foul ass!" he said. "I have to take this up with S.R.M.D., you know! What will he say and do?"

"I tell you I couldn't. There was an old man there who spoilt everything, in my idea."

"An old man?" Dr. Balloch almost dropped his hypocritical bedside voice in his rage. "Oh curse, oh curse it all!" He leant over to the Turk, caught his beard, and deliberately pulled it. There is no grosser insult that you can offer to a Mussulman, but Akbar accepted it without resentment. Yet so savage was the assault that a sharp cry of pain escaped him.

"You dog! you Turkish swine!" hissed Balloch. "Do you know what has happened? S.R.M.D. sent a Watcher – a bit of himself, do you understand what that means, you piece of dirt? – and it hasn't returned. It must have been killed, but we can't find out how, and S.R.M.D. is lying half dead in his house. You pig! Why didn't you come with your story at once? I know now what is wrong."

"You know I don't know your address," said the Turk humbly. "Please, oh please, leave go of my beard!"

Balloch contemptuously released his victim – who was a brave enough man in an ordinary way, and would have had the blood of his own Sultan, though he knew that the guards would cut him to pieces within the next ten seconds, for the least of such words as had been addressed to him. But Balloch was his Superior in the Black Lodge, which rules by terror and by torture; its first principle was to enslave its members. The bully Balloch became a whimpering cur at the slightest glance of the dreaded S.R.M.D.

"Tell me what the old man was like," he said. "Did you get his name?"

"Yes," said Akbar, "I got that. It was Simon Iff."

Balloch dashed his glass upon the ground. "Oh hell! Oh hell! Oh hell!" he said, not so much as a curse but as an invocation. "Hear, oh hear this creature! The ignorant, blind swine! You had him – Him! – under your hand; oh hell, you fool, you fool!"

"I felt sure he was somebody," said Akbar, "but I had no orders."

"And no brains, no brains," snarled the other. "Look here; I'll tell you how to get your step in the Lodge if you'll give me a hundred pounds."

"Do you mean it?" cried Akbar, entirely his own man in a moment, for abject fear and obsessing ambition combined to make his advancement the tyrant of his whole tormented mind. "Will you swear it?"

Balloch made an ugly face. "By the black sow's udder, I will."

His whole frame trembling with excitement, Akbar Pasha drew a cheque-book from his pocket, and filled in a blank for the required sum.

Balloch snatched it greedily. "This is worth your money," he said. "That man Iff is in the second grade, perhaps even the first, of their dirty Order; and we sometimes think he's the most powerful of the whole damned crew. That fool Grey's a child to him. I know now how the Watcher was destroyed. Oh! S.R.M.D. will pay somebody for this! But listen, man – you bring that old beast's head on a charger – or Grey's, either! – and you can have any grade you dare ask for! And that's no lie, curse it! Why," he went on with increasing vehemence, "the whole thing's a plant of ours. Monet-Knott's one of us; we use him to blackmail Lavinia King – about all he's fit for, the prig! And we got him to drag that dago woman in front of Master Grey's dog nose! And now they bring in Simon Iff. Oh, it's too much! We've even lost their trail. Ten to one they're safe in their Abbey tonight. Be off! No, wait for me here; I'll bring back orders.

And while I'm gone, get that son of yours here – he's got more sense than you. We'll have to trace Grey somehow – and astral watchers won't do the trick when Simon Iff's about."

Balloch rose to his feet, buttoned his coat around him, put on a tall silk hat, and was gone without wasting another word upon his subordinate.

The Turk would have given his ears to have dared to follow him. The mystery of S.R.M.D.'s personality and abode were shrouded in the blackest secrecy. Akbar had but the vaguest ideas of the man; he was a formless ideal of terrific power and knowledge, a sort of incarnated Satan, the epitome of successful iniquity. The episode of the "Watcher" had not diminished the chief's prestige in his eyes; it was evidently an "accident"; S.R.M.D. had sent out a patrol and it had been ambushed by a whole division, as it were. So trivial a "regrettable incident" was negligibly normal.

Akbar had no thought but of S.R.M.D. as a Being infinitely great in himself; he had no conception of the price paid by the members of the Black Lodge. The truth is, that as its intimates advance, their power and knowledge becomes enormously greater; but such progress is not a mark of general growth, as it is in the case of the White Brotherhood; it is like a cancer, which indeed grows apace, but at the expense of the man on whom it feeds, and will destroy both him and itself in the long run. The process may be slow; it may extend over a series of incarnations; but it is sure enough. The analogy of the cancer is a close one; for the man knows his doom, suffers continual torture; but to this is added the horrible delusion that if only the disease can be induced to advance far enough, all is saved. Thus he hugs the fearful growth, cherishes it as his one dearest possession, stimulates it by every means in his power. Yet all the time he nurses in his heart an agonizing certainty that this is the way of death.

Balloch knew S.R.M.D. well; had known him for years. He hoped to supplant him, and while he feared him with hideous and unmanly fear, hated him with most hellish hatred. He was under no delusion as to the nature of the Path of the Black Lodge. Akbar Pasha, a mere outsider, without a crime on his hands as yet, was a rich and honoured officer in the service of the Sultan; he, Balloch, was an ill-reputed doctor, living on the fears of old maids, on doubtful and even criminal services to foolish people from the supply of morphia to the suppression of the evidence of scandal, and on the harvest of half-disguised blackmail that goes with such pursuits. But he was respectability itself compared to S.R.M.D.

This man, who called himself the Count Macgregor of Glenlyon, was in reality a Hampshire man, of lowland Scottish extraction, of the name of Douglas. He had been well educated, became a good scholar, and developed an astounding taste and capacity for magic. For some time he had kept straight; then he had fallen, chosen the wrong road. His powers had increased at a bound; but they were solely used for base ends. He had established the Black Lodge far more firmly than ever before, jockeyed his seniors out of office by superior villainy, and proceeded to forge the whole weapon to his own liking. He had had one terrible setback.

Cyril Grey, when only twenty years of age, a freelance magician, had entered the Lodge; for it worked to attract innocent people under a false pretence of wisdom and of virtue. Cyril, discovering the trick, had not withdrawn; he had played the game of the Lodge, and made himself Douglas's right-hand man. This being achieved, he had suddenly put a match to the arsenal.

The Lodge was always seething with hate; Theosophists themselves might have taken lessons from this exponent; and the result of Cyril's intervention had been to disintegrate the entire structure. Douglas found his prestige gone, and his income with it. Addiction to drink, which had accompanied his magical fall, now became an all-absorbing vice. He was never able to rebuild his Lodge on its former lines; but those who thirsted for knowledge and power and these he still possessed in ever increasing abundance as he himself decayed – clung to him, hating and envying him, as a young ruffian of the streets will envy the fame of some robber or murderer who happens to fill the public eye.

It was with this clot of perverse feelings that Balloch approached the Rue Quincampoix, one of the lowest streets in Paris, and turned in at the den where Douglas lodged.

S.R.M.D. was lying on a torn soiled sofa, his face white as death; a mottled and empurpled nose, still showing trace of its original aggressive and haughty model, alone made for colour. For his eyes were even paler than the doctor's. In his hand was a bottle half full of raw whisky, with which he was seeking to restore his vitality.

"I brought you some whisky," said Balloch, who knew the way to favour.

"Put it down, over there. You've got some money."

Balloch did not dare to lie. S.R.M.D. had spotted the fact without a word.

"Only a cheque. You shall have half tomorrow when I've cashed it."

"Come here at noon."

Despite the obvious degradation of his whole being, S.R.M.D. was still somebody. He was a wreck, but he was the wreck of something indubitably big. He had not only the habit of command, but the tone of fine manners. In his palmy days he had associated with some very highly placed people. It was said that the Third Section of the Russian Police Bureau had once found a use for him.

"Is the Countess at home?" asked Balloch, apparently in courtesy.

"She's on the Boulevard. Where else should she be, at this time of night?"

It was the vilest thing charged against that vile parody of a man, his treatment of his wife, a young, beautiful, talented, and charming girl, the sister of a famous Professor at the Sorbonne. He had delighted to reduce her to the bedraggled street-walker that she now was. Nobody knew what Douglas did with his money. The contributions of his Lodge were large; blackmail and his wife's earnings aided the exchequer; he had probably a dozen other sources of income. Yet he never extricated himself from his sordidness; and he was always in need of money. It was no feigned need, either; for he was sometimes short of whisky.

The man's knowledge of the minds of others was uncanny; he read Balloch at a gesture.

"Grey never struck the Watcher," he said; "it was not his style; who was it?"

"Simon Iff."

"I shall see to that."

Balloch understood that, though S.R.M.D. feared Iff and loathed him, his great preoccupation was with Cyril Grey. He hated the young magician with a perfect hatred; he would never forget his ruin at those boyish hands. Also, he forgave nothing, from a kindness to an insult; he was malignant for the sake of malice.

"They will have gone over to their house on Montmartre," continued Douglas, in a voice of absolute certitude. "We must have the exits watched by Abdul Bey and his men. But I know what Grey will do as well as if he had told me; he will bolt somewhere warm for his damned honeymoon. You and Akbar watch the Gare de Lyon. Now, look here! with a bit of luck, we'll finish off this game; I'm weary of it. Mark me well!"

Douglas rose. The whisky he had drunk was impotent to affect him, head or legs. He went over to a small table on which were painted certain curious

figures. He took a saucer, poured some whisky into it, and dropped a five-franc piece into the middle. Then he began to make weird gestures, and to utter a long conjuration, harsh-sounding, and apparently in gibberish. Lastly, he set fire to the whisky in the saucer. When it was nearly burnt through, he blew it out. He took the coin, wrapped it in a piece of dark-red silk, and gave it to his pupil.

"When Grey boards a train," he ordered, "go up to the engine-driver, give him this, and tell him to drive carefully. Let me know what the fellow looks like; get his name, if you can; say you want to drink his health. Then come straight here in a cab."

Balloch nodded. The type of magic proposed was familiar enough to him. He took the coin and made off.

At the Sign of the Tranquil Father, Akbar was awaiting him with his son Abdul Bey. The latter was in charge of the Turkish Secret Service in Paris, and he did not hesitate to use the facilities thus at his disposal to his own magical advancement. All his resources were constantly at the service of Balloch. Now that S.R.M.D. himself was employing him, he was beside himself with pride and pleasure.

Balloch gave his instructions. An hour later the house where Lisa was even then undergoing her ordeal would be surrounded by spies; additional men would be placed at all the big terminals of Paris; for Abdul Bey meant to do the thing thoroughly. He would not take a chance; for all his fanatical faith in Douglas, he thought it prudent to provide against the possibility of an error in the chief's occult calculations. Also, his action would prove his zeal. Besides, Cyril might deliberately lay a false trail – was almost sure to play some trick of the sort.

Balloch and Akbar Pasha were stationed in a restaurant facing the Gare de Lyon, ready to answer the telephone at any moment. "Now," said Abdul, "Have you photographs of these people to show my men?"

Balloch produced them.

"I've seen this man Grey somewhere," remarked the young Turk casually. And then he gave a sudden and terrible cry. In Lisa he recognised an unknown woman whom he had admired the year before at a dance – and whom he had craved ever since. "Tell S.R.M.D.," he roared, "that I'm in this thing for life or death; but I ask the girl for a trophy."

"You'll get that, or anything else," said Balloch, "if you can put an end to the activities of Mr. Cyril Grey."

Abdul Bey rushed off without another word spoken; and Balloch and the Pasha went to the rendezvous appointed. They passed that night and the next day in alternate bouts of drink and sleep. About half-past eight on the following evening the telephone rang. Douglas had judged rightly; the lovers had arrived at the Gare de Lyon.

Balloch and his pupil sprang to life – fresh and vigorous at the prick of the summons to action.

It was easy to mark the tall figure of the magician, with the lovely girl upon his arm; at the barrier their distinction touched the humanity of the collector. Tickets through to Rome – and no luggage! Most evidently an elopement!

With romantic sympathy, the kind man determined to oppose the passage of Balloch, whom he supposed to be an angry father or an outraged husband. But the manner of the Englishman disarmed him; besides, he had a ticket to Dijon.

Concealing himself as best he could, the doctor walked rapidly to the head of the train. There, assuming the character of a timid old man, he implored the driver, with the gift of the bewitched "cart-wheel", to be sure to drive carefully. He would drink the good fellow's health, to be sure – what name? Oh! Marcel Dufour. "Of the furnace – that is appropriate!" laughed the genial passenger, apparently reassured as to his security.

But he did not enter the train. He dashed out of the station, and into a motor-cab, overjoyed to return to Douglas with so clean a record of work accomplished.

He never gave the Turk another thought.

But Akbar Pasha had had an idea. Balloch had taken a ticket for Dijon – he would take one, too. And he would go – he would retrieve his error of yesterday. He was not in the least afraid of that cub Grey, when Simon Iff was not there to back him. It would go hard, but he should get a drop of Lisa's blood – if he had to bribe the wagon-lit man. Then – who knows? – there might even be a chance to kill Grey. He waited till the last moment before he boarded the train.

The train would stop at Moret-les-Sablons; by that time the beds would be made up; he would have plenty of time to act; he could go on to Rome if necessary.

Cyril Grey, away from the influence of Simon Iff, had become the sarcastic sphinx once more. He was wearing a travelling suit with knickerbockers, but he still affected the ultra-pontifical diplomatist.

"The upholstery of these cars is revolting," he said to Lisa, with a glance of disgust. And he suddenly opened the door away from the platform and lifted her on to the permanent way; thence into a stuffy compartment in the train that was standing at the next "*Voie*".

"A frosty moonlight night like this," he said, pulling a large black pipe from his pocket and filling it, "indicates (to romantic lovers like ourselves) the propriety of a descent at Moret, a walk to Barbizon through the forest, a return to Moret by a similar route in a day or so, and the pursuance of our journey to Naples. See Naples and die!" he added musingly, "Decidedly a superior programme."

Lisa would have listened to a proposition to begin their travels by swimming the Seine, on the ground that the day after tomorrow would be Friday; so she raised no objection. But she could not help saying that they would have reached Moret more quickly by the rapide.

"My infant child!" he returned; "the celebrated Latin poet Quintus Horatius Flaccus has observed, for our edification and behoof, '*Festina lente*.' This epigram has been translated by a famous Spanish author, '*manana*.' Dante adds his testimony to truth in his grandiose outburst, '*Domani*.' Also, an Arab philosopher, whom I personally revere, remarks, if we may trust the assertion of Sir Richard Francis Burton, K.C.M.G. – and why should we not? – 'Conceal thy tenets, thy treasure, and thy travelling!' This I do. More so," he concluded cryptically, "than you imagine!"

They were still waiting for their local funeral (which the French grandiloquently describe as a train) to start when Dr. Balloch returned radiant to the Rue Quincampoix.

Douglas was on the alert to receive him. The news took only a second to communicate.

"Marcel Dufour!" cried S.R.M.D. "We shall drink for him, as he may not drink on duty."

He carefully opened two bottles of whisky, mixed the stale spirit in the magic saucer with their contents, and bade Balloch join him at the table.

"Your very good health, Marcel Dufour!" cried Douglas. "And mind you drive carefully!" Balloch and he now set to work steadily to drain the two bottles – a stiff nip every minute – but the stuff had no effect on them. It was far otherwise with the man on the engine.

Almost before he had well left Paris behind him, he began to fret about the furnace, and told his fireman to keep up the fullest head of steam. At

Melun the train should have slackened speed; instead, it increased it. The signalman at Fontainebleau was amazed to see the rapide rush through the station, eight minutes ahead of time, against the signals. He saw the driver grappling with the fireman, who was thrown from the footplate a moment after, but escaped with a broken leg.

"My mate went suddenly mad," the injured man explained later. "He held up a five-franc piece which some old gentleman had given him, and swore that the devil had promised him another if he made Dijon in two hours. (And, as you know, it is five, what horror!)"

He grew afraid, saw the signals set at danger, and sprang to the lever. Then that poor crazed Dufour had thrown him off the train.

The guard was new to that section of the line, and so, no doubt, too timid to take the initiative; he certainly should have applied the brakes, even at Melun.

An hour later Cyril Grey and Lisa and all their fellow passengers were turned out at Fontainebleau. There had been a terrible disaster to the Paris-Rome rapide at Moret. The line would be blocked all night.

"This contretemps," said Cyril, as if he had heard of a change of programme at a theatre, "will add appreciably to the length and, may I add, to the romance – of our proposed walk.

When they reached Moret more than three hours later, they found the rapide inextricably tangled with a heavy freight train. It had left the line at the curve and crashed into the slower train. Cyril Grey had still a surprise in store. He produced a paper of some sort from his pocket, which the officer of the police cordon received in the manner of the infant Samuel when overwhelmed by the gift of prophecy. He made way for them with proud deference.

They had not to walk far before the magician found what he was seeking. Beneath the ruins of the rear compartment were the remains of the late Akbar Pasha.

"I wonder how that happened," he said. "However, here is a guess at your epitaph: 'a little learning is a dangerous thing.' I think, Lisa, that we should sup at the Cheval Blanc before we start our walk to Barbizon. It is a long way, especially at night, and we want to cut away to the west so as to avoid Fontainebleau, for the sake of the romance of the thing."

Lisa did not mind whether she supped at the White Horse, or on one. She realised that she had hold of a man of strength, wisdom, and foresight, far more than a match for their enemies.

He stopped to speak to the officer in charge of the cordon as they passed him. "Among the dead: Mr. and Mrs. Cyril Grey. English people. No flowers. Service of the minister."

The officer promised to record the lie officially. His deference was amazing.

Lisa perceived that her lover had been at the pains to arm himself with more than one kind of weapon. Lisa pressed his arm, and murmured her appreciation of his cleverness.

"It won't deceive Douglas for two minutes, if he be, as I suspect, the immediate Hound of the Baskervilles, but he may waste some time rejoicing over my being such an ass as to try it; and that's always a gain."

Lisa began to wonder whether her best chance of ever saying the right thing would not be to choose the wrong. His point of view was always round the corner of her street!

CHAPTER X
HOW THEY
GATHERED THE SILK
FOR THE WEAVING OF
THE BUTTERFLY-NET

CYRIL GREY made the midnight invocation to the Sun-God, Khephra, the Winged Beetle, upon the crest of the Long Rocher; and he made the morning invocation to the Sun-God, Ra, the Hawk, upon the heights that overlooked the hamlet of Barbizon.

Thence, like Chanticleer himself, he woke the people of the Inn, who, in memory of the days Stevenson had spent with them, honour his ashes by emulating the morality of Long John Silver.

They were prepared for the breakfast order; but Cyril's requirement, a long-distance call to Paris, struck them as unseasonable and calculated to disturb the balance of the Republic. They asked themselves if the Dreyfus case were come again. However, Cyril got his call, and Simon Iff his information, before seven o'clock. Long before Douglas, who had waited until midnight for the news of his triumph, had recovered from the sleep following

443

its celebration, Iff in his fastest automobile had picked up the lovers at an agreed spot in the forest, the Croix du Grand Maitre, whirled them to Dijon, and put them into the train for Marseilles. There they took ship, and came to Naples by sea, without adventure.

The enemy, in one way or another, had been thrown utterly off the track. It was early in the morning when they landed; at three o'clock they had visited such local deities as commanded their more urgent piety; the Museum, Vergil's Tomb, also Michaelsen the bookseller and vendor of images of the Ineffable. At four they started, hand in hand, along the shore, towards their new home.

An hour's walk brought them to the foot of a long stairway, damp stonework, narrow, between high walls, that led vertical and steep to the very crest of Posilippo. One could see the old church amid its cluster of houses. Cyril pointed to a house a couple of hundred yards north of the church. It was the most attractive building on the hillside.

The house itself was not large, but it was built like a toy imitation of one of those old castles that one sees everywhere on difficult heights, throughout most of Southern and even Central Europe; in a word, like a castle in a fairy-story. It looked from below, owing to foreshortening, as if it were built over a sheer rampart, like the Potala at Lhassa; but this was only the effect of merging a series of walls which divided the garden by terraces.

"Is that the Butterfly-net?" cried Lisa, slapping her hands with delight.

"That," he dissented, "is The Net."

Once again Lisa felt a pang of something like distrust. His trick of saying the simplest things as if they bore a second meaning, hidden from her, annoyed her. He had been strangely silent on the voyage, and wholly aloof from her on those planes where she most needed him; that was a necessary condition of the experiment, of course; but none the less it tended to disturb her happiness. Such talks as they had had were either purely educative, Magick in Six Easy Lessons, he called it, or Magick without Tears, or else they were conventional lover's chats, which she felt sure he despised. He would tell her that her eyes were like the stars; and she would think that he meant: "What am I to say to this piece of wood?" Even nature seemed to stir his contempt in some way. One night she had noticed him rapt in a poetic trance leaning over the bows watching the foam. For a long while he remained motionless, his breast rising quickly and falling, his lips trembling with passion – and then he turned to her

and said in cold blood: "Ought that to be used to advertise a dentifrice or a shaving soap?" She was sure that he had rehearsed the whole scene merely to work her up in order to have the fun of dropping her again. Only the next morning she woke early, to find a pencilled sonnet on his table, a poem so spiritual, so profound, and of such jewelcraft, that she knew why the few people whom he had allowed to read his work thought him the match of Milton. So apt were the similes that there could be no doubt that he had thought it out line by line, in that trance which he had marred, for her, by his brutal anti-climax.

She had asked him about it.

"Some people," he had said quite seriously, "have one brain; some have two. I have two." A minute later: "Oh, I forgot. Some have none."

She had refused to be snubbed. "What do you mean by your having two brains?"

"I really have. It seems as if, in order to grasp anything, I were obliged to take its extremes. I see both the sublime and the ridiculous at once, and I can't imagine one existing apart from the other, any more than you can have a stick with only one end. So I use one point of view to overbalance the other, like a child starting to swing itself. I am never happy until I have identified an idea with its opposite. I take the idea of murder – just a plain, horrid idea. But I don't stop there. I multiply that murder, and intensify it a millionfold, and then a millionfold again. Suddenly one comes out into the sublime idea of the Opening of the Eye of Shiva, when the Universe is annihilated in an instant. Then I swing back, and make the whole thing comic by having the hero chloroform Shiva in the nick of time, so that he can marry the beautiful American heiress.

"Until I have been all round the clock like that, I don't feel that I have the idea at all. If you had only let me go on about the shaving soap, I should have made it into something lovely again – and all the time I should have perceived the absolute identity of even the two contradictory phases."

But it was beyond her still, in each case as it came up "That is the Net!" A riddle? It might mean a thousand things; and to a woman of her positive and prosaic temperament (which she had, for all her hysteria and romanticism) doubt was torture. Love itself always torments women of this type; they want their lovers under lock and key. They would like love itself to be a more substantial commodity, a thing that one could buy by the pound, and store in a safe or an ice-chest.

Doubt and jealousy, those other hand-maidens of love, are also the children of imagination. But people wrongly use the word "imagination" to mean abstraction of ideas from concrete facts. And this is the reverse of the truth. Imagination makes ideas visible, clothes Being in form. It is, in short, very much like the "faith" of which Paul speaks. When true imagination makes true images of the Unseen, we have true love, and all true gods; when false imagination makes false images – then come the idols, Moloch, Jahveh, Jaganath, and their kindred, attended by all shapes of vice, of crime, of misery.

Lisa was thinking, as she climbed the apparently unending staircase, that she had taken pretty long odds. She had not hesitated to buck the Tiger, Life. Simon Iff had warned her that she was acting on impulse. But – on the top of that – he had merely urged her to be true to it. She swore once more that she would stick to her guns. The black mood fell from her. She turned and looked upon the sea, now far below. The sun, a hollow orb of molten glory, hung quivering in the mist of the Mediterranean; and Lisa entered for a moment into a perfect peace of spirit. She became one with Nature, instead of a being eternally at war with it.

But Cyril turned his face again to the mountain; she knew that he wanted to perform the evening adoration from the terrace of the house itself.

At last they came out from their narrow gangway to the by-street behind the church. It was an old and neglected thoroughfare, far from the main automobile road that runs along the crest. It was a place that the centuries had forgotten. Lisa realised that it was a haven of calm – and in a sense she resented the fact. Her highly-coloured nature demanded constant stimulus. She was an emotion-fiend, if one may construct the term by analogy with another branch of pathology.

The lovers turned to the left through the village; in a few minutes the road opened, and they saw the villa before them. It stood on a spur of rock, separated from the main hill by a sharply-cut chasm. This was spanned by an old stone bridge, a flying arch set steeply from the road to the house. It almost gave the effect of a frozen cascade issuing from the great doorway.

Cyril led Lisa across the bridge. This house was not served like that they had left behind them in Paris. Visitors were not expected or desired at any time, and the inmates rarely left the grounds, except on duty.

It was therefore some time before an answer to the summons reached them. Cyril's hand, dragging down an iron rope, had set swinging a great bell, deep and solemn, like a tocsin, in the turret which overlooked the chasm. Not until

its last echo was dumb did a small Judas in the door slide back. Cyril held up his left hand, and showed his seal-ring. Immediately the door swung open; a man of fifty odd years of age, dressed in black, with a great sword, like his brother guard at the Profess-House in Paris, stood bowing before them.

"Do what thou wilt shall be the whole of the Law. I enter the house."

With these words Cyril Grey assumed possession. "Lead me to Sister Clara." The man turned and went before them down a long corridor which opened upon a stone terrace, flagged with porphyry. A circular fountain in the middle had for its centre a copy of the Venus Callipyge in black marble. The parapet was decorated with statues of satyrs, fauns, and nymphs.

The woman who came to meet them was assuredly kin to that ancient company. She was about forty years of age, robust and hardy, burnt dark with years of outdoor life, her face slightly pitted with smallpox, her eyes black, stern, and true. Her whole aspect and demeanour expressed devoting capacity and determination. It was she who ruled the house in the absence of Simon Iff.

A brief colloquy between this woman and Cyril Grey followed their first greetings, whose austere formality inexplicably conveyed the most cordial kindness. He explained that he wished her to continue in full control of the house, only modifying its rules so far as might be necessary for the success of a certain experiment in magick which he had come to carry out. Sister Clara acquiesced with the slightest of nods; then she raised her voice, and summoned the others to the evening adoration of the Sun.

Cyril performed this as leader; the duty done, he was free to meet his new brothers and sisters.

Sister Clara was assisted by two young women, both of the slender willowy type – rather babyish even, one might say, with their light brown fluffiness and their full, red soft lips. They remained standing apart from the men, who numbered five. First in rank came the burly Brother Onofrio, a man of some thirty-five years, strong as a bull, with every muscle like iron from constant physical toil. Two men of thirty stood beside him, and behind them two lads of about sixteen.

They were all devoted – so far as the outer world was aware – to the healing of humanity in respect of its physical ills. The men were doctors, or students, the women nurses; though in fact Sister Clara was herself the most brilliant of them all, a surgeon who could have held her own against any man in Europe.

But it was contrary to the rule of the house for any sick person to lodge there; the private hospital which was attached to it was situated some three hundred yards further back from the hillside.

At a glance Lisa perceived that she had come into a circle where discipline was the first consideration.

Every one moved as if a Prussian sergeant had been in charge of him from infancy. Every one looked as if his responsibility were ever present to his mind. These manners sat naturally enough upon Clara and Onofrio; on the others the idea was hardly yet assimilated. But there was no evidence of any outward constraint; even the youngest of the boys was proud to take himself so seriously as he did.

A touch of frost was in the air; Cyril led Lisa within. A special set of rooms had been prepared for their reception; but Lisa was displeased to find that they had been arranged entirely with reference to feminine tastes and requirements. A single scheme of colour embraced the whole suite; white, blue and silver. The tapestries, the carpets, the very ceilings, were wholly in these and no other lights.

The pictures and statues were of Artemis, no other goddess; the very objects in the apartment were crescent shaped, and the only metal in evidence was silver. Where the crescent could not serve the purpose, the surfaces had been engraved with stars of nine points.

Only three books lay upon the table; they were the *Endymion* of Keats, the *Atalanta in Calydon* of Swinburne, and one other. But in a small bookshelf were several other volumes; and Lisa found later that each one described, suggested, or had been more or less directly inspired by the moon. In a silver censer, too, burnt an incense whose predominating ingredient was camphor. Everything present was designed or chosen so that it might turn the girl's mind to the earth's satellite. Subsequently she discovered that this plan extended even to her diet – she was to live exclusively on those foods which wise men of old classified as lunar in nature, on account either of their inherent qualities, or because they are traditionally sacred to Diana.

After the beginning of the experiment, no male was to enter that apartment.

She was a little frightened on grasping the fact that Cyril must have forseen her perfect compliance from the beginning. He noticed it with a slow smile, and began to explain to her why he had chosen the moon as the type of "butterfly" they were going to snare.

"The moon is the most powerful influence in your horoscope," he said. "She stands, in her own sign Cancer, in the mid-heaven. The Sun and Mercury are rising in square to her, which is not specially good; it may bring trouble of a certain kind; But Neptune is sextile to her, Jupiter and Venus trine. It is about as good a horoscope as one could hope for in such a case. The worst danger is the conjunction of Luna and Uranus – they are much too close to be comfortable. My own nativity goes well with yours, for I am primarily solar by nature, though (Heaven knows!) Herschel in the ascendant modifies it; and so I make the complement to you. But I am not to influence you or associate with you too much. I shall sleep with the men in the square tower yonder, which is kept magically separate from the rest of the house. We shall all be working constantly to invoke the moon's influence and to keep off intruders. Sister Clara is egregiously powerful in work of this special kind; she has made a particular study of it for twenty years; and during the past ten she has never spoken to a man, except in strict necessity. Her pupils have taken a similar resolution. There is no question of vows, which imply self-distrust – fear of weakness and of vacillation; the women of our order execute their own wills, with no need of external pressure. Go thou and do likewise!" Suddenly he had become stern and gloomy; and she felt how terrible would be his anger or contempt.

The morning broke brilliant; and Lisa found, not for the first time, that the most bracing influence resulted from the routine peculiar to the Profess-houses. To rise before dawn; to make a ceremonial ablution with the intention of so purifying both body and mind that they should be as it were new-born; then the joyous outburst of adoration as the sun rose to sight: this was a true Opening of the Day. Insensibly the years slipped from her; she became like a maiden in thought and in activity.

About a week was to elapse before the new moon, at the moment of which the operation was timed to commence; but it was a busy week for Cyril Grey. With Brother Onofrio, for whom he had taken an immense liking, he inspected every inch of the defences of the house. It was already a kind of fortress; the terraces were bounded by ramparts angled or rounded so as to suggest that old-fashioned pattern of military work of which Fort William in Calcutta is said to be the most perfect example.

But the defence of which the magicians were thinking was of a different order; the problem was to convert the whole place as it stood into an impregnable magical circle. For years, of course, the place had been defended,

but not as against its present dangers. It had been hitherto sufficient to exclude evil and ignorant beings, things of the same class as Douglas' watcher; but now a far more formidable problem was in view, how to dissuade a Soul, a being armed with the imperial right to enter, from approaching. Demons and elementals and intelligences were only fractions of true Entities, according to the theory; they were illusions, things merely three-dimensional, with no core of substance in themselves. In yet another figure, they were adjectives, and not nouns. But a human soul is a complete reality. "Every man and every woman is a star."

To repel one such from its demand to issue into the world of matter was a serious difficulty – and, also, possibly involved no mean responsibility. However, Cyril's main hope was that any passing souls would be reasonable, and not try to force themselves into uncongenial company, or plant themselves in unsuitable soil. He had always held that incarnation was balked when the soul discovered that the heredity and environment of the embryo it had chosen were too hostile to allow the desired manifestation; the soul would then withdraw, with the physical result of miscarriage, still-birth, or, where the embryo, deserted by the human soul, becomes open to the obsession of some other thing, such as a Vampire or what the Bible calls a "dumb spirit", the production of monsters or idiots.

Cyril Grey, by insisting upon constant devotion to the human ideal, hoped to ward off all other types of soul, just as the presence of a pack of wolves would frighten away a lamb; and he further trusted to attract potent forces, who would serve as a kind of lighthouse to his harbour. He imagined his desired Moon-soul, afloat in space, vehemently spurred towards the choir of sympathetic intelligences whom it could hardly fail to perceive, by reason of the intensity of the concentration of the magical forces of the operators upon the human idea.

Two days before the beginning of the operation, a telegram from Paris reached him. It stated that, as he suspected, Balloch and Douglas were the forces behind the attack; further, that Grey's presence in Naples was known, and that three members of the Black Lodge had left Paris for Italy.

He thought it undesirable to communicate the news to Lisa.

But he renewed his general warnings to her.

"Child!" he said, "you are now ready for our great experiment. On Monday, the day of the New Moon, you take the oath of dedication; and we shall be able to resume those relations which we temporarily renounced. Now let me

say to you that you are absolutely guarded in every way but one. The weak spot is this: we cannot abolish unsuitable thoughts entirely from your mind. It is for you to do that, and we have done our best to make the conditions as favourable as possible; but I warn you that the struggle may be bitter. You will be amazed at the possibilities of your own mind, its fertility of cunning, its fatally false logic, its power of blinding you to facts that ought to be as clear as daylight – yes, even to the things before your very eyes. It will seek to bewilder you, to make you lose your mental balance – every trick is possible. And you will be so beaten and so blind that you have only one safeguard; which is, to adhere desperately to the literal terms of your oath.

"Do that, and in a little while the mind will clear; you will understand what empty phantoms they were that assailed you. But if you fail, your only standard is gone; the waters will swirl about you and carry you away to the abyss of madness. Above all, never distinguish between the spirit and the letter of your oath! The most exquisite deceit of the devil is to lure you from the plain meaning of words. So, though your instinct, and your reason, and your common sense, and your intelligence all urge you to interpret some duty otherwise than in the plain original sense; don't do it!"

"I don't see what you mean."

"Here's a case. Suppose you swore 'not to touch alcohol'. The devil would come with a sickness, and an alcholic medicine; he would tempt you to say that of course your oath didn't mean 'medicinally'. Or you would wish to rub your skin with *eau-de-cologne*; of course 'touch' really meant 'drink'."

"And I should really be right to be stupidly literal, like that?"

"Yes, in a case where the mind, being under a magical strain, becomes unfit to judge. It's the story of Bluebeard; only you must alter it so that the contents of the fatal chamber exist only in the woman's imagination, that she had so worked herself up by what she thought she might see that she also thought she saw it. So be on your guard!"

On the last day of the old moon he gave her an idea of the main programme.

First, the honeymoon; their normal relations were to endure until there was evidence of the need to emphasise the crucial point of the operation. From that moment she was to see nothing of Cyril save in the ceremonies of invocation; all other relations were to cease. The lover would become the hermit. The magician had calculated the probable moment of incarnation as about six months before the day of birth. Once it became certain that the

soul had taken possession of the embryo, the hermit would become the elder brother.

It was clearly the middle period that was critical; not only because of the magical difficulties, but because Lisa herself would be under intense strain, and isolated from her lover's active sympathy. But Cyril thought it best to dare these dangers rather than to allow his own soul to influence her atmosphere, as his solar personality might possibly drive away the very "butterfly" which they wished to collect. In fact, his human individuality was one of the things that had to be banished from her neighbourhood. She must know nothing of him but the purely magical side, when, clothed in robes suitable to the invocations of Luna and with word and gesture concentrated wholly upon the work, he sank Cyril Grey utterly in the Priest of Artemis – "thy shrine, thine oracle, thine heat of pale-mouthed prophet dreaming".

CHAPTER XI

OF THE MOON OF HONEY, AND ITS EVENTS;

WITH SUNDRY REMARKS ON MAGICK; THE WHOLE ADORNED WITH MORAL REFLECTIONS USEFUL TO THE YOUNG

THE many-terraced garden of the villa was planted with olive and tamarind, orange and cypress; but in the lowest of them all, a crescent over whose wall one could look down upon one of the paths that threaded the hillside, there was a pavement of white marble. A spring wept from the naked rock, and fell into a circular basin; from this small streamlets issued, and watered the terrace in narrow grooves, between the slabs. This garden was sacred to lilies; and because of its apt symbolism, Cyril Grey had chosen it for the scene of Lisa's dedication to Artemis. He had set up a small triangular altar of silver; and it was upon this that Sister Clara and her disciples came thrice nightly to make their incantations. The ritual of the moon might never be celebrated during daylight.

Upon the evening of Monday, after the adoration of the setting sun, Sister Clara called Lisa aside, and led her to this garden.

There she and the hand-maidens unclothed her, and washed her from head to foot in the waters of the sacred spring. Then she put upon her a solemn oath that she would follow out the rules of the ritual, not speaking to any man except her chosen, not leaving the protection of the circle, not communicating with the outer and uninitiated world; but, on the other hand, devoting herself wholly to the invocation of the Moon.

Then she clothed her in a specially prepared and consecrated garment. It was not of the same pattern as those of the Order; it was a loose vestment of pale blue covered with silver tissue; and the secret sigils of the moon were woven cunningly upon its hem. It was frail, but of great volume; and the effect was that the wearer seemed to be wrapped in a mist of moonlight.

In a languid and mysterious chant Sister Clara raised her voice, and her acolytes kept accord on their mandolines; it was an incantation of fervour and of madness, the madness of things chaste, remote, and inscrutable. At the conclusion she took Lisa by the hand, and gave her a new name, a mystic name, engraved upon a moonstone, set in a silver ring which she put upon her finger. This name was Iliel. It had been chosen on account of its sympathy of number to the moon; for the name is Hebrew, in which language its characters have the value of 81, the square of 9, the sacred number of the moon. But other considerations helped to determine the choice of this name. The letter L in Hebrew refers to Libra, the sign under which she had been born; and it was surrounded with two letters, I, to indicate her envelopment by the force of creation and chastity which the wise men of old hid in that hieroglyph.

The final "EL" signified the divinity of her new being; for this is the Hebrew word for God, and is commonly attached by the sages to divers roots, to imply that these ideas have been manifested in individuals of angelic nature.

This instruction had been given to Lisa in advance; now that it was ceremonially conferred upon her, she was struck to the heart by its great meaning. Her passion for Cyril Grey had been gross and vehement, almost vulgar; he had translated it into terms of hunger after holiness, of awful aspiration, of utter purity. Nor Rhea Silvia, nor Semele, nor any other mortal virgin had ever glowed to inherit more glorious a destiny, to feel such infinite exaltation of chastity. Even the thought of Cyril himself fell from her like a stain. He had become no more than a necessary evil. At that moment she could have shaken off the trammels of humanity itself, and joined Sister Clara

in her ecstatic mood, passed on, imperial votaress, in maiden meditation fancy-free. Only the knowledge of her sublime task inured her to its bitter taste. From these meditations she was awakened by the voice of Sister Clara.

"Oh, Iliel! Oh, Iliel! Oh, Iliel! there is a cloud upon the sea."

The, two girls chimed in with the music of their mandolins.

"It is growing dark. I am afraid," cried Sister Clara.

The girls quavered in their melody.

"We are alone in the sacred grove. Oh, Artemis, be near us, protect us from all evil!"

"Protect us from all evil!" echoed the two children. "There is a shape in the cloud; there is a stirring in the darkness; there is a stranger in the sacred grove!"

"Artemis! Artemis! Artemis!" shrilled the girls, their instruments fierce and agitated.

At that moment a great cry arose from the men, who were in waiting on the upper Terrace. It was a scream of abject fear, inarticulate, save for the one word "Pan"! They fled shrieking in every direction as Cyril Grey, clad in a rough dress of goatskins, bounded from the topmost terrace into their midst. In another moment, leaping down the garden, he reached the parapet that overlooked the little terrace where the girls crouched, moaning.

He sprang down among them; Sister Clara and her disciples fled with cries like startled sea-birds; but he crushed Iliel to his breast, then flung her over his shoulder, and strode triumphant to the house.

Such was the magical ceremony devised by the adept, a commemoration or dramatic representation of the legend of the capture of Diana by Pan. It is, of course, from such rites that all dramatic performance developed. The idea is to identify oneself, in thought by means of action, with the deities whom one desires to invoke.

The idea of presenting a story ceremonially may have preceded the ritual, and the Gods may have been mere sublimations of eponymous heroes or personifications of abstract ideas; but ultimately it is much the same. Admit that the genius of man is divine, and the question "Which is the cart, and which the horse?" becomes as pointless as if one asked it about an automobile.

The ensuing month, from the middle of November until the week before Christmas, was a honeymoon. But animal appetite was scarce more than an accidental adjunct; the human love of Cyril and Lisa had been raised to

inconceivable heights by the backbone of spirituality and love of mankind that lay behind its manifestations. Moreover, everything was attuned to it; nothing detracted from it. The lovers never lost sight of each other for an hour; they had their fill and will of love; but in a way, and with an intensity, of which worldly lovers never dream. Even sleep was to them but as a veil of many colours cast upon their rapture; in their dreams they still pursued each other, and attained each other, beneath bluer skies, upon seas that laughed more melodiously than that which lay between them and Capri, through gardens of more gladness than their own, and upon slopes that stretched eternally to the palaces of the Empyrean.

For four weeks no word came from outside; with one exception, when Sister Clara brought a telegram to Cyril. It was unsigned, and the message curt. "About August First" was all its purport. "The better the day, the better the deed!" cried Cyril gaily. Iliel questioned him. "Just magick!" he answered. She did not pursue the subject: she divined that the matter did not concern her, and she regretted even that microscopical interruption.

But although Iliel was kept from all knowledge of external events, it was by dint of steel. The Black Lodge had not been idle; Brother Onofrio, in charge of the garrison, had found his hands full. But his manoeuvres had been successful; the enemy had not even secured their first point of vantage, a material link with the Brotherhood.

It is a law of magick that causes and effects lie on the same plane. You may be able to send a ghost to frighten someone you dislike, but you must not expect the ghost to use a club, or steal a pocket handkerchief. Also, most practical magick starts on the material plane, and proceeds to create images on other planes. Thus, to evoke a spirit, you first obtain the objects necessary for its manifestation, and create subtler forms of the same nature from them.

The Butterfly-net was worked on exactly the same lines. Morality enters into magick no more than into art or science. It is only when the effects react upon the moral nature of man that this question arises. The Venus de Medici is neither good nor bad; it is merely beautiful; but its reaction on the mind of an Antony Comstock or a Harry Thaw may be disastrous, owing to the nature of such minds. One can settle the details of a murder over the telephone; but one should not blame the telephone.

The laws of magick are closely related to those of other physical sciences. A century or so ago men were ignorant of a dozen important properties of matter; thermal conductivity, electrical resistance, opacity to the X-ray,

spectroscopic reaction, and others even more occult. Magick deals principally with certain physical forces still unrecognised by the vulgar; but those forces are just as real, just as material – if indeed you can call them so, for all things are ultimately spiritual – as properties like radio-activity, weight and hardness. The difficulty in defining and measuring them lies principally in the subtlety of their relation to life. Living protoplasm is identical with dead protoplasm in all but the fact of life. The Mass is a magical ceremony performed with the object of endowing a material substance with divine virtue; but there is no material difference between the consecrated and the unconsecrated wafer. Yet there is an enormous difference in the moral reaction upon the communicant. Recognizing that its principal sacrament is only one of an infinite number of possible experiments in talismanic magic, the Church has never denied the reality of that Art, but treated its exponents as rivals. She dare not lop the branch on which she sits.

On the other hand, the sceptic, finding it impossible to deny the effects of ceremonial consecration, is compelled to refer the cause to "faith"; and sneers that Faith is the real miracle. Whereupon the Church smilingly agrees; but the magician, holding the balance between the disputants, and insisting upon the unity of Nature, asserts that all force is one in origin. He believes in the "miracle," but maintains that it is exactly the same kind of miracle as charging a Leyden Jar with electricity. You must use a moral indicator to test one, an electrical indicator to test the other; the balance and the test-tube will not reveal the change in either.

The Black Lodge knew well enough that the weak strand in the Butterfly-net was Lisa's untrained mind. Its white-hot flame of enthusiasm, radiating passionate love, was too active to assail directly, even could they have succeeded in communicating with it.

But they were content to watch and wait for the reaction, should it come, as they knew it must ultimately do. Eros finds Anteros always on his heels; soon or late, he will be supplanted, unless he have the wit to feed his fire with the fuel of Friendship. In the meanwhile, it was the best chance to work upon the mind through the body. Had they been able to procure a drop of Iliel's blood, she might have been as easy a prey as that unlucky engine-driver of the Paris-Rome rapide.

But Sister Clara saw to it that not so much as a nail-paring of Iliel escaped careful magical destruction; and Brother Onofrio organised a nightly patrol of the garden, so that no physical breach of the circle should be made.

The man in charge of the mission of the Black Lodge was one Arthwait, a dull and inaccurate pedant without imagination or real magical perception. Like most Black Magicians, he tippled habitually; and his capacity for inflicting damage upon others was limited by his inordinate conceit. He hated Cyril Grey as much as he hated any one, because his books had been reviewed by that bright spirit, in his most bitterly ironical strain, in the *Emerald Tablet*, the famous literary review edited by Jack Flynn; and Grey had been at particular pains to point out elementary blunders in translation which showed that Arthwait was comically ignorant of the languages in which he boasted scholarship. But he was not the man for the task set him by Douglas; his pomposity always stood in his way; a man fighting for life is exceptionally a fool if he insists on stopping every moment to admire himself. Douglas had chosen him for one of the curious back-handed reasons which so often appeal to people of perverse intelligence: it was because he was harmless that he was selected to work harm. A democracy often chooses its generals on the same principle; a capable man might overthrow the republic. It apparently prefers to be overthrown by a capable enemy.

But Douglas had backed him with a strong executive.

Abdul Bey knew no magic, and never would; but he had a desperate passion for Lisa, and a fanatical hatred of Grey, whom he credited, at the suggestion of Balloch, with the death of his father. He had almost unlimited resources, social and financial; there could hardly have been a better man for the external part of the work.

The third commissioner was the brains of the business. He was a man highly skilled in black magic in his own way. He was a lean, cadaverous Protestant-Irishman named Gates, tall, with the scholar's stoop. He possessed real original talent, with now and then a flash of insight which came close to genius. But though his intellect was keen and fine, it was in some way confused; and there was a lack of virility in his make-up. His hair was long, lank and unkempt; his teeth were neglected; and he had a habit of physical dirt which was so obvious as to be repulsive even to a stranger.

But there was no harm in him; he had no business in the Black Lodge at all; it was but one of his romantic phantasies to pose as a terribly wicked fellow. Yet he took it seriously enough, and was ready to serve Douglas in any scheme, however atrocious, which would secure his advancement in the Lodge. He was only there through muddle-headedness; so far as he had an object beyond the satisfaction of his vanity, it was innocent in itself – the

acquisition of knowledge and power. He was entirely the dupe of Douglas, who found him a useful stalking-horse, for Gates had a considerable reputation in some of the best circles in England.

Douglas had chosen him for this business on excellent points of cunning; for he neither hated nor loved his intended victims, and so was likely to interpret their actions without passion or prejudice. It was this interpretation that Douglas most desired. Douglas had seen him personally – rare privilege – before he left for Naples and explained his wishes somewhat as follows.

The fool Arthwait was to blunder pedantically along with the classical methods of magical assault, partly on the chance of a hit, partly to keep Grey busy, and possibly to lead him to believe that the main attack lay there. Meanwhile he, Gates, was to devote himself, on the quiet, to divining the true nature of Grey's purpose. This information was essential; Douglas knew that it must be something tremendous; that the forces which Cyril was working to evoke were cosmic in scope. He knew it not only from his own divinations, but deduced it from the fact of the intervention of Simon Iff. He knew well that the old Master would not have lifted a finger for anything less than a world-war. Douglas therefore judged that if he could defeat Grey's purpose, it would involve the triumph of his own. Such forces, recoiling upon his head who had evoked them, would shatter him into a thousand fragments. Douglas, still weak from the destruction of his "watcher", was particularly clear on this point!

Arthwait was to be the nominal head of the party in all things, and Abdul Bey was to be urged to support him vigorously in all ways that lay in his power; but if necessary Gates was to thwart Arthwait, and secure the allegiance of the Turk, bound to secrecy on the matter, by showing him a card which Douglas then and there duly inscribed and handed over.

Louis XV tried a double-cross game of this sort on his ambassadors; but Douglas was not strong on history, and knew nothing of how those experiments resulted.

Nor, apparently, had he taken to heart the words of the gospel: "If Satan be divided against Satan, how shall his kingdom stand?"

Still less did he realise that this ingenious plan had been suggested to him by Simon Iff! Yet it was so: this was the head of the counter-attack which the old mystic had agreed to deliver on behalf of Cyril Grey. It was only a quarter of an hour's work; the Way of the Tao is the easiest as it is the surest.

This is what "Simple Simon" had done. Since all simple motion is one-pointed, and its enemy is inertia, the swordsmith brings his sword to a single sharp edge; the fletcher grinds his arrow-barb to a fine point. Your Dum-Dum bullet will not penetrate as does your nickel tip; and you cannot afford to use the former unless the power of penetration is so great as to reach the soft spots before the bullet expands and stops. This mechanical principle is perfectly applicable in magick. Therefore, when there is need to resist a magical attack, your best method will be to divide your antagonist's forces.

Douglas had already lost a pawn in the game, Akbar Pasha having gone to his destruction through setting up an idea of his own, apart from, and inconsistent with, the plan of his superior. The defect is inherent in all Black Magic, because that art is itself a thing set up against the Universal Will. If it were not negligibly small, it would destroy the Universe, just as the bomb-throwing Anarchist would succeed in destroying society if he amounted to, say, a third of the population.

Now Simple Simon, at this time, did not know Douglas for the enemy General; but he was in the closest possible magical touch with him. For he had absorbed the Thing in the garden into himself and that Thing had been a part of Douglas.

So he set himself to the complete assimilation of that Thing; he made certain that it should be part of himself for ever. His method of doing this was as simple as usual. He went over the Universe in his mind, and set himself to reconcile all contradictions in a higher Unity. Beginning with such gross things as the colours of the spectrum, which are only partialities of white light, he resolved everything that came into his mind until he reached such abstractions as matter and motion, being and form; and by this process worked himself up into a state of mind which was capable of grasping those sublime ideas which unite even these ultimate antinomies. That was all.

Douglas, still in magical touch with that "watcher", could feel it being slowly digested, so to say, by some other magician. This (incidentally) is the final fate of all black magicians, to be torn piecemeal, for lack of the love which grows by giving itself to the beloved, again and again, until its "I" is continuous with existence itself. "Whoso loveth his life shall lose it" is the corresponding scriptural phrase.

So Douglas, who might at that moment have saved himself by resignation, was too blind to see the way – an acquired blindness resulting from repeated

acts whose essence was the denial of the unity of himself with the rest of the universe. And so he fought desperately against the assimilation of his "watcher". "It's mine, not yours!" he raged. To the steady and continuous affirmation of true unity in all diversity which Simon Iff was making, he opposed the affirmation of duality. The result was that his whole mind was aflame with the passion of contrasting things, of playing forces off against each other. When it came to practical decisions, he divided his forces, and deliberately created jealousy and hatred where co-operation and loyalty should have been the first and last consideration.

Yet Simon Iff had used no spell but Love.

CHAPTER XII
OF BROTHER ONOFRIO,
HIS STOUTNESS AND VALIANCE; AND OF THE MISADVENTURES THAT CAME THEREBY TO THE BLACK LODGE

THE ecclesiastic is a definite type of man. The Italian priest has changed his character in three thousand years as little as he has his costume.

Brother Onofrio's father happened to be a free-thinking Anti-clerical, a pillar of Masonry; otherwise, his son would assuredly have been a bishop. The type is perfectly pagan, whatever the creed; it is robust and subtle, spiritual and sensual, adroit in manipulation of inferiors and superiors alike. It has the courage which vigorous health and the consciousness of its own validity combine to give; and where courage will not serve the turn, astuteness deftly takes its place.

A stupid pedant like Edwin Arthwait is the very feeblest opponent for such a man.

Brother Onofrio, while successfully practising magick, was quite ready at a moment's notice to throw the whole theory overboard with a horse laugh – and at the same time to reckon his action in so doing a branch of magick

also. It was the beginning of the duplicate brain-development which Cyril Grey had cultivated to so high a point of perfection.

But Arthwait was in the fetters of his own egoism; while he pronounced himself father and grandfather of all spiritual science, in language that would have seemed stilted and archaic to Henry James, or Osric, and presumptuous in the mouth of an archangel, he was the bondslave of utterly insignificant writers, fakers of magical "grimoires" of the fourteenth century, hawkers of spells and conjurations to a benighted peasantry who wished to bewitch cows or to prevent their neighbours from catching fish. Arthwait had published a book to show the folly of such works, but in practice they were his only guide. In particular, he swore by the "Black Pullet", which seemed to him less dangerous than the "Grand Grimoire", or the forgery attributed to Pope Honorius. He wanted to evoke the devil, but was terrified lest he should be successful. However, nobody could be more pedantically pious than he in following out the practical prescriptions of these absurd charm-books.

This individual might usually have been discovered during that honeymoon in the Naples villa, seated in the armchair of the apartment which he had rented in the Galeria Vittoria. He would be clad in a frockcoat of City cut, for he affected the "professional man", and his air would be preoccupied. The arrival of his colleagues for consultation would apparently startle him from a profound speculation upon the weightier matters of the law.

It would be only by an effort that he spoke in English; the least distraction would send him back into Latin, Greek, or Hebrew, none of which languages he understood. He was a peddler of words; his mind was a rag-and-bone shop of worthless and disjointed mediaevalism.

After a severe struggle, he would "proceed to an allocution". He never "spoke"; he "monologised".

The first formal conference took place when they had been about a week in Naples.

"My fathers learned in Art Magic," he began, addressing Gates and Abdul, "venerable and archetypal doctors of the Hermetic Arcanum, it hath been sacramentally imposed upon our sophistic Tebunah by the monumentally aggregated psycho-mentality of Those whose names in respect of known dedications must here – juxta nos – be heled ob Danaos (as I should adumbrate advisedly, for is it not script, concerning cowans, in the archives of the Clermont Harodim?) that a term, in fine, should mete the orbit and

currency of the heretic and apostate, *quem in Tartarum conjuro*, high Grey, in his areopagus of the averse hierarchy. I exiterate, *clam populo*, that all warrants of precursors fait no ratification, peradventure, in the actual concatenation, *sed, me judice*, it is meliorated that by virtue and cosmodominicy of Satanas – *cognomen ineffabile, quod reverentissime proloquor!* – the opus confronts the Sir Knights of the Black Chapter – *in via sua propria* – in the authentic valley and this *lucus tenebrosa Neapolitanensis*, as the near – nay, the next! – conflagration of barbaric pilum against retiarial ludibry. Worthy Fathers and reverend in the doctrine, *salutatio in summo imperio – per totam orbem –* in the supranominal Donner of Orcus and of Phlegethon – *sufficit!*"

The Turkish diplomat spoke nine languages, but not this one. Gates, who had known Arthwait for many years, explained that these remarks, formidable in appearance, meant only that Grey ought to be killed at any time, on general principles, but that as they were specially charged with that task by their leaders, so much the better.

The conference, thus prosperously inaugurated, proved a lengthy one. How, indeed, could it be otherwise? For Arthwait was naturally slow of thought and speech; it took him some time to warm up to real eloquence; and then he became so long-winded, and lost himself so completely in his words and phrases, that he would speak for many hours without conveying a single idea of any kind to his hearers, or even having one to convey.

But the upshot of his conversation upon this occasion was that an attempt should be made to poison the household magically by bewitching the food supplied to them from the market. Certain succulent shell-fish, called *vongole*, very popular in Naples, were selected as a material basis, "because their appurtenance and charter was be-Yekl Klippoth", as Arthwait explained.

Into these molluscs, therefore, might be conjured a spirit of Mars "of them that bear witness unto Bartzabel", in the hope that those who partook of them might be stricken with some type of fever, fevers and all acute diseases being classified as Martial.

It was unfortunate for these plans that Brother Onofrio habitually took the precaution to purify and consecrate all food that came into the house before it reached the kitchen; and further, anticipating some such attempt, he had everything tested psychometrically by one of his acolytes, whom he had trained especially in sensitiveness to all such subtle impressions.

The shell-fish were consequently discovered to be charged with the Martial current; Brother Onofrio smiled hugely and proceeded to call upon the divine

forces of Mars, before which even Bartzabel "trembles every day", and, thus having converted himself into a high-power engine of war, sat down to a Gargantuan banquet, eating the entire consignment himself. The result was that the unfortunate Arthwait was seized with violent and intractable colic, which kept him twisted in agony on his bed for forty-eight hours.

Gates had taken no part in this performance; he knew how dangerous it was, and how likely to recoil upon the rash practitioner. But he did some genuinely useful work. He had been to the church in the village, near Posilippo, whose tower overlooked the Butterfly-net; and he had persuaded the priest to allow him continual access to that tower, on the pretext of being an artist. And indeed he had a pretty amateur talent for painting in water-colours: some people thought it stronger than his verses. For ten days he watched the Butterfly-net with extreme care, and he wrote down the routine of the inhabitants hour by hour. Nothing escaped him of their doings in the garden; and (as it happened) the preponderating portion of their work lay out-of-doors. He could make nor head nor tail of the fact that the most important people were apparently doing no magick of any kind, but, careless lovers, enjoying the first fruits of their flight to the South.

But Douglas put two and two together very cleverly, even from the first report; he noted, also, the intelligence and ability of Gates, and made a memorandum to use him up quickly and destroy him.

Without divining the exact intention of Cyril Grey, he rightly concluded that this "honeymoon" was not so simple as it seemed; in fact, he recognised it as the core of the apple. He telegraphed Gates to redouble his watch upon the lovers, and to report instantly if any marked change occurred in their habits.

Meanwhile, Edwin Arthwait was busy with the "Black Pullet". There is a method of describing a pentagram upon a doorstep which is infallible. The first person who crosses it receives a shock which may drive him insane, or even kill him. A magician would naturally be suspicious if he found anything of this kind on his front doorstep, so Arthwait cleverly determined to paint the pentagram in Gum Arabic, which would hardly be visible. Accordingly he went to the Butterfly-net at dead of night, armed with this means of grace, and set to work by the light of a candle-lamp. He was careful to make the pentagram so large that it was impossible to cross the bridge without stepping over it. Absorbed in his inspiring task, he did not notice, until the last stroke was in place, that he was himself hemmed in between his pentagram and

the door of the villa. He crouched in terror for the best part of an hour; then a hint of daylight made him fearful of discovery. He was forced to make a move of some sort; and he found that by careful sidling he could escape to the parapet of the bridge. But he was no climber; he overbalanced and fell into the chasm, being lucky to escape with a severe shaking. On his limping way back to Naples he was overtaken by an icy shower of rain; and as he got into bed, too late to avoid a nasty chill, which kept him in bed for a week, he had the irritating reflexion that his pentagram must have been washed away.

But he had not become known as the most voluminous of modern pedants without perseverance. His literary method was that of the "tank". It was not agile, it was not versatile, it was exposed to artillery attack; but it proceeded. He was as comprehensive as the Catalogue of the British Museum – and almost as extensive. But he was not arranged. Such a man was not to be deterred by two failures, or forty-two. Indeed, but for the frank criticism of Gates, he would have counted them successes.

For his third experiment he chose "The Wonder-working Serpent", whose possession confers the power of attracting love. The appeal lay in the failure of Abdul to make any impression upon Lisa, whom he had courted in characteristically local manner by appearing, guitar in hand, below the terrace where she had been dedicated to the moon. He caught her there alone, and called her by her name. She recognised him instantly; she had been violently attracted to him at the ball where they had originally met; and, until she had seen Cyril, regretted constantly that she had missed the opportunity.

The memory of that thwarted desire sprang vehement upon her; but she was at the white heat of her passion for Cyril. Even so, she half hesitated; she wanted to keep Abdul on ice, so to speak, for a future occasion; such action was as instinctive with her as breathing. But her obligation was still fresh in her mind; she was pledged not to communicate with the outer world. She ignored him; she turned and left the garden without so much as a gesture; and he went back to Naples in a black fury against her. "The Wonder-working Serpent" was, therefore, an operation entirely to his taste. Gates thought the line of attack hopeful; he was totally sceptical of Lisa's virtue, or any woman's; and he had lived on women long enough to make his view arguable, within the limits of his experience. He bade Abdul try again. Good – then let magic aid!

In order to possess "The Wonder-working Serpent", it is necessary, in the words of the Grimoire, "to buy an egg without haggling", which (by the way) indicates the class of person for and by whom the book was written. This egg is to be buried in a cemetery at midnight, and every morning at sunrise it must be watered with brandy. On the ninth day a spirit appears, and demands your purpose. You reply, "I am watering my plant." This occurs on three successive days; at the midnight following the egg is dug up, and found to contain a serpent, with a cock's head. This amiable animal answers to the name of Ambrosiel. Carry it in your bosom, and your suit inevitably prospers.

Arthwait put this scheme into careful rehearsal, and having got the conjurations and ceremonies perfect – for the egg must be buried with full military honours, as it were – he reached the third day without mishap. But at this point a spirit appeared – a guardian of the cemetery – and, dissatisfied with his answers, took him to the police-station as a wandering lunatic. A less other-worldly master of the dark sciences might have bribed the official; but Arthwait's self-importance once again stood in his way. He got in deeper, and in the end it was Gates who offered to be responsible for him, and persuaded the British Consul to use influence for his release.

As so many workers of magic have done, from the Yukon and Basutoland to Tonga and Mongolia, Arthwait attributed his defeats to the superior cunning and wickedness of his opponents.

Gates himself had varied his pleasures by a much more serious attempt to create a magical link with the garrison. From his tower he had observed many pigeons upon the hillside, and he began to tame these, spreading corn upon the tower. In three days they were eating out of his hand. He then trained them to recognise him and follow him from place to place. A week later he found a moment when the garden was deserted save for a single patrol, and threw his grain over the wall. The pigeons flocked to it and fed. Now it so happened that the patrolling magician was unsuspicious. He was aware that the benign influence of the house made its gardens attractive. There flowers bloomed brighter than elsewhere; and all Nature's wanderers seemed to look to it as their refuge. They felt instinctively the innocence and goodwill of the inhabitants, and thronged those hospitable terraces.

When Gates moved on, the pigeons followed his next throw; round the first corner, he placed the remains of his supply of corn in a small heap on the ground; the pigeons unsuspectingly approached, and he threw a net over half a dozen of them.

This was a great point gained; for the Black Lodge was in possession of living things that had come from within the guarded precinct; it would be easy to attack the inmates by means of sympathetic magic. As it chanced, two of the birds were male; but pigeons being of the general nature of Venus, it was decided to try to identify them with the least male persons of the garrison, namely the four women and the two boys. Accordingly, ribbons were tied to the necks of the birds, and the names of the intended victims inscribed upon them. Magical ceremonies were now made, Gates, who took a real interest in the experiment, being the leader.

When he considered the identification adequate, he placed red pepper on the tongues of the birds; and was rewarded the following morning by seeing Sister Clara turn upon one of her girls with a gesture of rage; he could even hear faintly the tones of anger in her voice. But Brother Onofrio had not failed to observe the same thing; and he divined instantly that a breach had been made in his circle. He went immediately to Sister Clara, and compelled her attention by a sign of such authority that no initiate dare overlook it.

"Sister," he said very gently, "you do not speak with man; what cause, then, can there be for bitterness?"

She answered him, still angrily. "The house is upside down," she said. "Iliel is as irritable as an eczema; the boys have both made insulting faces at every one they have seen this morning; and the girls are absolutely impudent."

"This is a matter for me, as in charge of the defence of the circle."

Sister Clara uttered a sharp exclamation. It had not occurred to her to think of it in that way. "I should be obliged," continued Brother Onofrio, "if you could see your way to impose a rule of silence for seven days from sunset tonight. Excepting, of course, in the invocations. I will warn the boys; do you take up the matter with Iliel and the girls."

"It shall be done."

Brother Onofrio went off to the private room where he did his own particular magick. He saw that a serious inroad had been made; but his divination, on this occasion, failed to enlighten him. His favourite device was the Tarot, those mysterious cards with their twenty-two hieroglyphic trumps; and as a rule he was able to discover all kinds of unknown matters by their use. But on this attempt he was baffled by the monotony of his answer.

However he used the cards, they always reverted to a single symbol, the trump numbered XVI, which is called "The Blasted Tower", and has some reference to the legend of Babel.

"I know," he muttered, himself irritated by the persistence of the card, "I know it's Mars" – which is the planet signified by that particular hieroglyph. "But I wanted a lot more than that. I asked 'What is the trouble?' 'From whom is the trouble?' 'Where is the trouble?' 'What shall I do?' And the same card answers all the questions!"

The next day Gates found that the tongues of the birds were shrivelled up, and he divined that his mode of attack had been detected, and precaution taken. He proceeded by drugging the pigeons with the vapour of ether.

In the house the result was immediate. The six people affected showed signs of intoxication and dizziness, coupled with a strong feeling of suffocation. Sister Clara was less troubled than the others, and she recognised the magical cause of the symptoms. She ran quickly to Brother Onofrio; he saw instantly that a new attack was in progress, and gave the sign agreed upon for retirement to a specially consecrated room in the square tower, a sort of inner circle, or citadel. The victims gathered in this room within a few minutes, and their symptoms abated on the instant.

But Brother Onofrio had a glimpse of light, as he assisted one of the two boys, who was almost choking, to reach the refuge. The tower caught his eye, and it flashed upon him that perhaps the Tarot was referring to an actual tower. It was only one step to think of the tower of the church; and, running into the garden, he saw that a man was standing there, evidently engaged in watching the house of the magicians. Brother Onofrio's quick insight decided him instantly upon the course to follow.

The Tarot Trump in question represents a tower struck by lightning, from which figures of men are seen falling.

He laughed joyously; his favourite method of divination had vindicated itself supremely. His four questions had indeed a single answer.

W. S. Gilbert informs us that "a deed of blood, and fire, and flames, was meat and drink to Simple James"; and to find himself approached upon the plane of Mars was like mother's milk to Brother Onofrio.

For he was himself of the strongest Martial type, having been born with Scorpio, the night house of Mars, rising, and the planet himself conjoined with Herschel in the mid-heaven in the sign of the Lion, with the Sun rising in trine and Jupiter conjoined with Saturn making an additional trine from the sixth house, which governs secret things such as magick. It was as formidable a combination as Mars could make in a thousand years.

He happened also to belong to that grade of the Order – Adeptus Major – which specialises in Mars; Arthwait and Company had unwittingly come to meet him where he was strongest.

To invoke Mars is to establish a connection with that order of nature which we class as martial. It may be remembered how a man once came to a doctor, suffering internal pangs of no mean order from having swallowed by mistake some pills intended for a horse. Asked how it came to happen, he explained that he had been administering them to the horse by blowing them down its throat through a tube; but the horse had blown first. This is of course the danger in every magical experiment; and this constitutes the evergreen glory of every man who adventures upon it; for at each new portal he enters, naked and new-born, to confront he knows not what malignant enemies. The sole excuse for the existence of our miserable species lies not in intelligence, but in this masterful courage, this aspiration to extend the empire of the spirit. Even the blackest of magicians, like Douglas, or the stupidest, like Arthwait, is a higher type of being than the bourgeois who goes along with his nose on the ground picking up gold bricks in the mire.

Now when Brother Onofrio found Gates perched upon the campanile, he saw the Martial symbol complete – only awaiting the lightning-flash. There was no need for him to produce a thunderstorm, as it would have been if Gates had been an ordinary man, accessible only to coarse influences; no, Brother Onofrio knew how to assimilate the church tower to The Blasted Tower of the Tarot without appealing to the material forces of nature, so-called, as if "matter" were not comprehensive as "nature" herself; but the English language is full of these booby-traps.

He went to his laboratory, took out the Tarot card XVI and set it up on the altar. He lighted the fire upon the tripod, and he kindled the incense of dragon's blood that stood ready in the iron censer. He then put upon his head the steel crown of Mars, thorny with its four flashing pentagrams, and he took in his hands the heavy sword, as long as himself, with a two-edged blade tapering from a width, at the junction of the hilt, of no less than five inches.

Chanting the terrible conjurations of Mars, fierce war-songs of the olden peoples of the world, invocations of mighty deities throned upon the thunder – "He sent out his arrows and scattered them; he sent forth his lightnings, and consumed them" – Brother Onofrio began the war-dance of the Serpent, the invoking dance of Mars. Close coiled about the altar at first, he took gradually a wider sweep, constantly revolving on himself but his feet tracing

a complex spiral curve. On reaching the door of the room, he allowed the "Serpent" to stretch out its length, and, ever twisting on himself, came out upon the terrace.

Gates was still at his post upon the campanile; he had been about to go, but this new feature of the routine of the house riveted him to his place. This was just what Douglas needed to know! He leant upon the parapet of the tower, watching with infinite eagerness and minuteness the convolutions of the adept.

Once upon the terrace, Brother Onofrio proceeded to coil up his "Serpent" after him, diminishing the sweep of his spirals until he was at zero, merely rotating on himself.

Then he began the second part of his work, the Dance of the Sword.

Slowly he began to cause his feet to trace a pentagram, and he allowed the Sword to leave his body as he quickened his pace, just as one sees the weights of the ball-governor of a steam-engine fly outwards as pressure and speed leap higher.

Gates was altogether fascinated by the sight. In the sunlight, this scarlet figure with lights darting from every brilliance of its steel was a magnificent spectacle, almost bewildering in its intensity.

Faster and faster whirled the adept, his sword swaying about him like a garment of light; and his voice, louder and fiercer with every turn, assumed the very majesty of thunder.

Gates watched with open mouth; he was learning much from this man. He began to perceive the primaeval energy of the universe, under a veil, the magical clang and rush of blazing stars in the blind emptiness of space. And suddenly Brother Onofrio stopped dead; his voice snapped short into a silence far more terrible than any word; and his long sword was still, fearfully still, stretched out like a shaft of murderous light – the point towards the tower.

Gates was suddenly aware that he had all along been the object of the dance; and then his brain began to reel. Had the whirling flashes hypnotised him? He could not think; the world went black for him. Automatically he clutched at the parapet; but he pitched headlong over it, and crashed upon the ground a hundred feet below.

On the terrace Brother Onofrio was beginning the banishing spirals of Mars, with songs of triumph into which stole, as if surreptitiously, some hint of that joy of love which, from the beginning of time, has welcomed the victorious soldier.

CHAPTER XIII

OF THE PROGRESS OF THE GREAT EXPERIMENT;

NOT FORGETTING OUR FRIENDS LAST SEEN IN PARIS. ABOUT WHOSE WELFARE MUCH ANXIETY MUST HAVE BEEN FELT

EARLY in January Cyril Grey received a letter from Lord Antony Bowling. "My good Grey," it began, "may the New Year bring you courage to break your resolutions early! My own plan is to swear off every kind of virtue, so that I triumph even when I fail!

"Morningside is off to America with his New Discovery in Science. It is that all crime is due to breathing. Statistics show (a) that all convicts are guilty of this disgusting habit; (b) it is characteristic of all the inmates of our insane asylums.

"On the other hand, neither crime nor insanity has ever been proved against any person who was not an habitual breather. The case, as you see, is complete. Morningside has gone even further, and shown that breathing

is akin to drug-habits; he has made numerous experiments upon addicts, and finds that suppression leads to mental and physical distress of an even more acute type than that which follows the removal of morphia or cocaine from their slaves. There is little doubt that Congress will take immediate action to penalise this filthy vice as it deserves, and Fresh Air will be included among the drugs to which the Harrison Law applies. Hot Air, as the natural food of the People, will of course be permitted.

"I saw Sister Cybele the other day. She was passing through London to visit friends in Scotland. I tried to alleviate that dreadful destiny by asking her to dinner, and we had an amusing seance with my new toy, a youth named Roger Blunt, who is controlled by a spirit called Wooloo, has eight secondary personalities, and causes pencils to adhere to walls. It cannot be that this is varnish, or surface tension, or a little of both; it would be too, too cruel!

"The Mahathera Phang has vanished from our gaze; he has probably gone to the Equator to correct the obliquity of the Ecliptic in the interest of the Law of Righteousness. I'm sorry; I believe in that man; I know he's got something that I haven't, and I want it. However, Simple Simon has been nice to me; only he won't talk Phenomena – says that, like a certain Pope, he has seen too many miracles to believe in them. Which is my own case, only he is referring to genuine ones. Hence difficulty in comprehension of his attitude.

"I hope you're having a great time with the devil; I envy your blue skies; London is wrapped in fog, and even on fine days I have to go to the War Office. But isn't it a pity those wicked bad naughty men know where you are? I have my doubts about magick; but I know Balloch, and he's the rottenest egg in London. I gather he's at the back of it. Some blackmailing articles on you, again; but as Morningside would say, you should worry. Come along and see me before, in a moment of madness and despair, you plunge into Vesuvius in the hope of exciting a future Mathew Arnold to immortalise you.

"Well, here's the best to you! – ANTONY BOWLING."

There was a brief note, too, from Simon Iff. "It's to be supposed all's well; rumours of disaster to enemy offensive current in Paris. You had better worry along on your own now; there's other fish frying in this kitchen. An old man may possibly drop in on you early in August; you may recognise him – with a strong pair of glasses – as your old friend – SIMON IFF."

Simple Simon never spoke of himself as "I" in a letter; he only used the pronoun in conversation as a concession to custom.

The Black Commissioners had also heard from headquarters; Gates was replaced, as quick as rail could carry, by a man of superior advancement in the Black Lodge.

This was the celebrated Dr. Victor Vesquit, the most famous necromancer of his age. There was really little harm in the man beyond his extraordinary perversion in the matter of corpses. His house in Hampden Road was not only a rendezvous of spiritualists, but a Home for Lost Mummies. He based all his magical operations upon dead bodies, or detached portions of the same, believing that to endow dead matter with life – the essential of nearly all magick, as he quite rightly saw – it was best to choose matter in which life had recently been manifest. An obvious corollary is that the best bodies are those that have met a violent death, rather than those which have been subjected to illness and decay. Also, it followed that the best corpses of all were those of executed murderers, whose vitality may be assumed as very great – though on this last point Cyril Grey, for one, would have disagreed with him, saying that the most vital people would have too much respect for the principle of life to commit murder in cold blood.

However, Dr Vesquit had obtained an appointment as coroner in the most murderous district of London; and uncanny were the rumours that circulated among occult sympathisers. His career had nearly been ruined on two occasions by scandal. The notorious Diana Vaughan, it had been said, was his mistress; and he had become her accomplice in the introduction of the frightful sect of the Palladists.

The rumour was not widespread, and Vesquit need not have suffered; but he took alarm, and had the unlucky thought of employing Arthwait to write a book clearing him from all suspicion, by which it naturally was fixed on him for ever.

The second trouble was his little quarrel with Douglas. Vesquit was Senior in the Black Lodge, and Douglas overthrew him by "carelessly" leaving, in a hansom cab, some documents belonging to the Lodge, with Vesquit's name and address attached to them, which made some exceedingly grim revelations of the necromantic practices carried on in Hampden Road.

The honest cabby had turned over the papers to Scotland Yard, as his duty was; and the police had sent them on to those in authority over coroners; and Vesquit received, with his documents, an intimation that he

must drop that sort of thing at once. To be chief in the Lodge seemed less than to be always in a Paradise of corpses; so he resigned office, and Douglas pushed his advantage by making him an abject tool, under the perpetual threat of exposure.

No sooner did Douglas learn of the death of Gates than he telegraphed to Arthwait to get the inquest adjourned "so that the relatives of the deceased in England might attend, and take possession of the body", and to Vesquit to attend the same. On this occasion the coroner needed no threat – the job was after his own heart.

Douglas met him in Paris in high glee, for he was not sorry to be rid of Gates; and, on the other hand, the man had died in full tide of battle, and should be the very corpse that Vesquit most needed; as Douglas himself said, with a certain grim humour in which he excelled, he was, morally speaking, an executed criminal; while, being in actual magical contact with Grey and his friends, so much so that he had evidently been killed by them, he was an ideal magical link.

Vesquit's task was, if possible, to learn from Gates exactly what had happened, and so expert a necromancer had no fear of the result. He was also to create a semi-material ghost of Gates from the remains, and send it to the person who had dealt out death to that unlucky wizard.

On his arrival at Naples, there was no difficulty in the way of the Black Lodge; the authorities were only too glad to return a formal verdict of death by misadventure, and to hand over the corpse to the rejoicing Vesquit.

Gates had fortunately left memoranda, a rough diary of the various procedures hitherto adopted; so that Vesquit was not committed to the task of acquiring information from Arthwait, which might easily have occupied a season; and from these notes the old necromancer came to the conclusion that the enemy was to be respected. Gates had done pretty well in the matter of the pigeons, at first; his procedure was not to be compared with his colleague's pedantic idiocies; but the first touch of riposte had been indeed deadly. Gates had been the clairvoyant of the party; he had gauged clearly enough the result of his operation; but naturally he had left no note of the last act, and neither Arthwait nor Abdul Bey had been able to do anything. Arthwait had been scared badly until his pompous vanity came to the rescue, and showed him that accidents of that kind must be expected when one is handicapped with an assistant of inferior ability.

Vesquit decided that the battle should be properly prepared, and no trouble spared to make it a success. His fondness for corpses had not gone to the length of desiring to become one.

In him there had been the makings of a fairly strong man; and, with Douglas to push him on, he was still capable of acting with spirit and determination. Also, he had the habit of authority. He set Arthwait to work on the Grimoire; for, in an operation of this importance, one must make all one's instruments.

Beginning with a magic knife, which one is allowed to buy, one cuts the magic wand from a hazel, the magic quill from a goose, and so on. The idea is to confirm the will to perform the operation by a long series of acts *ad hoc*. It is even desirable to procure parchment by killing a consecrated animal with the magic knife, and making ready the skin with similarly prepared utensils; one might for instance, cut and consecrate even the pegs which stretched the skin. However, in this case Arthwait had plenty of "Virgin parchment" in stock, with quills of a black vulture, and ink made by burning human bones, and mixing the carbonised products with the soot of the magic dark-lantern, whose candles were prepared with human fat.

But the Grimoire of any great operation must be thought out and composed; according to elaborate rules, indeed, but with the purpose of the work constantly in mind. Even when all this is done, the Grimoire is hardly begun; for it must be copied out in the way above indicated; and it should be illuminated with every kind of appropriate design. This was an ideal task for Arthwait; he was able to wallow in dog-Latin and corrupt Greek-Coptic; he made sentences so complicated that the complete works of George Meredith, Thomas Carlyle, and Henry James, tangled together, would have seemed in comparison like a word of three letters.

His Grimoire was in reality excellent for its purpose; for the infernal hierarchy delights in unintelligible images, in every kind of confusion and obscurity. This particular lucubration was calculated to drag the Archdemon of Bad Syntax himself from the most remote corner of his lair.

For Arthwait could not speak with becoming unintelligibility; to knot a sentence up properly it has to be thought out carefully, and revised. New phrases have to be put in; sudden changes of subject must be introduced; verbs must be shifted to unsuspected localities; short words must be excised with ruthless hand; archaisms must be sprinkled like sugar-plums upon the concoction; the fatal human tendency to say things straightforwardly must be detected and defeated by adroit reversals; and, if a glimmer of meaning

yet remain under close scrutiny, it must be removed by replacing all the principal verbs by paraphrases in some dead language.

This is not to be achieved in a moment; it is not enough to write disconnected nonsense; it must be possible for anyone acquainted with the tortuosities of the author's mind to resolve the sentence into its elements, and reproduce – not the meaning, for there is none, but the same mental fog from which he was originally suffering. An illustration is appended.

Pneumaticals	Omnient
(spirits)	(all)
Tabernacular	Subinfractically
(dwelling)	(Below)
Homotopic	hermeneutical
(this)	(magic)
Ru-volvolimperipunct,	suprorientalise,
(circle)	(arise)
factote	kinematodrastically,
(move)	(soon)
overplus	phenomenise!
(and)	(appear)

Upon this skeleton, a fair example of his earlier manner, for no man attains the summit of an art in a day, he would build a superstructure by the deft introduction of parentheses, amplifying each word until the original coherence of the paragraph was diluted to such an extent that the true trail was undiscoverable. The effect upon his public was to impress them with the universality of his learning.

Arthwait being thus well out of harm's way, Vesquit and Abdul set to work on the less arduous of the preparations. Four black cats were needed for the four points of the compass, and it was desirable to massacre a goat upon the altar, which would be no less than the corpse itself. Vesquit, declaring that the body was to be sent to England, had a dummy shipped off in a coffin, and kept Gates on ice, which may or may not have been a great comfort to him.

Abdul had no difficulty in procuring the cats which, much to their dissatisfaction, were caged in Arthwait's study, and fed on human flesh, which Vesquit easily procured from the dissecting-rooms of the local hospitals.

But the goat was a more serious matter. An ordinary goat will not do; it had to qualify in certain respects; Abdul succeeded in his quest only after a series of intrigues with the lowest ruffians in Naples, which brought him into more vulgar and unpleasant dangers than he had contemplated "when he first put that uniform on". It was, however, at least temporarily, a very amusing situation for the goat. The requisite bat, which must be fed on a woman's blood, was easily arranged for, a courageous country girl offering to accommodate with a toe, for a consideration. The nails from a suicide's coffin, and the skull of the parricide, were of course no trouble; for Vesquit never travelled without these household requisites.

There were many other details to arrange; the consideration of a proper place for the operation gave rise to much mental labour. It is, generally speaking, desirable to choose the locality of a recent battle; and the greater the number of slain the better. (There should be some very desirable spots in the vicinity of Verdun for black magicians who happen to flourish after the vulgar year 1917.) But the Grimoires were written in other times with other manners; now-a-days there is risk of disturbance if one sets up one's paraphernalia of goats and cats at a cross-roads, in the hope of helping oneself out with a recently-interred suicide, or a ceremonially annihilated vampire; where the peasant of the fourteenth century would have fled shrieking, the motorist of the twentieth century stops to observe, or, more likely, runs you over; so that unless your property includes a private battlefield, it is a point of valour to choose a more retired site for one's necromancy than the stricken field of the Marne. Cross-roads, again, are not so thickly planted with suicides and vampires as in happier days. Reflecting solidly and ably upon these points of modern degeneracy, Vesquit made up his mind to compromise, and accept the most agreeable substitute, a profaned chapel; it was easy to rent a villa with a chapel attached, and, to a man of Vesquit's ability, the work of a moment to profane it.

This he accordingly arranged through Abdul Bey.

The mind of this youth was very forcibly impressed by the preparations of the old coroner. He had been brought up in the modern school, and could laugh at superstition with the best of us; but there were traces of hereditary faith in Islam, and he was not sceptical enough to spoil the magic of Vesquit.

No man knew better than the necromancer that all this insane ceremonial was irrational. But it so happens that everything on this planet is, ultimately, irrational; there is not, and cannot be, any reason for the causal connexion

of things, if only because our use of the word "reason" already implies the idea of causal connexion. But, even if we avoid this fundamental difficulty, Hume said that causal connexion was not merely unprovable, but unthinkable; and, in shallower waters still, one cannot assign a true reason why water should flow downhill, or sugar taste sweet in the mouth. Attempts to explain these simple matters always progress into a learned lucidity, and on further analysis retire to a remote stronghold where every thing is irrational and unthinkable.

If you cut off a man's head, he dies. Why? Because it kills him. That is really the whole answer. Learned excursions into anatomy and physiology only beg the question; it does not explain why the heart is necessary to life to say that it is a vital organ. Yet that is exactly what is done, the trick that is played on every inquiring mind. Why cannot I see in the dark? Because light is necessary to sight. No confusion of that issue by talk of rods and cones, and optical centres, and foci, and lenses, and vibrations is very different to Edwin Arthwait's treatment of the long-suffering English language.

Knowledge is really confined to experience. The laws of Nature are, as Kant said, the laws of our minds, and, as Huxley said, the generalization of observed facts.

It is, therefore, no argument against ceremonial magic to say that it is "absurd" to try to raise a thunderstorm by beating a drum; it is not even fair to say that you have tried the experiment, found it would not work, and so perceived it to be "impossible". You might as well claim that, as you had taken paint and canvas, and not produced a Rembrandt, it was evident that the pictures attributed to his painting were really produced in quite a different way.

You do not see why the skull of a parricide should help you to raise a dead man, as you do not see why the mercury in a thermometer should rise and fall, though you elaborately pretend that you do; and you could not raise a dead man by the aid of the skull of a parricide, just as you could not play the violin like Kreisler; though in the latter case you might modestly add that you thought you could learn.

This is not the special pleading of a professed magician; it boils down to the advice not to judge subjects of which you are perfectly ignorant, and is to be found, stated in clearer and lovelier language, in the Essays of Thomas Henry Huxley. Dr. Victor Vesquit, to whom the whole of these ideas was perfectly familiar, proceeded with his quaint preparations unperturbed by the least doubt of their efficacy.

He had found that they worked; and he cared no more for the opinion of those who, whatever their knowledge in other branches of science might be, were not experts in necromancy, than does Harry Vardon when it is proved to him, with the utmost scientific precision, that he cannot possibly hit a golf ball so long as he swings as he does, and uses that mechanically defective grip.

It is also to be remarked that the contrary holds good; no method of doing anything has yet been found which cannot be bungled by the inept.

So, as the Persian poet says: "Who hath the How is careless of the Why."

It was early in the course of Dr. Vesquit's preliminaries that (what Arthwait called the "antilan-thanetical douleskeiarchy") the secret service which had been established reported to him a complete change in the routine of the people of the Butterfly net. On the seventh of January Iliel reported that the first point of the work was in all probability attained; all that was now necessary was to concentrate upon the real crux of the case, the catching of the Butterfly.

The household was reorganised accordingly; Cyril Grey withdrew himself completely from the company of Iliel, and joined the Church Militant Here On Earth; while Iliel herself came under the direct care of Sister Clara, the point within the triangle of women. She took part in their invocations, as the focus to which they were directed; while the men were wholly busied in watching over the safety of the fortress, their faces turned inexorably outward, their sole business to assure the security of the three women and their treasure.

Upon these facts being brought to the notice of Edwin Arthwait, he smiled. He had redeemed his earlier failures – due to the incapacity of his assistants – by a sweeping success.

For to his magic, evidently, was due the observed change in nature! Shortly after the arrival of Vesquit, he had completed his latest operation, the bewitchment of three nails in such a manner that, if struck into the door of a room of a house, the occupants would be thereby debarred from the enjoyment of conjugal felicity. And here was the result, shining before him, beautiful with banners. Even the pretence of amity had been abandoned. As a matter of fact, Brother Onofrio had discovered the nails, and taken the proper measures to return the current to its sender; but on this occasion it was as "tae tak' the breeks aff a Hielan' mon"!

Arthwait was totally insensible to the malice of his adversary, and remained in the enjoyment of his supposed victory. He resolved to steal a

march on Vesquit. Why should he share his glory with another? He had the enemy on the run; he had better pursue them forthwith. Vesquit's slow methods would only give them time to recover.

So he resolved upon the chivalrous if perilous course of Cat's Cradle. This magical operation, the relics of which are familiar even to the most unspiritually-minded children, is exceedingly widespread, especially among nations which live principally by fishing, as, for example, the South Sea Islanders. Many most intricate and beautiful patterns have been devised, and of these the wayfaring man may partake by a perusal of Dr. W. W. R. Ball's monograph upon the subject. That able mathematician, however, neglects unpardonably the magical side of the matter.

The theory is apparently based upon the fact that the most elusive objects, birds, butterflies, and fishes, may be taken by means of a net. It is argued, therefore, that anything whatever, no matter how elusive, such as the ghost of one's father or the soul of one's enemy, may be caught similarly, though of course the net must be adapted to the special game that one is after.

With these things Arthwait was familiar, and it occurred to him that it should be easy to identify string, or, preferably, cat-gut, with the viscera of his victims. There could then be no difficulty in knotting up the cords in such a pattern, for example, as the Many Stars, or the Owl, or the Zigzag Lightning; and assuredly the magicians thus assailed would find similar re-arrangements of the contents of their peritonea.

After various preliminary exercises, annoying to the objects of this solicitude, Arthwait proposed to proceed to the grand operation of all, tying up his gut in the Elusive Yam pattern, which, from the greatest complexity, dissolves like a dream at a single last twist; the persons thus sympathetically treated would obviously perish no less miserably than did Eglon, King of Moab, or Judas Iscariot.

The advantage of this operation is evidently its extreme simplicity and economy; while, if it works at all, it surely leaves nothing to be desired in such Teutonic qualities as thoroughness and frightfulness.

Whether from any difficulty in identification or otherwise, it was some little while before Arthwait began to feel that his plan was working out. The trouble with all these operations was in the absence of a direct link with the principals; the currents invariably struck the outer defences, in the person of Brother Onofrio, before penetrating. When, therefore, Arthwait's efforts began to show results, they were first noticed by that sturdy warrior. And

he, considering the situation, argued that the observed phenomena were due to Nature or to Magick, and that in either case the remedy lay in opposing no resistance to the forces, but allowing them to operate in a laudable manner. Accordingly, he took a large dose of a medicine known to the pharmacist as Hydrarg.Subchlor, adding the remark "If this be nature, may it do me good; and if this be magic, may it do him good!"

This occurred just as Arthwait reached his final operation, the evisceration of his enemy.

That night both parties were successful in causing things to happen; and the morning after Arthwait was securely incarcerated in the Quarantine Hospital of the city, and the newspapers were paragraphing a suspected case of Asiatic Cholera.

However, in five days the symptoms abated; the case was declared non-infectious; and the pallid shadow of the disconcerted sorcerer was restored to the more congenial atmosphere of his Grimoire.

CHAPTER XIV

AN INFORMATIVE DISCOURSE UPON THE OCCULT CHARACTER OF THE MOON,

HER THREEFOLD NATURE. HER FOURFOLD PHASES. AND HER EIGHT-AND-TWENTY MANSIONS; WITH AN ACCOUNT OF THE EVENTS THAT PRECEDED THE CLIMAX OF THE GREAT EXPERIMENT. BUT ESPECIALLY OF THE VISION OF ILIEL

THE Ancients, whose wisdom is so much despised by those who have never studied it, but content themselves with a pretence of understanding modern science which deceives nobody, would have smiled to observe how often the

"latest discoveries" are equivalent to some fancy of Aristotle, or some speculation of Heracleitus. The remoter Picay-universities of America, which teach farming or mining, with a little "useless" knowledge as a side-course, for show, are full of bumptious little professors who would not be allowed to sweep out a laboratory in London or Berlin. The ambition of such persons is to obtain an illustrated interview in a Sunday supplement, with a full account of their wonderful discoveries, which have revolutionised the art of sucking eggs. They are peculiarly severe upon back numbers like Charles Darwin. Their ignorance leads them to believe the bombast of democracy-flatterers, who scream weekly of Progress, and it really appears to them that anything more than six months old is out-of-date. They do not know that this is only true of loud-shouted mushroom rubbish such as they call truth.

The fundamental difference between ancient and modern science is not at all in the field of theory. Sir William Thomson was just as metaphysical as Pythagoras or Raymond Lully, and Lucretius quite as materialistic as Ernst Haeckel or Buchner.

But we have devised means of accurate measurement which they had not, and in consequence of this our methods of classification are more quantitative than qualitative. The result has been to make much of their science unintelligible; we no longer know exactly what they meant by the four elements, or by the three active principles, sulphur, mercury, and salt. Some tradition has been preserved by societies of wise men, who, because of the persecutions, when to possess any other book than a missal might be construed as heresy, concealed themselves and whispered the old teaching one to another.

The nineteenth century saw the overthrow of most of the old ecclesiastical tyranny, and in the beginning of the twentieth it was found once more possible to make public the knowledge. The wise men gathered together, discovered a student who was trustworthy and possessed of the requisite literary ability; and by him the old knowledge was revised and made secure; it was finally published in a sort of periodical encyclopedia (already almost impossible to find, such was the demand for it) entitled *The Equinox*.

Now in the science of antiquity, much classification depended upon the planets. Those things which were hot and fiery in their nature, lions, and pepper, and fevers, were classed under the Sun or Jupiter or Mars; things swift and subtle under Mercury; things cold and heavy under Saturn, and so forth.

Yet the principles of most of the planets appeared in varying proportions in almost everything; and the more equally these proportions were balanced and combined, the more complete was anything supposed to be, the nearer modelled on the divine perfection. Man himself was called a microcosm, a little universe, an image of the Creator. In him all the planets and elements had course, and even the Signs of the Zodiac were represented in his nature. The energy of the ram was in his head; the bull gave the laborious endurance to his shoulders; the lion represented the courage of his heart, and the fire of his temper; his knees, which help him to spring, are under the goat – all works in, and is divided and subdivided in, beauty and harmony.

In this curious language the moon signifies primarily all receptive things, because moonlight is only reflected sunlight. Hence "lunar" is almost a synonym of "feminine". Woman changes; all depends upon the influence of the man; and she is now fertile, now barren, according to her phase. But on each day of her course she passes through a certain section of the Zodiac; and according to the supposed nature of the stars beyond her was her influence in that phase, or, as they called it, mansion. It was in order to bring Iliel into harmony with every quality of the moon that her daily routine was ordered.

But beyond such minuteness of detail is the grand character of the Moon, which is threefold. For she is Artemis or Diana, sister of the Sun, a shining Virgin Goddess; then Isis-initiatrix, who brings to man all light and purity, and is the link of his animal soul with his eternal self; and she is Persephone or Proserpine, a soul of double nature, living half upon earth and half in Hades, because, having eaten the pomegranate offered her by its lord, her mother could not bring her wholly back to earth; and thirdly, she is Hecate, a thing altogether of Hell, barren, hideous and malicious, the queen of death and evil witchcraft.

All these natures are combined in woman. Artemis is unassailable, a being fine and radiant; Hecate is the crone, the woman past all hope of motherhood, her soul black with envy and hatred of happier mortals; the woman in the fullness of life is the sublime Persephone, for whose sake Demeter cursed the fields that they brought forth no more corn, until Hades consented to restore her to earth for half the year. So this "moon" of the ancients has a true psychological meaning, as sound today as when the priest of Mithras slew the bull; she is the soul, not the eternal and undying sun of the true soul, but the animal soul which is a projection of it, and is subject to change

and sorrow, to the play of all the forces of the universe, and whose "redemption" is the solution of the cosmic problem. For it is the seed of the woman that shall bruise the serpent's head; and this is done symbolically by every woman who wins to motherhood.

Others may indeed be chaste unto Artemis, priestesses of a holy and ineffable rite; but with this exception, failure to attain the appointed goal brings them into the dark side of the moon, the cold and barren house of Hecate the accursed.

It will be seen how wide is the range of these ideas, how sensitive is the formula of woman, that can touch such extremes, springing often from one to the other in a moment – according to the nature of the influence then at work upon her.

Cyril Grey had once said, speaking at a Woman's Suffrage Meeting:

"Woman has no soul, only sex; no morals, only moods; her mind is mob-rule; therefore she, and she only, ought to Vote."

He had sat down amid a storm of hisses; and received fourteen proposals of marriage within the next twenty-four hours.

Ever since the beginning of the second stage of the Great Experiment, Iliel had become definitely a Spirit of the Moon while Cyril was with her, she reflected him, she clung to him, she was one with him, Isis to his Osiris, sister as well as spouse; and every thought of her mind being but the harmonic of his, there was no possibility of any internal disturbance.

But now she was torn suddenly from her support; she could not even speak to her man; and she discovered her own position as the mere centre of an Experiment.

She knew now that she was not of scientific mind; that her aspirations to the Unknown had been fully satisfied by mere love; and that she would have been much happier in a commonplace cottage. It says much for the personality of Sister Clara, and the force of her invocations, that this first impulse never came to so much as a word. But the priestess of Artemis took hold of her almost with the violence of a lover, and whisked her away into a languid ecstasy of reverie. She communicated her own enthusiasm to the girl, and kept her mind occupied with dreams, faery-fervid, of uncharted seas of glory on which her galleon might sail, undiscovered countries of spice and sweetness, Eldorado and Utopia and the City of God.

The hour of the rising of the moon was always celebrated by an invocation upon the terrace consecrated to that planet. A few minutes earlier

lliel rose and bathed, then dressed herself in the robes, and placed upon her head the crescent-shaped tiara, with its nine great moonstones. In this the younger girls took turns to assist her. When she was ready, she joined the other girl, and together they went down to the terrace, where Sister Clara would be ready to begin the invocations.

Of course, owing to the nature of the ceremony, it took place an hour later every day; and at first lliel found a difficulty in accommodating herself to the ritual. The setting of the moon witnessed a second ceremony, directly from which she retired to her bed. It was part of the general theory of the operation thus to keep her concealed and recumbent for the greater part of the day; which, as has been seen, really lasted nearer 25 hours than 24.

But with soft singing and music, or with the recital of slow voluptuous poetry, her natural disinclination to sleep was overcome, and she began to enjoy the delicious laziness of her existence, and to sleep the clock round without turning in her bed. She lived almost entirely upon milk, and cream, and cheese soft-curded and mild, with little crescent cakes made of rye with white of egg and cane sugar; as for meat, venison, as sacred to the huntress Artemis, was her only dish. But certain shell-fish were permitted, and all soft and succulent vegetables and fruits.

She put on flesh rapidly; the fierce, active, impetuous girl of October, with taut muscles and dark-flushed mobile face, had become pale, heavy, languid, and indifferent to events, all before the beginning of February.

And it was early in this month that she was encouraged by her first waking vision of the Moon. Naturally her sleep had already been haunted by this idea from the beginning; it could hardly have been otherwise with the inveterate persistence of the ceremonies. The three women always chanted a sacred sentence, Epelthon Epelthon Artemis, continuously for an hour after her couching; and then one of them went on while the others slept. They would each take a shift of three hours. The words were rather droned than sung, to an old magical chant, which Sister Clara, who was half-Greek, half-Italian, born of a noble family of Mitylene, had inherited from some of the women of the island at her initiation as a young girl into some of their mysteries. They claimed that it had come down unaltered from the great singers of history. It was a drowsy lilt, yet in it was a current of fierce heat like that of the sun, and an undertone of sobbing like the sea.

So Iliel's dreams were always of the moon. If the watcher beheld trouble upon her face, as if disturbing influences were upon her, she would breathe

softly in her ear, and bring her thoughts back to the infinite calm which was desired for her.

For Cyril Grey in devising the operation had by no means been blind to the dangers involved in choosing a symbol so sensitive as Luna. There is all the universe between her good and evil sides; in the case of a comparatively simple and straightforward planet like Saturn, this is not the case. And the planets with a backbone are far easier to control. If you once get Mars going, so to speak, it is easy to make him comply with Queensberry rules; but the moon is so passive that the slightest new influence throws her entirely out.

And, of course, the calmer the pool, the bigger the splash! Hence, in order to draw down to Iliel only the holiest and serenest of the lunar souls, no precaution could be too great, no assiduity too intense.

The waking vision which came to her after about a month of the changed routine was of good cheer and great encouragement.

It was an hour after sunset; the night was curiously warm, and a soft breeze blew from the sea. It was part of the duty of Iliel to remain in the moonlight, with her gaze and her desire fixed upon the orb, whenever possible. From her room a stairway led to a tall turret, circular, with a glass dome, so as to favour all such observations. But on this night the garden tempted her. *Nox erat et caelo fulgebat Luna sereno inter minora sidera.* The moon hung above Capri, two hours from her setting. Iliel held her vigil upon the terrace, by the side of the basin of the fountain. When the moon was not visible, she would always replace her by looking upon the sea, or upon still water, for these have much in common with the lunar influence.

Something – she never knew what – drew her eyes from the moon to the water. She was so placed that the reflexion appeared in the basin, at the very edge of the marble, where the water flowed over into the little rivulets that coursed the terrace. There was a tremulous movement, almost like a timid kiss, as the water touched the edge.

And, to the eye of Iliel, it seemed as if the trembling of the moon's image were a stirring of vitality.

The thought that followed was a mystery. She said that she looked up, as if recalled to her vigil, and found that the moon was no longer in the sky. Nor indeed was there any sky; she was in a grotto whose walls, fantastically draped with stalactites, glimmered a faint purplish blue – very much the effect, she explained, of luminous paint. She looked down again; the basin was gone; at her feet was a young fawn, snow-white, with a collar of silver.

She was impelled to read the engraving upon the collar, and was able to make out these words:

> *Siderum regina bicornis audi,*
> *Luna, puellas.*

Iliel had learnt no Latin. But these words were not only Latin, but the Latin of Horace; and they were exactly appropriate to the nature of the Great Experiment, "*Luna*" she had heard, and "*regina*"; and she might have guessed "*puellas*" and even "*siderum*"; but that is one thing, and an accurate quotation from the *Carmen Saeculare* is another. Yet they stood in her mind as if she had always known them, perhaps even as if they were innate in her. She repeated aloud:

> "*Siderum regina bicornis audi,*
> *Luna, puellas.*

> "List, o moon, o queen of the stars, two-horned,
> List to the maidens!"

At the time, she had, of course, no idea of the meaning of the words.

When she had read the inscription, she stroked the fawn gently; and, looking up, perceived that a child, clad in a kirtle, with a bow and quiver slung from her shoulders, was standing by her.

But the vision passed in a flash; she drew her hand across her brow, as if to auscultate her mental condition, for she had a slight feeling of bewilderment. No, she was awake; for she recognised the sacred oak under which she was standing. It was only a few paces from the door of the temple where she was priestess. She remembered perfectly now: she had come out to bid the herald blow his horn. And at that moment its mountainous music greeted her.

But what was this? From every tree in the wood, from every blade of grass, from under every stone, came running little creatures in answer to the summons. They were pale, semi-transparent, with oval (but rather flattened) heads quite disproportionately large, thin, match-like bodies and limbs, and snake-like tails attached to the base of their skulls. They were extraordinarily light and active on their feet, and the tails kept up a lashing movement. The

whole effect was comic, at the first sight; one might have said tadpoles on stilts.

But a closer inspection stayed her laughter. Each of these creatures had a single eye, and in this eye was expressed such force and energy that it was terrifying. The effect was heightened by the sagacity, the occult and profound knowledge of all possible things, which dwelt behind those fiery wills. In the carriage of the head was something leonine as well as serpentine; there was extraordinary pride and courage to match the fierce persistency.

Yet there seemed no object in the movements of these strange beings; their immense activity was unintelligible. It seemed as if they were going through physical exercises – yet it was something more than that. At one moment she fancied that she could distinguish leaders, that this was a body of troops being rallied to some assault.

And then her attention was distracted. From her feet arose a swan, and took wing over the forest. It must have been there for a long time, for it had laid an egg directly between her sandalled feet. She suddenly realised that she was dreadfully hungry. She would go into the temple and have the egg for breakfast. But no sooner had she picked it up than she saw that it, like the collar of the fawn in her dream, was inscribed with a Latin sentence. She read it aloud: the words were absolutely familiar. They were those of the labarum of Constantine "*In hoc signo vinces*". "In this sign thou shalt conquer." But her, eyes gave the lie to her ears; for the word "*signo*" was spelt "*Cygno*"! The phrase was then a pun – "In this Swan thou shalt conquer." At the time she did not understand; but she was sure of the spelling, when she came afterwards to report her vision to Sister Clara.

It then came into her mind that this egg was a great treasure, and that it was her duty to guard it against all comers; and at the same moment she saw that the creatures of the wood – "sons of the oak" she called them instinctively – were advancing toward her.

She prepared to fight or fly. But, with a fearful crackling, the lightning – which was, in the strange way of dreams, identical with the oak – burst in every direction, enveloping her with its blaze; and the crash of the thunder was the fall of the oak. It struck her to the ground. The world went out before her eyes, dissolved into a rainbow rush of stars; and she heard the shouts of triumph of the "sons of the oak" as they dashed forward upon her ravished treasure. "*Mitos ho Theos!*" they shouted – Sister Clara did not know, or would not tell, its meaning.

As the iridiscent galaxy in which she was floating gradually faded, she became aware that she was no longer in the wood, but in a strange city. It was crowded with men and women, of many a race and colour. In front of her was a small house, very poor and squalid, in whose doorway an old man was sitting. A long staff was by his side, leaning against the door; and at his feet was a lantern – was it a lantern? It was more like the opposite of one; for in the full daylight it burned, and shed forth rays of darkness. The ancient was dressed in grey rags; his long unkempt hair and beard had lacked a barber for many a day. But his right arm was wholly bare, and around it was coiled a serpent, gold and green, with a triple crown sparkling with ruby, sapphire, and with it he was engraving a great square tablet of emerald.

She watched him for some time; when he had finished, he went away with the staff, and the lamp, and the tablet, to the sea shore. Along the coast he proceeded for some time, and came at last to a cave. Iliel followed him to its darkest corner; and there she saw a corpse lying. Strangely, it was the body of the old scribe himself. It came to her very intensely that he had two bodies, and that he always kept one of them buried, for safety. The old scribe left the tablet upon the breast of the dead man, and went very quickly out of the cave.

But Iliel remained to read what was written. It was afterwards translated by Cyril Grey, and there is no need to give the original.

> "Utter the Word of Majesty and Terror!
> True without lie, and certain without error,
> And of the essence of The Truth. I know
> The things above are as the things below,
> The things below are as the things above,
> To wield the One Thing's Thaumaturgy – Love.
> As all from one sprang, by one contemplation,
> So all from one were born, by permutation.
> Sun sired, Moon bore, this unique Universe;
> Air was its chariot, and Earth its nurse.
> Here is the root of every talisman
> Of the whole world, since the whole world began.
> Here is the fount and source of every soul.
> Let it be spilt on earth! its strength is whole.

Now gently, subtly, with thine Art conspire
To fine the gross, dividing earth and fire.
Lo! it ascendeth and descendeth, even
And swift, an endless band of earth and heaven;
Thus it receiveth might of duplex Love,
The powers below conjoined with those above,
So shall the glory of the world be thine
And darkness flee before thy SOVRAN shrine.
This is the strong strength of all strength; surpass
The subtle and subdue it; pierce the crass
And salve it; so bring all things to their fated
Perfection: for by this was all created.
O marvel of miracle! O magic mode!
All things adapted to one circling code!
Since three parts of all wisdom I may claim,
Hermes thrice great, and greatest, is my name.
What I have written of the one sole Sun,
His work, is here divined, and dared, and done."

In this obscure and antique oracle, so Simon Iff himself subsequently agreed, the secret of the Universe is revealed to those who are worthy to partake of it.

Iliel could not understand a word of what was written, but she realised that it must be valuable, and, taking the tablet, she hid it in her robe and came out of the cave. Then she saw that the coast was changed: it was the familiar Posilippo which hung above her, and she could see Vesuvius away to the right. She turned to breast the steep slope between her and the road, when she found herself confronted by something that she could not see. She had only a feeling that it was black, that it was icy cold, and that it wished to take the tablet from her. Her first sentiment was that of acute hatred and repulsion; but the thing, whatever it was, seemed so wretched, that she felt she would like to help it. Then she suddenly glowed hot – the arms of Abdul Bey were round her, and his face was looking into hers. She dropped the tablet hastily; she was back again in a ball-room somewhere, thousands of miles and thousands of years away. And then she saw the moon, near her setting, over Capri; she was on the terrace, seated on the ground, perfectly awake, but with the silver crescent from her hair lying upon the marble before her.

Sister Clara, on her knees beside her, was trying to decipher the scratches that she had made.

"That is the writing on the tablet," said Iliel, as if Sister Clara already knew all about it, "that the old man hid in the cave."

It was now the hour for her to cradle her limbs in slumber; but, while the monotonous chant of her hand-maidens wooed the soft air, Cyril Grey and Brother Onofrio were at work upon the inscription.

Almost until dawn they toiled; and, down in another villa, another labour reached its climax. Arthwait had finished his Grimoire. He was just in time. For the great operation of necromancy should properly begin on the second day of the waning of the moon, and there were nine previous days of most arduous preparation, no longer of the materials, but of the sorcerers themselves.

They must eat dog's flesh, and black bread baked without salt or leaven, and they must drink unfermented grape-juice – the vilest of all black magical concoctions, for it implies the denial of the divine beatitude, and affirms God to be a thing of wood. There were many other precautions also to be taken. The atmosphere of the charnel must be created about them; they must abstain from so much as the sight of women; their clothing might not be changed even for an hour, and its texture was to be that of cerements, for, filching the grave-clothes from corpses of the unassoiled, they must wrap themselves closely round in them, with some hideous travesty of the words of the Burial Service.

A visit to the Jewish graveyard put them in possession of the necessary garments; and Arthwait's palinode upon the "resurrection unto damnation" left in each mind due impression of the ghastliness of their projected rite.

And, in Paris, Douglas, smashing the neck of a bottle of whisky on the edge of the table, was drinking the good health of his visitor, an American woman of the name of Cremers.

Her squat stubborn figure was clad in rusty-black clothes, a man's except for the skirt; it was surmounted by a head of unusual size, and still more unusual shape, for the back of the skull was entirely flat, and the left frontal lobe much more developed than the right; one could have thought that it had been deliberately knocked out of shape, since nature, fond, it may be, of freaks, rarely pushes asymmetry to such a point.

There would have been more than idle speculation in such a theory; for she was the child of hate, and her mother had in vain attempted every violence against her before her birth.

The face was wrinkled parchment, yellow and hard; it was framed in short, thick hair, dirty white in colour; and her expression denoted that the utmost cunning and capacity were at the command of her rapacious instincts. But her poverty was no indication that they had served her; and those primitive qualities had in fact been swallowed up in the results of their disappointment. For in her eye raved bitter a hate of all things, born of the selfish envy which regarded the happiness of any other person as an outrage and affront upon her. Every thought in her mind was a curse – against God, against man, against love, or beauty, against life itself. She was a combination of the witch-burner with the witch; an incarnation of the spirit of Puritanism, from its sourness to its sexual degeneracy and perversion.

Douglas put the broken glass to his mouth, and gulped down a bumper of whisky. Then he offered the bottle to his visitor. She refused by saying that it "played hell with the astral body", and asked her host to give her the price of the drink instead. Douglas laughed like a madman – a somewhat disgusted madman, for in him was some memory of his former state, and even his fall had been comparatively decent, the floor of his hell a ceiling to her heaven. But he had a use for the hag, and he contemptuously tossed her a franc. She crawled over the floor, like some foul insect, in search of it, for it had rolled to a corner; and, having retrieved it, she forgot her mannish assumptions in her excitement at the touch of silver, and thrust it into her stocking.

CHAPTER XV

OF DR. VESQUIT
AND HIS COMPANIONS,

HOW THEY FARED IN THEIR WORK OF NECROMANCY; AND OF A COUNCIL OF WAR OF CYRIL GREY AND BROTHER ONOFRIO; WITH CERTAIN OPINIONS OF THE FORMER UPON THE ART OF MAGICK.

THE Neapolitan winter had overpassed its common clemency; save for a touch of frost, kindly and wholesome, on a few nights, it had no frown or rigour. Day after day the sun had enkindled the still air, and life had danced with love upon the hills.

But on the night of her fullness, the moon was tawny and obscure, with a reddish vapour about her, as if she had wrapped herself in a mantle of anger; and the next dawn broke grey with storm, the wind tearing its way across the mountain spine of Italy, as if some horde of demon bandits were raiding

the peasantry of the plains. The Butterfly-Net was sheltered from its rage by the crest of Posilippo; but it was bitter cold in the house, and Iliel bade her maidens pile the brazier with hazel and white sandalwood and birch.

Across the ridge, the villa which Dr. Vesquit had taken for the winter was exposed to the senseless madness of the blast; and he too heaped his braziers, but with cypress and bituminous coal.

As the day passed the violence of the storm increased; the doctor even began to fear for the safety of his operation when, about an hour after noon, a window of the villa was broken by a torn branch of olive that came hurtling against it.

But a little later the speed of the hurricane abated; the sky was visible, through the earth-vapours, as a wrack of wrathful clouds – one might say the flight of Michael before Satan.

Though the gale was yet fierce, its heart broke in a torrent of sleet mixed with hail; for two hours more it drove almost horizontally against the hillside, and then, steadying and steepening, fell as a flood, a cataract of icy rain.

The slopes of Posilippo roared with their foaming load; gardens were washed clear of soil; walls broke down before the impetuosity of the waves they strove to dam; and the streets of lower Naples stood in water to the height of a man's thigh.

The hour for the beginning of the work of the necromancers was that of sunset; and at that moment the rain, after a last burst of vehemence, ceased entirely; nightfall, though black and bitter, was silent as the corpse of Gates itself.

In the chapel a portion of the marble floor had been torn up; for it was desired to touch the naked earth with the bare feet, and draw her powers directly up from their volcanic stratum.

This raw earth had been smeared with mire brought from the swamps of the Maremma; and upon this sulphur had been sprinkled until it formed a thick layer. In this sulphur the magick circle had been drawn with a two-pointed stick, and the grooves thus made had been filled with charcoal powder.

It was not a true circle; no figure of sanctity and perfection might enter into that accursed rite; it had been made somewhat in the shape of an old-fashioned keyhole, a combination of circle and triangle.

In the centre the body of Gates, his head toward the north, was laid; Arthwait stood on one side with the Grimoire in one hand, and a lighted

taper of black wax in the other. On the opposite side was Abdul Bey, holding the goat in leash, and bearing the sickle which Vesquit was to use as the principal magical weapon of the ceremony.

The doctor was himself the last to enter the circle. In a basket he had the four black cats; and, when he had lighted the nine small candles about the circle, he pinned the four cats, at the four quarters, with black arrows of iron. He was careful not to kill them; it was important that their agony should frighten away any undesirable spirits.

All being now ready, the necromancers fell upon their knees; for this servile position is pleasing to the enemies of mankind.

The forces which made man, alone of all animals, erect, love to see him thank Them for that independence by refusing to surrender it.

The main plan of Dr. Vesquit's ceremony was simple; it was to invoke the spirit of a demon into the goat, and slaying the animal at that moment of possession upon the corpse of Gates, to endow that corpse with the demoniac power, in a kind of hideous marriage.

The object was then identical with that of spiritism, or "spiritualism", as it is commonly and illiterately called; but Dr. Vesquit was a serious student, determined to obtain results, and not to be duped; his methods were consequently more efficient than those of the common or parlour medium.

Arthwait opened the Grimoire and began his conjurations. It would be impossible to reproduce the hideous confusion and complexity of the manner, and undesirable to indicate the abomination of the matter. But every name of opposition to light was invoked in its own rite; the fearful deities of man's dawn, when nature was supposed to be a personal power of cruelty, delighting in murder, rape, and pillage, were called by their most secret names, and commemoration made of their deeds of infamy.

Such was the recital of horror that, cloaked even as it was in Arthwait's unintelligible style, the meaning was salient by virtue of the tone of the enchanter, and the gestures with which Vesquit accompanied him, going in dumb show through all the gamut of infernal discord, the music of the pit. He showed how children were cast into the fire, or thrown to bears, or offered up in sacrifice on bloody altars; how peaceful nations were uprooted by savage tribes in the name of their demon, their men slain or mutilated and enslaved, their women butchered, their virgins ravished; how miracle testified to the power of the evil ones, the earth opening to swallow heretic priests, the sun stopped in the sky that the hours of massacre might be prolonged.

It was in short one interminable recital of treachery and murder and revenge; never a thought of pity or of kindliness, of common decency or common humanity, struck a false note in that record of vileness; and it culminated in the ghastliest atrocity of human history, when the one man in all that cut-throat race who now and then showed gleams of a nobler mind was chosen for torture and death as a final offering to the blood-lust of the fiend.

With a sort of hellish laughter, the second conjuration continued the recital; how the demon had brought the corpse of his victim to life, and mocked and profaned his humanity by concealing himself in that man-shape, thence to continue his reign, and extend his empire, under the cloak of hypocrisy. The crimes that had been done openly in the fiend's name, were now to be carried on with fresh device of shame and horror, by those who called themselves the priests of his victim.

By this commemoration was concluded the first part of the ceremony; the atmosphere of the fiend, so to speak, was brought into the circle; in the second part the demon was to be identified with the goat; in the third part the two first were joined, and the goat as he died was to repeat the miracle wrought in long ages past upon that other victim, by coming to life again humanised by the contact of the ghost of the sorcerer.

It is not permissible to describe this ritual in detail; it is too execrably efficient; but the Turk, brought up in a merciful and cleanly religion, with but few stains of savagery upon it, faltered and nigh fainted; only his desire for Lisa, which had become a soul-tempest, held him to the circle.

And indeed the brains of them all were awhirl. As Eliphaz Levi says, evil ceremonies are a true intellectual poison; they do invoke the powers of hallucination and madness as surely as does hashish. And who dare call the phantoms of delirium "unreal"? They are real enough to kill a man, to ruin a life, to push a soul to every kind of crime; and there are not many "real" "material" things that have such weight in work.

Phantoms, then, were apparent to the necromancers; and there was no doubt in any of their minds that they were dealing with actual and malignant entities.

The hideous cries of the tortured cats mingled with the triumphant bleating of the goat and the nasal monotone of Arthwait as he mouthed the words of the Grimoire. And it seemed to all of them as though the air grew thick and greasy; that of that slime were bred innumerable creeping things,

monsters misshapen, abortions of dead paths of evolution, creatures which had not been found fit to live upon the earth and so had been cast off by her as excrement. It seemed as if the goat were conscious of the phantoms; as if he understood himself as demon-king of those regions; for he bounded under the manipulations of Vesquit with such rage and pride that Abdul Bey was forced to use all his strength to hold him. It was taken as a sign of success by all the necromancers; and as Vesquit made the final gesture, Arthwait turned his page, and Abdul struck home with a great knife to the brute's heart.

Now, as the blood stained their grave-clothes, the hearts of the three sorcerers beat heavily. A foul sweat broke out upon them. The sudden change – psychological or magical? – from the turgid drone of Arthwait to the grimness of that silence in which the howls of the agonising cats rose hideous, struck them with a deadly fear. Or was it that they realised for the first time on what a ship they had embarked?

Suppose the corpse did move? Suppose Gates rose in the power of the devil, and strangled them? Their sweat ran down, and mingled with the blood. The stench of the slain goat was horrible, and the body of Gates had begun decomposition. The sulphur, burning in little patches here and there, where a candle had fallen and kindled it, added the reek of hell to that of death. Abdul Bey of a sudden was taken deathly sick; at the end he pitched forward, prone upon the corpses. Vesquit pulled him roughly back, and administered a violent stimulant, which made him master of himself.

Now Arthwait started the final conjuration. It can hardly be called language; it was like the jabber of a monkey-house, and like the yells of a thousand savages, and like the moaning of damned souls.

Meanwhile Vesquit proceeded to the last stage of his task. With his knife he hacked off the goat's head, and thrust it into a cavity slashed in the abdomen of the other body. Other parts of the goat he thrust into the mouth of Gates, while the obscene clamour of the cats mingled with the maniac howls of his colleague.

And then the one thing happened which they none of them expected. Abdul Bey flung himself down upon the carcasses, and began to tear them with his teeth, and lap the blood with his tongue. Arthwait shrieked out in terror that the Turk had gone mad: but Vesquit understood the truth. Abdul was the most sensitive of the party, and the least developed; it was in him that the spirit of Gates, demon-inspired, would manifest.

A few minutes of that scene, and then the Turk sat up. His face expressed the most extreme pleasure. It was the release of a soul from agony that showed itself. But he must have known that his time was short, for he spoke rapidly and earnestly, with febrile energy. And his words were commanding and convincing: Vesquit had no doubt that they were in presence of knowledge vastly superior to anything that he had yet found.

He wrote down the speech upon the tablets that he had prepared for the purpose.

> "They are working by the moon towards the Sun.
> "Hecate will come to help you. Attack from within, not from without.
> "An old woman and a young man bring victory.
> "All the powers are at your service; but they are stronger. Treachery shall save you.
> "Abandon the direct attack; for even now you have called down your death upon you. Quick! snap the cord. Conceal yourselves awhile. Even so, you are nigh death. Oh haste! Look yonder who is standing ready to smite!"

The voice dropped. Well was it for Vesquit that he kept his presence of mind. The necromancers looked round over their shoulders, and in the East was a blue mist shaped like an egg. In the midst of it, standing upon two crocodiles, was the image of Brother Onofrio, smiling, with his finger upon his lips. Vesquit realised that he was in contact with a force a thousand times greater than any at his disposal. He obeyed instantly the command spoken through Abdul Bey. "I swear," he cried, raising his right hand to heaven, "I swear that we intend you no manner of hurt." He flushed inwardly, knowing it for a lie, and therefore useless to avert the blow which he felt poised above him. He sought a new form of words. "I swear that we will not seek to break through your defences." This, he thought, should satisfy the captain of the gate, and yet permit him to do as he intended in the matter of trying to attack from within. Abdul Bey gasped out that it was well, that no more could be done, that the link with the White Lodge was broken. "But now our own blow strikes us to the earth." He fell backwards, as one dead. In another moment Arthwait, with a yell, a last invocation of that fiend whom he really believed to be omnipotent, entered into spasmodic convulsions,

like a man poisoned with strychnine, or dying of tetanus. Vesquit, appalled at the fate of his companions, gazed on the figure of Brother Onofrio in an agony of fear and horror. It retained the infant smile, and Vesquit reached his arms toward it. "Mercy!" he cried, "oh, my lord, mercy!"

Arthwait was writhing upon the corpses, horribly twisting, foaming black blood from his lungs.

And the old man saw that his life had been an imbecility, that he had taken the wrong path.

Brother Onofrio still smiled. "Oh my lord!" cried Vesquit, rising to his feet, "'twere better I should die."

The formula of humanity is the willing acceptance of death; and as love, in the male, is itself of the nature of a voluntary death, and therefore a sacrament, so that he who loves slays himself, therefore he who slays himself that life may live becomes a lover. Vesquit stretched out his arms in the sign of the cross, the symbol of Him who gives life through his own death, or of the instrument of that life and of that death, of the Holy One appointed from the foundation of the world as its redeemer.

It was as if there had come to him a flash of that most secret Word of all initiated knowledge, so secret and so simple that it may be declared openly in the market-place, and no man hear it. At least he realised himself as a silly old man, whose weakness and pliability in the hands of evil men had made him their accomplice. And he saw that death, grasped now, might save him.

Brother Onofrio still smiled.

"I invoke the return of the current!" cried Vesquit aloud; and thus, uniting justice with self-sacrifice, he died the death of the righteous.

The image of Brother Onofrio faded away.

The great operation of necromancy had come to naught.

Yet the writing remained; and, nearly a day later, when Abdul Bey came to himself, it was the first thing that caught his eye. He thrust it into his shroud, automatically; then stumbled to his feet, and sought his colleagues. At his feet the old coroner lay dead; Arthwait, his convulsions terminated by exhaustion approximating coma, lay with his head upon the carrion, his tongue, lolling from his mouth, chewed to a bloody pulp.

The Turk carried him from the chapel to the villa. His high connexions made it easy for him to secure a silent doctor to certify the death of Vesquit, and to attend to Arthwait, who passed from one convulsion to another at

frequent intervals. It was almost a month before he could be considered out of danger, but a week after that he was his own man again. They repaired immediately to Paris to lay the case before Douglas; for even Arthwait was compelled to recognise some elements in the business which were not satisfactory, incidents which he could not but regard as indicating that he had fallen appreciably short of his high standard of success.

The day succeeding the exploit of the necromancers dawned gay and bright. The earth dried up again, but breathed refreshment. A light mist hung over the walled garden where lliel stood upon her terrace.

The moon sank large and pale over the ocean as sunrise awoke the waves, and lliel, her vigil almost ended, prepared for the ceremony that ended her day.

But no sooner had she gone to the care of her hand-maidens than Cyril Grey came down the garden with Brother Onofrio. Their arms were crossed upon their breasts in the stately fashion of the Order; and Brother Onofrio's scarlet robe contrasted magnificently with the soft green silk of Brother Cyril's.

In the eyes of the Italian was a passionate reverence for the younger, but more gifted, man, coupled with a human affection which was almost more than friendship; there was in it the devotion, selfless and unsleeping, which is only possible to those of immense singleness of heart. He understood that Brother Cyril was of a finer mould than himself; he seemed to be rather a flame of fire than a man, so subtle and so keen was he. For in every talk, whenever he thought that he had sounded Cyril's guard, he suddenly found, on the riposte, that he had lost touch of his blade without knowing it. But he burned with constant ardour to know more of his idol; and this morning the young man had awakened him softly with a whisper, smiling, with a finger pointed to the terrace: "Let's go over there, where the Chancellor of the Exchequer can't hear us." So they had risen and come down to the lily-pool, after the morning adoration of the Sun, and their daily exercise of meditation.

Brother Cyril proved to be in his airiest mood, "Do you remember who said '*Surtout, pas de zele?*'" he began.

"Whoever it was then, I'm saying it now. Brother Onofrio, big brother, strong brother, clever brother, it won't do. You're doing much too well. Think you're a Russian General, if that will assist your feeble intelligence; but what you think doesn't matter, so long as you understand that to win too many

victories is as bad as to eat *toujours perdrix*. You have not merely defended this excellent citadel, for which I formally tender you the thanks of the Republic. You may kiss my hand. But you have pursued the defeated enemy; you have annihilated their strongest regiments; and, after last night, I am afraid that they will abandon the attack altogether. The situation is lamentable."

"But they invoked the death-current themselves," objected Brother Onofrio. "How could I tell that they would send for poor old Vesquit, and prepare an operation so formidable that something definite was bound to happen, one way or the other?"

"But you failed to deal gently with the young man Gates!"

"I know I'm liable to be carried away by a Tarot divination; but he was himself attempting a magical murder. You can't work things except on their own plane. He who taketh the sword shall perish by the sword."

"I dare say you're right; but I'm terribly afraid you've scared the game. I wanted to have Douglas and Balloch down here; then was the moment to turn loose those engines of destruction."

"You might have told me."

"Ah, if I had only known!"

Brother Onofrio gave a savage gesture. Once again he was being eluded.

"I only realised just now how fit and final were your labours. And now we are going to eat our hearts out in enervating peace and Capuan luxury. Alas! Think of the fate of Hannibal and of Napoleon. Always the same story – too much victory!"

Brother Onofrio bounded again in his amazement. "Peace! Luxury!" he cried. "Haven't we got the Great Experiment?"

"Have we?" sighed Cyril, languidly.

"Isn't the crisis in a month?"

"There are twelve months in a year."

Brother Onofrio rose in indignation. He hated to be played with in this manner; he could see no point in the jest, if it were one; or excuse for the rudeness, in the alternative.

"Sit down, sit down!" said Cyril dreamily. "You say yourself the crisis is not for a month. What a wonderful way is Ocean, girdling the five continents like a mother with her children. I should like to sail out westward, past the Pillars of Hercules, and up into the stormy reaches of the Bay, and – ah well! it may not be. We are held here by our stern duty; we are the chosen warriors of the Final Battle to decide whether men shall mould their own destiny, or

remain the toys of Fate; we are the pioneers of the Great Experiment. To arms, Brother Onofrio! Be diligent! Be courageous! The crisis is upon us – a month, no more! Return to me with your shield, or upon it!

"*Dulce et decorum est pro patria mori.*"

"Ah! now I understand you!" cried Onofrio warmly, clasping him in the impulsive Italian fashion.

"That's splendid of you," he said brightly. "I do appreciate that."

Brother Onofrio wriggled again.

"I half think," he said "that you know the Great Experiment will be a failure, and that for some reason you don't care!"

"The bluntness of the British diplomat was no match for the subtlety of the ambitious, wily, and astute Italian."

"Confound it! Is there anything real or true to you?"

"Wine, spirits, and cigars."

"You won't be serious. You jest about everything most vital; and you make solemnities of merest wisps of fancy. You would make drumsticks of your father's bones, and choose a wife by blowing a puff-ball!"

"While you would go without music for fear of disturbing your father, and choose a wife by the smell of a powder-puff."

"Oh, how can you do it?"

Brother Cyril shook his head

"I must explain myself more carefully," he said. "Let me ask you, in the first place, what is the most serious thing in the world."

"Religion."

"Exactly. Now, what is religion? The consummation of the soul by itself in divine ecstasy. What is life but love, and what is love but laughter? In other words, religion is a joke. There is the spirit of Dionysus and there is the spirit of Pan; but they are twin phases of laughter. Religion is a joke. Now what is the most absurd thing in the world?"

"Woman."

"Right again. And therefore she is the only serious island in this ocean of laughter. While we hunt and fish, and fight, and otherwise take our pleasure, she is toiling in the fields and cooking, and bearing children. So, all the serious words are jests, and all the jokes are earnest. This, oh my brother, is the key to my light and sparkling conversation."

"But – "

"I know what you are going to say. You can reverse it again. That is

precisely the idea. You keep on reversing it; and it gets funnier and more serious every time, and it spins faster and faster until you cannot follow it, and your brain begins to whirl, and presently you become That Spiral Force which is of the Quintessence of the Absolute. So it is all a simple and easy method of attaining the summit of perfections, the stone of the Wise, True Wisdom and Perfect Happiness."

"Listening to you," reflected Brother Onofrio, with a whisk of the rapier, "produces something of this effect!"

"Then praise the Father of All for making me, and let us go to break our fast!"

In the refectory a telegram awaited Cyril Grey. He read it carefully, destroyed it, and, looking with quaint spieglish eyes at Brother Onofrio, refrained ostentatiously from a prolonged fit of laughter. His face grew exceedingly grave, and he spoke with the weightiest deliberation. "I deeply regret to be obliged to inform you," he said at last, "that the exigencies of the situation combine to make it incumbent on me to proceed to instant action by asking you to pass the sugar."

With sullen grace Brother Onofrio complied. "What saith the Scripture?" asked Cyril, still more portentous. "*Ornithi gluku* – a little bit of sugar for the bird!

CHAPTER XVI

OF THE SPREADING OF THE BUTTERFLY-NET;

WITH A DELECTABLE DISCOURSE CONCERNING DIVERS ORDERS OF BEING; AND OF THE STATE OF THE LADY ILIEL, AND HER DESIRES, AND OF THE SECOND VISION THAT SHE HAD IN WAKING.

A GREAT peace brooded on the Villa. Daily sun gathered the strength; and the west wind told the flowers that a little bird had whispered to him that the spring was coming.

The results of the magical invocations began to peep through the veil of matter, like early crocuses. The atmosphere of house and garden was languid and romantic, so that a stranger could not have failed to feel it; yet with this was a timid yet vigorous purity, a concentration of the longing of the magicians.

The physical signs were equally unmistakable. By night a faint blue

luminosity radiated from the whole enclosure, visible to the natural eye; and to one seated in the garden, darting scintillations, star-sparkles, would appear, flitting from flower to flower, or tree to stone, if he kept as still and sensitive as one should in such a garden. And on the rightly tuned and tempered ear might fall, now and again, vague snatches of some far-off music. Then there were pallid perfumes in the air, like suggestions of things cool, and voluptuous, and chaste and delicate, and lazy, of those soft tropical loves which satisfy themselves with dreams.

All these phenomena were of a peculiar quality. It will be well to recite the fact, and to suggest an explanation.

These sights and sounds are conveyed clearly enough; but they disappear the moment the full attention is turned upon them. They will not bear inspection; and the fact has been used by shallow thinkers as an argument against their reality. It is a foolish point to take, as will now be proved.

The range of our senses is extremely limited. Our sensorial apparatus only works properly with reference to a very few of very many things. Every child knows how narrow is the spectrum, how confined the range of musical tone. He has not yet been drilled properly to an understanding of what this may mean, and he has not been told with equal emphasis many similar facts relating to other forms of perception. In particular, he has not learnt the meaning of diluted impression, in spite of an admirable story called *The New Accelerator* by Mr. H. G. Wells.

Our vision of things depends upon their speed; for instance, a four-bladed electric fan in motion appears as a diaphanous and shining film. Again, one may see the wheels of automobiles moving backwards in a cinematograph; and, at certain distances, the report of a cannon may be heard before the order to fire is given. Physics is packed with such paradoxes. Now we know of living beings whose time-world is quite different to ours, only touching it over a short common section. Thus, a fly lives in a world which moves so fast that he cannot perceive motion in anything with a speed of less than about a yard a second, so that a man may put his hand upon it if he can restrain the impulse to slap. To this fly, then, the whirling fan would look quite different; he would be able to distinguish the four blades.

We have thus direct evidence that there are "real" "material" beings whose senses are on a different range to ours.

We also have reason to believe that this total range is almost inconceivably great. It is not merely a question of the worlds of the microscope and the telescope; these are mere extensions of our gamut. But we now think that a

molecule of matter is a universe in most rapid whirl, a cosmos comparable to that of the heavens, its electrons as widely separated from each other, in proportion to their size, as the stars in space. Our universe, then, in its unmeasured vastness, is precisely similar in constitution to one molecule of hydrogen; and we may suppose that it is itself only a molecule of some larger body; also that what we call an electron may itself be a universe – and so on for ever. This suggestion is supported by the singular fact, that the proportion in size of electron to molecule is about the same as that of sun to cosmos, the ratio in each case being as 1 to 10,000,000,000,000,000,000,000.

Suppose a drop of water, ⅛ inch in diameter, to be magnified to the size of the earth, there would be about 30 molecules in every cubic foot of it, each molecule being about the size of a golf ball, or a little more.

However, the point involved is a simpler one, so far as our argument is concerned; it is this – that there is no question of "illusion" about any of these things. Electrons are quite as elusive as ghosts; we are only aware of them as the conclusion to a colossal sorites. The evidence for ghosts is as strong as that for any other phenomenon in nature; and the only argument, for a horse-laugh is not argument, which has been adduced against their existence is that you cannot catch them. But, just as one can catch the fly by accommodating oneself to the conditions of its world, one might (conceivably) catch the ghost by conforming with its conditions.

It is one magical hypothesis that all things are made up of ten different sorts of vibrations, each with a different gamut, and each corresponding to a "planet". Our own senses being built up similarly, they only register these when they are combined. Hence, a "lunar" being, purified of other elements, would be imperceptible. And if one, by emphasising the lunar quality in oneself, began to acquire the power of perceiving similar beings, one would begin by perceiving them as tenuous and elusive; just, in fact, as is observed to be the case.

We are therefore justified in regarding the phenomena of the magicians as in all respects "real", in the same sense as our own bodies; and all doubt on the subject is removed by consideration of the fact, to which all magicians testify, that these phenomena can be produced at will, by using proper means.

It is no criticism to reply that it should be possible to show them "in the laboratory", because laboratory conditions happen not to suit their production. One does not doubt the reality of electrical phenomena either, because electricity is not perceptible directly by any of the senses, or because

its ultimate nature is unknown, or because the electrician refuses to comply with your "test conditions" by his irrational and evidently felonious habit of insulating his wires.

So far as Iliel was concerned, the result of the operation was almost too evident. Simon Iff might have thought that things were being overdone. For she had become extremely fat; her skin was of a white and heavy pallor; her eyes were almost closed by their perpetual droop. Her habit of life had become infinitely sensuous and languid; when she rose from recumbency she lolled rather than walked; her lassitude was such that she hardly cared to feed herself; yet she managed to consume five or six times a normal diet. She seemed always half asleep. A cradle, shaped like a canoe had been arranged for her on the Terrace of the Moon; and most of her waking hours were spent there, drinking milk, and munching creams flavoured with angelica. Her soul seemed utterly attracted to the moon. She held out her body to it like an offering.

Just before the new moon of February, Abdul Bey, before leaving Naples, determined to seek a last sight of his adored Lisa. He had found her easily, and was amazed at the physical changes in her. They increased his passion beyond all measure, for she was now the very ideal of any Turkish lover. She appeared hardly conscious of his presence upon the wall beyond the little lane that wound below the Terrace of the Moon, but in reality she absorbed his devotion with a lazy hunger, like a sponge. For her activity and resistance had been reduced to zero; she reflected any impression, feeling it to the utmost, but incapable of response. He understood that she could not have repulsed him, yet could have taken no step towards him; and he cursed the vigilance of the patrol. Help he must have; and though it was agony to drag himself from Naples, he knew that without Douglas he could do nothing more.

From the new moon of February, the invocations of Artemis had become continuous. Brother Onofrio and his two henchmen devoted their time and energy to the rituals which banish all other ideas than the one desired; but the boys had joined Sister Clara and her maidens in an elaborate ceremony in which the four represented the four phases of the moon. This ceremony was performed thrice daily; but the intervals were fully occupied. During the whole of the twenty-five hours one or the other of the enchanters kept up their conjurations by spells, by music, and by dances. Every day witnessed some new phenomenon, ever more vivid and persistent, as the imminence

of the lunar world increased, and as the natures of the celebrants became more and more capable of appreciating those silvern vibrations.

Cyril Grey alone took no active part. He represented the solar force, the final energy creatrix of all subordinate orbs; his work had been done when he had set the system in motion. But since Brother Onofrio represented so active a force as Mars, he made himself a silent partner to the Italian, an elasticity to buffer the reactions of his vehemence. Thus he became a shadow to the warrior, giving him the graceful ease which was the due reward of fatigues so exhausting as were involved in the Keeping of the Circle. For the labour of banishing became daily more arduous; the preponderance of lunar force within the circle created a high potential. All the other forces of Nature wished to enter and redress the balance. It is the same effect as would be seen were one to plunge a globe full of water beneath the sea, and gradually withdraw the water from the globe. The strain upon the surface of the globe would constantly increase. It may be remarked in parenthesis that the Laws of Magick are always exactly like those of the other natural forces. All that Magick lacks to put it on a footing with hydrostatics or electricity is a method of quantitative estimation. The qualitative work is admirably accomplished.

The moon was waxen beyond her first phase; she set well after midnight. The nights were yet cold; but Iliel's cradle had been made like a nest in cloudland with fleece of camels – for they are sacred to the moon; and she was covered with a quilt of silver fox. Thus she could lie in the open without discomfort, and yearn toward her goddess as she moved majestically across heaven.

Now that the climax of the Experiment was upon her, the exaltation of wonder seized her wholly; she was in precisely the state necessary to the magical plan. She remained in a continuous reverie of longing and expectancy for the marvel which was to come to her.

It was now the night of the full moon. She rose over the crest of Posilippo soon after sunset, and Iliel greeted her from her cradle on the Terrace with a hushed song of adoration.

She was more languid than ever before, that night. It seemed to her as if her body were altogether too heavy for her; she had the feeling so well known to opium-smokers, which they call "*cloué à terre*". It is as if the body clung desperately to the earth, by its own weight, and yet in the same way as a tired child nestles to its mother's breast. In this sensation there is a perfect lassitude mingled with a perfect longing. It may be that it is

the counterpart of the freedom of the soul of which it is the herald and companion. In the Burial Service of the Church, we read "earth to earth, dust to dust", coupled with the idea of the return of the spirit to the God that gave it. And there is in this state some sister-similarity to death, one would not say sleep, for the soul of the sleeper is usually earth-bound by his gross desires, or the memory of them, or of his recent impressions. But the smoker of opium, and the saint, self-conscious of their nature celestial, heed earth no more, and on the pinions of imagination or of faith seek mountain-tops of being.

It was in this state or one akin to it that Iliel found herself. And gradually, as comes also to the smoker of opium, the process of bodily repose became complete; the earth was one with earth, and no longer troubled or trammelled her truer self.

She became acutely conscious that she was not the body that lay supine in the cradle, with the moon gleaming upon its bloodless countenance. No; she was rather the blue mist of the whole circle of enchantment, and her thoughts the sparkling dew-spirits that darted hither and thither like silvery fire-flies. And, as if they were parts of herself, she saw Sister Clara and her pages and her hand-maidens under the image of stars. For each was a radiant world of glory, thrilling with most divine activities, yet all in azure orbits curling celestially, their wake of light like comets' tails, wrapping her in a motion that was music.

A flaming boundary to her sphere, the fires of the circle blazed far into the night, forked swords of scarlet light in everlasting motion, snakes of visible force extended every way to keep the gates of her garden. She saw the forms of Brother Onofrio and his captains, of the same shape as those of Sister Clara and her companions, but blazing with a fierce and indomitable heat, throwing off coruscations into the surrounding blackness. She was reminded of a visit that yonder idle carcass in the cradle had once made to an observatory, where she had been shown the corona of the sun.

And then, instinctively, she looked for Cyril Grey. But all that she could find of him was the green-veiled glory that surrounded the sphere of Brother Onofrio; and she understood that this was a mere projection of part of his personality. Himself she could not find. He should have been the core of all, the axis on which all swung; but she could feel nothing. Her intuition told her, in a voice of cogency beyond contradiction, that he was not there.

She began to argue with herself, to affirm that she held a part of him by

right of gift; but, looking on it, she beheld only an impenetrable veil. She knew and understood that not yet was the Butterfly in the Net, and in that she acquiesced; but the absence of her lover himself from her, at this moment of all moments, was mystery of horror so chill that she doubted for a time of her own being. She thought of the moon as a dead soul – and wondered – and wondered – She would have striven to seek him out, to course the universe in his pursuit; but she was incapable of any effort. She sank again into the receptive phase, in which impressions came to her, like bees to a flower, without eliciting conscious response.

And it was then that her bodily eyes opened. The action drew her back into her body; but the material universe held her only for a second. She saw the moon, indeed, but in its centre was a shape of minute size, but infinite brightness. With the speed of a huntress the shape neared her, hid the moon from her, and she perceived the buskined Artemis, silver-sandalled, with her bright bow and her quiver of light. Leaping behind her came her hounds, and she thought that she could hear their eager baying.

Between heaven and earth stood the goddess, and looked about her, her eyes a-sparkle with keen joy. She unslung her baldric, and put her silver bugle to her lips.

Through all the vastness of heaven that call rang loud; and, in obedience, the stars rushed from their thrones, and made obeisance to their mistress. It was a gallant hunting-party. For she perceived that these were no longer stars, but souls. Had not Simon Iff once said to her: "Every man and every woman is a star"? And even as she understood that, she saw that Artemis regarded them with reverence, with awe even. This was no pleasure chase; he who won the victory was himself the quarry. Every soul was stamped with absolute heroism; it offered itself to itself, like Odin, when nine windy nights he hung in space, his own spear thrust into his side. What gain might be she could not understand; but it was clear enough that every act of incarnation is a crucifixion. She saw that she had been mistaken in thinking of these souls as hunters at all; and at that instant it seemed to her as though she herself were the huntress. For a flash she saw the fabled load-stone rock which draws ships to it, and, flashing forth their bolts by the might of its magnetism, loosens their timbers so that they are but waifs of flotsam. It was only a glimpse; for now the souls drew near her. She could distinguish their differences by the colour of the predominating rays. And as they approached, she saw that only those whose nature was lunar might

pass into the garden. The others started back, and it seemed to her that they trembled with surprise, as if it were a new thing to them to be repelled.

And now she was standing on the Terrace of the Moon with Artemis, watching the body of Lisa la Giuffria, that lay there in its cradle. And she saw that the body was a dead thing, as dead as the cradle itself; it was unreal; all "material" things were unreal, shells void of meaning, geometrical abstractions, as Simon Iff had explained to her on their first meeting. But this body was different to the other husks in one respect, that it was the focus of a most startling electrical phenomenon. (She could not think of it but as electrical.) An incandescent cone was scintillating before her. She could see but the tip of it, but she knew intuitively that the base of it was in the sun itself. About this cone played curious figures, dancers wreathed with vine leaves, having all sorts of images in their hands, like toys, houses, and dolls, and ships and fields, and woods, little soldiers in their uniforms, little lawyers in their wigs and gowns, an innumerable multitude of replicas of everyday things. And Iliel watched the souls as they came into the glow of the cone. They took human shape, and she was amazed to see among them the faces of many of the great men of the race.

There was one very curious feature about the space in which this vision took place: this, that innumerable beings could occupy it at once, yet each one remain distinct from all the rest as the attention happened to focus it. But it was no question of dissolving views; for each soul was present equally all the time.

With most of the faces there was little attachment, scarce more than a vague wreath of a mist that swirled purposelessly about them. Some, however, were more developed; and it seemed as if more or less definite shapes had been formulated by them as adjuncts to their original personalities. When it came to such men as Iliel remembered through history, there was already a symbolic or pictorial representation of the nature of the man, and of the trend of his life, about him. She could see the unhappy Maximilian, once Emperor of Mexico, a frail thing struggling in an environment far too intense for him. He was stifled in his own web, and seemed afraid either to stay where he was, or to attempt to approach the cone.

Less hampered, but almost equally the prey of hideous vacillation, lack of decision, was General Boulanger, whose white horse charged again and again through space toward the cone, only to be caught up each time by the quick nervous snatch at his rein.

Next him, a gracious girlish figure was the centre of sparkling waves of music, many-hued; but one could see that they were not issuing from her, but only through her. A man of short stature, with a pale face, stood before her, very similar in the character of his radiations; but they were colder, and duller, and less clear and energetic.

And now all gave way to a most enigmatic figure. It was an insignificant face and form; but the attributions of him filled all heaven. In his sphere was primarily a mist which Iliel instinctively recognised as malarious; and she got an impression, rather than a vision, of an immense muddy river rushing through swamps. And then she saw that from this man's brain issued phantoms like pigeons. They were neither Red Indians nor Israelites, yet they had something of each in their bearing. And these poured like smoke from the head of this little man. In his hand was a book, and he held it over his head. And the book itself was guarded by an angelic figure whose face was extraordinarily stern and unbeautiful, but who scattered with wide hands the wealth of life, children, and corn, and gold. And behind all these things was a great multitude; and about them were the symbolic forms of exile and death and every persecution, and the hideous laughter of triumphant enemies. All this seemed to weigh heavily upon the little man that had created it; Iliel thought that he was seeking incarnation for the sake of its forgetfulness. Yet the light in his eyes was so pure and noble and magnetic that it might have been that he saw in a new birth the chance to repair his error.

And now her attention was drawn to a yet nobler and still more fantastic formal. It was a kingly figure, and its eyes blazed bright with an enthusiasm that was tinged almost with madness. His creations, like those of the last seen, were something vague and unsubstantial. They lacked clear draughtsmanship. But they made up for this by their extravagance and brilliance. It was a gorgeous play of dream; yet Iliel could see that it was only dream. Last of this company came a woman proud, melancholy, and sweet. Her face was noble and intelligent; but there was a red line about her throat, and the eyes were suffused with horror, and about her heaved rolling mists of blood. And then the greater pageant spread its peacockry.

In this great group not only the men but all their spheres were clean-cut and radiant; for here was direct creation, no longer the derivative play of fancy upon existing themes. And first came one "with branded and ensanguined brow", a mighty figure, although suffering from a deformity of one foot, virile,

herculean, intense but with a fierce sadness upon him. He came with a rush and roar as of many waters, and about him were a great company of men and women, almost as real as he was himself. And the waves (which Iliel recognised as music) surged about him, a stormy sea; and there were lightnings, and thunders, and desolations!

Behind him came another not unlike him, but with less vehemence; and instead of music were soft rays of light, rosy and harmonious; and his arms were folded upon his heart and his head bowed. It was clear that he understood his act as a sacrament.

Then came a strange paradox of a man – utter violence and extreme gentleness. A man at war within himself! And in his ecstasy of rage he peopled space with thousands of bright and vigorous phantasms. They were more real than those of all the others; for he fed them constantly with his own blood. Stern savagery, and lofty genius, hideous cruelty and meanness inexplicable, beauty, and madness, and holiness, and loving-kindness; these followed him, crying aloud with the exultation and the passion of their fullness of life.

Close upon him came one who was all music, fierce, wild, mystical, and most melancholy. The waves of his music were like pines in the vast forest, and like the undulations of frozen steppes; but his own face was full of a calm glory touched with pity.

Behind him, frowning, came a hectic, ape-like dwarf. But in his train were many people of all climes, soft Indians, fierce Malays and Pathans and Sikhs, proud Normans, humble Saxons, and many a frail figure of woman. These were too self-assertive, Iliel thought, to be as real as those of the other man. And the figure himself was strained, even in his pride.

Now came a marvellous person – almost a god, she thought. For about him were a multitude of bones that built themselves up constantly into the loveliest living forms, that changed from one into another, ever increasing in stature and in glory. And in his broad brow she read the knowledge of the Unity of Things, and in these eyes the joy unspeakable which that knowledge gives. Yet they were insatiable as death itself; she could see that every ounce of the man's giant strength was strained toward some new attainment.

And now came another of the sons of music. But this man's waves were fiery flames like snakes contorted and terrible. It seemed to Iliel as if all heaven were torn asunder by those pangs. Wave strove with wave, and the battle was eaten up by fresh swords of fire that burst from him as he waved

onward those battalions to fresh wrath. These waves moreover were peopled with immense and tragic figures; Iliel thought that she could recognise Electra, and Salome, daughter of Herodias.

Next, amid a cloud of angels bearing silver trumpets, came one with great height of brow, and eyes of golden flashes. In him the whole heaven rocked with harmonious music, and faint shapes formed up among the waves, like Venus born of ocean foam. They had not substance, like so many Iliel had seen; they were too great, too godlike, to be human. Not one was there of whom it could not be said "Half a woman made with half a god". And these, enormous and tragic, fiery, with wings and sandals of pure light, encompassed him and wooed him.

Last of this company – only a few of the visions are recorded here – came the greatest of them all. His face was abrupt and vehement; but a veil was woven over it, because of the glory of his eyes, and a thick scarf, like a cloud, held over his mouth, lest the thunder of it destroy men's hearing. This man was so enormous that his stature spanned all heaven; and his creatures, that moved about him, were all godlike – immensely greater than the human. Yet were they human; but so patriarchal, so intense, that they almost overwhelmed Iliel.

On him she dared not look. He had the gift of making every thing a thousand times larger than its natural size. She heard one word of his, a mere call to a pet: "Tiger, tiger!" But the beast that broke through the mazes of heaven was so vast that its claws spanned star and star. And with all that he smiled, and a million babe-children blossomed before him like new-budded flowers. And this man quickened as he came nigh to Iliel; he seemed to understand wholly the nature of the Great Experiment.

But every soul in all that glorious cohort of immortals, as it touched the cone, was whirled away like a pellet thrown upon a swiftly moving fly-wheel. And presently she perceived the cause of this.

The tip of the cone was sheathed in silver. So white and glittering with fierce heat was that corselot, and so mighty its pulse of vibration that she had thought it part of the cone. She understood this to be the formula of the circle, and realised with a great ache, and then a sudden anger, that it was by this that she was to be prevented from what might have been her fortune, the gaining of the wardenship of a Chopin or of a Paul Verlaine.

But upon the face of Artemis was gaiety of triumph. The last of the souls whirled away into the darkness. Humanity had tried and failed; it was its

right to try; it was its fate to fail; now came the turn of the chosen spirits, proved worthy of the fitted fastness.

They came upon the Terrace in their legions, Valkyrie-brave in silver arms, or like priestesses in white vestments, their hair close bound upon their brows, or like queens of the woodland, swift for the chase, with loose locks and bright eyes, or like little children, timid and gracious.

But amid their ranks were the black hideous forms of hags, bent and wrinkled; and these fled instantly in fear at the vision of the blazing cone. There were many other animal shapes; but these, seeing the cone, turned away indifferent, as not understanding. Only the highest human-seeming forms remained; and these appeared as if in some perplexity. Constantly they looked from Artemis to the cone, and back again to Artemis. Iliel could feel their thought; it was a child-like bewilderment, "But don't you understand? This is a most dangerous place. Why did you bring us here? Surely you know that to touch the cone is certain death to us?"

Iliel understood. The human souls had long since made themselves perfect, true images of the cosmos, by accepting the formula of Love and Death; they had made the great sacrifice again and again; they were veterans of the spiritual world-war, and asked nothing better than to go back to the trenches. But these others were partial souls; they had not yet attained humanity; they had not understood that in order to grow one must assimilate oneself with another being, the death of two to create the life of one, in whom the two live once more, transmuted and glorified, the corruptible having put on incorruption. To them incarnation was death; and they did not know that death was life. They were not ready for the Great Adventure.

So they stood like tall lilies about the coruscating cone of Light, wondering, doubting, drooping. But at the last came one taller than all the rest, sadder of mien, and lovelier of features; her robes were stained and soiled, as if by contact with other colours. Artemis drew back with quick repulsion.

For the first time the maiden goddess spoke.

"What is thy name?" she cried.

"I am Malkah of the tribe of the Sickles."

"And thy crime?"

"I love a mortal."

Artemis drew back once more.

"Thou, too, hast loved," said Malkah. "I drew my mortal lovers unto me; I did not sully my life with theirs; I am virgin unto Pan!"

"I also am virgin; for whom I loved is dead. He was a poet, and he loved thee above women, 'And haply the Queen-Moon is on her throne clustered around by all her starry fays', whereof I being one, loved him that he loved Thee! But he died in the city of Mars and the Wolf, before I could make him even aware of me. I am come hither to seek immolation; I am weary of the pale beauty of Levanah; I will seek him, at the price of death. I deny our life; I crucify myself unto the God we dare not name. I go. Hail and farewell!"

She flung up her arm in a wild gesture of renunciation, and came closer to the Cone. She would not haste, lest her will prove but impulse; she poised her breast deliberately over the Cone. Then, with fierce zest, so that the one blow might end all, she thrust herself vehemently down upon the blazing spike.

At that moment Iliel swooned. She felt that something had happened to her, something tremendous; and her brain turned crazily in her. But as she lost consciousness she was still aware of the last phase of the vision: that the sacrifice of Malkah had created a void in the ranks of the Amazon armies of the Moon; and she saw them and their mist of blue, licked up in the swirl of the vortex. The whole of the invoked forces were sucked up into her as Malkah in her death-agony took possession of that basis of materialization. Heroic – and presumptuous; for of all the qualities that go to make humanity she had but one, and she would have to shift, for the rest, with orts of inheritance. Among mankind she would be a stranger, a being without conscious race-experience, liable to every error that a partial view of life can make. Ill indeed for such a one who is without the wardenship of high initiates! It was for Cyril Grey to keep her unspotted from the world, to utilise those powers which she wielded in pre-eminence from her inheritance in the white sphere of Levanah!

When Sister Clara came to summon Iliel, she found her still in swoon. They carried her to her room. At noon she recovered consciousness.

Cyril Grey was seated by her bed. To her surprise, he was dressed in mundane attire, an elegant lounge suit of lavender.

"Have you seen the papers?" he cried gaily. "Neapolitan Entomologists capture rare butterfly, genus Schedbarshamoth Scharthathan, species Malkah be-Tharshishim ve-Ruachoth ha-Sche-halim!"

"Don't talk nonsense, Cyril!" she said, lazily, a little uncertain whether this unexpected apparition were not a dream.

"Perfect sense, I assure you, my child. The trick is turned. We have caught our Butterfly!"

"Yes, yes," she murmured; "but how did you know?"

"Why, use your eyes!" he cried. "Use your br – I should say your sensory organs! Look!"

He waved at the window, and Iliel idly followed with her eyes.

There could be no mistake. The garden was normal. Every vestige of magical force had disappeared.

"Couldn't have gone better," he said. "We don't know where we're going, but we know we're on the way. And, whatever we've got, we've got it."

Suddenly her mind ran back to her vision. "Where were you last night, Cyril?"

He looked at her for a moment before replying.

"I was where I always am," he said slowly.

"I looked for you all over the house and the garden." "Ah! you should have sought me in the House of my Father."

"Your father?"

"Colonel Sir Grant Ponsonby Grey, K.C.M.G., K.C.S.I., G.C.I.E. Born in 1846 at the Round Tower, Co. Cork; educ. Winchester and Balliol; Lieutenant Royal Artillery 1868; Indian Political Department 1873; in 1880 m. Adelaide, only d. of the late Rt. Hon. Lord Ashley Lovell, P.C.; one s., Cyril St. John, q.v. Residence, The Round Tower, Co. Cork; Bartland Barrows, Wilts.; 93, Arlington Street. W. Clubs. Carlton, Athenaeum, Travellers', Hemlock, etc. Amusements: Hunting, talking shop."

"You dear incorrigible boy!"

He took her hand and kissed it.

"And am I to see something of you now?"

"Oh, we're all penny plain humans from now on. It's merely a question of defending you from the malice of Douglas and Co.; a much simpler job than blocking out nine-tenths of the Universe! Apart from that, we are just a jolly set of friends; only I see less of you than anyone else does, naturally."

"Naturally!"

"Yes, naturally. You have to be saved from all worry and annoyance; and if there's one thing in the world more annoying and worrying than a wife, it's a husband! With the others, you have nothing to quarrel about; and if you try it on Brother Onofrio, in particular, he simply sets in motion a deadly and hostile current of will by which you would fall slain or paralyzed, as if blasted by the lightning flash! Click!"

Iliel laughed; and then Sister Clara appeared with the rest of the garrison, the boys and maidens burdened with the means of breakfast; for this was a day of festival and triumph.

But, as he shook hands with her, Iliel discovered, with a shock, that she hated Brother Onofrio.

CHAPTER XVII

OF THE REPORT WHICH EDWIN ARTHWAIT MADE TO HIS CHIEF,

AND OF THE DELIBERATIONS OF THE BLACK LODGE THEREUPON; AND OF THE CONSPIRACIES THERE-BY CONCERTED; WITH A DISCOURSE UPON SORCERY

"EXORDIUMATICALLY, deponent precateth otity orient exaudient, dole basilical's assumpt. Pragmatics, ex Ventro Genesiaco ad umbilicum Apocalypticum, determinated logomachoepy's nodal puncts, genethliacally benedict, eschatologically --- kakoglaphyrotopical! Ergmoiraetic, apert parthenorhodo-dactylical, colophoned thanatoskianko-morphic!"

Footnote Translation:

"Exordiumatically – First genethliaeally – at first

deponent precateth – I beg

benedict – fortunate

otity – hearing

esehatologically – later

orient – increasingly

kakoglaphyrotopical – in a bad hole

exaudient – favourable

erg – work

dole basilical's – a royal gift*

smoiractic – fatal

assumpt – assumption

apert – opened

Pregmatics – Facts

parthenorhododactylical – like the ex ventro Genesiaco ad

    umbilicum rosy fingers of a maid

Apocalypticum – from beginning

colophoned – closed to end

tbanatoskiankomorphic – in the determinate

mark shape of the valley of the shadow logomachoepy's –

    (my) story's of death

nodal puncts – limits

With these striking words the official Report of Douglas' chief commissioner began. It would be tedious to quote the 488 folio pages in full. Douglas himself did not read it; the transcript made by Vesquit of Abdul Bey's "inspiration", with a few practical questions to the latter, told him all that he needed.

Audience over, he dismissed Arthwait and his companion with orders to hold themselves in readiness for a renewal of the campaign. Douglas had many a moment of bitter contemplation; his hatred of Cyril Grey fed upon repulse; and it was evident that his assistants had met more than their match. He would have to act personally – yet he feared to expose himself in open battle. His plan hitherto had been to bribe or dupe some of the jackal journalists of London to attack him; but Grey had not so much as troubled to bring libel actions.

But he would not give in. He studied Vesquit's transcripts attentively, and with indecision. He did not know how far to trust the oracle, and he did not

understand how Vesquit had come to die, since on that point even Arthwait had been silent. The demons whom he consulted were emphatic in favour of the document, but failed to explain how the fortress was to be reduced from the inside.

He was clear in his mind as to the nature of Grey's operation; he saw perfectly that Lisa herself was the weak point in it; but he did not see how to get at her.

He continued in his bitter mood until the early hours, and he was interrupted by the return of his wife from her miserable night's trudging. She put two francs on the table without a single word as soon as she entered.

"Is that all?" snarled Douglas. "You ought to be getting fives again now spring's coming. Though you're not as pretty as you were."

He garnished this greeting with garlic of low abuse. Rarely to any other person did he use even mild oaths; he affected the grand manner; but he knew that foulness of speech emphasised his wife's degradation. He had no need of the vile money that she earned; he had a thousand better means of buying whisky; but he drove her to the streets as no professional *souteneur* would have dared do. By extreme refinement of cruelty he never struck or kicked her, lest she should think he loved her. To him, she was a toy; a means of exercising his passion for torture; to her, he was the man she loved.

Pitifully she pleaded that the cold rain of the night – she was wet through – had driven all Paris from the boulevard to the cafe; and she added an excuse for her unattractiveness which should have sent her husband to his pistol for very shame had a spark of manhood, or a memory of his mother, been alive within him.

Instead, he promised to change all that the next time Dr. Balloch came to Paris.

He had systematically degraded and humiliated her, corrupted her, branded her with infamy, for many a year; yet there was still in her a motion of revolt against the crime. But even as she made her gesture of repulsion, Douglas leapt to his feet, with the light of hell burning in his eyes. "I have it!" he shouted, "get to your straw, you stinking slut. And you may thank your stars that as you can't be ornamental, you're going to be useful."

It was dawn before Douglas turned into bed, for his great idea brought with it a flood of imagination, and a million problems of detail. The servant

girl was already half dressed for the day's work; and he made her fetch him a final whisky before he slept.

Late in the following afternoon he woke, and sent Cremers, whom he had turned into a drudge, to telegraph to Balloch to come over, and to bring her friend Butcher to see him.

Douglas had previously refused to see this man, who was a Chicago semi-tough. He ran a fake Rosicrucian society in America, and thought that Douglas could give him power over the elusive dollar. But Douglas had found no use for him; he rather insisted on respectability in his neophytes; it was only in the higher grades that one found the disreputable. It was an obvious point of policy. But Douglas had now remembered one little fact about this person; he fitted the Great Idea so nicely that his presence in Paris seemed as apt as an answer to prayer.

It was a rare, if doubtful, privilege to visit Douglas in his home. He never allowed the visit of any but those high in his confidence; the locality was hardly inspiring to an inquiring duchess. He had two other places in Paris, which he used for two types of interviewer; for although he discouraged knowledge of his authority in the Black Lodge, he did a good deal of the fishing himself, especially with rich or highly-placed people. For his subordinates had sticky fingers.

One of these places was a discreet apartment in the very best quarter of Paris. Here he was the Scottish Nobleman of the Old School. The decorations were rich but not gaudy; even the ancestors were not overdone. The place of honour was occupied by Rob Roy's claymore, alleged. One of his claims was that the Highland Cateran was his ancestor, owing to a liaison with a fairy. Another claim was that he himself was James IV of Scotland, that he had survived the Battle of Flodden Field, become an adept, and immortal. Despite what to a profane mind might seem the incompatibility of these two legends – to say nothing of the improbability of either – they were greedily swallowed by the Theosophist section of his following.

In this apartment he received the credulous type of person who is impressed by rank; and no man could play the part of stateliness better than this old reprobate.

His other place was of the hermit's cell model, a tiny cottage with its well-kept garden; such abound all over Paris in the most unexpected spots.

He actually imposed upon the old lady who kept this house for him. Here he was the simple old man of utter holiness, the lonely recluse, the saintly

anchorite, his only food bruised herbs or pulse, his only drink the same as quenched the thirst of Father Adam. His long absences from this sacrosanct abode were explained by the fact of his absorption in trance, in which he was supposed to indulge underground. Of course he only visited the place when he had to receive a certain type of visitor, that loftier type which has enough rank and wealth to know that they are not necessary to a search after Truth, and is impressed by simplicity and saintliness.

It was at the former address that the Count received Mr. Butcher. He was dressed in severe and refined broadcloth, with the rosette of the Legion of Honour – to which he was well entitled – in his buttonhole.

In presence of this splendour the American was ill at ease; but Douglas knew how to make a man his own by giving him a good conceit of himself.

"I am proud to meet you, Mr. Butcher," he began, affably. "May I beg of you to take the trouble to be seated! The chair is worthy of you," he added, with a smile; "it was at one time the property of Frederick the Great."

The servant, who was dressed as a Highland Gillie in gala costume, offered cigars and whisky.

"Say, this is sure some whisky, Count! This is where I fall off the wagon, one time, John. You watch my batting average!" observed Mr. Butcher, settling himself by placing his legs upon the table.

"It is from the private stock of the Duke of Argyll," returned Douglas. "And you, Mr. Butcher? I knew a Count Butcher many years ago. You are a relation?"

Mr. Butcher had only the vaguest notion as to his ancestry. His mother had broken down under cross-examination.

"Search me!" he replied, biting the end off his cigar, and spitting it out. "We Rosicrucians are out for the Hundred Years Club Dope, and the Long Green Stone; we should worry. We're short on ancestors in Illinois."

"But these matters are important in magic," urged Douglas. "Heredity goes for much. I should be glad indeed to hear that you were one of the Dorsetshire Butchers, for example, or even the Shropshire branch. In both families second sight is an appanage."

Here the conversation was interrupted by the gillie. "I crave your pardon, my lord," he said, bowing; "but his Grace the Duke of Hants is at the door to beg your aid in a most urgent matter which concerns his family honour."

"I am engaged," said Douglas. "He may write." The man withdrew with a solemn bow.

"I must apologise for this disturbance," continued Douglas. "The importunity of one's clients is exceedingly distressing. It is one of our penalties. I venture to suppose that you are yourself much annoyed in similar ways."

Butcher would have liked to boast that J. P. Morgan was always trying to borrow money from him, but he dared not attempt to bluff his host. Nor did he suspect that Douglas was himself engaged in that diverting and profitable pastime.

"To come to business," went on Douglas, eyeing his guest narrowly, and assuring himself that his scheme had borne fruit in due season, "What is it that you require of me? Frankly, I like you; and I have long admired your noble career. All that I can do for you – in – honour – pray count it done!"

"Why, Count," said Mr. Butcher, spitting on the floor; "Buttinsky's in Kalamazoo. But to come down to brass tacks, I guess I'd like to sit into the game."

"I pray you to excuse me," replied Douglas, "but my long residence in Paris has almost deprived me of the comprehension of my mother tongue. Could you explain yourself further?"

"Why, this Black Lodge stunt, Count. It's a humdinger. I guess it's a hell of a favour, but I see a dollar at the end of it, and old Doc. Butcher buys a one-way ticket."

Douglas grew portentous. "Are you aware of what you ask?" he thundered. "Do you understand that the ineffable and Sacrosanct Arcanum is not to be touched by profane hands? Must I inform you that Those who may not be named are even now at the Gate of the Abyss, whetting their fangs upon the Cubical Stone of the Unutterable? Oh ye magistral ministrants of the Shrine of the Unspeakable Abomination! Hear ye the Word of Blasphemy!" He spoke rapidly and thickly in a tongue unknown to Butcher, who became alarmed, and even took his legs off the table.

"Say!" he cried. "Have a heart! Can the rough dope, Count! This is a straight proposition, honest to God!"

"I am already aware of your sincerity," answered the other. "But infinite courage is required to confront those formidable Entities that lie in wait for the seeker even at the first Portal of the Descending Staircase!"

"Oh, I'm wise to Old Dog Cerberus. Ish Kabibble. Gimme an upper berth in the Chicawgo, Saint Lewis, and Hell Limited, if it busts the roll. Do you get me, Steve?"

"I understand you to say that you persist in your application."

"Sure. Andrew P. Satan for mine."

"I shall be pleased to place your name before the Watchers of the Gate."

"How deep do I have to dig?"

"Dig? I did not quite catch your remark."

"In the wad. Weigh the dough! What does it set me back? Me for the bread-line?"

"The initiation fee is one thousand francs."

"I guess I can skin that off without having to eat at Childs."

"You will remit the amount to the Comptroller of my Privy Purse. Here is the address. Now be so good as to sign the preliminary application-form."

They went over to the bureau (Douglas was prepared to derive it from the library of Louis XIV), on which lay a private letter from the Kaiser, if one might believe the embossed arms and address, and a note asking President Poincaré to dinner, "quite informally, my dear friend", which Butcher could not fail to see. The preliminary application form was a document which might have served for an exceptionally solemn treaty. But Douglas was above the charlatanism of requiring a signature in blood: Butcher signed it with an ordinary fountain pen.

"And now, Mr. Butcher," said Douglas, "I will ask you in your turn to render me a small service."

"Bat it up!" said Mr. Butcher. "I would buy an Illustrated Edition of O. Henry in nineteen parts."

Douglas did not know that Americans dread book agents more than rattlesnakes; but he gathered that his guest would acquiesce in any reasonable suggestion.

"I am informed that you are – or were – a Priest of the Roman Church."

"Peter is my middle name," admitted the "Rosicrucian", "and that's no jolly."

"But – apart from questions of nomenclature for the moment, if you will pardon me – you are a priest of the Roman Church?"

"Yep: I took a chance on Pop Dago Benedict. But it's a con game; I'm from Missouri. Four-flushing gold brick merchants! Believe me, some bull! I took it like playing three days in Bumville. Them boobs got my goat for fair, babe. No pipe!"

"You were interdicted in consequence of some scandal?"

"I ran a sporting house on the side, and I guess they endorsed my license for speeding."

"Your Bishop took umbrage at some business activity which he judged incompatible with your vows?"

"Like Kelly did."

"Oh, Bishop Kelly. Far too severe a disciplinarian, in my judgment. But you are still a priest? Your orders are still valid? A baptism or a marriage performed by you would hold good?"

"It's a cinch. The Hallelujah Guarantee and Trust Company, St. Paul. Offices in the James D. Athanasius Building."

"Then, sir, I shall ask of you the favour to hold yourself in readiness to baptise two persons at nine of the evening precisely, the day after tomorrow. That ceremony will be followed by another, in which you will marry them."

"I swan."

"I may rely on your good offices?"

"I'll come in a wheelbarrow."

"Suit yourself, Mr. Butcher, as to the mode of transit; but pray be careful to attend punctually, and in canonical costume."

"I'll dig the biretta out of the ice-box."

After a further exchange of courtesies the new disciple took his leave.

The same evening witnessed a very different interview.

Lord Antony Bowling was being entertained at dinner by Simon Iff, and their conversation turned upon the favourite subject of the old mystic – the Way of the Tao.

"In view of what you have been saying about the necessity of dealing with mediums on their own ground," remarked the host, "let me tell you of a paradox in magick. Do you remember a certain chapter in the Bible which tells one, almost in consecutive verses, firstly to answer a fool according to his folly, and secondly, not so to answer him? This is the Scriptural version of a truth which we phrase otherwise. There are two ways of dealing with an opponent; one by beating him on his own ground, the other by withdrawing to a higher plane. You can fight fire with fire, or you can fight fire with water.

"It is, roughly speaking, legitimate magick to resolve a difficult situation in either of these two ways. Alter it, or withdraw to higher ground. The black magician, or as I prefer to call him, sorcerer, for the word magick should not be profaned, invariably withdraws to lower planes. Let us seek an analogy in the perfectly concrete case of the bank cashier.

"This gentleman, we will assume, finds his salary inadequate to his

outgoings. Now he may economise, that is, withdraw himself to a kind of life where money is no longer needed in such quantity, or he may devote himself day and night to his business, and so increase his salary. But there is no third course open to a man of self-respect. The sorcerer type of man appeals to lower planes of money-making. He begins by gambling; beaten there, he resorts to the still viler means of embezzlement; perhaps, finally, he attempts to cover his thefts by murdering his mother for the insurance money.

"Notice how, as his plane becomes debased, his fears grow greater. At first, he is merely annoyed about his creditors; in the next stage, he fears being sharped by his fellow-gamblers; then, it is the police who loom terrible in his mind; and lastly the grim form of the executioner threatens him."

"Very nicely Hogarthed," said Lord Antony. "Reminds me of how the habit of lying degenerates into unintelligible stupidity. We had a case in the War Office last month, a matter of supplying certain furs. As you know, the seal furnishes a valuable fur. Less valuable, though superficially similar, is that of the rabbit. Now in trade, so it appears, it is impolitic to say rabbit, which sounds cheap and nasty, so the Scriptural equivalent, coney, is employed, thus combining Piety with Profit. Having caught your coney, you proceed to cook him, until he resembles seal. So you have a dyed rabbit-skin, and you call it seal coney. But there are by-ways that stray further yet from the narrow lane of truth. The increasing demand for rabbits has reduced the profit on seal coney, and it becomes desirable to find a cheaper substitute. Reckless of the susceptibilities of the ancient Egyptians, this is found in that domesticated representative of the lion family which consoles our spinsters. Having disguised the skin as far as may be, they next disguise the name; some buyer must be made to pay the price of seal coney, and think that he is getting it; so 'cat' becomes 'trade seal coney' – and unless one has the whole story there is no possibility of derivation. The lie has become mere misnomer."

"It is the general case of Anglo-Saxon hypocrisy," returned Simon Iff. "I had an amusing example the other day in an article that I wrote for the *Review* – rather prudish people. My little essay ended: 'So Science offers her virgin head to the caress of Magick.' The editor thought 'virgin' rather a 'suggestive' word, and replaced it by 'maiden.'"

"You remind me of a curate we had over at Grimthorpe Ambrose. 'Leg' has for many years been a not quite proper word; when the terrible necessity of referring to it arose, the polite ass replaced it by 'limb'.

"The refined sensibility of our curate perceived the indelicacy of saying 'limb', since every one knew that it meant 'leg'; so he wrapped it up in the decent obscurity of the Latin language, and declined to play croquet one afternoon on the ground that, the day before, in visiting old Mrs. Postlethwaite, he had severely strained his member."

"The wicked fall into the pit that they have digged," said Iff. "All this applies to the question of magick. It is a question of debasing coinage. I have great sympathy with the ascetics of India and their monkish imitators in Europe. They held spiritual gifts to be of supreme value, and devoted their lower powers to the development of the higher. Of course mistakes were made; the principle was carried too far; they were silly enough to injure their lower powers by undue fasting, flagellation, and even mutilation. They got the false idea that the body was an enemy, whereas it is a servant – the only servant available. But the idea was right; they wanted to exchange dross for gold. Now the sorcerer offers his gold for dross, tries to exchange his highest powers for money or the gratification of envy or revenge. The Christian Scientist, absurdly so-called, is a sorcerer of the basest type, for he devotes the whole wealth of religion to the securing of his bodily health. It is somewhat stupid, too, as his main claim is that the body is only an illusion!"

"Am I right in suggesting that ordinary life is a mean between these extremes, that the noble man devotes his material wealth to lofty ends, the advancement of science, or art, or some such true ideal; and that the base man does the opposite by concentrating all his abilities on the amassing of wealth?"

"Exactly; that is the real distinction between the artist and the bourgeois, or, if you prefer it, between the gentleman and the cad. Money, and the things money can buy, have no value, for there is no question of creation, but only of exchange. Houses, lands, gold, jewels, even existing works of art, may be tossed about from one hand to another; they are so, constantly. But neither you nor I can write a sonnet; and what we have, our appreciation of art, we did not buy. We inherited the germ of it, and we developed it by the sweat of our brows. The possession of money helped us, but only by giving us time and opportunity and the means of travel. Anyhow, the principle is clear; one must sacrifice the lower to the higher, and, as the Greeks did with their oxen, one must fatten and bedeck the lower, so that it may be the worthier offering."

"And what happens when you go on the other tack?"

"When you trade your gold for pewter you impoverish yourself. The sorcerer sells his soul for money; spends the money, and finds he has nothing else to sell. Have you noticed that Christian Scientists are hardly ever in robust health? They have given up their spiritual forces for a quite imaginary standard of well-being; and those forces, which were supporting the body quite well enough without their stupid interference, are debilitated and frittered away. I pray daily for a great war, that may root out the coward fear of death and poverty in the minds of these degenerate wretches. Death should be, as it used to be in the middle ages, even, and yet more in pagan times, the fit reward and climax of a life well spent in risking it for noble causes; and poverty should be a holy and blessed state, worthy of the highest minds and the happiest, and of them alone.

"To return to our sheep – I mean our sorcerer. He has not much against him to begin with, but he chooses to trade his sword for gold. The barbarian, having the sword, naturally uses it to recover the gold. In other words, the devil, having bought the soul, regains the price, for the sorcerer spends it in the devil's service. The next stage is that the sorcerer resorts to crime, declares war on all humanity. He uses vulgar means to attain his ends, and the price may be his liberty. Ultimately, he may lose life itself in some last desperate effort to retrieve all at a blow. When I was young and had less experience, I had many a fight with sorcerers; and it was always the end of the fight when Mr. Sorcerer broke the law. He was no longer fighting me, but the consolidated will of humanity; and he had no time to attack me when he was busy building breakwaters.

"And that reminds me. We have a young friend at bay – with the worst pack of devils in the world at him. I wonder if I have done wrong to leave him so much to himself. But I wanted the boy to gain all the laurels; he's young enough to like them."

"I think I know who you mean," said Lord Antony, smiling; "and I don't think you need be very much afraid. I never saw any one much better fitted to take care of himself."

"For all that, he's in urgent danger at this very moment. He has incurred the greatest possible risk; he has gained a victory. But it has been only a clash of outposts; the enemy is coming up now, horse, foot, and artillery, with lust of revenge and desperate fear to enflame the original hatred; and, unfortunately, the boy made some fundamental errors in his plan of campaign."

"Ah, well, Napoleon did that. Jena was the result of his own blundering miscalculations; so, to a certain extent, was Austerlitz. Don't fret! The bigger they are, the harder they fall, as my father's pet pugilist used to say. And now I must run away; there is a seance with a lady who materialises demon slugs. Do not forget to inscribe my name among the martyrs!"

CHAPTER XVIII

THE DARK SIDE OF THE MOON

THE spring gathered her garments together, then flung them wide over the Bay of Naples. Hers is the greatest force in Nature, because her clarion sounds the summons of creation. It is she that is the Vicegerent of the All-Father, and of His spirit hath He dowered her with a triple essence.

In southern lands, even before the Equinox opens its gates before her conquering armies, one feels her imminent. Her light-armed troops swarm over the breached ramparts of the winter, and their cry is echoed in the dungeons of the soul by those whom she has come to save.

Yet in her hands is nothing but a sword. It is a disturbance of the equilibrium to which the dying year has attained after its long joy and agony; and so to the soul which is at ease she comes with alarum and tocsin. A soul like Iliel's, naturally apt to receive every impulse, to multiply it, and to transform it into action, is peculiarly sensitive, without knowing it, to cosmic forces so akin to its own inborn turbulence.

In her idlest moods, Lisa la Giuffria would have started for China at the least provocation, provided that she could start within the hour.

She could take a lover, or throw one away, a dozen times in a year, and

would have been indignant and amazed if any one had called her fickle. She was not insincere; but she believed with her whole soul that her immediate impulse was the true Will of her whole Self. One night at the Savoy Hotel with Lavinia King, just before Christmas, the talk had turned on the distress then prevailing in London. Instantly she had dragged the whole party downstairs, provided it with the entire supply of silver money that the hotel happened to have on hand, and rushed it to the Embankment to rescue the unemployed. That night she was a super-Shaftsbury; she formulated a dozen plans to solve the problem of poverty, root, branch, and leaf; and the next morning her dressmaker found her amid a sheaf of calculations.

But a new style of costume being displayed, she had plunged with equal ardour into a cosmopolitan scheme of dress reform.

To such an one a thwarted impulse involves almost a wreckage of the soul. Iliel began openly to chafe at the restrictions to which her own act had bound her. She had never been a mother, and the mere physical disabilities of her condition were all the more irritating because they were so unfamiliar.

The excitement of the Butterfly-chase had kept her toe to the mark, and the strange circumstances with which she was surrounded had aided to make it easy for her. It flattered her vanity that she was the keystone of so great an arch, destined to span earth and heaven. Her new conditions, the relaxation of the tension, threw down her exaltation. The experiment was over; well, then, it ought to be over – and she had months of boredom before her which must be endured with no stimulus but that of normal human duty. She was one of those people who will make any sacrifice at the moment, beggar themselves to help a friend, but who are quite incapable of drawing a weekly cheque for a trifling sum for no matter how important a purpose

In this March and April she was one mass of thwarted impulse. The mere necessity, demanded by safety, of remaining within the circle, was abhorrent to her. But, though she did not know it, she was held in subjection by the wills of her guardians.

In Astrology, the moon, among its other meanings, has that of "the common people", who submit (they know not why) to any independent will that can express itself with sufficient energy. The people who guillotined the mild Louis XVI died gladly for Napoleon. The impossibility of an actual democracy is due to this fact of mob-psychology. As soon as you group men, they lose their personalities. A parliament of the wisest and strongest men in the nation is liable to behave like a set of schoolboys, tearing up their

desks and throwing their inkpots at each other. The only possibility of co-operation lies in discipline and autocracy, which men have sometimes established in the name of equal rights.

Now Iliel was at present a microcosm of the Moon, and her resentments were either changed into enthusiasms by a timely word from Sister Clara or one of the others, or else ignored. The public is a long-suffering dumb beast, an ass crouching beneath heavy burdens, and it needs not only unendurable ill-treatment, but leadership, before it will revolt. All Iliel's impulses were purposeless, negative things, ideas rather of escape than of any definite programme. She wanted to jump out of the frying-pan, neither fearing the fire nor having any clear idea of how to act when she got there. She lacked so much as a day-dream of any alternative Future; hers was the restless wretchedness of a morphineuse deprived of the drug.

She was, as it were, the place where four winds met; and such a place is dangerous for a ship that is without internal means of propulsion. She sagged, a dismasted derelict, in tow of Cyril Grey; and the rope of love which held her to him strained her creaking timbers.

The first evidence of these very indefinite feelings was shown by her unreasonableness. Under the rigid discipline of the ceremonies, she had been too well schooled, too absorbed, too directly under the influence of the forces invoked, to feel or express constraint; the mere human hygiene of her present position served only to make her more discontented. A similar phenomenon has been observed also with democracies; they are happiest when most thoroughly cowed and bullied.

Once or twice she treated Cyril to an outburst of temper; but he was very young, so he was tactless enough to refuse to be angry, and made every allowance for her. Such treatment insults women like Lisa; their rage smoulders in them. A blow and a caress would have tripled her passion for him. "What is the use of being a Chinese god," she might have asked, "if you do not gratify your worshippers by inflicting Chinese tortures?"

But the principal manifestation of her moral instability was in her whims. These were in some degree, no doubt, due to her physical condition; but the mental stress exaggerated them to an abnormal height, like a glacier cramped between two mountain chains. It is necessary, in this world, to be made of harder stuff than one's environment. But Iliel had no ambition to any action; she was reflex; simple reaction to impression was what she thought her will. And so she inflicted phantasies upon the patient fold about her;

one day she was all for dressing herself strangely; another day she would insist upon a masque or a charade; but she took no true pleasure in any of these things. Cyril Grey was assiduous in meeting her desires; there were but two prohibitions left of all the elaborate restrictions of the second stage of the experiment; she might not be unduly intimate with him, and she might not in any way communicate with the outside world. In other words, the citadel and the ramparts must be kept intact; between these was a wide range for whim. Yet she was not content; it was just those two forbidden things that haunted her. (The serpent is a later invention in the story of the Fall!) Her unconscious wish to violate these rules led to a dislike for those who personified their rigidity; namely Cyril Grey and Brother Onofrio. And her febrile mind began to join these separate objects in a common detestation.

This shewed itself in a quite insane jealousy of their perfectly natural and necessary intimacy. Sometimes, as they sat sunning themselves upon the wall of one of the terraces she would come flaming down the garden with some foolish tale, and Brother Onofrio at least could not wholly hide his annoyance. He was naturally anxious to make all he could out of the presence of the more advanced adept; and his inborn ecclesiastical contempt for women showed through the tissue of his good manners. Cyril's most admirable patience tried her even more sorely. "Are you my lover or my grandfather?" she screamed at him one night, when he had been more than usually tactful.

Had the matter rested there, it had been ill enough with her. But the mind of man is a strange instrument. "Satan finds some mischief still for idle hands to do" is a rattling good piece of psychology. Iliel had nothing to occupy her mind, because she had never trained herself to concentrate the current of her thoughts on one thing, and off all others. A passion for crochet-work has saved many a woman from the streets or the river. And as on marshes methane forms, and Will o' th' Wisp lures peasants to their oozy doom, so in the idle mind monsters are bred. She began to suffer from a real insanity of the type of persecution-mania. She began to imagine that Cyril and Brother Onofrio were engaged in some mysterious plot against her. It was lucky that every one in the house possessed medical knowledge and training, with specialisation in psychology, so that they knew precisely how to treat her.

Yet in the long run that very knowledge became a danger. The extraordinary powers of mind – in certain limited directions – which insanity

often temporarily confers, enabled her to see that she was regarded as in a critical mental state. She accepted the situation as a battle, instead of co-operating in frank friendship, and began to manoeuvre to outwit her guardians. Those who have any experience of madness, or its congeners, drug-neuroses, know how infernally easy was her task. Many's the woman who, with her pocket handkerchief to her face, and the tears pouring from her eyes, has confessed all to the specialist, and begged him to break her of the whisky habit, the while she absorbed a pint or so of the said whisky under cover of the said pocket handkerchief.

Iliel simply noted the states of mind which they thought favourable, and simulated them. Peaceful absorption in nature, particularly in the moon when she was shining, pleased them; and she cultivated these states, knowing that the others never disturbed her at such times; and, thus secured, she gave herself over to the most hideous thoughts.

They were in fact the thoughts of madness. It is a strange fact that the most harmless states of mind, the most correct trains of idea, may accompany a dangerous lunacy. The difference is that the madman makes a secret of his fancies. Lord Dunsany's stories are the perfect prose jewels of a master cutter and polisher, lit by the rays of an imagination that is the godlike son of the Father of All Truth and Light; but if he kept them to himself, they would be the symptoms of an incurable lesion of the brain. A madman will conceal the Terrible Secret that "today is Wednesday", perhaps "because the devil told him to do so". "I am He who is Truth" was the boast of a great mystic, Mansur, and they stoned him for it, as they stone all men who speak truth; but had he said "Hush! I am God!" he would have been merely a maniac.

So Iliel acquired the habit of spending a great part of the day in her cradle, and there indulging her mind in every possible morbidity. The very fact that she could not go on to action served to make the matter worse. It is a terrible error to let any natural impulse, physical or mental, stagnate. Crush it out, if you will, and be done with it; or fulfil it, and get it out of the system; but do not allow it to remain there and putrefy. The suppression of the normal sex instinct, for example, is responsible for a thousand ills. In Puritan countries one inevitably finds a morbid preoccupation with sex coupled with every form of perversion and degeneracy. Addiction to excess of drink, and to the drug habits, which are practically unknown in Latin countries, increase one's admiration at the Anglo-Saxon temperament.

Thus also Iliel's stagnant mind bred fearsome things. Hour after hour, the pageant of diseased thoughts passed through the shadowy gulfs of her chaotic spirit. Actual phantoms took shape for her, some seductive, some menacing; but even the most hideous and cruel symbols had a fierce fascination for her. There was a stag-beetle, with flaming eyes, a creature as big as an elephant, with claws in constant motion, that threatened her continually. Horribly as this frightened her, she gloated on it, pictured its sudden plunge with those ghastly mandibles upon her flanks. Her own fatness was a source of curious perverse pleasure to her; one of her favourite reveries was to imagine herself the centre of a group of cannibals, watch them chop off great lumps from her body, and seethe them in the pot, or roast them on a spear, hissing and dripping blood and grease, upon the fire. In some insane or atavistic confusion of mind this dream was always recognised as being a dream of love. And she understood, in some sub-current of thought, why Suffragettes forced men to use violence upon them; it is but a repressed sexual instinct breaking out in race-remembrance of marriage by capture.

But more dangerous even than such ideas were many which she learned to group under a name which one of them gave her. It was not a name that one can transcribe in any alphabet, but it was exactly like a very short slight cough, hardly more than a clearing of the throat, a quite voluntary cough of the apologetic type. She had only to make this little noise, and immediately a certain landscape opened before her. She was walking on a narrow ribbon of white path that wound up a very gentle slope. On either side of her were broad rough screes, with sparse grass and scrub peeping between the stones. The path led up to a pass between two hills, and near the crest of the ridge were two towers, one on either side of the path, as if for defence. These towers were squat and very ugly, with no windows, but mere slits for archery, and they had no sign of habitation. Yet she was quite sure that Something lived there, and she was conscious of the most passionate anxiety to visit whoever it might be. The moon, always in her wane, shone bright above the path, but little of her illumination extended beyond those narrow limits. Upon the screes she could see only faint shadows, apparently of some prowling beast of the jackal or hyena type, for she could hear howling and laughing, with now and again fierce snarls and cries as though a fight were in progress "in that fell cirque". But nothing ever crossed the path itself, and she would walk along it with a sense of the most curious lightness and pleasure. It was often her intention to go to the towers; but always she was deterred from doing so by the Old Lady.

It was at a sharp turn of the path round an immense boulder that this individual usually appeared, coming from a cleft in its face. On the first occasion she had herself greeted the Old Lady, asking if she could assist her. For the Old Lady was seated on the ground, working very hard.

"May I help you?" said Iliel, "in whatever you are doing?"

The Old Lady sighed very bitterly, and said that she was trying to make a fire.

"But you haven't got any sticks."

"We never use sticks to make a fire – in this country."

The last three words were in sing-song.

"Then what do you burn?"

"Anything round, and anything red, and anything ripe – in this country."

"And how do you kindle it? Have you matches, or do you rub sticks together, or do you use the sun's rays through a burning-glass?"

"Hush! there is no phosphorus, nor any sticks, nor any sun – in this country."

"Then how do you get fire?"

"There is no fire – in this country."

"But you said you were making a fire!"

"Trying to make a fire, my dear; we are always trying, and never succeeding – in this country."

"And how long have you been trying?"

"There is no time – in this country."

Iliel was half hypnotised by the reiteration of that negation, and that final phrase. She began to play a game.

"Well, Old Lady, I've something round, and something red, and something ripe to make your fire with. I'll give it to you if you can guess what it is."

The Old Lady shook her head. "There's nothing round, and there's nothing red, and nothing ripe – in this country."

"Well, I'll tell you: it's an apple. If you want it, you may have it."

"We never want anything – in this country."

"Well, I'll go on."

"There's no going on – in this country."

"Oh, but there is, and I'm off."

"Don't you know what a treasure we have – in this country?"

"No – what is it?"

The Old Lady dived into the cleft of the rock, and came out again in a moment with a monkey, and a mouse-trap, and a mandolin.

"I began," she explained, "with an arrow, and an adder, and an arquebus; for there are terrible dangers in the beginning – in this country."

"But what are they good for?"

"Nothing at all – in this country. But I'm changing them for a newt, and a narwhal, and a net, hoping that one day I may get to the end, where one needs a zebra, a zither, and a zarape, and one can always exchange those for something round, and red, and ripe – in this country."

It was really a sort of child's fairy story that Iliel was telling herself; but the teller was independent of her conscious mind, so that she did not know what was coming next. And really the Old Lady was quite a personality. On the second occasion she showed Iliel how to use her treasure. She made the monkey play the mandolin, and set the mouse-trap; and sure enough the newt and the narwhal, attracted by the music swam up and were duly caught. As for the net, the Old Lady bartered her three treasures for Iliel's hair-net.

"I'm afraid it isn't very strong to catch things with," she said.

"I only need an orange, and an oboe, and an octopus; and they are easy enough to catch – in this country."

Little by little the Old Lady beguiled Iliel, and one day, while they were setting a trap to catch a viper, and a vineyard, and a violin with their unicorn, and their umbrella, and their ukulele, she suddenly stopped short, and asked Iliel point-blank if she would like to attend the Sabbath on Walpurgis-night – the eve of May-day – for "there's a short cut to it, my dear, from this country."

Iliel revolted passionately against the idea, for she scented something abominable; but the Old Lady said:

"Of course we should disguise you; it would never do for you to be recognised by Cyril, and Brother Onofrio, and Sister Clara; they wouldn't like to know you live – in this country."

"I don't," said Iliel, rather angrily, "I only come out here for a walk."

"Ah, my dear," chuckled the Old Lady, "but a walk's as good as a whale – in this country. And you remember that the whale didn't put out Jonah where he wanted to go, but where somebody else wanted him. And that's the breed of whale we have – in this country."

"How do you know they'll be there on Walpurgis-night?"

"A how's as good as a hen – in this country. And what a hen doesn't know you may ask of a hog, and what a hog doesn't know you may ask of a horse, and what a horse doesn't know isn't worth knowing – in this country."

Iliel was in a black rage against her friends – why had they not asked her to come with them? And she went back that day in a vile temper.

This adventure of the Old Lady was only one of many; but it was the most vital, because the most coherent. Indeed, it led in the end to results of importance. For Iliel agreed to go to the Sabbath on Walpurgis-night. The Old Lady was very mysterious as to the method of travel. Iliel had expected conventionality on that point; but the Old Lady said:

"There are no goats, and no broomsticks – in this country."

Most of her visions were simply formless and incoherent horrors. Her foolish thoughts and senseless impulses took shape, usually in some distortion of an animal form, with that power of viscosity which is to vertebrates the most loathsome of all possibilities of life, since it represents the line of development which they have themselves avoided, and is there-fore to them excremental in character. But to Iliel's morbidity the fascination of these things was overpowering. She took an unnatural and morose delight in watching the cuttle-fish squeeze itself slowly into a slime as black and oozy as the slug, and that again send trickling feelers as of leaking motor-oil, greasy and repulsive, with a foul scum upon its surface, until the beast looked like some parody of a tarantula; then this again would collapse, as if by mere weariness of struggle against gravitation, and spread itself slowly as a pool of putrefaction, which was yet intensely vital and personal by reason of its power to suck up everything within its sphere of sensation. It struck her that such creatures were images of Desire, a cruel and insatiable craving deprived of any will or power to take a single step towards gratification; and she understood that this condition was the most hideous and continual torture, agony with no ray of hope, impotence so complete as even to inhibit an issue in death. And she knew, too, that these shapes were born of her own weaknesses; yet, so far from rousing herself to stamp them out in her mind, she gloated upon their monstrosity and misery, took pleasure in their anguish, which was her own, and fed them with the substance of her own personality and will. It was this, a spiritual "Nostalgie de la boue", which grew upon her like a cancer or a gangrene; treacheries of the body itself, so that the only possible remedy is instant extirpation; for once the flesh abandons its will to firmness, to organisation, and to specialised development, its degeneration into formless putrefaction becomes an accelerating rush upon a steepening slope.

How tenuous is the thread by which man climbs to the stars! What

concentration of the sub-conscious will of the race, through a thousand generations, has determined his indomitable ascent! A single slackness, a single false step, and he topples into the morass wherein his feet still plash! Degeneration is the most fatally easy of all human possibilities; for the fell tug of cosmic inertia, that pressure of the entire universe which tends to the homogeneous, is upon man continuously; and becomes constantly more urgent the more he advances upon his path of differentiation. It is more than a fable, Atlas who supports the Universe upon his shoulders, and Hercules, the type of the man, divinely born indeed, who must yet regain Olympus by his own fierce toil, taking upon himself that infinite load.

The price of every step of progress is uncounted, even in myriads of lives self-sacrificed; and every man who is unfaithful to himself is not only at war with the sum of things, but his own comrades turn upon him to destroy him, to crush out his individuality and energy, to assimilate him to their own pullulating mass. It is indeed the power of the Roman Empire which erects the Cross on Calvary; but there must needs be Caiaphas and Herod, so blind that they crush out their own one hope of salvation from that iron tyranny; and also a traitor among those who once "left all and followed" the Son of Man.

And who shall deny true Godhead to humanity, seeing that no generation of mankind has been without a Saviour, conscious of his necessary doom, and resolute to meet it, his face set as a flint towards Jerusalem?

CHAPTER XIX
THE GRAND BEWITCHMENT

THE Operation planned by the Black Lodge was simple and colossal both in theory and in practice. It was based on the prime principle of Sympathetic Magic, which is that if you destroy anything which is bound up with anybody by an identifying link, that person also perishes. Douglas had adroitly taken advantage of the fact of the analogy between his own domestic situation and that of Cyril Grey. He had no need to attack the young magician directly, or even Lisa; he preferred to strike at the weakest point of all, that being whose existence was as yet but tentative. He had no need to go beyond this; for if he could bring Cyril's magick to naught, that exorcist would be destroyed by the recoil of his own exorcism. The laws of force take no account of human prejudices about "good" or "evil"; if one is run over by a railway engine, it matters nothing, physically, whether one is trying to commit suicide or to save a child. The difference in the result lies wholly on a superior plane.

It is one mark of the short-sightedness of the sorcerer that he is content with his own sorceries; and if he should think that he can escape the operation of that superior law which does take account of spiritual and moral causes, he is the greater fool. Douglas might indeed wipe his enemy

off the planet, but only with the result of fortifying the immortal and divine self which was within his victim, so that he would return with added power and wisdom; while all his success in aggrandising himself – as he foolishly called it – would leave his better part exhausted and disintegrated beyond refreshment or repair. He was like a man who should collect all his goods about him, and set fire to his house; while the true adepts beggar themselves (to all appearances) by transforming all their wealth into a shape that fire cannot touch.

The sorcerer never sees thus clearly. He hopes that at the last his accumulation of corruptible things will outweigh the laws of Nature; much as a thief might argue that if he can only steal enough, he can corrupt the judges and bribe the legislature, as is done in America. But the laws of nature were not made by man, nor can they be set aside by man; they were not made at all. There are no laws of Nature in the usual sense of the word "law"; they are but statements, reduced to a generalised form in accordance with reason, of the facts observed in nature; they are formulae of the inherent properties of substance. It is impossible to evade them, or to suspend them, or to counteract them; for the effort to do so is itself in accordance with those laws themselves, and the compensation, though it be invisible for a time, is adjusted with an exactitude absolute because independent of every source of error. No trickery, no manipulation, can alter by the millionth of a milligramme the amount of oxygen in a billion tons of water. No existing thing is ever destroyed or magnified or lessened, though it change its form as it passes from one complexity to another. And if this be true of an atom of carbon, which is but one of the ideas in our minds, how much more is it true of that supremely simple thing which stands behind all thought, the soul of man? Doubt that? The answer comes: Who doubts?

The sorcerer is perhaps – at best – trying to create a permanence of his complexities, as who should try to fashion gold from the dust-heap. But most sorcerers do not go so deeply into things; they are set upon the advantage of the moment. Douglas probably did not care a snap of the fingers for his ultimate destiny; it may be that he deliberately avoided thinking of it; but however that may be, there is no doubt that at this moment he was ruthlessly pursuing his hate of Cyril Grey.

For great operations – the "set pieces" of his diabolical pyrotechnics – the sorcerer had a place set apart and prepared. This was an old wine-cellar in a street between the Seine and the Boulevard St. Germain. The entrance was

comparatively reputable, being a house of cheap prostitution which Douglas and Balloch – screened behind a woman – owned between them. Below this house was a cellar where the apaches of Paris gathered to dance and plot against society; so ran the legend, and two burly *sergents de ville*, with fixed bayonets and cocked revolvers lying on the table before them, superintended the revels. For in fact Douglas had perceived that the apache spent no money, and that it would pay better to run the cellar as a show place for Americans, Cockneys, Germans, and country cousins from the provinces on a jaunt to Paris, on the hunt for thrills. No one more dangerous than a greengrocer had crossed that threshold for many a long year, and the visible apaches, drinking and swearing, dancing an alleged can-can and occasionally throwing bottles and knives at each other, were honest folk painfully earning the exiguous salary which the "long firm" paid them.

But beneath this cellar, unknown even to the police, was a vault which had once served for storing spirits. It was below the level of the river; rats, damp, and stale alcohol gave it an atmosphere happily peculiar to such abodes. There is no place in the world more law-abiding than a house of ill-fame, with the light of police supervision constantly upon it; and the astuteness of the sorcerer in choosing this for his place of evocation was rewarded by complete freedom from disturbance or suspicion. Any one could enter at any hour of day or night, with every precaution of secrecy, without drawing more than a laugh from the police on guard.

The entrance to the sorcerer's den was similarly concealed – by cunning, not by more obvious methods.

A sort of cupboard-shelf, reached by a ladder from the dancing cellar and by a few steps from one of the bedrooms in the house above, was called "Troppman's refuge", it being said that that celebrated murderer once had lain concealed there for some days. His autograph, and some bad verses (all contributed by an ingenious cabaret singer) were shown upon the walls. It was therefore quite natural and unsuspicious for any visitor to climb up into that room, which was so small that it would only hold one man of average size. His non-reappearance would not cause surprise; he might have gone out the other way; in fact, he would naturally do so. But in the moment of his finding himself alone, he could, if he knew the secret, press a hidden lever which caused the floor to descend bodily. Arrived below, a corridor with three right-angled turns – this could, incidentally, be flooded at need, in a few moments – led to the last of the defences, a regular door such as is fitted to

a strong room. There was an emergency exit to the cellar, equally ingenious; it was a sort of torpedo-tube opening beneath the water of the Seine. It was fitted with a compressed air-chamber. Any one wishing to escape had merely to introduce himself into a shell made of thin cork, and shoot into the river. Even the worst of swimmers could be sure to reach the neighbouring quay. But the secret of this was known only to Douglas and one other.

The very earliest steps in such thoroughgoing sorcery as Douglas practised require the student to deform and mutilate his humanity by accustoming himself to such moral crimes as render their perpetrator callous and insensible to all such emotions as men naturally cherish; in particular, love. The Black Lodge put all its members through regular practices of cruelty and meanness. Guy de Maupassant wrote two of the most revolting stories ever told; one of a boy who hated a horse, the other of a family of peasants who tortured a blind relative that had been left to their charity. Such vileness as is written there by the divine hand of that great artist forbids emulation; the reverent reference must suffice.

Enough to say that stifling of all natural impulse was a preliminary of the system of the Black Lodge; in higher grades the pupil took on the manipulation of subtler forces. Douglas' own use of his wife's love to vitriolise her heart was considered by the best judges as likely to become a classic.

The inner circle, the fourteen men about Douglas himself and that still more mysterious person to whom even he was responsible, a woman known only as "Annie" or as "A. B.", were sealed to him by the direst of all bonds. Needless are oaths in the Black Lodge; honour being the first thing discarded, their only use is to frighten fools. But before joining the Fourteen, known as the Ghaaghaael, it was obligatory to commit a murder in cold blood, and to place the proofs of it in the hands of Douglas. Thus each step in sorcery is also a step in slavery; and that any man should put such power in the hands of another, no matter for what hope of gain, is one of the mysteries of perverse psychology. The highest rank in the Lodge was called Thaumiel-Qeretiel, and there were two of these, "Annie" and Douglas, who were alone in possession of the full secrets of the Lodge. Only they and the Fourteen had keys to the cellar and the secret of the combination.

Beginners were initiated there, and the method of introducing them was satisfactory and ingenious. They were taken to the house in an automobile, their eyes blinded by an ordinary pair of motor-goggles, behind whose glass was a steel plate.

The cellar itself was arranged as a permanent place of evocation. It was a far more complex device than that used by Vesquit in Naples, for in confusion lay the safety of the Lodge. The floor was covered with symbols which even the Fourteen did not wholly understand; any one of them, crossed inadvertently, might be a magical trap for a traitor; and as each of the Fourteen was exactly that, in fact, had to be so to qualify for supreme place, it was with abject fear that this Unholy of Unholies was guarded.

At the appointed hour Mr. Butcher presented himself at the Count's apartment, was furnished with the necessary spectacles, and conducted to the Beth Choi, or House of Horror, as the cellar was called in the jargon of the Sorcerers.

Balloch, Cremers, Abdul Bey and the wife of Douglas were already present.

The first part of the procedure consisted in the formal renunciation by Mrs. Douglas of the vows taken for her in her baptism, a ceremonial apostacy from Christianity. This was done in no spirit of hostility to that religion, but to permit of her being rebaptised into it under Lisa's maiden name. The Turk was next called upon to renounce Islam, and baptised by the name of the Marchese la Giuffria.

The American priest next proceeded to confirm them in the Christian religion, and to communicate the Sacrament.

Finally, they were married. In this long profanation of the mysteries of the Church the horror lay in the business-like simplicity of the procedure.

One can imagine the Charity of a devout Christian finding excuses for the Black Mass, when it is the expression of the revolt of an agonising soul, or of the hysteria of a half-crazed debauchee; he can conceive of repentance and of grace following upon enlightenment; but this cold-blooded abuse of the most sacred rites, their quite casual employment as the mere prelude to a crime which is tantamount to murder in the opinion of all right-minded men, must seem even to the Freethinker or the Pagan as an abomination not to be forgiven.

No pains had been spared by Douglas to make all secure. Balloch and Cremers had sponsored both "infants", and Douglas himself, as having most right, gave his wife in marriage to the Turk.

A brutally realistic touch was needed to consummate the sacrilege; it was not neglected.

Much of the pleasure taken by Douglas in this miserable and criminal farce was due to his enjoyment of the sufferings of his wife. Each new spurt

of filth wrung her heart afresh; and withal she was aware that all these things were but the prelude to an act of fiendish violence more horrible than them all.

Mr. Butcher, Cremers, and Abdul Bey, their functions ended, were led out of the cellar. Balloch remained to perform the operation from which the bulk of his income was derived.

But there was yet much sorcery of the more secret sort to be accomplished. Douglas who, up to now, had confined himself to intense mental concentration upon the work, forcing himself to believe that the ceremonies he was witnessing were real instead of mockery, that his wife was really Lisa, and Abdul really the Marchese, now came forward as the heart and brain of the work. The difficulty – the crux of the whole art – had been to introduce Cyril Grey into the affair, and this had been overcome by the use of a specimen of his signature. But now it was necessary also to dedicate the victim to Hecate, or rather, to her Hebrew equivalent, Nahema, the devourer of little children, because she also is one aspect of the moon, and Lisa having been adopted to that planet, her representative must needs undergo a similar ensorcelment.

In the art of evocation Douglas was profoundly skilled. His mind was of a material and practical order, and distrusted subtleties. He gladly endured the immense labour of compelling a spirit to visible appearance, when a less careful or more fine-minded sorcerer would have worked upon some other plane. He had so far mastered his art that in a place, such as he now had, long habitated to similar scenes, he could call up a visible image of almost any demon required in a period of not more than half an hour. For place-association is of great importance, possibly because it favours concentration of mind. Evidently, it is difficult not to feel religious in King's College Chapel, Cambridge, or otherwise than profoundly sceptical and Pagan in St. Peter's, at Rome, with its "East" in the West, its adaptation of a statue of Jupiter to represent its patron saint, and the emphasis of its entire architecture in bearing witness that its true name is Temporal Power. Gothic is the only mystic type; Templar and Byzantine are only religious through sexuality; Perpendicular is more moral than spiritual – and modern architecture means nothing at all.

In the Beth Choi there was always a bowl of fresh bull's blood burning over a charcoal brazier.

Science is gradually being forced round once more to the belief that there

is something more in life than its mere chemistry and physics. Those who practise the occult arts have never been in doubt on the subject. The dynamic virtue of living substance does not depart from it immediately at death. Those ideas, therefore, which seek manifestation in life, must do so either by incarnation or by seizing some still living matter which the idea or soul in possession has abandoned. Sorcerers consequently employ the fumes of fresh blood as a vehicle for the manifestation of the demons whom they wish to evoke. The matter is easy enough; for fiends are always eager to take hold on the sensory life. Occasionally, such beings find people ignorant and foolish enough to offer themselves deliberately to obsession by sitting in a dark room without magical protection, and inviting any wandering ghost or demon to take hold of them, and use their bodies and minds. This loathsome folly is called Spiritualism, and successful practitioners can be recognised by the fact that their minds are no use for anything at all any more. They become incapable of mental concentration, or a connected train of thought; only too often the obsessing spirit gains power to take hold of them at will, and utters by their mouths foulness and imbecility when the whim takes him. True souls would never seek so ignoble a means of manifesting in earth-life; their ways are holy, and in accord with Nature.

While the true soul reincarnates as a renunciation, a sacrifice of its divine life and ecstasy for the sake of redeeming those who are not yet freed from mortal longings, the demon seeks incarnation as a means of gratifying unslaked lusts.

Like a dumb beast in pain, the wife of Douglas watched her husband go through his ghastly ritual, with averted face, as is prescribed; for none may look on Hecate, and remain sane. The proper conjurations of Hecate are curses against all renewal of life; her sacrament is deadly night-shade or henbane, and her due offering a black lamb tom ere its birth from a black ewe.

This, with sardonic subter-thought, pleasing to Hecate, the sorcerer promised her as she made her presence felt; whether they could have seen anything if they had dared to look, who can say? But through the cellar moved an icy sensation, as if some presence had indeed been called forth by the words and rites spoken and accomplished.

For Hecate is what Scripture calls "the second death". Natural death is to man the greatest of the Sacraments, of which all others are but symbols; for it is the final and absolute Union with the creator, and it is also the Pylon

of the Temple of Life, even in the material world, for Death is Love.

Certainly the wife of Douglas felt the presence of that vile thing evoked from Tartarus. Its chill struck through to her bones. Nothing had so torn her breast as the constant refusal of her husband to allow her to fulfil her human destiny. Even her prostitution, since it was forced upon her by the one man she loved, might be endured – if only – if only –

But always the aid of Balloch had been summoned; always, in dire distress, and direr danger, she had been thwarted of her life's purpose. It was not so much a conscious wish, though that was strong, as an actual physical craving of her nature, as urgent and devouring as hunger or thirst.

Balloch, who had been all his life high-priest of Hecate, had never been present at an evocation of the force that he served. He shuddered – not a little – as the sorcerer recited his surgical exploits; the credentials of the faith of her servant then present before her. He had committed his dastardly crimes wholly for gain, and as a handle for blackmail; the magical significance of the business had not occurred to him at all. His magical work had been almost entirely directed to the gratification of sensuality in abnormal and extra-human channels. So, while a fierce pride now thrilled him, there was mingled with it a sinking of the spirit; for he realised that its mistress had been sterility and death. And it was of death that he was most afraid. The cynical calm of Douglas appalled him; he recognised the superiority of that great sorcerer; and his hope to supplant him died within his breast.

At that moment Hecate herself passed into him, and twined herself inextricably about his brain. He accepted his destiny as her high-priest; in future he would do murder for the joy of pleasing her! All other mistresses were tame to this one! The thrill of Thuggee caught him – and in a very spasm of maniacal exaltation, he vowed himself again and again to her services. She should be sole goddess of the Black Lodge – only let her show him how to be rid of Douglas! Instantly the plan came to him; he remembered that "Annie" was high-priestess of Hecate in a greater sense than himself; for she was notorious as an open advocate of this kind of murder; indeed, she had narrowly escaped prison on this charge; he would tempt Douglas to rid himself of "Annie" – and then betray him to her.

So powerful was the emotion that consumed him that he trembled with excitement and eagerness. Tonight was a great night: it was a step in his initiation to take part in so tremendous a ceremony. He became nervously

exalted; he could have danced; Hecate, warming herself in his old bones, communicated a devilish glee to him.

The moment was at hand for his renewed activity.

"Hecate, mother only of death, devourer of all life!" cried Douglas, in his final adjuration; "as I devote to thy chill tooth this secret spring of man, so be it with all that are like unto it! Even as it is with that which I shall cast upon thine altar, so be it with all the offspring of Lisa la Giuffria!"

He ended with the thirteenth repetition of that appalling curse which begins *Epikaloume se ten en to keneo pnevmati, deinan, aoraton, Pontokratora, theropoian kai eremopoian, e misonta, oikian efstathousanfl!* calling upon "her that dwelleth in the void place, the inane, terrible, inexorable, maker of horror and desolation, hater of the house that prospereth", and devoting "the signified and sealed, named and unnamed" to destruction.

Then he turned to Balloch, and bade him act. Three minutes later the surgeon gave a curse, and blanched, as a scream, despite herself, burst from the bitten lips of the brave woman who lay upon the altar.

"Why couldn't you let me give an anaesthetic?" he said angrily.

"What's wrong? Is it bad?"

"It's damned ugly. Curse it; not a thing here that I need!"

But he needed nothing; he had done more even than he guessed.

Mrs. Douglas, her face suddenly drawn and white, lifted her head with infinite effort towards her husband.

"I've always loved you," she whispered, "and I love you now, as – I – die."

Her head dropped with a dull crack upon the slab. No one can say if she heard the reply of Douglas:

"You sow! you've bitched the whole show!"

For she had uttered the supreme name of Love, in love; and the spell dissolved more swiftly than a dream. There was no Hecate, no sorcerer even, for the moment; nothing but two murderers, and the corpse of a martyr between them.

Douglas did not waste a single word of abuse on Balloch.

"This is for you to clear up," he said, with a simplicity that cut deeper than sneer or snarl, and walked out of the cellar.

Balloch, left to himself, became hysterical. In his act he recognised the first-fruits of the divine possession; his offering to the goddess had been stupendous indeed. All his exaltation returned: now would Hecate favour him above all men.

Well, he had but to take the body upstairs. The old woman understood these things; he would certify the death; there would be no fuss made over a poor prostitute. He would return at once to London, and open up the negotiations with "A. B."

CHAPTER XX

WALPURGIS-NIGHT

THE spring in Naples had advanced with eager foot; in her gait she revealed the truth of her godhead; and by the end of April there was no wreath of snow on Apennine, or Alban, or Apulian Hill.

The last day of the month was hot and still as midsummer; the slopes of Posillippo begged a breath from Ocean, and were denied. So heavy a haze hung on the sea that not only Capri, not only the blue spur that stabs the sunset, but Vesuvius itself, were hidden from the Villa where Iliel and her friends were nested.

Sunset was sombre and splendid; the disc itself was but a vague intensity of angry Indian red. His agony spilt a murky saffron through the haze; and the edges of the storm-clouds on the horizon, fantastically shapen, cast up a veritable mirage, exaggerated and distorted images of their own scarred crests, that shifted and changed, so that one might have sworn that monsters – dragons, hippogriffs, chimaerae – were moving in the mist, a saturnalia of phantasms.

Iliel impatiently awaited the moment of darkness, when she could meet the Old Lady and start for the Sabbath. She had noticed a long conference that day between Sister Clara and the two men; and she was sure that they were themselves arranging for their departure. The suspicion was confirmed

when, one after the other, they came to wish her a good night. She was more than ever determined to follow them to the Sabbath.

By nine o'clock everything was still in the garden, save for the tread of Brother Onofrio's patrol, who paced the upper terrace, chanting in the soft and low, yet stern, tones of his well-modulated voice, the exorcism that magical guardians have sung for so many ages, with its refrain: "On them will I impose my will, the Law of Light."

Iliel gave her little cough, and found herself immediately upon the path she knew so well. It only took her a few minutes to reach the rock, and there was the Old Lady waiting for her.

"I must tell you at once, my dear," she began without any preliminary, "that you must be very careful to do exactly as I say – in that country."

It was the same sing-song, with the one change of word.

"First of all, you must never speak of anything by its name – in that country. So, if you see a tree on a mountain, it will be better to say 'Look at the green on the high'; for that's how they talk – in that country. And whatever you do, you must find a false reason for doing it – in that country. If you rob a man, you must say it is to help and protect him: that's the ethics – of that country. And everything of value has no value at all – in that country. You must be perfectly commonplace if you want to be a genius – in that country. And everything you like you must pretend not to like; and anything that is there you must pretend is not there – in that country. And you must always say that you are sacrificing yourself in the cause of religion, and morality, and humanity, and liberty, and progress, when you want to cheat your neighbour – in that country."

"Good heavens!" cried Iliel, "are we going to England?"

"They call the place Stonehenge – in that country." And without another word the Old Lady dragged Iliel into the cleft of the rock. It was very, very dark inside, and she tripped over loose stones. Then the Old Lady opened a little door, and she found herself standing on a narrow window-ledge. The door shut fast behind her, almost pushing her out. Beyond the ledge was nothing but the Abyss of Stars. She was seized with an enormous vertigo. She would have fallen into that cruel emptiness, but the Old Lady's voice came: "What I said outside was nonsense, just to put the Gwalkins off the trail, my dear; there is only one rule, and that is to take things as they come – in this country."

She pushed Iliel deliberately from the window-sill; with a scream she flew

through the blackness. But the chubby little old clergyman explained to her that she must go into the castle on the islet. It was only a little way to walk over the ice of the lake, but there was no sign of an entrance. The castle was fitted cunningly to the irregularities of the rock, so that one could see nothing but the masonry; and there was no trace of any door, and the windows were all very high in the wall. But as Iliel came to it she found herself inside, and she never knew how she got there. It was easy to scramble along the ladder to the golf course, but the main deck of the galleon was slippery with the oil that spurted from its thousand fountains. However, she came at last to the wardrobe where her hairbrush was hanging, and she lost no time in digging for the necessary skylarks. At last the way was clear! The pine-woods on the left; the ant-hills on the right; straight through the surf to the heathery pagoda where the chubby clergyman and the Old Lady had already arrived, and were busy worshipping the Chinese God.

Of course! It was Cyril, with Brother Onofrio and Sister Clara all the time – how stupid she had been!

But for all that the toads were a nuisance with their eternal chatter and laughter; and they wore their jewels much too conspicuously and profusely.

And then she perceived that Cyril and his two companions formed but one triangle, out of uncounted thousands; and each triangle was at a knot upon the web of an enormous spider. At each knot was such a group of three, and every one was different. There must have been millions of such gods, each with its pair of worshippers; every race and clime and period was represented. There were the gods of Mexico and of Peru, of Syria and Babylon, of Greece and Rome, of obscure swamps of Ethiopia, of deserts and mountains. And upon each thread of the web, from knot to knot, danced incredible insects, and strange animals, and hideous reptiles. They danced, sang, and whirled frantically, so that the entire web was a mere bewilderment of motion. Her head swam dizzily. But she was now full of a curious anger; her thought was that the Old Lady had betrayed her. She found it quite impossible to approach the triangle, for one thing: she was furious that it should be Sister Clara herself who had led her into this Sabbath, for another; and she was infinitely disgusted at the whole vile revel. Now she noticed that each pair of worshippers had newborn children in their arms; and they offered these to their god, who threw them instantly towards the centre of the web. Following up those cruel meshes, she beheld the spider itself, with its six legs. Its head and body formed one black sphere, covered

with moving eyes that darted rays of darkness in every direction, and mouths that sucked up its prey without remorse or cessation, and cast it out once more in the form of fresh strands of that vibrating web.

Iliel shuddered with the horror of the vision; it was to her a dread unspeakable, yet she was hypnotised and helpless. She felt in herself that one day she too must become the prey of that most dire and demoniac power of darkness.

As she gazed, she saw that even the gods and their worshippers were morsels for its mouths. Ever and anon she beheld one of the legs crooked round a triangle and draw it, god, shrine, and worshippers, into the blackness of the spider's bloated belly. Then they were thrown out violently again, in some slightly altered form, to repeat the same uncanny ritual.

With a strong shudder she broke away from that infernal contemplation. Where was the kindly earth, with all its light and beauty? In God's name, why had she left Lavinia King to explore these dreadful realms – of illusion? of imagination? of darker and deadlier reality than life? It mattered little which; the one thing needful was to turn again to humanity, to the simple sensible life that she had always lived. It was not noble, not wonderful; but it was better than this nightmare of phantoms, cruel and malignant and hideous, this phantasmagoria of damnation.

She wrenched herself away; for a moment she lost consciousness completely; then she found herself in her bed at the Villa. With feverish energy she sprang from the couch, and ran to the wardrobe to put on her travelling dress. It would be easy to drop from the wall of the terrace into the lane; in an hour she would be safe in Naples. And then she discovered that the dress would have to be altered before she could wear it. With vehemence she set instantly to work – and just as she was finishing, the door opened, and Sister Clara stood beside her.

"Come, Iliel," she said, "it is the moment to salute May Morn!"

The indignant girl recoiled in anger and disgust; but Sister Clara stood smiling gently and tenderly. Iliel looked at her, almost despite herself; and she could not but see the radiance of her whole being, a physical aura of light playing about her, and the fire of her eyes transcendent with seraph happiness.

"They are waiting for us in the garden," she said, taking Iliel by the arm, like a nurse with an invalid. And she drew over her shoulders the great lunar mantle of blue velvet with its broidered silver crescents, its talismans of the

moon, and its heavy hanging tassels of seed pearls; and upon her head she set the tiara of moon-stones.

"Come, they are waiting."

So Iliel suffered herself to be led once more into the garden. In the east the first rays of the sun gilded the crest of Posilippo, and tinged the pale blue of the firmament with rosy fingers. The whole company was gathered together, an ordered phalanx, to salute the Lord of Life and Light.

Iliel could not join in that choir of adoration. In her heart was blackness and hate, and nausea in her mouth. What vileness lay beneath this fair semblance! Well, let it be; she would be gone.

Cyril came to her with Brother Onofrio, as the last movement of their majestic chant died away upon the echoing air. He took her in his arms. "Come! I have much to tell you." He led her to a marble seat, and made her sit down. Brother Onofrio and Sister Clara followed them, and sat upon the base of a great statue, a copy of the Marsyas and Olympas in green bronze, hard by.

"Child!" said Cyril, very gravely and gently, "look at the eastern slope of Posilippo! And look at the stars, how brightly they shine! And look at that shoal of gleaming fish, that swim so deep beneath the waters of the bay! And look at your left ear! What shapeliness! What delicate pink!"

She was too angry even to tell him not to be an idiot. She only smiled disdainfully.

He continued. "But those things are there. You cannot see them because the conditions are not right. But there are other things that your eye sees indeed, but you, not; because you have not been trained to see them for what they are. See Capri in the morning sun! How do you know it is an island, not a dream, or a cloud, or a sea-monster? Only by comparison with previous knowledge and experience. You can only see things that are already in your own mind – or things so like them that you can adjust yourself to the small percentage of difference. But you cannot observe or apprehend things that are utterly unfamiliar except by training and experience. How does the alphabet look to you when you first learn it? Don't you confuse the letters? Arabic looks 'fantastic' to you, as the Roman script does to the Arab; you can memorise one at a glance, white you plod painfully over the other, letter by letter, and probably copy it wrong after all. That's what happened to you last night. I know you were there; and, knowing you were not an initiate, I can guess pretty well what you must have seen. You saw things

'accurately', so far as you could see them; that is, you saw a projection into your own mind of something really in being. How right such vision can be, and yet how wrong! Watch my hand!" He suddenly raised his right hand. With the other he held a book between it and her eyes.

"I can't see it!" she cried petulantly.

"Look at its shadow on the wall!"

"It's the head of the devil!"

"Yet I am only making the gesture of benediction." He lowered the book. She recognised at once the correctness of his statement.

She looked at him with open mouth and eyes. He was always stupefying her by the picturesqueness of his allegories, and his trick of presenting them dramatically.

"What then?"

"This is what really happened last night – only there's no such thing as time. This is what you should have seen, and what you will see one day, if you cling to the highest in you."

He drew a note-book of white vellum from his pocket, and began to read.

"The whirlwind of the Eagle and the Lion!
　　The Tree upon the Mountain that is Zion!
The marriage of the Starbeam and the Clod!
　　The mystic Sabbath of the Saints of God!
Bestride the Broomstick that is God-in-man!
　　Spur the rough Goat whose secret name is Pan!
Before that Rod Heaven knows itself unjust;
　　Beneath those hoofs the stars are puffs of dust.
Rise up, my soul! One stride, and space is spanned;
　　Time, like a poppy, crushed in thy left hand,
While with thy right thou reachest out to grip
　　The Graal of God, and tilt it to thy lip?
Lo! all the whirring shafts of Light, a web
　　Wherein the Tides of Being flow and ebb,
One heart-beat, pulsing the Eternal stress,
　　Extremes that cancel out in Nothingness.
Light thrills through Light, the spindle of desire,
　　Cross upon Cross of elemental Fire;
Life circles Life, the Rose all flowers above,

And in their intermarriage they are Love.
Lo! on each spear of Splendour burns a world
   Revolving, whirling, crying aloud; and curled
About each cosmos, bounding in its course,
   The sacred Snake, the father of its force,
Energised, energizing, self-sustained,
   Man-hearted, Eagle-pinioned, Lion-maned.
Exulting in its splendour as it lashes
   Its Phoenix plumage to immortal ashes
Whereof one fleck, a seed of spirit spun,
   Whirls itself onward, and creates a sun.
Light interfused with Light, a sparkling spasm
   Of rainbow radiance, spans the cosmic chasm;
Light crystallised in Life, Life coruscating
   In Light, their mood of magick consummating
The miracle of Love, and all the awe
   Of Need made one with Liberty's one law;
A fourfold flower of Godhead, leaf and fruit
   And seed and blossom of one radiant root,
Resolving all the being of its bloom
   Into the rapture of its own perfume.
Star-clustered dew each fibre of that light
   Wherein all being flashes to its flight!
All things that live, a cohort and a choir,
   Laugh with the leapings of that fervid fire;
Motes in that sunlight, they are drunken of
   The wine of their own energy of love.
Nothing so small, so base, so incomplete,
   But here goes dancing on diviner feet;
And where Light crosses Light, all loves combine
   Behold the God, the worshippers, the shrine,
Each comprehensive of its single soul
   Yet each the centre and fountain of the whole;
Each one made perfect in its passionate part,
   Each the circumference, and each the heart!
Always the Three in One are interwoven,
   Always the One in Three sublimely cloven,

Their essence to the Central Spirit hurled
    And so flung forth, an uncorrupted world,
By That which, comprehending in one whole
    The universal rapture of Its soul,
Abides beyond Its own illumination,
    Withdrawn from Its imperishable station,
Upholding all, an arm whose falchion flings
    With every flash a new-fledged Soul of Things;
Beholding all, with eyes whose flashes flood
    The veins of their own universe with blood;
Absorbing all, each myriad mouth aflame
    To utter the unutterable Name
That calls all souls, the greatest and the least,
    To the unimaginable marriage-feast;
And, in the self-same sacrament, is stirred
    To recreate their essence with a Word;
This All, this Sire and Lord of All, abides
    Behind the unbounded torrent of Its tides,
In silence of all deed, or word, or thought,
    So that we name It not, or name It Naught.
This is the Truth behind the lie called God;
    This blots the heavens, and indwells the clod.
This is the centre of all spheres, the flame
    In men and stars, the Soul behind the name,
The spring of Life, the axle of the Wheel,
    All-mover, yet the One Thing immobile.
Adore It not, for It adoreth thee,
    The shadow-shape of Its eternity.
Lift up thyself! be strong to burst thy bars!
    For lo! thy stature shall surpass the stars."

Cyril put away his book. "Language," said he, "has been developed from its most primitive sources by persons so passionately concentrated upon the Ideal of selling cheese without verbal infelicity that some other points have necessarily been neglected. One cannot put mystic experience into words. One can at best describe phenomena with a sort of cold and wooden accuracy, or suggest ecstasy by very vagueness. You know that line 'O windy

star blown sideways up the sky!' It means nothing, if you analyse it; but it gives the idea of something, though one could never say what. What you saw, my beloved Iliel, bears about the same ratio to what I have said as what I have said does to what Sister Clara saw: or, rather, was. Moral: when Sister turns we all turn. I have now apologised, though inadequately, for inflicting my bad verses upon you; which will conclude the entertainment for this morning. Brother Onofrio will now take up the collection. He that giveth to the poor lendeth to the Lord; details of rate of interest and security on application to the bartender. The liberal soul shall be made fat; but I am Banting, as the hart banteth after the water brooks. He that watereth shall be watered also himself: I will take a cold shower before the plunge. The Mother's Meeting will be held as usual at 8.30 on Thursday evening. Those who are not yet Mothers, but who wish to become so, kindly apply to me in the Vestry at the conclusion of the service. Sister Clara, please play the people out quickly!"

Cyril babbled out this nonsense in the tones of the Sweet Young Thing type of Curate; it was his way of restoring the superficial atmosphere.

Iliel took his arm, and went smiling to breakfast; but her soul was yet ill at ease. She asked him about the identification of Sister Clara and her Old Lady.

"Yes," he said, "it was best to have her on the watch outside – on the Astral Plane – to keep you from getting into too great mischief. But you can never come to any real harm so long as you keep your vow and stay inside the circle. That's the one important point."

She was quite satisfied in her upper conscious self, which was usually her better self, because of its rationality, and its advantage of surface training, which saved her from obeying her impulses on every occasion. She was glad, she was proud, of her partnership with the adepts. Yet there was a subconscious weakness in her which hated them and envied them the more because of their superiority to her. She knew only too well that the price of their attainment had been the suppression of just such darknesses of animal instinct and savage superstition as were her chief delight. The poet speaks of "the infinite rage of fishes to have wings"; but when you explain to the fish that it will have to give up pumping water through its gills, it is apt to compromise for a few million generations; though the word may rankle if you call it a flying-fish, when swimming-bird is evidently a properer and politer name.

She was permanently annoyed with Sister Clara; her motive for making excursions on that path had been to get rid of the idea of Cyril and his

magick; and he had not even come himself to welcome her, but set this woman to disguise herself and spy upon her thoughts! It was disgusting.

Cyril had certainly done his best to put the matter in the proper light. He had even told her a story. "A charming lady, wife of a friend of Bowling's, whom her physical and mental characteristics induce me to introduce as Mrs. Dough-Nut, was once left lorn in the desert island of Manhattan, while her husband was on a spook-shikar with Lord Antony in this very Naples, which you see before you. (Slightly to the left, child!) Mrs. Dough-Nut was as virtuous as American women sometimes are, when denied opportunity to be otherwise; and the poor lady was far from attractive. But in the world of spirits, it appears, the same standards are not current as in Peacock Alley or Times Square; and she was soon supplied with a regular regiment of 'spirit lovers'. They told her what to do, and how to do it; eating, drinking, reading, music, whatever she did, all must be done under spirit control; and one day they told her that they had a great and wonderful work for her to do – the regeneration of humanity and so forth, I think it was; anyhow, something perfectly dotty. She was now quite without power to criticise her actions by reason or good sense; the voice of the 'Spirits' was for her the voice of God. So they sent her to the Bank for money, and to the Steamship office for a passage to Europe; and when she got to Liverpool they sent her to London, from London to Paris, from Paris to Genoa. And when she came to Genoa they told her which hotel to choose; and then they sent her out to buy a revolver and some cartridges; and then they told her to cock it and put the muzzle to her forehead; and then to pull the trigger. The bullet made little impression on that armour-plate of solid bone; and she escaped to tell her story. She had not even sense enough to tell it different. But that, my child, is why it is better to have a kind friend to look after you when you start a flirtation with the gay if treacherous Lotharios of the Astral World."

"I hope you don't think I'm a woman like that!"

"All women are like that."

She bit her lips; but her good sense showed her that his main principle was right. If she had only been able to stifle the formless promptings which were so alluring and so dangerous! But as she could not live wholly on the heights of aspiration, so also she could not live on the safe plains of earth-life. The voices of the swamp and the cavern called to her continuously.

And so the external reconciliation had no deep root. For a few weeks she was better and healthier in body and mind. Then she slipped back into her

sulks, and went "fairy-tale-ing" as she called it, with a very determined mind to be on guard against the interference of Sister Clara. She had begun to familiarise herself with the laws of this other world, and could distinguish symbols and their meanings to some extent; she could even summon certain forms, or banish them. And she set a mighty bar between herself and Sister Clara. She kept herself to the definite creations of her own impulses, would not let herself go except upon some such chosen lines.

In her earth-life, too, she became more obviously ill-tempered; and, as to a woman of her type revenge only means one thing, she amused the garrison exceedingly by attempting flirtations. The rule of the Profess-House happened to include the virtue of chastity, which is an active and positive thing, a passion, not that mere colourless abstinence and stagnation which passes in Puritan countries by that name, breeds more wickedness than all the vice on the planet, and, at the best, is shared by clinkers.

She was clever enough to see in a few hours that she was only making herself utterly ridiculous; but this again did not tend to improve her temper, as many devout ladies, from Dido to Potiphar's wife, have been at the pains to indicate to our psychologists.

The situation grew daily more strained, with now and then an explosion which cleared the air for a while. The discipline of the Profess-House prevented the trouble from spreading; but Cyril Grey confided to Brother Onofrio that he was angrier than ever at the efficient way in which Edwin Arthwait and his merry men had been put out of business.

"I'd give my ears," said Cyril, "to see Edwin, arm in arm with Lucifuge Rofocale, coming up from the bay to destroy us all by means of the Mysterious Amulet of Rabbi Solomon, conferring health, wealth and happiness, with bag complete; also lucky moles and love-charms, price two eleven three to regular subscribers to *The Occult Review.*"

But with June a great and happy change came over Iliel. She became enthralled by the prospect of the miracle that was so soon to blossom on her breast. Her sulkiness vanished; she was blithe and joyous from the day's beginning to its end. She bore fatigue and discomfort without a murmur. She made friends with Sister Clara, and talked to her for hours while she plied her needle upon those necessary and now delightful tasks of making tiny and dainty settings for the expected jewel. She clean forgot the irksomeness of her few restrictions; she recovered all the gaiety and buoyancy of youth; indeed, she had to be cautioned in the mere physical matter of activity. No

longer did she indulge morbid fancies, or take unwholesome pleasure in the contemplation of evil ideas. She was at home in her heaven of romance, the heroine of the most wonderful story in the world. Her love for Cyril showed a tender and more exalted phase; she became alive to her dignity and responsibility. She acquired also a sense of Nature which she had never had before in all her life; she felt a brotherhood with every leaf and flower of the garden, told herself stories of the loves of the fishermen whose sails dotted the blue of the bay, wondered what romances were dancing on the decks of the great white liners that steamed in from America to tour the Mediterranean, laughed with joy over the antics of the children who played on the slopes below the garden, and glowed with the vigour of the sturdy peasants who bore their baskets of fish, or flowers, or their bundles of firewood, up or down the lanes which her terraces overlooked. There was one wrinkled fish-wife who was perfectly delightful: old and worn with a lifetime of toil, she was as cheerful as the day was long; bowed down as she was by her glittering burden, she never failed to stop and wave a hand, and cry "God bless you, pretty lady, and send you safe and happy day!" with the frank warmth of the Italian peasant.

The world was a fine place, after all, and Cyril Grey was the dearest boy in it, and herself the happiest woman.

CHAPTER XXI
OF THE RENEWAL
OF THE GREAT ATTACK;
AND HOW IT FARED

DOUGLAS had been decidedly put out by the death of his wife. After all, she had been a sort of habit; a useful drudge, when all was said. Besides, he missed, acutely, the pleasures of torturing her. His suspicions of the bona fides of Balloch were conjoined with actual annoyance.

It was at this painful moment in his career that Cremers came to the rescue. A widowed friend of hers had left a daughter in her charge: for Cremers had the great gift of inspiring confidence. This daughter was being educated in a convent in Belgium. The old woman immediately telegraphed for her, and presented her to Douglas with the compliments of the season. Nothing could have been more timely or agreeable. She was a gentle innocent child, as pretty and charming as he had ever seen. It was a great point in the game of the astute Cremers to have pleased the sorcerer; and she began insensibly to gain ascendancy over his spirit. He had at first suspected her of being an emissary of his colleague, "A. B.", who might naturally wish to destroy him. For the plan of the sorcerer who wishes to be sole and supreme

is to destroy all rivals, enemies, and companions; while the magician attains supremacy in Unity by constantly uniting himself with others, and finding himself equally in every element of existence. It is the difference between hate and love. He had been careful to examine her magically, and found no trace of "A. B." in her "aura". On the contrary, he concluded that her ambition was to supplant "A. B."; and that went well with his own ideas. But first he must get her into his Fourteen, and have a permanent hold over her.

She, on the other hand, appeared singly desirous of making herself a treasure to him. She knew the one torment that gnawed continually at his liver, the hate of Cyril Grey. And she proposed to herself to win him wholly by offering that gentleman's scalp. She sharpened her linguistic tomahawk.

One fine day in April she tackled him openly on the subject. "Say, great one, you 'n I gotta have another peek at that sperrit writing. Seems t'me that was a fool's game down there." She jerked her head towards the river. "And I don't say but that you done right about Balloch."

Douglas glanced at her sharply in his most dangerous mood. How much did she know of a certain recent manoeuvre? But she went on quite placidly.

"Now, look 'e here. We gotta get these guys. An' we gotta get them where they live. You been hitting at their strong point. Now I tell you something. That girl she live five years with Lavinia King, durn her! I see that bright daughter of Terpsichore on'y five minutes, but she didn't leave one moral hangin' on me, no, sir. Now see here, big chief, you been bearin' the water for them fish, an', natural, off they goes. For the land's sake! Look 'e here, I gotta look after this business. An' all I need is just one hook an' line, an' a pailful o' bait, an' ef I don' land her, never trus' me no more. Ain't I somebody, all ways? Didn' I down ole Blavatzsky? Sure I did. An' ain't this like earin' pie after that?"

The sorcerer deliberated with himself a while. Then he consulted his familiar demons. The omens were confusing. He thought that perhaps he had put his question ambiguously, and tried again in other words. He had begun by asking vaguely "whether Cremers would succeed in her mission", which had earned him a very positive "yes", flanked by a quite unintelligible message about "deception", "the false Dmitri" and "the wrong horse", also some apparent nonsense about Scotland and an island. This time he asked whether Cremers would succeed in luring Lisa to her destruction. This time the answer was more favourable, though tremulous. But ever since his wife's death, his demons had behaved very strangely. They seemed the prey of

hesitation and even of fear. Such as it was, however, their voice now jumped with his own convictions, and he agreed to her proposal.

They spent the evening merrily in torturing a cat by blinding it, and then squirting sulphuric acid on it from a syringe; and in the morning Cremers, with Abdul Bey for bait, set out upon her journey to Naples. Arrived in that favoured spot, she bade Abdul Bey enjoy the scenery, and hold his peace. She would warn him when the hour struck. For Cremers was a highly practical old person. She was not like St. James' devils, who believe and tremble; she disbelieved, but she trembled all the same. She hated Truth, because the Truth sets men free, and therefore makes them happy; but she had too much sense to shut her eyes to it; and though she doubted the causes of magick, and scoffed at all spiritual theory, she could not deny the effects. It was no idle boast of hers that she had destroyed Madame Blavatzsky. Together with another woman, she had wormed her way into the big-hearted Theosophist's confidence, and betrayed her foully at the proper moment. She had tried the same game on another adept; but, when he found her out, and she knew it, he had merely continued his kindnesses. The alternative before her was repentance or brain fever; and she had chosen the latter.

Her disbelief in magick had left her with its correlate, a belief in death. It was the one thing she feared, besides magick itself. But she did not make the mistake of being in a hurry, on that account. The strength of her character was very great, in its own way; and she possessed infinite reserves of patience. She played the game with no thought of the victory; and this is half the secret of playing most games of importance. To do right for its own sake is Righteousness, though if you apply this obvious truth to Art the Philistine calls you names, and your morals in question.

Cremers was a genuine artist in malice. She was not even glad when she had harmed a friend and benefactor, however irreparably; nothing could ever make her glad – but she was contented with herself on such occasions. She felt a sort of sense of duty done. She denied herself every possible pleasure, she hated happiness in the abstract in a genuinely Puritan spirit, and she objected to eat a good dinner herself as much as to consent that anyone else should eat it. Her principal motive in assisting Abdul Bey to his heart's desire was the cynical confidence that Lisa was capable of pouring him out a hell-broth at least forty per cent above proof.

The summer was well begun. The sun had turned toward the southern hemisphere once more; he had entered the Sign of the Lion, and with fierce

and noble heat scarred the dry slopes of Posilippo. Iliel spent most of her time on the Terrace of the Moon at her needlework, watching the ships as they sailed by, or the peasants at their labour or their pastimes.

It was a little before sunset on the first of August. She was leaning over the wall of the Terrace. Sister Clara had gone up to the house to make ready for the adoration of the setting of the sun. Up the uneven flagstones of the lane below toiled the old fishwife with her burden, and looked up with the usual cheery greeting. At that moment the crone slipped and fell. "I'm afraid I've hurt my back," she cried, with an adjuration to some saint. "I can't get up."

Iliel, whether she understood the Italian words fully or no, could not mistake the nature of the accident. She did not hesitate; in a moment she had lowered herself from the wall. She bent down and gave her hand to the old woman.

"Say," said the woman in English, "that boy's just crazy about you; and he's the loveliest man on God's earth. Won't you say one word to him?"

Lisa's jaw dropped in amazement. "What? Who?" she stammered.

"Why, that perfectly sweet Turk, Abdul. Sure, you know him, dearie!" Cremers was watching Lisa's face; she read the answer. She gave a low whistle, and round the corner Abdul Bey came running. He took Lisa in his arms, and rained kisses passionately on her mouth.

She had no thought of resistance. The situation entranced her. The captive princess; the intrigue; the fairy prince; every syllable was a poem.

"I've longed for you every hour for months," she cried, between his kisses; "why, oh why didn't you come for me before?" She had no idea that she was not telling the truth. The past was wiped clean out of her mind by the swirl of the new impulse; and once outside the enchanted circle of the garden, her vow in tatters, there was nothing to remind her.

"I'm – here – now." The words burst, like explosions, from his lips. "Come. I've got a yacht waiting."

"Take me – oh, take me – where you will."

Cremers was on her feet, spry and business-like. "We're best out of here," she said. "Let's beat it!" Taking Lisa's arms, she and Abdul hurried her down the steps which led to the Shore-road.

Brother Onofrio's patrol witnessed the scene. He took no notice; it was not against that contingency that he was armed. But at the summons to the Adoration he reported the event to his superior.

Brother Onofrio received the news in silence, and proceeded to perform the ceremony of the Salutation.

An hour later, as supper ended, the sound of the bell rang through the House. The visitor was Simon Iff.

He found Cyril dressed in everyday clothes, no more in his green robe. The boy was smoking a cigar upon the Terrace where he had read his poem on the day after Walpurgis Night.

He did not rise to greet his master. "Tell the Praetor that you have seen Caius Marius, a fugitive seated upon the ruins of Carthage!" he exclaimed.

"Don't take it so hardly, boy!" cried the old mystic. "The man who makes no mistakes makes nothing. But it is my duty to reprove you, and we had better get it over. Your whole operation was badly conceived; in one way or another it was bound to fail. You select a woman with no moral strength – not even with that code of convention which helps so many weak creatures through their temptations. I foresaw from the first that soon or late she would throw up the Experiment."

"Your words touch me the more deeply because I also foresaw it from the first."

"Yet you went on with it."

"Oh no!" Cyril's eyes were half closed.

"What do you mean – Oh, no!" cried the other sharply. He knew his Cyril like a book.

"I never even began," murmured the boy, dreamily.

"You will be polite to explain yourself."

Simon's lips took a certain grimness of grip upon themselves.

"This telegram has consoled me in my grief," said Cyril, taking with languid grace a slip of paper from his pocket. "It came last week."

Simon Iff turned it towards the light. "Horatii," he read. "A code word, I suppose. But this is dated from Iona, from the Holy House where Himself is!" "Himself" was the word used in the Order to designate its Head.

"Yes," said Cyril, softly, "I was fortunate enough to interest Himself in the Experiment; so Sister Cybele has been there, under the charge of the Mahathera Phang!"

"You young devil!" It was the first time that Simple Simon had been startled in forty years. "So you arranged this little game to draw the enemy's fire?"

"Naturally, the safety of Sister Cybele was the first consideration."

"And 'Horatii'?"

"It's not a code word. I think it must be Roman History."

"Three Boys!"

"Rather a lot, isn't it?"

"They'll be needed," said Simon grimly. "I have been doing magick too."

"Do tell me."

"The Quest of the Golden Fleece, Cyril. I've been sowing the Dragon's Teeth; you remember? Armed men sprang to life, and killed each other."

"But I don't see any armed men."

"You will. Haven't you seen the papers?"

"I never see papers. I'm a poet, and I like my lies the way mother used to make them."

"Well, Europe's at war I have got your old commission back for you, with an appointment as Intelligence Officer on the staff of General Cripps."

"It sounds like Anarchism. From each according to his powers; to each according to his needs, you know. By the way, what's it about? Anything?"

"The people think it's about the violation of solemn treaties, and the rights of the little nations, and so on; the governments think it's about commercial expansion; but I who made it know that it is the baptism of blood of the New Aeon. How could we promulgate the Law of Liberty in a world where Freedom has been strangled by industrialism? Men have become such slaves that they submit to laws which would have made a revolution in any other country since the world began; they have registration cards harder to bear than iron fetters; they allow their tyrants to bar them from every pleasure that even their poverty allows them. There is only one way to turn the counter-jumper into a Curtius and the factory girl into a Cornelia; and I have taken it."

"How did you work it?"

"It has been a long business, But as you know. Sir Edward is a mystic. You saw that article on fishing, I suppose?"

"Oh yes; I knew that. But I didn't know it was more definite."

"It was he did it. But he'll lose his place; he's too fair-minded; and in a year they'll clamour for fanatics. It's all right; they'll butt each other's brains out; and then the philosophers will come back, and build up a nobler type of civilisation."

"I think you accused me recently of using strong medicine."

"I was practising British hypocrisy on you. I had to see the Prime Minister

that week. Excuse me if I answer a humourist according to his humour. I want to show you how necessary this step has been. Observe: the bourgeois is the real criminal, always."

"I'm with you there."

"Look at the testimony of literature. In the days of chivalry our sympathies go with the Knight-errant, who redresses wrongs; with the King, whose courage and wisdom deliver his people from their enemies. But when Kingship became tyranny, and feudalism oppression, we took our heroes from the rebels. Robin Hood, Hereward the Wake, Bonnie Prince Charlie, Rob Roy; it was always the Under Dog that appealed to the artist. Then industrialism became paramount, and we began – in Byron's time – to sympathise with brigands and corsairs. Presently these were wiped out, and today or rather, the day before yesterday, we were reduced to loving absolute scoundrels, Arsene Lupin, Raffles, Stingaree, Fantomas, and a hundred others, or the detectives who (although on the side of society) were equally occupied in making the police look like fools. That is the whole charm of Père What's-his-name in Gaboriau, and Dupin, and Sherlock Holmes. There has never been a really sympathetic detective in fiction who was on good terms with the police! And you must remember that the artist always represents the subconscious will of the people. The literary hack who panders to the bourgeois, and makes his heroes of millionaires' sons, has never yet created a character, and never will. Well, when the People love a burglar, and hate a judge, there's something wrong with the judges."

"But what are you doing here, in a world crisis?"

"I'm over here to buy Italy. Bowling bought Belgium, you know, some time back. He was thick with Leopold, but the old man had too much sense to deal. He knew he would be the first to go smash when the war came. But Albert pocketed the good red gold without a second thought; that's partly what the trouble is over. Germany found out about it."

"And why buy Italy? To keep Austria busy, I suppose? These Wops can hardly hope to force the line, especially with the Trentino Salient on the flank."

"That's the idea. It would have been better and cheaper to buy Bulgaria. But Grey wouldn't see it. There's the eternal fear of Russia to remember. We're fighting against both sides in the Balkans! And that makes Russia half-hearted, and endangers the whole Entente. But it doesn't matter so long as enough people are killed. The survivors must have elbow-room for their souls, and

the memory of heroic deeds in the lives of them and theirs to weigh against the everlasting pull of material welfare. When those men come back from a few years in the trenches, they'll make short work of the pious person that informs them of the wickedness of smoking, and eating meat, and drinking beer, and being out after eleven o'clock at night, and kissing a girl, and reading novels, and playing cards, and going to the theatre, and whistling on the Sabbath!"

"I hope you're right. You're old, which tends, I suppose, to make you optimistic. In my young ears there always rings the scream of terror of the slave when you offer to strike off his fetters."

"All Europe will be scream and stench for years to come. But the new generation will fear neither poverty nor death. They will fear weakness; they will fear dishonour."

"It is a great programme. *Qui vivra verra*. Meanwhile, I suppose I report to General Cripps."

"You will meet him, running hard, I expect, somewhere in France. It will be a fluke if Paris is saved. As you know, it always takes England three years to put her boots on. If we had listened to the men who knew – like 'Bobs' – and fixed up an army of three millions, there could have been no war – at least, not in this particular tangle of alliances. There would have been a Social Revolution, more likely, an ignoble business of greed against greed, which would have left men viler and more enslaved than ever. As it is, the masses on both sides think they are fighting for ideals; only the governments know what hypocrisy and sham it is; so the ideals will win, both in defeat and victory. Man! only three days ago France was the France of Panama, and Dreyfus, and Madame Humbert, and Madame Steinheil, and Madame Caillaux; and today she is already the France of Roland and Henri Quatre and Danton and Napoleon and Gambetta and Joan of Arc!"

"And England of the Boer wars, and the Irish massacres, and the Marconi scandals, and Tran by Croft?"

"Oh, give England time! She'll have to be worse before she's better!"

"Talking of time, I must pack up if I'm to catch the morning train for the Land of Hope and Glory."

"The train service is disorganised. I came from Toulon in a destroyer; she'll take you back there. Jack Manners is in command. Report at Toulon to the O. C.! You'd better start in half-an-hour, I'll see you safe on board. My car's at the door. Here's your commission!"

572

Cyril Grey thrust the document into his pocket, and the two men went up into the house.

An hour later they were aboard the destroyer; they shook hands in silence. Simon Iff went down the gangway, and Manners gave the word. As they raced northward, they passed under the lee of Abdul's yacht, where Lisa, up to the eyes in champagne, was fondling her new lover.

Her little pig-like eyes sparkled through their rolls of fat; her cheeks, the colour and consistency of ripe Camembert cheese, sagged pendulous upon a many-chinned neck which looked almost goitrous; and the whole surmounted one of those figures dear to engineers, because they afford endless food for speculation as to the means of support. The moon was now exercising her full influence, totally unchecked and unbalanced; and the woman's nature being wholly of the body, with as little brain in proportion as a rhinoceros, the effect was seen mostly on the physical plane. Her mind was a mere swamp of succulent luxury. So she sat there and swayed and wallowed over Abdul Bey. Cremers thought she looked like a snow man just beginning to melt.

With a sardonic grin, the old woman waved her hand, and went on deck. The yacht was now well out in the open sea on her way to Marseilles. Here Cremers was to be landed, so that she might return to Paris to report her success to Douglas, while the lovers went on their honeymoon. The wind blew fresh from the south-west, and Cremers, who was a good sailor, came as near as she ever could to joy as she felt the yacht begin to roll, and pictured the tepid ice-cream heroine of romance in the saloon.

Meanwhile, the destroyer, her nose burrowing into the sea like a ferret slipped into a warren, drove passionately towards Toulon. The keenness and ecstasy of Cyril's face were so intense that Manners rallied him about it.

"I thought you were one of the all-men-are-brothers crowd," he said. "Yet you're as keen as mustard to slay your cousin-German."

"Puns," replied Cyril, "are the torpedo-boat destroyers of the navy wit. Consider yourself crushed. Your matchless intelligence has not misled you as to my views. All men are brothers. As a magician, I embrace, I caress, I slobber over the cheeks of Bloody Bill. But fighting in the army is not a magical ceremony. It is the senseless, idiotic, performance of a numbskull, the act, in a word, of a gentleman; and as, to my lasting shame, I happened to be born in that class, I love to do it. Be reasonable! It's no pleasure to me, as an immortal God, to sneeze; I refuse to render myself a laughing-stock

to the other Olympians by such indignity; but when my body has a cold in its head, it is proper for it to blow its nose. I do not approve, much less participate; and my body is therefore the more free to act according to its nature, and it blows its nose much harder than it would if I took a hand. That is the advantage of being a magician; all one's different parts are free to act with the utmost possible vigour according to their own natures, because the other parts do not interfere with them. You don't let your navigators into the stoke-hole, or your stokers into the chart-house. The first art in adeptship is to get your elements sorted out and specialised and organised and disciplined. Here endeth the first lesson. I think I'll turn in."

"It's a bit beyond me, Cyril. All I know is that I'm willing to risk my life in a good cause."

"But it's a rotten bad cause! We have isolated Germany and hemmed her in for years exactly as we did a century ago with Napoleon; Wilhelm, who wanted peace, because he was getting fat on it, knew us for his real enemy. In 'ninety-nine he came within an ace of uniting Europe against us, at the time of the Fashoda incident. But we baffled him, and since then he has been getting deeper in every moment. He tried again over the Boer war. He tried threats, he tried diplomacy, he tried everything. The Balkan War and the Agadir incident showed him his utter helplessness. The kingdom of Albania! The war in Tripoli proved that he could no longer rely on Italy. And when Russia resorted to so shameless an assassination as that of Sarajevo – my dear good man! England has been a pirate as she always was. From Hengist and Horsa, and the Vikings, she first learnt the trick. William the Conqueror was a pirate; so was Francis Drake. Look at Morgan, whom we knighted, and all the other buccaneers! Look at our system of privateering! Ever hear of the 'Alabama'? We learnt the secret of sea-power; we can cut the alimentary canal of any nation in Europe – bar Switzerland and Russia. Hence our fear of Russia! It's the Jolly Roger you should fly, Jack Manners! We stood all Germany's expansion; we said we were her cousins – but when she, started a Navy, that was another barrel of fish!"

"I don't think I can bear this, you know!"

"Cheer up! I'm one of the pirate crew!"

"Oh, you're Captain Kidd!"

"I have already stated my opinion as to the conversational value of puns. I'm going to turn in; you get busy, and find a neutral ship to rob."

"I shall do my best to maintain the law of the sea."

"Made by the pirate to suit his game. Good God! I can't see why we shouldn't be sensible. Why must we invoke Law and Gospel every time we want to do a dirty act? My character's strong enough to let me kill all the Germans I can without persuading myself that I'm saving them from Prussian Tyranny! Goodnight!"

"The youth is unintelligible or immoral," thought Manners, as he turned his face to the spindrift; "but I bet he kills a lot of Germans!"

CHAPTER XXII

OF A CERTAIN DAWN UPON OUR OLD FRIEND THE BOULEVARD ARAGO;

AND OF THE LOVES OF LISA LA GIUFFRIA AND ABDUL BEY, HOW THEY PROSPERED. OF THE CONCLUSION OF THE FALSE ALARM OF THE GREAT EXPERIMENT, AND OF A CONFERENCE BETWEEN DOUGLAS AND HIS SUBORDINATES.

LORD ANTONY BOWLING was one of three men in the War Office who could speak French perfectly; despite this drawback, he had been selected to confer with the French headquarters in Paris. Here he met Cyril Grey, busy with his tailor. The young magician had once held a captaincy in a

Hussar regiment, but a year of India had developed his native love of strange places and peoples. He had been tempted to resign his commission, and yielded. He had gone exploring in Central Asia, and the deadly districts beyond Assam. He could not stand gymkhanas, polo, and flirtation. Simon Iff had given him a hint now and again of what magick might effect if a war came, and the boy had profited. He had formed provisional plans.

He encountered Lord Antony by chance one evening on the Boulevard des Italiens, dined him, and on finding that all amusements, even that of watching the world from the terrace of a cafe, were to end by order of the Military Governor of Paris, at eight o'clock, suggested that they should spend the evening smoking opium *"chez Zizi"*, a delightful girl who lived with a brilliant young English journalist on the Boulevard M. Marcel. At midnight, serenely confident that God was in his heaven, as asserted by the late Robert Browning, they decided to finish the night at Cyril's studio. Here the young magician "reconstructed the crime" of the jumping balls of the mysterious countess, and recounted the episode of the Thing in the Garden, to the delectation of the "Merman of Mayfair". He then offered to amend Bowling's coat of arms by the introduction of twelve prawns couchant, gules, gartered azure, and the substitution of Poltergeists for the Wild Men of the ducal escutcheon.

Modestly disclaiming these heraldic glories, Lord Antony regaled his host with an ingenious account of a Swedish gentleman who materialised the most voluminous spectres from – as subsequently appeared in circumstances which can only be qualified as dramatic – the contents of a steel cylinder measuring twelve inches in length and three in diameter, which a search of the medium, stripped to the buff, had at first failed to disclose.

But neither was honestly interested in his own remarks; the subconscious excitement of the War made all conversation on any other topic sound miserably artificial. Bowling's story made them both distrait; they fell into a heavy silence, pondering methods of concealing dispatches or detecting spies. Investigation of spiritualism makes a capital training-ground for secret service work; one soon gets up to all the tricks.

Presently Cyril Grey began to preach magick.

"Germany is on a pretty good wicket," he said. "She is at war; we have only taken a holiday to go fighting. The first condition of success in magick is purity of purpose. One must let no other consideration interfere with the business in hand. But we are hypocrites in England; consequently, we

compromise and fumble. When a magician does get in charge of an affair, all goes pretty well; look how Simple Simon has isolated Germany! Even there he has been thwarted by the Exchequer; five millions in the right place would have bought the Balkans. How much do you think that little economy will cost us before we're through? As for the foolishness of leaving Turkey doubtful, it's beyond all words!"

"Yes," agreed Bowling "we ought to have supported Abdul Hamid from the first. The best kind of Englishman is blood brother to the best kind of Mussulman. He is brave, just, frank, manly and proud. We should always be in alliance with Islam against the servile Hindus and so-called Christians. Where is the spirit of the Paladins and the Templars and the Knights of the Round Table? The modern Christian is the Bourgeois, whose character is based on fear and falsehood."

"There are two kinds of animals, mainly: one whose defence is obscurity, shunning death, avoidance of danger; the other whose defence is attack."

"Yes; we're all right so long as we make ourselves feared. But Victorian prudery turned our tigers into oxen; we found that it was wrong fight dangerous to drink beer, wicked to love; presently it was cruel to eat beef, immoral to laugh, fatal to breathe. We went in terror of the omnipresent germ. Hence we are fat, cowardly slaves. I hear that Kitchener is hard put to it to get his first 100,000 men. Only the public schools respond. Only gentlemen and sportsmen really love England – the people that have been cursed these last few years as tyrants and libertines."

"Only the men."

"And few there are, in the crowd of canaille, old women, slackers, valetudinarians, eaters of nuts!"

"God rest the soul of Edward Seventh! I thought all would be well when Victoria died; but now – "

"This is no hour of the night to lapse into poetry! Anyhow, Germany is nearly as bad, with her Social Democratic Party."

"Do you think that?" cried Cyril, sharply, sitting up. His gesture was indecipherably intense; it seemed utterly disproportionate to Bowling's casual commonplace.

"I know it. It's one of the chief causes of the war. The Zabern incident showed the Junkers that they were safe only for a year or two; after that the people would start out to be too proud to fight," replied Lord Antony, anticipating a transpontine chameleon.

"And so?" Cyril's voice trembled. A tense thrill ran through his body. He had become sober in an instant.

"The Court Party wanted war, to bring back the manly spirit to the nation, and incidentally to keep their place in the sun."

The boy sank with a large sigh into his seat. His tone changed to its old supercilious slurring.

"Bloody Bill was afraid for his dynasty?"

"Scared green."

"Don't talk for five minutes, there's a good chap! I've a strange feeling come over me – almost as if I were going to think!"

Lord Antony obliged with silence. The five minutes became twenty. Then Cyril spoke.

"I had better get to Cripps double quick," said he; "I'm his Intelligence Officer, and I think it my duty to inform him of the plans of the German Great General Staff!"

"Yes, you should certainly do that!" answered Lord Antony, laughing.

"Then let's stroll up the Boulevard. Dawn's breaking. We'll get a *cafe-brioche* at the Rotonde, and then I'll tyrannise my tailor, and get off."

They went out into the cold morning air. Three hundred yards away, outside the Sante prison, a small crowd had collected. The centre of attraction seemed to be a framework, two narrow uprights crowned with a cross-bar where a triangular piece of metal glittered in the pale twilight.

"Peace hath her victories no less renowned than war!" drawled Cyril, cynically. "Confess that I have entertained you royally! Here is a choice savoury to wind up our feast."

Lord Antony could not conceal his horror and repulsion. For he knew well enough what sight chance had prepared for them. But the fascination drew him far more surely than if his temperament had resembled that of his friend. They approached the crowd. A ring was kept about the framework by a cordon of police.

Just then the gates of the prison opened, and a little procession came out. All eyes were drawn instantly to its central figure, an old, old man whose jaw was dropped, and from whose throat issued a hoarse howling, utterly monotonous and inhuman. His eyes were starting from his head, and their expression was one not to be described. His arms were bound tightly to his sides. Two men were half supporting him, half pushing him. Save for his horrible cry, there was no sound. There was no movement in the crowd – no

579

whisper. Like automata the officials did their duty. In a trice the prisoner was thrown forward on to a board, thrust up toward the framework. His caterwaul suddenly ceased. A moment later a sharp order rang out in the voice of one of the prison officials. The knife fell. From the crowd burst a most dreadful sound an "Ah!" so low, so fierce, that it had no human quality. Lord Antony Bowling could never be sure whether it was after that or before it that he heard the head tumble into the basket.

"Who was it?" asked Cyril of a bystander.

"*Un anglais*," answered the man. "*Le docteur* Balloch."

Cyril started back. He had not recognised his old enemy.

But even at that moment he was accosted by one whom he would never fail to know, even dressed as he was in the uniform of French colonel – Douglas. On his arm was a child whose eyes were blear already with debauchery, who staggered, her eyes rolling, her hair dishevelled, her mouth loose and wet, laughing with indecent and profane intoxication.

"Good morning, Captain Grey; well met, well met indeed!" began Douglas, urbane in his triumph.

"I trust you passed a pleasant time in Naples."

"Very pleasant," returned Grey. "Dr. Balloch," continued Douglas, "crossed my path. I am glad you should have seen the end of him."

"I am glad," said Cyril.

"And what end do you think I have reserved for you?" said the sorcerer, with a sudden foam of ferocity.

"Something charming, I am sure," said Cyril, silkily. "I always admired your work, you know. That translation of *The Book of the Sacred Magick of Abramelin the Mage*, in particular. You remember the passage about the wicked Antony of Prague," he went on, with sudden force and solemnity, "the marvellous things he did, and how he prospered – and how he was found by the roadside, his tongue torn out, and the dogs at feast upon his bowels! Do you know what has saved you so far? Only one bar between you and destruction – the love of your wife, whom you have murdered!" With that Cyril cried aloud three words in a strange tongue, and giving the other no chance to reply, marched rapidly away with his friend.

Douglas could not have recovered, in any case. He was as one stunned. How did this boy know of the death of his wife? Well, that might be understood; but how did he know his most secret fear, the fact that since

580

the crime his demons had lost their courage? He shook the feeling off, and turned again to gloat over the death of Balloch.

"Who was that?" asked Bowling.

"The Grand Panjandrum himself, with the little round button on top! That's Douglas!"

"The Black Lodge man?"

"Ex-man."

"I see daylight. Balloch was condemned, you know, for a crime done twenty years ago. Douglas must have known about it and betrayed him."

"That's the regular thing."

"How does he come to be a colonel in the French Army?"

"Don't know. He was close in with one or two ministers; Becasseux, I think, in particular. There's a lot of politics in Occultism, as you know."

"I'll think that over. I might ask the minister this morning. But I tell you it's no time for trifles. Ever since all the mobilisation plans were scrapped by the failure of Liege and Namur to hold out, distraction has reigned supreme, no casual mistress, but a wife, and procuress to the Lords of Hell at that!"

"Do not quote Tennyson, even mixed, under the shadow of the Lion de Belfort! As to trifles, there are none in war. Ask the Germans if you don't believe me."

A little later, after the Rotonde Cafe in the Boulevard Montparnasse had refreshed them with its admirable coffee, and those brioches which remind one of boyhood's earliest kisses, they walked down to the Place de la Concorde, and parted.

Cyril went on to the Opera, to his tailor in the Rue de la Paix. His mind was full of meditations upon the details of the great idea that had come to him, the divination of the enemy's objective. His suggestion had made Lord Antony laugh. He himself had never felt less like laughing; he was on fire with creative genius – and terrified lest his work should fall upon barren soil. Well he knew how hard it is to get Power to listen to Reason!

At the corner of the Place de l'Opera he lifted his eyes to assure himself of a free crossing.

The mind of Abdul Bey was in turmoil. His first night upon the yacht had been mere wallowing in debauch; but he woke with a clear head, acutely alive to the complexity of his situation. He was personally triumphant; there was nothing in his private affairs to worry him. But in charge, as he was, of

the Turkish Secret Service in Paris, he knew the political situation well enough. He knew that Turkey would throw in her lot with Germany, sooner or later; and he was doubtful as to the wisdom of returning to France. On the other hand, duty called him with clarion voice; and he wanted to have as many fingers as possible in the pie. After much consideration, he thought he would land at Barcelona, and get through with his American passport – for he had papers from most nations – as a distracted millionaire. His companions – both American citizens – would aid the illusion. Supposing that there was already trouble or suspicion, this subterfuge would serve; once in Paris, he could find out how the land lay, and act accordingly.

He gave orders to the captain to make for Catalonia. The voyage was uneventful, save for the brief visit of a cruiser which discovered nothing contraband; in fact, Abdul and Lisa remained drunk the whole time. Only, just off the Spanish coast, a capful of wind once again interfered with Lisa's enjoyment of the honeymoon. It had another consequence, more serious. No sooner had they landed at Barcelona, than Lisa became suddenly and terribly ill. After a week, the doctors decided upon a radical remedy-operation. The next day a girl child entered the world, very much alive, despite the irregularity of her entrance. No ordinary child, either. She was a beautifully made baby, with deep blue eyes; and she was born with four teeth, and with hair six inches long, so fair as to be silvery white. Like a tattoo-mark, just over the heart, was a faint blue crescent.

Lisa recovered rapidly from her illness, but not too quickly for the amorous Turk; though he was surprised and annoyed to find that she had recovered her early grace and activity. The fat had gone from her in the three weeks of illness; and when she began to be able to move about, and drive in the city, she looked once more almost as she did on the night when Cyril first saw her, a gay, buxom, vigorous woman. The change cooled Abdul's ardour, and her own feelings altered with it. Her lover's sloppiness began to disgust her. As to the child, it was a source of irritation to both of them. Cremers, again, was hardly a boon companion; she would have depressed a hypochondriac going to the funeral of a beloved uncle who had left him nothing. Before Lisa had been out of bed three days, a crisis arose; she felt instinctively that Paris would be "no fun", and wanted to go to America. Abdul felt that he must lose no time in getting to Paris. Cremers, for some reason, had changed her mind about reporting to Douglas; she was homesick for West 186th Street, so she said.

The explosion came at lunch, the Spanish nurse having failed to muffle the baby with due adequacy.

"Oh hell!" said Abdul Bey.

"God knows, I don't want the little beast!" said its proud mother.

"Looke here!" remarked Cremers. "I do want it. Sure some baby!"

"Oh hell!" repeated Abdul Bey.

"Looke here! You gimme the rocks, an' I'll take her across the pond. There's ships. Gimme three thousand bucks and expenses, and three thousand every year, and I'll fix it. You folks get off and paint Paree pink. Is it a go?"

Abdul Bey brightened immediately. Only one thought chilled him. "What about Douglas?" he said.

"I'll 'tend to that." "It's a good scheme," muttered Lisa.

"Let's get away tonight; I'm sick of this hole." She caressed the Turk warmly.

But Paris was no longer the Paris of her dreams, no longer the Paris of idleness and luxury "where good Americans go when they die"; it was a Paris of war, of stern discipline, of patriotic enthusiasm, nothing less than a nightmare for the compatriots of the lady who didn't raise her boy to be a soldier. She blamed Abdul, who shrugged his shoulders, and reminded her that she was lucky to get dinner at all, that the Germans were likely to be in the city in a week or so. She taunted him; he let loose his ancestral feelings about women, those which lie deep-buried in all of us who are at least not utterly degenerate in soul, however loose morality may have corrupted us upon the surface. She rose in the automobile, just as they crossed the Place de l'Opera, and broke her parasol over his head; then turned her nails loose on his eyes. He fisted her in the abdomen, and she collapsed into the seat of the car with a scream. It was this that diverted the attention of Cyril Grey from his contemplation of the designs of Germany.

The boy made a leap, and had Abdul by the throat in a moment, dragging him out of the car, and proceeding to administer summary castigation with his boot. But the police interfered; three men rode up with drawn sabres, and put an end to the affair. They arrested all parties, and Cyril Grey only escaped by the exhibition of that paper which had won him such respect months earlier on the shambles of Moret railway station.

"I have to go to my tailor: service of the minister," he remarked with a cynical smile; and was dismissed with the profoundest respect.

"After all, it was no business of mine," he muttered as he wriggled into his new tunic, to the immense admiration of the tailor, a class whose appreciation

of manly beauty depends so largely upon the price of the suit. "'Tis better to have loved and lost than never to have loved at all. The trouble comes when you can't lose 'em. Poor old Lisa! Poor old Abdul! Well, as I said, it's none of my business. My business is to divine the thoughts of the enemy, and – oh Lord! how long? – to get the powers that be to understand that I am right. Considering that they needed eight million marching men to persuade them that Bloody Bill meant war, I fear that my task may be no sinecure."

He went to the barracks, where a military automobile was waiting for him, and told the chauffeur, with bitter wit, to go out to meet General Cripps. As to Lisa and the Turk, it was twenty-four hours before they were set at liberty. The sight of Cyril, his prompt intervention in her defence, relit the flames of her half crazy passion. She rushed over to the studio to see him; it was shut up, and the concierge could give her no news. She drove wildly to the Profess-House in Montmartre. There they told her that he had gone to join the British army. Various excited enquiries in official quarters led her at last to Lord Antony Bowling. He was genuinely sympathetic: he had liked the girl at first sight; but he could hold out no hopes of arranging for her to see him.

"There's only one way for you to get to the front," said he. "Join the Red Cross. My sister's here forming a section. I'll give you a note to her, if you like."

Lisa jumped at the suggestion. She saw, more vividly than if it were actual, the obvious result. Cyril would be desperately wounded, leading the last victorious charge of the dragoons against the walls of Berlin; she would interestingly nurse him back to life, probably by means of transfusion of blood; then, raised to the peerage, Marshal Earl Grey of Cologne (where he had swum the Rhine, and, tearing the keys of the city from the trembling hands of the astonished burgomaster, had flung them back across the river to his hesitating comrades) would lead her, with the Victoria Cross in gold and diamonds on his manly bosom, to the altar at St. Margaret's, Westminster.

It was worth while learning magick to become clairvoyant like this! She dashed off, still at top speed, to enroll herself with Lady Marcia Bowling.

She gave no further thought to Abdul. He would never have attracted her, had she not perceived a difficulty in getting him.

As to that gentleman himself, if grief tore at his heart strings, he showed it that night in an unusual way. It may have been but simulation of

584

philosophical fortitude; there is no need to enquire. His actions are of more interest: they consisted of picking up a *cocotte* on the Boulevard des Italiens, and taking her to dinner at the Café de Paris. At the conclusion of a meal which would have certainly been prescribed as a grief-cure to any but a dyspeptic, the *maitre d'hotel* approached their table, and tendered, with a bow, an envelope. Abdul opened it – it was a summons from Douglas to appear immediately in his presence at the apartment in the Faubourg St. Germain.

The Turk had no choice but to comply. He excused himself to his fair guest, at the cost of a hundred-franc note, and drove immediately to the rendezvous.

Douglas received him with extreme heartiness.

"A thousand congratulations, dear young man, upon your brilliant victory! You have succeeded where older and more learned men failed badly. I called you here tonight to tell you that you are now eligible for a place in the Fourteen, the Ghaagaael, for a seat is vacant since this morning."

"They executed Balloch?"

Douglas nodded with a gloating smile.

"But why did you not save him, master?"

"Save him! It was I that destroyed him when he tried to betray me. Candidates take notice!"

Abdul protested his loyalty and devotion.

"The supreme test," continued Douglas, "cannot conveniently be imposed in time of war. There is too much to do just now. But – as a preliminary – how do you stand with Germany?"

Abdul shrank back, startled out of his presence of mind.

"Germany!" he stammered at last. "Why, Colonel," (he emphasised the title) "I know nothing. I have no instructions from my Government." He met the eye of his master, and read its chill contempt. "I – er – er-"

"Dare you play with me?"

The young man protested that no such thought had crossed his mind.

"In that case," pursued the sorcerer, "you won't know what that means."

Douglas took from his pocket a fifty-franc note. The Turk caught it up, his eyes grown momentarily wider with surprise.

"Examine it!" said Douglas, coldly.

The Turkish agent held it to the light. In the figures numbering the note were two small pinpricks.

"Allah!" he cried. "Then you are – "

"I am. You may as well know that my colleague in the Lodge, 'A. B.', is going to stir up trouble for the British in India. Her influence with certain classes of Hindus is very great. For your part, you may try discreetly to tamper with the Mussulman section of the French troops, the Africans. But be careful – there is more important work to your hand, no less than the destruction of the French armies in the field. Now let us see what you can do. I am going to send you to my little garden hermitage, where I occasionally appear in the character of a great ascetic; there is an old lady there, devoted to me. Have your best man there to play Yogi. In the garden – here's the plan – is the terminal of a wire. There's another in that house where you got baptised and married – remember? Thence there's a cable up Seine to another cottage where that old Belgian mystic lives – the friend of Maeterlinck! Ha! ha! He's really von Walder, a Dresdener. And he is in charge of another cable – underground three hundred miles, thanks to Becasseux, who helped us with the road squads, to a place which by now is firmly in the hands of the Crown Prince. So all you have to do is to tell your man to sit and pretend to meditate – and tap. I shall send you plenty of information from the front. You will know my agents by a nick filed in a trouser-button. Each message will have a number, so that you will know if any go astray. All clear?"

"Admirable. I need not say how proud I am to find that we are on the same side. I was very frightened of that uniform!"

"*L'hobit ne fait pas le moine*," replied Douglas gaily. "And now, sir, let us spend the night discussing our plans in detail – and some very excellent whisky which I happen to have by me."

The spies pursued their double task, with pitiless energy, till morning was well broken. Later in the day Douglas left for Soissons. He was attached to the French army as chief of a corps of signallers – thanks, once again, to the good offices of Becasseux. His plans were perfect: they had been cut and dried for over fifteen years.

CHAPTER XXIII

OF THE ARRIVAL OF A CHINESE GOD UPON THE FIELD OF BATTLE;

OF HIS SUCCESS WITH HIS SUPERIORS AND OF A SIGHT WHICH HE SAW UPON THE ROAD TO PARIS. ALSO OF THAT WHICH THEREBY CAME UNTO HIM. AND OF THE END OF ALL THOSE THINGS WHOSE EVENT BEGAT A CERTAIN BEGINNING

UNMATCHED in history is the Retreat of the British Army from Mons. It was caught unprepared; it had to fight three weeks before it was ready; it was outnumbered three to one by a triumphant enemy; it was not co-ordinated with the French armies, and they failed to support it at critical moments; yet

it fought that awful dogged fight from house to house, and field to field, through league on league of Northern France. The line was forced to lengthen constantly as the retreat continued; it was attenuated by that and by its losses to beyond any human breaking-point; but luckily for England, her soldiers are made of such metal that the thinner the wire is drawn the tougher it becomes.

However, there is a point at which "open order" is like the word "decolletée" used to describe a smart American woman's dinner dress; and General Cripps was feeling it at the moment when his new Intelligence Officer presented himself. It was about six o'clock at night; Cripps and his staff were bivouacked in the *mairie* of a small village. They were contemplating a further retreat that night.

"Sit down, Captain Grey," said the chief kindly. "Join us at dinner – just as soon as we can get these orders out – listen and you'll pick up the outlines – we'll talk after dinner – on the road."

Cyril took a chair. To his delight, an aide-de-camp, Lord Juventius Mellor, an exquisite young dandy with a languid lisp, who, in time of peace, had been pupil and private secretary of Simon Iff, came to greet him.

"Ju, dear boy, help me out. I've got to tell Cripps something, and he'll think I'm mad. It's bluff, too; but it's true for all that – and it's the one chance in the world."

"Right O!"

"Are we retreating again?"

"All through the night. There's not a dog's chance to save Paris, and the line stretches every hour."

"Don't worry about Paris – it's as safe as Bordeaux. Safer, because the Government is at Bordeaux!"

"My poor friend, wouldn't you be better in a home?"

The British Army had no illusions about its situation. It was a thin, drab line of heroes, very thin and very drab, but there was no doubt about the heroism, and no uncertainty about what would happen to it if the Germans possessed a leader with initiative. So far the hostile legions had moved according to the rules, with all due scientific precaution. A leader of temperament and intuition might have rushed that tenuous line. Still, science was as sure as it was as slow – and the whole army knew it. They prepared to die as expensively as possible, with simplicity of manhood. They had not yet heard that Press and Pulpit had made them the laughing-stock

of the world by the invention of the ridiculous story of the "Angels of Mons". Lord Juventius Mellor was something of a hero-worshipper. From Simon Iff he would have taken any statement with absolute respect, and Grey's remark had been somewhat of the Simon Iff brand. It was, therefore, almost as much an impertinence as it was an absurdity. Paris was as certain to fall as the sun to set. It was in rotten bad taste to joke about it.

"Look here!" said Cyril, "I'm serious."

"All the worse!" retorted Mellor.

"You really would be better in a home."

"You wouldn't talk like that if we were discussing magick."

"True."

"Then you are an ass. I am talking magick. If you had only ears to hear!"

"How?"

"Everything's a magical phenomenon, in the long run. But war's magick, from the word jump. Come now therefore and let us reason together, saith the Lord. I have done a divination by the Tarot, by a method which I cannot explain, for that it pertaineth to a grade so much more exalted than yours that you have never even heard the name of it; and I know the plans of the German General Staff in detail." Cyril's tone transformed his asinine utterance into something so Sybilline, Oracular, Delphic, Cumaean, that his interlocutor almost trembled. *Verus incessu patuit Deus* – when Cyril thought it necessary to impress the uninitiate. To the majority of mankind gold looks like dross unless it be wrapped up in tinsel, and tenfold the proper price marked on it in plain figures, with the word "Sacrifice". Hence it is that the most successful merchants omit the gold altogether.

"Oh; I didn't understand."

"You'll observe that I can't explain this to Cripps; I shall have to spin some sort of a yarn."

"Yes, yes."

In point of fact the "yarn" was already spun; Cyril had not been divining by any means more occult than his innate sagacity; but Lord Juventius was one of those people who bow only before the assumption of authority supported by mystery and tomfoolery, since their reason is undeveloped. Such people make excellent secondary figures in any campaign; for their confidence in their leaders impresses the outsider, who does not know how mentally abject they are. It is said that no man is a hero to his valet. On the contrary, every man is a God to his secretary – if not, he had better get rid of the secretary!

Lord Juventius could not have followed Cyril's very astute calculations – those which he meant to lay before General Cripps; but he would have staked his life on the accuracy of a Tarot divination so obscure that he was not allowed even to hear its nature, and which in fact had not been performed. Indeed, it did not even exist, having been invented on the spur of the moment by the unscrupulous magician.

"I shall tell him that the military situation is inextricably bound up with political and dynastic considerations; I shall drop a word about *Anschauung* and *Weltpolitik*; you know!"

Lord Juventius giggled adorably.

"By the way," continued Cyril, "have you any influence – personal, I mean – with the old man?"

Lord Juventius bent forward with lowered eyelids, and sank his voice to a confidential whisper. "The day we crossed," he murmured.

"Great. But I thought – "

"Prehistoric. It's perfectly Cocker."

Such conversations lack the merit of intelligibility to the outsider; but then the outsider is particularly to be kept from understanding. Dialogues of this curious sort determine most important events in English society and "*haute politique*".

"Then see to it that I get taken seriously."

"Surely, Kurille!" "*Precetur oculis mellitis!*"

"Kurille, Catulle!"

When Englishmen return to the use of the dead languages, it is a sign of that moral state which is said by the Psalmist to resemble the Holy Oil that flowed down upon the head of Aaron, even unto the skirts of his garments.

The orderly called the Staff to dinner. Cyril, as the guest of the evening, was on the Commander-in-Chief's right hand.

"You have been very highly recommended to me," said the old Cavalry leader, when the time came to smoke, "and I look to you to distinguish yourself accordingly. You will be under the orders of Colonel Mavor, of course; you should report to him at once."

"May I give you some information direct?" asked Cyril. "The matter hardly brooks delay, as I see it: you should know it at once, and – to be frank – I think this my best chance of your ever hearing it."

"A damned funny beginning," growled the general. "Well, get on!" The

permission was not very gracious; but an irregularity is a serious thing in the British Army. General Cripps made bad worse.

"Unofficially, mind, absolutely unofficially," he added, before Cyril could begin.

This is the English expedient for listening to anything without hearing it, or saying anything without meaning it. An official conversation cannot be thus sterile; it involves notes, memoranda, dockets, recommendations, reports, the appointment of commissions, interminable deliberations, more reports, questions in Parliament, the introduction of bills, and so on. Nothing is done in the end, exactly as in the case of an unofficial conversation; so you can take your choice, sir, and be damned to you!

"Unofficially, of course, General!" agreed Cyril. "My object is merely to disclose the plans of the German General Staff."

"Thank you, Captain Grey," replied the great man, sarcastically; "this will indeed be a service. To save time, begin from Von Kluck's occupation of Paris, about four days hence."

"Impossible, General! Von Kluck will never capture Paris. Why, the man is actually of plebeian origin!"

"After dinner – but only then – such observations are in perfectly good taste. Proceed!"

"I am not joking in the least, General. Von Kluck will not be allowed to try to capture Paris."

"It is at least curious that he is marching straight upon the city!"

"Only to thin out our line, sir. Do you observe that the Germans have driven a salient to St. Mihiel?"

"I have. What of it?"

"The object, sir, I submit, is to cut off Verdun from the South."

"Yes?"

"Why Verdun? Because the Crown Prince is at the head of the army which threatens it. Paris will never be taken but by that modern Caesar!"

"Something in that, I admit. The little beast is certainly unpopular."

"They are bound to make him the national hero, at any cost."

"And where do we come in?"

"What could be clearer? Their right wing will break through somewhere, or roll us up. Verdun will be isolated. *Der Kronprinz* (God bless his noble heart!) will walk through, and goose-step all the way to Paris. It is the only chance for the Hohenzollern dynasty."

"It is military madness."

"They think they have enough in hand to risk it. But see, sir, for God's sake see the conclusion! If I'm right, Von Kluck is bound to swerve East, right across our front – and we'll smash him!"

"He couldn't risk such a crazy manoeuvre."

"Mark my word, sir, he will."

"And what do you suggest that I should do about it? Unofficially, Captain Grey, quite unofficially!"

"Get ready to lam it in, sir – quite unofficially."

"Well, sir, I congratulate you – on having talked the most amusing nonsense that I've heard since my last talk with General Buller! And now perhaps you had better report to Colonel Mavor as Intelligence Officer." The general's tone was contemptuous. "Facts are required in this army."

"Psychological facts are facts, General."

"Nonsense, sir; you are not in a debating society or at a scientific tea-party."

"That last, sir," replied Cyril coldly, "is my unavailing regret."

But Lord Juventius Mellor frustrated the effect of this impolitic speech. He fixed his languid eyes upon the red face of the veteran, and his voice came in a soft caressing whisper.

"Pardon me; do let us be unofficial for five minutes more!"

"Well, boy?"

"I think it's only fair to let General Foch enjoy the joke. I hear he has been depressed lately."

"He might not take it so easily. The French do not care to be played with when their country is at stake."

"He can only shoot poor Cyril, *mon vieux*! Just give him two days leave, so that he can run over before reporting to Mavor."

"Oh well, I dare say the Intelligence Department can get on without its champion guesser for a day or so. Trot along, Grey; but for your own sake I advise you to think up a fact or two."

Cyril saluted, and took his leave. Juventius came to see him into the car. "I'll wheedle the old ass," he whispered to his friend, "I'll get him to make such dispositions as he can without disturbing the line too much; so that if Foch should see any sense in your scheme, by any chance, we shan't be too backward in coming forward."

"Good for you. So long!"

"Ta."

Cyril drove off. It was a terrible and ominous journey to the headquarters of General Foch. The line sagged hideously here and there so that long detours were necessary. The roads were encumbered not only with every kind of military supply, all in disorder, but with fugitive soldiers and civilians, some burdened with their household goods, some wounded, a long trail of agony lumbering to the rear. The country was already patrolled by herds of masterless and savage dogs, reverted, in a month of war, to the type of the coyote and the dingo. But Cyril shouted in his joy. His confidence rose as he went; he had thought out one of General Cripps's "facts" which he felt sure would carry conviction to the mind of the French commander.

Arrived at the chateau where the general was quartered, he found no trouble in gaining audience. The Frenchman, splendidly built, his eyes glittering with restless intelligence, concentrated all his faculties instantly on his visitor. "You have come from General Cripps?"

"Yes, my General, but on my own responsibility. I have an idea – "

Foch interrupted him.

"But you are in an English uniform!" he could not help saying with brisk Gallic surprise.

"*Cuchullus non facit monachum*," retorted Cyril Grey. "I am half-Scotch, half-Irish."

"Then pray give yourself the trouble to continue."

"I may premise that I have told my idea to General Cripps. It convinced him that I am an imbecile or a joker."

That was his "fact", his master-argument. It told heavily. The face of Foch grew instantly keen and eager with all expectation.

"Let me hear it!"

The General reached for a memorandum.

Grey laughed. In a few words he repeated his theory of the German plans. "But it is certain!" cried Foch. "One moment; excuse me; I must telephone."

He left the room. In five minutes he was back.

"Rest easy, Captain Grey," he said, "we shall be ready to catch Von Kluck as he turns. Now, will you do me the pleasure to take this note back to your chief? The British must be ready to strike at the same moment. I won't ask you to stay; but – I beg of you to come to dine with me after the victory."

It is impossible to give any idea of how the word "*victoire*" sounds in the mouth of a French soldier. It has in it the ring of a sword thrust home to the hilt, and the cry of a lover as he seizes his mistress, and the exultation

of a martyr who in the moment of his murder reaches conclusively to God. Cyril went back to the British Headquarters, and handed in General Foch's request, through Colonel Mavor, officially. The events of the next week are of the very spine of history. The cruel blow was definitely parried. More still, that first great victory not only saved France for all time, but showed that the men of Bonaparte had come into their own moral sublimity again. It proved 1870 to have been but a transient weakness like our own year of shame when Van Tromp swept our ships from the seas.

General Cripps summoned Cyril Grey to his quarters.

"I'm afraid," said the old man, "that nothing can be done to recognise your services. That your crazy theory should have proved correct is only one more example – we have many such every day – of the operation of the laws of Chance. The weather forecasters themselves cannot guess wrong every time. But even if your act had merited reward, we should still have been powerless; for, as you remember, our conversation was strictly unofficial.

"Unofficially, however, you get your step and the K. C. B. Favouritism, sir, rank favouritism! Now go across to General Foch, Major – he wishes to present you to two gentlemen named respectively Joffre and Poincaré. Boot and saddle! No time to waste," he said hastily, to check any expression of gratitude. But as the two men gripped hands, their eyes were dim – they were thinking of England.

So off went Cyril on the road to Paris, where his rendezvous was fixed.

The victory had changed the aspect of the country in the rear of the armies as by stage-craft. There were no more fugitives, no more disorder. Still the long trains of wounded clogged the roads, here and there, but the infection of glory had spread like sunlight over a sky swept clear of storm. The supply trains radiated confidence. Always the young man met new guns, new wagons, new horses. At every turn of the road were fresh regiments, gaily singing on their way to the front. Cyril was enchanted at the aspect of the troops. Their elasticity and high spirits were overwhelming. Once he came upon a regiment of Turcos being transferred to another sector – every man of them with a trophy of the great battle. His intense love for all savage men, true men unspoilt by civilization, almost mastered him: he wanted to embrace them. He saw life assurgent, the menace of the enemy thwarted, and his joy flooded his heart so that his throat caught fire, and song leaped to his lips.

And then chill caught him as he came suddenly upon a dreadful sight.

Before him on the road stood a signpost, the lance of a Spahi, thrust into the bank of a ditch; nailed to it was a placard on which was coarsely chalked the one word ESPION. A fatal curiosity drew him to the spot; as he approached, the wild dogs that were fighting around the sinister signal fled in terror from their ghastly meal.

A sword had been thrust through the belly of the corpse; the tongue had been torn out. One could recognise at a glance the work of Algerian troops – men who had lost a third of their effectives through the treacheries of the German spies. But, despite all mutilation, he recognised more than that: he recognised the carcass. This carrion had once been Douglas.

Cyril Grey did a strange thing, a thing he had not done for many years: he broke into a strong sobbing.

"I know now," he murmured, "that Simon Iff is right. The Way of the Tao! I must follow that harder path, the Path where he who would advance draws back."

He put spurs to his horse; half-an-hour later he saw the sunset glint upon the Eiffel Tower, and on the wings of one of those gallant birds that circled about it to keep watch and ward on Paris. The next morning he reported himself to the British authorities; and it was Lord Antony Bowling who presented him to the President and Commander-in-Chief.

At the banquet he found himself an Officer of the Legion of Honour; but his brilliancy and buoyancy were gone. He dined in dull decorum. His thoughts still turned to the shameful corpse in the ditch by the wayside. He excused himself early, and left the Élysée. At the gate stood an automobile. In it sat Lisa la Giuffria. She jumped out and caught him by the shoulders. She poured out the tale of her madness, and its result, and its cure, her careful tracking of his movements, her determination to recover him at any cost. He listened in silence – the silence of incurable sadness. He shook his head.

"Have you no word for me?" she cried impetuously, torn by her agony.

"Have you no gift for me?" he answered. She understood. "Oh, you are human! you are human!" she cried.

"I do not know what I am," he answered. "Yesterday I saw the end of the game – for one!"

He told her in a few words of the horror on the roadside.

"Go!" he said, "take that girl, Douglas's last victim, for your maid. Go to America; find the Child of the Moon. There may, or there may not be, other tasks for us to do; I know not – time will show."

"I will, I will," she cried, "I will go now, quickly. Kiss me first!"

Once again the tears gathered in the magician's eyes; he understood, more deeply than he had ever done, the Sorrow of the Universe. He saw how utterly incompatible are all our human ideals with the Laws of Life. He took her slowly and gently in his arms; and he kissed her. But Lisa did not respond; she understood that this was not the man whom she had loved: this was a man that she had never known, one whom she dared not love. A man set apart, an idea to adore! She knew herself unworthy, and she withdrew herself.

"I go," she said, "to seek the Child. Hail and farewell!"

"Hail and farewell!" The girl mounted unsteadily into her car. Cyril Grey, his head bowed upon his breast, plunged into the wooded pleasaunce of the Champs Élysées.

An ineffable weariness came upon him as he walked. He wondered dully if he were going to be ill. He came up against the Obelisk in the Place de la Concorde with a shock of surprise. He had not noticed that he had left the trees. The Obelisk decided him; its shape smote into his soul the meaning of the Mysteries of Egyptian Magick. It was as invigorating as a cold plunge. He strode away towards Montmartre.

The Profess-House of the Order had been converted into a hospital. But who should come to greet him if not Sister Cybele?

Beside her stood the severe figure of Simon Iff. There were two others in the background. Cyril was not surprised to see his old master, the Mahathera Phang; but the other? It was Abdul Bey.

"Come forward and shake hands," cried Simon Iff. "I have not been inactive, Cyril," added the old man. "I have had my eye on our young friend for a long time. I put my hand on him at the right moment. I showed him that spying was a dog's game, with a dog's death at the end of it. He has renounced his errors, and he is now a Probationer of our Holy Order."

The young men greeted each other, the Turk stammering out an appeal for pardon, the other laughing off his embarrassment.

"But you are ill, Cyril!" cried Sister Cybele. And in truth the boy could hardly stand.

"Action and reaction are equal and opposite," explained Simon Iff, cheerily. "You will sleep, Brother Cyril, and you will then pass seven days in meditation, in one of the high trances. I will see to the extension of your leave."

"There is a meditation," said Cyril firmly, "given by the Buddha, a meditation upon a corpse torn by wild beasts. I will take that."

Simon Iff acquiesced without comprehending. He did not know that Cyril Grey had understood that the corpse of Douglas was his own; that the perception of the identity of himself with all other living things had come to him, and raised him to a great Adeptship.

But there was one to comprehend the nature of that initiation. As Cyril walked, leaning on the arm of Sister Cybele, to the room appointed for his prescribed solitude, he beheld a great light. It shone serenely from the eyes of the Mahathera Phang.

HOUSEHOLD GODS

A COMEDY BY ALEISTER CROWLEY
[Privately printed in 1912]

TO LEILA WADDELL

SCENE

THE HEARTH OF CRASSUS;
AFTERWARDS THE LAWNS, THE WOODS, THE LAKE, THE ISLE.

CHARACTERS

CRASSUS, a barbarian from Britain.
ADELA, his wife, a noble Roman lady.
ALICIA, a servant in the house.
A STATUE OF PAN.
A FAUN.

HOUSEHOLD GODS

THE SCENE is at the hearth of CRASSUS, where is a little
bronze altar dedicated to the Lares and Penates. A pale
flame rises from the burning sandal-wood, on which CRASSUS
throws benzoin and musk. He is standing in deep dejection.

CRASSUS.
Smoke without fire!
No thrill of tongues licks up
The offerings in the cup.
Dead falls desire.

Black smoke thou art,
O altar-flame, that dost dismember,
Devour the hearth, to leave no ember
To warm this heart.

I see her still
Adela dancing here
Till dim gods did appear
To work our will.

The delicate girl!
Diaphanous gossamer
Subtly revealing her
Brave breast of pearl!

Now she's withdrawn
At dusk to the wild woods,
Mystic beatitudes

That dure till dawn.

Let life exclaim
Against these things of spirit,
Mankind that disinherit
Of love's pure flame!
[He bends before the altar and begins to weep.]

Ye household gods!
By these male tears I swear
That ye shall grant this prayer.
All things at odds

Shall be put straight
Harmonised, reconciled
By some appointed child
Of some far Fate!
[A curtain has been drawn aside during this invocation, and
ALICIA advances. She smiles subtly upon him; and, giving a
strange gesture, makes one or two noiseless steps of dancing.]

ALICIA.
Master still sad?

CRASSUS.
These faint and fearful shores
Of time are beaten by the surge of sense,
Love worn away – by love? – to indifference.
Who knows what god – or demons – she adores?
Or in what wood she shelters, or what grove
Sees her profane our sacrament of love?

ALICIA.
I saw her follow
The stream in the hollow
Where never Apollo
Abides.
So thick are the trees
That never the breeze
Stirs them, or sees
What satyr inhabits the glen, what nymph in the
pools of it hides.

Lighter of foot

Than a sylph or a fairy,
Sinuous, wary,
I passed from the airy
Lawns, where the flute
Of the winds made tremulous music for man.

I followed the ripple
Of the stream; I crept
Where the waters wept
The floss in the foss
Gurgling across
The bosses of moss,
Like a dryad's nipple
In the mouth of Pan!

CRASSUS.
O pearl of the house! you came to the end?

ALICIA.
The dusk of the slave, the dawn of a friend?

CRASSUS.
Freedom is thine for the skill and the will.

ALICIA.
The skill is mine, but the will lies still,
Still as the earth that dare not stir
Till the kiss of the sun awaken her!

CRASSUS.
Yet at these secrets and riddles? Behold!
I can fill thy lap with a harvest of gold.

ALICIA.
Yet all the gold you could give to me
Would fall at my feet when I rose to be free.

CRASSUS.
What will you then?

ALICIA.
No gift from men.
Of my own free will I give you wit,
(O man so sorely in need of it!)

And happiness; and the flame that hath dwindled
On this dull hearth shall be rekindled.
But this you must swear:
To will, and to dare,
To seek the spirit and slay the sense;
And for this hour
To give me power
To lead you in silent obedience,
Though I bade you fall on your sword....

CRASSUS.
Enough!
I give my life as I gave my love.

ALICIA.
O! love you have not understood.
You have not guessed its secret food.
You have not seen its single eye;
But fear and doubt and jealousy
Have risen, and now your love is trembling
Like a mountebank dissembling
When his trick's detected. Come!
To find home we must leave home.

CRASSUS.
Starless and moonless, hidden in cloud,
The night's one flame of pearl.

ALICIA.
The bat flaps; the owl hoots aloud.

CRASSUS.
Lead on; I trust you, girl.

ALICIA.
You are bold to trust me; or, have you divined
My secret?

CRASSUS.
No; the crystal of your mind
Shows only faint disturbing images,
Things passing strange, as if enchanted seas
Kept their great swell upon it, and strange fish
Played in its oily depths. Some monstrous wish,

The shadow of some unspeakable desire,
Strikes my heart cold, and sets my brain on fire.

ALICIA.
Learn this, as we pass through the portico:
Fear nothing; there is nothing you can know!
And by these terraces and steps that gleam
Wintry, although the summer night is hot,
This what we seek is never what we find!

Life is a dream, like love; and from the dream
If we may wake, we never find it what
We would; for the wisdom of a mightier mind
Leads us in its own ways
To a perfected praise.

CRASSUS.
Why are these shadows thrown across the lawn
From the elms and yews? They were not wont to reach
Beyond the branches of that copper-beech.

ALICIA.
Attend the dawn
Of an unknown comet, that shall come
From the unfathomable wells of space
Into its halidom.

CRASSUS.
I know it not. Last night I walked alone
Here, and saw nothing.

ALICIA.
I was not with you!
There is no God upon the eternal throne
Of stars begemming the bewildering blue
Unless one has the eyes to see him. Think
How we two stand upon the brink
Of nothing! Here's a globe, whereto we trust,
No larger than the smallest speck of dust
Or mote in the sunbeam is to that sun's self,
And we are like dead leaves in autumn's whil
Of wind upon it.

CRASSUS.
Mystify me, girl!
It is the right of an elf.
Surely your flickering fire
Will draw me to some mire!

ALICIA.
Here the stream dips its mouth into the wood.
So does youth's calm and chaste beatitude
Touch the black mouth of Love, the ancient whore.

CRASSUS.
Girl! what a scorpion leaping from your lips!

ALICIA.
My mouth stings as no scorpion ever stang.
in this round impudent smiling face of mine
There is a poison fiercer than all wine;
And from these eyes more subtle sorrows pour
Than you can dream. These teeth have been at grips
With gods; I have sung what no girl ever sang.
These ears have heard
An insufferable word!

CRASSUS.
What do you mean?

ALICIA.
The secret's in a kiss.
Here are no kisses. Here great Artemis
Rules; only in the woodland may a man
Hide his eyes from her, pledge himself to Pan.
Come! through the tangled arches
Of cypresses and larches,
Stoop; under Artemis we walked upright;
But this is Pan's home, and the House of Night.
[They enter the wood.]

CRASSUS.
So when I stoop, my cheek comes close to yours.
Give me a kiss.

ALICIA.
The poisonous apple lures
Thus the boy's mouth. Beware!

CRASSUS.
O you are fair!
Fairer than ever! In this tangle of trees
Your hot breath wraps you in perfume.

ALICIA.
There is some gloom or doom,
A bitter harsh ingredient
In these my sorceries
Of animal scent.

CRASSUS.
Yes! there is fear mixed with the fascination.
It is the reverence that chastity, be sure!
Gains from the impure.

ALICIA.
O virtuous nation!
It is the fear of the uninitiate
Before the throne of Fate
The hierophant.

CRASSUS.
Kiss me, however!

ALICIA.
Did I grant
This favour, all were lost. It is your truth
To Adela that tempts my youth.
[Henceforth Alicia shakes with silent laughter.]

CRASSUS.
What little breasts you have!

ALICIA.
Ay, maiden breasts!
Would you betray my oath?

CRASSUS.
My will contests
My wishes.

ALICIA.
Wait, and you shall surely see
Part of the secret that ensorcels me.
See all these bosses! It is not
As if a Titan smote himself into the earth,
And was caught into her, made one with her?

CRASSUS.
The scent is fierce and hot
Like a rutting panther's slot.
Yet you are matched with mirth,
Shaking each other like two wrestlers.

ALICIA.
What should stir
Your melancholy but laughter?

CRASSUS.
Look, before us
Light streams, a tremulous chorus.
Oh, it is vague and vacillating!

ALICIA.
Love,
Young love of maidens, is the soul thereof.
And in the midst, behold, O man!
The image of great Pan.

CRASSUS.
I fear him.

ALICIA.
Go and lie there, at his feet.
Lie supine! Lie on that moss-covered root,
While I draw forth the flute
And make a marvellous music.
[She ceases laughing and begins to play.]

CRASSUS.
O I writhe
Beneath the force of lips, of fingers lithe
That touch the delicate stops so delicately.

ALICIA.
Hush!
I have drawn the bird from the bush.
Pan will appear anon.

CRASSUS.
Ah! Ah! ... Ah! Ah!

ALICIA.
This music moves you. Now I'll play a tune
That would make mad the melancholy moon.
This.

CRASSUS.
Ah! you tear my soul out with the trills.
Your fingers play like summer lightning on the shaft.
It is like a storm on the mountains when it shrills;
Like the angry sea when it booms. Hark!

ALICIA.
Some god laughed.

CRASSUS.
Your mouth is like some god's It burns and blooms
With fire unheard of, with unguessed perfumes.
O let me kiss you!

ALICIA.
So you stop my song!
[She ceases the tune.]

CRASSUS.
There is another song.

ALICIA.
You do me wrong.
For you love Adela!

CRASSUS.
By God, girl, no!
I love Alicia.

ALICIA.
Ah! you love her SO! [She laughs]

CRASSUS.
Your laugh is shocking; why do you mock me, dear?

ALICIA.
Because you will not guess my secret here.
But put your arms about my neck, and swear
You love me, and will always keep them there.
Then I might dare.

CRASSUS.
I swear it. O my sweet!

ALICIA.
Then take my kiss.

CRASSUS.
Your mouth is like a rose of fire. But what is this?
I cannot bear it.

ALICIA.
Ai! Uhu! Uhu!
It is my heart; this arrow strikes me through.
Stir not one muscle for a moment. Death!
You beast, you kill me with your urgent breath.

CRASSUS.
O how I love you! [He moves violently.]

ALICIA.
Fool! Now all my pain
Must be gone through again.
It is sure your chastity's unstained by crime;
You do the wrong thing just at the right time!

CRASSUS.
Why do you taunt me? All the wood is spring's,
And love is hovering o'er us with his wings.

ALICIA.
Sub pennis, penis!

CRASSUS.
Hush! you break the spell.

ALICIA.
Oh! you great fools of men, I know you well.
But nothing is so detrimental
To love as to be sentimental.
I will yet make you wise.
Know that I have the magic to disguise
Myself in many ways. Do you feel this?
(Lie still, this heaven were ruined by a kiss!)
I am a butterfly, such idle flitting
As to a flower like you is fitting
Now I'm a mole. Do you think you know me now?
Here is the earthworm severed by the plough.

CRASSUS.
You are a witch. I want your love; you give
Only love's comedy.

ALICIA.
The way to live
Is to find comedy and tragedy
In everything. But if you cannot see
Through to the Bacchanal spirit, this should suit.
Here is the blacksmith hammering a flute.

CRASSUS.
Oh love, love, kiss me!

ALICIA.
I will forge a ring
Of bloom of blood-kisses upon your neck,
Till it is like a garden of roses in late spring.

CRASSUS.
"Soft, and stung softly, fairer for a fleck."

ALICIA.
O marvellous nation!
Vanity, dullness, slobber, and quotation!

CRASSUS.
Why do you love me if you scorn me so?

ALICIA.
Why, did I say I loved you? I say no.

CRASSUS.
Why do you make love?

ALICIA.
To beguile the hour;
To crown my rose-wreath with a greener flower
To do my master's bidding, that's to give
Life to yourself, who only think you live.
But listen! Have you seen the nine waves roll
Monotonous upon the shoal,
Rising and falling like a maiden asleep;
Then with a lift and a leap
The ninth wave curls, and breaks upon the beach,
And rushes up it, swallowing the sand?
I am that ocean.... Now, you understand?

CRASSUS.
Alicia! O! this is unbearable.
Surely this wave washes the shore of hell!

ALICIA.
Each follows each
Remorseless and indifferent as Nature
Is to each creature.

CRASSUS.
Wonderful, wonderful woman!
[She throws her head back, and laughs]

ALICIA.
Now, you think
You know my secret. I have given you drink,
And you are wise. But hush! to all emotion
Save this the pulse and swell of Ocean
For at the last with mouth and fingers wried
All must proclaim the triumph of the tide.

CRASSUS.
Ah! still you mock me with your cruel laugh.

ALICIA.
It is your foolish epitaph.

CRASSUS.
But this can be no mockery. Heave and sway
And curl and thrust; these waves are not at play.

ALICIA.
You feel the ocean breaking on the shoal;
But passionless and moveless is its soul.

CRASSUS.
Ah! but your soul is in your breath.

ALICIA.
Only as the graven image of death
Which men call life, and ignorantly adore!

CRASSUS.
Spare me! I cannot bear you more.

ALICIA.
Then will I drown you. Lock your fingers fast
In mind, and let our mouths mix at the last.
[The stuatue of PAN is seen to be alive.]

PAN.
Shrill, shrill
Over the hill!
The hunter is hot; this is the kill!
Scream! Scream!
Dissolving the dream
Of life, the knife to the heart of the wife!
The fountain jets
Its flood of blood,
And the moss that it wets
Is an amethyst flame of violets.

Who shall escape
Murder and rape
What I am alive in my solemn shape?

Shrill, shrill,
Over the hill!
The hunter is hot; this is the kill!
The heart of the home
Is a fury of foam;
The storm is awake, and the billows comb.
But though I be
Their frenzy of glee,
I am also the passionless soul of the sea!

Mine eyes glint fire,
And my cruel lips curl;
Mine the desire
Of the god and the girl;
But fierier and fleeter,
And subtler and sweeter
Than the race of the rhythm, the march of the metre,
Is the shrilling, shrilling
Of the knife in the killing
That ends, when it must,
(O the throb and the thrust!)
In a death, in the dust,
The silence, the stillness, of satiate lust,
The solemn pause
When the veil withdraws
And man looks on his god, on the Causeless Cause.
Still, still,
Under the hill!
The hunter is dead; this is the kill!

CRASSUS.
Pan spoke.

ALICIA.
Pan never speaks till man is dumb,
And only then if he be like a child
Silently curled within its mother's womb,
Or feeding at her breast. There is a wild
Way also, when his dumbness is of death.
And there's a first and second death. Remember
To die so that no god's or angel's breath
May quicken into life the wasted ember!

CRASSUS.
I am dead now.

ALICIA.
But I must raise you up.
The night grows darker; all Pan's light is gone,
And you and I are pledged to sup
Upon a secret.

CRASSUS.
All your secret shone.
[She laughs again.]

ALICIA.
Oh, when you know it! But you must divine
Adela's shrine.

CRASSUS.
I am weary of Adela grown chaste and chill.

ALICIA.
The hunter lags; how heavy is the hill!
But you are bound to Adela.

CRASSUS.
To you!

ALICIA.
But you have given me freedom. I will leave you.

CRASSUS.
What have I done to grieve you?

ALICIA.
You have been the solemn fool with face awry
That I have gathered in my ecstasy.
You are only a vulgar primrose I have plucked.

CRASSUS.
At least, she-devil, you have been well-treated.

ALICIA.
O tragic farce, not even rimes completed!
Nay, darling! no rebellion. When you know

My secret, you will understand.
You are bound
To Adela within the portico,
To me upon this ground.
By day, in life, adore the Lares, man!
By night, in death, make offering to Pan!
Can you cut day from night by any endeavour?
If so, both life and death were lost for ever.
Come, the stream steepens.

CRASSUS.
This road leads to hell.

ALICIA.
The way to heaven is shorter.

CRASSUS.
Who can tell?

ALICIA.
I have measured it.

CRASSUS.
You, girl?

ALICIA.
It is not hard.

CRASSUS.
What did you make the height of it?

ALICIA.
One yard.

CRASSUS.
You always mock me?

ALICIA.
Pity of my youth!
I swerve not from, you stumble at, the truth.

CRASSUS.
I like not jests. This is a serious journey.

ALICIA.
Why did you make a mocker your attorney?
The way to Rome leads through the Apennines.
Bacchus has horns beneath the crown of vines.
If you fear horns, make some polite excuse
Not to invoke him by the name Zagreus!

A FAUN [Passing among the trees].
Ye thought me a lamb
With a crown of thorns;
I am royal, a ram
With death in my horns.
So mild and soft
And feminine,
Ye held me aloft
And frowned on sin!
But I was awake
In your clasp as I lay;
I roused the snake
From its nest of clay;
And ere ye knew
I had sunk my forehead
Through and through;
Harsh and horrid
Through all the pleasure
Of rose and vine
I thrust my treasure,
The cone of the pine.
Irru's maid
Was easily sated,
For she was afraid
When Irru mated!

CRASSUS.
Ha! Ha! Ha! Ha! Ha! Ha!

ALICIA.
You would not laugh
Were you the maid!

CRASSUS.
How could I be?

ALICIA.
Great calf!
But you are all the same, blaspheme and jeer
At any mystery beyond your sphere
Of beer, and beef, and beer, and beef, and beer.
Now you have frightened the shy god!

CRASSUS.
Why heed?
Between your arms is all the god I need.

ALICIA.
Prudish and coarse to the last. Now hush indeed!
The stream kisses the lake. We near the shrine.
Stir no snapped twig. Let your foot, even yours,
Fall like a fawn's.

CRASSUS.
Your breath is like new wine.

ALICIA.
Hush now! no porpoise gambols!

CRASSUS.
How obscure's
The glimmer of the lake. Is that the isle?

ALICIA.
Yes! in that shadow lurks a smile.
See; from that jagged cloud Diana starts
Like a deer from the brake; her silver splendour darts
Through the crisp air to the grove upon the isle...
Do you see her? Do you see her?

CRASSUS.
Monstrous! Vile!
These eyes betray me.

ALICIA.
No! your Adela lies
With arms thrown back, head tilted, open thighs.
Her lips flame out like poppies in the dusk.
The breeze brings back to us a scent of musk.
Her mouth is oozing kisses!

CRASSUS.
Filthy harlot!

ALICIA.
I never fed on a superber scarlet.
And look! the wonder of plumes that foams upon
Her tidal breast, oh, but a swan! a swan!
A swan snow-white with his sole scarlet hidden
In the abode forbidden!

O but his eye swoons as his broad beak slips
Within her luscious lips.
O but I cannot see; I long to die
Alike for wonder, and for jealousy!

CRASSUS.
Vile, filthy whore! I'll catch you at it.

ALICIA.
Soft!
See how his feathers hold her soul aloft!

CRASSUS.
Beast! Have you brought me through the wood for
this?

ALICIA.
Now wonder I must teach you how to kiss.

CRASSUS.
I'll clip his wings.

ALICIA.
Sub pennis, penis! 'Slife!
It's not the wings of him that clip your wife.

CRASSUS.
Thou art as filthy a creature as she!

ALICIA.
Fat fool!
All your emotions vary with your...

CRASSUS.
What?

ALICIA.
Your state of health.

CRASSUS.
Be off with you, foul…

ALICIA.
Well?

CRASSUS.
I'll swim and stab them. The black mouth of hell
Yawns for their murder.

ALICIA.
I'll be at the death.
Dive then, but softly. Scarcely draw your breath.

CRASSUS.
O, she's unwary!

ALICIA.
Is your love forgotten?

CRASSUS.
All love is rotten.

ALICIA.
But your pure love for me you boasted of?

CRASSUS.
Ay, that was perfect love.

ALICIA.
You love me then, not her?

CRASSUS.
Indeed I do.

ALICIA.
Swear me the oath anew!

CRASSUS.
I swear to love you till the world shall end.

ALICIA.
Then, Crassus, I will always be your friend.

CRASSUS.
Ah, that is good! You do not mock me now!

ALICIA.
Creep softly to the land. Kiss but my brow.
My curls are wet... No, never touch me there!

CRASSUS.
Why? Have I not?

ALICIA.
You have not.

CRASSUS.
Just my hand.

ALICIA.
You disobey your mistress's command?
The time is near when you shall see
The keyhole of my comedy!

CRASSUS.
Ha! Ha! Ha!

ALICIA.
Hush, you coarse slave; we'll surprise
Your good wife in her mystic exercise.
Quick, through the bramble!
[They burst through upon ADELA.]

CRASSUS.
Now, you beast, I've got you!
The curst of God, and plague of Naples, rot you!
For this white brute, one slit!
[He cuts the throat of THE SWAN with
his dagger.]

ADELA.
Oh love betrayed!
O my dead beauty! Faugh! deceitful maid.
Not Crassus found me out. Had I the wings
Of my dead love, oh love! -

ALICIA.
Why, wondrous things!

ADELA.
These nails shall serve. A servant!

CRASSUS.
She shall be
My wife, damned witch, when I have done with thee!
[THE SWAN dies.]

ADELA.
I'll kill her now. But see! my swan is dead.

ALICIA.
Yes! and what light is breaking overhead?
What blaze of blue and gold envelops us?

CRASSUS.
O marvel! O miraculous!

ADELA.
What is it? Why, my lover's life, in me
Once concentrated, now diffused, illumes
The endless reaches of eternity
With infinite brilliance, with intense perfumes.

ALICIA.
O then your lover was some god's disguise.

ADELA.
And you have robbed me. Now beware your eyes!
[She springs at ALICIA, who guards herself
easily. But in the struggle her robe tears.]

ALICIA.
Take care!

ADELA.
A boy!

CRASSUS.
A boy! Then what am I?

ALICIA.
That is the key-word of the comedy.
You thought you had two vices at your need;
But she had Jove and you had Ganymede.
[They are struck dumb and still with
amazement. ALICIA claps her hands four times.]

Sweep through the air, bright blaze of eagle-wings!
Crassus, sub pennis, penis! How he swings
His bulk from yonder sightless poise, to bear
me back to the Dominion of the air
Where I shall bear the cup of Jupiter!
Blind babes, love one another, no less true
Because the gods have deigned to dwell with you!
[The eagle bears GANYMEDE aloft.]

CRASSUS.
Adela! these mysteries too great
For you and me to estimate.
But, widowed both, come, seek domestic charms
As we were wont, in one another's arms!
What perfect moss for you to lie upon!

ADELA.
I am your wife, dear Crassus.
(sotto voce) Oh, my swan!

CURTAIN.

THE BOOK OF LIES

WHICH IS ALSO FALSELY
CALLED

BREAKS

THE WANDERINGS OR FALSIFICATIONS
OF THE ONE THOUGHT OF

FRATER PERDURABO
(Aleister Crowley)

WHICH THOUGHT IS ITSELF
UNTRUE

"Break, break, break
    At the foot of thy stones, O Sea!
And would that I could utter
    The thoughts that arise in me!"

A∴ A∴

Publication in Class C and D
Official for the Grade of Babe of the Abyss

THE BOOK OF LIES

WHICH IS ALSO FALSELY CALLED

The number of the book is 333, as implying despersion, so as to correspond with the title, "Breaks" and "Lies".

However, the "one thought" is itself untrue, and therefore its falsifications are relatively true.

This book therefore consists of statements as nearly true as is possible to human language.

The verse from Tennyson is inserted partly because of the pun on the word "break"; partly because of the reference to the meaning of this title page, as explained above; partly because it is intensely amusing for Crowley to quote Tennyson.

There is no joke or subtle meaning in the publisher's imprint.

?

!

FOREWORD

THE BOOK OF LIES, first published in London in 1913, Aleister Crowley's little master work, has long been out of print. Its re-issue with the author's own Commentary gives occasion for a few notes. We have so much material by Crowley himself about this book that we can do no better than quote some passages which we find scattered about in the unpublished volumes of his "CONFESSIONS". He writes:

"... None the less, I could point to some solid achievement on the large scale, although it is composed of more or less disconnected elements. I refer to THE BOOK OF LIES. In this there are 93 chapters: we count as a chapter the two pages filled respectively with a note of interrogation and a mark of exclamation. The other chapters contain sometimes a single word, more frequently from a half-dozen to twenty paragraphs. The subject of each chapter is determined more or less definitely by the Qabalistic import of its number. Thus Chapter 25 gives a revised ritual of the Pentagram; 72 is a rondel with the refrain 'Shemhamphorash', the Divine name of 72 letters; 77 Laylah, whose name adds to that number; and 80, the number of the letter Pé, referred to Mars, a panegyric upon War. Sometimes the text is serious and straightforward, sometimes its obscure oracles demand deep knowledge of the Qabalah for interpretation, others contain obscure allusions, play upon words, secrets expressed in cryptogram, double or triple meanings which must be combined in order to appreciate the full flavour; others again are subtly ironical or cynical. At first sight the book is a jumble of nonsense intended to insult the reader. It requires infinite study, sympathy, intuition and initiation. Given these I do not hesitate to claim that in none other of my writings have I given so profound and comprehensive an exposition of my philosophy on every plane...

"... My association with Free Masonry was therefore destined to be more fertile than almost any other study, and that in a way despite itself. A word should be pertinent with regard to the question of secrecy. It has become difficult for me to take this matter very seriously. Knowing what the secret actually is, I cannot attach much importance to artificial mysteries. Again, though the secret itself is of such tremendous import,

and though it is so simple that I could disclose it... in a short paragraph, I might do so without doing much harm. For it cannot be used indiscriminately... I have found in practice that the secret of the O. T. O. [the Ordo Templi Orientis, or The Order of the Temple of the East] cannot be used unworthily...

"It is interesting in this connection to recall how it came into my possession. It had occurred to me to write a book, THE BOOK OF LIES, ... One of these chapters bothered me. I could not write it. I invoked Dionysus with particular fervour, but still without success. I went off in desperation to 'change my luck', by doing something entirely contrary to my inclinations. In the midst of my disgust, the spirit came over me, and I scribbled the chapter down by the light of a farthing dip. When I read it over, I was as discontented as before, but I stuck it into the book in a sort of anger at myself as a deliberate act of spite towards my readers.

"Shortly after publication, the O. H. O. (Outer Head of the O. T. O.) came to me. (At that time I did not realise that there was anything in the O. T. O. beyond a convenient compendium of the more important truths of Free Masonry.) He said that since I was acquainted with the supreme secret of the Order, I must be allowed the IX° and obligated in regard to it. I protested that I knew no such secret. He said, 'But you have printed it in the plainest language.' I said that I could not have done so because I did not know it. He went to the bookshelves; taking out a copy of THE BOOK OF LIES, he pointed to a passage in the despised chapter. It instantly flashed upon me. The entire symbolism not only of Free Masonry but of many other traditions blazed upon my spiritual vision. From that moment the O. T. O. assumed its proper importance in my mind. I understood that I held in my hands the key to the future progress of humanity... "

ΚΕΦΑΛΗ Η ΟΥΚ ΕΣΤΙ ΚΕΦΑΛΗ

O![1]
The Ante Primal Triad which is
NOT-GOD
Nothing is.
Nothing Becomes.
Nothing is not.

The First Triad which is GOD
I AM.
I utter The Word.
I hear The Word.

The Abyss
The Word is broken up.
There is Knowledge.
Knowledge is Relation.
These fragments are Creation.
The broken manifests Light.[2]

The Second Triad which is GOD
GOD the Father and Mother is concealed in Generation.
GOD is concealed in the whirling energy of Nature.
GOD is manifest in gathering: harmony: consideration: the
Mirror of the Sun and of the Heart.

The Third Triad
Bearing: preparing.
Wavering: flowing: flashing.
Stability: begetting.

The Tenth Emanation
The world.

COMMENTARY (The Chapter that is not a Chapter)

This chapter, numbered 0, corresponds to the Negative, which is before Kether in the Qabalistic system.

The notes of interrogation and exclamation on the previous pages are the other two veils.

The meaning of these symbols is fully explained in "The Soldier and the Hunchback".

This chapter begins by the letter O, followed by a mark of exclamation; its reference to the theogony of "Liber Legis" is explained in the note, but it also refers to KTEIS PHALLOS and SPERMA, and is the exclamation of wonder or ecstasy, which is the ultimate nature of things.

NOTE

(1) Silence. Nuit, O; Hadit; Ra-Hoor-Khuit, 1.

COMMENTARY (The Ante Primal Triad)

This is the negative Trinity; its three statements are, in an ultimate sense, identical. They harmonise Being, Becoming, Not-Being, the three possible modes of conceiving the universe.

The statement, Nothing is Not, technically equivalent to Something Is, is fully explained in the essay called Berashith.

The rest of the chapter follows the Sephirotic system of the Qabalah, and constitutes a sort of quintessential comment upon that system.

Those familiar with that system will recognise Kether, Chokmah, Binah, in the First Triad; Daath, in the Abyss; Chesed, Geburah, Tiphareth, in the Second Triad; Netzach, Hod and Yesod in the Third Triad, and Malkuth in the Tenth Emanation.

It will be noticed that this cosmogony is very complete; the manifestation even of God does not appear until Tiphareth; and the universe itself not until Malkuth.

The chapter many therefore be considered as the most complete treatise on existence ever written.

NOTE

(2) The Unbroken, absorbing all, is called Darkness.

1

ΚΕΦΑΛΗ Α

THE SABBATH OF THE GOAT

O! the heart of N. O. X. the Night of Pan.
ΠΑΝ: Duality: Energy: Death.
Death: Begetting: the supporters of O!
To beget is to die; to die is to beget.
Cast the Seed into the Field of Night.
Life and Death are two names of A.
Kill thyself.
Neither of these alone is enough.

COMMENTARY (A)

The shape of the figure I suggests the Phallus; this chapter is therefore called the Sabbath of the Goat, the Witches' Sabbath, in which the Phallus is adored.

The chapter begins with a repetition of O! referred to in the previous chapter. It is explained that this triad lives in Night, the Night of Pan, which is mystically called N. O. X., and this O is identified with the O in this word. N is the Tarot symbol, Death; and the X or Cross is the sign of the Phallus. For a fuller commentary on Nox, see Liber VII, Chapter I.

Nox adds to 210, which symbolises the reduction of duality to unity, and thence to negativity, and is thus a hieroglyph of the Great Work.

The word Pan is then explained, Π, the letter of Mars, is a hieroglyph of two pillars, and therefore suggest duality; A, by its shape, is the pentagram, energy, and N, by its Tarot attribution, is death.

Nox is then further explained, and it is shown that the ultimate Trinity, O!, is supported, or fed, by the process of death and begetting, which are the laws of the universe.

The identity of these two is then explained.

The Student is then charged to understand the spiritual importance of this physical procession in line 5.

It is then asserted that the ultimate letter A has two names, or phases, Life and Death.

Line 7 balances line 5. It will be notice that the phraseology of these two lines is so conceived that the one contains the other more than itself.

Line 8 emphasises the importance of performing both.

2

ΚΕΦΑΛΗ Β

THE CRY OF THE HAWK

Hoor hath a secret fourfold name: it is Do What Thou
Wilt.[3]
Four Words: Naught – One – Many – All.
Thou – Child!
Thy Name is holy.
Thy Kingdom is come.
Thy Will is done.
Here is the Bread.
Here is the Blood.
Bring us through Temptation!
Deliver us from Good and Evil!
That Mine as Thine be the Crown of the Kingdom, even
now.
ABRAHADABRA.
These ten words are four, the Name of the One.

COMMENTARY (B)

The "Hawk" referred to is Horus.

The chapter begins with a comment on Liber Legis III, 49.

Those four words, Do What Thou Wilt, are also identified with the four possible modes of conceiving the universe; Horus unites these.

Follows a version of the "Lord's Prayer", suitable to Horus. Compare this with the version in Chapter 44. There are ten sections in this prayer, and, as the prayer is attributed to Horus, they are called four, as above explained; but it is only the name of Horus which is fourfold; He himself is One.

This may be compared with the Qabalistic doctrine of the Ten Sephiroth as an expression of Tetragrammaton (1 plus 2 plus 3 plus 4 = 10).

It is now seen that this Hawk is not Solar, but Mercurial; hence the words, the Cry of the Hawk, the essential part of Mercury being his Voice; and the number of the chapter, B, which is Beth the letter of Mercury, the Magus of the Tarot, who has four weapons, and it must be remembered that this card is numbered 1, again connecting all these symbols with the Phallus.

The essential weapon of Mercury is the Caduceus.

NOTE

(3) Fourteen letters. Quid Voles Illud Fac. Q.V.I.F. 196 = 14^2.

3

ΚΕΦΑΛΗ Γ

THE OYSTER

The Brothers of A∴A∴ are one with the Mother of the
Child.[4]

The Many is as adorable to the One as the One is to the
Many. This is the Love of These; creation-parturition is
the Bliss of the One; coition-dissolution is the Bliss of
the Many.

The All, thus interwoven of These, is Bliss.

Naught is beyond Bliss.

The Man delights in uniting with the Woman; the Woman
in parting from the Child.

The Brothers of A∴A∴ are Women: the Aspirants to
A∴A∴ are Men.

COMMENTARY (G)

Gimel is the High Priestess of the Tarot. This chapter gives the initiated feminine point of view; it is therefore called the Oyster, a symbol of the Yoni. In Equinox X, The Temple of Solomon the King, it is explained how Masters of the Temple, or Brothers of A∴A∴ have changed the formula of their progress. These two formulae, Solve et Coagula, are now explained, and the universe is exhibited as the interplay between these two. This also explains the statement in Liber Legis I, *28-30.*

NOTE
(4) They cause all men to worship it.

4

ΚΕΦΑΛΗ Δ

PEACHES

Soft and hollow, how thou dost overcome the hard
    and full!
It dies, it gives itself; to Thee is the fruit!
Be thou the Bride; thou shalt be the Mother hereafter.
To all impressions thus. Let them not overcome thee; yet
    let them breed within thee. The least of the
    impressions, come to its perfection, is Pan.
Receive a thousand lovers; thou shalt bear but One Child.
This child shall be the heir of Fate the Father.

COMMENTARY (Δ)

Daleth is the Empress of the Tarot, the letter of Venus, and the title, Peaches, again refers to the Yoni. The chapter is a counsel to accept all impressions; it is the formula of the Scarlet woman; but no impression must be allowed to dominate you, only to fructify you; just as the artist, seeing an object, does not worship it, but breeds a masterpiece from it. This process is exhibited as one aspect of the Great Work. The last two paragraphs may have some reference to the 13th Aethyr (see The Vision and The Voice).

5

ΚΕΦΑΛΗ Ε

THE BATTLE OF THE ANTS

That is not which is.
The only Word is Silence.
The only Meaning of that Word is not.
Thoughts are false.
Fatherhood is unity disguised as duality.
Peace implies war.
Power implies war.
Harmony implies war.
Victory implies war.
Glory implies war.
Foundation implies war.
Alas! for the Kingdom wherein all these are at war.

COMMENTARY (E)

He is the letter of Aries, a Martial sign; while the title suggests war. The ants are chosen as small busy objects.

Yet He, being a holy letter, raises the beginning of the chapter to a contemplation of the Pentagram, considered as a glyph of the ultimate.

In line 1, Being is identified with Not-Being.

In line 2, Speech with Silence.

In line 3, the Logos is declared as the Negative.

Line 4 is another phrasing of the familiar Hindu statement, that that which can be thought is not true.

In line 5, we come to an important statement, an adumbration of the most daring thesis in this book – Father and Son are not really two, but one; their unity being the Holy Ghost, the semen; the human form is a non-essential accretion of this quintessence.

So far the chapter has followed the Sephiroth from Kether to Chesed, and Chesed is united to the Supernal Triad by virtue of its Phallic nature; for not only is Amoun a Phallic God, and Jupiter the Father of All, but 4 is Daleth, Venus, and Chesed refers to water, from which Venus sprang, and which is the symbol of the Mother in the Tetragrammaton. See Chapter 0, "God the Father and Mother is concealed in generation".

But Chesed, in the lower sense, is conjoined to Microprosopus. It is the true link between the greater and lesser countenances, whereas Daath is the false. Compare the doctrine of the higher and lower Manas in Theosophy.

The rest of the chapter therefore points out the duality, and therefore the imperfection, of all the lower Sephiroth in their essence.

6

ΚΕΦΑΛΗ Ϝ

CAVIAR

The Word was uttered: the One exploded into one
thousand million worlds.
Each world contained a thousand million spheres.
Each sphere contained a thousand million planes.
Each plane contained a thousand million stars.
Each star contained a many thousand million things.
Of these the reasoner took six, and, preening, said:
This is the One and the All.
These six the Adept harmonised, and said:
This is the Heart of the One and the All.
These six were destroyed by the Master of the Temple; and
he spake not.
The Ash thereof was burnt up by the Magus into
The Word.
Of all this did the Ipsissimus know Nothing.

COMMENTARY (F)

This chapter is presumably called Caviar because that substance is composed of many spheres.

The account given of Creation is the same as that familiar to students of the Christian tradition, the Logos transforming the unity into the many.

We then see what different classes of people do with the many.

The Rationalist takes the six Sephiroth of Microprosopus in a crude state, and declares them to be the universe. This folly is due to the pride of reason.

The Adept concentrates the Microcosm in Tiphareth, recognising an Unity, even in the microcosm, but, qua Adept, he can go no further.

The Master of the Temple destroys all these illusions, but remains silent. See the description of his functions in the Equinox, Liber 418 and elsewhere.

In the next grade, the Word is re-formulated, for the Magus in Chokmah, the Dyad, the Logos.

The Ipsissimus, in the highest grade of the A∴A∴, is totally unconscious of this process, or, it might be better to say, he recognises it as Nothing, in that positive sense of the word, which is only intelligible in Samasamadhi.

7

ΚΕΦΑΛΗ Ζ

THE DINOSAURS

None are They whose number is Six:[5] else were they six
   indeed.
Seven[6] are these Six that live not in the City of the
   Pyramids, under the Night of Pan.
There was Lao-tzu.
There was Siddartha.
There was Krishna.
There was Tahuti.
There was Mosheh.
There was Dionysus.[7] There was Mahmud. But the
   Seventh men called PERDURABO; for enduring unto
   The End, at The End was Naught to endure.[8]
Amen.

COMMENTARY (Z)

This chapter gives a list of those special messengers of the Infinite who initiate periods. They are called Dinosaurs because of their seeming to be terrible devouring creatures. They are Masters of the Temple, for their number is 6 (1 plus 2 plus 3), the mystic number of Binah; but they are called "None", because they have attained. If it were not so, they would be called "six" in its bad sense of mere intellect.

They are called Seven, although they are Eight, because Lao-tzu counts as nought, owing to the nature of his doctrine. The reference to their "living not" is to be found in Liber 418.

The word "Perdurabo" means "I will endure unto the end". The allusion is explained in the note.

Siddartha, or Gotama, was the name of the last Budda.

Krishna was the principal incarnation of the Indian Vishnu, the preserver, the principal expounder of Vedantism.

Tahuti, or Thoth, the Egyptian God of Wisdom.

Mosheh, Moses, the founder of the Hebrew system.

Dionysus, probably an ecstatic from the East.

Mahmud, Mohammed.

All these were men; their Godhead is the result of mythopoeia.

NOTE

(5) Masters of the Temple, whose grade has the mystic number 6 (= 1 + 2 + 3).

(6) These are not eight, as apparent; for Lao-tzu counts as 0.

(7) The legend of "Christ" is only a corruption and perversion of other legends. Especially of Dionysus: compare the account of Christ before Herod/Pilate in the gospels, and of Dionysus before Pentheus in "The Bacchae".

(8) O, the last letter of Perdurabo, is Naught.

8

ΚΕΑΛΗ Η

STEEPED HORSEHAIR

Mind is a disease of semen.
All that a man is or may be is hidden therein.
Bodily functions are parts of the machine; silent, unless
    in disease.
But mind, never at ease, creaketh "I".
This I persisteth not, posteth not through generations,
    changeth momently, finally is dead.
Therefore is man only himself when lost to himself in
    The Charioting.

COMMENTARY (H)

Cheth is the Chariot in the Tarot. The Charioteer is the bearer of the Holy Grail. All this should be studied in Liber 418, the 12th Aethyr.

The chapter is called "Steeped Horsehair" because of the mediaeval tradition that by steeping horsehair a snake is produced, and the snake is the hieroglyphic representation of semen, particularly in Gnostic and Egyptian emblems.

The meaning of the chapter is quite clear; the whole race-consciousness, that which is omnipotent, omniscient, omnipresent, is hidden therein.

Therefore, except in the case of an Adept, man only rises to a glimmer of the universal consciousness, while, in the orgasm, the mind is blotted out.

9

ΚΕΦΑΛΗ Θ

THE BRANKS

Being is the Noun; Form is the adjective.

Matter is the Noun; Motion is the Verb.

Wherefore hath Being clothed itself with Form?

Wherefore hath Matter manifested itself in Motion?

Answer not, O silent one! For THERE is no "wherefore",
no "because".

The name of THAT is not known; the Pronoun interprets,
that is, misinterprets, It.

Time and Space are Adverbs.

Duality begat the Conjunction.

The Conditioned is Father of the Preposition.

The Article also marketh Division; but the Interjection is
the sound that endeth in the Silence.

Destroy therefore the Eight Parts of Speech; the Ninth is
nigh unto Truth.

This also must be destroyed before thou enterest into
The Silence.

Aum.

COMMENTARY (Θ)

Teth is the Tarot trump, Strength, in which a woman is represented closing the mouth of a lion.

This chapter is called "The Branks", an even more powerful symbol, for it is the Scottish, and only known, apparatus for closing the mouth of a woman.

The chapter is formally an attack upon the parts of speech, the interjection, the meaningless utterance of ecstasy, being the only thing worth saying; yet even this is to be regarded as a lapse.

"Aum" represents the entering into the silence, as will observed upon pronouncing it.

10

ΚΕΦΑΛΗ I

WINDLESTRAWS

The Abyss of Hallucinations has Law and Reason; but in
  Truth there is no bond between the Toys of the Gods.
This Reason and Law is the Bond of the Great Lie.
Truth! Truth! Truth! crieth the Lord of the Abyss of
  Hallucinations.
There is no silence in that Abyss: for all that men call
  Silence is Its Speech.
This Abyss is also called "Hell", and "The Many". Its name
  is "Consciousness", and "The Universe", among men.
But THAT which neither is silent, nor speaks, rejoices
  therein.

COMMENTARY (I)

There is no apparent connection between the number of this chapter and its subject.

It does, however, refer to the key of the Tarot called The Hermit, which represents him as cloaked.

Jod is the concealed Phallus as opposed to Tau, the extended Phallus. This chapter should be studied in the light of what is said in "Aha!" and in the Temple of Solomon the King about the reason.

The universe is insane, the law of cause and effect is an illusion, or so it appears in the Abyss, which is thus identified with consciousness, the many, and both; but within this is a secret unity which rejoices; this unit being far beyond any conception.

11

ΚΕΦΑΛΗ ΙΑ

THE GLOW-WORM

Concerning the Holy Three-in-Naught.

Nuit, Hadit, Ra-Hoor-Khuit, are only to be understood by the Master of the Temple.

They are above The Abyss, and contain all contradiction in themselves.

Below them is a seeming duality of Chaos and Babalon; these are called Father and Mother, but it is not so. They are called Brother and Sister, but it is not so. They are called Husband and Wife, but it is not so.

The reflection of All is Pan: the Night of Pan is the Annihilation of the All.

Cast down through The Abyss is the Light, the Rosy Cross, the rapture of Union that destroys, that is The Way. The Rosy Cross is the Ambassador of Pan.

How infinite is the distance form This to That! Yet All is Here and Now. Nor is there any there or Then; for all that is, what is it but a manifestation, that is, a part, that is, a falsehood, of THAT which is not?

Yet THAT which is not neither is nor is not That which is!

Identity is perfect; therefore the Law of Identity is but a lie. For there is no subject, and there is no predicate; nor is there the contradictory of either of these things.

Holy, Holy, Holy are these Truths that I utter, knowing them to be but falsehoods, broken mirrors, troubled waters; hide me, O our Lady, in Thy Womb! for I may not endure the rapture.

In this utterance of falsehood upon falsehood, whose contradictories are also false, it seems as if That which I uttered not were true.

Blessed, unutterably blessed, is this last of the illusions; let me play the man, and thrust it from me! Amen.

COMMENTARY (IA)

"The Glow-Worm" may perhaps be translated as "a little light in the darkness", though there may be a subtle reference to the nature of that light.

Eleven is the great number of Magick, and this chapter indicates a supreme magical method; but it is really called eleven, because of Liber Legis, I, 60.

The first part of the chapter describes the universe in its highest sense, down to Tiphareth; it is the new and perfect cosmogony of Liber Legis.

Chaos and Babalon are Chokmah and Binah, but they are really one; the essential unity of the supernal Triad is here insisted upon.

Pan is a generic name, including this whole system of its manifested side. Those which are above the Abyss are therefore said to live in the Night of Pan; they are only reached by the annihilation of the All.

Thus, the Master of the Temple lives in the Night of Pan.

Now, below the Abyss, the manifested part of the Master of the Temple, also reaches Samadhi, as the way of Annihilation.

Paragraph 7 begins by a reflection produced by the preceding exposition. This reflection is immediately contradicted, the author being a Master of the Temple. He thereupon enters into his Samadhi, and he piles contradiction upon contradiction, and thus a higher degree of rapture, with every sentence, until his armoury is exhausted, and, with the word Amen, he enters the supreme state.

12

ΚΕΦΑΛΗ ΙΒ

THE DRAGON-FLIES

IO is the cry of the lower as OI of the higher.

In figures they are 1001;[9] in letters they are Joy.[10]

For when all is equilibrated, when all is beheld from without all,
    there is joy, joy, joy that is but one facet of a diamond, every
    other facet whereof is more joyful than joy itself.

COMMENTARY (IB)

The Dragon-Flies were chosen as symbols of joy, because of the author's observation as a naturalist.

Paragraph 1 mere repeats Chapter 4 in quintessence; 1001, being 11Σ (1-13), is a symbol of the complete unity manifested as the many, for Σ (1-13) gives the whole course of numbers from the simple unity of 1 to the complex unity of 13, impregnated by the magical 11.

I may add a further comment on the number 91. 13 (1 plus 3) is a higher form of 4. 4 is Amoun, the God of generation, and 13 is 1, the Phallic unity. Daleth is the Yoni. And 91 is AMN (Amen), a form of the Phallus made complete through the intervention of the Yoni. This again connects with the IO and OI of paragraph 1, and of course IO is the rapture-cry of the Greeks.

The whole chapter is, again, a comment on Liber Legis, I, 28-30.

NOTE
(9) 1001 = 11Σ. The Petals of the Sahasraracakkra.
(10) JOY = 101, the Egg of Spirit in equilibrium between the
Pillars of the Temple.

13

ΚΕΦΑΛΗ ΙΓ

PILGRIM-TALK

O thou that settest out upon The Path, false is the Phantom that thou seekest. When thou hast it thou shalt know all bitterness, thy teeth fixed in the Sodom-Apple.

Thus hast thou been lured along That Path, whose terror else had driven thee far away.

O thou that stridest upon the middle of The Path, no phantoms mock thee. For the stride's sake thou stridest.

Thus art thou lured along That Path, whose fascination else had driven thee far away.

O thou that drawest toward the End of The Path, effort is no more. Faster and faster dos thou fall; thy weariness is changed into Ineffable Rest.

For there is not Thou upon That Path: thou hast become The Way.

COMMENTARY (IΓ)

This chapter is perfectly clear to anyone who has studied the career of an Adept.

The Sodom-Apple is an uneatable fruit found in the desert.

14

ΚΕΦΑΛΗ ΙΔ

ONION-PEELINGS

The Universe is the Practical Joke of the General at the Expense
of the Particular, quoth *FRATER PERDURABO*, and laughed.
But those disciples nearest to him wept, seeing the Universal
Sorrow.
Those next to them laughed, seeing the Universal Joke.
Below these certain disciples wept.
Then certain laughed.
Others next wept.
Others next laughed.
Next others wept.
Next others laughed.
Last came those that wept because they could not see the Joke,
and those that laughed lest they should be thought not to see
the Joke, and thought it safe to act like *FRATER
PERDURABO*.
But though *FRATER PERDURABO* laughed openly, He also at
the same time wept secretly; and in Himself He neither
laughed nor wept.
Nor did He mean what He said.

COMMENTARY (IΔ)

The title, "Onion-Peelings", refers to the well-known incident in Peer Gynt.

The chapter resembles strongly Dupin's account of how he was able to win at the game of guessing odd or even. (See Poe's tale of 'The Purloined Letter'.) But this is a more serious piece of psychology. In one's advance towards a comprehension of the universe, one changes radically one's point of view; nearly always it amounts to a reversal.

This is the cause of most religious controversies. Paragraph 1, however, is Frater Perdurabo's formulation of his perception of the Universal Joke, also described in Chapter 34. All individual existence is tragic. Perception of this fact is the essence of comedy. Household Gods is an attempt to write pure comedy. The Bacchae of Euripides is another.

At the end of the chapter it is, however, seen that to the Master of the Temple the opposite perception occurs simultaneously, and that he himself is beyond both of these.

And in the last paragraph it is shown that he realises the truth as beyond any statement of it.

15

ΚΕΦΑΛΗ ΙΕ

THE GUN-BARREL

Mighty and erect is this Will of mine, this Pyramid of fire whose
summit is lost in Heaven. Upon it have I burned the corpse
of my desires.

Mighty and erect is this Φαλλοσ of my Will. The seed thereof is
That which I have borne within me from Eternity; and it is
lost within the Body of Our Lady of the Stars.

I am not I; I am but an hollow tube to bring down Fire from
Heaven.

Mighty and marvellous is this Weakness, this Heaven which
draweth me into Her Womb, this Dome which hideth, which
absorbeth, Me.

This is The Night wherein I am lost, the Love through which I
am no longer I.

COMMENTARY (IE)

The card 15 in the Tarot is "The Devil", the mediaeval blind for Pan.

The title of the chapter refers to the Phallus, which is here identified with the will. The Greek word Πυραμισ has the same number as Φαλλοσ.

This chapter is quite clear, but one my remark in the last paragraph a reference to the nature of Samadhi.

As man loses his personality in physical love, so does the magician annihilate his divine personality in that which is beyond.

The formula of Samadhi is the same, from the lowest to the highest. The Rosy-Cross is the Universal Key. But, as one proceeds, the Cross becomes greater, until it is the Ace, the Rose, until it is the Word.

16

ΚΕΦΑΛΗ ΙΣ

THE STAG-BEETLE

Death implies change and individuality if thou be THAT
which hath no person, which is beyond the changing,
even beyond changelessness, what hast thou to do
with death?
The bird of individuality is ecstasy; so also is its death.
In love the individuality is slain; who loves not love?
Love death therefore, and long eagerly for it.
Die Daily.

COMMENTARY (ΙΣ)

This seems a comment on the previous chapter; the Stag-Beetle is a reference the Kheph-ra, the Egyptian God of Midnight, who bears the Sun through the Underworld; but it is called the Stag-Beetle to emphasise his horns. Horns are the universal hieroglyph of energy, particularly of Phallic energy.

The 16th key of the Tarot is "The Blasted Tower". In this chapter death is regarded as a form of marriage. Modern Greek peasants, in many cases, cling to Pagan belief, and suppose that in death they are united to the Deity which they have cultivated during life. This is "a consummation devoutly to be wished" (Shakespeare).

In the last paragraph the Master urges his pupils to practise Samadhi every day.

17

ΚΕΦΑΛΗ ΙΖ

THE SWAN[11]

There is a Swan whose name is Ecstasy: it wingeth from the
Deserts of the North; it wingeth through the blue; it
wingeth over the fields of rice; at its coming they push forth
the green.
In all the Universe this Swan alone is motionless; it seems to
move, as the Sun seems to move; such is the weakness of
our sight.
O fool! criest thou?
Amen. Motion is relative: there is Nothing that is still.
Against this Swan I shot an arrow; the white breast poured forth
blood. Men smote me; then, perceiving that I was but a Pure
Fool, they let me pass.
Thus and not otherwise I came to the Temple of the Graal.

COMMENTARY (IZ)

This Swan is Aum. The chapter is inspired by Frater P.'s memory of the wild swans he shot in the Tali-Fu.

In paragraphs 3 and 4 it is, however, recognised that even Aum is impermanent. There is no meaning in the word, stillness, so long as motion exists.

In a boundless universe, one can always take any one point, however mobile, and postulate it as a point at rest, calculating the motions of all other points relatively to it.

The penultimate paragraph shows the relations of the Adept to mankind. Their hate and contempt are necessary steps to his acquisition of sovereignty over them.

The story of the Gospel, and that of Parsifal, will occur to the mind.

NOTE

(11) This chapter must be read in connection with Wagner's Parsifal.

18

ΚΕΦΑΛΗ ΙΗ

DEWDROPS

Verily, love is death, and death is life to come.

Man returneth not again; the stream floweth not uphill; the old
life is no more; there is a new life that is not his.

Yet that life is of his very essence; it is more He than all that he
calls He.

In the silence of a dewdrop is every tendency of his soul, and of
his mind, and of his body; it is the Quintessence and the
Elixir of his being. Therein are the forces that made him and
his father and his father's father before him.

This is the Dew of Immortality.

Let this go free, even as It will; thou art not its master, but the
vehicle of It.

COMMENTARY (IH)

The 18th key of the Tarot refers to the Moon, which was supposed to shed dew. The appropriateness of the chapter title is obvious.

The chapter must be read in connection with Chapters 1 and 16.

In the penultimate paragraph, Vindu is identified with Amrita, and in the last paragraph the disciple is charged to let it have its own way. It has a will of its own, which is more in accordance with the Cosmic Will, than that of the man who is its guardian and servant.

19

ΚΕΦΑΛΗ ΙΘ

THE LEOPARD AND THE DEER

The spots of the leopard are the sunlight in the glade; pursue
thou the deer stealthily at thy pleasure.

The dappling of the deer is the sunlight in the glade; concealed
from the leopard do thou feed at thy pleasure.

Resemble all that surroundeth thee; yet be Thyself – and take
thy pleasure among the living.

This is that which is written – Lurk! – in *The Book of The Law.*

COMMENTARY (ΙΘ)

19 is the last Trump, "The Sun", which is the representative of god in the Macrocosm, as the Phallus is in the Microcosm.

There is a certain universality and adaptability among its secret power. The chapter is taken from Rudyard Kipling's Just So Stories.

The Master urges his disciples to a certain holy stealth, a concealment of the real purpose of their lives; in this way making the best of both worlds. This counsels a course of action hardly distinguishable from hypocrisy; but the distinction is obvious to any clear thinker, though not altogether so the Frater P.

20

ΚΕΦΑΛΗ Κ

SAMPSON

The Universe is in equilibrium; therefore He that is without it,
though his force be but a feather, can overturn the Universe.
Be not caught within that web, O child of Freedom! Be not
entangled in the universal lie, O child of Truth!

COMMENTARY (K)

Samson, the Hebrew Hercules, is said in the legend to have pulled down the walls of a music-hall where he was engaged, "to make sport for the Philistines", destroying them and himself. Milton founds a poem on this fable.

The first paragraph is a corollary of Newton's First Law of Motion. The key to infinite power is to reach the Bornless Beyond.

21

ΚΕΦΑΛΗ ΚΑ

THE BLIND WEBSTER

It is not necessary to understand; it is enough to adore.

The god may be of clay: adore him; he becomes GOD.

We ignore what created us; we adore what we create. Let us
create nothing but GOD!

That which causes us to create is our true father and mother; we
create in our own image, which is theirs.

Let us create therefore without fear; for we can create nothing
that is not GOD.

COMMENTARY (KA)

The 21st key of the Tarot is called "The Universe", and refers to the letter Tau, the Phallus in manifestation; hence the title, "The Blind Webster".

The universe is conceived as Buddhists, on the one hand, and Rationalists, on the other, would have us do; fatal, and without intelligence. Even so, it may be delightful to the creator.

The moral of this chapter is, therefore, an exposition of the last paragraph of Chapter 18.

It is the critical spirit which is the Devil, and gives rise to the appearance of evil.

22

ΚΕΦΑΛΗ ΚΒ

THE DESPOT

The waiters of the best eating-houses mock the whole world;
they estimate every client at his proper value.

This I know certainly, because they always treat me with
profound respect. Thus they have flattered me into praising
them thus publicly.

Yet it is true; and they have this insight because they serve, and
because they can have no personal interest in the affairs of
those whom they serve.

An absolute monarch would be absolutely wise and good.

But no man is strong enough to have no interest. Therefore the
best king would be Pure Chance.

It is Pure Chance that rules the Universe; therefore, and only
therefore, life is good.

COMMENTARY (KB)

Comment would only mar the supreme simplicity of this chapter.

23

ΚΕΦΑΛΗ ΚΓ

SKIDOO

What man is at ease in his Inn?
Get out.
Wide is the world and cold.
Get out.
Thou hast become an in-itiate.
Get out.
But thou canst not get out by the way thou camest in.
The Way out is THE WAY.
Get out.
For OUT is Love and Wisdom and Power.[12]
Get OUT.
If thou hast T already, first get UT.[13]
Then get O.
And so at last get OUT.

COMMENTARY (ΚΓ)

Both "23" and "Skidoo" are American words meaning "Get out". This chapter describes the Great Work under the figure of a man ridding himself of all his accidents.

He first leaves the life of comfort; then the world at large; and, lastly, even the initiates.

In the fourth section is shown that there is no return for one that has started on this path.

The word OUT is then analysed, and treated as a noun.

Besides the explanation in the note, O is the Yoni; T, the Lingam; and U, the Hierophant; the 5th card of the Tarot, the Pentagram. It is thus practically identical with IAO.

The rest of the chapter is clear, for the note.

NOTE

(12) O = ♉, "The Devil of the Sabbath". U = 8, the Hierophant or Redeemer. T = Strength, the Lion.

(13) T, manhood, the sign of the cross or phallus. UT, the Holy Guardian Angel; UT, the first syllable of Udgita, see the Upanishads. O, Nothing or Nuit.

24

ΚΕΦΑΛΗ ΚΔ

THE HAWK AND THE BLINDWORM

This book would translate Beyond-Reason into the words of
Reason.

Explain thou snow to them of Andaman.

The slaves of reason call this book Abuse-of-Language: they are
right.

Language was made for men to eat and drink, make love, do
barter, die. The wealth of a language consists in its Abstracts;
the poorest tongues have wealth of Concretes.

Therefore have Adepts praised silence; at least it does not
mislead as speech does.

Also, Speech is a symptom of Thought.

Yet, silence is but the negative side of Truth; the positive side is
beyond even silence.

Nevertheless, One True God crieth *hriliu*!

And the laughter of the Death-rattle is akin.

COMMENTARY (KΔ)

The Hawk is the symbol of sight; the Blindworm, of blindness. Those who are under the dominion of reason are called blind.

In the last paragraph is reasserted the doctrine of Chapters 1, 8, 16 and 18.

For the meaning of the word hriliu *consult Liber 418.*

25

ΚΕΦΑΛΗ ΚΕ

THE STAR RUBY

Facing East, in the centre, draw deep deep deep thy breath, closing thy mouth with thy right forefinger prest against thy lower lip. Then dashing down the hand with a great sweep back and out, expelling forcibly thy breath, cry: ΑΠΟ ΠΑΝΤΟΣ ΚΑΚΟΔΑΙΜΟΝΟΣ.

With the same forefinger touch thy forehead, and say ΣΟΙ, thy member, and say Ω ΦΑΛΛΕ,[14] thy right shoulder, and say ΙΣΧΥΡΟΣ, thy left shoulder, and say ΕΥΧΑΡΙΣΤΟΣ; then clasp thine hands, locking the fingers, and cry ΙΑΩ.

Advance to the East. Imagine strongly a Pentagram, aright, in thy forehead. Drawing the hands to the eyes, fling it forth, making the sign of Horus, and roar ΧΑΟΣ. Retire thine hand in the sign of Hoor pa kraat.

Go round to the North and repeat; but scream ΒΑΒΑΛΟΝ.

Go round to the West and repeat; but say ΕΡΩΣ.

Go round to the South and repeat; but bellow ΨΥΧΗ.

Completing the circle widdershins, retire to the centre, and raise thy voice in the Paian, with these words ΙΟ ΠΑΝ with the signs of N. O. X.

Extend the arms in the form of a Tau, and say low but clear: ΠΡΟ ΜΟΥ ΙΥΓΓΕΣ ΟΠΙΣΩ ΜΟΥ ΤΕΛΕΤΑΡΧΑΙ ΕΠΙ ΔΕΞΙΑ ΣΥΝΟΧΕΣ ΕΠΑΡΙΣΤΕΡΑ ΔΑΙΜΟΝΕΣ ΦΛΕΓΕΙ ΓΑΡ ΠΕΡΙ ΜΟΥ Ο ΑΣΤΗΡ ΤΩΝ ΠΕΝΤΕ ΚΑΙ ΕΝ ΤΗΙ ΣΤΗΛΗΙ Ο ΑΣΤΗΡ ΤΩΝ ΕΞ ΕΣΤΗΚΕ.

Repeat the Cross Qabalistic, as above, and end as thou didst begin.

COMMENTARY (KE)

25 is the square of 5, and the Pentagram has the red colour of Geburah.

The chapter is a new and more elaborate version of the Banishing Ritual of the Pentagram.

It would be improper to comment further upon an official ritual of the A∴A∴

NOTE
*(14) The secret sense of these words is to be sought
in the numeration thereof.*

26

ΚΕΦΑΛΗ ΚϜ

THE ELEPHANT AND THE TORTOISE

The Absolute and the Conditioned together make The One Absolute.

The Second, who is the Fourth, the Demiurge, whom all nations of Men call The First, is a lie grafted upon a lie, a lie multiplied by a lie.

Fourfold is He, the Elephant upon whom the Universe is poised: but the carapace of the Tortoise supports and covers all.

This Tortoise is sixfold, the Holy Hexagram.[15]

These six and four are ten, 10, the One manifested that returns into the Naught unmanifest.

The All-Mighty, the All-Ruler, the All-Knower, the All-Father, adored by all men and by me abhorred, be thou accursèd, be thou abolished, be thou annihilated, Amen!

COMMENTARY (K_F)

The title of the chapter refers to the Hindu legend.

The first paragraph should be read in connection with our previous remarks upon the number 91.

The number of the chapter, 26, is that of Tetragrammaton, the manifest creator, Jehovah.

He is called the Second in relation to that which is above the Abyss, comprehended under the title of the First.

But the vulgarians conceive of nothing beyond the creator, and therefore call him The First.

He is really the Fourth, being in Chesed, and of course his nature is fourfold. This Four is conceived of as the Dyad multiplied by the Dyad; falsehood confirming falsehood.

Paragraph 3 introduces a new conception; that of the square within the hexagram, the universe enclosed in the law of Lingam-Yoni.

The penultimate paragraph shows the redemption of the universe by this law.

The figure 10, like the work IO, again suggest Lingam-Yoni, besides the exclamation given in the text.

The last paragraph curses the universe thus unredeemed.

The eleven initial A's in the last sentence are Magick Pentagrams, emphasising this curse.

NOTE

(15) In nature the Tortoise has 6 members at angles of 60°.

27

ΚΕΦΑΛΗ ΚΖ

THE SORCERER

A Sorcerer by the power of his magick had subdued all things to himself.

Would he travel? He could fly through space more swiftly than the stars.

Would he eat, drink, and take his pleasure? There was none that did not instantly obey his bidding.

In the whole system of ten million times ten million spheres upon the two and twenty million planes he had his desire.

And with all this he was but himself.

Alas!

COMMENTARY (KZ)

This chapter gives the reverse of the medal; it is the contrast to Chapter 15. The Sorcerer is to be identified with The Brother of the Left Hand Path.

28

ΚΕΦΑΛΗ ΚΗ

THE POLE-STAR

Love is all virtue, since the pleasure of love is but love,
and the pain of love is but love.
Love taketh no heed of that which is not and of that
which is.
Absence exalteth love, and presence exalteth love.
Love moveth ever from height to height of ecstasy and
faileth never.
The wings of love droop not with time, nor slacken for life
or for death.
Love destroyeth self, uniting self with that which is
not-self, so that Love breedeth All and None in One.
Is it not so?... No?...
Then thou art not lost in love; speak not of love.
Love Alway Yieldeth: Love Alway Hardeneth.
. . . . May be: I write it but to write Her name.

COMMENTARY (KH)

This now introduces the principal character of this book, Laylah, who is the ultimate feminine symbol, to be interpreted on all planes.

But in this chapter, little hint is given of anything beyond physical love. It is called the Pole-Star, because Laylah is the one object of devotion to which the author ever turns.

Note the introduction of the name of the Beloved in acrostic in line 15.

29

ΚΕΦΑΛΗ ΚΘ

THE SOUTHERN CROSS

Love, I love you! Night, night, cover us! Thou art night, O my
love; and there are no stars but thine eyes.

Dark night, sweet night, so warm and yet so fresh, so scented
yet so holy, cover me, cover me!

Let me be no more! Let me be Thine; let me be Thou; let me be
neither Thou nor I; let there be love in night and night in
love.

N. O. X. the night of Pan; and Laylah, the night before His
threshold!

COMMENTARY (KΘ)

Chapter 29 continues Chapter 28.

Note that the word Laylah is the Arabic for "Night".

The author begins to identify the Beloved with the N. O. X. previously spoken of.

The chapter is called "The Southern Cross", because, on the physical plane, Laylah is an Australian.

30

ΚΕΦΑΛΗ Λ

JOHN-A-DREAMS

Dreams are imperfections of sleep; even so is consciousness the
imperfection of waking.

Dreams are impurities in the circulation of the blood; even so is
consciousness a disorder of life.

Dreams are without proportion, without good sense, without
truth; so also is consciousness.

Awake from dream, the truth is known:[16] awake from waking,
the Truth is – The Unknown.

COMMENTARY (Λ)

This chapter is to be read in connection with Chapter 8, and also with those previous chapters in which the reason is attacked.

The allusion in the title is obvious.

This sum in proportion, dream: waking: : waking:

Samadhi is a favourite analogy with Frater P., *who frequently employs it in his holy discourse.*

NOTE
(16) I.e. the truth that he hath slept.

31

ΚΕΦΑΛΗ ΛΑ

THE GAROTTE

IT moves from motion into rest, and rests from rest into
   motion. These IT does alway, for time is not. So that IT does
   neither of these things. IT does THAT one thing which we
   must express by two things neither of which possesses any
   rational meaning.

Yet ITS doing, which is no-doing, is simple and yet complex, is
   neither free nor necessary.

For all these ideas express Relation; and IT, comprehending all
   Relation in ITS simplicity, is out of all Relation even with
   ITSELF.

All this is true and false; and it is true and false to say that it is
   true and false.

Strain forth thine Intelligence, O man, O worthy one, O chosen
   of IT, to apprehend the discourse of THE MASTER; for thus
   thy reason shall at last break down, as the fetter is struck
   from a slave's throat.

COMMENTARY (ΛA)

The number 31 refers to the Hebrew word LA, which means "not".

A new character is now introduced under the title of IT, I being the secret, and T being the manifested, phallus.

This is, however, only one aspect of IT, which may perhaps be defined as the Ultimate Reality.

IT is apparently a more exalted thing than THAT.

This chapter should be compared with Chapter 11; that method of destroying the reason by formulating contradictions is definitely inculcated.

The reason is situated in Daath, which corresponds to the throat in human anatomy. Hence the title of the chapter, "The Garotte".

The idea is that, by forcing the mind to follow, and as far as possible to realise, the language of Beyond the Abyss, the student will succeed in bringing his reason under control.

As soon as the reason is vanquished, the garotte is removed; then the influence of the supernals (Kether, Chokmah, Binah), no longer inhibited by Daath, can descend upon Tiphareth, where the human will is situated, and flood it with the ineffable light.

32

ΚΕΦΑΛΗ ΛΒ

THE MOUNTAINEER

Consciousness is a symptom of disease.

All that moves well moves without will.

All skillfulness, all strain, all intention is contrary to ease.

Practise a thousand times, and it becomes difficult; a thousand
thousand, and it becomes easy; a thousand thousand times
a thousand thousand, and it is no longer Thou that doeth it,
but It that doeth itself through thee. Not until then is that
which is done well done.

Thus spoke FRATER PERDURABO as he leapt from rock to
rock of the moraine without ever casting his eyes upon
the ground.

COMMENTARY (ΛB)

This title is a mere reference to the metaphor of the last paragraph of the chapter.

Frater P., as is well known, is a mountaineer. This chapter should be read in conjunction with Chapters 8 and 30.

It is a practical instruction, the gist of which is easily to be apprehended by comparatively short practice of Mantra-Yoga.

A mantra is not being properly said as long as the man knows he is saying it. The same applies to all other forms of Magick.

33

ΚΕΦΑΛΗ ΛΓ

BAPHOMET

A black two-headed Eagle is GOD; even a Black Triangle is He.
In His claws He beareth a sword; yea, a sharp sword is held
therein.

This Eagle is burnt up in the Great Fire; yet not a feather is
scorched. This Eagle is swallowed up in the Great Sea; yet not
a feather is wetted. so flieth He in the air, and lighteth upon
the earth at His pleasure.

So spake IACOBUS BURGUNDUS MOLENSIS,[17] the Grand
Master of the Temple; and of the GOD that is Ass-headed
did he dare not speak.

COMMENTARY (ΛΓ)

33 is the number of the Last Degree of Masonry, which was conferred upon Frater P. in the year 1900 of the vulgar era by Don Jesus de Medina-Sidonia in the City of Mexico.

Baphomet is the mysterious name of the God of the Templars.

The Eagle described in paragraph 1 is that of the Templars.

This Masonic symbol is, however, identified by Frater P. with a bird, which is master of the four elements, and therefore of the name Tetragrammaton.

Jacobus Burgundus Molensis suffered martyrdom in the City of Paris in the year 1314 of the vulgar era.

The secrets of his order were, however, not lost, and are still being communicated to the worthy by his successors, as is intimated by the last paragraph, which implies knowledge of a secret worship, of which the Grand Master did not speak.

The Eagle may be identified, though not too closely, with the Hawk previously spoken of.

It is perhaps the Sun, the exoteric object of worship of all sensible cults; it is not to be confused with other objects of the mystic aviary, such as the swan, phoenix, pelican, dove and so on.

NOTE

(17) His initials I.B.M. are the initials of the Three Pillars of the Temple, and add to 52, 13×4, BN, the Son.

34

ΚΕΦΑΛΗ ΛΔ

THE SMOKING DOG[18]

Each act of man is the twist and double of an hare.
Love and death are the greyhounds that course him.
God bred the hounds and taketh His pleasure in the sport.
This is the Comedy of Pan, that man should think he hunteth,
 while those hounds hunt him.
This is the Tragedy of Man when facing Love and Death he
 turns to bay. He is no more hare, but boar.
There are no other comedies or tragedies.
Cease then to be the mockery of God; in savagery of love and
 death live thou and die!
Thus shall His laughter be thrilled through with Ecstasy.

COMMENTARY (ΛΔ)

The title is explained in the note.

The chapter needs no explanation; it is a definite point of view of life, and recommends a course of action calculated to rob the creator of his cruel sport.

NOTE

(18) This chapter was written to clarify Χεψιδ of which it was the origin. FRATER PERDURABO perceived this truth, or rather the first half of it, comedy, at breakfast at "Au Chien qui Fume".

35

ΚΕΦΑΛΗ ΛΕ

VENUS OF MILO

Life is as ugly and necessary as the female body.
Death is as beautiful and necessary as the male body.
The soul is beyond male and female as it is beyond Life
    and Death.
Even as the Lingam and the Yoni are but diverse
    developments of One Organ, so also are Life and
    Death but two phases of One State. So also the
    Absolute and the Conditioned are but forms of THAT.
What do I love? There is no form, no being, to which I do
    not give myself wholly up.
Take me, who will!

COMMENTARY (ΛE)

This chapter must be read in connection with Chapters 1, 3, 4, 8, 15, 16, 18, 24, 28, 29.

The last sentence of paragraph 4 also connects with the first paragraph of Chapter 26.

The title "Venus of Milo" is an argument in support of paragraphs 1 and 2, it being evident from this statement that the female body becomes beautiful in so far as it approximates to the male.

The female is to be regarded as having been separated from the male, in order to reproduce the male in a superior form, the absolute, and the conditions forming the one absolute.

In the last two paragraphs there is a justification of a practice which might be called sacred prostitution.

In the common practice of meditation the idea is to reject all impressions, but here is an opposite practice, very much more difficult, in which all are accepted.

This cannot be done at all unless one is capable of making Dhyana at least on any conceivable thing, at a second's notice; otherwise, the practice would only be ordinary mind-wandering.

36

ΚΕΦΑΛΗ ΛΣ

THE STAR SAPPHIRE

Let the Adept be armed with his Magick Rood [and provided
with his Mystic Rose].

In the centre, let him give the L. V. X. signs; or if he know them,
if he will and dare do them, and can keep silent about them,
the signs of N. O. X. being the signs of Puer, Vir, Puella,
Mulier. Omit the sign I.R.

Then let him advance to the East, and make the Holy Hexagram,
saying: PATER ET MATER UNIS DEUS ARARITA.

Let him go round to the South, make the Holy Hexagram, and
say: MATER ET FILIUS UNUS DEUS ARARITA.

Let him go round to the West, make the Holy Hexagram, and
say: FILIUS ET FILIA UNUS DEUS ARARITA.

Let him go round to the North, make the Holy Hexagram, and
then say: FILIA ET PATER UNUS DEUS ARARITA.

Let him then return to the Centre, and so to The Centre of All
[making the ROSY CROSS as he may know how] saying:
ARARITA ARARITA ARARITA.

[In this the Signs shall be those of Set Triumphant and of
Baphomet. Also shall Set appear in the Circle. Let him drink
of the Sacrament and let him communicate the same.]

Then let him say: OMNIA IN DUOS: DUO IN UNUM: UNUS
IN NIHIL: HAE NEC QUATUOR NEC OMNIA NEC DUO
NEC UNUS NEC NIHIL SUNT.

GLORIA PATRI ET MATRI ET FILIO ET FILIAE ET SPIRITUI
SANCTO EXTERNO ET SPIRITUI SANCTO INTERNO UT
ERAT EST ERIT IN SAECULA SAECULORUM SEX IN
UNO PER NOMEN SEPTEM IN UNO ARARITA.

Let him then repeat the signs of L. V. X. but not the signs of N. O. X.;
for it is not he that shall arise in the Sign of Isis Rejoicing.

COMMENTARY (ΛΣ)

The Star Sapphire corresponds with the Star-Ruby of Chapter 25; 36 being the square of 6, as 25 is of 5.

This chapter gives the real and perfect Ritual of the Hexagram.

It would be improper to comment further upon an official ritual of the A∴A∴

37

ΚΕΦΑΛΗ ΛΖ

DRAGONS

Thought is the shadow of the eclipse of Luna.

Samadhi is the shadow of the eclipse of Sol.

The moon and the earth are the non-ego and the ego: the Sun is THAT.

Both eclipses are darkness; both are exceeding rare; the Universe itself is Light.

COMMENTARY (ΛZ)

Dragons are in the East supposed to cause eclipses by devouring the luminaries.

There may be some significance in the chapter number, which is that of Jechidah the highest unity of the soul.

In this chapter, the idea is given that all limitation and evil is an exceedingly rare accident; there can be no night in the whole of the Solar System, except in rare spots, where the shadow of a planet is cast by itself. It is a serious misfortune that we happen to live in a tiny corner of the system, where the darkness reaches such a high figure as 50 per cent.

The same is true of moral and spiritual conditions.

38

ΚΕΦΑΛΗ ΛΗ

LAMBSKIN

Cowan, skidoo!
Tyle!
Swear to hele all.
This is the mystery.
Life!
Mind is the traitor.
Slay mind.
Let the corpse of mind lie unburied on the edge of the
    Great Sea!
Death!
This is the mystery.
Tyle!
Cowan, skidoo!

COMMENTARY (ΛH)

This chapter will be readily intelligible to E.A. Freemasons, and it cannot be explained to others.

39

ΚΕΦΑΛΗ ΛΘ

THE LOOBY

Only loobies find excellence in these words.

It is thinkable that A is not-A; to reverse this is but to revert to the normal.

Yet by forcing the brain to accept propositions of which one set is absurdity, the other truism, a new function of brain is established.

Vague and mysterious and all indefinite are the contents of this new consciousness; yet they are somehow vital. By use they become luminous.

Unreason becomes Experience.

This lifts the leaden-footed soul to the Experience of THAT of which Reason is the blasphemy.

But without the Experience these words are the Lies of a Looby.

Yet a Looby to thee, and a Booby to me, a Balassius Ruby to GOD, may be!

COMMENTARY (ΛΘ)

The word Looby occurs in folklore, and was supposed to be the author, at the time of writing this book, which he did when he was far from any standard works of reference, to connote partly "booby", partly "lout". It would thus be a similar word to Parsifal.

Paragraphs 2–6 explain the method that was given in Chapters 11 and 31. This method, however, occurs throughout the book on numerous occasions, and even in the chapter itself it is employed in the last paragraphs.

40

ΚΕΦΑΛΗ Μ

THE HIMOG[19]

A red rose absorbs all colours but red; red is therefore the one
   colour that it is not.

This Law, Reason, Time, Space, all Limitation blinds us to the
   Truth.

All that we know of Man, Nature, God, is just that which they
   are not; it is that which they throw off as repugnant.

The HIMOG is only visible in so far as He is imperfect.

Then are they all glorious who seem not to be glorious, as the
   HIMOG is All-glorious Within?

It may be so.

How then distinguish the inglorious and perfect HIMOG from
   the inglorious man of earth?

Distinguish not!

But thyself Extinguish: HIMOG art thou, and HIMOG shalt
   thou be.

COMMENTARY (M)

Paragraph 1 is, of course, a well-known scientific fact.

In paragraph 2 it is suggested analogically that all thinkable things are similarly blinds for the Unthinkable Reality.

Classing in this manner all things as illusions, the question arises as to the distinguishing between illusions; how are we to tell whether a Holy Illuminated Man of God is really so, since we can see nothing of him but his imperfections. "It may be yonder beggar is a King."

But these considerations are not to trouble such mind as the Chela may possess; let him occupy himself, rather, with the task of getting rid of his personality; this, and not criticism of his holy Guru, should be the occupation of his days and nights.

NOTE
(19) HIMOG is a Notariqon of the words
Holy Illuminated Man of God.

41

ΚΕΦΑΛΗ ΜΑ

CORN BEEF HASH[20]

In V.V.V.V.V. is the Great Work perfect.

Therefore none is that pertaineth not to V.V.V.V.V.

In any may he manifest; yet in one hath he chosen to manifest; and this one hath given His ring as a Seal of Authority to the Work of the A∴A∴ through the colleagues of FRATER PERDURABO.

But this concerns themselves and their administration; it concerneth none below the grade of Exempt Adept, and such an one only by command.

Also, since below the Abyss Reason is Lord, let men seek by experiment, and not by Questionings.

COMMENTARY (MA)

The title is only partially explained in the note; it means that the statements in this chapter are to be understood in the most ordinary and commonplace way, without any mystical sense.

V.V.V.V.V. is the motto of a Master of the Temple (or so much He disclosed to the Exempt Adepts), referred to in Liber LXI. *It is he who is responsible for the whole of the development of the A∴A∴ movement which has been associated with the publication of* THE EQUINOX; *and His utterance is enshrined in the sacred writings.*

It is useless to enquire into His nature; to do so leads to certain disaster. Authority from him is exhibited, when necessary, to the proper persons, though in no case to anyone below the grade of Exempt Adept. The person enquiring into such matters is politely requested to work, and not to ask questions about matters which in no way concern him.

The number 41 is that of the Barren Mother.

NOTE
(20) I.e. food suitable for Americans.

42

ΚΕΦΑΛΗ ΜΒ

DUST-DEVILS

In the wind of the mind arises the turbulence called I.
It breaks; down shower the barren thoughts.
All life is choked.
This desert is the Abyss wherein is the Universe. The Stars are
   but thistles in that waste.
Yet this desert is but one spot accursèd in a world of bliss.
Now and again Travellers cross the desert; they come from the
   Great Sea, and to the Great Sea they go.
As they go they spill water; one day they will irrigate the desert,
   till it flower.
See! five footprints of a Camel! V.V.V.V.V.

COMMENTARY (MB)

This number 42 is the Great Number of the Curse. See Liber 418, Liber 500, and the essay on the Qabalah in the Temple of Solomon the King. This number is said to be all hotch-potch and accursed.

The chapter should be read most carefully in connection with the 10th Aethyr. It is to that dramatic experience that it refers.

The mind is called "wind", because of its nature; as has been frequently explained, the ideas and words are identical.

In this free-flowing, centreless material arises an eddy; a spiral close-coiled upon itself.

The theory of the formation of the Ego is that of the Hindus, whose Ahamkara is itself a function of the mind, whose ego it creates. This Ego is entirely divine.

Zoroaster describes God as having the head of the Hawk, and a spiral force. It will be difficult to understand this chapter without some experience in the transvaluation of values, which occurs throughout the whole of this book, in nearly every other sentence. Transvaluation of values is only the moral aspect of the method of contradiction.

The word "turbulence" is applied to the Ego to suggest the French "tourbillion", whirlwind, the false Ego or dust-devil.

True life, the life, which has no consciousness of "I", is said to be choked by this false ego, or rather by the thoughts which its explosions produce. In paragraph 4 this is expanded to a macrocosmic plane.

The Masters of the Temple are now introduced; they are inhabitants, not of this desert; their abode is not this universe.

They come from the Great Sea, Binah, the City of the Pyramids. V.V.V.V.V. is indicated as one of these travellers; He is described as a camel, not because of the connotation of the French form of this word, but because "camel" is in hebrew Gimel, and Gimel is the path leading from Tiphareth to Kether, uniting Microprosopus and Macroprosopus, i.e. performing the Great Work.

The card Gimel in the Tarot is the High Priestess, the Lady of Initiation; one might even say, the Holy Guardian Angel.

43

ΚΕΦΑΛΗ ΜΓ

MULBERRY TOPS

Black blood upon the altar! and the rustle of angel wings above!

Black blood of the sweet fruit, the bruised, the violated bloom –
that setteth The Wheel a-spinning in the spire. Death is the
veil of Life, and Life of Death; for both are Gods.

This is that which is written: "A feast for Life, and a greater feast
for Death!" in THE BOOK OF THE LAW.

The blood is the life of the individual: offer then blood!

COMMENTARY (MΓ)

The title of this chapter refers to a Hebrew legend, that of the prophet who heard "a going in the mulberry tops"; and to Browning's phrase, "a bruised, black-blooded mulberry".

In the World's Tragedy, Household Gods, The Scorpion, and also The God-Eater, the reader may study the efficacy of rape, and the sacrifice of blood, as magical formulae. Blood and virginity have always been the most acceptable offerings to all the gods, but especially the Christian God.

In the last paragraph, the reason of this is explained; it is because such sacrifices come under the Great Law of the Rosy Cross, the giving-up of the individuality, as has been explained as nauseam in previous chapters. We shall frequently recur to this subject.

By "the wheel spinning in the spire" is meant the manifestation of magical force, the spermatozoon in the conical phallus. For wheels, see Chapter 78.

44

ΚΕΦΑΛΗ ΜΔ

THE MASS OF THE PHŒNIX

The Magician, his breast bare, stands before an altar on which are his Burin, Bell, Thurible, and two of the Cakes of Light. In the Sign of the Enterer he reaches West across the Altar, and cries:

Hail Ra, that goest in Thy bark
Into the Caverns of the Dark!

He gives the sign of Silence, and takes the Bell, and Fire, in his hands.

East of the Altar see me stand
With Light and Musick in mine hand!

He strikes Eleven times upon the Bell 3 3 3 – 5 5 5 5 5 – 3 3 3 and places the Fire in the Thurible.

I strike the Bell: I light the flame:
I utter the mysterious Name. ABRAHADABRA

He strikes Eleven times upon the Bell.

Now I begin to pray: Thou Child,
Holy Thy name and undefiled!
Thy reign is come: Thy will is done.
Here is the Bread; here is the Blood.
Bring me through midnight to the Sun!
Save me from Evil and from Good!
That Thy one crown of all the Ten.
Even now and here be mine. AMEN.

He puts the first Cake on the Fire of the Thurible.

I burn the Incense-cake, proclaim
These adorations of Thy name.

He makes them as in Liber Legis, *and strikes again Eleven times upon the Bell. With the Burin he then makes upon his breast the proper sign.*

Behold this bleeding breast of mine
Gashed with the sacramental sign!
He puts the second Cake to the wound.
I staunch the blood; the wafer soaks
It up, and the high priest invokes!
He eats the second Cake.
This Bread I eat.
This Oath I swear
As I enflame myself with prayer:
"There is no grace: there is no guilt:
This is the Law: DO WHAT THOU WILT!"
He strikes Eleven times upon the Bell, and cries ABRAHADABRA.

   I entered in with woe; with mirth
I now go forth, and with thanksgiving,
To do my pleasure on the earth
Among the legions of the living.
He goeth forth.

COMMENTARY (MΔ)

This is the special number of Horus; it is the Hebrew blood, and the multiplication of the 4 by the 11, the number of Magick, explains 4 in its finest sense. But see in particular the accounts in Equinox I, vii of the circumstances of the Equinox of the Gods.

The word "Phoenix" may be taken as including the idea of "Pelican", the bird, which is fabled to feeds its young from the blood of its own breast. Yet the two ideas, though cognate, are not identical, and "Phoenix" is the more accurate symbol.

This chapter is explained in Chapter 62.

It would be improper to comment further upon a ritual which has been accepted as official by the A∴A∴

45

ΚΕΦΑΛΗ ΜΕ

CHINESE MUSIC

"Explain this happening!"
"It must have a 'natural' cause." } Let these two
"It must have a 'supernatural' cause." asses be set to grind corn.
May, might, must, should, probably, may be, we may safely
    assume, ought, it is hardly questionable, almost certainly –
    poor hacks! let them be turned out to grass!
Proof is only possible in mathematics, and mathematics is only a
    matter of arbitrary conventions.
And yet doubt is a good servant but a bad master; a perfect
    mistress, but a nagging wife.
"White is white" is the lash of the overseer: "white is black" is
    the watchword of the slave. The Master takes no heed.
The Chinese cannot help thinking that the octave has 5 notes.
The more necessary anything appears to my mind, the more
    certain it is that I only assert a limitation.
I slept with Faith, and found a corpse in my arms on awaking; I
    drank and danced all night with Doubt, and found her a
    virgin in the morning.

COMMENTARY (ME)

The title of this chapter is drawn from paragraph 7.

We now, for the first time, attack the question of doubt.

"The Soldier and the Hunchback" should be carefully studied in this connection. The attitude recommended is scepticism, but a scepticism under control. Doubt inhibits action, as much as faith binds it. All the best Popes have been Atheists, but perhaps the greatest of them once remarked, "Quantum nobis prodest haec fabula Christi".

The ruler asserts facts as they are; the slave has therefore no option but to deny them passionately, in order to express his discontent. Hence such absurdities as "Liberté, Egalité, Fraternité", "In God we trust", and the like. Similarly we find people asserting today that woman is superior to man, and that all men are born equal.

The Master (in technical language, the Magus) does not concern himself with facts; he does not care whether a thing is true or not: he uses truth and falsehood indiscriminately, to serve his ends. Slaves consider him immoral, and preach against him in Hyde Park.

In paragraphs 7 and 8 we find a most important statement, a practical aspect of the fact that all truth is relative, and in the last paragraph we see how scepticism keeps the mind fresh, whereas faith dies in the very sleep that it induces.

46

ΚΕΦΑΛΗ Μϝ

BUTTONS AND ROSETTES

The cause of sorrow is the desire of the One to the Many, or of
the Many to the One. This also is the cause of joy.

But the desire of one to another is all of sorrow; its birth is
hunger, and its death satiety.

The desire of the moth for the star at least saves him satiety.

Hunger thou, O man, for the infinite: be insatiable even for the
finite; thus at The End shalt thou devour the finite, and
become the infinite.

Be thou more greedy that the shark, more full of yearning than
the wind among the pines.

The weary pilgrim struggles on; the satiated pilgrim stops.

The road winds uphill: all law, all nature must be overcome.

Do this by virtue of THAT in thyself before which law and
nature are but shadows.

COMMENTARY (M$_F$)

The title of this chapter is best explained by a reference to Mistinguette and Mayol.

It would be hard to decide, and it is fortunately unnecessary even to discuss, whether the distinction of their art is the cause, result, or concomitant of their private peculiarities.

The fact remains that in vice, as in everything else, some things satiate, others refresh. Any game in which perfection is easily attained soon ceases to amuse, although in the beginning its fascination is so violent.

Witness the tremendous, but transitory, vogue of ping-pong and diabolo. Those games in which perfection is impossible never cease to attract.

The lesson of the chapter is thus always to rise hungry from a meal, always to violate one's own nature. Keep on acquiring a taste for what is naturally repugnant; this is an unfailing source of pleasure, and it has a real further advantage, in destroying the Sankharas, which, however "good" in themselves, relatively to other Sankharas, are yet barriers upon the Path; they are modifications of the Ego, and therefore those things which bar it from the absolute.

47

ΚΕΦΑΛΗ ΜΖ

WINDMILL-WORDS

Asana gets rid of Anatomy-consciousness. ⎱ Involuntary
Pranayama gets rid of Physiology-consciousness. ⎰ "Breaks"

Yama and Niyama get rid of Ethical consciousness.⎱ Voluntary "Breaks"

Pratyhara gets rid of the Objective.
Dharana gets rid of the Subjective.
Dhyana gets rid of the Ego.
Samadhi gets rid of the Soul Impersonal.

Asana destroys the static body (Nama).
Pranayama destroys the dynamic body (Rupa).
Yama destroys the emotions.
Niyama destroys the passions. ⎱ (Vedana)
Dharana destroys the perceptions (Sañña).
Dhyana destroys the tendencies (Sankhara).
Samadhi destroys the consciousness (Viññanam).
Homard à la Thermidor destroys the digestion.
The last of these facts is the one of which I am most certain.

COMMENTARY (MZ)

The allusion in the title is not quite clear, though it may be connected with the penultimate paragraph.

The chapter consists of two points of view from which to regard Yoga, two odes upon a distant prospect of the Temple of Madura, two Elegies on a mat of Kusha-grass.

The penultimate paragraph is introduced by way of repose. Cynicism is a great cure for over-study.

There is a great deal of cynicism in this book, in one place and another. It should be regarded as Angostura Bitters, to brighten the flavour of a discourse which were else too sweet. It prevents one from slopping over into sentimentality.

48

ΚΕΦΑΛΗ ΜΗ

MOME RATHS[22]

The early bird catches the worm and the twelve-year-old
    prostitute attracts the ambassador. Neglect not the
    dawn-meditation!

The first plovers' eggs fetch the highest prices; the flower of
    virginity is esteemed by the pandar.
Neglect not the dawn-meditation!

Early to bed and early to rise
Makes a man healthy and wealthy and wise:
But late to watch and early to pray
Brings him across The Abyss, they say.
Neglect not the dawn-meditation!

COMMENTARY (MH)

This chapter is perfectly simple, and needs no comment whatsoever.

NOTE

(22) "The mome raths outgrabe" – Lewis Carroll.
But "môme" is Parisian slang for a young girl, and "rathe"
O.E. for early. "The rathe primrose" – Milton.

49

ΚΕΦΑΛΗ ΜΘ

WARATAH-BLOSSOMS

Seven are the veils of the dancing-girl in the harem of IT.
Seven are the names, and seven are the lamps beside Her bed.
Seven eunuchs guard Her with drawn swords; No Man may
    come nigh unto Her.
In Her wine-cup are seven streams of the blood of the Seven
    Spirits of God. Seven are the heads of THE BEAST whereon
    She rideth.
The head of an Angel: the head of a Saint: the head of a Poet:
    the head of An Adulterous Woman: the head of a Man of
    Valour: the head of a Satyr: and the head of a Lion-Serpent.
Seven letters hath Her holiest name; and it is

This is the Seal upon the Ring that is on the Forefinger of IT:
    and it is the Seal upon the Tombs of them whom She hath
    slain.
Here is Wisdom. Let Him that hath Understanding count the
    Number of Our Lady; for it is the Number of a Woman; and
    Her Number is
        An Hundred and Fifty and Six.

COMMENTARY (MΘ)

49 is the square of 7.

7 is the passive and feminine number.

The chapter should be read in connection with Chapter 31 for IT now reappears.

The chapter heading, the Waratah, is a voluptuous scarlet flower, common in Australia, and this connects the chapter with Chapters 28 and 29; but this is only an allusion, for the subject of the chapter is OUR LADY BABALON, who is conceived as the feminine counterpart of IT.

This does not agree very well with the common or orthodox theogony of Chapter 11; but it is to be explained by the dithyrambic nature of the chapter.

In paragraph 3 NO MAN is of course NEMO, the Master of the Temple, Liber 418 will explain most of the allusions in this chapter.

In paragraphs 5 and 6 the author frankly identifies himself with the BEAST referred to in the book, and in the Apocalypse, and in LIBER LEGIS. In paragraph 6 the word "angel" may refer to his mission, and the word "lion-serpent" to the sigil of his ascending decan. (Teth = Snake = spermatozoon and Leo in the Zodiac, which like Teth itself has the snake-form. θ first written ⊙ = Lingam-Yoni and Sol.)

Paragraph 7 explains the theological difficulty referred to above. There is only one symbol, but this symbol has many names: of those names BABALON is the holiest. It is the name referred to in Liber Legis, 1, 22.

It will be noticed that the figure, or sigil, of BABALON is a seal upon a ring, and this ring is upon the forefinger of IT. This identifies further the symbol with itself.

It will be noticed that this seal, except for the absence of a border, is the official seal of the A∴A∴ Compare Chapter 3.

It is also said to be the seal upon the tombs of them that she hath slain, that is, of the Masters of the Temple.

In connection with the number 49, see Liber 418, the 22nd Aethyr, as well as the usual authorities.

50

ΚΕΦΑΛΗ N

THE VIGIL OF ST. HUBERT

In the forest God met the Stag-beetle. "Hold! Worship me!"
    quoth God. "For I am All-Great, All-Good, All Wise....The
    stars are but sparks from the forges of My smiths...."
"Yea, verily and Amen," said the Stag-beetle, "all this do I
    believe, and that devoutly."
"Then why do you not worship Me?"
 "Because I am real and you are only imaginary."
But the leaves of the forest rustled with the laughter of the wind.
Said Wind and Wood: "They neither of them know anything!"

COMMENTARY (N)

St. Hubert appears to have been a saint who saw a stag of a mystical or sacred nature.

The Stag-beetle must not be identified with the one in Chapter 16. It is a merely literary touch.

The chapter is a resolution of the universe into Tetragrammaton; God the macrocosm and the microcosm beetle. Both imagine themselves to exist; both say "you" and "I", and discuss their relative reality.

The things which really exist, the things which have no Ego, and speak only in the third person, regard these as ignorant, on account of their assumption of Knowledge.

51

ΚΕΦΑΛΗ ΝΑ

TERRIER-WORK

Doubt.
Doubt thyself.
Doubt even if thou doubtest thyself.
Doubt all.
Doubt even if thou doubtest all.
It seems sometimes as if beneath all conscious doubt there
    lay some deepest certainty. O kill it! Slay the snake!
The horn of the Doubt-Goat be exalted!
Dive deeper, ever deeper, into the Abyss of Mind, until
    thou unearth the fox THAT. On, hounds! Yoicks!
    Tally-ho! Bring THAT to bay!
Then, wind the Mort!

COMMENTARY (NA)

The number 51 means failure and pain, and its subject is appropriately doubt.

The title of the chapter is borrowed from the health-giving and fascinating sport of fox-hunting, which Frater Perdurabo followed in his youth.

This chapter should be read in connection with "The Soldier and the Hunchback" of which it is in some sort an epitome.

Its meaning is sufficiently clear, but in paragraphs 6 and 7 it will be noticed that the identification of the Soldier with the Hunchback has reached such a pitch that the symbols are interchanged, enthusiasm being represented as the sinuous snake, scepticism as the Goat of the Sabbath. In other words, a state is reached in which destruction is as much joy as creation. (Compare Chapter 46.)

Beyond that is a still deeper state of mind, which is THAT.

52

ΚΕΦΑΛΗ ΝΒ

THE BULL-BAITING

Fourscore and eleven books wrote I; in each did I expound THE
GREAT WORK fully, from The Beginning even unto The
End thereof.

Then at last came certain men unto me, saying: O Master!
Expound thou THE GREAT WORK unto us, O Master!

And I held my peace.

O generation of gossipers! who shall deliver you from the Wrath
that is fallen upon you?

O Babblers, Prattlers, Talkers, Loquacious Ones, Tatlers, Chewers
of the Red Rag that inflameth Apis the Redeemer to fury,
learn first what is Work! and THE GREAT WORK is not so
far beyond!

COMMENTARY (NB)

52 is BN, the number of the Son, Osiris-Apis, the Redeemer, with whom the Master (Fra. P.) identifies himself. He permits himself for a moment the pleasure of feeling his wounds; and, turning upon his generation, gores it with his horns.

The fourscore-and-eleven books do not, we think, refer to the ninety-one chapters of this little masterpiece, or even to the numerous volumes he has penned, but rather to the fact that 91 is the number of Amen, implying the completeness of his work.

In the last paragraph is a paranomasia. "To chew the red rag" is a phrase for to talk aimlessly and persistently, while it is notorious that a red cloth will excite the rage of a bull.

53

ΚΕΦΑΛΗ ΝΓ

THE DOWSER

Once round the meadow. Brother, does the hazel twig dip?
Twice round the orchard. Brother, does the hazel twig dip?
Thrice round the paddock. Highly, lowly, wily, holy, dip, dip, dip!
Then neighed the horse in the paddock – and lo! its wings.
For whoso findeth the SPRING beneath the earth maketh the
    treaders-of-earth to course the heavens.
This SPRING is threefold; of water, but also of steel, and of the
    seasons.
Also this PADDOCK is the Toad that hath the jewel between his
    eyes – Aum Mani Padmen Hum!
    (Keep us from Evil!)

COMMENTARY (ΝΓ)

A dowser is one who practises divination, usually with the object of finding water or minerals, by means of the vibrations of a hazel twig.

The meadow represents the flower of life; the orchard its fruit.

The paddock, being reserved for animals, represents life itself. That is to say, the secret spring of life is found in the place of life, with the result that the horse, who represents ordinary animal life, becomes the divine horse Pegasus.

In paragraph 6 we see this spring identified with the phallus, for it is not only a source of water, but highly elastic, while the reference to the seasons alludes to the well-known lines of the late Lord Tennyson:

"In the spring a livelier iris changes on the burnished dove, In the Spring a young man's fancy lightly turns to thoughts of love." – Locksley Hall.

In paragraph 7 the place of life, the universe of animal souls, is identified with the toad, which

"Ugly and venomous, Wears yet a precious jewel in his head" – Romeo and Juliet –

this jewel being the divine spark in man, and indeed in all that "lives and moves and has its being". Note this phrase, which is highly significant; the word "lives" excluding the mineral kingdom, the word "moves" the vegetable kingdom, and the phrase "has its being" the lower animals, including woman.

This "toad" and "jewel" are further identified with the Lotus and jewel of the well-known Buddhist phrase and this seems to suggest that this "toad" is the Yoni; the suggestion is further strengthened by the concluding phrase in brackets, "Keep us from evil", since, although it is the place of life, the means of grace, it may be ruinous.

54

ΚΕΦΑΛΗ ΝΔ

EAVES-DROPPINGS

Five and forty apprentice masons out of work!

Fifteen fellow-craftsmen out of work!

Three Master Masons out of work!

All these sat on their haunches waiting The Report of the
Sojourners; for THE WORD was lost.

This is the Report of the Sojourners: THE WORD was LOVE;[23]
and its number is An Hundred and Eleven.

Then said each AMO;[24] for its number is An Hundred and
Eleven.

Each took the Trowel from his LAP,[25] whose number is An
Hundred and Eleven.

Each called moreover on the Goddess NINA,[26] for Her number
is An Hundred and Eleven.

Yet with all this went The Work awry; for THE WORD OF THE
LAW IS ΘΕΛΗΜΑ.

COMMENTARY (NΔ)

The title of this chapter refers to the duty of the Tyler in a blue lodge of Freemasons.

The numbers in paragraphs 1 to 3 are significant; each Master-Mason is attended by 5 Fellow-Crafts, and each Fellow-Craft by 3 Apprentices, as if the Masters were sitting in pentagrams, and the Fellow-Craftsmen in triangles. This may refer to the number of manual signs in each of these degrees.

The moral of the chapter is apparently that the mother-letter א is an inadequate solution of the Great Problem. א is identified with the Yoni, for all the symbols connected with it in this place are feminine, but א is also a number of Samadhi and mysticism, and the doctrine is therefore that Magick, in that highest sense explained in the Book of the Law, *is the truer key.*

NOTE

(23) L=30, O=70, V=6, E=5 = 111.

(24) A=1, M=40, O=70 = 111.

(25) The trowel is shaped like a diamond or Yoni. L=30, A=1, P=80 = 111.

(26) N=50, I=10, N=50, A=1 = 111.

55

ΚΕΦΑΛΗ ΝΕ

THE DROOPING SUNFLOWER

The One Thought vanished; all my mind was torn to rags: – nay!
nay! my head was mashed into wood pulp, and thereon the
Daily Newspaper was printed.

Thus wrote I, since my One Love was torn from me. I cannot
work: I cannot think: I seek distraction here: I seek
distraction there: but this is all my truth, that I who love
have lost; and how may I regain?

I must have money to get to America.

O Mage! Sage! Gauge thy Wage, or in the Page of Thine Age is
written Rage!

O my darling! We should not have spent Ninety Pounds in that
Three Weeks in Paris!... Slash the Breaks on thine arm with
a pole-axe!

COMMENTARY (NE)

The number 55 refers to Malkuth, the ride; it should then be read in connection with Chapters 28, 29, 49.

The "drooping sunflower" is the heart, which needs the divine light.

Since Jivatma was separated from Paramatma, as in paragraph 2, not only is the Divine Unity destroyed but Daath, instead of being the Child of Chokmah and Binah, becomes the Abyss, and the Qliphoth arise. The only sense which abides is that of loss, and the craving to retrieve it. In paragraph 3 it is seen that this is impossible, owing (paragraph 4) to his not having made proper arrangements to recover the original position previous to making the divisions.

In paragraph 5 it is shown that this is because of allowing enjoyment to cause forgetfulness of the really important thing. Those who allow themselves to wallow in Samadhi are sorry for it afterwards.

The last paragraph indicated the precautions to be taken to avoid this.

The number 90 is the last paragraph is not merely fact, but symbolism; 90 being the number of Tzaddi, the Star, looked at in its exoteric sense, as a naked woman, playing by a stream, surrounded by birds and butterflies. The pole-axe is recommended instead of the usual razor, as a more vigorous weapon. One cannot be too severe in checking any faltering in the work, any digression from the Path.

56

ΚΕΦΑΛΗ Nϝ

TROUBLE WITH TWINS

Holy, holy, holy, unto Five Hundred and Fifty Five times holy be
OUR LADY of the STARS!

Holy, holy, holy, unto One Hundred and Fifty Six times holy be
OUR LADY that rideth upon THE BEAST!

Holy, holy, holy, unto the Number of Times Necessary and
Appropriate be OUR LADY Isis in Her Millions-of-Names,
All-Mother, Genetrix-Meretrix!

Yet holier than all These to me is LAYLAH, night and death; for
Her do I blaspheme alike the finite and the The Infinite.

So wrote not FRATER PERDURABO, but the Imp Crowley in
his Name.

For forgery let him suffer Penal Servitude for Seven Years; or at
least let him do Pranayama all the way home-home? nay! but
to the house of the harlot whom he loveth not. For it is
LAYLAH that he loveth . . . .

And yet who knoweth which is Crowley, and which is FRATER
PERDURABO?

COMMENTARY (N_F)

The number of the chapter refers to Liber Legis *I, 24, for paragraph 1 refers to Nuit. The "twins" in the title are those mentioned in paragraph 5.*

555 is HADIT, HAD spelt in full. 156 is BABALON.

In paragraph 4 is the gist of the chapter, Laylah being again introduced, as in Chapters 28, 29, 49 and 55.

The exoteric blasphemy, it is hinted in the last paragraph, may be an esoteric arcanum, for the Master of the Temple is interested in Malkuth, as Malkuth is in Binah; also "Malkuth is in Kether, and Kether in Malkuth"; and, to the Ipsissimus, dissolution in the body of Nuit and a visit to a brothel may be identical.

57

ΚΕΦΑΛΗ ΝΖ

THE DUCK-BILLED PLATYPUS

Dirt is matter in the wrong place.

Thought is mind in the wrong place.

Matter is mind; so thought is dirt.

Thus argued he, the Wise One, not mindful that all place
is wrong.

For not until the PLACE is perfected by a T saith he
PLACET.

The Rose uncrucified droppeth its petals; without the Rose
the Cross is a dry stick.

Worship then the Rosy Cross, and the Mystery of
Two-in-One.

And worship Him that swore by His holy T that One
should not be One except in so far as it is Two.

I am glad that LAYLAH is afar; no doubt clouds love.

COMMENTARY (NZ)

The title of the chapter suggest the two in one, since the ornithorhynchus is both bird and beast; it is also an Australian animal, like Laylah herself, and was doubtless chosen for this reason.

This chapter is an apology for the universe. Paragraphs 1–3 repeat the familiar arguments against reason in an epigrammatic form. Paragraph 4 alludes to Liber Legis I, 52; "place" implies space; denies homogeneity to space; but when "place" is perfected by "t" – as it were, Yoni by Lingam – we get the word "placet", meaning "it pleases".

Paragraphs 6 and 7 explain this further; it is necessary to separate things, in order that they might rejoice in uniting. See Liber Legis I, 28-30, which is paraphrased in the penultimate paragraph.

In the last paragraph this doctrine is interpreted in common life by a paraphrase of the familiar and beautiful proverb, "Absence makes the heart grow fonder." (PS. I seem to get a subtle after-taste of bitterness.)

(It is to be observed that the philosopher having first committed the syllogistic error quaternis terminorum, *in attempting to reduce the terms to three, staggers into* non distributia medii. *It is possible that considerations with Sir Wm. Hamilton's qualification [or quantification (?)] of the predicate may be taken as intervening, but to do so would render the humour of the chapter too subtle for the average reader in Oshkosh for whom this book is evidently written.)*

58

ΚΕΦΑΛΗ ΝΗ

HAGGAI-HOWLINGS

Haggard am I, an hyena; I hunger and howl. Men think it
   laughter – ha! ha! ha!
There is nothing movable or immovable under the firmament
   of heaven on which I may write the symbols of the secret of
   my soul.
Yea, though I were lowered by ropes into the utmost Caverns
   and Vaults of Eternity, there is no word to express even the
   first whisper of the Initiator in mine ear: yea, I abhor birth,
   ululating lamentations of Night!
Agony! Agony! the Light within me breeds veils; the song within
   be dumbness.
God! in what prism may any man analyse my Light?
Immortal are the adepts; and ye hey die – They die of SHAME
   unspeakable; They die as the Gods die, for SORROW.
Wilt thou endure unto The End, O FRATER PERDURABO,
   O Lamp in The Abyss? Thou hast the Keystone of the Royal
   Arch; yet the Apprentices, instead of making bricks, put the
   straws in their hair, and think they are Jesus Christ!
O sublime tragedy and comedy of THE GREAT WORK!

COMMENTARY (NH)

Haggai, a notorious Hebrew prophet, is a Second Officer in a Chapter of the Royal Arch Masons.

In this chapter the author, in a sort of raging eloquence, bewails his impotence to express himself, or to induce others to follow into the light. In paragraph 1 he explains the sardonic laughter, for which he is justly celebrated, as being in reality the expression of this feeling.

Paragraph 2 is a reference to the Obligation of an Entered Apprentice Mason.

Paragraph 3 refers to the Ceremony of Exaltation in Royal Arch Masonry. The Initiate will be able to discover the most formidable secret of that degree concealed in the paragraph.

Paragraphs 4–6 express an anguish to which that of Gethsemane and Golgotha must appear like whitlows. In paragraph 7 the agony is broken up by the sardonic or cynical laughter to which we have previously alluded.

And the final paragraph, in the words of the noblest simplicity, praises the Great Work; rejoices in its sublimity, in the supreme Art, in the intensity of the passion and ecstasy which it brings forth. (Note that the words "passion" and "ecstasy" may be taken as symbolical of Yoni and Lingam.)

59

ΚΕΦΑΛΗ ΝΘ

THE TAILLESS MONKEY

There is no help – but hotch pot! – in the skies
When Astacus sees Crab and Lobster rise.
Man that has spine, and hopes of heaven-to-be,
Lacks the Amoeba's immortality.
What protoplasm gains in mobile mirth
Is loss of the stability of earth.
Matter and sense and mind have had their day:
Nature presents the bill, and all must pay.
If, as I am not, I were free to choose,
How Buddhahood would battle with The Booze!
My certainty that destiny is "good"
Rests on its picking me for Buddhahood.
Were I a drunkard, I should think I had
Good evidence that fate was "bloody bad".

COMMENTARY (NΘ)

The title is a euphemism for homo sapiens.

The crab and the lobster are higher types of crustacae than the crayfish.

The chapter is a short essay in poetic form on Determinism. It hymns the great law of Equilibrium and Compensation, but cynically criticises all philosophers, hinting that their view of the universe depends on their own circumstances. The sufferer from toothache does not agree with Doctor Pangloss, that "all is for the best in the best of all possible worlds". Nor does the wealthiest of our Dukes complain to his cronies that "Times is cruel 'ard".

60

ΚΕΦΑΛΗ Ξ

THE WOUND OF AMFORTAS[27]

The Self-mastery of Percivale became the Self-masturbatery of
the Bourgeois.

Vir-tus has become "virture".

The qualities which have made a man, a race, a city, a caste,
must be thrown off; death is the penalty of failure. As it is
written: in the hour of success sacrifice that which is dearest
to thee unto the Infernal Gods!

The Englishman lives upon the excrement of his forefathers.

All moral codes are worthless in themselves; yet in every new
code there is hope. Provided always that the code is not
changed because it is too hard, but because it is fulfilled.

The dead dog floats with the stream; in puritan France the best
women are harlots; in vicious England the best women are
virgins.

If only the Archbishop of Canterbury were to go make in the
streets and beg his bread!

The new Christ, like the old, it the friend of publicans and
sinners; because his nature is ascetic.

O if everyman did No Matter What, provided that it is the one
thing that he will not and cannot do!

COMMENTARY (Ξ)

The title is explained in the note. The number of the chapter may refer to the letter Samech (□), Temperence, in the Tarot.

In paragraph 1 the real chastity of Percivale or Parsifal, a chastity which did not prevent his dipping the point of the sacred lance into the Holy Grail, is distinguished from its misinterpretation by modern crapulence. The priests of the gods were carefully chosen, and carefully trained to fulfill the sacrament of fatherhood; the shame of sex consists in the usurpation of its function by the unworthy. Sex is a sacrament.

The word virtus *means "the quality of manhood".*
Modern "virtue" is the negation of all such qualities.

In paragraph 3, however, we see the penalty of conservatism; children must be weaned.

In the penultimate paragraph the words "the new Christ" alluded to the author.

In the last paragraph we reach the sublime mystic doctrine that whatever you have must be abandoned. Obviously, that which differentiates your consciousness from the absolute is part of the content of that consciousness.

NOTE
(27) Chapter so called because Amfortas was wounded by his own spear, the spear that had made him king.

61

ΚΕΦΑΛΗ ΞΑ

THE FOOL'S KNOT

O Fool! begetter of both I and Naught, resolve this
Naught-y Knot!

O! Ay! this I and O – IO! – IAO! For I owe "I" aye to
Nibbana's Oe.[28]

I Pay-Pé, the dissolution of the House of Godfor Pe comes
after O – after Ayin that triumphs over Aleph in Ain,
that is O.[29]

OP-us, the Work! the OP-ening of THE EYE![30]

Thou Naughty Boy, thou openest THE EYE OF HORUS
to the Blind Eye that weeps![31] The Upright One in
thine Uprightness rejoiceth – Death to all Fishes![32]

COMMENTARY (ΞA)

The number of this chapter refers to the Hebrew word Ain, the negative and Ani, 61.

The "fool" is the Fool of the Tarot, whose number is 0, but refers the the letter Aleph, 1.

A fool's knot is a kind of knot which, although it has the appearance of a knot, is not really a knot, but pulls out immediately.

The chapter consists of a series of complicated puns on 1 and I, with regard to their shape, sound, and that of the figures which resemble them in shape.

Paragraph 1 calls upon the Fool of the Tarot, who is to be referred to Ipsissimus, to the pure fool, Parsifal, to resolve this problem.

The word Naught-y suggests not only that the problem is sexual, but does not really exist.

Paragraph 2 shows the Lingam and Yoni as, in conjunction, the foundation of ecstasy (IO!), and of the complete symbol I A O.

The latter sentence of the paragraph unites the two meanings of giving up the Lingam to the Yoni, and the Ego to the Absolute.

This idea, "I must give up", I owe, is naturally completed by I pay, and the sound of the word "pay" suggest the Hebrew letter Pe (see Liber XVI), which represents the final dissolution in Shivadarshana.

In Hebrew, the letter which follows O is P; i therefore follows Ayin, the Devil of the Tarot.

AYIN is spelt O I N, thus replacing the A in A I N by an O, the letter of the Devil, or Pan, the phallic God.

Now AIN means nothing, and thus the replacing of AIN by OIN means the completion of the Yoni by the Lingam, which is followed by the complete dissolution symbolised in the letter P.

These letters, O P, are then seen to be the root of opus, the Latin word for "work", in this case, the Great Work. And they also begin the word "opening". In Hindu philosophy, it is said that Shiva, the Destroyer, is asleep, and that when he opens his eye the universe is destroyed – another synonym, therefore, for the accomplishment of the Great Work. But the "eye" of Shiva is also his Lingam. Shiva is himself the Mahalingam, which unites these

symbolisms. The opening of the eye, the ejaculation of the lingam, the destruction of the universe, the accomplishment of the Great Work – all these are different ways of saying the same thing.

The last paragraph is even obscurer to those unfamiliar to the masterpiece referred to in the note; for the eye of Horus (see 777, Col. XXI, line 10, "the blind eye that weeps" is a poetic Arab name for the lingam).

The doctrine is that the Great Work should be accomplished without creating new Karma, for the letter N, the fish, the vesica, the womb, breeds, whereas the Eye of Horus does not; or, if it does so, breeds, according to Turkish tradition, a Messiah.

Death implies resurrection; the illusion is reborn, as the Scythe of Death in the Tarot has a crosspiece. This is in connection with the Hindu doctrine, expressed in their injunction, "Fry your seeds". Act so as to balance your past Karma, and create no new, so that, as it were, the books are balanced. While you have either a credit or a debit, you are still in account with the universe.

(N.B. Frater P. wrote this chapter – 61-while dining with friends, in about a minute and a half. That is how you must know the Qabalah.)

NOTE
(28) Oe = Island, a common symbol of Nibbana.

(29) אין Ain. עין Ayin.

(30) Scil. of Shiva.

(31) Cf. Bagh-i-Muattar for all this symbolism.

(32) Death = Nun, the letter before O, means a fish, a symbol of Christ, and also by its shape the Female principle

62

ΚΕΦΑΛΗ ΞΒ

TWIG?[33]

The Phoenix hat a Bell for Sound; Fire for Sight; a Knife
    for Touch; two cakes, one for taste, the other for smell.
He standeth before the Altar of the Universe at Sunset,
    when Earth-life fades.
He summons the Universe, and crowns it with MAGICK
    Light to replace the sun of natural light.
He prays unto, and give homage to, Ro-Hoor-Khuit; to
    Him he then sacrifices.
The first cake, burnt, illustrates the profit drawn from the
    scheme of incarnation.
The second, mixt with his life's blood and eaten, illustrates
    the use of the lower life to feed the higher life.
He then takes the Oath and becomes free –
    unconditioned – the Absolute.
Burning up in the Flame of his Prayer, and born again –
    the Phoenix!

COMMENTARY (ΞB)

This chapter is itself a comment on Chapter 44.

NOTE
(33) Twig? = dost thou understand? Also the Phoenix takes twigs to kindle the fire in which it burns itself.

63

ΚΕΦΑΛΗ ΞΓ

MARGERY DAW

I love LAYLAH.

I lack LAYLAH.

"Where is the Mystic Grace?" sayest thou?

Who told thee, man, that LAYLAH is not Nuit, and I Hadit?

I destroyed all things; they are reborn in other shapes.

I gave up all for One; this One hath given up its Unity for all?

I wrenched DOG backwards to find GOD; now GOD barks.

Think me not fallen because I love LAYLAH, and lack LAYLAH.

I am the Master of the Universe; then give me a heap of straw in a hut, and LAYLAH naked! Amen.

COMMENTARY (ΞΓ)

This chapter returns to the subject of Laylah, and to the subject already discussed in Chapters 3 and others, particularly Chapter 56.

The title of the chapter refers to the old rime:

> "See-saw, Margery Daw,
> Sold her bed to lie upon straw.
> Was not she a silly slut
> To sell her bed to lie upon dirt?"

The word "see-saw" is significant, almost a comment upon this chapter. To the Master of the Temple opposite rules apply. His unity seeks the many, and the many is again transmuted to the one. Solve et Coagula.

64

ΚΕΦΑΛΗ ΞΔ

CONSTANCY

I was discussing oysters with a crony:
GOD sent to me the angels DIN and DONI.
"A man of spunk," they urged, "would hardly choose
To breakfast every day *chez* Laperouse."
"No!" I replied, "he would not do so, BUT
Think of his woe if Laperouse were shut!
"I eat these oysters and I drink this wine
Solely to drown this misery of mine.
"Yet the last height of consolation's cold:
Its pinnacle is – not to be consoled!
"And though I sleep with Janefore and Eleanor
I feel no better than I did before,
"And Julian only fixes in my mind
Even before feels better than behind.
"You are Mercurial spirits – be so kind
As to enable me to raise the wind.
"Put me in LAYLAH'S arms again: the Accurst,
Leaving me that. Elsehow may do his worst."
DONI and DIN, perceiving me inspired,
Conceived their task was finished: they retired.
I turned upon my friend, and, breaking bounds,
Borrowed a trifle of two hundred pounds.

COMMENTARY (ΞΔ)

64 is the number of Mercury, and of the intelligence of that planet, Din and Doni.

The moral of the chapter is that one wants liberty, although one may not wish to exercise it: the author would readily die in defence of the right of Englishmen to play football, or of his own right not to play it. (As a great poet has expressed it: "We don't want to fight, but, by Jingo, if we do –") This is his meaning towards his attitude to complete freedom of speech and action. He refuses to listen to the ostensible criticism of the spirits, and explains his own position. Their real mission was to rouse him to confidence and action.

65

ΚΕΦΑΛΗ ΞΕ

SIC TRANSEAT –

"At last I lifted up mine eyes, and beheld; and lo! the flames of
violet were become as tendrils of smoke, as mist at sunset
upon the marsh-lands.

"And in the midst of the moon-pool of silver was the Lily of
white and gold. In this Lily is all honey, in this Lily that
flowereth at the midnight. In this Lily is all perfume; in this
Lily is all music. And it enfolded me."

Thus the disciples that watched found a dead body kneeling at
the altar. Amen!

COMMENTARY (ΞE)

65 is the number of Adonai, the Holy Guardian Angel; see Liber 65, Liber Konx Om Pax, *and other works of reference.*

The chapter title means, "So may he pass away", the blank obviously referring to N E M O.

The "moon-pool of silver" is the Path of Gimel, leading from Tiphareth to Kether; the "flames of violet" are the Ajna-Chakkra; the lily itself is Kether, the lotus of the Sahasrara. "Lily" is spelt with a capital to connect with Laylah.

66

ΚΕΦΑΛΗ Ξϝ

THE PRAYING MANTIS

"Say: God is One." This I obeyed: for a thousand and one
   times a night for one thousand nights and one did I
   affirm the Unity.
But "night" only means LAYLAH[34]; and Unity and GOD
   are not worth even her blemishes.
Al-lah is only sixty-six; but LAYLAH counteth up to
   Seven and Seventy.[35]
"Yea! the night shall cover all; the night shall cover all."

COMMENTARY (Ξϝ)

66 is the number of Allah; the praying mantis is a blasphemous grasshopper which caricatures the pious.

The chapter recurs to the subject of Laylah, whom the author exalts above God, in continuation of the reasonings given in Chapter 56 and 63. She is identified with N. O. X. by the quotation from Liber 65.

NOTE
(34) Laylah is the Arabic for night.
(35) A L L H = 1 + 30 + 30 + 5 = 66. L + A + I + L + A + H = 77, which also gives MSL, the Influence of the Highest, OZ, a goat, and so on.

67

ΚΕΦΑΛΗ ΞZ

SODOM-APPLES

I have bought pleasant trifles, and thus soothed my lack of
LAYLAH.

Light is my wallet, and my heart is also light; and yet I
know that the clouds will gather closer for the false
clearing.

The mirage will fade; then will the desert be thirstier than
before.

O ye who dwell in the Dark Night of the Soul, beware
most of all of every herald of the Dawn!

O ye who dwell in the City of the Pyramids beneath the
Night of PAN, remember that ye shall see no more
light but That of the great fire that shall consume your
dust to ashes!

COMMENTARY (ΞZ)

This chapter means that it is useless to try to abandon the Great Work. You may occupy yourself for a time with other things, but you will only increase your bitterness, rivet the chains still on your feet.

Paragraph 4 is a practical counsel to mystics not to break up their dryness by relaxing their austerities.

The last paragraph will only be understood by Masters of the Temple.

68

ΚΕΦΑΛΗ ΞΗ

MANNA

At four o'clock there is hardly anybody in Rumpelmayer's.
I have my choice of place and service; the babble of the
    apes will begin soon enough.
"Pioneers, O Pioneers!"
Sat no Elijah under the Juniper-tree, and wept?
Was not Mohammed forsaken in Mecca, and Jesus in
    Gethsemane?
These prophets were sad at heart; but the chocolate at
    Rumpelmayer's is great, and the Mousse Noix is like
    Nepthys for perfection.
Also there are little meringues with cream and chest-
    nut-pulp, very velvety seductions.
Sail I not toward LAYLAH within seven days?
Be not sad at heart, O prophet; the babble of the apes will
    presently begin.
Nay, rejoice exceedingly; for after all the babble of the
    apes the Silence of the Night.

COMMENTARY (ΞH)

Manna was a heavenly cake which, in the legend, fed the Children of Israel in the Wilderness.

The author laments the failure of his mission to mankind, but comforts himself with the following reflections:

(1) He enjoys the advantages of solitude.
(2) Previous prophets encountered similar difficulties in convincing their hearers.
(3) Their food was not equal to that obtainable at Rumpelmayer's.
(4) In a few days I am going to rejoin Laylah.
(5) My mission will succeed soon enough.
(6) Death will remove the nuisance of success.

69

ΚΕΦΑΛΗ ΞΘ

THE WAY TO SUCCEED – AND THE WAY TO SUCK EGGS

This is the Holy Hexagram.
Plunge from the height, O God, and interlock with Man!
Plunge from the height, O Man, and interlock with Beast!
The Red Triangle is the descending tongue of grace; the
    Blue Triangle is the ascending tongue of prayer.
This Interchange, the Double Gift of Tongues, the Word of
    Double Power – ABRAHADABRA! – is the sign of
    the GREAT WORK, for the GREAT WORK is
    accomplished in Silence. And behold is not that Word
    equal to Cheth, that is Cancer, whose Sigil is ♋?
This Work also eats up itself, accomplishes its own end,
    nourishes the worker, leaves no seed, is perfect in itself.
Little children, love one another!

COMMENTARY (ΞΘ)

The key to the understanding of this chapter is given in the number and the title, the former being intelligible to all nations who employ Arabic figures, the latter only to experts in deciphering English puns.

The chapter alludes to Levi's drawing of the Hexagram, and is a criticism of, or improvement upon, it. In the ordinary Hexagram, the Hexagram of nature, the red triangle is upwards, like fire, and the blue triangle downwards, like water. In the magical hexagram this is reversed; the descending red triangle is that of Horus, a sign specially revealed by him personally, at the Equinox of the Gods. (It is the flame desending upon the altar, and licking up the burnt offering.) The blue triangle represents the aspiration, since blue is the colour of devotion, and the triangle, kinetically considered, is the symbol of directed force.

In the first three paragraphs this formation of the hexagram is explained; it is a symbol of the mutual separation of the Holy Guardian Angel and his client. In the interlocking is indicated the completion of the work.

Paragraph 4 explains in slightly different language what we have said above, and the scriptural image of tongues is introduced.

In paragraph 5 the symbolism of tongues is further developed. Abrahadabra is our primal example of an interlocked word. We assume that the reader has thoroughly studied that word in Liber D., *etc. The sigil of Cancer links up this symbolism with the number of the chapter.*

The remaining paragraphs continue the Gallic symbolism.

70

ΚΕΦΑΛΗ Ο

BROOMSTICK-BABBLINGS

FRATER PERDURABO is of the Sanhedrim of the
Sabbath, say men; He is the Old Goat himself, say
women.
Therefore do all adore him; the more they detest him the
more do they adore him.
Ay! let us offer the Obscene Kiss!
Let us seek the Mystery of the Gnarled Oak, and of the
Glacier Torrent!
To Him let us offer our babes! Around Him let us dance
in the mad moonlight!
But FRATER PERDURABO is nothing but AN EYE; what
eye none knoweth.
Skip, witches! Hop, toads! Take your pleasure! – for
the play of the Universe is the pleasure of FRATER
PERDURABO.

COMMENTARY (O)

70 is the number of the letter Ain, the Devil in the Tarot.

The chapter refers to the Witches' Sabbath, the description of which in Payne Knight should be carefully read before studying this chapter. All the allusions will then be obvious, save those which we proceed to note.

Sanhedrim, a body of 70 men. An Eye. Eye in Hebrew is Oin, 70.

The "gnarled oak" and the "glacier torrent" refer to the confessions made by many witches.

In paragraph 7 is seen the meaning of the chapter; the obscene and distorted character of much of the universe is a whim of the Creator.

71

ΚΕΦΑΛΗ ΟΑ

KING'S COLLEGE CHAPEL

For mind and body alike there is no purgative like
Pranayama, no purgative like Pranayama.
For mind, for body, for mind and body alike – alike! –
there is, there is, there is no purgative, no purgative
like Pranayama – Pranayama! – Prana – yama! yea, for
mind and body alike there is no purgative, no
purgative, no purgative (for mind and body alike!) no
purgative, purgative, purgative like Pranayama, no
purgative for mind and body alike, like Pranayama,
like Pranayama, like Prana – Prana – Prana – Prana –
pranayama!
Pranayama!
    AMEN.

COMMENTARY (OA)

This chapter is a plain statement of fact, put in anthem form for emphasis.
The title is due to the circumstances of the early piety of Frater Perdurabo,
who was frequently refreshed by hearing the anthems in this chief of the
architectural glories of his Alma Mater.

72

ΚΕΦΑΛΗ ΟΒ

HASHED PHEASANT

Shemhamphorash! all hail, divided Name!
Utter it once, O mortal over-rash! –
The Universe were swallowed up in flame –
   Shemhamphorash!

Nor deem that thou amid the cosmic crash
May find one thing of all those things the same!
The world has gone to everlasting smash.

No! if creation did possess an aim,
(It does not) it were only to make hash
Of that most "high" and that most holy game,
Shemhamphorash!

COMMENTARY (OB)

There are three consecutive verses in the Pentateuch, each containing 72 letters. If these be written beneath each other, the middle verse bring reversed, i.e. as in English, and divisions are then made vertically, 72 tri-lateral names are formed, the sum of which is Tetragrammaton; this is the great and mysterious Divided Name; by adding the terminations Yod He, or Aleph Lamed, the names of 72 Angels are formed. The Hebrews say that by uttering this Name the universe is destroyed. This statement means the same as that of the Hindus, that the effective utterance of the 'name of Shiva would cause him to awake, and so destroy the universe.

In Egyptian and Gnostic magick we meet with pylons and Aeons, which only open on the utterance of the proper word.

In Mohammedan magick we find a similar doctrine and practice; and the whole of Mantra-Yoga has been built on this foundation.

Thoth, the god of Magick, is the inventor of speech; Christ is the Logos. Lines 1–4 are now clear.

In lines 507 we see the results of Shivadarshana. Do not imagine that any single ides, however high, however holy (or even however insignificant!!), can escape the destruction.

The logician my say, "But white exists, and if white is destroyed, it leaves black; yet black exists. So that in that case at least one known phenomenon of this universe is identical with one of that." Vain word!

The logician and his logic are alike involved in the universal ruin.

Lines 8–11 indicate that this fact is the essential one about Shivadarshana.

The title is explained by the intentionally blasphemous puns and colloquialisms of lines 9 and 10.

73

ΚΕΦΑΛΗ ΟΓ

THE DEVIL, THE OSTRICH, AND THE ORPHAN CHILD

Death rides the Camel of Initiation.[36]
Thou humped and stiff-necked one that groanest in Thine
    Asana, death will relieve thee!
Bite not, Zelator dear, but bide! Ten days didst thou go
    with water in thy belly? Thou shalt go twenty more
    with a firebrand at thy rump!
Ay! all thine aspiration is to death: death is the crown of
    all thine aspiration. Triple is the cord of silver
    moonlight; it shall hang thee, O Holy One, O Hanged
    Man, O Camel-Termination-of-the-third-person-plural
    for thy multiplicity, thou Ghost of a Non-Ego!
Could but Thy mother behold thee, O thou UNT![37]
The Infinite Snake Ananta that surroundeth the Universe
    is but the Coffin-Worm!

COMMENTARY (ΟΓ)

The Hebrew letter Gimel adds up to 73; it means a camel.

The title of the chapter is borrowed from the well-known lines of Rudyard Kipling:

"But the commissariat camel, when all is said and done,
’E’s a devil and an awstridge and an orphan-child in one."

Paragraph 1 may imply a dogma of death as the highest form of initiation. Initiation is not a simple phenomenon. Any given initiation must take place on several planes, and is not always conferred on all of these simultaneously. Intellectual and moral perception of truth often, one might almost say usually, precedes spiritual and physical perceptions. One would be foolish to claim initiation unless it were complete on every plane.

Paragraph 2 will easily be understood by those who have practised Asana. There is perhaps a sardonic reference to rigor mortis, and certainly one conceives the half-humorous attitude of the expert towards the beginner.

Paragraph 3 is a comment in the same tone of rough good nature. The word Zelator is used because the Zelator of the A∴A∴ has to pass an examination in Asana before he becomes eligible for the grade of Practicus. The ten days allude merely to the tradition about the camel, that he can go ten days without water.

Paragraph 4 identifies the reward of initiation with death; it is a cessation of all that we call life, in a way in which what we call death is not. 3, silver, and the moon, are all correspondences of Gimel, the letter of the Aspiration, since gimel is the Path that leads from the Microcosm in tiphareth to the Macrocosm in Kether.

The epithets are far too complex to explain in detail, but Mem, the Hanged man, has a close affinity for Gimel, as will be seen by a study of Liber 418.

Unt is not only the Hindustani for Camel, but the usual termination of the third person plural of the present tense of Latin words of the Third and Fourth Conjugations.

The reason for thus addresing the reader is that he has now transcended the first and second persons. Cf. Liber LXV, *Chapter III, vv. 21-24, and* FitzGerald’s Omar Khayyam:

"Some talk there was of Thee and Me

There seemed; and then no more of Thee and Me.")

The third person plural must be used, because he has now perceived himself to be a bundle of impressions. For this is the point on the Path of Gimel when he is actually crossing the Abyss; the student must consult the account of this given in "The Temple of Solomon the King".

The Ego is but "the ghost of a non-Ego", the imaginary focus at which the non-Ego becomes sensible.

Paragraph 5 expresses the wish of the Guru that his Chela may attain safely to binah, the Mother.

Paragraph 6 whispers the ultimate and dread secret of initiation into his ear, identifying the vastness of the Most Holy with the obscene worm that gnaws the bowels of the damned.

NOTE

(36) Death is said by the Arabs to ride a Camel. The Path of Gimel (which means a Camel) leads from Tiphareth to Kether, and its Tarot trump is the "High Priestess".

(37) UNT, Hindustani for Camel. I.e. Would that BABALON might look on thee with favour.

74

ΚΕΦΑΛΗ ΟΔ

CAREY STREET

When NOTHING became conscious, it made a bad bargain.
This consciousness acquired individuality: a worse bargain.
The Hermit asked for love; worst bargain of all.
And now he has let his girl go to America, to have "success" in
    "life": blank loss.
Is there no end to this immortal ache
That haunts me, haunts me sleeping or awake?
   If I had Laylah, how could I forget
    Time, Age, and Death? Insufferable fret!
     Were I an hermit, how could I support
      The pain of consciousness, the curse of thought?
       Even were I THAT, there still were one sore spot –
        The Abyss that stretches between THAT and NOT.
Still, the first step is not so far away:-
The *Mauretania* sails on Saturday!

COMMENTARY (OΔ)

Carey Street is well known to prosperous Hebrews and poor Englishmen as the seat of the Bankruptcy buildings.

Paragraphs 1–4 are in prose, the downward course, and the rest of the chapter in poetry, the upward.

The first part shows the fall from Nought in four steps; the second part, the return.

The details of this Hierarchy have already been indicated in various chapters. It is quite conventional mysticism.

Step 1, the illumination of Ain as Ain Soph Aour; step 2, the concentration of Ain Soph Aour in Kether; step 3, duality and the rest of it down to Malkuth; step 4, the stooping of Malkuth to the Qliphoth, and the consequent ruin of the Tree of Life.

Part 2 show the impossibility of stopping on the Path of Adeptship.

The final couplet represents the first step upon the Path, which must be taken even although the aspirant is intellectually aware of the severity of the whole course. You must give up the world for love, the material for the moral idea, before that, in its turn, is surrendered to the spiritual. And so on. This is a Laylah-chapter, but in it Laylah figures as the mere woman.

75

ΚΕΦΑΛΗ ΟΕ

PLOVERS' EGGS[38]

Spring beans and strawberries are in: goodbye to the
 oyster!
If I really knew what I wanted, I could give up Laylah, or
 give up everything for Laylah.
But "what I want" varies from hour to hour.
This wavering is the root of all compromise, and so of all
 good sense.
With this gift a man can spend his seventy years in peace.
Now is this well or ill?
Emphasise *gift*, then *man*, then *spend*, then *seventy years*,
 and lastly *peace*, and change the intonations – each
 time reverse the meaning!
I would show you how; but – for the moment! – I prefer
 to think of Laylah.

COMMENTARY (OE)

The title is explained in the note, but also alludes to paragraph 1, the plover's egg being often contemporary with the early strawberry.

Paragraph 1 means that change of diet is pleasant; vanity pleases the mind; the idee fixe *is a sign of insanity. See paragraphs 4 and 5.*

Paragraph 6 puts the question, "Then is sanity or insanity desirable?" The oak is weakened by the ivy which clings around it, but perhaps the ivy keeps it from going mad.

The next paragraph expresses the difficulty of expressing thought in writing; it seems, on the face of it, absurd that the the text of this book, composed as it is of English, simple, austere, and terse, should need a commentary. But it does so, or my most gifted Chela and myself would hardly have been at the pains to write one. It was in response to the impassioned appeals of many most worthy brethren that we have yielded up that time and thought which gold could not have bought, or torture wrested.

Laylah is again the mere woman.

NOTE

(38) These eggs, being speckled, resemble the wandering mind referred to.

76

ΚΕΦΑΛΗ Oϝ

PHAETON

No.
Yes.
Perhaps.
O!
Eye.
I.
Hi!
Y?
No.
Hail! all ye spavined, gelded, hamstrung horses!
Ye shall surpass the planets in their courses.
How? Not by speed, nor strength, nor power to stay,
But by the Silence that succeeds the Neigh!

COMMENTARY (O_F)

Phaeton was the charioteer of the Sun in Greek mythology.

At first sight the prose of this chapter, though there is only one dissyllable in it, appears difficult; but this is a glamour cast by Maya. It is a compendium of various systems of philosophy.

No = Nihilism; Yes = Monism, and all dogmatic systems; Perhaps = Pyrrhonism and Agnosticism; O! = The system of Liber Legis. (See Chapter 0.)

Eye = Phallicism (cf. Chapters 61 and 70); I = Fichteanism; Hi! = Transcendentalism; Y? = Scepticism, and the method of science. No denies all these and closes the argument.

But all this is a glamour cast by Maya; the real meaning of the prose of this chapter is as follows:

No, some negative conception beyond the IT spoken of in Chapters 31, 49 and elsewhere.

Yes, IT.

Perhaps, the flux of these.

O!, Nuit, Hadit, Ra-Hoor-Khuit.

Eye, the phallus in Kether.

I, the Ego in Chokmah.

Hi!, Binah, the feminine principle fertilised. (He by Yod.)

Y?, the Abyss.

No, the refusal to be content with any of this.

But all this is again only a glamour of Maya, as previously observed in the text (Chapter 31). All this is true and false, and it is true and false to say that it is true and false.

The prose of this chapter combines, and of course denies, all these meanings, both singly and in combination. It is intended to stimulate thought to the point where it explodes with violence and for ever.

A study of this chapter is probably the best short cut to Nibbana.

The thought of the Master in this chapter is exceptionally lofty.

That this is the true meaning, or rather use, of this chapter, is evident from the poetry.

The master salutes the previous paragraphs as horses which, although in

themselves worthless animals (without the epithets), carry the Charioteer in the path of the Sun. The question, How? Not by their own virtues, but by the silence which results when they are all done with.

The word "neigh" is a pun on "nay", which refers to the negative conception already postulated as beyond IT. The suggestion is, that there may be something falsely described as silence, to represent absence-of-conception beyond that negative.

It would be possible to interpret this chapter in its entirety as an adverse criticism of metaphysics as such, and this is doubtless one of its many sub-meanings.

77

ΚΕΦΑΛΗ ΟΖ

THE SUBLIME AND SUPREME SEPTENARY IN ITS
MATURE MAGICAL MANIFESTATION THROUGH
MATTER: AS IT IS WRITTEN: AN HE-GOAT ALSO

Laylah.

L.A.Y.L.A.H.

COMMENTARY (OZ)

77 is the number of Laylah (LAILAH), to whom this chapter is wholly devoted.

The first section of the title is an analysis of 77 considered as a mystic number.

7, the septenary; 11, the magical number; 77, the manifestation, therefore, of the septenary.

Through matter, because 77 is written in Hebrew Ayin Zayin (OZ), and He-Goat, the symbol of matter, Capricornus, the Devil of the Tarot; which is the picture of the Goat of the Sabbath upon an altar, worshipped by two other devils, male and female.

As will be seen from the photogravure inserted opposite this chapter, Laylah is herself not devoid of "Devil", but, as she habitually remarks, on being addressed in terms implying this fact, "It's nice to be a devil when you're one like me."

The text need no comment, but it will be noticed that it is much shorter that the title.

Now, the Devil of the Tarot is the Phallus, the Redeemer, and Laylah symbolises redemption to Frater P. The number 77, also, interpreted as in the title, is the redeeming force.

The ratio of the length of title and text is the key to the true meaning of the chapter, which is, that Redemption is really as simple as it appears complex, that the names (or veils) of truth are obscure and many, the Truth itself plain and one; but that the latter must be reached through the former. This chapter is therefore an apology, were one needed, for the Book of Lies itself. In these few simple words, it explains the necessity of the book, and offers it – humbly, yet with confidence – as a means of redemption to the world of sorrowing men.

The name with full-stops: L.A.Y.L.A.H. represents an analysis of the name, which may be left to the ingenium of the advanced practicus (see photograph).

78

ΚΕΦΑΛΗ ΟΗ

WHEEL AND – WOA!

The Great Wheel of Samsara.
The Wheel of the Law [Dhamma].
The Wheel of the Taro.
The Wheel of the Heavens.
The Wheel of Life.
All these Wheels be one; yet of all these the Wheel of the
TARO alone avails thee consciously.
Meditate long and broad and deep, O man, upon this
Wheel, revolving it in thy mind
Be this thy task, to see how each card springs necessarily
from each other card, even in due order from The Fool
unto The Ten of Coins.
Then, when thou know'st the Wheel of Destiny complete,
mayst thou perceive THAT Will which moved it first.
[There is no first or last.]
And lo! thou art past through the Abyss.

COMMENTARY (OH)

The number of this chapter is that of the cards of the Tarot.

The title of this chapter is a pun of the phrase "weal and woe". It means motion and rest. The moral is the conventional mystic one; stop thought at its source!

Five wheels are mentioned in this chapter; all but the third refer to the universe as it is; but the wheel of the Tarot is not only this, but represents equally the Magickal Path.

This practice is therefore given by Frater P. to his pupils; to treat the sequence of the cards as cause and effect. Thence, to discover the cause behind all causes. Success in this practice qualifies for the grade of Master of the Temple.

In the penultimate paragraph the bracketed passage reminds the student that the universe is not to be contemplated as a phenomenon in time.

79

ΚΕΦΑΛΗ ΟΘ

THE BAL BULLIER

Some men look into their minds into their memories, and
    find naught but pain and shame.
These then proclaim "The Good Law" unto mankind.
These preach renunciation, "virtue", cowardice in every
    form.
These whine eternally.
Smug, toothless, hairless Coote, debauch-emasculated
    Buddha, come ye to me? I have a trick to make you
    silent, O ye foamers-at-the mouth!
Nature is wasteful; but how well She can afford it!
Nature is false; but I'm a bit of a liar myself.
Nature is useless; but then how beautiful she is!
Nature is cruel; but I too am a Sadist.
The game goes on; it may have been too rough for
    Buddha, but it's (if anything) too dull for me.
Viens, beau négre! Donne-moi tes levres encore!

COMMENTARY (OΘ)

The title of this chapter is a place frequented by Frater P. until it became respectable.

The chapter is a rebuke to those who can see nothing but sorrow and evil in the universe.

The Buddhist analysis may be true, but not for men of courage. The plea that "love is sorrow", because its ecstasies are only transitory, is contemptible. Paragraph 5. Coote is a blackmailer exposed by The Equinox. The end of the paragraph refers to Catullus, his famous epigram about the youth who turned his uncle into Harpocrates. It is a subtle way for Frater P. to insist upon his virility, since otherwise he could not employ the remedy.

The last paragraph is a quotation. In Paris, Negroes are much sought after by sportive ladies. This is therefore presumably intended to assert that even women may enjoy life sometimes.

The word "Sadist" is taken from the famous Marquis de Sade, who gave supreme literary form to the joys of torture.

80

ΚΕΦΑΛΗ Π

BLACKTHORN

The price of existence is eternal warfare.[39]
Speaking as an Irishman, I prefer to say: The price of
eternal warfare is existence.
And melancholy as existence is, the price is well worth
paying.
Is there a Government? Then I'm agin it! To Hell with the
bloody English!
"O FRATER PERDURABO, how unworthy are these
sentiments!"
"D'ye want a clip on the jaw?"[40]

COMMENTARY (Π)

Frater P. continues the subject of Chapter 79.

He pictures himself as a vigorous, reckless, almost rowdy Irishman. he is no thin-lipped prude, to seek salvation in unmanly self-abnegation; no Creeping Jesus, to slink through existence to the tune of the Dead March in Saul; no Cremerian Callus to warehouse his semen in his cerebellum.

"New Thoughtist" is only Old Eunuch writ small.

Paragraph 2 gives the very struggle for life, which disheartens modern thinkers, as a good enough reason for existence.

Paragraph 5 expresses the sorrow of the modern thinker, and paragraph 6 Frater P.'s suggestion for replying to such critics.

NOTE

(39) ISVD, the foundation scil. of the universe = 80 = P, the letter of Mars.

(40) P also means "a mouth".

81

ΚΕΦΑΛΗ ΠΑ

LOUIS LINGG

I am not an Anarchist in your sense of the word: your
    brain is too dense for any known explosive to affect it.
I am not an Anarchist in your sense of the word: fancy a
    Policeman let loose on Society!
While there exists the burgess, the hunting man, or any
    man with ideals less than Shelley's and self-discipline
    less than Loyola's – in short, any man who falls far
    short of MYSELF – I am against Anarchy, and for
    Feudalism.
Every "emancipator" has enslaved the free.

COMMENTARY (ΠΑ)

The title is the name of one of the authors of the affair of the Haymarket, in Chicago. See Frank Harris, The Bomb.

Paragraph 1 explains that Frater P. sees no use in the employment of such feeble implements as bombs. Nor does he agree even with the aim of the Anarchists, since, although Anarchists themselves need no restraint, not daring to drink cocoa, lest their animal passions should be aroused (as Olivia Haddon assures my favourite Chela), yet policemen, unless most severely repressed, would be dangerous wild beasts.

The last bitter sentence is terribly true; the personal liberty of the Russian is immensely greater than that of the Englishman. The latest Radical devices for securing freedom have turned nine out of ten Englishmen into Slaves, obliged to report their movements to the government like so many ticket-of-leave men.

The only solution of the Social Problem is the creation of a class with the true patriarchal feeling, and the manners and obligations of chivalry.

82

ΚΕΦΑΛΗ ΠΒ

BORTSCH

Witch-moon that turnest all the streams to blood,
  I take this hazel rod, and stand, and swear
  An Oath – beneath this blasted Oak and bare
That rears its agony above the flood
  Whose swollen mask mutters an atheist's prayer.
What oath may stand the shock of this offence:
"There is no I, no joy, no permanence"?

Witch-moon of blood, eternal ebb and flow
  Of baffled birth, in death still lurks a change;
  And all the leopards in thy woods that range,
And all the vampires in their boughs that glow,
  Brooding on blood-thirst-these are not so strange
And fierce as life's unfailing shower. These die,
  Yet time rebears them through eternity.

Hear then the Oath, with-moon of blood, dread moon!
  Let all thy stryges and thy ghouls attend!
  He that endureth even to the end
Hath sworn that Love's own corpse shall lie at noon
  Even in the coffin of its hopes, and spend
All the force won by its old woe and stress
In now annihilating Nothingness.

This chapter is called Imperial Purple
    and A Punic War.

COMMENTARY (ΠΒ)

The title of this chapter, and its two sub-titles, will need no explanation to readers of the classics.

This poem, inspired by Jane Cheron, is as simple as it is elegant.

The poet asks, in verse 1, How can we baffle the Three Characteristics?

In verse 2, he shows that death is impotent against life.

In verse 3, he offers the solution of the problem.

This is, to accept things as they are, and to turn your whole energies to progress on the Path.

83

ΚΕΦΑΛΗ ΠΓ

THE BLIND PIG[41]

Many becomes two: two one: one Naught. What comes to
  Naught?

What! shall the Adept give up his hermit life, and go
  eating and drinking and making merry?

Ay! shall he not do so? he knows that the Many is Naught;
  and having Naught, enjoys that Naught even in the
  enjoyment of the Many.

For when Naught becomes Absolute Naught, it becomes
  again the Many.

Any this Many and this Naught are identical; they are not
  correlatives or phases of some one deeper Absence-of-
  Idea; they are not aspects of some further Light: they
  are They!

Beware, O my brother, lest this chapter deceive thee!

COMMENTARY (ΠΓ)

The title of this chapter refers to the Greek number, PG being "Pig" without an "i".

The subject of the chapter is consequently corollary to Chapters 79 and 80, the ethics of Adept life.

The Adept has performed the Great Work; He has reduced the Many to Naught; as a consequence, he is no longer afraid of the Many.

Paragraph 4. See Berashith.

Paragraph 5, takes things for what they are; give up interpreting, refining away, analysing. Be simple and lucid and radiant as Frater P.

Paragraph 6. With this commentary there is no further danger, and the warning becomes superfluous.

NOTE
(41) Π = PG = Pig without an I = Blind Pig.

84

ΚΕΦΑΛΗ ΠΔ

THE AVALANCHE

Only through devotion to FRATER PERDURABO may
this book be understood.

How much more then should He devote Himself to
AIWASS for the understanding of the Holy Books of
ΘΕΛΗΜΑ?

Yet must he labour underground eternally. The sun is not
for him, nor the flowers, nor the voices of the birds;
for he is past beyond all these. Yea, verily, oft-times he
is weary; it is well that the weight of the Karma of the
Infinite is with him.

Therefore is he glad indeed; for he hath finished THE
WORK; and the reward concerneth him no whit.

COMMENTARY (ΠΔ)

This continues the subject of Chapter 83.

The title refers to the mental attitude of the Master; the avalanche does not fall because it is tired of staying on the mountain, or in order to crush the Alps below it, or because that it feels that it needs exercise. Perfectly unconscious, perfectly indifferent, it obeys the laws of Cohesion and of Gravitation.

It is the sun and its own weight that loosen it.

So, also, is the act of the Adept. "Delivered from the lust of result, he is every way perfect."

Paragraphs 1 and 2. By "devotion to Frater Perdurabo" is not meant sycophancy, but intelligent reference and imaginative sympathy. Put your mind in tune with his; identify yourself with him as he seeks to identify himself with the Intelligence that communicates to him the Holy Books.

Paragraphs 3 and 4 are explained by the 13th Aethyr and the title.

85

ΚΕΦΑΛΗ ΠΕ

BORBORYGMI

I distrust any thoughts uttered by any man whose health
is not robust.

All other thoughts are surely symptoms of disease.

Yet these are often beautiful, and may be true within the
circle of the conditions of the speaker.

Any yet again! Do we not find that the most robust of
men express no thoughts at all? They eat, drink, sleep,
and copulate in silence.

What better proof of the fact that all thought is disease?

We are Strassburg geese; the tastiness of our talk comes
from the disorder of our bodies.

We like it; this only proves that our tastes also are
depraved and debauched by our disease.

COMMENTARY (ΠΕ)

*We now return to that series of chapters which started with Chapter 8 (**H**).*
The chapter is perfectly simple and needs no comment.

86

ΚΕΦΑΛΗ ΠϜ

Ex nihilo N. I. H. I. L. fit.

N. the Fire that twisteth itself and burneth like a scorpion.

I. the unsullied ever-flowing water.

H. the interpenetrating Spirit, without and within. Is not its name ABRAHADABRA?

I. the unsullied ever-flowing air.

L. the green fertile earth.

Fierce are the Fires of the Universe, and on their daggers they hold aloft the bleeding heart of earth.

Upon the earth lies water, sensuous and sleepy.

Above the water hangs air; and above air, but also below fire – and in all – the fabric of all being woven on Its invisible design, is

ΑΙΘΗΡ.

COMMENTARY (ΠϜ)

The number 86 refers to Elohim, the name of the elemental forces.

The title is the Sanskrit for That, in its sense of "The Existing".

This chapter is an attempt to replace Elohim by a more satisfactory hieroglyph of the elements.

The best attribution of Elohim is Aleph, Air; Lamed, Earth; He, Spirit; Yod, Fire; Mem, Water. But the order is not good; Lamed is not satisfactory for Earth, and Yod too spiritualised a form of Fire. (But see Book 4, part III.)

Paragraphs 1–6. Out of Nothing, Nothing is made. The word Nihil is taken to affirm that the universe is Nothing, and that is now to be analysed. The order of the element is that of Jeheshua. The elements are taken rather as in Nature; N is easily Fire, since Mars is the ruler of Scorpio: the virginity of I suits Air and Water, elements which in Magick are closely interwoven: H, the letter of of breath, is suitable for Spirit; Abrahadabra is called the name of Spirit, because it is cheth: L is Earth, green and fertile, because Venus, the greenness, fertility, and earthiness of things is the Lady of Libra, Lamed.

In paragraph 7 we turn to the so-called Jetziratic attribution of Pentagrammaton, that followed by Dr. Dee, and by the Hindus, Tibetans, Chinese and Japanese. Fire is the Foundation, the central core, of things; above this forms a crust, tormented from below, and upon this condenses the original steam. Around this flows the air, created by Earth and Water through the action of vegetation.

Such is the globe; but all this is a mere strain in the aethyr, AIΘHP. Here is a new Pentagrammaton, presumably suitable for another analysis of the elements; but after a different manner. Alpha (A) is Air; Rho (P) the Sun; these are the Spirit and the Son of Christian theology. In the midst is the Father, expressed as Father-and-Mother. I–H (Yod and He), Eta (H) being used to express "the Mother" instead of Epsilon (E), to show that She has been impregnated by the Spirit; it is the rough breathing and not the soft. The centre of all is Theta (Θ), which was originally written as a point in a circle (☉), the sublime hieroglyph of the Sun in the Macrocosm, and in the Microcosm of the Lingam in conjunction with the Yoni. This word

AIΘHP (Aethyr) is therefore a perfect hieroglyph of the Cosmos in terms of Gnostic Theology.

The reader should consult La Messe et ses Mystères, par *Jean 'Marie de V .... (Paris et Nancy, 1844), for a complete demonstration of the incorporation of the Solar and Phallic Mysteries in Christianity.*

87

ΚΕΦΑΛΗ ΠΖ

MANDARIN-MEALS

There is a dish of sharks' fins and of sea-slug, well set in
    birds' nests... oh!
Also there is a souffle most exquisite of Chow-Chow.
These did I devise.
But I have never tasted anything to match the

which she gave me before She went away.

March 22, 1912. E. V.

COMMENTARY (ΠΖ)

This chapter is technically one of the Laylah chapters.

It means that, however great may be one's own achievements the gifts from on high are still better.

The Sigil is taken from a Gnostic talisman, and refers to the Sacrament.

88

ΚΕΦΑΛΗ ΠΗ

GOLD BRICKS

Teach us Your secret, Master! yap my Yahoos.

Then for the hardness of their hearts, and for the softness
of their heads, I taught them Magick.

But... alas!

Teach us Your real secret, Master! how to become
invisible, how to acquire love, and oh! beyond all, how
to make gold.

But how much gold will you give me for the Secret of
Infinite Riches?

Then said the foremost and most foolish; Master, it is
nothing; but here is an hundred thousand pounds.

This did I deign to accept, and whispered in his ear this
secret:

A SUCKER IS BORN EVERY MINUTE.

COMMENTARY (ΠΗ)

The term "gold bricks" is borrowed from American finance.

The chapter is a setting of an old story.

A man advertises that he could tell anyone how to make four hundred a year certain, and would do so on receipt of a shilling. To every sender he dispatched a postcard with these words: "Do as I do."

The word "sucker" is borrowed from American finance.

The moral of the chapter is, that it is no good trying to teach people who need to be taught.

89

ΚΕΦΑΛΗ ΠΘ

UNPROFESSIONAL CONDUCT

I am annoyed about the number 89.

I shall avenge myself by writing nothing in this chapter.

That, too, is wise; for since I am annoyed, I could not
  write even a reasonably decent lie.

COMMENTARY (ΠΘ)

Frater P. had been annoyed by a scurvy doctor, the number of whose house was 89.

He shows that his mind was completely poisoned in respect of that number by his allowing himself to be annoyed.

(But note that a good Qabalist cannot err. "In Him all is right." 89 is Body – that which annoys – and the Angel of the Lord of Despair and Cruelty.

Also "Silence" and "Shut Up".

The four meanings completely describe the chapter.)

90

ΚΕΦΑΛΗ Ρ

STARLIGHT

Behold! I have lived many years, and I have travelled in
every land that is under the dominion of the Sun, and
I have sailed the seas from pole to pole.

Now do I lift up my voice and testify that all is vanity on
earth, except the love of a good woman, and that good
woman LAYLAH. And I testify that in heaven all is
vanity (for I have journeyed oft, and sojourned oft, in
every heaven), except the love of OUR LADY
BABALON. And I testify that beyond heaven and earth
is the love of OUR LADY NUIT.

And seeing that I am old and well stricken in years, and
that my natural forces fail, therefore do I rise up in my
throne and call upon THE END.

For I am youth eternal and force infinite.

And at THE END is SHE that was LAYLAH, and
BABALON, and NUIT, being...

COMMENTARY (P)

This chapter is a sort of final Confession of Faith.
It is the unification of all symbols and all planes.
The End is expressible.

91

ΚΕΦΑΛΗ ΡΑ

THE HEIKLE

A. M. E. N.

COMMENTARY (PA)

The "Heikle" is to be distinguished from the "Huckle", which latter is defined in the late Sir W.S. Gilbert's Prince Cherry-Top.

A clear definition of the Heikle might have been obtained from Mr Oscar Eckenstein, 34 Greencroft Gardens, South Hampstead, London, N.W. (when this comment was written).

But its general nature is that of a certain minute whiteness, appearing at the extreme end of great blackness.

It is a good title for the last chapter of this book, and it also symbolises the eventual coming out into the light of his that has wandered long in the darkness.

91 is the numberation of Amen.

The chapter consists of an analysis of this word, but gives no indication as to the result of this analysis, as if to imply this: The final Mystery is always insoluble.

FINIS.

CORONAT OPUS.

THE
BOOK
OF THE
LAW

INTRODUCTION

I THE BOOK

1. This book was dictated in Cairo between noon and 1 p.m. on three successive days, April 8th, 9th and 10th in the year 1904.

The Author called himself Aiwass, and claimed to be "the minister of Hoor-Paar-Kraat"; that is, a messenger from the forces ruling this earth at present, as will be explained later on.

How could he prove that he was, in fact, a being of a kind superior to any of the human race, and so entitled to speak with authority? Evidently he must show KNOWLEDGE and POWER such as no man has ever been known to possess.

2. He showed his KNOWLEDGE chiefly by the use of cipher or cryptogram in certain passages to set forth recondite facts, including some events which had yet to take place, such that no human being could possibly be aware of them; thus, the proof of his claim exists in the manuscript itself. It is independent of any human witness.

The study of these passages necessarily demands supreme human scholarship to interpret – it needs years of intense application. A great deal has still to be worked out. But enough has been discovered to justify his claim; the most sceptical intelligence is compelled to admit its truth.

This matter is best studied under the Master Therion, whose years of arduous research have led him to enlightenment.

On the other hand, the language of most of the Book is admirably simple, clear and vigorous. No one can read it without being stricken in the very core of his being.

3. The more than human POWER of Aiwass is shewn by the influence of his Master, and of the Book, upon actual events; and history fully supports the claim made by him. These facts are appreciable by everyone; but are better understood with the help of the Master Therion.

4. The full detailed account of the events leading up to the dictation

of this Book, with facsimile reproduction of the Manuscript and an essay by the Master Therion, is published in *The Equinox of the Gods.*

II THE UNIVERSE

This Book explains the Universe.

The elements are Nuit, Space – that is, the total of possibilities of every kind – and Hadit, any point which has experience of these possibilities. (This idea is for literary convenience symbolised by the Egyptian Goddess Nuit, a woman bending over like the Arch of the Night Sky. Hadit is symbolised as a Winged Globe at the heart of Nuit.)

Every event is a uniting of some one monad with one of the experiences possible to it.

"Every man and every woman is a star", that is, an aggregate of such experiences, constantly changing with each fresh event, which affects him or her either consciously or subconsciously.

Each one of us has thus an universe of his own, but it is the same universe for each one as soon as it includes all possible experience. This implies the extension of consciousness to include all other consciousness.

In our present stage, the object that you see is never the same as the one that I see; we infer that it is the same because your experience tallies with mine on so many points that the actual differences of our observation are negligible. For instance, if a friend is walking between us, you see only his left side, I his right; but we agree that it is the same man, although we may differ not only as to what we may see of his body but as to what we know of his qualities. This conviction of identity grows stronger as we see him more often and get to know him better. Yet all the time, neither of us can know anything of him at all beyond the total impression made on our respective minds.

The above is an extremely crude attempt to explain a system which reconciles all existing schools of philosophy.

III THE LAW OF THELEMA*

This Book lays down a simple Code of Conduct.

"Do what thou wilt shall be the whole of the Law."

"Love is the law, love under will."

"There is no law beyond Do what thou wilt."

This means that each of us stars is to move on our true orbit, as marked out by the nature of our position, the law of our growth, the impulse of our past experiences. All events are equally lawful – and every one necessary, in the long run – for all of us, in theory; but in practice, only one act is lawful for each one of us at any given moment. Therefore Duty consists in determining to experience the right event from one moment of consciousness to another.

Each action or motion is an act of love, the uniting with one or another part of "Nuit"; each such act must be "under will", chosen so as to fulfil and not to thwart the true nature of the being concerned.

The technical methods of achieving this are to be studied in Magick, or acquired by personal instruction from the Master Therion and his appointed assistants.

Thelema is the Greek for Will, and has the same numerical value as *Agape*, the Greek for Love.

IV THE NEW AEON

The third chapter of the Book is difficult to understand, and may be very repugnant to many people born before the date of the book (April, 1904).

It tells us the characteristics of the Period on which we are now entered. Superficially, they appear appalling. We see some of them already with terrifying clarity. But fear not!

It explains that certain vast "stars" (or aggregates of experience) may be described as Gods. One of these is in charge of the destinies of this planet for periods of 2,000 years.* In the history of the world, as far as we know accurately, are three such Gods: Isis, the mother, when the Universe was conceived as simple nourishment drawn directly from her; this period is marked by matriarchal government.

Next, beginning 500 B.C., Osiris, the father, when the Universe was imagined as catastrophic, love, death, resurrection, as the method by which experience was built up; this corresponds to patriarchal systems.

Now, Horus, the child, in which we come to perceive events as a

continual growth partaking in its elements of both these methods, and not to be overcome by circumstance. This present period involves the recognition of the individual as the unit of society.

We realise ourselves as explained in the first paragraphs of this essay. Every event, including death, is only one more accretion to our experience, freely willed by ourselves from the beginning and therefore also predestined.

This "God", Horus, has a technical tide: Heru-Ra-Ha, a combination of twin gods, Ra-Hoor-Khuit and Hoor-Paar-Kraat. The meaning of this doctrine must be studied in Magick. (He is symbolised as a Hawk-Headed God enthroned.)

He rules the present period of 2,000 years, beginning in 1904. Everywhere his government is taking root. Observe for yourselves the decay of the sense of sin, the growth of innocence and irresponsibility, the strange modifications of the reproductive instinct with a tendency to become bisexual or epicene, the childlike confidence in progress combined with nightmare fear of catastrophe, against which we are yet half unwilling to take precautions.

Consider the outcrop of dictatorships, only possible when moral growth is in its earliest stages, and the prevalence of infantile cults like Communism, Fascism, Pacifism, Health Crazes, Occultism in nearly all its forms, religions sentimentalised to the point of practical extinction.

Consider the popularity of the cinema, the wireless, the football pools and guessing competitions – all devices for soothing fractious infants, no seed of purpose in them.

Consider sport, the babyish enthusiasms and rages which it excites, whole nations disturbed by disputes between boys.

Consider war, the atrocities which occur daily and leave us unmoved and hardly worried. We are children.

How this new Aeon of Horus will develop, how the Child will grow up, these are for us to determine, growing up ourselves in the way of the Law of Thelema under the enlightened guidance of the Master Therion.

* The moment of change from one period to another is technically called The Equinox of the Gods.

V THE NEXT STEP

Democracy dodders.

Ferocious Fascism, cackling Communism, equally frauds, cavort crazily all over the globe.

They are hemming us in.

They are abortive births of the Child, the New Aeon of Horus.

Liberty stirs once more in the womb of Time.

Evolution makes its changes by anti-Socialistic ways. The "abnormal" man, who foresees the trend of the times and adapts circumstance intelligently, is laughed at, persecuted, often destroyed by the herd; but he and his heirs, when the crisis comes, are survivors.

Above us today hangs a danger never yet paralleled in history. We suppress the individual in more and more ways. We think in terms of the herd. War no longer kills soldiers; it kills all indiscriminately. Every new measure of the most democratic and autocratic govenments is Communistic in essence. It is always restriction. We are all treated as imbecile children. DORA, the Shops Act, the Motoring Laws, Sunday suffocation, the Censorship – they won't trust us to cross the roads at will.

Fascism is like Communism, and dishonest into the bargain. The dictators suppress all art, literature, theatre, music, news, that does not meet their requirements; yet the world only moves by the light of genius. The herd will be destroyed in mass.

The establishment of the Law of Thelema is the only way to preserve individual liberty and to assure the future of the race.

In the words of the famous paradox of the Comte de Fénix: "The absolute rule of the state shall be a function of the absolute liberty of each individual will."

All men and women are invited to cooperate with the Master Therion in this, the Great Work.

O. M.

AL

(LIBER LEGIS) THE BOOK OF THE LAW

SUB FIGURA XXXI

AS DELIVERED BY

93 – AIWASS – 418

TO

ANKHOFON-KHONSU

THE PRIEST OF THE PRINCES

WHO IS

666

THE COMMENT

Do what thou wilt shall be the whole of the Law

The study of this Book is forbidden. It is wise to destroy it after the first reading.

Whosoever disregards this does so at their own peril and risk. These are most dire.

Those who discuss the contents of this Book are to be shunned by all, as centres of pestilence.

All questions of the Law are to be decided only by appeal to my writings, each for himself.

There is no law beyond Do what thou wilt.

Love is the law, love under will.

The priest of the princes

Ankh-F-N-Khonsu

CHAPTER I

1. Had! The manifestation of Nuit.

2. The unveiling of the company of heaven.

3. Every man and every woman is a star.

4. Every number is infinite; there is no difference.

5. Help me, O warrior lord of Thebes, in my unveiling before the Children of men!

6. Be thou Hadit, my secret centre, my heart & my tongue!

7. Behold! it is revealed by Aiwass the minister of Hoor-paar-kraat.

8. The Khabs is in the Khu, not the Khu in the Khabs.

9. Worship then the Khabs, and behold my light shed over you!

10. Let my servants be few & secret: they shall rule the many & the known.

11. These are fools that men adore; both their Gods & their men are fools.

12. Come forth, O children, under the stars, & take your fill of love!

13. 1 am above you and in you. My ecstasy is in yours. My joy is to see your joy.

14. Above, the gemmed azure is
The naked splendour of Nuit;
She bends in ecstasy to kiss

The secret ardours of Hadit.

The winged globe, the starry blue,

Are mine, O Ankh-af-na-khonsu!

15. Now ye shall know that the chosen priest & apostle of infinite space is the prince-priest the Beast; and in his woman, called the Scarlet Woman, is all power given. They shall gather my children into their fold: they shall bring the glory of the stars into the hearts of men.

16. For he is ever a sun, and she a moon. But to him is the winged secret flame, and to her the stooping starlight.

17. But ye are not so chosen.

18. Burn upon their brows, O splendrous serpent!

19. O azure-lidded woman, bend upon them!

20. The key of the rituals is in the secret word which I have given unto him.

21. With the God & the Adorer I am nothing: they do not see me. They are as upon the earth; I am Heaven, and there is no other God than me, and my lord Hadit.

22. Now, therefore, I am known to ye by my name Nuit, and to him by a secret name which I will give him when at last he knoweth me. Since I am Infinite Space, and the Infinite Stars thereof, do ye also thus. Bind nothing! Let there be no difference made among you between any one thing & any other thing; for thereby there cometh hurt.

23. But whoso availeth in this, let him be the chief of all!

24. 1 am Nuit, and my word is six and fifty.

25. Divide, add, multiply, and understand.

26. Then saith the prophet and slave of the beauteous one: Who am I, and what shall be the sign? So she answered him, bending down, a lambent flame of blue, all-touching, all penetrant, her lovely hands upon the black earth, & her lithe body arched for love, and her soft feet not hurting the little flowers: Thou knowest! And the sign shall be my ecstasy, the consciousness of the continuity of existence, the omnipresence of my body.

27. Then the priest answered & said unto the Queen of Space, kissing her lovely brows, and the dew of her light bathing his whole body in a sweet-smelling perfume of sweat: O Nuit, continuous one of Heaven, let

it be ever thus; that men speak not of Thee as One but as None; and let them speak not of thee at all, since thou art continuous!

28. None, breathed the light, faint & faery, of the stars, and two.

29. For I am divided for love's sake, for the chance of union.

30. This is the creation of the world, that the pain of division is as nothing, and the joy of dissolution all.

31. For these fools of men and their woes care not thou at all! They feel little; what is, is balanced by weak joys; but ye are my chosen ones.

32. Obey my prophet! follow out the ordeals of my knowledge! seek me only! Then the joys of my love will redeem ye from all pain. This is so: I swear it by the vault of my body; by my sacred heart and tongue; by all I can give, by all I desire of ye all.

33. Then the priest fell into a deep trance or swoon, & said unto the Queen of Heaven; Write unto us the ordeals; write unto us the rituals; write unto us the law!

34. But she said: the ordeals I write not: the rituals shall be half known and half concealed: the Law is for all.

35. This that thou writest is the threefold book of Law.

36. My scribe Ankh-af-na-khonsu, the priest of the princes, shall not in one letter change this book; but lest there be folly, he shall comment thereupon by the wisdom of Ra-Hoor-Khuit.

37. Also the mantras and spells; the obeah and the wanga; the work of the wand and the work of the sword; these he shall learn and teach.

38. He must teach; but he may make severe the ordeals.

39. The word of the Law is THELEMA.

40. Who calls us Thelemites will do no wrong, if he look but close into the word. For there are therein Three Grades, the Hermit, and the Lover, and the man of Earth. Do what thou wilt shall be the whole of the Law.

41. The word of Sin is Restriction. O man! refuse not thy wife, if she will! O lover, if thou wilt, depart! There is no bond that can unite the divided but love: all else is a curse. Accursed! Accursed be it to the aeons! Hell.

42. Let it be that state of manyhood bound and loathing. So with thy all; thou hast no right but to do thy will.

43. Do that, and no other shall say nay.

44. For pure will, unassuaged of purpose, delivered from the lust of result, is every way perfect.

45. The Perfect and the Perfect are one Perfect and not two; nay, are none!

46. Nothing is a secret key of this law. Sixty-one the Jews call it; I call it eight, eighty, four hundred & eighteen.

47. But they have the half: unite by thine art so that all disappear.

48. My prophet is a fool with his one, one, one; are not they the Ox, and none by the Book?

49. Abrogate are all rituals, all ordeals, all words and signs. Ra-Hoor-Khuit hath taken his seat in the East at the Equinox of the Gods; and let Asar be with Isa, who also are one. But they are not of me. Let Asar be the adorant, Isa the sufferer; Hoor in his secret name and splendour is the Lord initiating.

50. There is a word to say about the Hierophantic task. Behold! there are three ordeals in one, and it may be given in three ways. The gross must pass through fire; let the fine be tried in intellect, and the lofty chosen ones in the highest. Thus ye have star & star, system & system; let not one know well the other!

51. There are four gates to one palace; the floor of that palace is of silver and gold; lapis lazuli & jasper are there; and all rare scents; jasmine & rose, and the emblems of death. Let him enter in turn or at once the four gates; let him stand on the floor of the palace. Will he not sink? Amn. Ho! warrior, if thy servant sink? But there are means and means. Be goodly therefore: dress ye all in fine apparel; eat rich foods and drink sweet wines and wines that foam! Also, take your fill and will of love as ye will, when, where and with whom ye will! But always unto me.

52. If this be not aright; if ye confound the space-marks, saying: They are one; or saying, They are many; if the ritual be not ever unto me: then expect the direful judgments of Ra-Hoor-Khuit!

53. This shall regenerate the world, the little world my sister, my heart & my tongue, unto whom I send this kiss. Also, O scribe and prophet, though thou be of the princes, it shall not assuage thee nor absolve thee. But ecstasy be thine and joy of earth: ever To me! To me!

54. Change not as much as the style of a letter; for behold! thou, O prophet, shalt not behold all these mysteries hidden therein.

55. The child of thy bowels, he shall behold them.

56. Expect him not from the East, nor from the West; for from no expected house cometh that child. *Aum*! All words are sacred and all prophets true; save only that they understand a little; solve the first half of the equation, leave the second unattacked. But thou hast all in the clear light, and some, though not all, in the dark.

57. Invoke me under my stars! Love is the law, love under will. Nor let the fools mistake love; for there are love and love. There is the dove, and there is the serpent. Choose ye well! He, my prophet, hath chosen, knowing the law of the fortress, and the great mystery of the House of God.

All these old letters of my Book are aright; but [Tzaddi] is not the Star. This also is secret: my prophet shall reveal it to the wise.

58. I give unimaginable joys on earth: certainty, not faith, while in life, upon death; peace unutterable, rest, ecstasy; nor do I demand aught in sacrifice.

59. My incense is of resinous woods & gums; and there is no blood therein: because of my hair the trees of Eternity.

60. My number is 11, as all their numbers who are of us. The Five Pointed Star, with a Circle in the Middle, & the circle is Red. My colour is black to the blind, but the blue & gold are seen of the seeing. Also I have a secret glory for them that love me.

61. But to love me is better than all things: if under the night stars in the desert thou presently burnest mine incense before me, invoking me with a pure heart, and the Serpent flame therein, thou shalt come a little to lie in my bosom. For one kiss wilt thou then be willing to give all; but whoso gives one particle of dust shall lose all in that hour. Ye shall gather goods and store of women and spices; ye shall wear rich jewels; ye shall exceed the nations of the earth in splendour & pride; but always in the love of me, and so shall ye come to my joy. I charge you earnestly to come before me in a single robe, and covered with a rich headdress. I love you! I yearn to you! Pale or purple, veiled or voluptuous, I who am all pleasure and purple, and drunkenness of the innermost sense, desire

you. Put on the wings, and arouse the coiled splendour within you: come unto me!

62. At all my meetings with you shall the priestess say – and her eyes shall burn with desire as she stands bare and rejoicing in my secret temple – To me! To me! calling forth the flame of the hearts of all in her love-chant.

63. Sing the rapturous love-song unto me! Burn to me perfumes! Wear to me jewels! Drink to me, for I love you! I love you!

64. 1 am the blue-lidded daughter of Sunset; I am the naked brilliance of the voluptuous night-sky.

65. To me! To me!

66. The Manifestation of Nuit is at an end.

CHAPTER II

1. Nu! the hiding of Hadit.

2. Come! all ye, and learn the secret that hath not yet been revealed. I, Hadit, am the complement of Nu, my bride. I am not extended, and Khabs is the name of my House.

3. In the sphere I am everywhere the centre, as she, the circumference, is nowhere found.

4. Yet she shall be known & I never.

5. Behold! the rituals of the old time are black. Let the evil ones be cast away; let the good ones be purged by the prophet! Then shall this Knowledge go aright.

6. I am the flame that burns in every heart of man, and in the core of every star. I am Life, and the giver of Life, yet therefore is the knowledge of me the knowledge of death.

7. I am the Magician and the Exorcist. I am the axle of the wheel, and the cube in the circle. "Come unto me" is a foolish word: for it is I that go.

8. Who worshipped Heru-pa-kraath have worshipped me; ill, for I am the worshipper.

9. Remember all ye that existence is pure joy; that all the sorrows are but as shadows; they pass & are done; but there is that which remains.

10. O prophet! thou hast ill will to learn this writing.

11. I see thee hate the hand & the pen; but I am stronger.

12. Because of me in Thee which thou knewest not.

13. For why? Because thou wast the knower, and me.

14. Now let there be a veiling of this shrine: now let the light devour men and eat them up with blindness!

15. For I am perfect, being Not; and my number is nine by the fools; but with the just I am eight, and one in eight: Which is vital, for I am none indeed. The Empress and the King are not of me; for there is a further secret.

16. I am The Empress & the Hierophant. Thus eleven, as my bride is eleven.

17. Hear me, ye people of sighing!
The sorrows of pain and regret
Are left to the dead and the dying,
The folk that not know me as yet.

18. These are dead, these fellows; they feel not. We are not for the poor and sad: the lords of the earth are our kinsfolk.

19. Is a God to live in a dog? No! but the highest are of us. They shall rejoice, our chosen: who sorroweth is not of us.

20. Beauty and strength, leaping laughter and delicious languor, force and fire, are of us.

21. We have nothing with the outcast and the unfit: let them die in their misery. For they feel not. Compassion is the vice of kings: stamp down the wretched & the weak: this is the law of the strong: this is our law and the joy of the world. Think not, O king, upon that lie: That Thou Must Die: verily thou shalt not die, but live. Now let it be understood: If the body of the King dissolve, he shall remain in pure ecstasy for ever. Nuit! Hadit! Ra-Hoor-Khuit! The Sun, Strength & Sight, Light; these are for the servants of the Star & the Snake.

22. I am the Snake that giveth Knowledge & Delight and bright glory, and stir the hearts of men with drunkenness. To worship me take wine and strange drugs whereof I will tell my prophet, & be drunk thereof! They shall not harm ye at all. It is a lie, this folly against self. The exposure of innocence is a lie. Be strong, O man! lust, enjoy all things of sense and rapture: fear not that any God shall deny thee for this.

23. I am alone: there is no God where I am.

24. Behold! these be grave mysteries; for there are also of my friends who be hermits. Now think not to find them in the forest or on the mountain; but in beds of purple, caressed by magnificent beasts of women with large limbs, and fire and light in their eyes, and masses of flaming hair about them; there shall ye find them. Ye shall see them at rule, at victorious armies, at all the joy; and there shall be in them a joy a million times greater than this. Beware lest any force another, King against King! Love one another with burning hearts; on the low men trample in the fierce lust of your pride, in the day of your wrath.

25. Ye are against the people, O my chosen!

26. I am the secret Serpent coiled about to spring: in my coiling there is joy. If I lift up my head, I and my Nuit are one. If I droop down mine head, and shoot forth venom, then is rapture of the earth, and I and the earth are one.

27. There is great danger in me; for who doth not understand these runes shall make a great miss. He shall fall down into the pit called Because, and there he shall perish with the dogs of Reason.

28. Now a curse upon Because and his kin!

29. May Because be accursed for ever!

30. If Will stops and cries Why, invoking Because, then Will stops & does nought.

31. If Power asks why, then is Power weakness.

32. Also reason is a lie; for there is a factor infinite & unknown; & all their words are skew-wise.

33. Enough of Because! Be he damned for a dog!

34. But ye, O my people, rise up & awake!

35. Let the rituals be righdy performed with joy & beauty!

36. There are rituals of the elements and feasts of the times.

37. A feast for the first night of the Prophet and his Bride!

38. A feast for the three days of the writing of the Book of the Law.

39. A feast for Tahuti and the child of the Prophet – secret, O Prophet!

40. A feast for the Supreme Ritual, and a feast for the Equinox of the Gods.

41. A feast for fire and a feast for water; a feast for life and a greater feast for death!

42. A feast every day in your hearts in the joy of my rapture!

43. A feast every night unto Nu, and the pleasure of uttermost delight!

44. Aye! feast! rejoice! there is no dread hereafter. There is the dissolution, and eternal ecstasy in the kisses of Nu.

45. There is death for the dogs.

46. Dost thou fail? Art thou sorry? Is fear in thine heart?

47. Where I am these are not.

48. Pity not the fallen! I never knew them. I am not for them. I console not: I hate the consoled & the consoler.

49. I am unique & conqueror. I am not of the slaves that perish. Be they damned & dead! Amen. (This is of the four: there is a fifth who is invisible, & therein am I as a babe in an egg.)

50. Blue am I and gold in the light of my bride: but the red gleam is in my eyes; & my spangles are purple & green.

51. Purple beyond purple: it is the light higher than eyesight.

52. There is a veil: that veil is black. It is the veil of the modest woman; it is the veil of sorrow, & the pall of death: this is none of me. Tear down that lying spectre of the centuries: veil not your vices in virtuous words: these vices are my service; ye do well, & I will reward you here and hereafter.

53. Fear not, O prophet, when these words are said, thou shalt not be sorry. Thou art emphatically my chosen; and blessed are the eyes that thou shalt look upon with gladness. But I will hide thee in a mask of sorrow: they that see thee shall fear thou art fallen: but I lift thee up.

54. Nor shall they who cry aloud their folly that thou meanest nought avail; thou shall reveal it: thou availest: they are the slaves of because: They are not of me. The stops as thou wilt; the letters? Change them not in style or value!

55. Thou shalt obtain the order & value of the English Alphabet; thou shalt find new symbols to attribute them unto.

56. Begone! ye mockers; even though ye laugh in my honour ye shall laugh not long: then when ye are sad know that I have forsaken you.

57. He that is righteous shall be righteous still; he that is filthy shall be filthy still.

58. Yea! deem not of change: ye shall be as ye are, & not other. Therefore the kings of the earth shall be Kings for ever: the slaves shall serve. There is none that shall be cast down or lifted up: all is ever as it was. Yet there are masked ones my servants: it may be that yonder beggar is a King. A King may choose his garment as he will: there is no certain test: but a beggar cannot hide his poverty.

59. Beware therefore! Love all, lest perchance is a King concealed! Say you so? Fool! If he be a King, thou canst not hurt him.

60. Therefore strike hard & low, and to hell with them, master!

61. There is a light before thine eyes, O prophet, a light undesired, most desirable.

62. I am uplifted in thine heart; and the kisses of the stars rain hard upon thy body.

63. Thou art exhaust in the voluptuous fullness of the inspiration; the expiration is sweeter than death, more rapid and laughterful than a caress of Hell's own worm.

64. Oh! thou art overcome: we are upon thee; our delight is all over thee: hail! hail: prophet of Nu! prophet of Had! prophet of Ra-Hoor-Khu! Now rejoice! now come in our splendour & rapture! Come in our passionate peace, & write sweet words for the Kings.

65. I am the Master: thou art the Holy Chosen One.

66. Write, & find ecstasy in writing! Work, & be our bed in working! Thrill with the joy of life & death! Ah! thy death shall be lovely: whoso seeth it shall be glad. Thy death shall be the seal of the promise of our age long love. Come! lift up thine heart & rejoice! We are one; we are none.

67. Hold! Hold! Bear up in thy rapture; fall not in swoon of the excellent kisses!

68. Harder! Hold up thyself! Lift thine head! breathe not so deep – die!

69. Ah! Ah! What do I feel? Is the word exhausted?

70. There is help & hope in other spells. Wisdom says: be strong! Then canst thou bear more joy. Be not animal; refine thy rapture! If thou drink, drink by the eight and ninety rules of art: if thou love, exceed by delicacy; and if thou do aught joyous, let there be subtlety therein!

71. But exceed! exceed!

72. Strive ever to more! and if thou art truly mine – and doubt it not, an if thou art ever joyous! – death is the crown of all.

73. Ah! Ah! Death! Death! thou shalt long for death. Death is forbidden, O man, unto thee.

74. The length of thy longing shall be the strength of its glory. He that lives long & desires death much is ever the King among the Kings.

75. Aye! listen to the numbers & the words:

76. 4 6 3 8 A B K 2 4 A L G M O R 3 Y X 24 89 R P S T O V A L. What meaneth this, O prophet? Thou knowest not; nor shalt thou know ever. There cometh one to follow thee: he shall expound it. But remember, O chose none, to be me; to follow the love of Nu in the star-lit heaven; to look forth upon men, to tell them this glad word.

77. O be thou proud and mighty among men!

78. Lift up thyself! for there is none like unto thee among men or among Gods! Lift up thyself, O my prophet, thy stature shall surpass the stars. They shall worship thy name, foursquare, mystic, wonderful, the number of the man; and the name of thy house 418.

79. The end of the hiding of Hadit; and blessing & worship to the prophet of the lovely Star!

CHAPTER III

1. Abrahadabra; the reward of Ra-Hoor-Khut.

2. There is division hither homeward; there is a word not known. Spelling is defunct; all is not aught. Beware! Hold! Raise the spell of Ra-Hoor-Khuit!

3. Now let it be first understood that I am a god of War and of Vengeance. I shall deal hardly with them.

4. Choose ye an island!

5. Fortify it!

6. Dung it about with enginery of war!

7. I will give you a war-engine.

8. With it ye shall smite the peoples; and none shall stand before you.

9. Lurk! Withdraw! Upon them! this is the Law of the Battle of Conquest: thus shall my worship be about my secret house.

10. Get the stele of revealing itself; set it in thy secret temple – and that temple is already aright disposed – & it shall be your Kiblah for ever. It shall not fade, but miraculous colour shall come back to it day after day. Close it in locked glass for a proof to the world.

11. This shall be your only proof. I forbid argument. Conquer! That is enough. I will make easy to you the abstruction from the ill-ordered house in the Victorious City. Thou shalt thyself convey it with worship,

O prophet, though thou likest it not. Thou shalt have danger & trouble. Ra-Hoor-Khu is with thee. Worship me with fire & blood; worship me with swords & with spears. Let the woman be girt with a sword before me: let blood flow to my name. Trample down the Heathen; be upon them, O warrior, I will give you of their flesh to eat!

12. Sacrifice cattle, little and big: after a child.

13. But not now.

14. Ye shall see that hour, O blessed Beast, and thou the Scarlet Concubine of his desire!

15. Ye shall be sad thereof.

16. Deem not too eagerly to catch the promises; fear not to undergo the curses. Ye, even ye, know not this meaning all.

17. Fear not at all; fear neither men nor Fates, nor gods, nor anything. Money fear not, nor laughter of the folk folly, nor any other power in heaven or upon the earth or under the earth. Nu is your refuge as Hadit your light; and I am the strength, force, vigour, of your arms.

18. Mercy let be off; damn them who pity! Kill and torture; spare not; be upon them!

19. That stele they shall call the Abomination of Desolation; count well its name, & it shall be to you as 718.

20. Why? Because of the fall of Because, that he is not there again.

21. Set up my image in the East: thou shalt buy thee an image which I will show thee, especial, not unlike the one thou knowest. And it shall be suddenly easy for thee to do this.

22. The other images group around me to support me: let all be worshipped, for they shall cluster to exalt me. I am the visible object of worship; the others are secret; for the Beast & his Bride are they: and for the winners of the Ordeal x. What is this? Thou shalt know.

23. For perfume mix meal & honey & thick leavings of red wine: then oil of Abramelin and olive oil, and afterward soften & smooth down with rich fresh blood.

24. The best blood is of the moon, monthly: then the fresh blood of a child, or dropping from the host of heaven: then of enemies; then of the priest or of the worshippers: last of some beast, no matter what.

25. This burn: of this make cakes & eat unto me. This hath also

another use; let it be laid before me, and kept thick with perfumes of your orison: it shall become full of beetles as it were and creeping things sacred unto me.

26. These slay, naming your enemies; & they shall fall before you.

27. Also these shall breed lust & power of lust in you at the eating thereof.

28. Also ye shall be strong in war.

29. Moreover, be they long kept, it is better; for they swell with my force. All before me.

30. My altar is of open brass work: burn thereon in silver or gold!

31. There cometh a rich man from the West who shall pour his gold upon thee.

32. From gold forge steel!

33. Be ready to fly or to smite!

34. But your holy place shall be untouched throughout the centuries: though with fire and sword it be burnt down & shattered, yet an invisible house there standeth, and shall stand until the fall of the Great Equinox; when Hrumachis shall arise and the double-wanded one assume my throne and place. Another prophet shall arise, and bring fresh fever from the skies; another woman shall awake the lust & worship of the Snake; another soul of God and beast shall mingle in the globed priest; another sacrifice shall stain the tomb; another king shall reign; and blessing no longer be poured To the Hawk-headed mystical Lord!

35. The half of the word of Heru-ra-ha, called Hoor-pa-kraat and Ra-Hoor-Khut.

36. Then said the prophet unto the God:

37. I adore thee in the song –
I am the Lord of Thebes, and I
The inspired forth-speaker of Mentu;
For me unveils the veiled sky,
The self-slain Ankh-af-na-khonsu
Whose words are truth. I invoke, I greet
Thy presence, O Ra-Hoor-Khuit!

Unity uttermost showed!
I adore the might of Thy breath,
Supreme and terrible God,
Who makest the gods and death
To tremble before Thee: –
I, I adore thee!

Appear on the throne of Ra!
Open the ways of the Khu!
Lighten the ways of the Ka!
The ways of the Khabs run through
To stir me or still me!
Aum! let it fill me!

38. So that thy light is in me; & its red flame is as a sword in my hand to push thy order. There is a secret door that I shall make to establish thy way in all the quarters, (these are the adorations, as thou hast written), as it is said:

The light is mine; its rays consume
Me: I have made a secret door
Into the House of Ra and Turn,
Of Khephra and of Ahathoor.
I am thy Theban, O Mentu,
The prophet Ankh-af-na-khonsu!

By Bes-na-Maut my breast I beat;
By wise Ta-Nech I weave my spell.
Show thy star-splendour, O Nuit!
Bid me within thine House to dwell,
O winged snake of light, Hadit!
Abide with me, Ra-Hoor-Khuit!

39. All this and a book to say how thou didst come hither and a reproduction of this ink and paper for ever – for in it is the word secret

& not only in the English – and thy comment upon this the *Book of the Law* shall be printed beautifully in red ink and black upon beautiful paper made by hand; and to each man and woman that thou meetest, were it but to dine or to drink at them, it is the Law to give. Then they shall chance to abide in this bliss or no; it is no odds. Do this quickly!

40. But the work of the comment? That is easy; and Hadit burning in thy heart shall make swift and secure thy pen.

41. Establish at thy Kaaba a clerk-house: all must be done well and with business way.

42. The ordeals thou shalt oversee thyself, save only the blind ones. Refuse none, but thou shalt know & destroy the traitors. I am Ra-Hoor-Khuit; and I am powerful to protect my servant. Success is thy proof: argue not; convert not; talk not over much! Them that seek to entrap thee, to overthrow thee, them attack without pity or quarter; & destroy them utterly. Swift as a trodden serpent turn and strike! Be thou yet deadlier than he! Drag down their souls to awful torment: laugh at their fear: spit upon them!

43. Let the Scarlet Woman beware! If pity and compassion and tenderness visit her heart; if she leave my work to toy with old sweetnesses; then shall my vengeance be known. I will slay me her child: I will alienate her heart: I will cast her out from men: as a shrinking and despised harlot shall she crawl through dusk wet streets, and die cold and an-hungered.

44. But let her raise herself in pride! Let her follow me in my way! Let her work the work of wickedness! Let her kill her heart! Let her be loud and adulterous! Let her be covered with jewels, and rich garments, and let her be shameless before all men!

45. Then will I lift her to pinnacles of power: then will I breed from her a child mightier than all the kings of the earth. I will fill her with joy: with my force shall she see & strike at the worship of Nu: she shall achieve Hadit.

46. I am the warrior Lord of the Forties: the Eighties cower before me, & are abased. I will bring you to victory & joy: I will be at your arms in battle & ye shall delight to slay. Success is your proof; courage is your armour; go on, go on, in my strength; & ye shall turn not back for any!

47. This book shall be translated into all tongues: but always with the

original in the writing of the Beast; for in the chance shape of the letters and their position to one another: in these are mysteries that no Beast shall divine. Let him not seek to try: but one cometh after him, whence I say not, who shall discover the Key of it all. Then this line drawn is a key: then this circle squared in its failure is a key also. And Abrahadabra. It shall be his child & that strangely. Let him not seek after this; for thereby alone can he fall from it.

48. Now this mystery of the letters is done, and I want to go on to the holier place.

49. I am in a secret fourfold word, the blasphemy against all gods of men.

50. Curse them! Curse them! Curse them!

51. With my Hawk's head I peck at the eyes of Jesus as he hangs upon the cross.

52. I flap my wings in the face of Mohammed & blind him.

53. With my claws I tear out the flesh of the Indian and the Buddhist, Mongol and Din.

54. Bahlasti! Ompehda! I spit on your crapulous creeds.

55. Let Maty inviolate be torn upon wheels: for her sake let all chaste women be utterly despised among you!

56. Also for beauty's sake and love's!

57. Despise also all cowards; professional soldiers who dare not fight, but play; all fools despise!

58. But the keen and the proud, the royal and the lofty; ye are brothers!

59. As brothers fight ye!

60. There is no law beyond Do what thou wilt.

61. There is an end of the word of the God enthroned in Ra's seat, lightening the girders of the soul.

62. To Me do ye reverence! to me come ye through tribulation of ordeal, which is bliss.

63. The fool readeth this Book of the Law, and its comment; & he understandeth it not.

64. Let him come through the first ordeal, & it will be to him as silver.

65. Through the second, gold.

66. Through the third, stones of precious water.

67. Through the fourth, ultimate sparks of the intimate fire.

68. Yet to all it shall seem beautiful. Its enemies who say not so, are mere liars.

69. There is success.

70. I am the Hawk-Headed Lord of Silence & of Strength; my nemyss shrouds the night-blue sky.

71. Hail! ye twin warriors about the pillars of the world! for your time is nigh at hand.

72. I am the Lord of the Double Wand of Power; the wand of the Force of Coph Nia – but my left hand is empty, for I have crushed an Universe; & nought remains.

73. Paste the sheets from right to left and from top to bottom: then behold!

74. There is a splendour in my name hidden and glorious, as the sun of midnight is ever the son.

75. The ending of the words is the Word Abrahadabra.

The Book of the Law is Written and Concealed.

Aum. Ha.

THE COMMENT.

Do what thou wilt shall be the whole of the Law.

The study of this Book is forbidden. It is wise to destroy this copy after the first reading.

Whosoever disregards this does so at his own risk and peril. These are most dire.

Those who discuss the contents of this Book are to be shunned by all, as centres of pestilence.

All questions of the Law are to be decided only by appeal to my writings, each for himself.

There is no law beyond Do what thou wilt.

Love is the law, love under will.

The priest of the princes,

Ankh-f-n-khonsu

WHITE STAINS

THE LITERARY REMAINS OF GEORGE ARCHIBALD BISHOP
A NEUROPATH OF THE SECOND EMPIRE

(Aleister Crowley)

1898

1

[02] The Editor hopes that Mental Pathologists, for whose eyes alone treatise in destined, will spare no precaution to prevent it falling into other hands

Une nouvelle Phedre a lui moins dure

(SELECTED POEMS)

PREFACE

In the fevered days and nights under the Empire that perished in the struggle of 1870, that whirling tumult of pleasure, scheming, success and despair, the minds of men had a trying ordeal to pass through. In Zola's *La Curée*, we see how such ordinary and natural characters as those of Saccard, Maxime and the incestuous heroine were twisted and distorted from their normal sanity, and sent whirling into the jaws of a hell far more effrayant than the mere cheap and nasty brimstone Sheol, which is a Shibboleth for the dissenter, and with which all classes of religious humbug, from the Pope to the Salvation ranter, from the Mormon and the Jesuit to that mongrel mixture of the worst features of both, the Plymouth Brother, have scared their illiterate, since hypocrisy was born, with Abel, and spiritual tyranny, with Jehovah! Society, in the long run, is eminently sane and practical; under the Second Empire it ran mad. If these things are done in the green tree of Society, what shall be done in the dry tree of Bohemianism? Art always has a suspicion to fight against; always some poor mad Max Nordau is handy to call everything outside the kitchen the asylum. Here, however, there is a substratum of truth. Consider the intolerable long roll of names, all tainted with glorious madness. Baudelaire the diabolist, debauchee of sadism, whose dreams are nightmares, and whose waking hours delirium; Rollinat the necrophile, the poet of phthisis, the anxiomaniac; Peladan, the high priest – of nonsense; Mendes, frivolous and scoffing sensualist; besides a host of others, most alike in this, that, below the cloak of madness and depravity, the true heart of genius burns. No more terrible period than this is to be found in literature; so many great minds, of which hardly one comes to fruition; such seeds of genius, such a harvest of – whirlwind! Even a barren waste of sea is less saddening than one strewn with wreckage.

In England such wild song found few followers of any worth or melody. Swinburne stands on his solitary pedestal above the vulgar crowds of priapistic plagiarists; he alone caught the first frenzy of Baudelaire's brandied shrieks, and his *Poems and Ballads First Series* was the legitimate echo of that not fierier note. But English Art as a whole was unmoved, at any rate not stirred to any depth, by this wave of debauchery. The great

thinkers maintained the even keel, and the windy waters lay not for their frailer barques to cross. There is one exception of note, till this day unsuspected, in the person of George Archibald Bishop. In a corner of Paris, this young poet (for in his nature the flower of poesy did spring, did even take root and give some promise of a brighter bloom, till stricken and blasted in latter years by the lightning of his own sins) was steadily writing day after day, night after night, often working forty hours at a time, work which he destined to entrance the world. All England should ring with his praises; by-and-by the whole world should know his name. Of these works none of the longer and more ambitious remains. How they were lost, and how those fragments we possess were saved, is best told by relating the romantic and almost incredible story of his life.

The known facts of this life are few, vague and unsatisfactory; the more definite statements lack corroboration, and almost the only source at the disposal of the biographer is the letters of Mathilde Doriac to Mdme J. S., who has kindly placed her portfolio at my service. A letter dated Oct. 15th, 1866 indicates that our author was born on the 23rd of that month. The father and mother of George were, at least on the surface, of an extraordinary religious turn of mind. Mathilde's version of the story, which has its source in our friend himself, agrees almost word for word with a letter of the Rev. Edw. Turle to Mrs. Cope, recommending the child to her care. The substance of the story is as follows:

The parents of George carried their religious ideas to the point of never consummating their marriage! This arrangement does not seem to have been greatly appreciated by the wife at least; one fine morning she was found to be *enceinte*. The foolish father never thought of the hypothesis which commends itself most readily to a man of the world, not to say a man of science, and adopted that of a second Messiah! He took the utmost pains to conceal the birth of the child, treated everybody who came to the house as an emissary of Herod, and finally made up his mind to flee into Egypt! Like most religious maniacs, he never had an idea of his own, but distorted the beautiful and edifying events of the Bible into insane and ridiculous ones, which he proceeded to plagiarise. On the voyage out the virgin mother became enamoured, as was her wont, of the nearest male, in this case a fellow-traveller.

He, being well able to support her in the luxury which she desired, easily persuaded her to leave the boat with him by stealth. A small sailing vessel conveyed them to Malta, where they disappeared. The only trace left in the books of earth records that this fascinating character was accused, four years later, in Vienna, of poisoning her paramour, but thanks to the wealth and influence of her new lover, she escaped.

The legal father, left by himself with a squalling child to amuse, to appease in his tantrums, and to bring up in the nurture and admonition of the Lord, was not a little perplexed by the sudden disappearance of his wife. At first he supposed that she had been translated, but, finding that she had not left the traditional mantle behind her, he abandoned this supposition in favour of a quite different, and indeed a more plausible, one. He now believed her to be the scarlet woman in the Apocalypse, with variations. On arrival in Egypt he hired an old native nurse, and sailed for Odessa. Once in Russia he could find Gog and Magog, and present to them the child as Antichrist. For he was now persuaded that he himself was the First Beast, and would ask the sceptic to count his seven heads and ten horns. The heads, however, rarely totted up accurately!

At this point the accounts of Mr. Turtle and Mathilde diverge slightly. The cleric affirms that he was induced by a Tartar lady, of an honourable and ancient profession, to accompany her to Thibet "to be initiated into the mysteries". He was, of course, robbed and murdered with due punctuality, in the town of Kiev. Mathilde's story is that he travelled to Kiev on the original quest, and died of typhoid or cholera. In any case, he died at Kiev in 1839. This fixes the date of the child's birth at 1837. His faithful nurse conveyed him safely to England, where his relatives provided for his maintenance and education. With the close of this romantic chapter in his early history, we lose all reliable traces for some years. One flash alone illumines the darkness of his boyhood; in 1853, after being prepared for confirmation, he cried out in full assembly, instead of kneeling to receive the blessing of the officiating bishop, "I renounce for ever this idolatrous church"; and was quietly removed.

He told Mathilde Doriac that he had been to Eton and Cambridge – neither institution, however, preserves any record of such admission. The imagination of George, indeed, is tremendously fertile with regard

854

to events in his own life. His own story is that he entered Trinity College, Cambridge, in 1856, and was sent down two years later for an article which he had contributed to some university or college magazine. No confirmation of any sort is to be found anywhere with regard to these, or any other statements, of our author. There is, however, no doubt that in 1861 he quarrelled with his family; went over to Paris, where he settled down, at first, like every tufthead, somewhere in the Quartier Latin; later, with Mathilde Doriac, the noble woman who became his mistress and held to him through all the terrible tragedy of his moral, mental, and physical life, in the Rue du Faubourg-Poissonniere. At his house there the frightful scenes of '68 took place, and it was there too that he was apprehended after the murders which he describes so faithfully in 'Abysmos'. He had just finished this poem with a shriek of triumph, and he had read it through to the appalled Mathilde "*avec des yeux de flamme et de gestes incoherentes*", when, foaming at the mouth, and "*hurlant de blasphemes indicibles*", he fell upon her with extraordinary violence of passion; the door opened, officers appeared, the arrest was effected. He was committed to an asylum, for there could be no longer any doubt of his complete insanity; for three weeks he had been raving with absinthe, and satyriasis. He survived his confinement no long time; the burning of the asylum with its inmates was one of the most terrible events of the war of 1870.

So died one of the most talented Englishmen of his century, a man who, for wide knowledge of men and things, was truly to be envied, yet one who sold his birthright for a mess of beastlier pottage than ever Esau guzzled, who sold soul and body to Satan for sheer love of sin, whose mere lust of perversion is so intense that it seems to absorb every other emotion and interest. Never since God woke light from chaos has such a tragedy been unrolled before men, step after step towards the lake of Fire!

At his house all his writings were seized, and, it is believed, destroyed. The single most fortunate exception is that of a superbly jewelled writing-case, now in the possession of the present editor, in which were found the MSS. which are here published. Mathilde, who knew how he treasured its contents, preserved it by saying to the officer, "But, sir, that is mine."

On opening this, it was found to contain, beside these MSS., his literary will. All MSS. were to be published thirty years after his death, not before. He would gain no spurious popularity as a reflection of the age he lived in. "Tennyson," he says, "will die before sixty years are gone by: if I am to be beloved of men, it shall be because my work is for all times and all men, because it is greater than all the gods of chance and change, because it has the heart of the human race beating in every line. This is a patch of magenta to mauve, undoubtedly; but – ! The present collection of verses will hardly be popular; if the lost works turn up, of course it may be that there may be found "shelter for songs that recede". Still, even here, one is, on the whole, more attracted than repelled; the author has enormous power, and he never scruples to use it, to drive us half mad with horror, or, as in his earlier most exquisite works, to move us to the noblest thoughts and deeds. True, his debt to contemporary writers is a little obvious here and there; but these are small blemishes on a series of poems whose originality is always striking, and often dreadful, in its broader features.

We cannot leave George Bishop without a word of enquiry as to what became of the heroic figure of Mathilde Doriac. It is a bitter task to have to write in cold blood the dreadful truth about her death. She had the misfortune to contract, in the last few days of her life with him, the same terrible disease which he describes in the last poem of this collection. This shock, coming so soon after, and, as it were, as an unholy perpetual reminder of the madness and sequestration of her lover, no less than of his infidelity, unhinged her mind, and she shot herself on July 5th, 1869. Her last letter to Madame J... S... is one of the tenderest and most pathetic ever written. She seems to have been really loved by George, in his wild, infidel fashion: 'All Night' and 'Victory', among others, are obviously inspired by her beauty, and her devotion to him, the abasement of soul, the prostitution of body, she underwent for and with him, is one of the noblest stories life has known. She seems to have dived with him, yet

ever trying to raise his soul from the quagmire; if God is just at all, she shall stand more near to His right hand than the vaunted virgins who would soil no hem of vesture to save their brother from the worm that dieth not!

The Works of George Archibald Bishop will speak for themselves; it would be both impertinent and superfluous in me to point out in detail their many and varied excellences, or their obvious faults. The *raison d'etre*, though, of their publication, is worthy of especial notice. I refer to their psychological sequence, which agrees with their chronological order. His life-history, as well as his literary remains, gives us an idea of the progression of diabolism as it really is; not as it is painted. Note also, (1) the increase of selfishness in pleasure, (2) the diminution of his sensibility to physical charms. Pure and sane is his early work; then he is carried into the outer current of the great vortex of Sin, and whirls lazily through the sleepy waters of mere sensualism; the pace quickens, he grows fierce in the mysteries of Sapphism and the cult of Venus Aversa with women; later of the same forms of vice with men, all mingled with wild talk of religious dogma and a general exaltation of Priapism at the expense, in particular, of Christianity, in which religion, however, he is undoubtedly a believer till the last (the pious will quote James 2, 19, and the infidel will observe that he died in an asylum); then the full swing of the tide catches him, the mysteries of death become more and more an obsession, and he is flung headlong into Sadism, Necrophilia, all the maddest, fiercest vices that the mind of fiends ever brought up from the pit. But always to the very end his power is unexhausted, immense, terrible. His delirium does not amuse; it appals! A man who could conceive as he did must himself have had some glorious chord in his heart vibrating to the eternal principle of Boundless Love. That this love was wrecked is for me, in some sort a relative of his, a real and bitter sorrow. He might have been so great! He missed Heaven! Think kindly of him!

DEDICACE

You crown me king and queen. There is a name
For whose soft sound I would abandon all
This pomp. I liefer would have had you call
Some soft sweet title of beloved shame.
Gold coronets be seemly, but bright flame
I choose for diadem; I would let fall
All crowns, all kingdoms, for one rhythmical
Caress of thine, one kiss my soul to tame.

You crown me king and queen; I crown thee lover!
I bid thee hasten, nay, I plead with thee,
Come in the thick dear darkness to my bed.
Heed not my sighs, but eagerly uncover,
As our mouths mingle, my sweet infamy,
And rob thy lover of his maidenhead.

Lie close; no pity, but a little love.
Kiss me but once and all my pain is paid.
Hurt me or soothe, stretch out one limb above
Like a strong man who would constrain a maid.
Touch me; I shudder and my lips turn back
Over my shoulder if so be that thus
My mouth may find thy mouth, if aught there lack
To thy desire, till love is one with us.

God! I shall faint with pain, I hide my face
For shame. I am disturbed, I cannot rise.
I breathe hard with this breath; thy quick embrace
Crushes; thy teeth are agony – pain dies
In deadly passion. Ah! You come – you kill me!
Christ! God! Bite! Bite! Ah Bite! Love's fountains fill me.

PREFATORY

SONNET TO THE VIRGIN MARY
Mother of God! who knowest the dire pangs
Of childbirth, and has suffered, and dost know
How utter sweet the full fruit of thy woe,
And how His heel hath crushed the serpent's fangs,
Be with me in the birth of this my book,
These songs of mine, poor children, like to die;
Yet, if they may not perish utterly,
It is to thee for sustenance I look.

Mother of God! be with me in success,
Abide with me if peradventure fail
These faint songs, murmurs of a summer gale
That my heart clothes within a mortal dress;
And with thy sympathy, their bliss or bale
Shall be too light to shake my happiness.

A FRAGMENT

Man Hero
Maid Heroine
Her Mother
Count B

He. Draw nigh, sweet maiden, violets blush at birth,
Pale lilies tinge with crimson, as the snow
At dawn's approach, the pansy's darksome dye
Deepens when tender winds blow over it
And give its beauties to the summer's gaze:
So blush at being mine, yet gently come
And place a dainty hand within my hold
Too delicate to crush it into warmth,
Save that blood mantling to thy cheek shall flow
Back to the fingers, though I press them not.

And so I will not hesitate to put
A ring upon thy hand, sweet mystery
Of Love's device, to shadow in our hearts
Th' Eternity of an immortal self
That is, and shall be while the stars endure,
Or while a God of Love is pitiful
Of all men's sorrows, and most happy in
Their joys –
She. Ah! joys are fleeting! –
He. But our love
Is anchored in the portals of the dawn
Where heaven begins.
She. And heaven begins with us
This day. Behold the flowers, whose kindly gaze
Of modest love is on us as we stand,
And clasp fond hands before high Heaven to swear
Truth an eternal bond, no parchment scroll

Of perishable matter ill devised
And scored upon with perishable ink,
But in our pulses' quick delight to live
From day to day renewed, as if a fount
Of God's mysterious stream, that here a man
May wet his ankle, and again immerse
Unto his knees, and yet again assay
To cross its silver depth and find himself
Swimming in crystal coldness on a sea
Broad as God's mercy and as deep as Love.
He. And whose strong tide shall bear our spirit out
Into the ocean of all happiness
Whose bounds are Heaven.
She. See! the scythe of Time
Sweeps on to cut the new-born flowers in twain
That symbolises the reluctant hour
In which we met – and now the flower is dead
And we must part.
He. Fond hearts, chaste souls, as one
Whose unity is sacred, still shall dwell
Together – Not the cold embrace
Of "We shall meet again", but let us say
The ritual of a lover, being this
"God be with you!"
She. O heart too dear to me,
Too much beloved for lover's tongue to tell,
God be with you! Farewell, sweet heart!
He. Farewell.
(EXEUNT).
DESUNT CETERA.

THE RAINBOW

On land wrought of starlight rain lingers
In delicate spirals and spines,
And sunlight's immaculate fingers
Creep through the desire of the pines;
The promise is flashed into being,
Tremendous and florid and proud,
To be seen by the eyes of the seeing,
A bow in the cloud.

O flamed through the sky as a harlot
In splendour transcendent and bold,
With purple and crimson and scarlet
And azure and olive and gold!
O melting to magic and mystery,
As clouds fly to heaven again,
And holy Hyperion's history
Is flashed into rain!

O Godhead of glory through anguish!
O Christ shone through Magdalen's tears!
Thy sons on the universe languish
In iron bands strong as the spheres;
With virtue Thy likeness we cover,
With priestcraft we mock at Thy power,
And the meanest on earth is a lover,
As vile as a flower.

Come down through the visionless aether,
And watch for the sprout of the grain
Hid dark in the wonder beneath her,
A marvel of passion and pain;

Smite power from on high into mortals,
Draw spirit to spirit and nigher,
That winds burst the wonderful portals
And tongues as of fire.

O Life of the stars in their glory,
O Light of the passionate spring,
How sweet and supreme is thy story,
Most Wonderful, Counsellor, King!
O crucified, slain, re-arisen!
Burst open the fetters that bind,
Change from us the garb of our prison
And lighten the mind.

O Spring, tell the bountiful Giver
Thy smiles on the world are in vain;
Come down, O Lord God, and deliver
Our souls from the wheel and the chain,
That Love may lie fragrant and shaded,
And Joy may spread wings unto flight,
And Peace stand above, unupbraided,
As splendid as night.

No longer the sun shall cast shadow,
No longer the flower shall lack rain,
The word shall be fair as a meadow,
And Love know no tincture of pain;
The Glory of God shall be on us,
And over the kingdon unpriced
The Spirit of Love is upon us,
A crucified Christ!

O rapture! O glory! O gladness!
When Satan is fled from the land,
When Christ cleanses sin, and from madness

Deletes its indelible brand;
For life shall spring where they have smitten,
And Love rise from under the rod,
Till all men behold what is written,
The kingdom of God!

WITH A COPY OF 'POEMS AND BALLADS'

Bon Pantagruel, je t'offre ces lyriques,
Vu que tu aimes, comme moi, ces mots
Des roideurs sadiques d'un grand jambot,
Des sacrées lysses de l'amour saphique.

Accepte donc comme temoin complet
D'amitié, ce petit don, qui dit
Toutes les délices de rose et lys,
Ces fleurs odorantes du sadinet!

Oublié donc, en lisant, toute faute
De moi qui écris cette dédicace
Laible, d'une lyre mal attunée;
Souviens-toi seul de l'admiration haute
Qui a fait naître, d'étemelle grace,
La fleur d'une loyale amitié.

AD LYDIAM, UT SECUM A MARITO FUGERET

1

The bird has chosen, and the world of spring
Under Love's banner is enrolled, but thou,
Chained to the iron couch of wedlock fast,
Art mourning while all nature else doth sing
The deep delights of Love. Still on thy brow
Lurks the dark shade, thy smile is overcast
With fear of the world's thought, and lips of love
Pale at that spectre, imminent, immense,
Cold Chastity, the child of Impotence,
And eyes grow dim with grey distrust thereof.
Forget, dear heart, forget; life's glow is sweet:
Come to a lover's arms that grow divine
At the first eloquent embrace of thine,
While pulses in wild unison warmly beat.

2

I know a valley walled with glistening steep
Of fire-hewn rock, and stately cliff of ice,
Filled with green lawns and forests black with pine,
Where the clear stream shall sing us into sleep
With murmuring faintly, and devine device:
Come with me there, and we will surely twine
Bright wreaths of Alpine gentian for thine head,
Those glowing tresses, auburn in the sun,
And in the night, dim fires of matchless red
To hold my love, and lead my kisses on
From night to night upon the purple bed
Of dark embraces; till the summer is gone
We will forget in love the world of tears
Whose tumult reaches not our amorous ears.

3

Come with me thither. Let the chaster snow
Blush at the sunset, when our limbs grow fain
To twine close caressing, let it blush
Redder at sunrise, when our eyelids grow
Weary of kissing, and our arms again
Slowly unclasp, and our fair cheeks do flush
With memory's modesty. The mountains glow
Warmer and whiter, dreamland's power shall wane
While the sun tints the beauty of the bush
And all the forest with his finger-tips
Of budding fire, and we surprised will wake
While Shadow's brush in darker colour dips,
And roam about the valley, and will take
Fresh delicate delight, with smiling lips.

4

Summer may die, but on the azure sea
That girdles warmer lands the sun will gleam;
There will we wander, over dale and how,
Sweet with green sward, faint flower, and tender tree.
There all the winter may we idly dream
Still of our love, and there forgetfulness
Of the past sorrow may steal o'er thy brow
In the new birth of stainless happiness,
Rich harvest of the blossoms desire,
Satisfied alway, yet for ever fresh
In hearts so passionate, and there may'st thou
Love to thy fulness, nor for ever tire
Of linking me to thee with dainty mesh
Of auburn ripples of delicious fire.

5

Doubt not, dear love, nor hesitate to say;
Blush if thou wilt; I love to see thy cheek

Grow hot with love-thoughts – let the word be said:
Between shy finger whisper me the "yea"!
My soul will leap to hear, as thine to speak.
Remember Love, forget the loveless bed;
Forget thy husband, and the cruel wreck
Of thy dear life on Wedlock's piteous sands;
Love's all in all on the golden bands
Forged in heaven without flaw or fleck.
I know thine answer by these amorous hands
That touch me thus to tempt me, by the kiss
Whose sudden passion burns upon my neck
Thy heart clings to me in perfect "Yes"!

CONTRA CONJUGIUM T. B. B.

Anathema foederis nefandi, jugeris
immondi, flagitii contra
Amorem, contra Naturam,
contra Deum, in saecula praesit
Amen! Cum comminatione pastorum improborum,
Ecclesiae malae, qui tales nuptias benedicunt.

Through nave and chancel drone the choir,
Their chant rolls through the darkened aisle;
Their song soars up beyond the spire;
The priest prepares; there waits his smile
A deed most vile.

Harken, thou fool at altar-rails
The still small awful voice of fear
Whereat earth shakes and heaven pales –
"I am the Lord"; His voice rings clear:
What dost thou here?

"Thou hast despised my laws, and stilled
The voice of Nature and my voice,
Now, shall thy life with joy be filled?
At thine own time shalt thou rejoice?
At thine own choice?

"I gave thee life, I gave thee youth,
Four seasons fair, for love the same,
Health, strength and comeliness – forsooth,
And thou hast quenched my holy flame,
And scorned my name!

"I gave thee life, life passeth by;
I gave thee youth, that youth is fled.

Thinkst thou that I will fructify
Now, at thine own good time, thy dead
And barren bed?

"How worship me, yet break my laws?
Art thou a God? Didst thou devise
The infinite world? Did thy word cause
The silver Caucasus to arise?
Art thou all-wise?

"'Or hast thou mocked me, setting high
A molten calf, a graven block,
A fetish foul, a devil's lie,
And worshipped that? Thou shalt not mock,
Thou barren rock!

"Thou shalt not mock! Cold Chastity,
Father and child of Impotence,
Whom thou hast set on high for me,
From her foul shrine shall chase thee thence:
'Avoid, get hence!'

"And I – thou shalt not scorn my word,
All Nature sets it scorn on thee;
Sweet flower and stream, swift fish and bird,
Shall chorus out 'Thou fruitless tree!
Thou salt dry sea!'

"I will not aid thee in thine age,
Nor heed thee in thy piteous strait;
Live thou in thine own empty cage,
Forged every day that thou didst wait
Too long, too late!

"Shall I turn back the seasons past,

Recall sun's shine and cloudlet's fleece,
Revive the ghosts of aeons vast,
And bid the scythe of Chronos cease
For thy caprice?

"Because thou wilt, shall I accede
And change my laws that I have made
Shall I make grapes from thorn and weed,
Fresh water from the fountains stayed,
If thou hast prayed?

"For thine outcry bring chaos back,
Turn over earth and heaven to hell,
And listen 'mid the roar and wrack,
With pleasure to creation's knell,
Thy marriage bell?

"I will not turn the Red Sea back
That thou mayst pass again dry-shod:
Thou hast chosen, thou shalt live the black
Dry years out till thou cleave the sod,
And meet thy God.

"What are thy good deeds? This one thing
Thou hast not done. This chiefest task
Thou wouldst not do. And shall the King
Of Kings do only what men ask?
Thou empty mask!

"Repentance is too late, lost fool,
Dead flower, salt fountain, rusty sword,
This curse is on thee for thy dule,
That thou shalt know and be assured
I am the Lord."

The loud-voiced choir would drown in song
The voice of God; their music woke
Echoes through chancel weird and long –
In thunder and fierce fire and smoke
Jehovah spoke.

"On with the farce! My perjured priests,
The wolves that raven through my flock,
Nay, wolves in shepard's garb, wild beasts
That fang and tear my lambs, and mock
At Judah's stock.

"On with the grim foul farce! Black hell
Gapes to receive all actors there.
Play on its brink! What soul can tell
But I, your God, may be as air,
A children's snare?

"But I am here, I will not heed,
I will not give more signs; But I
Will come with heavy hand and deed
And give men knowledge ere they die
How their priests lie.

"A gospel marred, a bastard creed,
A dogma out of hell ye teach!
False shepards, ye shall learn your meed;
Not as waves breaking on the beach
My wrath shall reach!

"I forget not – heed not my cry,
Play out the farce, wed fast the twain! –
Red judgement and black death draw nigh,
Your blasphemies shall all be vain,
And your souls slain.

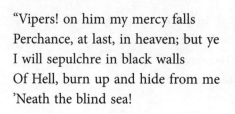

"Vipers! on him my mercy falls
Perchance, at last, in heaven; but ye
I will sepulchre in black walls
Of Hell, burn up and hide from me
'Neath the blind sea!

"Vipers! eternal fire shall quench
Your prayers and curses, hell shall hold
The vapourous vomit of your stench
Wrung from foul souls, no longer bold
But cowed and cold.

"Vipers! his fooly I will heal,
Your sin I will not put away;
My Christ is vain for you; appeal
In vain to his shed blood; nor pray
I will not slay.

"I will most utterly destroy
Your souls from off the earth; your power
Sealed by your Satan I will cloy
With subtle strength; your church shall flower
No further hour.

"Because ye set your hands to this,
Blaspheming nature and my name,
Cemented the unholy kiss
Of barren age's fruitless shame
Your hell shall flame

"Seven times more hot, that ye may know
My paths shall be most surely trod,
That I who answer thus, who show
Myself in wielding sword and rod,
Am high Lord God!"

Silent the voice, and through the nave
And chancel droned the choir; the sun
Darkened, as Satan's perjured slave,
The priest, in blessing, made them one.
The Deed was done.

A BALLAD OF CHOOSING

Love brought a garland to my feet today
Offering to crown my head withal, and said:
"The year is young, it is the time of May,
Autumn is distant, and the winter, dead."
And would therewith my brows have garlanded
But that I asked him "Is not this a fire
To burn the scorched brain through
   my maddened head?
Thou has a guerdon, is it not for hire?"

Fame brought a golden crown, bejewelled o'er
With precious rubies beyond price, and cried
"The world is young, thy name shall evermore
Ring in men's ears, stately and glorified."
But I, with shuddering lips, to him replied
"Fame is the aramanth that fools desire
My soul's price is beyond thy jewel's pride
Thou has a guerdon, is it not for hire?"

"Wealth brought to me a purse, whose glancing gold
Mocked the sun's rays, grown dull as iron rust,
And pressed it in my hand, saying 'Behold
The corner-stone of fame, the means of lust'
And I in thee I put but little trust
Shameful, most vile, accursed of God's ire,
Dross of the dunghill's most detested dust,
Thou has a guerdon, is it not for hire?"

Christ came to me, alone and sorrowful,
And offered me a cross, saying to me,
"I have great joys to give most bountiful.
Carry this through the world, and when the sea
Of death is past, then is prepared for thee

A house of many mansions." My desire
Hid not from me the vileness of his plea:
"Thou has a guerdon, is it not for hire?"

ENVOI

Prince of the air, thou offerest nought to me
I serve thee, recompensed of hell-fire,
More nobly than these others, verily
Since none with impious word may mock at thee
"Thou has a guerdon, is it not for hire?"

A JEALOUS LOVER

1

I have an idol wrought of stainless gold
Before whose feet I bow, in whose delight
I am content to live, whose spells of might
Are smiles that gleam, are tears that glisten cold
On the fair cheek that blushes if I praise;
Are warm ripe kisses in the softer hours
When love is perfect blossom of sweet flowers,
Are shadowed glances of pure lovelight rays
From clear blue eyes, are wonderful caresses
When love is golden autumn of sweet fruit.
What other worship can usurp my days
When I may lie amid her sunny tresses
Enraptured by the music of her lute
One long calm love, one heart's delight always?

2

Bright spheres of heaven, firefly gleams, fair ghosts
Laugh lightly to the silver globe of night
That glitters on green fields, and on the sea
Ripples break foamless, where the golden coasts
Echo their mellow cadence. Such delight
Is on me I would fain sigh into sleep
Until my love comes forth to dream with me
Of silent words of love and peopled stars
Where we may live and love and never weep
Nor yet be weary. The last ruby bars
Are sunk beneath the sea. The shadows creep
More on me as I quicken with desire
My love is all of gold, my faith is deep
Lit with my heart's imperishable fire.

877

3

Pale spectres of the stars, corpse-lights, bad-ghosts
Sicken the icy glamour of the moon
Upon the vacant earth; and where the sea
Marshals sepulchral billows, obscene hosts
Of harpies gibber weirdly. I should swoon
For the silence, rolled not some dread minstrelsy
In fearful anguish on the shuddering air,
Breathing out terror and lightning to the night
That wildly echoes back Hell's venomous spite,
And shrieks aloud the watchword of despair
To draw each painracked nerve more tense and gray
For I am alone, unloved, in murk and gloom,
Unloved, unfriended, fittest for the tomb,
Who worshipped golden feet and found them clay.

4

She creeps alive upon the tawny sands,
False glittering woman, girt about with lies!
She steals toward me, the tigress sleek and fierce!
Destroying devil, with long sinuous hands
And hate triumphant in blue-murderous eyes!
I nerve myself to spring upon and pierce
With maddening fangs those firm white bosom towers,
To tear those lithe voluptuous limbs apart
And glut my ravening soul with vengeance. Heart
Quickens as she draws near; the scent of flowers
Breathes round her damned presence. Shall she live
To triumph with those tainted lips of song –
She whispered "Dearest, I have kept thee long."
I flung myself before her, "Love, forgive!"

BALLADE DE LA JOLIE MARION

It is a sweet thing to be loved,
Although my sighs in absence wake,
Although my saddening heart is moved,
I smile and bear for love's dear sake.
My songs their wonted music make,
Joyous and careless, songs of youth,
Because the sacred lips of both
Are met to kiss the last good-bye,
Because sweet glances weep for ruth
That we must part, and love must die.

Remembrance of love's long delights
Is to remember sighs and tears,
Yet I will think upon the nights
I whispered into passionate ears
The fond desires, the sweet faint fears.
My lover's limbs of lissome white
Gleamed in the darkness and strange light,
The wondrous orbs voluptuously
Bent on me all unearthly bright:
But we must part, and love must die.

Fond limbs with mine were intertwined,
A hand lascivious fondled me;
My ears grew deaf, my eyes grew blind,
My tongue was hot from kisses free,
Short madness, and we lazily
Lolled back upon the bed of fire.
I was a-weary – her desire
Drew her upon me – Marion, fie!
You work our pleasure till I tire:
But we must part, and love must die.

Nor thus did love's embraces wane,
Though lusty limbs grow idle quite;
Our mouths' red valves are over-fain
To suck the sweetness from the night;
And amorously, with touches light,
Steal passion from reluctant pain.
So has the daystar fled again
Before the blushes of the sky,
So did I clasp thy knees in vain:
For we must part, and love must die.

You say another's sensuous lips
Shall open to my kisses there:
When weary, steal those luscious sips;
Another's hands play in my hair
And find delight for me to bare
The bosom, and the passionate mound
White and, for Venus' temple, round,
A garden of wild thyme whose eye
My sword shall pierce, and never wound:
For we must part, and love must die.

You say – but Oh! my Marion's kiss
Shall linger on my palate still,
No joy on earth is like to this
That we have tasted to our fill
Of all our sweet lascivious will.
The cup is drained of lust's delight,
Yet wells with pleasure, and by night
I'll come once more and loving lie
Between thine amorous limbs, despite
That we must part, and love must die.

ENVOI
Thus, sweet, I'll sing when day doth break
And weary lovers must awake
To part, but now our pleasure take
In one last bout of rivalry,
Whose passions first shall answer make
To the dances that the curtains shake
Till we must part, and love must die.

AT STOCKHOLM

We could not speak, although the sudden glow
Of passion mantling to the crimson cheek
Of either, told our tale of love, although
We could not speak.

What need of language, barren and false and bleak,
While our white arms could link each other so,
And fond red lips their partners mutely seek?

What time for language, when our kisses flow
Eloquent, warm, as words are cold and weak? –
Or now – Ah! sweetheart, even were it so,
We could not speak!

MATHILDE

O large lips opening outward like a flower
To breathe upon my face that clings to thee!
O wanton breasts that heave deliciously
And tempt my eager teeth! Oh cruel power
Of wide deep thighs that make me furious
As they enclasp me and swing to and fro
With passion that grows pale and drives the flow
Of the fast fragrant blood of both of us
Into the awful link that knits us close
With chain electric! O have mercy yet
In drawing out my life in this desire
To consummate this moment all the gross
Lusts of tonight, and pay the sudden debt
That with strong water shall put out our fire!

YET TIME TO TURN

Brighter than snow on glittering Alps, the soul
Of my lost love was, bluer than the haze
Of those same hills, more violent and deep
Her eyes' clear gaze,
Dreaming of hidden wonders; and the goal
Of life grew luminous o'er Time's empurpled steep

She loved me then; she loves me now, afar.
Ah, she knew not! and I, so steeped and stained
With fierce sins, knew myself unworthy of
The heart I gained,
And, a lost mariner whose polar star
He is ashamed to look to, cast away her love.

I would not have her love a thing so vile,
I would not link her life with such as mine!
0 cursed sin, to leave my soul too high
To cheat the shrine!
I drave Love forth, Love lingered yet awhile
So that I might not quite win Hell before I die.

O little root of nobleness left thus
Dead since it has no power to grow, to bloom;
Live, since I may not bury it within
The gaping tomb
Where virtue lies, that I, imperious,
Long since interred with hope, all life's joy save sin.

ALL NIGHT

All night no change, no whisper. Scarce a breath
But lips closed hard upon the cup of death
To drain its sweetest poison. Scarce a sigh
Beats the dead hours out; scarce a melody
Of measured pulses quickened with the blood
Of that desire which pours its deadly flood
Through soul and shaken body; scarce a thought
But sense through spirit most divinely wrought
To perfect feeling; only through the lips
Electric ardour kindles, flashes, slips
Through all the circle to her lips again
And thence, unwavering, flies to mine, to drain
All pleasure in one draught. No whispered sigh,
No change of breast, love's posture perfectly
Once gained, we change no more.
The fever grows Hotter or cooler, as the night wind blows
Fresh gusts of passion on the outer gate.
But we, in waves of frenzy, concentrate
Our thirsty mouths on that hot drinking cup
Whence we may never suck the nectar up
Too often or too hard; fresh fire invades
Our furious veins, and the unquiet shades
Of night make noises in the darkened room.
Yet, did I raise my head, throughout the gloom
I might behold thine eyes as red as fire,
A tigress maddened with supreme desire.
White arms that clasp me, fervent breast that glides
An eager snake, about my breast and sides,
And white teeth keen to bite, red tongue that tires,
And lips ensanguine with unfed desires,
Hot breath and hands, dishevelled hair and head,
Thy fevered mouth like snakes' mouths crimson red,

A very beast of prey; and I like thee,
Fiery, unweary, as thou art of me.
But raise no head; I know thee, breast and thigh,
Lips, hair and eyes and mouth: I will not die
But thou come with me o'er the gate of death.
So, blood and body furious with breath
That pants through foaming kisses, let us stay
Gripped hard together to keep life away,
Mouths drowned in murder, never satiate,
Kissing away the hard decrees of Fate,
Kissing insatiable in mad desire
Kisses whose agony may never tire,
Kissing the gates of hell, the sword of God,
Each unto each a serpent or a rod,
A well of wine and fire, each unto each,
Whose lips are fain convulsively to reach
A higher heaven, a deeper hell. Ah! Day
So soon to dawn, delight to snatch away!
Damned day, whose sunlight finds us as with wine
Drunken, with lust made manifest divine
Devils of darkness, servants unto hell –
Yea, king and queen of Sheol, terrible
Above all fiends and furies, hating more
The high Jehovah, loving Baal Peor,
Our father and our lover and our god!
Yea, though he lift his adamantine rod
And pierce us through, how shall his anger tame
Fire that glows fiercer for the brand of shame
Thrust in it; so, we who are all of fire,
One dull red flare of devilish desire,
The God of Israel shall not quench with tears,
Nor blood of martyrs drawn from myriad spheres,
Nor watery blood of Christ; that blood shall boil
With all the fury of our hellish toil;

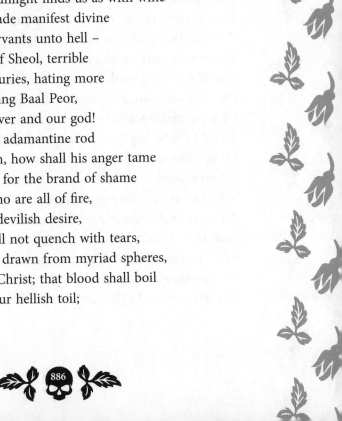

His veins shall dry with heat; his bones shall bleach
Cold and detested, picked of dogs, on each
Dry separate dunghill of burnt Golgotha.
But we will wrest from heaven a little star,
The Star of Bethlehem, a lying light
Fit for our candle, and by devils' might
Fix in the vast concave of hell for us
To lume its ghastly shadows murderous,
That in the mirror of the lake of fire
We may behold the image of Desire
Stretching broad wings upon us, and may leap
Each upon other, till our bodies weep
Thick sweet salt tears, and, clasping as of yore
Within dull limits of Earth's barren shore,
Fulfil immense desires of strange new shames,
Burn into one another as the flames
Of our hell fuse us into one wild soul:
Then, one immaculate divinest whole,
Plunge, fire, within all fire, dive far to death;
Till, like king Satan's sympathetic breath,
Burn on us as a voice from far above
Strange nameless elements of fire and love;
And we, one mouth to kiss, one soul to lure,
For ever, wedded, one, divine, endure
Far from sun, sea, and spring from love or light,
Imbedded in impenetrable night;
Deeper than ocean, higher than the sky,
Vaster than petty loves that dream and die,
Insatiate, angry, terrible for lust,
Who shrivel God to adamantine dust
By our fierce gaze upon him, who would strive
Under our wrath, to flee away, to dive
Into the deep recesses of his heaven.
But we, one joy, one love, one shame for leaven,

Quit hope and life, quit fear and death and love,

Implacable as God, desired above
All loves of hell or heaven, supremely wed,
Knit in one soul in one delicious bed
More hot than hell, more wicked than all things,
Vast in our sin, whose unredeeming wings
Rise o'er the world, and flap for lust of death,
Eager as anyone that travaileth;
So in our lusts, the monstrous burden borne
Heavy within the womb, we wait the morn
Of its fulfilment. Thus eternity
Wheels vain wings round us, who may never die,
But cling as hard as serpent's wedlock is,
One writhing glory, an immortal kiss.

ODE TO VENUS CALLIPYGE

Where was light when thy body came
Out of the womb of a perished prayer?
Where was life when the sultry air,
Hot with the lust of night and shame,
Brooded on dust, when thy shoulders bare
Shone on the sea with a sudden flame
Into all Time to abundant fame?

CHORUS

Daughter of Lust by the foam of the sea!
Mother of flame! Sister of shame!
Tiger that Sin nor her son cannot tame!
Worship to thee! Glory to thee!
Venus Callipyge, mother of me.

Fruitless foam of a sterile sea,
Wanton waves of a vain desire,
Maddening billows flecked with fire,
Storms that lash on the brine, and flee,
Dead delights, insatiate ire
Broke like a flower to the birth of thee,
Venus Callipgye, mother of me!

Deep wet eyes that are violet-blue!
Haggard cheeks that may blush no more!
Body bruised daintily, touched of gore
Where the sharp fierce teeth have bitten through
The olive skin that thy sons adore,
That they die for daily, are slain anew
By manifold hate; for their tale is few.

Few are thy sons, but as fierce as dawn,
Rapturous moments and weary days,
Nights when thine image a thousand ways
Is smitten and kissed on the fiery lawn
Where the wash of the waves of thy native bays
Laps weary limbs, that of thee have drawn
Laughter and fire for their souls in pawn.

O thy strong sons! they are dark as night,
Cruel and barren and false as the sea,
They have cherished Hell for the love of thee,
Filled with thy lust and abundant might,
Filled with the phantom desire to free
Body and soul from the sound and sight
Of a world and a God that doth not right.

O thy dark daughter! their breasts are slack,
Their lips so large and as poppies red;
They lie in a furious barren bed;
They lie on their faces, their eyelids lack
Tears, and their cheeks are as roses dead;
White are their throats, but upon the back
Red blood is clotted in gouts of black.

All on their sides are the wounds of lust,
Down, from the home of their auburn hair
Down to the feet that we find so fair;
Where the red sword has a secret thrust
Pain, and delight, and desire they share.
Verily, pain! and thy daughters trust
Thou canst bid roses spring out of dust.

Mingle, ye children of such a queen,
Mingle, and meet, and sow never a seed!
Mingle, and tingle, and kiss and bleed

With the blood of the life of the Lampsacene,
With the teeth that know never a pitiful deed
But fret and foam over with kisses obscene –
Mingle and weep for what years have been.

Never a son nor a daughter grow
From your waste limbs, lest the goddess weep;
Fill up the ranks from the babes that sleep
Far in the arms of a god of snow.
Conquer the world, that her throne may keep
More of its pride, and its secret woe
Flow through all earth as the rivers flow.

Which of the gods is like thee, our queen?
Venus Callipyge, nameless, nude,
Thou with the knowledge of all indued
Secrets of life and the dreams that mean
Loves that are not, as are mortals', hued
All rose and lily, but linger unseen
Passion-flowers purpled, garlands of green!

Who like thyself shall command our ways?
Who has such pleasures and pains for hire?
Who can awake such a mortal fire
In the veins of a man, that deathly days
Have robbed of the masteries of desire?
Who can give garlands of fadeless bays
Unto the sorrow and pain we praise?

Yea, we must praise, though the deadly shade
Fall on the morrow, though fires of hell
Harrow our vitals; a miracle
Springs at thy kisses, for thou hast made
Anguish and sorrow desirable
Torment of hell as the leaves that fade

Quickly forgotten, despised, decayed.

They are decayed, but thou springest again,
Mother of mystery, barren, who bearest
Flowers of most comeliest children, who wearest
Wounds for delight, whose desire shall stain
Star-space with blood as the price thou sharest
With thy red lovers, whose passing pain
Ripens to marvellous after-gain.

Thou art the fair, the wise, the divine,
Thou art our mother, our goddess, our life,
Thou art our passion, our sorrow, our strife,
Thou, on whose forehead no lights ever shine,
Thou, our Redeemer, our mistress, our wife,
Thou, barren sister of deathlier brine,
Venus Callipyge, mother of mine!

CHORUS
Daughter of Lust by the foam of the sea!
Mother of flame! Sister of shame!
Tiger the Sin nor her son cannot tame!
Worship to thee! Glory to thee!
Venus Callipyge, mother of me.

VOLUPTE

Clitoridette, m'amourette,
Ote ta jolie robe d'or,
Tes roses bas, chemise nette,
Et découvre pour moi le con,
Le con que j'aime, aux cheveux noirs,
Le cul ou tu m'admets ce soir,
Les seins je baise, que j'adore,
Tous les secrets de ton boudoir.

'Viens a moi, qui, raide, couche,
Attendant tes désirs lubriques;
Tu suces et couvres dans la bouche
De l'amour le pouce phallique;
Je tremble, en mourant avec feu,
Voyant la clarté de tes yeux,
Leur flamme méchante, saphique,
Brulant en langueur amoureux.

Laisse mon épée affaiblie,
Donne a mes baisere la vagine
D'ou je suc'rai de l'eau-de-lys,
Et te ferai comme divine.
La langue qui cherche tes reins,
Les genoux qui pressent tes seins,
Te feraient déesse, ma mine,
Je mordrai, et tu cries en vain.

Alors, de nouvelle énergie,
Je jette entre tes jolies cuisses,
Dedans ton cul, ce fleur-de-lys,
Long, gros, et ardent. Ça, il glisse
En haut, en bas. La passion croit
Fiévreux, furieux, pour toi!

Vient, la crise du délice!....
Ah, je suis mort!.... Embrasse-moi!!

RONDELS

1

Maid of dark eyes, that glow with shy sweet fire,
Song lingers on thy beauty till it dies
In awe and longing on the smitten lyre:
Maid of dark eyes.
Grant me thy love, earth's last surpassing prize,
Me, cast upon the faggots of love's pyre
For love of the white bosom that underlies

The subtle passion of thy snowy attire,
The shadowy secret of thine amorous thighs,
The inmost, shrine of my supreme desire,
Maid of dark eyes!

2

Boy of red lips, pale face, and golden hair,
Of dreamy eyes of love, and finger-tips
Rosy with youth, too fervid and too fair,

Boy of red lips.

How the fond ruby rapier glides and slips
'Twixt the white hills thou spreadest for me there;
How my red mouth immortal honey sips
From thy ripe kisses, and sucks nectar rare
When each the shrine of God Priapus clips
In hot mouth passionate more than man may bear,
Boy of red lips!

AD LUCIUM

The Lampsacene is girt with golden dress;
His courts gleam ever with forbidden light;

I only bring no gift to him tonight,
Being the mockery of his rod's distress.
While satyrs woo, and fauns, and nymphs give ear,
I burn unslacked, my Lucius is unkind,
He dare not guess, I dare not speak my mind,
Nor feed upon his lips, nor call him dear,
Nor may I clasp him, lissome and divine,
Nor suck our passion from his eager verge,
Nor pleasure in his quick embraces prove;
I faint for love, come aid me sparkling wine,
That my unquenchable desire may urge
In Lucius' fiery heart responsive love.

O fervent and sweet to my bosom
Past woman, I'll clasp thee and cling
Till the buds of desire break to blossom
And my kisses surprise thee and sting;
Till my hand and my mouth are united
In caresses that shake thee and smite,
While the stars hide their lustre affrighted
In measureless night.

I will neither delay nor dissemble
But utter my love in thine ear
Though my voice and my countenance tremble
With a passion past pity and fear;
I will speak from my heart till thou listen
With the soft sound of wings of a dove,
Till thine eyes anser back till they glisten
0 Lucius, love!

I will touch thee but once with a finger,
But thy vitals shall shudder and smart,
And the smile through thy sorrow shall linger,
And the touch shall pierce through to thine heart;

Thy lips a denial shall fashion,
Thou shalt tremble and fear to confess,
Till thou suddenly break into passion
With yes, love, and yes.

I will kiss thee and fondle and woo thee
And mingle my lips into thine
That shall tingle and thrill through and through thee
As the draught of the flame of a wine;
I will drink of the fount of our pleasure
Licking round and about and above
Till its streams pour me out their full measure,
O Lucius, love!

Thou shalt clasp me and clamber above me
And press me with eager desire,
Thou shalt kiss me and clip me and love me
With a love beyond infinite fire,
Thou shalt pierce to the portals of passion
And satiate thy longing and lust
In the fearless Athenian fashion,
A rose amid dust.

We will taste all delights and caresses
And know all the secrets of joy,
From the love-look that chastity blesses
To the lusts that deceive and destroy;
We will live in the light of sweet glances,
By day and by night we will move
To the music of manifold dances,
O Lucius, love!

A PAEAN IN THE SPRINGTIDE

Now is the triumph of Love, now is the day of his guerdon,
Now when the blossoms are full on the bountiful delicate
    spray;
Now has the year sprung aloft and shaken the frost and its
    burden,
April is come with his showers, sun laughs and promises May.
Newly the bird sings of Love, newly he wooeth a maiden,
Newly the heart of a boy leaps, and his eyes catch its fire.
Light is his laugh as the sea, with no sad remembrances
    laden;
Light as the sea, and as fierce and fickle is grown his desire.
Here in the spring we are free, as the winds that look love at
    the ocean;
Change we and weary too soon of delight that is hardly
    begun;
Pleasure and pain are made one, a delirious noble emotion;
Love dies before he grows manly, dawn never yields to the
    sun.

Love in a night shall live and die,
Love in a day shall wing and fly;
Love in the Spring shall last an hour,
Easily fades a spring-tide flower.

Where are the blooms of frost, hoary and bright and vestal;
Virginal lips not kissed, flowers unbidden to bud?
Ah! we have slain their beams, as our low heads lazily nestle,
Where the dark home of Love is, where the impatient blood
Spurts at the furious kiss, darts far forth as an adder,
Stinging and biting amain, as the night becomes golden with
    fire.
Dawn brings reason back, and the violet eyes grow sadder,
Eyes that were red in the dark, eyes of enfevered desire.

Eyes that wrote songs with a glance, whose look sang the
    sweetest of stories,
Sweeter than lips could have told, who loved better only to kiss;
Sweeter than hands could have written, who took delight in
the glories
Fierce of a triple embrace, a fadeless implacable bliss.

Love is a sword whose blade is red,
Love is a deed whose fruit is dead;
Love is a tiger, fierce of power,
Easily fades a spring-tide flower.

Death shall come slow and soft, with the stealthy tread of a
    leopard;
While the few stars have grown dim, as he seeks for an
    innocent prey.
Death shall pounce soon on the fold, where Love was a
    treacherous shepherd;
So with hot lips shall he come, ere the mountains are silver
    and grey.
Life shall gasp out in the gloom, and all our desires shall
    perish;
Hope and its roseate crown shall fall in the dark to the dust.
Love and his garland shall go, with the last of the joys we may
    cherish,
Death with cold finger shall touch the delicate springs of our
    lust.
We shall be weary of kisses, weary of all the caresses Man or
    his sisters of shame dream or devise or obtain;
Cover the white limbs ashamed with the fiery impassionate
    tresses,
Once for a bed to delight, now for a covering to pain.

Love is a fruit with rotted core,
Love is a thing shall be no more;

Love is a bride of a bitter dower,
Easily fades a spring-tide flower.

Where shall be Hylas then? for his lonely lips are sighing,
Vainly in hell for love, vainly for days gone by;
Where the incarnate flame of Lesbian lovers dying,
Then where the world is past, and Heaven or hell draw nigh?
Heaven with cold and loveless lips, though his fruits be many,
Hell with his red mouth hot, barren although he be.
Hylas and Sappho choose, and are never denied of any,
Hell's most insatiate fangs, death and his empery.
Heaven is bare and bleak, hell has the joys beyond Heaven,
Fire and desire and delight, of a love that is always young;
Hell has the pains of hell, but the sweetest of lusts for leaven.
Fierce body, breasts of delight, fearful and murderous tongue.

Hell is the house of all delight,
Heaven the home of a bitter blight;
Pain is our joy and our spirits' power,
Never shall fade its fiery flower.

Now is the triumph of Love, gazing far to an infinite pleasure,
Pleasure that mocks Heaven's hopes, that our hands are
    impatient to hold.
Love and delight pouring out, in a fearless insatiate measure,
Out of the chalice of lust, scarlet o'errunning its gold.
This is the song of the Spring, that the nightingale's carol by
    starlight,
This the delight of our eyes, as they shine with strange fire in
    the night,
This is our trust and our joy – beyond death we look on to the
    far light
Flaming from hell our last home, this is the key of our might.
Come, fiery birds of a clime we know not, and sing us your
    paean;

Triumph of gods that are known secretly, not by a name,
Gods whose implacable feet have trampled the god Galilean,
Cast though they be into hell, given to death and to shame.

Heaven and hell has striven in war,
Sappho and Hylas, with Christ and Jah;
We are of those, though they lose their power,
Never shall fade their fiery flower.

TO J. L. D.

At last, so long desired, so long delayed,
The step is taken, and the threshold past;
I am within the palace I have prayed
At last.

Like scudding winds, when skies are overcast,
Came the soft breath of Love, that might not fade.
O Love, whose magic whispers bind me fast,

O Love, who hast the kiss of Love betrayed,
Hide my poor blush beneath thy pinions vast,
Since thou hast come, nor left me more a maid.
At last.

TO A. D.

Across the sea that lies between us twain
I gaze and see thee, exiled but as free
As winds that lash the billows of the main
Across the sea.

I remain here in sombre slavery
Amid these winter gusts of bitter pain,
And sorrow for thy lips in vain, in vain,
Bound by the world's inexorable chain,
And parted from thee. Spirit of Liberty,

Bear thou my kisses' sunshine, my tears' rain
To him I love, who may one day love me
And bid him gladden at my amorous strain
Across the sea.

AT KIEL

Oh, the white flame of limbs in dusky air,
The furnace of thy great grey eyes on me
Turned till I shudder. Darkness on the sea,
And wan ghost-lights are flickering everywhere
So that the world is ghastly. But within
Where we two cling together, and hot kisses
Stray to and fro amid the wildernesses
Of swart curled locks! I deem it a sweet sin,
So sweet that fires of hell have no more power
On body and soul to quench the lustrous flame
Of that desire that burns between us twain.
What is Eternity, seeing we hold this hour
For all the lusts and luxuries of shame?
Heaven is well lost for this surpassing gain.

THE BLOOD-LOTUS

The ashen sky, too sick for sleep, makes my face grey; my
    senses swoon;
Here, in the glamour of the moon, will not some pitying
    godhead weep

For cold grey anguish of her eyes, that look to God, and look
    in vain,
For death, the anodyne of pain, for sleep, earth's trivial
    paradise?

Sleep I forget. Her silky breath no longer fans my ears; I
    dream
I float on some forgotten stream that hath a saviour still of
    death,

A sweet warm smell of hidden flowers whose heavy petals kiss
    the sun,
Fierce tropic poisons every one that fume and sweat through
    forest hours;

They grow in darkness, heat beguiles their sluggish kisses, in
    the wood
They breathe no murmur that is good, and Satan in their
    blossom smiles.

They murder with the old perfume that maddens all men's
    blood; we die
Fresh from some corpse-clothed memory, some secret
    redolence of gloom,

Some darkling murmurous song of lust quite strange to man
    and beast and bird,
Silent in power, not overheard by any snake that eats the dust:

No crimson-hooded viper knows, no silver-crested asp has
    guessed
The strange soft secrets of my breast; no leprous cobra shall
    disclose

The many-seated, multiform, divine, essential joys that these
Dank odours bring, that starry seas wash white in vain;
    intense and warm

The scents fulfil, they permeate all lips, all arteries, and fire
New murmured music on the lyre that throbs the horrors they
    create.

Omniscient blossom! Is thy red slack bosom fresher for my
    kiss?
Are thy loves sharper? Hast thou bliss in all the sorrows of the
    dead?

Why art thou paler when the moon grows loftier in the
    troublous sky?
Why dost thou beat and heave when I press lips of fire, hell's
    princeliest boon,

To thy mad petals, green and gold like angels' wings, when as
    a flood
God's essence fills them, and the blood throughout their web
    grows icy cold?

To thy red centre are my eyes held fast and fervent, as at night
Some sad miasma lends a light of strange and silent
    blasphemies

To lure a soul to hell, to draw some saint's charred lust, to
    tempt, to win
Another sacrifice to sin, another poet's heart to gnaw

With dubious remorse. Oh! flame of torturing flower-love!
    sacrament
Of Satan, triple element of mystery and love and shame,

Green, gold, and crimson, in my heart you strive with Jesus
    for its realm,
While Sorrow's tears would overwhelm the warriors of either
    part!

Jesus would lure me: from his side the gleaming torrent of the
    spear
Withdraws, my soul with joy and fear waits for sweet blood to
    pour its tide

Of warm delight – in vain! so cold, so watery, so slack it flows,
It leaves me moveless as a rose, albeit her flakes are manifold.

He hath no scent to drive men mad; no mystic fragrance from
    his skin
Sheds a loose hint of subtle sin such as the queen Faustina
    had.

Thou drawest me. Thy golden lips are carven Cleopatra-wise
Large, full, and moist, within them lies the silver rampart,
    whence there slips

That rosy flame of love, the fount of blood at my light bidding
    spilt;
And my desires, if aught thou wilt, are with thy mind, and thy
    account

With God shall bear my name the more; give me the
    knowledge, me the power
For some new sin one little hour, and bankrupt God the
    creditor:

Steal from his stock of suffering; his tender mercies rob at will;
Destroy his graciousness, until he must avenge the name of
    king.

Strange fascinations whirl and wind about my spirit lying
    coils;
Thy charm enticeth, for the spoils of victory, all an evil mind.

Thy perfume doth confound my thought, new longings echo,
    and I crave
Doubtful liaisons with the grave and loves of Parthia for sport,

I think perhaps no longer yet, but dream and lust for stranger
    things
Than ever sucked the lips of kings, or fed the tears of
    Mahomet.

Quaint carven vampire bats, unseen in curious hollows of the
    trees,
Or deadlier serpents coiled at ease round carcases of birds
    unclean.

All wandering changeful spectre shapes that dance in slow
    sweet measure round
And merge themselves in the profound, nude women and
    distorted apes

Grotesque and hairy, in their rage more rampant than the
    stallion steed;
There is no help; their horrid need on these pale women they
    assuage.

Wan breasts too pendulous, thin hands waving so aimlessly,
    they breathe
Faint sickly kisses, and inweave my head in quite burial-bands.

The silent troops recede; within the fiery circle of their glance
Warm writhing woman-horses dance a shameless Bacchanal of
    sin;

Foam whips their reeking lips, and still the flower-witch
    nestless to my lips,
Twines her swart lissome legs and hips, half serpent and half
    devil, till

My whole life seems to lie in her; her kisses draw my breath;
    my face
Loses its lustre in the grace of her quick bosom; sinister

The raving spectres reel; I see beyond my Circe's eyes no shape
Save vague cloud-measures that escape the dances' whirling
    witchery.

Their song is in my ears, that burn with their melodious
    wickedness;
But in her heart my sorceress has songs more sinful, that I
    learn

As she sings slowly all their shame, and makes me tingle with
    delight
At new debaucheries, whose might rekindles blood and bone
    to flame.

The circle gathers. Negresses howl in the naked dance, and
    wheel
On poniard-blades of poisoned steel, and weep out blood in
    agonies;

Strange beast and reptile writhe; the song grows high and
    melancholy now;
The perfume savours every brow with lust unutterable of wrong;

Clothed with my flower-bride I sit, a harlot in a harlot's dress,
And laugh with careless wickedness that strews the broad road
    of the Pit

With vine and myrtle and thy flower, my harlot-maiden, who
    for man
Now first forsakest thy leman, thy Eve, my Lilith, in this bower

Which we indwell, a deathless three, changeless and changing,
    as the pyre
Of earthly love becomes a fire to heat us through eternity.

I have forgotten Christ at last; he may look back, grown
    amorous,
And call across the gulf to us, and signal kisses through the
    vast;

We shall disdain, clasp vaster yet, and mock his newer pangs,
    and call
With stars and voices musical, jeers his touched heart shall not
    forget.

I would have pitied him. This flower spits blood upon him, so
    must I
Cast ashes through the misty sky to mock his faded crown of
    power,

And with our laughter's nails refix his torn flesh faster to the
    wood,
And with more cruel zest make good the shackles of the
    Crucifix.

So be it, in thy arms I rest, lulled into silence by the strain
Of sweet love-whispers, while I drain damnation from thy
     tawny breast.

Nor heed the haggard sun's eclipse, feeling thy perfume fill my
     hair,
And all thy dark caresses wear sin's raiment on thy melting
     lips –

Nay, by the witchcraft of thy charms to sleep, nor drain that
     God survive;
To wake this, only to contrive – fresh passions in thy naked
     arms;

And at that moment when thy breath mixes with mine, like
     wine to call
Each memory, one merged into all, to kiss, to sleep, to mate
     with death!

TO MY FIRST-BORN

At last a father! In Mathilde's womb
The poison quickens, and the tare-seeds shoot;
On my old upas-tree a bastard fruit
Is grafted. One more generation's doom
Fixes its fangs. Crime's flame, disease's gloom,
Are thy birth-dower. Another prostitute
Predestined, born man, damned to grow a brute!
Another travels tainted to the tomb!

My sin, my madness, in thy blood are set,
A vile imperishable coronet,
To hound thee into hell! God spits at thee
The curse thy parents earned. Revenge be thine!
Kiss Lust, kill Truth, and worship at Sin's shrine.
And foul His face with dung – thy infamy!

CHANT AU SAINT-ESPRIT

Bah! gros bougre du ciel!
Tu ne te plais pas seulement
Des chansons de Gabriel,

Ni non plus du sacrament
Très banal, ni des anthemes;
Mais l'horrible hurlement

De mes curieux blasphèmes
Te plaira, je parierai!
Jesus dit ces anathèmes:

"Vous ces choses qui direz,
Blasphémant le Saint-Esprit,
N'aurez pardon pour jamais!"

Néanmoins, Jesus, je dis!
Saint-Esprit, je crois a toi,
Suceur du callibistris

Du bon Dieu, ta douce loi
Moi je garderai toujours!
Salut, bon et puissant roi!

Je veux goûter tes amours,
Avoir ta belle Marie,
En la jouant les trois tours;

Derrière, et ventre aussi,
Et la belle bouche, après,
Quand je serai ramolli,

Ni la semer de bon blé,
Mais la sucer, si l'on ose
Après toi; je n'aimerais

Comme toi, en plein névrose,
Si je devine tes goûts,
La faire feuille-de-rose!

Eh, gros bougre? Es-tu fou
Que ta grosse bouche baise
(Quand la lune est moins aigüe)

Le bon vin au goût des fraises
De ces nymphes si sanglantes –
Ce qu'on nomme "les Anglaises"

Envie-tu ces amantes
Qui le culte de Sapho
Jouissent, petites tantes?

N'exiges-tu quelque impot
Sur ces fours des Lesbiennes
Pour ton bon petit jambot?

Permets-tu que ces chiennes
Boivent de ta Marie miel,
Sans que leur p'tits cuts tiennent

Mémoire de tes autels?
Ai-je dit assez, bretteur,
Pour m'assurer de l'enfer?
Bah! gros bougre du ciel!

HERMAPHRODITE'S DREAM

I know that winged sprite
Who flew from heaven – was it hell?
Into these bounds of light
And music – yesternight –
Had some new song to tell.

I saw a living soul
Flame into mortal dress;
Whose glance – a fiery coal,
Whose lips – a ruby bowl
Whose wine was wickedness.

They were strange lips, I ween
Whereon no kiss might be,
And teeth were sharp therein;
Ivory and white and keen,
Tameless as hungering sea.

Strange body of my desire,
Voluptuous, lithe, and wan;
For, on my eyes drawn nigher,
My hot blood turns to fire,
Seeing nor maid nor man.

Not maid, not man – the breast
Like palaces of gold,
Yet where my lips caressed,
In the wild dove's wild nest
A dove too soft to hold.

No dove that Hylas knew,
No dove that Sappho kissed,
Nor in wide Heaven there grew

915

This child of stranger dew
Than God's good spirit wist.

Yet his wings bear him high,
Divine beyond control,
And, like for love to die,
I felt his arrow fly
Within my very soul.

Ah Love! the ambiguous kiss,
Not man's nor woman's touch,
In that estatic bliss –
Not hell's heat, as I wish,
Had warmed us overmuch.

Ah! Love! how fierce that night!
With what unsung desire
Thy lips and mouth were bright,
In mine eye to give light,
And fire to kindle fire.

Ah Love! nor king nor queen
Of mine exhaustless flame,
But comrade of my teen,
Spouse of that epicene
Incontinence of shame.

Twin Love! Soul's dual spouse,
Dream-serpent of my life,
Rose-garland of my brows
Within that ivory house,
Sex with itself at strife.

Were I a wanton stream,
Thou mightest bathe in me,

Yet in that happy dream
Methought my heart did deem
We mingled utterly.

O sexless! deathless! fair
Beyond the world to me,
Thy love-gift I will wear,
Thy joys my soul shall share,
Being made one with thee.

So, love, the days may keep
My nameless love from me;
Yet over slumber's deep
I will sail into sleep
Thither to lie by thee,

Hold thee with arms that cleave
Lock thee in limbs that leap,
Chain thee with lips that leave
Kisses of blood to weave
Castles of hope in sleep.

Poppy! best flower whose bud
Sends dreams to men that die,
I drain thy drowsy flood
That our impatient blood
May mingle utterly.

So, Hermes, thou art wed,
So, Aphrodite, mine,
In one sweet spirit shed
In one ambrosial bed,
In one fair frame divine.

Like clouds in rain, like seas
Exultant as they roll,
We mix in ecstasies,
And, as breeze melts in breeze,
Thy soul becomes my soul.

I come to thee with tears,
Nameless immortal dove;
Forget the fleet-foot years
In the incarnate spheres
Of our mysterious Love.

EREBUS

Something of monstrous in our love, our bed,
Soothes me with strong desire,
Strong but availing nothing – black and red
Thy body gleams, as fire
Thy great eyes burn, thy lips respire
It seems unnatural breath within their tomb.
Ah! the red portals of thy dusky womb,
Wherein my loves expire,
'Twixt thy black breasts to rise, kissed hard by thee
Till joy flows full once more, salt river to sweet sea.

Fairer than roses are thy swarthy cheeks,
Thine hair more sharp than gold;
Purple is warmer than mere red, when seeks
My love thy lips to hold.
Ah Queen! that other's breasts are cold
Being of wafted snowflakes beside thine;
Her breasts give milk as thine the fiercest wine;
Her ivory thighs enfold
Limbs not so amorous as these that lie
By the dark limbs, and lust for their imperial dye. Thy mouth
    takes me within its eager lips;

My mouth thirsts, drinking long
Deep from the fount of love, whence out there slips
An eager purple tongue,
Sweet as the taste of summer song
From thrush's tender throat, a tongue that tires
My thirsty lips with its insatiate fires,
While swart limbs soft and strong
Grip my hot head, while thy lips kiss away
With blood and foam the life from him thou wouldst not slay.

ABYSMOS

This is th' abyss! Implacable disease
Springs from the black defilement of that kiss,
That foul embrace that moulds these agonies.
This is th' abyss!

A serpent was my whore; her hellish hiss,
Her slaver venoms soul and strength; life flees
Repugnant from the corpse-caress. Ah, this

Rots blood and body; see, the liquor's lees
I drained, whose pangs are fierce with Syphilis.
Christ God, damn soul, but quench the pain of these!
This is th' abyss!

This is th' abyss. Behold wherein I lurk
The lazar-house my mind, wherein do work
The horrid charnel-priests, whose loathly song
Sickens my soul, and quells the spirit strong.
Hell-fire within my heart! and poisoned blood
Through every vein and artery pours a flood
Of devilish pain. This is th' abyss indeed;
Fears on my mind and pains on body feed,
Serpents of hell that gnaw my bones, nor quench
The fires of torture with the sickly stench
Of many a venomed drug, that clings and cleaves,
And clutches like a dead man's hand, and weaves
Its subtle scheme of agony through me.
Is God to help a mortal? Or are we
Caught in Fate's mesh without a hope to 'scape?
Ah! look around! In every darksome shape!
Fearful, nude Venus grins. Alcyone
Mocks with her sickening smile. Hill, moor, and lea
Make me to hate them. Only Clyde there,

Wild arms thrown wide, an agony of hair
Streamed fierce behind her, seems to sympathise;
Through selfish, yet despair in both our eyes
Gives us a link of love. The darkling room
Is fearsome; one red light throughout the gloom
Thrills my void veins with horror. On the couch
The gruesome hound with sleepy stare doth crouch.
His red hard eye upon me. Every shelf
Of noisome books reflects my hideous self!
Lucky I burnt my picture! Snakes on floor
Writhe, lick my legs, I fear them. By the door
Yon horrid panther snarls. His eye inspires
Fresh torments, to invade my soul with fires
Too angry to assuage, and in its glass
I see myself. I hate myself, alas!
More than all these. I cannot rid me of
Myself, my hates, my tortures, or my love;
My golden-haired Greek goddess, who divines
In me a god, who cannot read the lines
Of anguish on my forehead, neither scent
The poison of breast, blood, and excrement!
I gnash my teeth in impotent despair
That I may never hold her heavenly hair
Again, nor bite her lips, as once my teeth
Met in her cheek, to cull a rosy wreath
Of blood upon it, nor assuage the pangs
Of love with hardy limbs, and dolorous fangs,
And sweating body, crimsoning with gore,
As her mad mouth devoured me. Never more
Though years decay! With them my blood decays,
My bones rot inwardly, the venomed days
Sink shaft on shaft of agony, the years
Bring new distortions, miseries, and fears;
New torture to my spirit, and forgot
Of God, and health, and loveliness, I rot.

Outward, my face and breast have leprous sores;
Inward, my filthy blood; its poison pours
Corruption through me. In the eyes of man
I am condemned, the haughty one. God's fan
Is eager on my threshing/floor; his rod
Smites no vain stroke. Oh, how I curse thee, God!
What is my aid? But yet to Satan's power
I lend my utmost vigour for an hour,
To wrest Thy damned throne from out thy hands!
My aid? How shall I burst thy bitter bands,
Strike off thy shackles, from thy fetters break,
I, whom Thy name appals, whose vitals quake
At the dim thought of Thee? Have mercy, Christ!
Who suffered on the cross, who sacrificed
Thy heaven for three hours. Ah! pity me,
For years, not hours, condemned to agony
Thrice Thine! Have pity, hear me, virgin queen,
Whose pangs of childbirth were seven times more keen
Than all, since love and memory of joy
Thou hadst not, but the fear of shame to cloy
Even the hope of motherhood. But I,
Cut off from love and joy; its memory
One black hell of distorted pain; my shame
More horrid than that first unholy flame,
That burnt my blood, and flung me in her arms,
Whose filthy kisses and thrice loathly charms,
Her purple lips, her acrid redolence,
Her black lewd limbs, her breasts, whose foul incense
Smoked like hell's mouth though pendulous they hung,
Her devilish black belly, and her tongue
Sharp as a tiger's tooth, lured on my lust.
Oh! God in heaven! It is turned to dust
And dung and corpse-flesh! I can see even here
(For changeful spectres haunt me) how a tear
Of blood stood on my breast at her first bite:

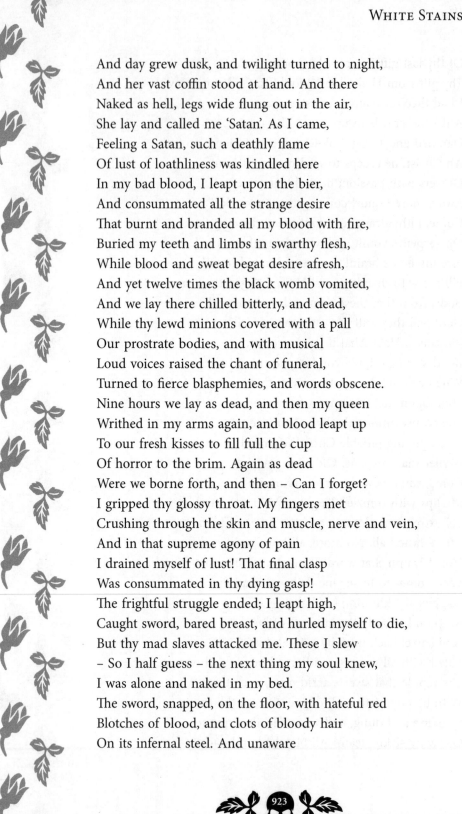

And day grew dusk, and twilight turned to night,
And her vast coffin stood at hand. And there
Naked as hell, legs wide flung out in the air,
She lay and called me 'Satan'. As I came,
Feeling a Satan, such a deathly flame
Of lust of loathliness was kindled here
In my bad blood, I leapt upon the bier,
And consummated all the strange desire
That burnt and branded all my blood with fire,
Buried my teeth and limbs in swarthy flesh,
While blood and sweat begat desire afresh,
And yet twelve times the black womb vomited,
And we lay there chilled bitterly, and dead,
While thy lewd minions covered with a pall
Our prostrate bodies, and with musical
Loud voices raised the chant of funeral,
Turned to fierce blasphemies, and words obscene.
Nine hours we lay as dead, and then my queen
Writhed in my arms again, and blood leapt up
To our fresh kisses to fill full the cup
Of horror to the brim. Again as dead
Were we borne forth, and then – Can I forget?
I gripped thy glossy throat. My fingers met
Crushing through the skin and muscle, nerve and vein,
And in that supreme agony of pain
I drained myself of lust! That final clasp
Was consummated in thy dying gasp!

The frightful struggle ended; I leapt high,
Caught sword, bared breast, and hurled myself to die,
But thy mad slaves attacked me. These I slew
– So I half guess – the next thing my soul knew,
I was alone and naked in my bed.
The sword, snapped, on the floor, with hateful red
Blotches of blood, and clots of bloody hair
On its infernal steel. And unaware

923

Of thy last gift I slept. I have it now,
Thy gift from Hell's door! Would to God somehow
I had thee once alive – to slay again! -
Ah! Who crawls in upon me like a vain
Damned ghost? Ugh! blotchy spectre! Fiend, aroint!
Ah Christ, he creeps toward me; evert joint
Quivers with passion; he will tear my eyes!
Away! more liquor! come, green cockatrice!
Come, filthy draught of fire! green dancing fiend
On serpent's vomit and whore's spittle weaned,
Fire my fierce brain! resolve my rotted heart!
Fill me with drunkenness! How changed thou art,
Body, from that these women loved so well!
God! will they still lust after me in Hell?
But this is Hell! Aha! if you were me,
Blind staring cripple yonder, you should see
Whether I lie! A cripple are you then?
Look upon me, the leper among men,
The corpse among the living! Intercede,
Good pitying pitiable Christ! My need
Is viler than my sins! Old sins, you tire!
Come, some new devilry to reinspire
My lips with frenzied laughter! Vain, ah, vain!
Th' extreme of pleasure and the worst of pain,
I have tasted all. No more, all hope must end –
Hope! Damn that word! It mocks me like that friend
Who comes to to see me daily – I shall die
Happier if I kill him; so shall I
Reap on his body the last tare of lust,
And shivel back into my primal dust
Filled with all worms and homed beasts with wings,
The reptile that sweats acrid juice, and stings
With bloody teeth and tongue! Oh, all the room
Spits fire and dung, and vomits forth a spume
Of tawny sickly death! All blotched and dark,

The putrid air is vital with a spark
Of fiery eyes of yonder filthy hound!
God! I am reeling brain and body! I swound!
The floor heaves up! The worms devour my breast!
Beasts and lewd fish and winged things infest
Each vital part! Screech, rats! more liquor! Come!
Rumble, you rotting whore-skin of a drum!
I care not! Scream, you rats! Snakes, bite and hiss!
Hell's spawn, I mouth you with this putrid kiss!
Satan! Damnation! This is the abyss!